THE GROTTO

By the same author

RINGARRA
SWEET ALICE
FELICITY

THE GROTTO

Coral Lansbury

ALFRED A. KNOPF
NEW YORK
1989

THIS IS A BORZOI BOOK
PUBLISHED BY ALFRED A. KNOPF, INC.

 Published in the United States by Alfred A. Knopf, Inc., New York. Distributed by Random House, Inc., New York. Originally published in Great Britain by The Bodley Head, London

Grateful acknowledgment is made to Angus & Robertson (UK) for permission to reprint an extract from "Five Bells" from *Selected Poems* by Kenneth Slessor. Reprinted by permission of Angus & Robertson (UK).

Library of Congress Cataloging-in-Publication Data
Lansbury, Coral.
The grotto / Coral Lansbury.—1st American ed.
p. cm.
ISBN 0-394-57438-9
I. Title
PR9619.3.L36G76 1989
823—dc19 88-23830
CIP

Manufactured in the United States of America
First American Edition

For Malcolm

1

Trapani

One

There is a special curse on the child of a great love. Tradition did not dictate that lovers should die young in order to spare them the inevitable disappointments of marriage or to sever the bridge that time sets between passion and friendship, but to spare the children. Would Romeo and Juliet have made good parents? Or can you see Heloise and Abelard leaving each other's arms to cradle the child that is crying in another room? Great lovers are monsters of selfishness who break every social bond and discard all ties of family to live in a world that reflects nothing but the other. "I live for your father," my mother used to say, but what she meant was that she lived in him, and he in her, and there was no place for me in either of them. My mother must once have carried me in her womb, but I know she did it grudgingly, as though I were some kind of unwanted parcel that had been thrust on her at the worst possible time.

If my mother and father had been young so that I could have seen them as children a little taller than myself, playing in the sand, splashing water like some of the parents I saw on the beach at Trapani, they would not have seemed so strange. For six years my best friend was Bessie Victoria Chambers whose parents came every summer and lived *en pension* at the Villa d'Athena. Mr Chambers had been wounded in the War and one arm ended in a pink, puckered stub at the elbow, but often he would pick Mrs Chambers up on his back and gallop along the beach with her shouting "Tally-ho!"—and we would all follow him pretending to be hounds and barking. The lean local dogs would sit silent and watch us from a distance, but you could not really expect a Sicilian dog to understand foxhunting. Once he went down on his knees in the sand, balancing on his one hand; Mrs Chambers knelt on his shoulders, Bessie climbed on her mother's back and Colonel Whitlow took a photograph of them all before Bessie fell off screaming with laughter. I was seven when Bessie became my friend, and it was then that I realized how different my parents were.

"Is that really your mother, or your grandmother?" Bessie asked me as we decorated a wall of wet sand with shells, and when I replied in surprise that of course it was my mother, Bessie said that she had a friend in Manchester who called her grandparents mother and father because her real father had been killed at Ardennes and her mother died of influenza. She said that her own real father had died at sea in the first year of the War and Mr Chambers was her stepfather, but since she could not really remember her real father, only that everyone cried when he went away and cried again when the news came that he was dead, Mr Chambers was her father and she had been given his name to avoid complications. It all sounded very satisfying and orderly as Bessie told it, for "complications" was an impressive word that only adults used.

The thought that my parents were unlike anyone else's had never occurred to me at that time. My mother did not seem angry or even disturbed when I told her what Bessie had said; instead she simply said matter-of-factly, "Well, of course she would think I'm your grandmother. I'm old enough to be your grandmother, heaven only knows. You were certainly a big surprise, I can tell you that." And it did not sound like the kind of surprise that came wrapped in coloured paper accompanied with shrieks of delight. Yet before I was seven I don't remember feeling any sense of loss or that my parents were odd.

That was the time when I first began to wonder if I had been adopted; if perhaps my real parents, who had been young and playful like Bessie's, were dead. Yet even then a certain logic told me that my mother and father would never have adopted a child, not even if I had been left on their doorstep wrapped in a satin blanket embroidered with a coronet and with a gold locket around my neck. I know what I wanted to believe at that time, but I could never pretend that I was a lost princess raised by shepherds. Even though I can smile now at the dreadfully serious and pompous child I was then, my yearning to be Bessie's sister and the desire to make her parents mine was a lasting anguish.

When I look back I know that, in spite of my desire to reveal the truth about myself, I am adjusting and altering the meaning of this history: memory is like the puppet master who makes the marionettes move a little differently every time he takes up the strings. What I am now is not the way I shall see myself ten or twenty years from now, and if I am foolish enough then to try to write another story of my life, it will not be the same as this. Perhaps I will not have gold in my hands as I do now. But there will be certain people and some events that will remain fixed. From Trapani you can see three fishing islands that change every day according to the light: in the early morning they float above the water like silver galleons in a dream, they vanish during storms, and at noon in summer they are etched so sharply against the sky that every bush seems to be carved into the light. Memory and mood can reshape the past but it can never alter the substance.

At seven I was suddenly convinced as I examined my life that I was a very unfortunate little girl who did not return to England at the end of summer like Bessie and the other children, or even go to school. It did not seem the same when I told them that my mother gave me lessons, or a little later, that my parents were teaching me Greek and Latin. Yet before the day that Bessie asked me about my mother I was not particularly unhappy, or happy, as I recall. I never thought about myself or measured my life by anyone else's, and surely happiness or the lack of it is the result of choice and the awareness of others. At first I thought the whole world was contained in the *bagghiu*, the walled court of our house and its fountain, a triton holding a dolphin from whose nostrils water spouted into a basin where three terrified goldfish occasionally flickered out from crevices in the stone. They were always being hunted by the neighbourhood cats, and one of my earliest duties was to rush out shouting at some wretched, starving cat raking the water with its paw. The tallest *giarra* held a gardenia tree that bloomed all the year round, there were a pomegranate and a fig in earthenware pots against the sunniest wall of the court, and grapes were trained across one corner so that it was always a place of deep shade in the summer. The *zibbibbu* grapes hung in long golden clusters dripping sweetness and I would lie on my back and watch them circled by clouds of tiny glittering wasps. A drop of sugar fell to the stones, the wasps followed it, and a brilliant green lizard darted forward and swallowed a wasp and the sugar in one quick gulp. Assunta kept herbs in ranked jars on each side of the kitchen steps and on the other side of the court my mother grew roses. I used to stand beside her as she complained about the lack of fragrance in the teas: "They look like blowsy washerwomen in this climate. Those Horace Vernets should be a dark velvet red but they fade to that dingy mauve before the petals are even open. I really should throw the lot of them out and grow peonies. One day I'll take you to Russell Morton and then you'll see such roses!"

Russell Morton was my mother's home in Shropshire, but she was never allowed to go back there after she married my father. It was one of the prices that had to be paid for a great love. The story of that day, the 23rd of June, 1910, when my mother and my father fell in love on the steps to the Greek temple at Segesta, was the legend of my life: it held me and controlled me in the same way that religion shapes every thought and action in the lives of other people. My mother, Evelyn Harcourt, had graduated from London University in Classics and become an archaeologist. She never actually conducted a dig on her own, but she had helped on several expeditions in the Mediterranean and that year she was working as an assistant to Joseph Whittaker on the island of Mothya, where he had built a mansion and discovered one of the earliest Phoenician settlements in Sicily.

"How can I describe it?" she used to say. "I was bending down measuring the base of the column when I felt someone staring at me. I looked up, and it was your father. At first I couldn't make out his face because he was standing against the sun, but I shaded my eyes with my hand, and then he spoke to me. It was as though we had spent all our lives waiting for that moment."

My mother was always silent at that point and then she would say slowly, "It was as if we had recognized each other and the joy of our meeting was all the more wonderful because we had both waited so long for it."

That always gave the legend its particular meaning, because my mother never spoke in superlatives. Her voice was clipped and almost laconic and one of her favourite pieces of advice to me was, "Eliminate all the adjectives and you may find yourself with an approximate truth."

After another pause she said that she felt a sudden jolt of fear because she had been of two minds whether to go to Segesta that day or finish cataloguing a tray of potsherds for Mr Whittaker. "I went there almost on impulse with no particular project in mind except that I had promised myself to do a comparative study of the unfinished temple at Segesta and the ruins of the temple of Demeter Malophoros at Selinunte. There was no urgency, none at all, and yet I knew I must go to Segesta."

My father had not taken her hand and kissed it, which Bessie and I considered to be the appropriate beginning to any courtship. He introduced himself and then said simply that having seen her he was born into a new life.

Bessie told me that her parents had met during the War in an army hospital where her mother was a nurse and she had been with Mr Chambers when his arm was cut off. We often talked about that and we played a game in which we took turns being nurse and patient. I would lie writhing on the sand with one arm tucked underneath me and crying how terrible the pain was. Bessie would place a wet towel over my head and say, "There, there, the pain will go and I shall always love you even if you only have one arm."

It was a marvellous game with a number of elaborate variations. I enjoyed being the surgeon and with a stick I sawed away at Bessie's arm while she screamed and rolled around on the sand in agony. There was always a ceremony then while we buried the arm and said a prayer over it. Since I already knew some Latin I would recite the Paternoster with my hands folded and my eyes closed. Afterwards, I was the nurse again, wrapping the elbow in the towel and stroking Bessie's red hair. Mr Chambers came up quietly to us once and we went on playing without noticing him. Bessie rolled over, crying out, "The pain! Oh, the terrible pain! I can't bear it!" And found herself on her father's feet. He leaned over and said very softly, "That's how it was, Bessie. That's exactly how it was." We felt afraid without knowing why, but he took us both up to have lemonade at their changing shed that stood in the middle of the row of tourists' cabins at the English end of the beach. Assunta came to the esplanade and called for me and Mr Chambers walked me back towards her. He held my hand and as we passed by the place where we had been playing he said, "Can you show me where you buried my arm, Gwen?"

I never knew how to play my mother's story and when I told Bessie she sat back on her heels and looked at me and sniffed disdainfully. "That's not a proper love story. That's nothing at all."

How could it possibly have been a love story when my parents were both so old? My mother was forty-three in 1910 and my father was exactly fifty. My father was Enrico di Marineo and he had enraged his parents when he refused either to become a priest or to marry after he had studied at the University of Milan, and instead had become secretary to Leonard Burgoyne, a rich English archaeologist. Burgoyne retired to Sicily when he was sixty, built a magnificent baroque villa in Trapani on the Via Nausica, and bought the plot of ground outside the town where he had discovered an Elymian settlement that he dated to a thousand years BC. Burgoyne did not have the wealth of Whittaker or Sir Alexander Hardcastle of Agrigento but he was respected as an archaeologist and at his death he left his house in Trapani as a museum with my father as permanent curator. The museum was my home.

The reception and dining rooms were now lined with glass cases and Mr Burgoyne's own study, with a rack of his carved meerschaum pipes on the wall beside the door, was a library where I used to do my lessons every morning. The curator's room opened out on to the *bagghiu* and that was where my mother and father sat across from each other at a long table repairing pots and tabulating the fragments of pottery and metal that people had once used like the china bowls and copper pans in Assunta's kitchen. The bedrooms were all upstairs: my own little room that looked down on to the vines, my parents' bedroom from which you could see the bay, and another bedroom that was now a sitting room with my mother's piano and all her family photographs. The English community regularly held musical evenings and I remember my mother singing George Butterworth's renditions of *A Shropshire Lad* with my father sitting beside her, turning the pages. Over the mantelpiece was a large watercolour in a gold frame of Russell Morton against the sunset reflected in an ornamental lake with two women in the foreground holding parasols. My mother had painted it when she was twenty. On the other side of the courtyard was a long tiled kitchen and behind it a stable opening on to the next street where my parents' Austin car was kept and polished every day by Miki. Nobody seemed to know where Miki had come from or what he really was because he had been inherited from Leonard Burgoyne. Miki was a mute and must have been very old, but whether he was Sicilian or Italian, it was impossible to say. He made himself understood by a variety of grunts and coughs and gestures that mimicked every human and animal sound and movement: birds crying at dusk and brawling cats, motor cars and creaking carts, and without words he could imitate the call of the milk vendor who led his cow to the stable door every morning. Most people bought milk from the goats that were taken from door to door, but my mother and the other English residents insisted on cow's milk, so an old brindle cow was walked from the Villa d'Athena at one end of the town to Colonel Whitlow's home at the Villa d'Eschia. Colonel Whitlow said that by the time the cow reached him it was so tired that even with curses and kicks the cowman could barely drag a cup of milk from its bruised udder. Indeed, one day the cow did drop dead on his doorstep and for a week we had powdered milk until the cowman found another, even older beast.

My mother insisted that Miki must be from the north because he was honest and worked every minute of the day. The car was polished and cleaned before the sun was up, then he would scuffle around, sweeping and weeding in the courtyard, or polishing and dusting. "No Sicilian," my mother always said, "ever works like that, and there is no Sicilian born who can ever tell the truth." She refused to have a Sicilian servant and relied upon Hilda Brunner at the Villa d'Athena to supply her with trained northern Italians who could speak reasonable English. Assunta had come to us from the Villa d'Athena when she had a falling out with Frau Brunner's temperamental Swiss chef.

The museum ran between two streets and the stable had one small door that opened on to the Via delle Arti. Assunta slept in a large sprawling room next to the kitchen and Miki lived somewhere over the stable in a sort of loft that he reached by a ladder. Every night Assunta locked and bolted her door because she was terrified of the Sicilians who were all thieves and murderers. My mother would pooh-pooh most of Assunta's fears, but she understood them, and when Assunta told her that she had a dream of the *banditi* coming down from the Montagna Grande and murdering them all in their beds, my mother shook her head and said she thought we were all safe enough in Trapani.

Every Sunday morning when Assunta went to Mass my father drove us to Canon Burnside's for morning service. There was no Anglican church in Trapani so Canon Burnside had turned one of the rooms in his old villa into a chapel with a plain wooden altar and a cross that did not have a Christ hanging in agony from it. "Thank God," Colonel Whitlow said, "we don't have to put up with any of that Romish nonsense from old Burnsie. Just a few sensible words, a hymn and you're set for the rest of the week." Colonel Whitlow had been gassed at the Somme and he generally ran out of breath before we finished singing the hymn and we would hear him wheezing through the last verses.

All the English residents together with Frau Brunner and her Swiss chef came to Canon Burnside's on Sunday morning, and later I realized what a strange service it was. There was the lesson for the day that Mr Chambers, or one of the other men, read from a large gilt-clasped Bible, and then Canon Burnside would stand in front of the altar and deliver a sermon. Bessie said it was not in the least like any of the sermons she heard from the Reverend Harkness in Manchester, or from Dr Tindall at her school. Canon Burnside always smiled when the lesson had been read, stretched out his hands and said, "We can all appreciate the beauty and the truth of that, can't we?" People nodded and Colonel Whitlow said "Hear! Hear!" and then Burnside would speak about what really interested everyone. An amateur archaeologist himself, Burnside had the latest news about every dig in the Mediterranean. He corresponded with Arthur Evans and Mortimer Wheeler and kept in touch with the Americans who were excavating in Turkey and Egypt; when he concluded by reading a letter from Dale Mitchener at Hyksos, he would look around at us all and say, "And thus we work to the greater glory of God to recover a nobler and a finer world than this. Amen." And announce the hymn for the day.

My father drove us to Canon Burnside's but he never sat with us during the first part of the service, preferring to stand on the balcony admiring the view of the mountains. He made it quite clear that he was not refusing to pray with us because it was an Anglican service but because he was an agnostic. However, the moment Canon Burnside began to give his sermon, my father would come and sit at the back of the room. Nobody seemed to be offended by this, and I heard Canon Burnside once say to Mr Chambers, "I have every sympathy with the poor little chap. After all, he was brought up a Roman like the rest of those benighted souls out there. I say it does him credit. Shows a lot of moral fibre, if you ask me. Do you know his family wanted him to be a priest?"

Frau Brunner always left first with the chef and we stood around and chatted while Mrs Burnside served tea on the balcony. Bessie and I led the rest of the children down into the garden which was full of old Roman statues: satyrs leering out from under ferns, Pan playing his pipes under a lemon tree, Aphrodite stepping from a shell at the edge of a lily pond. My father said most of them were fakes but not to mention this to Canon Burnside who had collected them when he once owned a villa in Florence and before he moved to Sicily because Italy had become too expensive.

There were always half a dozen children, and in the summer one or two students who came to my father's dig and to work with him in the museum. They were all like grown men to me at that age and I scarcely remember them. But I can see Bessie now with her thick red plaits and a butterfly of tiny freckles across her nose. Bessie used to weep over her freckles and once I carefully rubbed a piece of chalk over them to please her. That same night I remember taking a red pencil and drawing a butterfly of freckles over my own nose because I thought they were beautiful. One day, Bessie, we'll find each other again and try to remember for each other every one of those days on the beach and the way we used to pretend to be nymphs among the lilies in Canon Burnside's garden. It was many years before I realized how happy I was then.

When everyone had finished tea the cars were brought round and we were all driven to the Villa d'Athena. "It was," my mother said, "one of the most theatrical palazzi in Sicily." A vast white Spanish palace on marble terraces that stood high above Trapani looking from the salt fields to the south along the bay to the jutting promontory to the north, the Villa d'Athena was now a hotel owned by Frau Brunner. Even in the off season, she had guests who paid for the comfort of clean rooms, fine French food and a staff who all spoke English.

Canon Burnside's garden was like a jungle compared with Frau Brunner's terraces and fountains. Bougainvillaea hung in shawls of coral and magenta from the terraces and along the front wall with its fat ornamental urns there were topiary bougainvillaeas that looked as though they were about to pick up their skirts and waltz down to the town. In March the wisteria cascaded over marble archways and to my mother's chagrin, Frau Brunner's white roses never lost their shape or perfume even when the sirocco blew in the summer. The secret of the garden was quite simple according to Frau Brunner who always said, "I have never had a Sicilian gardener. Only Tuscans know how to keep a garden. Tuscans or the English," she would add, but who could hope to find English gardeners in Sicily?

Frau Brunner served an English Sunday dinner of roast beef or chicken, cooked vegetables and baked puddings with table napkins folded like swans that everyone in Trapani attended. She was a woman of great importance, for not only had some of the older residents known her parents when they bought the palazzo from a local prince and restored it to a glory he had never known, but she was the source of our north Italian servants.

We never played so freely in the garden of the Villa d'Athena because there were always gardeners brandishing their rakes and shouting at you if you tried to make castles in the gravel or throw the pebbles into the fountains. After lunch the English would either sit on the terrace talking or play cards in what was called the Whist Room, a huge cavern lined with red damask, and lit by chandeliers and gilt Nubian statues holding candelabra. Late in the afternoon the others would arrive. I never saw one of them before dusk and Bessie, who lived at the Villa, said that they remained there playing cards and gambling all night. The first to arrive was always the Principessa dell'Orino, an old woman with frizzed yellow hair wrapped in black satin and wearing shoes with diamanté heels and buckles. She was accompanied by a woman even older who, even in the middle of summer, wore moulting furs that showed bare skin and who was introduced as her sister, another princess. The Duca di Sciascia came with two sons who never seemed to raise their eyes from the ground. The smaller one combed his hair over his eyes in a thin black sweep of hair that left his bulging forehead exposed and the other had a rash of acne, and a red silk handkerchief trailing from his top pocket. One afternoon we counted two princes, four princesses, five dukes and a baron. They would stop as they passed us and there would be a little stiff conversation with the English before they drifted into the Whist Room.

"Parasites," my father would mutter.

I knew what parasites were, and I always thought of them afterwards as the bronze and gold beetles that came to feed on my mother's roses, or the mottled caterpillars that left the vine leaves in lacy shreds. Once, at the end of summer, a tall white-haired man in a white silk suit arrived with the Principessa di Modica and my father bowed awkwardly to him. The white-haired man stared at him and then walked past without speaking. At the door he turned and for a moment he looked back at me, then beckoned and I went slowly across to him. He smelt of jasmine and he leaned on a slender ivory stick with a handle shaped like a crouching, snarling monkey; there were heavy jewelled rings on the long fingers that held the monkey. When he smiled two gold teeth shone between his pale lips. I looked up at him and he said in English, "A pretty daughter of Sicily." And touched the lobe of my ear with his forefinger.

I did not know how to reply, but he did not seem to expect an answer and, turning, had taken the hand of a fat woman in tangerine silk and was laughing at something she had just said to him.

"Who was that?" I asked my father.

"The noble head of my family," Father said drily. "The Barone di Marineo."

"I didn't know you were related to a baron," I said excitedly and stared after the old man who was now listening to another baron.

"I would sooner be related to a sulphur miner in Capo di Monte," my father replied.

Later, I asked my mother about the Barone di Marineo and she laughed and said he belonged to a pantomime aristocracy, not like the aristocracy of England. We always left when they arrived, and Colonel Whitlow said he wished they'd either wash more or use less perfume. Bessie said that her mother told her that every Sicilian was related to somebody or other who was a duke or a baron. "Can you imagine our Prince Edward looking like one of those frights?" she said, and I had to agree with her.

Three days later a small box was delivered to the door with my name on it. I had never received anything but letters from Bessie and two of my other friends when they went home to England for the winter. But this was summer and nothing ever came for me in summer. When I opened the box it had a pair of small gold earrings in it. I showed them to my father and he left the room without speaking. My mother glared at them as though they represented something disgusting. She read the card slowly. "They are from the Barone di Marineo and you must send them back to him with a polite note. He must understand that while Sicilian girls may have their ears pierced for earrings when they are babies and before they can walk, it is not customary for an English girl to wear jewellery of any kind until she is sixteen or older."

When I told Bessie she said that the Barone had probably fallen in love with me and wanted to marry me, but even though we tried we could not play a love story from this. Bessie pretended to be the Barone and rolled her eyes and said, "I luvva you, I luvva you with all ovva my heart." But I shouted at her and began to cry, I was so angry, so we never played it again. She must have said something to her mother, because afterwards Mrs Chambers sat down beside me on the beach and said, "You must be very, very careful of these old Sicilian men, Gwen. Don't talk to them, and never, never let them touch you. When you're older, I'll tell you about the White Slave Trade."

Assunta didn't understand when I asked her in English so I translated it into Italian for her, and then she began to scream so loudly that my mother came across the court and I had to tell her. Nothing was ever frightening when my mother explained it, but this time I could feel a chill of fright in my stomach: "Girls, some of them very young, are kidnapped and sold into houses of ill fame in North Africa. Betty Chambers was quite right to speak to you about it. Some very nasty things have happened to little girls in Sicily."

Bessie had not heard about houses of ill fame and we spent weeks imagining what they were and what people did in them. I was convinced that I would be tortured and eaten in them, while Bessie thought it was more likely that the little girls were slowly starved. Bessie was plump and she ate cream cake and ice cream with such relish that she often had a white moustache and her father called her "Whiskers."

Even though I was so young I realized that my parents were angry that anyone should think I was Sicilian. Bessie was called "Whiskers," but sometimes when Assunta complained that I was arguing her to distraction, my mother said I was a regular Boadicea. I was English, even though my father was Sicilian and related to a baron, and I never mentioned the earrings again to Bessie or my parents. After that incident my parents always left the Villa d'Athena before the aristocrats began to arrive.

Bessie knew so much more about the Villa d'Athena than I did because she lived there all through the summer and she seemed to have a talent for finding out things. It was agreed between us that I was wise, but she was clever. I was reading Virgil when I was nine, but Bessie found out about the roulette wheel and the baccarat table that appeared in the Whist Room when the aristocrats arrived. Her father told her that the parasites lost millions and millions of lire gambling and Frau Brunner was probably one of the richest women in Sicily. And I never knew Frau Brunner was married until Bessie told me that she had overheard her parents discussing it.

"It's a terrible scandal," Bessie said frowning and shook her head.

"What kind of scandal?" I asked. It was not a word I had heard used very often.

Bessie knew how to frown with a raised eyebrow and put her head on one side exactly like her mother.

"I can't tell you."

There were times when Bessie almost reduced me to tears of vexation because she would hint at a special secret and then keep me in suspense for days. I begged her to tell me, but she only shook her head and said it was too awful a scandal to tell anyone.

When we were driving home in the car I leaned forward and asked my mother if Frau Brunner had been married.

"Yes, she was," my mother replied abruptly.

"Where is Mr Brunner now?"

"Do not ask personal questions, Gwen. Gentlefolk discuss things, only servants talk about people."

I sat back devoured with curiosity as my father stopped the car for a procession carrying a statue of the Virgin on a brilliantly painted catafalque covered with flowers and candles.

"Oh dear, I thought they'd finished with all that at Easter," my mother said.

"The opiate of the people," my father replied.

"Why do they worship the Virgin Mary?" I asked. "We don't worship her."

"They worship her," my mother said, "because Sicily is the Island of Persephone and what you have there is a racial and cultural memory. Don't look at the people, Gwen, look at the past. The beauty and the truth of Sicily is in its remains."

I knew that was right because everyone came to Sicily to see the remains. Colonel Whitlow and his wife specialized in Byzantine mosaics and architecture and Bessie's mother loved to sketch the ruins, while Mr Chambers often went out and helped my father at his dig.

The little smiling Virgin seemed to be dancing in the air as the men rocked the poles of the catafalque from side to side; a group of black-shawled women were counting their rosaries and praying; behind them came the *penitenti* in white pointed cowls with slits for their eyes and mouths. The scent of incense filled the car.

"It's all they have," my father said bitterly. "They have no bread or hope, only religion."

"And that doll instead of Persephone," said my mother, pointing to the Virgin.

Persephone was snatched away by Pluto, the god of the underworld, and she lived with him in Hades for six months of the year, mourned by her mother, Demeter. My father told me that if you examined the rites of Catholicism in Sicily you could always find the ancient beliefs of the Greeks: the grief of Demeter was Mary's sorrow for the death of her son, and Persephone could be either Christ or Mary according to the ceremony. You had to look beyond the surface to what lay buried and there you would find the reality.

I watched the procession and found myself thinking of the Barone di Marineo and wondering if perhaps I was Persephone and he was Pluto bent on abducting me. I had seen my father dust away the earth from a stone at the dig and there would be the wall of a house, and he could stand and draw the outlines of an Elymian temple from the tumbled earth. This was the way all the English looked at things and I was learning to do the same. I had never guessed that Frau Brunner was married, but Bessie had found out, and now I must discover that secret and the even greater secret of my parents. I was sure that if Bessie came to live with me in the museum she would understand what had made my parents fall in love. She used to listen to her parents, but mine never said anything when I was with them, or if they did talk it was about nothing of importance. Mostly they were silent when they were together, working opposite each other at the long table, where I was able to watch them from a dark corner under the vines. Once I saw something so strange that I shivered.

My mother reached across the table and gave my father a fragment of pot. He took her hand and held it and then she leaned across and he took her other hand. They sat like that gazing at each other and I suddenly saw that my father was crying. I wanted to run in and ask him what was wrong but I knew they disliked being interrupted when they were working. Neither of them moved, and then, almost in a single motion, they stood up and I heard them go upstairs and the bedroom door closed.

Two

Bessie and I used to quarrel like jealous lovers, but we knew as we teased and tormented each other that it was all part of a game: the end was always an hysterical reconciliation of tears and declarations that we would be best friends until we died. We argued about which would be the best way to kill ourselves if we were ever parted. Bessie preferred poison but I would point to the highest peak of Monte San Giuliano and say that I would throw myself from it and then haunt her for the rest of her life. I am not sure if it was the prospect of my committing suicide that made her tell me, or the thought of my appearing at the end of her bed like a moaning transparent sheet, but after three days of pleading and threats she finally whispered, "Frau Brunner was married to a Sicilian rotter."

"A Sicilian? Like my father?" I said falteringly.

"Not like your father. My mother says he's the exception that proves the rule."

Bessie could always make a cliché sound like an addition to the Decalogue, and I sat back suitably impressed.

"He was the living end, and he tried to take all her money and get the hotel from her, and there were all sorts of problems with Other Women, so she threw him out."

"Where is he now?"

Bessie shrugged eloquently and fluttered her hands.

"Who knows what happens to a man when he's thrown out? He ends in the gutter or goes to the dogs."

I thought of houses of ill fame and a bar down by the waterfront that Assunta hurried me past, trying to place a hand over my eyes. Frau Brunner's husband was probably in a place like that.

"But she had a son," Bessie continued.

I could not imagine Frau Brunner with a child or anything small because she always seemed so big to me. When she kissed me I felt that I would be lost forever under the cliff of her bosom, and even her face seemed larger than anyone else's. Wide-browed, with plucked eyebrows and shingled blonde hair in perfectly symmetrical waves, Frau Brunner surveyed the world across the rampart of a bosom that seemed without division. When I was younger I used to wonder if she had one gigantic breast that stretched from armpit to armpit with a cameo brooch in the middle to mark the place of her nipple.

"Is her son dead?" I asked.

"No—" Bessie breathed deeply and I knew the revelation was at hand.

"He is a Jesuit," Bessie said.

My father sometimes spoke about the Jesuits and I had heard Canon Burnside refer to them as the black limbs of Satan.

"She must wish her son was dead," I said.

"Every day of her life. Oh Gwen, just think, if when we're married, one of our children decides to become a Jesuit. What would we do?"

"Kill ourselves," I said firmly, because at that age death was another game we played like getting married, or having an arm cut off by the army surgeon. One of us would lie on the beach with hands folded and eyes closed, and the other would pray, and then bury the sad corpse with sand and place wreaths of seaweed on top.

I can scarcely remember what I did during the winter except wait for Bessie to return in the spring. There were letters every week but hers were always so much more interesting than mine, with news of going to the cinema and school dances and titbits of information about film stars: Douglas Fairbanks and Mary Pickford who were like Zeus and Hera, and Rudolf Valentino who was more handsome than Apollo. I had never seen a film. All the Greek gods were real to me: I had been to Aphrodite's temple at Erice and I knew that the goddess had been born of sea foam and carried by nymphs to the shore; Demeter's beautiful daughter, Persephone, was carried off by Pluto at Enna and my father showed me the spot by the Cyane River where he split the earth with his two-pronged fork and carried her down into the underworld. Every rock and tree was sacred to the memory of a god, or saints who were like the pale children of the old gods, and when there was no memory of gods or saints there was always the history of the invaders of Sicily: Greeks and Phoenicians, Carthaginians and Romans, Byzantines and Normans, Arabs and French and Spanish.

Bessie introduced me to another pantheon called film stars who lived in an Olympus known as Hollywood. They made love and quarrelled just like the Greek gods, and sometimes an ordinary boy or girl was discovered and made into a star just as Zeus found Ganymede and Europa and made them gods. I longed for Bessie's letters and yet I hated reading them because she would mention girls at her school, and being invited to parties and learning how to dance. But her letters would always end: "Your ever best and most loving friend, Bessie Chambers." And then I would sit and cry for hours because I missed her and loved her so much.

When we were nine Mr and Mrs Chambers said they would take us on a camping tour with tents and sleeping bags. My mother refused at first because she said that some of the places where we were going were not safe, particularly for travellers out of doors at night. Mr Chambers laughed and said he would be taking a rifle and a pistol and he thought he was a match for any Sicilian bandit. Reluctantly my mother agreed but only after she had persuaded Mr Chambers to take Miki with us. I think they were quite glad to have the extra help and Mr Chambers said it gave the trip a little tone to be travelling with a manservant.

We went in a large touring car with all the bags strapped to the back and Miki sitting on top of them.

"How's the mascot back there?" Mr Chambers called and Miki would grin and pretend he was a bird perched on the luggage. But every night he managed to get the tents up and the fire lit before we had climbed out of the car and stretched.

We made a camp at Segesta and spent all day walking around the temple and the theatre. Mr Chambers gave us a performance, pretending to be Charlie Chaplin, and I recited the lines from the second *Olympian* where Pindar speaks of the good who wear an equal splendour through all their nights and days and who dwell in the islands of the blessed. When I had finished Mr Chambers patted me on the head and said I was going to be a regular scholar like my parents, while Miki nodded furiously and clapped. Bessie and I lay awake talking that night and she said that she intended to get married when she was eighteen and have three children, two boys and a girl.

"That's only nine years from now!" I cried despairingly.

"I am not going to be an old maid or left on the shelf," Bessie said firmly.

"But what will I do then? You know I won't get married like you."

"You'll come and live with us," Bessie said and put her arms round me, "and you can help with the children and we'll be best friends just as we are now."

I was so happy I thought I was going to burst into tears and then we heard Bessie's parents arguing.

"It's always about the same thing," Bessie whispered.

"At least we're saving money," Mr Chambers said.

"I wish you'd stop talking about saving money and start making some, Edgar."

"We're managing, Betty. All we have to do is watch the pennies. Come here—"

"No, I don't feel like it. We shouldn't be taking such long holidays every year. You should spend more time at the factory."

"Damn the factory! It's breaking even. And look at it this way—we're going to show a profit this summer. Hilda wants curtains for the whole ground floor of the hotel, and I think I can talk her into refurnishing the other floors too."

"One sale won't put you in the black, Edgar. You can't expect the business to run itself."

"It did for my father. I am not going to become a grubby-fingered little clerk poring over the books. Chambers Cotton Laces are known worldwide, we have a competent manager and a good staff. I always wanted to be an archaeologist and this is my chance to enjoy myself and do something useful. God help us, Betty, it's not as though I'm drinking or gambling."

"Edgar, I'm not complaining about you, it's just that I wish you'd spend a little more time thinking about the business."

"Fine, I've thought about it. Now, I want a cuddle."

"Oh, all right, but be very quiet, the girls are probably wide awake."

They didn't talk any more but we listened and heard sounds and sighs, and Bessie whispered that they were making love. We strained to hear but the sounds did not come together in the way that Miki's grunts and whistles made pictures we could all recognize. Bessie went to sleep and I wondered why Mrs Chambers should be worried about money when my mother said that half the lace curtains in England came from his factory. An owl woke me before it was light and I began to think about my parents and their great love. My shoulder was damp from Bessie's breathing but she did not stir when I climbed out of my sleeping bag. I put a cardigan over my nightgown and walked barefoot up to the temple and stood on the steps. This was where they had met and where my father said he had been born into a new life. Had Demeter been responsible? I was standing in the temple that was sacred to her rites.

A little breeze rustled through the asphodel and in the half light it seemed brushed with silver and luminous. Red poppies opened like eyes as the sky flushed from apricot to gold, and one long grey cloud lying across the hills suddenly glowed to a deep purple fringed with burning scarlet. The whole world was being changed before me. Somewhere behind me a sheep bell chinked once and, as if it were a signal, the swallows flew high above my head, chittering like the souls of the dead through the columns and open roof of the temple. I tried to reach out to the ghosts of my parents. They must be here if only I had the power to penetrate the stones to the place where their memory was still engraved like the image of a photograph. I could easily imagine Bessie's mother and father making love, but I had never seen my parents together in their bedroom or heard a sound from that place. Did they close the door behind them and face each other with outstretched hands, then slowly and delicately step out of their old bodies as they would out of ragged clothes and become young and beautiful lovers? I shut my eyes and leaned against the rough stone of the column trying to imagine what my parents must really be like. Only if I could see them as they appeared to each other would I ever be able to understand their great love.

The asphodel was rustling all around me and a bird flew so close to my face that I almost stumbled and fell forward. The sun blinded me and when I put down my head it seemed as if my bare feet had become flames that were leaping up my white nightgown. I heard a crying and shading my face with my hand I looked down the slope. Bessie was stumbling through the asphodel calling for me and when she saw me she ran towards me sobbing.

"Oh Gwen, I woke and you weren't there and I was so scared!"

We held each other and in that instant I felt something rush through me like a wind.

"I know who I am," I said. "I'm Demeter, and you're Persephone."

Bessie rubbed the tears from her face and looked up at me.

"She was young and very pretty, wasn't she?"

"Oh yes, Pluto fell in love with her at first sight and she became the queen of the underworld, and Demeter only saw her for six months every year."

And that became another game for us. For six months every year I mourned the loss of my Persephone and we signed our letters with our new names.

We tried to keep it a secret but everyone seemed to know about it, and Colonel Whitlow said that I didn't look matronly enough to be Demeter.

"After all, she's the goddess of fertility, of corn and harvests, and all that sort of thing," he said.

I knew he was deliberately making a joke about my flat chest and scowled. Bessie was becoming a woman with little breasts and a narrow waist while I was like a thin, scrawny boy. All I seemed to do was get taller, with bony shoulder blades like prehistoric wings, and when my mother measured me she would sigh and tell me I was costing her a fortune in clothes. Twice a year she wrote to Swan and Edgar's and then we would go to the shipping agent at the port and collect a box of dresses and shoes. Everything was very good and very plain and I used to shrivel with envy when Persephone arrived in the spring with her flowered muslins and ruffled silks.

She was now taking dancing lessons and when I went up to the Villa d'Athena to visit her she made me carry a gramophone on to the terrace and practise. Because I was so tall I always had to take the boy's part and Bessie would lightly place her left hand on my shoulder and tell me not to step on her feet. I was naturally clumsy and it took weeks for me to learn the simplest steps but soon we were foxtrotting and tangoing and some of the hotel guests who saw us strolled over and applauded. Bessie loved that and would give them all a graceful curtsey but I couldn't bear to be watched. She said I was such a gawk because I spent too much time with old people and perhaps she was right. It was agreed that I knew everything about history and archaeology but she understood Life.

There were always other children at the Villa d'Athena but we ignored most of them, particularly if they were foreigners, and there seemed to be more Germans and Swiss and fewer English every year. One summer the Chamberses arrived with two friends and their daughter, a girl a year younger than we. Her name was Margaret Moglen and she had a very pale face and wispy brown hair that always looked wet. Bessie said she was detestable and we resolved to make her as miserable as we possibly could. We said that it was only natural to hate her because she was stupid and ugly, but I know it was because she wanted to share our love. Bessie laughed at her lank hair and I asked her if she knew Latin. She shook her head and I stood in front of her and conjugated *odi* through all its parts.

When Mrs Chambers told us to play with Margaret we would dutifully take her down into the garden and pinch her, defying her to tell on us. But she never did. It infuriated both of us that anyone would dare to think she could become our friend, or that she might hope to join our games. One morning we told her to wait for us by the lower fountain on the terrace and we would fetch her in half an hour. We went off and spent the day at the beach, and when we arrived back in the afternoon she was still standing there with long tear stains down her cheeks.

"You are a stupid girl," I said.

"Stupid! Stupid!" Bessie shouted and slapped her.

We talked of very little except ourselves and once spent a whole day making up our faces with a tube of old lipstick that Mrs Chambers had thrown out, and spent hours walking on our toes to be ready for the time when we would be allowed to wear high heels. When Bessie became convinced that her eyelashes were getting thinner, I counted every one of them each day for a week. Bessie, have you ever found a lover who was as devoted to you as I was? Who admired the shape of your toenails, who combed and plaited your hair and marvelled that you had a tiny freckle at the side of your mouth like a beauty spot?

When we were not admiring each other or talking about ourselves we whispered about sex. Bessie was afflicted by the curse when she was eleven and that summer for at least three days every month she told me she was dying and how excruciating the pain was, and could I see a speck of blood on the back of her dress? On those particular days I used to walk a little behind her to make sure there were no telltale signs on her skirt. I knew she was keeping another secret from me because when she spoke about falling in love and getting married, she said that there was more to it than that.

"What do you mean?"

"If you don't know I can't possibly discuss it with you."

"Persephone! Don't be so beastly."

"It's what people do when they're in love. And I suppose you think it's just kissing and all that mushy stuff."

"I may know a whole lot more than you think."

"How could you?"

"I just might."

We were in the museum because my parents had both gone out to the dig with their student, David Maybrick.

"Gwen, you know that you couldn't learn anything about Life in a museum."

"Sometimes, you can find things in a museum that nobody would ever dream of putting on show."

I could see that Bessie was considering this and I pretended to be rapt in thought.

"All right, I'll tell you. It's my Uncle Travis—he's engaged."

"Mmm—"

"Well, he came with his fiancée and stayed with us for a weekend."

I was silent and Bessie became irritated.

"Mother put Nancy in my room and Travis took the spare bedroom, but in the night I heard them together in his room. I got out of bed very quietly and I crept down the hall and climbed on the hall stand so I could look through the fanlight. The moon was shining directly into the room and I saw them—doing it."

As Bessie was speaking and waiting for me to ask her what her uncle and his fiancée had done, I went to a cupboard at the end of the museum. It was always locked, but I had discovered that the key was kept on a small ledge underneath the bottom drawers. Bessie followed me, complaining fretfully that I simply wasn't old enough to understand what she was saying. I unlocked the door and pulled out a deep, heavy drawer. It was full of squat painted vases and I passed one to her. I was glad I kept my hand under it because she almost dropped it in shock.

"It's filthy!" she shrieked.

"Isn't that what they were doing?" I asked calmly.

"Yes, but—it wasn't like that."

"Oh, this is exaggerated, but exaggeration is part of the whole style in Phlyax vases."

The leering man had an enormous penis that he was gleefully about to insert in a fat woman with a gaping vagina.

Bessie asked me to turn it so she could see the other side, and then wanted to know if there were any others in the drawer.

"A few."

"Let's see them."

"Oh, but you know everything, Persephone."

"I didn't mean to tease you, Demeter."

As she examined the vases, gasping, I told her about Roman farces and how these early Italian vases from Paestum showed scenes from them. There were women caressing women with bulging breasts and hanging stomachs, men with men and men with animals, but invariably the men had gigantic organs that stood out in front of them like horns.

"I think your parents are quite right to keep these locked up," Bessie said primly. "It would never do for children to see them."

"I only found the key by accident," I said and added that when I'd asked my mother about the cupboard she told me it was full of broken pots that did not belong in the collection.

"I read some articles on Phlyax vases and some of them must be much dirtier than these, Bessie."

She looked at me in wonder and shook her head.

"You found out all that in a museum?"

"I just don't know what's supposed to be so marvellous about it, Bessie. I mean, a man and a woman joined together with that—that thing."

"It's not like that in real life and yet—" She admitted that this was what she had seen.

We had both seen little boys piddling against walls or flourishing their penises on the beach, but here were paintings of burly men dwarfed by their huge organs. When we talked about falling in love or looked at Bessie's film magazines we could produce shivers of delight in ourselves, yet the vases and what Bessie had seen did not seem to have any relation to all that we imagined and felt. If this was Life then where was there any place in it for Love?

"What's in the other drawers?" Bessie asked.

She did not believe me when I told her that all they held were simply uncatalogued pieces, or objects that had no provenance. She insisted that I pull out the drawers and then carefully examined everything.

"What's that?" she asked, pointing to a long bronze blade or pin that curved to a hook. The handle was a humped figure that could have been a man or a woman.

"I don't know what it is," I said. "I've seen it before. My father bought it last year but when he couldn't find out what it was, he put it away here. He said it was probably Elymian."

"It's a knife," Bessie said.

"That's what I thought, but he said it wasn't designed to cut anything. And why should it have such a funny little hook on the end? Some of the archaeologists think it might be a strigil, but strigils were flesh scrapers, and it's not really the right shape for that. My mother said it was a weaving tool, but neither of them really knows. Father showed it to the director of the Palermo Museum when he was here and he said it could be a sacrificial knife."

"Sacrificing what?"

"I don't know."

Bessie was practising falling in love and when David Maybrick came back to have tea with us she sat opposite him and gave him languishing glances from under the long eyelashes that she was darkening with coffee.

"Do you have sore eyes?" he asked her solicitously. "You must be careful of the flies here. My mother gave me a special ointment to use if I had any inflammation."

I wanted to laugh but I could see that Bessie was turning scarlet with rage. Even my mother seemed amused.

Miki drove her back to the Villa d'Athena and David asked me if I would help him with some Greek inscriptions he was trying to translate. I was continually amazed at how little he knew for someone who was studying at Cambridge, and I told him so.

"You are exceptionally bright, Gwen."

I shrugged and wondered why he was looking at me so intently.

"You know, I'd like to come back and see you when you're a little older."

"I shall probably know much more then."

"That's not quite what I meant—"

"Were you deliberately making fun of my friend this afternoon?"

"Your friend? That fat little girl with the red hair? No, I don't think so."

"How dare you speak about Bessie like that! Why—why, everyone knows she's a—she's the Clara Bow of Sicily. Red hair is the most fashionable colour of all and some girls would die to have hair like Bessie's."

He was laughing at me and saying that he hoped he could have a friend like me one day. I cannot remember what he looked like except that he was tall and had spectacles that were always smeary. No matter what he said after that I refused to speak to him for the rest of the summer. He left a parcel of books for me when he went back to England, but I did not even open them. I didn't care what they were or what happened to them and for all I know Assunta threw them away.

Assunta seemed as much a part of the house to me as the triton in the *bagghiu* that I was sure must be shrinking every year. My mother had told me that Assunta's fiancé was in Lucca and one day they planned to get married when they had saved enough money. I used to enjoy bullying her or reducing her to terrified screams. Assunta lived in daily fear that the Sicilian *banditi* were going to attack the house, or that some sinister mafioso would climb through the windows with a razor and cut off her head. She read the newspaper moving her lips as though she were eating, darting back and forth from her cleaning to a page that she kept open above the sink. Sometimes I offered to read to her and then I would invent stories of servants who were cut to pieces, or terrify her with an account of one Italian housekeeper in Palermo who was drowned in her own clothes tub by a pack of thieves.

When she was sent to fetch us from the Villa, Bessie and I would run through the gardens and walk home alone. My mother had forbidden this and said that we must always be escorted, but we preferred to walk together, particularly at dusk when the piazza was full of strolling men. We knew that they were all staring at us and I would scowl at the ground, wishing I had Bessie's aplomb. "Look at them," she whispered to me. "They'd all like to do it to us." Her eyes became narrow blue slits, her nose wrinkled and she puckered her top lip so that her two front teeth were bared. I tried to copy this expression of belligerent contempt in the mirror but I looked as though I were about to be sick.

"They treat their women like Oriental slaves," Bessie muttered, glaring balefully around her.

Whenever we managed to escape Assunta, we stalked home across the piazza to the museum, feeling like two avenging Furies vindicating the rights of all those Sicilian women locked up in their miserable dark houses. If we chanced to see any women in the streets they would always be hurrying along in black shawls as though ashamed to be seen abroad. Occasionally one might be seen shaking some bedding from a balcony, or an old woman would be sitting over her needlework in front of a doorway with her face to the wall for it was considered immodest if a woman showed her face outside the family. How righteous Bessie and I felt as we defied these tyrannical customs! Besides, there was always the comforting awareness that Assunta was following us, and that before we reached the corner of our street we would hear her calling to us.

"Mussolini thinks he's going to change all this," Bessie jeered. "What a hope! Are any of them following us?"

It was the frisson of excitement that really led us to run the gauntlet of the *passeggiata*: I knew how it thrilled Bessie to have a crowd of men staring at her. When I complained and said I felt silly, Bessie told me it was good training, like learning how to dance.

"You must learn how to keep men at arm's length, Gwen. Every girl needs a killing glance."

It was Hilda Brunner who finished that game. One afternoon we'd seen Assunta coming across the terrace and were running through the card room when Frau Brunner loomed up in front of us.

"Gwen, Bessie—how old are you?"

We grudgingly admitted to twelve and she told us that we were no longer children and must learn to behave like young ladies.

"We're not doing any harm," Bessie said in a plaintive little voice.

"You are playing games you do not understand. I've heard about your parading through the town. Nothing goes unnoticed here. This is Sicily and there are people—men out there who could take advantage of your innocence and your stupidity."

"We are not stupid!" I said angrily because I was very proud of my learning.

"Women—young women particularly, never leave their houses alone, not even to go to Mass. This is the custom in Sicily."

"But we're English."

"One day the men here might choose to see you as women."

"They'd never dare!" Bessie said furiously.

"If you ever go off alone again I shall speak to your parents." Frau Brunner paused and then said slowly, "You have no notion how vile the Sicilian male can be. Nothing governs him except lust. In this heat the blood boils in his veins. He's like a prowling cat in the night, a dog who smells a bitch in heat. What he can't take he kills."

Even Bessie was cowed by Frau Brunner's sombre, accented voice and we told her that we would never run away again.

"May you both be spared," she said and gave us each a kiss.

Assunta seemed to have become a different person by the end of that summer. Her red hair was now pinned in curls at the back of her head instead of being twisted in a knot and she was wearing a garnet necklace.

"I shall be going home at the end of the year to be married," she announced.

Bessie and I looked at each other in amazement. I had never thought about Assunta's age except to see her as a part of the house like Miki or the triton in the *bagghiu*.

"Paolo has been made a stationmaster and with his salary and what I have saved we can afford to marry."

"But what will we do?"

"Frau Brunner will find you another servant."

"I don't think you should leave us," I said firmly. "You won't be happy anywhere else but here."

Assunta only laughed and poked a finger through one of the fat round curls. I could see that my mother was irritated but she said that Assunta had waited a long time to get married.

"Isn't she too old now?" I asked.

"My dear Gwen, she is not a Sicilian. Assunta has had the good sense to delay her marriage until she can afford to have a family. She's not like the women here who marry when they're children and have a brood of starving babies by the time they're twenty."

"I shall miss her."

"I'll speak to Frau Brunner on Sunday. Assunta is not leaving us until Christmas, so it may even be possible for the new servant to move in before she goes, and then Assunta could help train her."

Bessie returned tearfully to England and I wept with grief and envy that she would be greeting her school friends and going to see films and plays. I began writing to her almost immediately. My mother wrote every week to my grandmother at Russell Morton but while my letters often crossed with Bessie's, my mother never received any word from her family. Yet I knew that I had a married aunt as well as my grandmother at Russell Morton. There were solicitors' letters and letters from friends addressed to my mother but it was as if Russell Morton was a black well and not a house in Shropshire. I tried to talk to my mother about it but she would always cut me short, or say that you paid for everything in life, and no sacrifice had been too great for the love of my father.

Whenever I asked my mother if I could go back to England to school she shook her head and said that if anything happened to her there must be someone here to look after my father. I was not simply translating unending passages of Greek and Latin every morning, I was also learning how to live with loneliness. It was like a dull pain in my chest those first few weeks without Bessie, and I think it was my father who took pity on me and said I could help him sort a tray of potsherds. Perhaps it was because my eyes were young that I was able to see at once which pieces fitted together, and when my mother came downstairs she was amazed at what I had done.

"You have a good eye," she said.

"Not like yours," my father replied gently, smiling at my mother, and I could feel the conversation being pulled away from me and circling round themselves.

At least I could sit with them as they worked together at the long table and soon I was assembling the broken fragments and watching the form of a beaker or a jar take shape in my hands. I learned how to use plaster of Paris to fill in the empty places, but when I wanted to paint over them and make the jar seem whole again, my father told me that restoration was not re-creation. You could bring fragments of the past together, but you must never try to invent what had been lost. Generally my father was a silent man, speaking only when he talked about his dig or the museum, and there were very few occasions when I was alone with him. I was already taller than he was and I could see that the top of his head had only a feathering of white hair over the brown skin.

Frau Brunner must have known about Assunta's marriage plans before any of us because the following Sunday she assured my mother that she already had a well-trained domestic in mind.

"That woman is a godsend," my mother said as we drove back that afternoon. "It would be impossible to live here without her."

"Does she ever see her son?" I asked.

"I haven't the faintest idea," my mother replied, and immediately changed the subject.

When Miki brought in the mail the next day there was a fat envelope from Bessie for me, some official-looking letters for my mother and one small triangular sealed letter for my father. He frowned when he examined the crest and opened and read it slowly. I was so engrossed with Bessie's news that I was not aware of the sudden silence in the room. I heard my mother's shocked cry and then she said, "It's out of the question. The man's audacity is beyond belief."

When I asked what was in the letter I saw my mother mouth something silently to my father and she turned and told me to go down and help Assunta. I complained vigorously, but I knew better than to argue with my mother when I heard that flinty tone in her voice. As I went down the stairs very slowly, sliding my hand down the cool mahogany banister, I could hear my mother's voice crack with anger, but just as I was about to creep back and listen at the door she flung it open and said, "We'll answer him now and Miki can deliver it to him by hand since he's staying at the Villa."

Bessie had sent me cuttings about Rudy Vallee who was her favourite crooner and this was far more interesting than the letter my father had received that morning. The following day I had completely forgotten it. I am not certain what woke me, but I was shivering and wondered if I'd had a nightmare. It was still dark as I fumbled out of the mosquito net and looked down into the *bagghiu*. Everything was still. Puzzled, I opened my door and went across the landing to the top of the stairs. I saw what had happened at the same moment as Assunta began to scream.

There was no longer a front door to the museum and the dawn light was pouring through the gaping opening: every case and statue was outlined in the main room because all the shutters had vanished from the windows.

Three

The front door of the house had been taken from its hinges and lay at the bottom of the steps: the shutters from the four long windows were piled on top of it. Nothing seemed to have been disturbed in the museum but I knew where a small collection of gold coins and jewellery was kept in a corner cabinet and I ran to see if it was safe. Assunta had thrown her apron over her head and was kneeling in a corner, begging the Virgin to protect her, while Miki crept slowly out into the street shaking his head. I scarcely noticed my father as he walked down the stairs and stood gazing at the heavy oak door. He took off his gold-rimmed spectacles, polished them carefully with the sash of his dressing gown, pinched them firmly on the bridge of his nose and walked around the neat wooden pile. How could anybody have taken down the door so silently, and who would have the strength to unbolt the engraved iron hinges that were rusted into the jamb?

My mother called from the top of the stairs, "What have they stolen, Enrico?"

"Nothing. Nothing at all," my father replied. "I'll have the door replaced this morning. No one has touched anything in the museum."

He went up to her and I heard them whispering. Miki was grunting as he lifted up the shutters and placed them against the house. I tried to help him and he put his finger to his lips and then across his throat, glancing quickly over his shoulder.

"Were they thieves, Miki? Did I wake in time to stop them?"

Mike shook his head and covered his ears with his hands.

"Were they *banditi*?"

Assunta heard me and began to gabble a rosary, kissing each bead with such ferocity that I thought she might swallow it. I shouted to her to be quiet and get the coffee ready and when she still remained huddled in the corner I went over and shook her.

"Do you know who they were?" I asked.

"Mafiosi."

The word seemed to inspire fresh hysteria and she stuffed a length of the rosary in her mouth. I slapped her hard to stop her screaming again.

"We are English, Assunta. Don't forget that. We are English in this house and the Mafia only persecutes Sicilians."

The words seemed to comfort her a little and, still praying, she stumbled off to the kitchen. Soon I could smell coffee and Miki and I tried to lift the door and place it against the wall of the house. It was too heavy for us.

"Was it really the Mafia?" I asked him.

Miki looked at me, his small black eyes almost lost in a web of wrinkles. He nodded and motioned for me to go upstairs.

As I was dressing in my room I remembered the odd triangular letter with its red wax seal and recalled that I had seen something like it once before. I knew instinctively that my mother's reply to the Barone di Marineo had been responsible for whatever had happened during the night. My parents were in the *bagghiu* drinking coffee and, without thinking, I leaned out of my window and said, "It was the Barone. He did it, didn't he? What was in the letter, Father?"

My father did not raise his head but my mother glared up and told me not to shout from the window like a Sicilian fishwife. They refused to discuss it with me and I stormed off to the kitchen to question Assunta. She was cutting bread with the rosary dangling from her wrist.

"Do you think the Barone di Marineo could have done this, Assunta?"

"Who else?"

"Why?"

"Because he has a black Sicilian heart and he hates your father."

"Nobody hates my father."

This was the truth. There were times when my father was so self-effacing that you wondered if he were in the room. At Sunday lunch at the Villa he talked about the museum and discussed archaeological finds, but he always seemed happiest when he could stand at my mother's side and listen to her. He had never once spoken angrily to me; indeed, before I was twelve, I hardly remember him talking to me about anything except history or mythology. There were times when he looked at me and frowned, apparently puzzled, as though he had walked into the room and found a stranger sitting at his table.

I think one of the reasons he was so well liked was because he always deferred to my mother, who was a Harcourt, and because his English had only the slightest accent. Bessie's father said that no one would ever take him for a foreigner and when Colonel Whitlow organized a cricket match in the main park of Trapani, my father offered to score and Whitlow slapped him on the back and said he was a good chap. The match was to be the event of the summer but just as the first batsman, an Embassy clerk from Palermo, hit the ball wide, it was seized by a stray dog who bolted into a side street with it. The same thing happened to the next four balls and then play was abandoned. The following day there were scraps of chewed leather down all the Trapani alleys where starving dogs had tried to make a meal of the cricket balls.

Assunta told me that Miki had been running from the Villa d'Athena to the Villa d'Eschia carrying messages and my mother had ordered sandwiches and scones for a meeting that afternoon.

"What sort of meeting?"

"*Non lo so.*"

Assunta shrugged miserably and went on cutting bread. Two carpenters came later in the morning to hang the door and replace the shutters. It took all three of them with Miki's help to hang the door again. It was still a mystery how it could have happened: I was known to be a light sleeper and yet nothing had woken me during the night.

I could not understand why the Barone di Marineo had ordered this mad joke, for what else was it? Bessie often told me of the pranks they played at her school with pails of water suspended over doors and elastic bands tied to the knob. This seemed to be the same and yet there had been so much work involved. There must have been half a dozen men working silently outside the house during the night, and yet since the museum was a public building, the street was always patrolled by the *carabinieri.*

My mother was clearly at a loss to know how I could be kept out of the way when the English arrived. I decided to help her and asked if I could walk round to the Museo Pepoli. It was only three streets away and I thought she might break her rule about my going out alone.

"Wear your hat and walk quickly. If anyone speaks to you don't answer but walk faster."

She looked worried and kept tugging at her short grey hair. I assured her that I would behave myself like an English lady and she smiled briefly.

"An Englishwoman can go anywhere in the world because she never forgets that she is a lady."

I met Colonel and Mrs Whitlow at the front door and watched him examining the iron hinges and whistling.

"Jolly bad show, Demeter," he said as his wife nudged his elbow.

"Ah, off somewhere?"

"Yes," I said and walked purposefully to the corner and then ran round to the stable door. I climbed up to Miki's room and he held a chair so I could clamber through a small window outside his door, across to the ledge and over to my own room.

There was a starched white cloth on a long table in the *bagghiu* and I could see several plates on it covered with table napkins to protect them from the flies. Colonel Whitlow was directly underneath me and it was as if he was shouting in my ear.

"Mussolini keeps saying he's going to wipe out the Mafia, but I haven't seen any changes."

"Give him time," his wife murmured. "He's a strong man but this is Sicily."

I heard other voices and soon they were all gathered around the table and my mother was pouring tea, while Assunta handed around the cups.

"It's all right," my mother said. "She doesn't understand enough English to follow us and Gwen has gone to the Pepoli."

They all looked so old to me as I stared down at them: white and grey heads scattered along either side of the table like driftwood and dried seaweed, and so few of them. The Robinsons had left last year, and two months later the Norton-Frazers had returned to England, and they had been permanent residents of Trapani. It was true what everyone was saying: the foreigners were buying up the old villas and the English were getting older or leaving altogether.

Canon Burnside coughed and said that he doubted if much could be accomplished until Hilda arrived. I could see my father next to my mother: every few minutes she took his hand and smiled at him and he looked at her and nodded.

"Might as well tuck into the tea instead of just waiting," Colonel Whitlow said encouragingly, and the white cloths were whisked from the plates.

Canon Burnside coughed again and said it was a sad business but something like it had happened to him three years ago when he needed new guttering. He was quite prepared to use a local man but an agent for some firm in Palermo had come to the door and asked for the job, and when he was told that he already had an agreement with local tradesmen, this Palermo fellow told him that the Trapani boys had pulled out. Of course, he knew the Mafia was behind it, but he got his guttering done at a fair price and that was all that concerned him. You had to respect local customs, he said, and spilled some tea down his shirt front. Mrs Burnside was mopping him down when Frau Brunner arrived and immediately the courtyard brimmed over in a tide of pink linen with a huge rose-smothered hat floating on top of it.

She sat down apologizing for being late and drank her tea while everyone waited for her to speak.

"He was as foxy as ever. Kept asking me who could have committed such a wanton act against a museum."

"Who indeed!" My mother was leaning over the table with her right fist clenched.

"He said that anybody could have walked into the museum, smashed all the cases and taken whatever he wanted."

"Well, wasn't that the whole idea?" Colonel Whitlow had lit his pipe and the smoke was floating past my nose like a blue streamer. "It's a show of strength on his part."

"We have never had a Sicilian servant in this house," my mother said.

"The Barone assured me that Rosalia is a jewel, and he would never have dreamed of parting with her if he had not been selling his apartment in Naples."

"I'm glad we're not the only ones who've had to retrench," Mrs Burnside murmured.

"But it's the insult to Enrico—and to me," my mother said.

"I think that was what he intended," my father said, so quietly that I had to lean forward to hear him.

"However, I have friends in Naples." Frau Brunner put her head back and smiled up as though God were among her immediate acquaintances. "And they assure me that this Rosalia is a treasure. She used to care for the Barone's two elder sisters."

"She is also Enrico's cousin—or aunt, or something or other," my mother retorted. "Can you imagine what it will be like having a relation—a Sicilian in-law—over there in the kitchen?"

"If she's decent, I don't see what you can do about it, Evelyn." Colonel Whitlow blew another plume of smoke into the air. "I mean, this is a show of superior force and all that sort of thing. Gunboat stuff. In effect, he's telling you exactly what he can do if he feels so inclined."

"You've already said that," my mother replied bitterly. "I was hoping for your support and your advice."

"Local customs," Canon Burnside said.

"My dear Evelyn, it's not so bad really." His wife was leaning across to my mother. "It's not as though this Rosalia has a bad reputation. I think you should humour the Barone and tell him you'll be delighted to accept his housekeeper."

"Who is related to my husband, Edith."

"All Sicilians are related, my dear. It's not as though you're being called upon to treat her like one of the family."

"I am concerned with Enrico's feelings."

"What do you say, old chap?" Colonel Whitlow was now blowing his smoke at my father.

"We have no choice," my father said. "The most important thing is not our feelings, our convenience, or the Barone's honour, but the museum. He has shown us his strength—if we defy him he may well destroy the whole collection."

"You think he'd go as far as that?" Colonel Whitlow sounded impressed.

"For him it has now become a question of honour."

"In that case—enough said."

"I sincerely believe we should all rejoice that this matter has been settled so satisfactorily." Canon Burnside was addressing everyone now. "Evelyn, I hope you can teach this Rosalia to make cucumber sandwiches like Assunta's. Our Sylvia measures the doorstep and then the cucumber. But you all know that, don't you?"

They began to chat among themselves and I felt as though I were reading a book with missing pages. But when I told Assunta that we were going to have a Sicilian housekeeper she said that we would all be poisoned and the *carabinieri* would have to break into the house when they smelt our bodies bloating in our beds. I think she was having her revenge on me for all the times I had frightened her, but she may well have believed it.

Twice a week my father used to get up before dawn and go down to meet the fishing boats. We ate very little meat except when Assunta bought some from the chef of the Villa, for nobody except a Sicilian would go to any of the local butchers. You could hear the throbbing buzz of flies before you saw the moving blue-black swarms dangling from hooks. Bessie and I stood amazed when we first saw the butcher smack the flies from a joint and slice off a piece of dark flesh for one of his customers. We both said we were going to be ill on the spot, but later we became accustomed to that sight and others like it.

My father always went alone to buy our fish but the day after the door and shutters had been taken down, I heard him on the stairs before it was light. I was dressed in seconds and followed him.

"Please, can I go with you? I've never seen the boats come in, father."

He hesitated and I reached out for the basket.

"I can carry the basket for you."

He smiled then and said I could go if I behaved like a lady and did not try to carry the basket on my head.

"You should still be sleeping," he said to me.

"I don't need much sleep."

"I was like that at your age. I used to study all day and work by candlelight through the night. When I could not afford candles, I used to light splinters of wood."

"Were you very poor?"

He did not answer and we walked through the dark streets to the beach. Two cats were squalling behind a wall and a dog began to bark. Furtive and trembling, the stray dogs slipped through the darkness, and I could hear them snuffling and digging in every pile of garbage. But there was no food for them. Once when I was much younger a kitten wandered into the *bagghiu* and lapped some water from the fountain. It seemed so tiny that I did not try to frighten it away. I was eating some bread and cheese under the vines and the kitten smelt the cheese and stiffened with excitement. I held out a piece to it, but no matter how I coaxed it, the kitten did not seem to see what I was holding. Assunta was watching and told me to drop the cheese on the ground. The kitten pounced and the cheese was gone. She told me that the kitten had already learned the most important lesson of a cat's life: expect nothing but blows and cruelty from a human hand. When she threw the kitten into the street I cried, but what she told me then was true: every street was full of starving animals, and starving people.

My father was a reserved man except when he was with my mother and then they talked and laughed together as if they had just met. Now I waited for him to answer.

"They said that candles cost money."

Even at that age I could sense how it hurt him to speak about his parents and I remembered Canon Burnside saying that they had wanted him to become a priest. He never really spoke about his own past and yet he made the buried past seem more real to me than the present. I came to know exactly what lay hidden beneath the landscape around me but I never understood what was buried in my father. Sometimes in winter we made trips to other museums where my father traded some of the finds from his area for Elymian artefacts, and wherever we stopped he made every rock and stream seem alive with the spirit of a god. Now as we walked along the shadowy esplanade and looked for the boats he did not mention his childhood again but instead he told me that below our feet were the bones of giant deer and the pigmy elephants that had grazed along this shore before the first Elymians made their settlement. He always spoke softly and yet his words almost made me see those prehistoric shapes in the dawn's grainy reflecting light.

"What did the Elymians look like?" I asked him.

"They were not African, and I doubt if they were Trojans escaping from the fall of Troy." He laughed a little. "We all like to think we're descended from gods or heroes. I think they were probably like me—small and dark with round heads."

I always thought of him after that as the last Elymian, and whenever I held one of their pots with its animal handle and waved patterns, I could see my father, and I wondered whether he had been the historian of his people, or the village potter. Perhaps he would have been happy to be a priest of the Elymians, for I could never imagine my father as a warrior or a king.

The sun was still not up but the horizon was now defined by a dazzling yellow line and the sea suddenly darkened to a deep purplish red. Homer's wine-dark sea was before us, and I was just about to tell my father this when I saw the men spreading out the nets. I had turned and was pointing to them when two figures of such horror rose up before me that I almost screamed. They were covered in blood and stank of blood, fresh blood and old caked blood that had soaked into their clothes and was cracking on their skin. My father greeted them and they began to speak in Sicilian.

I stood back and felt myself shivering although the air had lost its morning chill. My father turned to me. "The *mattanza* was good last night. The tunny filled the net, but there are plenty of mackerel and other fish."

The two men walked off to the *tonnara* factory and my father told me that when he was a boy he had gone out on one of the boats for the *mattanza* and watched the men gaff the tunny and drag them into the boat.

"It's a dangerous life, and sometimes they are injured by the struggling fish. I remember when I went out with them that there was so much blood from the fish on the deck that I almost slipped over the side and into the net. If they had not pulled me back I could have ended up in a tin and been served for *antipasto* in some fine restaurant."

The tunny were being carried up to the factory in sacks and the other fish had been sorted and spread out on the sand: dark blue mackerel, silvery grey squid, pink and brown octopus and flying fish—some still gasping, spreading their fins and trying to throw themselves into the air. There were other people there with baskets, a few men and two women huddled in black shawls.

The fishermen were greeting my father like an old friend as he walked among them shaking their hands and laughing. I had never seen him like this and I stood back trying to follow their Sicilian. Then something that must have been born in the sea lurched forward and threw his arms around my father. They seemed to be the same height but this man looked like some ancient crab that had grown barnacles and weed. His bare legs were twisted and scarred, his neck so thick that his head seemed to burst from his shoulders into a bloodstained cap that could have been the body of a drowned cat. They kissed and embraced each other and I guessed by the way the other men deferred to him that this must be the *rais*, the captain of the boat. My father beckoned to me, and he introduced me to Turiddu Matteo.

In awkward Italian, Turiddu said that he had sat next to my father in school, "but he was the genius, and I was the bonehead." He laughed and knocked his forehead with his fist. "The *bella signorina* must choose a fish for her own *colazione*," he said and waved across the ranks of dying fish.

My father nodded his approval as I hesitated and I stepped through the writhing squid and across two thick rays to the flying fish. One had thrown itself a little apart from the others and I picked it up. The fish was still trying to spread its fins as I walked down to the edge of the water, reached out and placed it on a receding wave.

"Gwen, what are you doing?"

That was my father speaking to me in English but I did not turn round. The fish floated for a moment and I thought it was dying but suddenly it righted itself and plunged forward. The wave turned and it flew with outstretched wings shimmering blue and iridescent green in the sunlight. It was gone.

My father was at my side. "Gwen, that was rude and foolish of you. Fish are food, and you were given that as a gift from my friend."

Turiddu was shaking his head and grinning and said something in Sicilian to my father that I could not follow, then he swung round to me and his teeth were jagged like those of a fish.

"She has made an offering to the sea and the sea will not forget. The sea has a long memory."

My father lined the basket with seaweed and placed the fish in it, covering them with more weed, and we walked home in silence. He did not ask me why I had set the flying fish free and I could not have explained had I tried, but even now I can see those dull grey fins change to shimmering wings of light above the water. After that morning I always woke in time to go down with my father to meet the fishing boats and once Turiddu gave me a piece of red coral that had been caught in the net. He told me it was a piece large enough to carve.

It surprised me when my father spoke disparagingly of Mussolini. When the English were not laughing at him—and Mr Chambers did a marvellous imitation of him—they all said he would pull Italy into the twentieth century.

"He imitates the past but he can never be anything more than a clownish parody. The memory of Garibaldi was profaned when Mussolini marched on Rome, and now that the bully boy has proclaimed himself Il Duce, the ghost of Caesar Augustus must be weeping."

As we walked through the darkness to the beach my father told me that Mussolini had come to power by means of treachery and murder: Giacomo Matteotti assassinated and the workers beaten into submission.

"Sicily has never been free, Gwen. There have always been foreign oppressors here, and the Sicilians have always cast out one invader to be conquered by another."

I knew about the great slave revolts in the second century BC when the Romans crucified thousands of rebellious slaves until the whole island was a forest of stakes hung with dying men, and the Sicilian Vespers when the towns rose against the French and all the revolutions in Palermo and Messina where the Sicilians had tried to overthrow the Spanish.

"Now we are conquered by Rome, and others will follow Rome because poverty must always have a master and poverty will always try to rebel."

He told me about Marx and Lenin and said that when I was older he would give me *Das Kapital* to read. I was beginning to understand why he had called the Barone di Marineo and his friends "parasites," because they owned the great estates, the *latifundia*, where the peasants worked like serfs.

"There will never be prosperity here while Mussolini supports the aristocracy. The parasites feed on the land and the bodies of the peasants, and they will never permit industry to flourish here. With industry you have unions and men who can think for themselves. But the Communist Party is growing no matter how Mussolini's blackshirts try to crush it."

"Why don't the people revolt?"

My father laughed sourly. "To revolt, you must first combine, and the Sicilian trusts no one because he has always been betrayed. The Sicilian has only his family and the family is his prison."

There was a great deal that I did not understand or even hear because I was more intent on trying to discover my father. While he was speaking of Matteotti and Gramsci I was searching for his past as I had learned to do with the landscape around me. I asked him when he had first studied politics and he said it was when he was starving. The thought that my father had once lacked food was so horrifying to me that I did not ask him any more. I also guessed that his friends the fishermen belonged to a part of his life that I knew nothing about. After we had walked some distance along the beach he spoke about Turiddu Matteo.

"He is a hero—a triton."

I laughed because the triton in the *bagghiu* now seemed like a toy frozen in crumbling stone to me.

"When you hear the surf against the cliffs remember that Turiddu is probably at sea trying to ride out the storm. And remember too why this *tonnara* is one of the few prosperous tunny factories in Sicily."

"Because of his bravery?"

"Because he made the fishermen cooperate."

"Was that so difficult?"

"If you were Sicilian, Gwen, you would say that it is impossible. Only a man like Turiddu Matteo has the strength to make them work together." He paused and said, almost as an afterthought, "After the bombing he had them in his hand."

This time I did not have to ask, or wait for him to continue. I could hear the excitement in his voice.

"Eight years ago the fishing was being ruined here because one of the fishermen was dropping grenades into the water. Turiddu called the men together, but no one knew who it was although everyone suspected it was Rosario Urzi. Then another began using grenades and soon the sea was floating with dead fish, but the next season it was empty when they put down their nets. One night the nets were dropped and they felt a weight dragging against the mesh. They pulled in the head of Rosario Urzi. There was never any bombing again and the fishermen here now have a cooperative."

"Turiddu cut off the man's head?"

"That is a question no one asked—and neither should you."

"Why must we take this Rosalia as our housekeeper?"

My father seemed surprised that I should have made this abrupt association. He paused and I could see him hunch his shoulders in the way that he did when he was worried.

"They say she is a good servant."

"Would you like to cut off the Barone's head, father?"

I expected him to laugh but instead he said almost to himself, "I am not Turiddu Matteo. I am not a hero."

Assunta left early in the morning three weeks before Christmas, and my mother told me that Rosalia would be arriving before evening. I knew that I was going to miss Assunta but whenever I began to cry I thought about Rosalia and the expectation of meeting this relation of my father filled my mind with curiosity. Assunta's last words to me were to get a cat or a dog and before every meal give it some of the food Rosalia had cooked for us, because she would assuredly try to poison us and steal all the valuables from the house while we lay dying. Miki followed the cart that was carrying Assunta's baggage until she waved and shouted to him to go back, and later I found him in a corner of the kitchen weeping into one of her old aprons.

My mother sat down in front of me with her hands clasped and with her thumbs twisting round in circles as though she could not keep them still.

"Gwen, I never objected to your associating with Assunta because she was Italian and quite trustworthy. But this woman is Sicilian and we must keep her at a distance. If she once—if she ever dares to presume on her relationship with your father, you must put her down immediately."

"You don't think she'll try to poison us, do you, mother?"

She smiled only slightly and said that she was more afraid of presumption than poison.

Bessie had just written to me about her new school in Cheshire and I asked my mother when I could go to England to study.

"You're receiving a perfectly good education here," she said abruptly.

"I'm not. Bessie's learning heaps of things that I know nothing about."

"You are going to be a classical scholar."

"What if I don't want to be a classical scholar?"

She was about to answer when Miki brought in the letters and she told me not to bother her with any more questions.

"There's nothing here from Bessie," she said sharply, dismissing me, and began opening her letters.

"Everyone is going back to England except us, mother. You say I'm English, well, how can I ever be English when I've never seen my own country?"

I must have said this a hundred times to her and no matter what her response was; lack of money and the fact that I was being taught by two fine scholars, the real reason was that she expected me to look after my father if anything should ever happen to her. Yet every letter from Bessie seemed to be stamped in a country that was becoming stranger to me every year.

"People say it's wrong for someone of my age to spend so much time with old people," I cried desperately.

"Don't be so melodramatic, and you can tell your well-meaning friends to keep their psychological nonsense to themselves."

She continued to open her letters. What, I wondered, could possibly happen to my mother when she was younger and so much stronger than my father? The thought of losing him and being left alone with her filled me with dread.

We heard a cart rattling in the street outside and Miki ran through to the stable door as my mother slowly read a letter from her solicitor. I saw her frown and then she began to shake. I was about to follow Miki when I stopped and asked her if anything was wrong.

"My mother died three weeks ago," she said in a stifled voice. "My sister did not write—no one told me. They let the solicitor inform me."

She stood up abruptly and said she was going upstairs to her room and that I should greet Rosalia.

Four

My mother should have been there to meet Rosalia. That was what she intended, only just as the carter was asking Miki to help him with a box, I heard her walk slowly up the stairs, stumbling once, and then her bedroom door was closed. I knew that my father was at a meeting of antiquarians at the Pepoli, and I could not send for him, so it was in that moment of indecision, of wondering whether I should help my mother or go across to the kitchen and greet Rosalia, that the little dark woman stepped down between Assunta's potted herbs and took possession of the house.

"You are Gina," she said and smiled.

"My name is Gwen Harcourt di Marineo," I replied and knew that I had reddened because no one had ever translated my English Gwen into an Italian Gina. Without bothering to conceal my anger I said that I was sorry my mother was not here but she had just received word that her mother was dead.

Rosalia bowed her head and made the sign of the cross. Out of the corner of my eye I saw Miki peering round the kitchen door, his features contracted into an expression of terror. He pointed to Rosalia and made the *mano cornuta*, the sign of horns, with his fingers.

Did Rosalia have the evil eye? In that instant of my looking away from her she suddenly appeared servile, and to have actually grown smaller.

"Ah, your poor mother," she said, "I must take her some tea at once. Only tea can help the English when they suffer such a loss."

I did not know whether she was laughing at me and I frowned and told her I thought that was a good idea. At least she could speak Italian, but I was accustomed to being addressed as the *signorina*, not by a variation of my first name. It was just as my mother had feared. This woman was going to take liberties because she was related to my father.

When my mother did not answer my knock, I opened the door and went into her bedroom. It was always a strange room to me because I had so seldom been inside it and on every occasion when I was there I had the sensation of being in someone else's house. My mother was sitting at a small desk by the window with a box of photographs spread out in front of her. I asked if I could do anything to help but when I tried to touch her on the arm she flinched so I sat down opposite her.

"Rosalia's here," I said awkwardly.

"I disappointed my mother, and she disappointed me."

I did not know how to answer and remained silent as she sorted the photographs aimlessly.

"I had a right to marry, just as she had. But she wouldn't even meet Enrico."

She was now sorting the photographs into little piles but I could not see any order to them.

"Eleanor was allowed to marry, and what kind of a marriage was that? The family was Australian and there was money, but no breeding. Jumped-up shopkeepers the lot of them. Probably descended from convicts. My mother could have stopped her marrying, but she did nothing and overnight the house was swarming with Australian Wigrams."

"Everybody likes my father," I said quietly. "Even the fishermen."

She was not listening to me and began to shuffle the photographs from pile to pile. I could see my grandmother among them with her two daughters, Eleanor and my mother. There were several pictures of my uncles, George and Michael, who had died at sea in the War. All the photographs were a faded sepia and some were cracked. I knew I had two cousins, Edith and Frederick, but I could not see any pictures of them.

Rosalia had entered the room so quietly that neither of us heard her, and to my astonishment she spoke English as she gently placed a tray of tea in front of my mother.

"The *bella Signora* has suffered a blow to the heart." She asked permission to pour the tea and when my mother nodded Rosalia took charge of the table as though she were the mistress of the house. It was when my mother reached out to take the cup that I noticed her right hand was trembling. Rosalia saw it too and carefully placed the cup on the desk in front of her. My mother raised it to her lips with both hands but she seemed to have difficulty swallowing.

"Your mother should rest now," Rosalia said and went over to turn down the bed. "Later I shall bring the *bella Signora* up a little soup and soft bread."

Again my mother did not seem to hear her and Rosalia bustled with the bedcovers. I was ignored by both of them so I trailed off downstairs to the kitchen. Miki was crouched in a corner and when he saw me he covered his head as though in fright, pointed upstairs and made the sign of horns again.

"I don't believe in the evil eye, Miki."

Miki nodded furiously and performed a pantomime of bringing the letters to my mother, and followed that with the way she had opened one and frowned. Miki's imitations of all us were sometimes like seeing ourselves in a looking glass, and this was my mother, the tightening of her mouth and then the trembling.

"Rosalia didn't kill my grandmother," I laughed.

Miki was still for a moment and then he suddenly clutched himself between the legs and pointed to me. I was horrified until he made the *mano cornuta* again, and I realized that this was another way to ward off the evil eye. Reaching down into his shirt he pulled up a cord with a gold horn and a large piece of garlic tied to it. I shook my head and smiled for, as I had just decided to tell Bessie in my next letter, Rosalia was a pushy old witch who obviously thought she had the right to take over the house, and it would be my job to put her in her place.

If there was any witchcraft Rosalia used it in her cleaning. She never appeared to hurry but everything was polished so brightly that the whole house soon seemed full of mirrors, even the staircase captured broken reflections of my skirt when I went up and down, and there was a ghostly image of myself in my old cherry wardrobe. Every time Rosalia saw my father she curtseyed and her tone was so obsequious that I could see it was beginning to irritate him too.

My mother remained in bed for the next three days and when Dr Polcari examined her he said it was simply a case of nervous exhaustion and she must rest. The shock of hearing about her mother's death had been too much for her nervous system. Rosalia was in and out of her room all the time carrying trays and sponging her but when I went in to see my mother she did not mention her family or Russell Morton again except to say that her income would remain exactly the same.

"I knew my mother would cut me out of her will, but she could never touch my own inheritance. That is mine as long as I live."

"Perhaps if you went back and saw your family, when you felt better I mean, there would be a reconciliation, Mother." I wanted to add, "Please take me with you when you go."

"I went back once," she said sharply, and I saw how the trembling in her hand was a constant fluttering now. "Gwen, I'm sure there's work for you to do downstairs. Send Rosalia to me."

"Are you satisfied with Rosalia?" I asked.

My mother seemed surprised.

"We should always be guided by Hilda Brunner in these domestic affairs. Hilda said the woman was a jewel and she is."

I was beginning to sense my parents' mortality and felt that only Bessie would understand my fears. What would become of me if my mother died and then something happened to my father? I could contemplate my mother's death without pain, but I loved my father, and the long walks down to the fishing boats had made me feel that he now saw me as his daughter. The knowledge that at heart he was a revolutionary amazed me, and his friendship with Turiddu Matteo and the other fishermen revealed something to me about him that I had never imagined before. But how could I ask him what would happen to me when he was dead? It was only to Bessie that I could speak of what terrified me: where would I be and what would I do if my parents died?

When my mother was ill my father seldom left her alone and I opened the museum on Tuesday and Thursday afternoons and showed three Germans and a Swedish couple around the collection. They asked stupid questions and wanted to know if the Elymians were Africans and cannibals. I explained that the Elymians were an indigenous people who were later absorbed by the Greeks and the Phoenicians. The Swedish man offered me a tip and I gave it back to him.

For almost a week I had been looking for the piece of coral that Turiddu had given me. Because I knew it was valuable I had placed it in the cupboard where the Phlyax vases were kept. Now it was gone, and I suspected that Rosalia had stolen it. Before I accused her I decided to ask Miki about it and he waved his hands and grinned, pointing to himself.

"Do you have it, Miki?"

He nodded and when I asked him why, he circled his fingers as a sign that I should wait.

"It was a gift to me from Turiddu Matteo, and I'd hate to lose it."

Miki pointed to the clock and turned around twice.

"All right, two days, but I want it back."

My mother had a slight limp when she eventually made her way downstairs to the *bagghiu* where my father had filled a chair with cushions for her. From my bedroom I heard him talking about a trip to a specialist in Palermo but my mother said she was feeling better every day and time would cure the shock of hearing about her mother's death. I knew that people died of grief, but was it possible to die for someone you did not love? My mother had never once spoken of her own mother with affection, and more than once I heard her say, as much to herself as to me, that she had always done her duty as a daughter, writing every week and never forgetting birthdays or Christmas.

My parents would sit together for hours under the grapevine, sometimes talking, more often silent, and once I saw something that made me so angry I wanted to shout at them to stop and behave like ordinary people. My father was kneeling beside my mother with his head in her lap as she stroked his hair. I could feel the blood throbbing in my face and I was about to walk out from the shadows of the curator's room and confront them when I felt a hand on my elbow and Rosalia pulled me back. Without a word she turned me round and pushed me back into the museum.

Somewhere Rosalia had learned to make a few English dishes so we had blancmange and rice pudding for dessert and my mother said we should really have a dinner party because she was feeling just like her old self again. Rosalia was never still, and even when she was waiting to receive instructions from my mother she was polishing silver or crocheting. I was not sure whether it was crochet, but she used tiny scraps of ribbon and material and wound them round her thumb with a long needle: a twist and a flat knot was made to which she added another so that it became a circle or any other kind of shape.

She saw me watching her and smiled.

"English hands cannot do this."

"English hands haven't tried," I replied sharply because I detested Rosalia and told Bessie in my next letter that she was a slyboots.

"Not even Sicilians can do this."

"Really?"

I pretended indifference.

"It is a craft of the old Saracens and now I am the only woman in Sicily who knows the secret. When I am dead the art will be buried with me."

I watched her closely and that night I practised in my room with a length of hair ribbon, but the loops slipped from my thumb and when I thought I had made a knot it pulled apart.

Miki whistled from his room and signalled for me to crawl over to his window. He was crouched on the ledge like a grizzled monkey. I climbed over quietly and he helped me through and on to the landing. On the other side there was a small round window through which you could see the street. Rosalia was down there with two women. She had a book in her hand and from this distance I could not see what it was, but the women were talking and Rosalia turned the pages and spoke. They gave her some money and Rosalia came back into the house.

"What was she doing?" I asked Miki.

He closed his eyes as if he were sleeping then kicked and twitched and fluttered his eyelids.

"Dreaming?"

He wet his finger and drew numbers on the wall.

"Rosalia tells fortunes!"

Miki nodded furiously and I laughed. So Rosalia was nothing but a *smorfiatora*, an old woman who interpreted people's dreams by numbers so they could win a prize in the lottery. My mother used to say that a Sicilian would buy a lottery ticket before he bought food. Rosalia had obviously picked up some English when she was working for the Barone's two sisters in Naples, and she knew how to cook and clean. But at heart she was as superstitious as all the Sicilians who thought every dream had a meaning and that meaning could tell you the numbers to pick in the lottery. I even found the book she used between the kitchen dresser and the wall, and I laughed as I read it. Dreaming of a black pig meant the number eight, a wedding was nineteen and a hearse was seven. One morning I told her that I had dreamed of an old woman who put her head in a bucket and drowned and should I go and buy a ticket in the lottery?

"It's foolish to dream when you are awake," she said and went on scrubbing the red tiled floor until it glittered.

But no matter how I watched her I could not make that looping double knot over my thumb. Every night I tried and during the day I pretended not to notice how deftly Rosalia produced a flat, dense fabric. Once I thought I had almost succeeded but there was a loose end sticking out like a bristle: Rosalia's knot concealed it and her weaving was so tight that all the different coloured threads were bound together.

When we next went down to the beach to meet the fishermen I asked my father about the evil eye and he told me it was an ancient superstition known to the Greeks and the Egyptians. No one with any sense believed such rubbish now, but when reality was too oppressive people took refuge in magic. Sometimes, he said, the water around the fishing boats was blood red as the men washed down the decks and occasionally an old woman would come down alone or with a child and bathe fully clothed in the bloody water as a cure for some sickness. I had seen this and thought the women were simply looking for scraps of fish. My father said that when he was a boy there would often be a dozen or more women, some of them with children, and a few old men too.

"It is a most interesting custom and Canon Burnside is planning to write an article about it one day. Undoubtedly, it is derived from a literal acceptance of Christian doctrine in which the blood of Christ represents salvation. As you know, Gwen, the fish was one of the earliest symbols of Christian art, because the letters of the Greek *ichthys* were taken as an acrostic for *Ieosus Christos Theou Hyios Soter*, Jesus Christ, of the God the

Son, Saviour. Remember always what your mother says; look behind the customs of the people and you will find the buried past."

He paused and shook his head. "Ah, the poor—if you cannot afford doctors and medicine you make do with magic and superstition."

While my father was choosing our fish and covering them with wet seaweed I stared at Turiddu's boat: it was painted black but on either side of the prow there was a brilliant blue and white eye.

"Is Turiddu superstitious?" I asked my father.

"No, but his men are and if he did not have St Lucia's eyes on his ship to help find the tunny, they would not be happy to sail with him."

My father was more silent than usual that morning and I knew he was worrying about my mother. She laughed about her "problem," as she called it, but the trembling never stopped and I could see that she was dragging her foot as though it did not belong to her.

I asked my father if he would answer a very difficult question for me. He laughed a little and said he hoped it wasn't politics because I never listened when he discussed that.

"It's not politics. What—what will become of me if anything happens to you and mother?"

My father did not seem surprised and looked up at me, smiling. "My dear child, you will go back to your family in England, and I hope they appreciate what a fine scholar you have become."

I felt exactly as I did when I was a little girl pretending to be dead and Bessie dug me out of my grave of wet sand.

"Did you ever go to Russell Morton, father?"

"No, they would not accept a Sicilian Catholic—even one who does not believe in the Church or its teachings. But you are a Protestant, christened by Canon Burnside—"

"He said he'd confirm me on my fourteenth birthday."

"So you see—you belong at Russell Morton."

Everything seemed very clear to me then. It was only because of my mother's great love for my father that I was being kept here in Trapani, but my real home was in England with Bessie. Her letters were now full of news about her uncle's wedding and how she was to be a bridesmaid. Nancy's father was a Canadian widower, so the wedding reception was being held in Manchester with an orchestra and a banquet for one hundred and seventy guests. I told Bessie about my plans to get rid of Rosalia and how I proposed to get Frau Brunner to help me.

Miki was as watchful of Rosalia as I was and that morning I gathered from him that she had been out in the street again, telling fortunes. I decided to tell my mother but when I had finished my story, she simply sighed and told me that I must be more tolerant and never to forget what Canon Burnside said about local customs. Fortune-telling to a Sicilian, my mother said, was like black cats and not walking under ladders to the English working class.

I came downstairs feeling betrayed and Miki beckoned to me from the museum. He took my hand and pressed something into it. At first I did not recognize it, but it was my coral carved into a horn with a gold crown: a talisman to protect me from Rosalia and the evil eye. Miki nodded towards the kitchen and made the *mano cornuta*. I thanked him for his gift and told him that I would always wear it—as I have to this day.

It was exactly six weeks before Bessie and her parents were due to arrive. We were at Canon Burnside's for Sunday service and just as we were all having tea, Mrs Burnside suddenly got up and said, "My dear, you must hurry. Evensong—it's time for Evensong," and she started to walk down the steps to the garden.

Mrs Whitlow hurried after her and brought her back to the house, murmuring to her. Canon Burnside was flustered and said that Maud was beginning to wander—in mind and body. Last week he had found her in the piazza trying to find her way to the lending library in Deepdene.

Frau Brunner was sighing and staring at Mrs Burnside when I sat down beside her and told her that Rosalia was a sneak and a fortune-teller, and I really didn't think she was a good housekeeper. Before I had finished she was scowling and said it was not my place to complain, and I should be grateful we had found such a good servant. She wished that her staff at the Villa d'Athena were all so honest and reliable. As for fortune-telling, that was just a local custom and it was like other people collecting shells or butterflies. She paused and said slowly, "Do not upset Rosalia. She has important friends."

I knew Frau Brunner was referring to the Barone, but before I could answer she had got up and was speaking to Mrs Burnside, who was laughing nervously into her handkerchief.

"I really don't know what comes over me. I suppose it's old age and there's no cure for that, is there."

The day Bessie arrived I was waiting on the terrace of the Villa for her, and I could see she was full of secrets. We hugged and kissed and cried and Mr Chambers said that if we didn't calm down he'd throw us in the nearest fountain.

I spent the next two nights with her at the Villa and the third day she came home with me on the painted Sicilian cart that Frau Brunner used to bring baggage and an occasional guest from the station in Trapani. Miki sat next to Benno Sciafa and went "Stt" between his teeth and frowned every time Benno spoke to us. My mother used to laugh at Benno and said he looked like the tenor in a provincial production of *Cavalleria Rusticana*, but we admired his black cloak and embroidered waistcoat and his smouldering glances through half-shut eyes always made us giggle. Bessie said that Benno was just like Ramon Novarro and when I asked her who Novarro was she screamed with laughter and even Benno looked over his shoulder and laughed with us. He took us to the corner of the street and I saw Rosalia waiting at the door for us with folded hands and a black shawl over her head.

"She's worse than Assunta," I muttered.

When we were in my room I rattled the bolt fast on my door and Bessie showed me a white leather-covered book full of photographs of the wedding, with a hand-coloured one of Travis and Nancy in the front.

"She's tall and very thin, like you, but you'd never guess that when she's dressed. Everyone said her bridal gown was daring because it barely touched her knees but I thought it was fabulous. I'm going to have one exactly like it when I'm married."

Bessie named everyone in the photos for me, and I said she looked like an English princess in her flounced lace dress. Her Uncle Travis was very handsome and Nancy's father was a tall, grim man with a moustache, who refused to smile for the photographer.

"He's a millionaire," Bessie said, "and he has mines and things like that in Canada. He gave all the bridesmaids a bracelet."

Bessie held out her wrist and showed me a gold link bracelet with a heart attached to it.

"There's something for you, Demeter," she said and I saw a brown parcel in her suitcase.

"For me? But I don't know any of these people."

"It's not a real present," Bessie said carefully. "It's something I saved for you. I didn't buy it, or anything like that. It's something that Nancy didn't want."

"What is it?"

"Open it."

Bessie dropped the parcel into my lap and I slowly unfolded the paper. Inside was a pale blue cotton dress with a handkerchief-pleated skirt that fell in points. I had never seen anything quite so beautiful, but I could also tell that it was brand new. I looked at Bessie and there were tendrils of scarlet climbing up her throat.

"Nancy didn't want it, Demeter. She said so."

"Why?"

"Because—" Her tone was elaborately offhand and I knew she was lying

—"Because it's meant to have a dark blue scarf under the collar, and well—the scarf was lost. Everyone looked for it but Nancy said she couldn't wear it without the scarf so she threw the whole dress away."

"Persephone—"

"It wasn't stealing, Demeter. Not really stealing. She had heaps and heaps of clothes in her trousseau, and she'll never miss it. And I wanted you to have something."

I really felt as if my heart were going to burst and then her arms were round me and she was crying.

"It's not fair that you should never have anything nice!"

"I can't keep it if it's stolen," I said.

"Oh yes, you can," she shouted. "I wanted you to be at the wedding so badly." She paused and I knew she had another secret. "They're fighting all the time now."

"Your parents?"

"People aren't buying lace curtains. They're not in fashion anymore. My mother said we might not be able to have any more holidays."

"You mean—you might not come back next year?"

I could barely speak I was so frightened.

"That's what my mother said—but father said he'd come here for the summer if he had to pawn the silver. He knows about us, Demeter, and he likes you so much."

I knew this was true and my dread began to subside a little.

"Nothing will ever separate us," Bessie said.

She saw the coral horn around my neck when I was trying on her aunt's dress and I told her about Rosalia and her fortune-telling.

"Would she tell ours?" Bessie asked breathlessly.

"I don't think I'd care to ask her," I retorted stiffly.

What I wanted to say was that I felt as though Rosalia was beginning to fill every corner of the house and suffocating me. I could tell my father did not like her, but even he had to praise her cooking. As for my mother, she kept saying we had found a jewel, as if she had forgotten how Rosalia had been forced on us by the Barone.

Rosalia made an enormous fuss of Bessie that evening, touching her hair and saying it was like Greek gold. I could see that Bessie was fascinated by the prying old woman, so I was deliberately rude to her, but Rosalia seemed deaf to everything I said and after dinner, when my parents had gone upstairs and we were sitting by the fountain, she brought out a bandeau of green and white ribbon for Bessie. Before I could stop her Bessie had pulled it over her hair and was admiring herself in the fountain.

"Remember what happened to Narcissus," I said.

Rosalia began to show her how she knotted the ribbons and before she finished I said that anybody could crochet like that. I snatched the needle and thread from her hand and made a double loop, pulled it tight and then made another.

"You see," I said, "it's nothing. A child could do it, so please don't tell my friend all this rubbish about lost Saracen arts."

I half expected Rosalia to be angry but instead she stared at me and then she smiled.

"You have the hands of your family. There is Saracen blood in the di Marineos."

"Perhaps that's where you got your black hair, Demeter," Bessie said and I could have shrieked with rage.

"Could you tell our fortunes?" Bessie asked Rosalia. I stood up abruptly.

"I don't believe in fortune-telling. They used to burn witches in the olden days."

"Don't be such a spoilsport, Demeter. It's only fun, isn't it, Rosalia. All the girls at school read their stars every day. I'm a Cancer with a Taurus ascendant."

"*Destino* is not always pleasant," Rosalia said drily.

"But you'll tell our fortunes, won't you?"

"This evening I am busy. Perhaps another time," and she began to clear the dishes from the table.

"Should we help?" Bessie whispered.

"No, she's a servant," I said loudly enough for her to hear.

Even Frau Brunner came out to admire my new dress when I wore it at the Villa next day and I was careful to dust my chair on the terrace before I sat down. Mrs Chambers told Bessie to fetch her a cardigan and pulled her chair next to mine.

"Gwen, I've seen your mother, and I'm desperately sorry, dear."

I said she was feeling much better and Mrs Chambers looked at me sharply.

"My dear, people don't recover from a stroke. Believe me, I was a nurse and I know. If you have one stroke, it's generally followed by another, and then you pray that you're not left totally paralysed."

I stared at her uncomprehending.

"Now dear, I want you to remember this, so pay attention."

I could not have moved or taken my eyes from her face had I tried.

"If anything happens to your mother, and I'm not saying it will, but one must be prepared, you must come to us."

"To you—and Bessie?"

"And live with us. I don't know what other family you have in England but we can sort all that out when you're with us. Heaven knows, I've often thought of you with those two old people in that museum and worried myself sick about you."

I sat there feeling a tide of quiet joy sweep over me and I knew I was blushing. Mrs Chambers seemed concerned that she might have offended me, but I was only thinking how beautiful Bessie's mother was with her light red hair and bright blue eyes.

"I always wished you were my mother," I blurted out.

"I know, dear. I know," and she leaned forward and kissed me on the cheek.

The four of us played tennis on the courts at the Villa that afternoon and two Frenchwomen stopped to look at us and pointed up to the sky with their sunshades. "*Les Anglais*!" they said and shook their heads.

"English sweat," Mr Chambers said, mopping his face, "Foreigners stink." And Bessie and I almost collapsed laughing because I think the Frenchwomen heard him.

Mrs Chambers had partnered me and when we won she danced up to the net and told Mr Chambers that he should take lessons in winning. I knew he was hurt because he laughed in an odd way and said that playing the game was more important than winning. Bessie looked at me with raised eyebrows and her mouth pulled down, yet even though I tried to seem sympathetic I felt that her parents were more like real people than my own. It was awkward when they snapped at each other in front of us, but we were not embarrassed by them and I felt strangely comforted when Bessie squeezed my hand and said that she would never speak to her husband like that when she was married.

Late in the afternoon we all went swimming and as we walked along the beach I told them about the fishing boats and the old women who came down to bathe in blood.

"Ghastly! How horrible!" Bessie cried and ran ahead waving her hands.

Mrs Chambers followed her, laughing, and I was left with Bessie's father. Usually he was full of jokes but he was as quiet as my father now as we walked between the ridges of bleached white seaweed watching the gulls wheeling and turning over our heads.

"You are going to come back next year, aren't you?" I asked him.

"Wild horses wouldn't keep me away," he said. "Did you know my parents owned a villa up there?"

I shook my head.

"I often walk round and look at the garden. It's owned by a Swiss family now. I must say everything looks tidier than the way I remembered it. I often tell myself I should walk up to the front door, introduce myself and ask to look around inside the house, but I never do. It's probably full of cuckoo clocks."

"All the English seem to be leaving Trapani."

"Just a few of us left to show the flag. You win a war and people like those fat Swiss walk off with the prize. We should be top of the heap now but—there are too many foreigners in the world, Gwen."

I laughed with him and he stood looking up to the mountains and Erice.

"Whenever I come back here I feel—I feel like myself."

We walked on. Mrs Chambers and Bessie were now trying to balance on a pile of seaweed.

"Times will change—you get these slumps in the market. Lace fabrics will come back into fashion."

He took my arm and pulled it through his.

"You're a good listener, Gwen."

"Bessie's my best friend," I said lamely.

"I had some good friends—lost them in the War. Still, remember Harry Lauder?" He began to sing, "Keep right on to the end of the road, keep right on to the end . . ."

Bessie and I passed our time between the Villa and the museum. Whenever Rosalia saw Bessie she would begin to fawn and say that we must have taken the oath of San Giovanni which made us closer than sisters. No matter what I said, Bessie kept asking Rosalia to tell our fortunes, and Rosalia kept saying "*Domani*," or that she was too busy.

"She won't tell us, because she can't," I told Bessie.

"Miki thinks she has the evil eye, you said so, Demeter."

"Miki is an old, old man. Of course, he's superstitious. He's not educated like us."

"I think it would be fun and I don't see why you're so nasty to her all the time."

"She's trying to take over."

Bessie shrugged and said she'd love to know her future. When I asked her why, she said it was because she knew it was full of wonderful things and expecting something nice was almost as good as having it.

We had walked from the museum to the Villa and were just climbing the steps to the terrace. There was a current of irritability between us and I knew it was because of Rosalia.

"If you asked her, Demeter, I know she'd do it for us."

How could I refuse my friend? I was mumbling something about asking her the next day when we both heard a voice and looked up. Standing on the steps above us was a boy in a cream suit with a flowing lilac cravat and a wide panama hat on the side of his yellow hair.

"Hello there. Are you two gels guests of the Villa?"

I could feel myself gaping because the boy's accent was so absurd. He was trying to imitate an Oxford accent, and we both looked at each other and giggled.

"Don't know what's so dem funny about it, you gels." He struck an attitude and showed us his profile. "I am the English Lord Marchmont."

At this we howled and I had to sit down on the side of the steps.

"Excuse me, please, a moment—"

We could not believe what we were seeing. The boy slowly unbuttoned his fly, turned sideways and we watched a golden arc rise in the sunshine and splash into the fountain.

Five

Bessie gasped and covered her eyes as the boy gracefully piddled into the fountain.

"You—you disgusting beast!" she screeched. "I'm going to tell Frau Brunner about you! She'll have you arrested!"

The boy began to laugh as Bessie flew up the stairs, screaming Frau Brunner's name at the top of her voice. He fastened his buttons without looking and called after her, "My mother won't believe you. She'll think I did something much worse to you."

Bessie was on the next terrace and when she heard that, she looked over her shoulder at him in disbelief and almost tripped and fell backwards. She steadied herself, screamed again and ran up the next flight of steps, followed by his jeering laughter. Without thinking, I threw myself on top of the yellow-haired boy and pushed him into the fountain. I was sitting on his chest trying to force his head under the water and yelling at him when Frau Brunner thumped down the steps and pulled me back by my hair.

"You wretched girl! Stop it! Stop it! You'll kill him!"

I was suddenly ashamed of behaving like a child and I tried to apologize, but Frau Brunner had the boy in her arms and was cradling him like a baby.

"*Armer kleiner Teufel*," she said over and over again and Bessie looked at me bemused.

"I told her, Gwen. I told her exactly what he did."

The boy had his face against Frau Brunner's shoulder and as she rocked him he reached up and stroked her face with the back of his hand. His face was impassive and although his eyes were half open he seemed to be asleep.

Bessie was beginning to lose her temper and she stamped her foot. "I told you what he did, Frau Brunner, and I don't see why you should be making such a fuss over him. I think I'd better speak to my father and he'll give that—that pervert the hiding of his life."

Frau Brunner rocked the boy back and forth and we could see that she was crying. "Bessie, please, I beg you, don't tell anyone about him. Everybody knows enough bad things about him already. He cannot help it—it is his father in him."

My Persephone was about to walk away, but she was also inquisitive and with a little shrug, as though it was more important to humour Frau Brunner than to punish the boy, she turned back and stood beside me.

"His father was a terrible man—a pervert—yes, that is the right word to use, and this poor child takes after him."

"He can't go round weeing in public whenever he feels like it," Bessie said frowning. "He only did it because we laughed at him."

"He has done worse, Bessie, much, much worse. But it is not his fault, you must believe me. If you were both older I would tell you what I had to endure from his father. The shame and the pain of it all killed my poor parents. I married a Sicilian and he was the devil incarnate."

The boy's lips were parted and he now looked as if he were fast asleep except for the stroking of his mother's cheek.

"He will try to be good, I promise you. Dolfi!" She shook the boy gently and her voice was brokenly husky. "Dolfi, promise me you will be good."

The boy sighed and smiled and Frau Brunner got up slowly, almost lifting him to his feet. Her arm was still around him and he rested his head against her shoulder.

"Dolfi will be a good boy, I promise you, and he will take you both to afternoon tea where he will behave like a perfect little gentleman, won't you, Dolfi?"

The boy yawned languidly and the two went up towards the Villa. We gaped after them.

"You told me her son was a Jesuit," I said to Bessie.

"Everybody said he was."

"He's our age. He couldn't possibly be a Jesuit."

"Perhaps she has another son."

We considered the likelihood of this and then abandoned it.

"I think we should refuse Frau Brunner's invitation," I said firmly, but Bessie was shaking her head.

"We'll go and give him the shrieking bird. We'll talk to each other and ignore him no matter what he says to us."

I could see that curiosity was getting the better of Bessie and, no matter how I invoked every principle of decorum and dignity, she insisted that we would never find out about his being a Jesuit unless we had afternoon tea with him.

Usually, Bessie and I went around to the side terrace and one of the maids brought tea to us there on a tray, but this afternoon there was a table set for us with all the grown-up guests under one of the orange umbrellas on the main terrace. We sat down and prepared to be haughty, waiting for Dolfi who finally appeared in a pale blue suit with his yellow hair in damp curls on his forehead. Our resolve to snub him did not have its desired effect because no matter how brilliantly we chatted about the Manchester wedding in particular and film stars in general, he drank and ate in moody silence, staring down the hill to the town and the sea. We looked from each other to him and I could see Bessie's expression changing. Suddenly she leaned towards him and asked him pointblank if he was a Jesuit.

Dolfi did not answer immediately, drinking slowly and putting down the cup as though abstracted by a problem that reduced everything apart from his own thoughts to a trivial irrelevance. Our plan was to cut him dead but he had made us talk in spite of our determination to ignore him.

Bessie was beginning to turn scarlet and I asked him quietly if he would like me to punch him again. At this he laughed and said I was a savage.

"But you're half Sicilian too, so naturally you have a taste for murder."

I was speechless and could not answer him.

"My friend was only trying to protect me," Bessie retorted.

"From what? I didn't put my prick anywhere near you."

Bessie almost choked, spluttering a mouthful of tea, and I kicked her under the table.

"People say you're a Jesuit." Bessie recovered quickly, not permitting him to shock her, and pointedly ignored his comment.

"I have just been expelled from a Jesuit college in Rome. They said I would spread corruption through the whole Society of Jesus if I stayed there."

"How old are you?" I asked him.

"I'm the same age as you—sixteen."

I didn't tell him I was almost two years younger.

"I don't see how you could corrupt the Jesuits," Bessie said. "Everyone knows they're the most wicked and depraved of all the priests."

Dolfi shrugged and said he was acquainted with most of the orders and the Jesuits were no worse than the Dominicans and the Augustinians.

"Why did you go to a Catholic school?" I asked because I knew Frau Brunner was Protestant.

"Because when I was ten the Protestants said I was uncontrollable."

"What—what did you do?" Bessie whispered.

Dolfi smiled at her, and I felt a tiny shiver run through my body because I had once seen the same delighted ferocity on the faces of a group of boys who were torturing a dog in a doorway near the museum. Assunta tried to hurry me past them but I ran across to see what they were doing. The most terrible thing had been that the dog was whimpering and trying to lick the hands of the boy who had the knife. Miki kicked the boys and freed the dog, but Assunta said it would be best to kill it quickly. She covered my face and took me round the corner of the street and I never saw what Miki did. Now, Dolfi was smiling at Bessie, and I realized that in spite of the watchful cruelty in his face, he was extraordinarily handsome. Not handsome like Benno Sciafa, who combed his hair every five minutes and wore perfume. This boy glowed as the sunlight cast an aureole around his head and made his dark blue eyes flash and burn. Even his skin was ardent with a light that caused a vein at his wrist to pulse like a gold spring.

There were people at the other tables who were admiring him too and one fat man by a marble baluster adjusted his chair and grimaced as he squinted through a monocle. A plump German woman stopped in front of us and said in frightful Italian that she had never seen so much beauty at one small table, but she got the nouns in the wrong order and I laughed. Dolfi was still gazing at Bessie and I could see the two bright patches of scarlet in her cheeks and how quickly she was breathing.

"Blasphemy," Dolfi said softly and Bessie hesitated as if she were afraid to ask another question.

His English was so poor that I wondered if he understood what he was saying, so I translated the word into Italian and he smiled radiantly at me.

"Are you going to teach me English? I would so like to speak it with a perfect accent—not like hers."

"You are the rudest, most ill-mannered boy," Bessie said and bit her lip to prevent herself crying.

He bent over and kissed the crook of her arm murmuring, "I shall make you love me with all your heart."

Bessie and I came home to the museum that afternoon and bolted the door of my room. Twice I mentioned Dolfi Brunner and on each occasion Bessie gestured dismissively and said that he was beneath contempt and the very sound of his name made her feel sick. We heard Rosalia in the *bagghiu* and Bessie looked out of my window.

"Are you going to ask her this evening?" Bessie demanded.

I was still reluctant but she was insistent, no matter how many times I told her that Sicilian fortune-telling wouldn't work for English people.

"I don't see why not."

"We'd have to tell her our dreams and then she'd look them up in that stupid book of hers. We could do that ourselves."

Bessie, who was sitting cross-legged with her hands on her knees, said solemnly, "I bet she uses a *planchette* or a ouija board and gets in touch with spirits."

"Oh—I don't believe any of that stuff."

"Mother has a friend who gets messages from her son who was killed in the War."

"All right—I'll ask her and then you'll see how stupid it all is."

Rosalia was becoming more hateful to me every day because I knew she was watching me. She seemed to know when I was planning to go to the Villa with Bessie and what I had done there. No matter what time we came home to the museum she would be outside the door waiting for us with a black shawl over her head and her hands folded across her waist. Benno Sciafa saw her one afternoon, standing there like a black stone, and he made the *mano cornuta*, but she said nothing to him and spoke only to Bessie and to me. It was as if we had been carried home by an invisible driver in a cart of air.

That evening my parents went to the Whitlows' for a bridge party and Rosalia gave us pasta and fruit under the vine. As she placed the fruit in front of us she sighed deeply and said that only the blessed Madonna could help Frau Brunner bear the sorrows of her son. I wondered if she crept upstairs when I was with Bessie and listened outside on the landing.

"Dolfi? Do you know about him?"

I was astounded because Bessie had just told me that she never wanted to hear Dolfi's name or see him again and now she was almost jumping from her chair with excitement. Even before Rosalia could answer she was helping her gather up the plates.

"We don't want any of this fruit now. Gwen and I will help you in the kitchen."

"There is no need, these hands take joy in serving you," Rosalia said sweetly.

"I always help at home. We only have a cook and a daily now. When I was little we had five servants."

Bessie was busily stacking the plates and I was forced to help her, seething with resentment because I had caught a sidelong glance of triumph from Rosalia's black eyes.

We sat down at the table under the vine and, although I feigned boredom by yawning, I too wanted to know more about Dolfi Brunner.

"He is a child of the devil," Rosalia said and made the sign of the cross. As though to protect herself further she reached down into her dress and pulled up a large crucifix and kissed the body of Christ stretched out in agony on it.

"Who was his father?" I asked.

"A cousin of your grandmother," Rosalia said calmly, and pushed the crucifix down into her dress.

"He's no relation of mine!" I cried.

"All Sicilians are related, you know that," Bessie said matter-of-factly.

"I am your great-aunt," Rosalia said quietly to me.

"I called Nancy's two sisters Auntie after the wedding, and her father said I should call him Uncle Bob. It doesn't mean anything," Bessie said quickly. "But tell us about Dolfi."

"He went to an English school in Switzerland first, then to other schools, but it was always the same."

"He said he was expelled for blasphemy."

Both of us thought that blasphemy meant taking the Lord's name in vain, but Dolfi had made it sound much worse than that.

"The devil is in him," Rosalia said bluntly.

"I think he's probably very spoiled because he's so good-looking," I said.

"Do you really think so?" Bessie was frowning at me.

"It's not—" I wanted to say that I did not think Dolfi looked quite human, but I saw the opportunity to impress them both with my learning. "The Greeks made statues of gold and ivory—none of these chryselephantine works exist today, although there are descriptions of them. Dolfi looks like one of those statues."

"A Greek god," Bessie murmured.

"A child of the devil," Rosalia said and produced a pack of cards from a pocket in her skirt. "Who wants to know what *destino* has in store for her?" she asked playfully.

"Me please," Bessie said.

Rosalia shuffled the cards three times, muttering something to herself, and I tried to catch Bessie's attention with a supercilious sneer but she was intent on the cards.

"Oh, they're tarot cards!" she said delightedly. "Helen Bertram brought a pack to school but it was confiscated."

Rosalia told Bessie to pick a card and place it face down in front of her. It was a woman with a sword and scales. Swiftly, she set out nine different cards and then she began to laugh.

"Well?"

With one finger Rosalia touched the cards and then pointed to Bessie's. "Oh, it is a most fortunate aspect."

"Is there love in it?" Bessie asked in a small voice.

"So much love that you will be ready to die of it."

"And money?"

"More money than you could wish."

Bessie seemed unsatisfied and asked if Rosalia could tell her more.

"Will I always be pretty?"

"You will never be ugly."

"I think it's all nonsense," I said abruptly.

"Would you like me to give your San Giovanni sister the key to her tarot?"

I felt she was challenging me in some strange way.

"Please, tell me—" Bessie said.

"You will always get exactly what you deserve. And that is the most fortunate of all readings."

Bessie sat back and smiled contentedly but I suspected that Rosalia was laughing at her. She had shuffled the cards and now held them out to me.

"I don't want to know," I said.

Bessie accused me of being a spoilsport and reluctantly I took a card. It was a hanged man and Bessie sighed sympathetically.

Rosalia was frowning as she set out the cards and moved them into place with her forefinger. She looked at me and I saw her lips framing words that were inaudible to me. I was not frightened.

"I don't care what you say, Rosalia. Whatever you tell me will be superstitious nonsense."

"It's good you should think that."

"I want to know!" Bessie said urgently. "Whatever happens to Gwen will happen to me."

Rosalia shook her head. "It is not a future of joy—"

I knew Rosalia was punishing me for my rudeness, so I stood up and told her that I had no interest in her cards or any of her other Sicilian arts.

Dolfi became our companion at the Villa that summer. I am not sure how he came to be with us so much but Bessie was fascinated by him. Some days she said that she could not bear the sight of him and then, for no reason, she would insist that he play tennis with us, or walk down to the beach. He was a better mimic than Mr Chambers and we collapsed laughing when he imitated some of the older guests at the Villa. If he pulled in his chin and pushed out his stomach he was Mussolini, and even some Italian delegates to a Fascist rally in Trapani had to laugh when they saw him orating from a chair by the swimming pool. He mocked everything and I soon discovered that he was an outrageous liar and appallingly ignorant.

"What did you do at school?" I asked him and he told us stories of summoning Satan and his minions to a class in trigonometry, or taking a troupe of ghouls on a spree around the town.

"You have to be careful with ghouls," he said solemnly. "They cannot hold their liquor because it runs through the holes in their feet."

One morning we walked across the rocks, with the cliff on one side and the sea on the other, and pretended we could see the coast of Africa. Dolfi was making a great show of helping Bessie over the rougher places, leaving me to scramble along on my own. He was unlike anyone I had ever known, not because he lied and tormented people, but because he could make a person love him without making any effort to please. We both knew how a prospective suitor should behave, and we had contemplated enough courting couples at the Villa to appreciate the refinements of seduction. Nobody was more critical of boorish behaviour and rudeness than Bessie, yet she allowed Dolfi to insult and abuse her and all she did was find excuses for him. Now, her hand was in his and she was about to jump across a cleft between two boulders when she suddenly stopped and asked him what was the blasphemy he had committed at school.

They stood there, hands locked, Dolfi smiling and Bessie very serious.

"I murdered God."

Bessie cried out involuntarily and he pulled her across to him.

"He's only trying to shock you," I said and clambered up to join them.

Bessie was shivering in the sunlight and I put my arm around her.

"Don't listen to him, Bessie. He wants to frighten you."

She stared at him and then in a small voice asked him what he meant.

Dolfi put his hands over his head as if he were trying to touch the sky, stretched and yawned.

"I killed a priest," he said flatly. "I didn't mean to do it, but he kept insisting I study philosophy, so one afternoon when he wouldn't stop talking about Aquinas and Benedict I picked up a stool and smashed it on his head. His brains splattered on the wall and one of his eyes fell out at my feet."

"I hope you picked it up for him," I said drily but Bessie did not laugh.

"A priest is God's image on earth, so you see, Bessie, I was telling you the truth despite what my wicked cousin is saying. She'd like you to think that I only murdered a priest, but the truth is that I killed God."

Bessie shivered again. "Some of your jokes are horrible," she said.

"That was my blasphemy." Dolfi smiled. "The priests had to hush it up and pretend it was an accident, otherwise the boys would have turned on them and murdered the lot of them."

Nobody seemed to know anything about his father, but I could almost believe Rosalia was right when she said that Dolfi was a child of the devil. He played obscene tricks on the servants at the Villa and used words that I had never heard before in front of the guests. Instead of punishing him, Frau Brunner showered him with kisses, implored people to forgive her little Dolfi and said it was his father's wicked blood. He urinated whenever he felt like it, generally into one of the terrace fountains when there were some women guests passing. The remarkable thing was that after they had screamed and complained to Frau Brunner they were always the first to forgive him and I heard some of them saying that the poor boy really should be pitied. Even Mr Chambers used to refer to him as that "pathetic little swine," and told everyone that Dolfi was the living proof of what Jesuits did in the name of education.

What angered me most was that before Dolfi came, Bessie used to spend as much time at the museum as she did at the Villa, but towards the end of summer she hardly came home with me at all. She said it was because there was more to do at the Villa now that Frau Brunner had built a swimming pool, but I knew it was because of Dolfi.

"I don't know how you can like him so much!" I cried over and over again.

"I don't—" Bessie always turned scarlet when I challenged her about him.

"It's not as though he's the sort of boy we should be meeting."

"Frau Brunner asked us to look after him."

"He's sixteen and we're barely fifteen."

"You said he was a Greek god."

"I never did. And who'd want to meet a Greek god? They were mischievous and wicked. Homer blamed all human troubles upon the gods. I think Dolfi could be a satyr but he's certainly not a god."

We were sitting by the edge of Frau Brunner's new marble pool watching Dolfi swim lazily back and forth. He rolled over in the water almost at our feet and spouted water at us.

"That's a change," I said and saw Bessie's cheeks flush as she watched him.

"You're in love with him, Bessie."

"It's a sort of crush," she replied faintly.

It was in her eyes—the same expression I had seen when my mother looked at my father: a gaze that excluded everything but the object of that devouring vision. I beat my fists against the stone edge of the pool and ground my teeth to stop myself from screaming with rage and dismay.

"Gwen—there's blood on your hands."

Bessie's voice sounded like the echo of another voice that I had once known, but it was not my Persephone, so I opened my eyes and tried to breathe evenly. My knuckles were scraped and bloodied.

"I didn't mean to fall for him," Bessie said. "It just happened to me."

"No, it didn't happen like that at all. You try to fall in love with every boy you meet. Do you remember David Maybrick?"

I was about to tell Bessie what he had said about her but she was making tiny ripples with her toes in the water and murmuring dreamily, "Do you think he likes me?"

"I don't think he cares for anyone except himself. We ought to call him Narcissus."

Dolfi emerged at the far end of the pool and the fat man with a monocle heaved himself out of a deck chair and shuffled over to him like a walrus. It was impossible for us to hear what the man was saying, but suddenly Dolfi turned and laughed in his face. The fat man began to shake with embarrassment or anger and Dolfi walked slowly round the pool and sat down beside us.

"Do you know who that is?"

Bessie shook her head and I stared down into the water, wondering if I would ever be able to speak to Dolfi again without cursing him to his face. It annoyed me when Bessie flirted with every man she met, from Benno Sciafa to all of the waiters, but I knew it was an exercise with her, like practising the tango. Over the summer I had watched her change from someone who prided herself on conquering men with her killing glance to something less than a child who burst into frightened giggles or tears whenever Dolfi Brunner appeared. She told me that nothing would ever change our friendship, but once there had only been the two of us and how fiercely we had driven off anyone who tried to join us! Now she was turning away from me to listen to Dolfi.

"That is the Baron von Breiterhauf."

Neither of us was impressed by aristocratic titles unless they were English.

"He lives at Taormina and he collects boys."

"All right, Dolfi!" I shouted. "Tell us that he pickles boys in bottles or that he sells them for slaves."

Dolfi sighed and put his head on Bessie's shoulder. "Oh Bessie, I'm so glad I don't have to put up with my nasty cousin all the time. It's so good to have you."

"Dolfi—" Bessie shifted slightly but she did not push him away as I would have done.

He looked at me but I glared at the water and the tremble and glimmer of our reflections.

"No, the Baron does not pickle boys, he photographs them—naked."

Bessie was blushing and this time she did move away from Dolfi.

"Why—why should he do that?" she asked faintly.

"Oh, he says it's because he's making an anthropophalous study and collecting racial types: Arab types, Norman and Spanish."

"Did the anthropologist recognize your type?" I said sneering.

"Oh yes—he said I was divine—divinely Greek."

"You're not going to pose for him, are you?" Bessie looked imploring.

"Not unless he pays me ten thousand lire."

Every day was becoming a torment to me because of Dolfi. I also saw that whenever I attacked him, Bessie would defend him. My only consolation was that she was just as miserable as I was because Dolfi had never once told her that he loved her.

Bessie, I anguished about you that summer because I did not know then the pain of loving and not being loved in return. All I felt was that I had lost you, not to England and all your friends there, but to someone who seemed an abomination to me. I began to think of killing Dolfi, and there were nights when I lay awake planning his death in a dozen different ways that would not make me seem the murderer. Preferably, some way that would make you think that I had tried to save Dolfi's life at the risk of my own; and then I hated myself because I felt I was becoming like one of the Furies, with snakes in my hair and a lusting for blood. You told me that you would always love me as your best and dearest friend, but I knew it would never mean quite the same because in my heart it was not Dolfi I raged against, but time. Although Demeter prided herself on being mature and learned, I was the child throughout that summer and you were already a woman.

There were times when Dolfi mysteriously disappeared, always without warning and leaving his mother frantically sending messages to Messina and Palermo. When he came back to the Villa he never gave any explanation of where he had been or what he had done, and when Bessie pressed him he told fantastic stories of carousing with the devil or being invited to a convent of lascivious nuns. I secretly hoped that he would never return, but when I foolishly said this to Bessie she became hysterical and said that I had no feeling for anyone except myself. This was what my mother said to me one afternoon when I trailed into the *bagghiu* and found her propped up with cushions in a reclining chair. I was surprised to find her without my father, but she told me that he was out at the dig with Mr Chambers and some visiting archaeologists from Germany.

My mother's sickness was getting worse. She walked with a dragging limp and always held her trembling left hand by the wrist as though it were a bird trying to escape from the cage of her body. The only book she cared to read was her old copy of Housman's poems, although she knew every line of *A Shropshire Lad* by heart.

"Sit down," she said peremptorily when I said something about going up to my room.

"Your friend is not here?"

I said that Bessie and her mother were playing tennis. I did not tell her that I had been arguing with Bessie all morning and we had parted in a storm of tears.

"Your father says you have not been to the fishing boats with him recently."

"I've been at the Villa."

"You seem to forget this is your home."

Water was trickling in two green streams from the cracked and broken nostrils of the dolphin and I felt a sudden twinge of pain that I had neglected my father.

"She'll write to you when I'm gone. She'll send for you!"

My mother's tone was always peculiarly emphatic, but now there was a note of hysteria in her voice. She released the fluttering hand and placed the other on my arm. How could she possibly have known about Mrs Chambers and the promise she had made me?

"Eleanor has been waiting for this. She'll never speak to me but she'll want you at Russell Morton where she can choke you with money and blind you to your duty to your father. You do love him, don't you?"

Her passion was so intense that she was shaking me and I told her that I did not understand what she was saying.

"My sister Eleanor will punish me by leaving your father alone here and by taking his only child from him—my child."

I remained silent because I knew what Mrs Chambers and my father had both promised me. If my mother died, I would not remain here in the *bagghiu* watching the triton crumble down into the basin of the fountain.

"I cannot bear to think of your father alone here, with no one to care for him."

That was my mother's only concern, and I realized that she had no regard and no love for me. At least Bessie was prepared to give me some place in her heart, but my mother's only thought was for my father.

"I shall do whatever Father wants," I said coldly.

"Eleanor will take you to Russell Morton," my mother said dully. "She will tell you that your father is an evil man who married me for my money. And he will be here alone—oh Gwen, I cannot bear to think of that."

Her passion and the depth of her love frightened me, and I tried to move away.

"Russell Morton will be a curse to you as it was to me!" she cried.

"I don't believe in curses," I said evenly. "I am not a Sicilian."

Six

The day before Bessie and her parents left for England, the sirocco, laden with dust and sand from Africa, began to gust through the streets. Within hours the whole parched country was like an old abandoned house cluttered with furniture that conscientious servants had covered with dingy sheets: every colour in the sky and on the earth was bleached by the wind to a uniform pallor so that houses seemed suspended in dusty clouds and their shadows were cast at improbable angles by an invisible sun. The towers of the cathedral were suddenly propped against each other, the bells sounding from beneath the ground or from every point of the town while the street curled back upon itself. It was not the heat that drove people mad but this new landscape of strange and unfamiliar shapes. Every sense was altered as the sand sifted between eyelids and even food and drink tasted different: whenever I swallowed, a burning grit rasped my tongue. Alongside the road, the prickly pears took on the shape of writhing creatures trying to assume human form through the eddying dust, while people staggered along with their heads down like walking tree stumps. Every window at the Villa was shuttered and at noon it felt like midnight with all the lamps lit. I had helped Mrs Chambers pack and stayed with her while Benno carried her cases down to the cart.

"You'll remember the plans we've made, won't you, dear?" she said and hugged me to her.

I felt then as I often had before, if only Mrs Chambers had been my mother I would have said I lived in heaven. One of Canon Burnside's favourite hymns was "Abide with Me" and whenever we sang it on Sunday morning I looked across to Mrs Chambers' bright copper hair and blue eyes and prayed for her to be my mother and Bessie my sister. Now she said quietly, "I've always regarded you as my second daughter."

I found it difficult to speak because I could not bear to see Bessie go, and, because of Dolfi, it had been such a wretched summer.

"If we can't manage to come back next summer, we'll send Bessie."

Even smiling seemed to twist my mouth in all the wrong directions and I tried to answer her but failed.

"She won't find it so grand staying with you, Gwen, but I'm sure Hilda will let you both use the tennis courts and the swimming pool here."

Mrs Chambers went out to look for her husband and I wandered along the corridor, doing my best not to cry. Bessie was in her room sitting on the edge of her bed and staring at her shoes. I sat down beside her and she put her head against mine.

"I thought he'd come and say goodbye to me," she said wanly.

"I don't even know if he's here."

"Oh, yes he is. I heard Frau Brunner speaking to him a few minutes ago."

"Bessie, your mother says that if they can't afford to come next summer, they'll send you. Would you mind not staying at the Villa?"

"I wouldn't mind where I went so long as you were there—and I could see Dolfi."

At that moment it was again in my heart to kill Dolfi for I could feel Bessie's pain as though it were my own.

"I tell myself all the time that I've got to get over him, that there are heaps of boys in Manchester who are wild about me, but I can't, Gwen—I just can't. I know he's terrible—"

"I understand," and what a lie that was, because Bessie's infatuation with Dolfi affronted me like my parents' great love.

"It's been a horrible summer," she sighed, and that was true. Mr and Mrs Chambers had quarrelled, sometimes publicly, and he had taken to wandering off to his family's old villa. "Mooning around the front gate like the village idiot," Mrs Chambers had said.

We were sitting together with our hands clasped, too miserable to speak, when the door was suddenly flung open and Dolfi pranced in carrying a huge bouquet of flowers. He ignored me and knelt in front of Bessie.

"Bessie *bellissima*, the little queen of Trapani, for you, with my heart."

I felt the passion like a current of electricity running through Bessie's body but she did not cry. Instead she took the flowers from him and handed them to me, saying stiffly, "They're very pretty, Dolfi, thank you, but I'm leaving in five minutes and they'd die outside in the sirocco. Gwen will take them home for me—"

The bouquet of roses and orange lilies was in my lap when Frau Brunner burst into the room and snatched it from me. She stared at Dolfi for a moment and then wailed, "Must you steal the floral decorations? Oh Dolfi, you break my heart. Your father stole everything from me, must you do the same?"

I began to laugh as Frau Brunner rushed off with the flowers and Dolfi stretched himself out at Bessie's feet, his deep blue eyes fixed on her.

"So, I stole the flowers, Bessie, but you was stealing my heart."

"Oh, don't be ridiculous, Dolfi," she said but there were tides of delight flowing through her.

We kissed goodbye at the bottom of the steps in the swirling dust. Her last words to me were, "I'll come back, Gwen, I'll always come back to you." Then my Persephone was gone.

I turned and Dolfi was leaning against the wall, grinning. "I am saying that to her only to make you happy, cousin. I didn't want you to be miserable for the rest of the year."

Screaming with rage I tried to punch him, but he was too fast and I heard his laughter ascending from the terraces above my head.

I made an effort to pity my mother as she stumbled around the house, always with my father or Rosalia to support her. For some reason she never liked me to touch her and once when I offered to hold her arm as she faltered on the stairs, she brushed me aside and said the banister was sufficient. I tried to avoid her as much as I could because no matter what I said to her she would begin to shake with a kind of hysteria and accuse me of wanting to go to her sister Eleanor at Russell Morton.

"She'll buy you, promise you a private income, anything to punish me. You'll be given my old room with the dormer windows that look down to the lake, and she'll let you have your pick of any horse in the stables. I used to enjoy riding so much when I was your age, but of course, never with the local hunt. It was against my mother's religious principles to kill for sport, but I rode point to point on my dapple grey pony and he used to take the jumps before all the other horses. Spring Heel Jack they used to call him." Her eyes would look beyond me to Russell Morton as she spoke about every room, describing it so vividly that I could see the patterned chintz on the wicker-backed chairs in the sun room, and the shape of the silver epergne with carved peacocks surmounted by one with its tail outspread. "So beautiful when it was decorated with fruit and flowers and asparagus fern—the purple of the grapes and the soft reflections of the silver. It was supposed to be mine, so Eleanor will make you take it. And you won't spare a thought for your father here."

The moment she mentioned my father's name the edge of hysteria would enter her voice and tears filled her eyes.

"You have no heart, Gwen, no feeling for him."

"Mother, it seems pointless to talk about something that hasn't happened."

"If she writes to you—promise me you'll let me see the letter."

"If it's addressed to me, I don't see why—"

"She won't wait until I'm dead! She'll want you now!"

If I argued, she screamed at me and Rosalia would come and try to soothe her with a "*Calma! Calma! Signora.*"

I felt as though my mother was piling stones against the wall that enclosed me. What she did not understand was that beyond that wall was neither Russell Morton nor Trapani, but the home that Mrs Chambers had promised me. My mother thought I had only one choice to make, for I never spoke to her about Manchester. She made every room at Russell Morton familiar to me, but I knew every inch of the Chamberses' house from what Bessie had told me. If I closed my eyes I could watch myself walking into Bessie's room: the cream enamelled chest of drawers to the right, with five dolls and two stuffed pink rabbits on top of it, and the kidney-shaped dressing table with a muslin frill on the left. The spare bedroom where Nancy and Travis had slept was to be mine and Bessie and I had already discussed how we would change the curtains and rearrange the furniture. So, hugging this secret to myself, I could afford to accept my mother's demands and yet all the time I writhed with anger that she had so little regard for me.

"All right! You can read all my letters! But when, Mother, when do you ever think of me?"

My mother was staring at me as though I were someone whose name she had momentarily forgotten.

"Did you ever once think of me or is it always Father?"

"I cannot bear to think of your father here alone," she said forlornly, and tried to wipe away her tears but her fluttering hand brushed the air and her hair.

I went into the museum and sat down at my books. I was translating some articles from the *Notizie Scavi* into English—why, I am not sure, but my parents said the articles would reach a wider audience in English. Who that audience was or where it could be found I never discovered. I know that Colonel Whitlow read the articles but where they went from him I had no idea. The pain of losing Bessie at the end of summer was still like iron bands around my chest and as I wrote I pressed against the edge of the table to ease the heavy ache. There was a film of dust across my books: slanting light passed through air as dense as liquid stone and outside the grapevine seemed afflicted with a spectral blight. I turned the page and instinctively sensed there was someone else at the other end of the table. Looking up, I expected to see my father, but it was Dolfi reading a Latin grammar book. If I had found him at the end of my bed I could not have felt more outraged.

"There is no point of you to be angry, *cara mia*, your father said for me to be here, to sit here and read this book until you were ready for teaching me."

"Me! Your teacher!"

"I cannot go back to school so my mother has spoken to your father and you and he are to be tutoring me."

I heard my father's voice upstairs and I stormed up the stairs, demanding to know why Dolfi was with us.

"It's very little return for all that Hilda Brunner has done for us, Gwen," my father said.

"You always complained about being lonely here," my mother interjected.

"He's not a friend. I dislike him."

"He has not had an easy life," my father said. "His mother wants him prepared for the *liceo*."

"But he's ignorant and immoral."

"Thinking of yourself and your own pleasures," my mother said, and half rose from her chair. "Your selfishness is inhuman. Have you never heard of Christian charity?"

My father was polishing his spectacles and he spoke very softly.

"It will be a great kindness to help this boy, Gwen, and I would be grateful if you would do so. Of course, if it is too much I shall teach him myself."

I muttered something under my breath and stamped downstairs. Dolfi had opened the cupboard and was turning a Phlyax vase over in one hand while with the other he languidly scratched his back with the long Elymian strigil.

"How dare you pry into that cupboard!"

Dolfi looked quizzically at the little figures and then placed the vase back with the others.

"Did Bessie tell you about them?"

"Bessie loves me," he said complacently. "As you will be loving me," he added. "I can make anybody love me."

"Love you! You're detestable!"

"That is why you will love me."

I sat very still and stared at him as he closed the cupboard and lounged opposite me. Perhaps it was because he was so young that the fine down on his skin made him seem as though he were dusted with gold and again I had the feeling that he was not quite human. He smiled and let me see the tip of his tongue at the corner of his mouth.

"No, I'll never love you, Dolfi."

He laughed and his eyes were half closed.

"You'd be happy if I loved you as much as Bessie does, wouldn't you, Dolfi?"

"More—much more," he said.

"You'd enjoy seeing us fight over you."

"Or be of an agreement to share me."

"Dolfi—I'll stand on your grave and dance the tarantella before I say I love you."

Neither of us saw Rosalia at the door but we both knew she had been listening. She nodded approvingly at me.

"Are you going to curse me?" Dolfi asked her playfully.

"You are already cursed," Rosalia replied and placed a tray of lemon water on the table.

My father was not a patient teacher. I had often heard him snap at one of the summer students who had stumbled over a translation, but he was extraordinarily gentle with Dolfi. I realized in half an hour that Dolfi's Latin was nonexistent and he had no notion of the parts of speech in any language. His ignorance astounded me but when I slammed the grammar book down on the table and told him that he was an illiterate savage, my father came into the room and pulled out the chair alongside him.

"Why have you learned so little in all the years you have been at school?"

Dolfi hesitated, looked up at my father, and replied quietly, "Because when I was beaten I would not learn. How else can you rebel against a teacher?"

My father placed his hand on Dolfi's shoulder. "I remember those schools. I have a friend who is now a fisherman and one day he refused to open his book. The teacher cut his back open with a cane but Turiddu never cried out once, even though he fainted from the pain. I was never such a hero," he added wryly, "and I became a scholar."

"I would be liking that—to talk like a proper English gentleman."

My father went upstairs and came down with a volume of Dickens.

"You can read *Pickwick Papers* and Gwen will explain any difficult words to you."

In this fashion we spent the next weeks. I would sit mending pots or translating grimly on one side of the table while Dolfi read Dickens. He was restive at first and I never knew whether he would be there: sometimes he vanished for days and then Frau Brunner would stand sobbing in the museum while my father tried to soothe her, telling her that Dolfi would come back, which he always did, much to my chagrin.

At first I had to explain every paragraph to Dolfi but he began to read more easily and often he would rock back in his chair laughing. "This Carlo Dickens, I like him! He is a Sicilian, he knows how to make you laugh while he twists your gut."

Bessie's letters arrived every week and she always asked about Dolfi. It gave me great satisfaction to tell her that he was stupid, lazy, ignorant, depraved and that he hardly mentioned her name. At least she was not jealous of me: I was taller than Dolfi and we both knew it was impossible to fall in love with a man who barely reached one's ear. My mother was taller than my father but we had discussed that and said it did not count because old people were always different. Nothing I wrote seemed to cool Bessie's passion, not even when I told her how disgusting it was to sit opposite someone who was reading and picking his nose so that the snot fell on the table.

The only ally I had in the house was Rosalia. She would stand silently at the door behind him, her whole face a mask of disapproval. I wished she were a real witch and did have the power to turn Dolfi into a lizard or a toad and then I could have stamped him into the ground. Often I stood in the middle of the kitchen reciting a litany of his failings, with Rosalia nodding approvingly at each fresh iniquity while Miki shrugged helplessly in the background. I was outraged by Miki's behaviour because he chortled and cackled whenever Dolfi appeared. At the sight of Miki, Dolfi would give a low bow and try to kiss his hand as though he were paying homage to some grand signor, making Miki caper and laugh delightedly.

"He's making fun of you. He mocks everyone. Can't you see that?" I shouted at Miki, but he only bobbed his head and grinned when Dolfi's name was mentioned.

Nothing made Rosalia sneer more than Dolfi's determination to be an English gentleman and once when he vanished she said he was probably in Palermo with one of the English guests from the Villa. I thought this was quite possible. The day before he told me how he had seized the breakfast tray from a maid and carried it up himself to a lady's room. "I took off all my clothes," he said gleefully, "and placed the tray on her bed."

"Did she call for the servants?" I asked.

"No." He laughed. "She asked me to stay for lunch and dinner."

Dolfi had a store of stupid jokes like this, but sometimes I wondered if he did not treat these jokes as little plays, forcing people to act in them against their will. If he could make you laugh, he had controlled you as surely as though he had bewitched you. The worse the joke, and the more it humiliated people, the greater pleasure it gave Dolfi. Sometimes, when he had poor Miki doubled up with laughter and with tears streaming from his eyes, he would pause and lean forward to examine him critically as though measuring the kind of joke needed to produce this effect. But no matter what Dolfi said or did, I never laughed.

He had been gone for two days and Frau Brunner had just finished weeping all over the museum.

"It is his father," she wailed. "Why should I expect my *armer kleiner* Dolfi to be different. His father was unfaithful, he was a thief. My dear Gwen, you must help him. You are his age—make him see that he can be a good boy even though his father is Sicilian."

She then gave me a typewriter to help with my translating. It stood tall and black on the table and when I pressed one of the keys the carriage jumped. I was delighted because Bessie had just written to tell me that she was now taking secretarial courses at school and was learning touch-typing with a little cloth over the keys.

"Help my poor Dolfi," Frau Brunner wept and dabbed her face with eau de cologne.

The typewriter and the blue dress were the two best presents I had ever received. I sat enthralled, reading the little book that told you to type as though you were playing the piano—by touch and not by sight.

Rosalia coughed behind me and when I looked round I saw that she had a shawl over her head and pinned to her chest with a silver brooch.

"Your parents have gone to a reception at the Pepoli and I am going to the *teatrino* this afternoon," she said and her voice was alive with excitement. "Would you—perhaps you would like to see the *opera di pupei*?"

I shrugged and said I had heard about the marionettes but I had never seen them. Mrs Burnside used to say that it was the puppet theatre that gave the Sicilians a morbid fascination with violence and when they saw the paladins battling the Saracens or killing each other they rushed out of the theatre and did the same to each other. "Can you imagine," she said, "what the English working class would be like if they lived on a diet of the *Faerie Queen* and *Orlando Furioso*?" Nonetheless, I was prepared to humour Rosalia because she was the only person who listened to me when I denounced Dolfi as an ignorant savage.

She wanted me to wear a shawl on my head when we went out but I refused and put my straw hat squarely over my forehead. I told her there was no need for an English girl to look like a Sicilian peasant when she went to see the marionettes. We walked across the town and through streets that I had never seen before, where ragged washing trailed over our heads and half-naked children played in gutters oozing with a viscid slime that made me cover my nose with a handkerchief.

The puppet theatre was in an old shed advertised by a tattered banner daubed with scenes of battling paladins and a grinning black ogre on the point of losing his head to the sword of a moustachioed knight. I was about to walk through the door but Rosalia took me by the elbow and told me that the men sat together downstairs—there was a special place upstairs for women. Creaking steps led up to an opening no larger than a window and we climbed through this and found ourselves on a dark balcony. I stepped forward and felt a shape move and grunt angrily, and when my eyes grew accustomed to the light I saw the whole space was crammed with women in long black shawls, some of them shelling and crunching peanuts. Rosalia squeezed a place for us and told me in whispers that her father had been one of the greatest puppet masters in Sicily.

"Ah, he was a genius who could take any voice and often several at once. My uncle made puppets that were so human that people started when they came on stage, and my brothers worked the wires so deftly that everyone wept when a single tear fell from Bradamante's eye."

"A tear?" I said smiling, wondering whether I would be asphyxiated in the hot reek of bodies around me and the acrid stink of tobacco and oranges from the men below us.

"It was a pearl on a wire so fine that a spider could not have spun it."

A young man came out and recited a long prologue in Sicilian with a little Italian intermixed: the noble Ferrau was going to kill Medoro and Medoro's wife, Angelica, would then commit suicide. However, Angelica deserved her fate because she had spread discord among the paladins and Sacripante and the Duca d'Avilla had both fallen in love with her and killed each other in a duel over her. There were going to be several battles and many deaths, including the beheading of a giant by the magic sword, la Durlandina, which Carlo Magno had given Orlando.

At first I watched the strings on the marionettes, intent on discovering how they moved, contemptuous of the painted backdrops that were not as skilfully designed as the boards on Benno Sciafa's cart and waiting for a hand to appear as a paladin glided on to the little stage. Whenever one of the paladins died the men below us would suck their oranges in unison and groan and all of them seemed to know exactly what was going to happen next. The women around us were murmuring their own commentary and when Malagigi the magician appeared they all made the *mano cornuta*.

It must have been the lack of air and the heat that sapped my concentration, because soon I was no longer aware of the strings and the marionettes seemed part of a drama that was as real as one of the street brawls that I occasionally glimpsed from the car or from Benno's painted cart.

Bradamante and her sister-in-law, the Empress Marfisa, were dressed like warriors with bare legs, only their pretty rouged faces distinguished them from the paladins. They fought bravely but Bradamante could not save her husband from the treachery of Conte Gano.

"She will die of grief," Rosalia whispered to me.

There was a confusion of battles and a head flew from a Turk's head and almost rolled into the audience; la Durlandina flashed and a red-eyed ogre was dismembered at a blow. Then the scene changed and it was a wood and Marfisa appeared on a white caparisoned horse that hopped rather than galloped around the stage. The empress rode up and down seated cross-legged on her steed, looking for her sister-in-law, who had retired from the world to die of grief in an obscure grotto.

Again and again Marfisa called Bradamante's name, speaking of her beauty, her virtue and how her brother Ruggiero da Risa had lived for love of her and died speaking her name. Everything was very still and then we saw Bradamante in the *grotta oscura*, lying on her side with her head supported on her hand. Marfisa rushed to her calling "*Dolce cognata*," beloved sister-in-law, over and over again, but Bradamante seemed too weak to hear her. Marfisa wept and struck the ground with her feet so that the wooden boards of the stage trembled and now I could hear men sobbing below me and a woman in front of me began to moan as she rocked back and forth.

Bradamante was in Marfisa's arms; she slowly lifted her hand and pointed to heaven. "I am dying," she whispered. "Here in this dark grotto I wait for death to claim me. Oh, dear sister, do not weep for me. Our beloved Ruggiero is leaning across the bar of heaven, his hands outstretched to greet me. I can see his shining face."

As the audience wept and some of them begged her to live, Bradamante fell back in Marfisa's arms and a small white angel came down, took the soul from her lips, and flew up to heaven. The curtain was drawn and *lui che parla*, the narrator, came out and announced the next day's programme of battles and betrayals. I felt my face wonderingly because it was wet with tears.

The magic was not shaken from my head when we went backstage and I saw the wooden puppets hanging up in rows on nails along the wall. Rosalia was being greeted like a sister by the puppet master and his family and I gathered that her father had sold his theatre to the present operators when he grew too crippled with rheumatism to work the strings. I also discovered what the odd little shapes of crochet were that she was always working. Every paladin wore a tunic of chain mail under his tin breastplate, and that chain mail was Rosalia's crochet lacquered with gold paint.

I walked along the rows of puppets looking for one in particular and eventually I found Bradamante. She had golden curls under her helmet, large black eyes and her round red lips were parted in a half smile.

"Ah, you should have seen the Bradamante that my brother made," Rosalia said. "She was a great beauty and whenever she died such a tear fell from her eyes it was like an angel weeping."

We strolled home across the town with Rosalia clucking angrily if any man stared or walked too close to us. I felt clumsy and confused, as though I had just woken from sleeping in the sun, irritated that wooden dolls had produced such emotions in me. Even when I saw the puppet master's hand and the strings glittered in the light, I had not been able to control the feeling that I was dying with Bradamante and everyone would weep for me. It was as strangely absurd as though I had sat on a block of ice and suddenly been overcome with a burning heat.

We stopped at the square as a funeral cortège made its way to the church, and Rosalia told me that it was good luck to see a hearse. Provided, she added, there was a coffin. Nothing was more unfortunate than to meet an empty hearse on the road because that was a sign you would die within the week.

"I shall be buried in a white coffin like a little child, or a nun, because I am a virgin," she said with great satisfaction. "I have kept my honour as spotless as one of the holy sisters and the blessed Mother of God will find a special place for me in heaven."

Rosalia was old, much older than Assunta, but she was inordinately proud that her face was not wrinkled like those of most old women whose skin fell into pleats and folds as if the flesh had been crushed and left to dry in the sun. Instead, you could see the bones under skin that was dragged taut as though every morning she pinned it up under her hair.

"A woman's honour," she said as the aroma of the swinging censers filled the square and people stopped to bless themselves or say a quick Hail Mary, "a woman's honour can only be sacrificed to God or to her husband. God will reward me for my gift more generously than any man."

I went back twice to see the marionettes with Rosalia but it was not the same without Bradamante, even though I saw a dozen different paladins fight and die. When I told Dolfi where I had been he sneered and said he preferred the marionettes in Palermo who were as big as ordinary people, and the puppet masters who worked them had arms and shoulders like wrestlers. I accused him of lying but Rosalia said that for once Dolfi was speaking the truth. I am sure it was the only occasion and then it must have been by accident.

Every time Frau Brunner came to the museum she brought me a little gift, sometimes a box of handkerchiefs or some chocolates, and I could not understand why she was so kind to me. I had certainly not been able to teach Dolfi very much, although his English had improved. It annoyed me that he still did not know the parts of speech, but his accent was better and he was not making so many grammatical mistakes when he spoke.

One day Frau Brunner told me that she wanted me to help her with the bookkeeping at the Villa.

"It is important that you should know these things, Gwen," she said to me. "Dolfi will never learn."

So, I worked at the museum in the morning and in the afternoon Benno would call for us and Dolfi and I rode back to the Villa or, if the weather was fine, we walked. It did not once occur to me that Frau Brunner had anything more in mind than to teach me something in return for the English lessons I gave Dolfi and it was a relief to get away from my mother who seemed to be getting weaker every day. She seemed to accept now that I would go back to Russell Morton and her only concern was that I should get everything that had rightfully been hers.

I had just closed the museum door one Thursday afternoon when I heard her stumbling towards me.

"The Nonsuch chest," she said. "You must insist on that being yours, Gwen. It was always passed down on the female line and even though Eleanor may want Edith to have it, you must insist on it. Mother always said it was mine."

I enjoyed Frau Brunner's lessons in bookkeeping and found I had quite a talent for mathematics, something I had never studied before. I was also amazed at how much money Frau Brunner made at the Villa. Of course, I had always known about the gambling, but now the Villa seemed to be flourishing because the Fascists were using it for meetings. Every week there seemed to be more uniforms at the hotel and in the town, and I no longer bothered to correct some of the young officers who saluted me in the corridors and addressed me as Signorina Brunner.

"She thinks you're going to marry me," Dolfi said one day as we walked up to the Villa.

I stopped and looked at him in blank disgust.

"We're cousins after all," he said, and grinned at me.

"I hate you," I said passionately.

"That's why she thinks you'd make a good wife," Dolfi said.

I knew it was another of his stupid jokes and reached out to slap him but he swerved away from me, laughing.

Seven

I felt like Christian beset with temptations. On one side was Frau Brunner teaching me how to keep the Villa's books and saying that one day everything would belong to me: the gardens, the fountains and terraces, every room with its marble tiles and Persian rugs; on the other, my mother gave me a daily inventory of all that was rightfully mine at Russell Morton. But I had my eyes fixed on the heavenly kingdom of Bessie's home in Manchester and I knew that was the goal and haven of my life. I no longer had the nightmare of suddenly waking terrified in a place of absolute darkness with a void under my feet and an emptiness all around me. Rosalia always pulled the curtain across my window in the late afternoon but I opened it before I went to bed so that whenever I woke during the night or in the early morning I could see where I was. I was not afraid now of what would become of me if my parents died. Bessie said she had spoken to her teachers about my coming to live with her and they were expecting me at the school and her mother had even promised to buy a new carpet for the spare bedroom.

At first my mother grumbled when I told her that I would be going up to the Villa to help Frau Brunner and she reminded me that I had been carefully trained for a profession in classical archaeology. I tried to explain to her that I wanted to do something more than mend pots and translate articles so dull I felt as though I were sifting ashes from dust. Bessie was taking secretarial courses and I felt I was doing the same at the Villa where Frau Brunner was now letting me type her business letters. Everything I did for her seemed a thousand times more interesting than the long succession of dingy articles about Elymian beaker handles or the frequency of the key motif in incised pottery. My mother took this dislike of translating as a personal affront and insisted on addressing me as Boadicea. If it were not for Rosalia my life would have been a misery, but she always managed to calm my mother when she started to cry at the thought of my father being left alone.

"*Calma! Calma! Signora*," she would say. "I shall not leave this house while the *Dottore* lives."

Then my mother would smile and tell me that without Rosalia's care she would have died long ago. Perhaps it was Rosalia, or perhaps because my mother did seem stronger with the coming of spring, but she no longer railed at me as an undutiful daughter, saying instead, "Rosalia will remain here with your father and Eleanor will undoubtedly let you do whatever you like at Russell Morton."

When I spoke about this to my father as we walked down to the beach in the early morning for our fish he smiled, and said that everyone knew my mother's health was improving, but that if God were truly merciful he would take both of them together. Even though I knew my father loved me, I felt that they would both have gladly gone away and left me just as Bessie and I had abandoned Margaret Moglen in the garden of the Villa. Bessie wrote that it was like old people to think about themselves and no one else, and my parents should remember that I was young and had my own life to live—I could hear her mother's voice in those lines. I was angry with my father because he seemed to think that I could go back to Russell Morton without a single regret for him and for my home in Trapani. My mother's only concern seemed to be that I should inherit her share of the property.

If my parents took it for granted that Russell Morton held my future, Frau Brunner was equally certain that it was in Trapani at the Villa d'Athena.

"This—this will be for you to manage when I am old," she would say, extending her arms wide. "Of course, you and Dolfi are both too young to think of marriage now, but one day—when he has finished his military training—"

"I hate Dolfi, Frau Brunner," I always replied and this seemed to give her greater satisfaction than if I had praised him. Smiling, she told me that marriage had nothing to do with love and she would be a happy woman today if only she had kept that in mind when she married Dolfi's father.

"Dolfi will never break your heart, Gwen, and since you will have charge of the money he will have to pretend to be good."

When I told Rosalia about Frau Brunner she shrugged and said it would not be for me or Dolfi to say when we would get married.

"Oh, I think I can make up my own mind when that will happen," I said sharply, because I felt that I might take after my mother and be an old woman before I ever fell in love. I did not tell Bessie about Frau Brunner's plans because I knew how it would hurt her.

Dolfi was now reading *The Old Curiosity Shop* and he had become infatuated with Quilp. It was bad enough when he jumped over chairs imitating Sam Weller; as Quilp, he howled and barked and pretended to bite me.

"Little Nell is an idiot—she should kill her grandfather."

"She is not a savage," I said.

"But her grandfather is an evil man who drinks and gambles and who would sell her for money. He should die." Dolfi shrugged as though murder was as casual a gesture as combing one's hair.

It irritated me that Dolfi and Miki had become such friends. When Dolfi was supposed to be reading and improving his English, he encouraged Miki to imitate every sound in the house and the street outside and then the two of them would face each other and shriek like old women quarrelling or cats fighting. I told Miki that Dolfi was making fun of him but Miki only bobbed and grinned and clapped his hands over his head as though his infirmities had at last been recognized as theatrical talents. I was the audience Dolfi could never impress or entertain and this seemed to produce a kind of frenzy in him. When we walked back to the Villa he capered and cried to make me laugh and once he lay down in the middle of the road, kicking his legs, and pretended to be dying from an agonizing poison, but nothing he did touched me. Whenever I looked at Dolfi I saw him through Bessie's tears.

Spring came early and within a week the whole country was a tapestry of flowers. On either side of the road to the Villa the bank was thick with daffodils and purple iris, a white star-like flower on fragile stems and a bluebell that my mother said carpeted the woods near Russell Morton. Dolfi was singing a disgusting song about a peasant girl who kept her skirts over her head so that everyone could admire her most attractive part while I ignored him and picked flowers, arranging them in circles of colour. From the road we saw Frau Brunner talking to two of the gardeners on the lower terrace and on impulse I handed the flowers to Dolfi.

"Give them to your mother," I said.

Dolfi looked at me sideways and I could not read his expression, but he was not smiling. Quietly, almost diffidently, he walked up to his mother and offered her the flowers.

For an instant she stared at him blankly, then slapped his face and told him not to bring weeds into the garden. I tried to explain that I had picked the bouquet but she was gone, leaving Dolfi and me among the tumbled and broken flowers. Dolfi kicked them aside.

"You see—she only kisses me when I am wicked because then I am like my father."

Frau Brunner often invited me to have tea in her own apartment at the back of the Villa. The only view from her little balcony was high above my head to Erice and when I stood out there looking up I had the feeling that the whole cliff was about to fall down on top of me.

"I have no time to look at the view," she would say. "It is guests who pay for views."

There were photos of her parents on the cluttered mantelpiece, one of them showing two stout elderly people in Bavarian peasant costume, and a large silver-framed picture of a young man in a tweed jacket and plus-fours leaning against a baluster at the front of the Villa. I thought this must be Dolfi's father and wondered how he could have been so wicked when he looked so gentle and refined, as though he were listening to poetry or soft music.

One afternoon a maid came in screaming that Dolfi had upset the whole kitchen and a scullery maid had just fainted. It seemed that he had been sidling up to the girls and pushing a banana into their hands; most of them had laughed and pretended to slap him, but when he came to Fulvia it was not a banana but something else she found in her hand and the girl had toppled over in a dead faint and cut her head. Frau Brunner rushed off to comfort Dolfi and I picked up the silver-framed picture and again wondered how such a sensitive and elegant young man could have been the fiend that married Frau Brunner.

I was gazing at the photo when she came back weeping.

"How can I punish him? They all say he should be flogged but I know it is not his fault. It is in his blood to do these things."

She paused and took the photo from my hands.

"Ah, he was my love."

"Dolfi's father?" I said in surprise.

"Dolfi's father!" she screamed. "Do you think Carmelo Rossi had eyes like that? I have burned every photo of him."

"Who—?" I did not like to question her, but she continued without hearing me.

"Randolph Achurch, the heir of Lord Courtney. We were promised to each other in marriage but he went to India and he died there of a fever. Ah, my heart was broken, so I married quickly to try to forget the pain. Why do you think I have always had such sympathy for the English in Trapani? When I hear an English voice I think of my beloved Randolph who would have married me and made me a lady of title."

"Carmelo Rossi—" I prompted her tentatively.

"He was a fellow of no importance who worked here in the office for my father."

"Is he dead too?"

"I do not know where he is—I do not care. My father told him to go and he went."

This was a mystery that I related to Bessie in my next letter and she replied that she was sure now that Dolfi was the son of an English lord, but not on the right side of the blanket. Frau Brunner must have got in the family way with an English aristocrat and his family prevented him marrying her so she had to find someone to give Dolfi a father. She had just seen a film starring Ronald Colman with a plot exactly like that. Why else was Dolfi so fair? Bessie's new conviction was not mine: I knew dozens of Sicilians who were as blond as Dolfi and everyone said they were the descendants of the Normans, but I could see nothing of the slender and gentle young man of the photograph in Dolfi.

Every week more Fascists in uniform arrived at the Villa and from the bottom of the hill it looked as though a great white wedding cake, like Miss Havisham's at Satis House, had suddenly been infested with black beetles scurrying up and down the terraces. There was to be a rally in Trapani and until a few days before the event we were all told that Mussolini himself was going to be staying at the Villa. Every curtain was taken down and washed, Frau Brunner ordered fresh linens from Paris for the tables in the dining room and the royal suite was redecorated. At the last moment we were informed that only Roberto Farinacci would be there, and Frau Brunner was mortified, for the secretary was not to be compared with the Duce himself.

It was plain that trouble was expected in the town from the Communists—every day bunting and flags were set out by the Fascists and by the next morning they would have either disappeared or been replaced with red banners. One morning the statue of Garibaldi in the main square was wearing a red shirt and a hammer and sickle had been painted on the base. Truckloads of soldiers began to arrive and there was talk of people being arrested before dawn and taken to Palermo.

I was never able to find out exactly what happened, but two days before the parade there was another meeting at the museum: from what I could piece together it seemed that Colonel Whitlow had been slapped by a young Fascist officer for refusing to salute him after the colonel had insisted on crossing the street in front of an official Fascist car. Canon Burnside said it was time to bring in the English consul from Palermo to deliver an official rebuke to the local Fascists. I arrived back from the Villa just as they were all leaving and Colonel Whitlow announced that he would show these damned Fascists the mettle of an English officer. He was going to carry his old service revolver whenever he went out and he would shoot the next Fascist officer who had the audacity to approach him.

"It's all right. Everything will be all right when Roger comes," Mrs Whitlow said, and I gathered that she had written to their nephew.

My father was very silent that night and my mother asked me to play the piano for them.

"I don't feel in the mood," I said, not because I disliked the piano but because my mother always complained about my touch and reminded me what a fine pianist she had been before she lost the strength in her hand.

"You must not leave the house tomorrow," my father said abruptly to me.

"Frau Brunner expects me. Farinacci arrives this evening and she has asked me to take care of the office while she receives everyone."

"Farinacci!" My father was standing and almost shaking with rage. "My poor Sicily has known tyrants before this but nothing like these jackbooted bullies who steal every liberty from the people in the name of order. They promise the poor bread but they give nothing but parades."

Reluctantly, I agreed to stay indoors and early the next morning Miki put up all the shutters on the windows. I heard the bands and the cheering throughout the day and towards evening I climbed up on to the roof but all I could see were the crowds at the end of the street. Suddenly, directly below me, I saw two men in red shirts, then another, until it seemed there were more than a hundred drawn up in ranks in front of the museum. When I leaned out I was just able to glimpse the man in front who unfurled a red flag: it was Turiddu Matteo. A cap was pulled over his head and a scarf tied across the bottom of his face but I would have recognized his bow legs anywhere. He gave a signal and the men began to march forward up the street singing the Internationale. The crowd parted in front of them and I glimpsed a swaying catafalque with a gilded saint in the procession, a group of children and the *penitenti* in their peaked, hooded robes.

I could not see what happened next as the redshirts joined the procession and the crowd closed in again at the end of the street. After a few moments I heard shouting, the sound of gunfire and the air was bulging with smoke. The redshirts were running back down the street, some turning to stand and throw rocks at the Fascist troops. I felt a piece of stone strike my hand and at the same instant Rosalia took hold of my ankle and dragged me back across the roof.

"*Stupida*!" she cried. "Do you want to be shot and killed."

I crawled back across the roof and slipped down through the window. Rosalia was trembling with anger and pointed to the street. "There will be men dying there. Would you like to be killed with them?"

"What is it? Why?"

"The Communists—they wanted to march with the procession, to show the people their true leaders."

We heard footsteps, shouts and more shots from the street. The sound of bullets striking the walls of the museum was like wood being split. When I went downstairs my father was pacing up and down in the museum and for once he seemed to have lost his English.

"I should be with them—out there with my brothers!" he said in Italian.

Miki was in a corner with his hands over his ears and Rosalia went over and shook him.

"The Signora will need some tea. Put on some water to boil."

My father looked upstairs. "I must go to her. She will be afraid."

But my mother had already joined us and she seemed undisturbed.

"You know the arrangements, Miki," she said sharply and Miki nodded. "Yes, we shall sit here in the *bagghiu* and have tea."

My mother found her cushioned chair and took up a magazine. I wanted to ask a thousand questions but she told me to be silent and turned the pages, pausing to look across to her garden.

"The roses have never been so beautiful," she said as there was a staccato cracking against the wall outside and a man began to scream. "Rosalia has green fingers. Even Hilda was amazed when she saw the colour of the Horace Vernets this year."

We sat there drinking tea until everything was quiet outside and black shadows stood in every corner of the *bagghiu*. I wanted to climb up on the roof again to see what had happened but my mother told me to remain where I was. It grew dark and Rosalia brought a lamp out to the table because there was no electricity. Miki was at the top of the kitchen steps with three fingers raised and my father got up instantly and joined him. A few moments later Turiddu Matteo and two other men were in the kitchen. There was blood on one man's shoulder and Turiddu's red shirt was hanging in smoky tatters.

"Now you can do something to assist instead of gaping and asking silly questions," my mother said briskly, and she let me help her up.

There was a pile of sheets already cut in strips on the kitchen table and I passed them to Rosalia and my mother as they cleaned and bound the wounds. Turiddu had his grizzled head in his hands and was crying.

"We had no hope. They were ready for us."

"Were you recognized?" my father asked him.

Turiddu shook his head.

"Next time we shall fight like the *banditi*," my father said quietly. "At night and by stealth. That was my advice from the beginning."

"We expected the people would join us," Turiddu said passionately. "But they did nothing. Nothing to help us."

Rosalia was giving them brandy and then we heard the sound of a car stopping outside.

"Upstairs—my daughter's room. One under the bed, two in the wardrobe. Quickly, take them," my father said to me.

The men stumbled after me and I opened the wardrobe and watched while two of them climbed in among my clothes and Turiddu vanished under the bed. There was a hammering at the front door as I came down and joined my parents in the *bagghiu*. Rosalia had made a fresh pot of tea and was just pouring it when we heard Miki unbolt the front door to the sound of voices. My father got up slowly and went through to the museum. He returned with two Fascist officers and two young militiamen who must have been my age or a little older. My mother barely glanced up from her magazine as she said that she hoped the military had come to tell us it was safe to take down the shutters.

I recognized one of the officers from the Villa, a tall, fair man with a wispy moustache and polished boots that creaked. He smiled as though surprised to see me there. They said it was a formality that they had been given orders to search all the houses in the street. My father protested that the house was a museum, but we heard the boots echoing up the stairs and doors being opened. Within moments they had come downstairs and the tall officer in charge was apologizing for the intrusion. I dared not look up because I had heard the vine rustling over my head and knew that Turiddu and his men must have climbed out of my window and were on the ledge outside.

My mother asked the officers if they would like tea but they refused and left, apologizing again for disturbing us. Impassively, Rosalia ushered them to the door and Turiddu and his companions climbed down into the *bagghiu*.

I knew without being told that what I had seen must never be repeated, not even to Bessie, and when Dolfi asked me about the shooting next day I told him only that we had heard shouting and the sound of gunfire from the street outside. We had been inside drinking tea. Still, I wished my parents had let me know what they expected that night. Rosalia had helped my mother prepare the bandages, even Miki had been instructed what to do, but I was told nothing.

There were arrests throughout the town but when next my father and I went down to the beach in the early morning, Turiddu was there sorting the fish and complaining about the catch. He had saved a basket of little round pink fish no longer than a finger for my mother.

"These will make her strong," he said, giving me the basket.

"They're her favourite," I said.

"And yours too," he said to me and grinned.

"Poor men," my father muttered as we walked back through the town. "They believed that the people would follow the red flag of Garibaldi and defy the Fascists. Instead, most of them are in hiding now and three of them are dead."

"How did Turiddu escape?" I asked and for once I was not told to be silent.

"His boat was at sea but we arranged for a little skiff to be moored behind the cliff. He joined that with his friends and sailed out to meet his boat. The militia were here waiting for him on the beach when he came in at dawn, but it was clear to everyone that Turiddu had been at sea when the demonstration took place."

"What will happen next?"

My father shrugged and I saw that over the last few months he had become so stooped that his shoulders now seemed higher than his head.

"The Church and the Fascists have joined forces and many people who would revolt against the blackshirts are afraid of angering Rome."

My father was right when he said that for all of Mussolini's promises nothing had really changed in Sicily: the *latifundia* were still in the hands of the aristocrats and there seemed to be just as many poor people in the streets and begging in front of the churches.

"Nothing will change this country because you cannot alter the Sicilian," Frau Brunner said to me. "The Sicilian is treacherous, violent and subject to all the worst passions devised by the devil in hell." She now wore tiny gold-framed spectacles on the end of her nose and she squinted at me, frowning. "I hope that these are only rumours I hear about your father and his friends among the fishermen."

I shrugged and looked stupid.

"The Fascists will crush the Communists—that is their mission and they will succeed."

"I don't care about politics," I said and bent over the long accounts book.

"Your father should not be involved in politics either," Frau Brunner said. "The Fascists are bringing discipline to Sicily and they are doing a lot to bring tourists here. People like to know they will be safe from *banditi* when they are travelling. The Sicilian must be controlled—it is not in his nature to be able to govern himself. The Villa has doubled in value since the Fascists came to power and that is proof how everything has improved here."

"My father's only concern is for my mother," I replied and told Frau

Brunner that we were going to Palermo so that she could see a specialist. "My father is going to take us to the opera," I added.

"Very thoughtful," Frau Brunner said and went to look for Dolfi, who had disappeared.

Rosalia was flushed with excitement when I told her that we were going to the Opera House in Palermo.

"You must wear a beautiful dress," she said emphatically.

"I only have one, but I'll put some flowers at the waist. Frau Brunner will let me have some from the hothouse."

I had already decided exactly how I would refurbish Nancy's blue voile dress with a belt of knotted silver ribbon. When I told Rosalia what I was planning, she clapped her hands and ran off to her room, returning with rolls of shining silver thread.

"The Saracens will have to wait for new corselets." She smiled, handing the silver stuff to me.

My mother was confident that the specialist in Palermo would be able to prescribe some medicine or treatment to cure the incessant trembling in her hand. I tried to believe that she was not dragging her foot quite so badly and I laughed with her when she told me that Eleanor would not be sending for me just yet.

"She'll have to wait and with a little luck I may well outlive her."

I put my arms around my mother and hugged her before she had a chance to push me away with an embarrassed laugh.

"For heaven's sake, Gwen, don't be so emotional. You're behaving like a proper Sicilian."

I had often seen my father embrace her and she never thrust him away.

Critically, with her lips pursed so tightly that her mouth was like a tiny crinkled starfish, Rosalia examined the silver cord I had made and finally announced delightedly and with all the lines vanishing that she could not have done as well herself.

"It is in your hands," she said finally. "You have the Saracen arts."

The dress was washed and ironed and folded in tissue paper together with my best black shoes, polished by Miki until they glittered. I had new white stockings and Frau Brunner gave me an embroidered evening purse in the shape of a satin flower. At the last moment she begged me to search Palermo for Dolfi.

"There was an American woman who left two days ago. One of the maids said she used to see Dolfi leaving her room just before breakfast. I know she is in Palermo at the Hotel des Palmes. Oh, Gwen, you will be there and you must ask for him. See if Dolfi is with her."

"What should I do if he is?" I asked.

"Tell him that he is tearing his mother's heart from her breast," she shrieked and pounded her massive chest with her fists.

Bessie was due to arrive in two weeks, and this time I would have exciting news to tell her about Palermo and the opera. In her last letter she wrote that her parents were getting on much better and they had decided on one last trip to Trapani. "After that," she wrote, "you'll have to come to us because Mother says we will be bankrupt."

My father took the wheel of the car to Miki's great disappointment and we set off for Palermo. When I looked back Miki was standing beside Rosalia and waving forlornly at the door of the museum. As we turned the corner I saw two old women shuffle up to Rosalia and I knew they were coming to have their dreams interpreted so they could pick lucky numbers in the lottery. I never heard of any of her clients winning. My father used to say that misery and dreams were the natural diet of the Sicilians and I think he was right.

We were staying at the Hotel des Palmes on the Via Roma and I did not feel in the least like some *contadina* who had just arrived from the country to see the city. I knew what a great hotel was like from the Villa d'Athena, and I was able to examine the service critically as I felt Frau Brunner would have done. We were leaving the dining room when I saw Mrs Emmet Forester, the American woman, about to pay her account at the front desk. She smiled when she saw me and her braying voice echoed round the foyer.

"Well, fancy seeing you here, honey."

I went up and shook hands and after a few pleasantries I asked her if she had seen my cousin, Dolfi.

"I never knew he was a cousin of yours. You sure don't look alike. No, the last I saw of him he was charming the ladies at the Villa—and that included me." She laughed. "That boy is a regular caution. I reckon he's going to be a real problem for his mother."

I scarcely remembered the Teatro Politeama. Assunta had shown it to me one morning as a child when my parents were visiting the archaeological museum. Now, at night, it was like a great ship riding out into the piazza, with banners streaming and multicoloured lamps flashing circles of fire. The chariot and the rearing horses on the pediment seemed triumphantly alive, tensely held back in the instant before they lunged up into the smoking air. Already there were carriages and cars arriving with people so beautifully dressed that they could have floated down on jewelled clouds from another world. Occasionally, I recognized someone from the gambling salon at the Villa and when I mentioned this to my father he said drily that the Politeama was the favourite place for all the parasites to gather and admire each other's riches. My father was wearing an evening suit that seemed to be a strange shade of green under the light and my mother had on a dress of pleated violet taffeta that I had not seen for years. I noticed people looking at us and I suddenly felt that we were out of place and ridiculous. At the hotel I was sure that my blue voile with its silver cord was enchanting, yet now, without meeting anyone's eyes, I was conscious that people were staring at me. I tried to gaze at my shoes but in spite of my embarrassment I kept glancing up, for I was fascinated by the glittering crowd, the musky perfumes, the shimmering marbles and golden candelabra surrounding me.

The opera was *Madama Butterfly* and from the moment that Madama Butterfly appeared on a little painted bridge under a canopy of cherry blossom, my soul was lost to the music. At the interval everyone paraded around the vast foyer in an aristocratic *passeggiata*, lorgnettes and monocles winking at each other, but I could see nothing except the Japanese girl offering her love to Lieutenant Pinkerton and hear nothing except voices like bells that were still ringing in my head. I was not even aware that someone was standing in front of me and speaking to me until I saw the snarling ivory monkey under a ringed hand.

"The child has become a great beauty," he said, and I recognized the Barone di Marineo wearing a row of medals and with a blue sashed ribbon across his velvet evening suit.

My father nodded curtly to him but the Barone merely smiled at me and then walked away to join a group of feathered and jewelled people.

"What did he say to you?" my mother asked sharply.

"I don't remember."

"Don't remember? But he just spoke to you!"

"I wasn't listening."

How could I tell her what I felt at that moment? The idea that people were staring at me because I was beautiful had never once occurred to me. I thought they were sneering because my shoes were not pointed and beaded like those of the other women, or because my dress was cotton and not silk, or perhaps at the silver cord that must have appeared home-made. That anyone should think I was beautiful amazed me. Even Dolfi used to call me the beanpole and ask me when I was going to become a boy, because I had no breasts.

It was a night of such tumultuous emotions that I could not sleep, and lay awake listening to the noise of the city, still hearing Puccini's music and burying my face in my pillow to stifle my sobs when I began to cry again over Madama Butterfly's death. If only I were beautiful like Bessie then perhaps I too could fall in love and someone tall in a white naval uniform would love me and it would not matter if he deserted me and married another so long as I could feel the passion of love. I was glad I had not repeated the Barone's words to my parents because I was sure now that he had been making fun of me. Madama Butterfly had died for love like Bradamante and later I dreamed of her riding cross-legged on a white stiff-gaited horse through a forest of cherry blossom, finding her way to the *grotta oscura* where she could lay her head down on the earth and die.

Next morning my parents gave me instructions on how to find my way to the museum while they went to see a famous nerve specialist who had studied at Paris and Vienna.

"Wear your blue serge skirt, don't speak if anyone addresses you and remember that you are an English lady," my mother said and made me repeat aloud the directions to the museum.

The music was still surging through me as I strolled unthinking across the piazza, almost expecting Lieutenant Pinkerton to walk towards me with hands outstretched. I knew I should have turned to the right but somehow I had missed the street and I felt certain that if I went to the next corner I would find it. I was not even sure how long I had been walking. The next corner led into a little square of cracked cobblestones in front of a church and I decided to turn back and retrace my steps, hurrying because suddenly there were no longer fashionable shops on either side of the street, but old warehouses with dark alleys between them. Hastily I turned back again because I could see masts ahead of me and knew I was making my way down towards the port. Two men began to follow me and I quickened my step. They spoke to me in Sicilian but I pretended I could not understand them and clutched my purse to my side with both hands.

The street spilled into another little square with a crumbling church stained with a spreading yellow lichen and I wondered if I should go inside and ask help of the priest, to at least find out where I was. There was a group of men lounging on the steps and I decided to walk back across the square and avoid them because they were staring at me and laughing. The street turned and abruptly I found myself in a market with rotten vegetables under my feet and carts piled with sacks and squealing pigs. Chickens croaking with fear and thirst were hung up by their feet in bedraggled bundles, a kid bleated shrilly in thin, sharp cries and ragged children fought and screamed.

People were jostling and pushing against me and suddenly I felt hands on my purse and three boys were dragging it from me. I shouted at them but my voice was swallowed up in the clamour of noises around me. They darted off between some tables of broken china and tattered books and I tried to follow, stumbling in the garbage, aware that people were pointing at me and someone was dragging at my sleeve. I saw two of the boys once more as they slipped into an alley and then I found myself in a maze of laundry hung from ropes and strings, with screaming babies covered with sores spilling from the doors and an old man with a gaping black mouth and a cavernous hole for a nose who suddenly rose up in front of me, begging for food. The alley was stinking with filth, and hands like birds' claws were stretching out on either side. Through the tattered sheets I could see a porticoed wall with a broken frieze of cornucopia and vine leaves and two little naked children like grey skeletons leaning from a window.

Terrified, I pushed my way through the dripping clothes and a woman shouted angrily at me and began to beat my back. There was a fragment of light ahead of me and I rushed forward through dank rags and clutching hands until I found myself in the ruined court of an old palace. In the middle was a fountain with a slimy stream oozing from something that may once have been a god or river deity, but that now no longer had shape or meaning except decay and ruin. Children dabbled in the muck of the pool and more rags hung from every corner, dangling like the ghosts of clothes and bed linen. I stood, turning, for I could no longer see the alley or any way out of the court and some men who had been crouched against a wall playing with bones now stood up slowly and began to walk towards me, smiling.

I could hear myself screaming and tried to force my way across the court through the forest of rags when there was another voice at my elbow. "My rosy, posy little Nell," it said. "I would like to eat you all up, I would, I would."

Eight

I knew you'd be angry and that would stop you screaming," Dolfi said, laughing, and pushed me ahead of him down a passage so narrow that I felt my elbows scraping the walls on either side. There were windows behind elaborate carved pillars to my right and through one recess, half-naked children as thin as spiders played among tumbled wreckage; at the next, a man hammered at a shoe in front of a peeling fresco of nymphs in billowing pink robes and in another, two old women in black brocade dresses sat motionless with folded hands, facing each other across a little table in a room of frayed velvet chairs and satin curtains blotched with age. We went quickly and the passage opened into a flight of stairs worn down to such a hollow that one step slid to the next and we were scrambling through a slimy trough. Across a street and down another alley, through a square with four dishevelled poplars and suddenly I saw part of the main town below us.

"What were you doing in the old city?" Dolfi asked and I gaped as I looked at him more carefully. He was dressed like a bandit with a wide sash and a scarf around his neck, an embroidered jacket and trousers that buttoned at the ankle.

"I bet you were robbed." He grinned.

"Your mother told me to look for you."

"In the old city? I don't believe it. She thought I was with the American woman."

I was very confused and tired and we went a little farther and sat down near a children's park where some girls in starched dresses were spinning a hoop along a gravel path.

"I was going to the museum and I got lost, I don't know how, Dolfi, and three *ragazzi* stole my purse."

"Naturally. What would you expect in the old city?"

"I was supposed to go to the museum, but I—"

"You think you're so clever but you're no better than one of those *bambini*," Dolfi jeered, pointing to the little girls in their white frilled pinafores.

"I lost my way. Anyone can do that."

"In the old city? I heard there was a stupid-faced English girl as tall as a lamp-post wandering around and I knew it must be you. If it had not been for me, what would have become of you? I tell you, Gwen, you should be grateful to your very soul for me. There are people in the old city who would murder you for the sake of your shoelaces."

"I think you're loathsome, Dolfi," I said and then I paused. "What were you doing there dressed like a bandit?"

"I am," Dolfi said slowly, "the leader of the most important band of *banditi* in Sicily. I come to the old city to give my men their orders."

"You are a liar," I retorted.

Dolfi shrugged and pulled horrible faces at a little girl who had stopped inquisitively in front of us. She ran away crying with fright and he pounded his knees laughing.

"I shall tell your mother that I saw you, Dolfi."

"Oh, it's all right. I'll come back with you in your father's car."

His audacity left me speechless and I realized that he still had not told me what he had been doing in the old city.

The trip back from Palermo was joyful because my parents had received good news from the specialist.

"That fool in Trapani," my mother said, "recommending all the wrong treatment. What I have to do now is keep the arm in a sling until it's rested and take Sanatogen regularly."

Dolfi was on his best behaviour and listened quietly as my father brought the landscape to life with stories about the Elymians, the Greeks and the Phoenicians.

"Is it true," Dolfi asked politely, "that the Phoenicians sacrificed children to their gods?"

My father told him about the graves that his friend Mr Whittaker had found on the island of Mothya—graves of babies and little children buried with the corpses of dogs and cats.

"The Phoenicians were very sensible people," Dolfi said seriously. "There are too many starving children in Sicily, not to speak of the dogs and cats. It would be better if their parents sacrificed them like the Phoenicians."

I waited for my father to rebuke Dolfi but instead I saw his head nodding as the road swung down towards Trapani.

"Sacrifice might be kinder than starvation, Dolfi. But don't you think it would be better to have a society where people could earn enough money to feed their children?"

"Where is that society? In heaven? That's what the priests used to tell us—in heaven everyone will rejoice and be forever happy because there will be no bodies to feed, only spirits that can live on air. Is that where we are going to find this society of the blessed?"

"In Russia—the new Russia that has been born of revolution and war," my father said quietly, and I saw my mother glance sharply at him and murmur, "Not in front of the children."

I could have leaned forward and shaken her.

My parents did not think it at all extraordinary that Dolfi should have been wandering around Palermo in a bandit's costume.

"One day, perhaps, you will be an actor," my father said to Dolfi.

"Perhaps," Dolfi said, and yawned. "But I wouldn't enjoy being on stage with a lot of people saying things that other people have written. I would like to be there alone with everyone watching me. Like Mussolini," he added.

My father chuckled and I wanted to interject and say that laughing at his stupidities only made Dolfi worse. I frowned and glared out of the window. Even my mother turned and smiled at Dolfi.

"How will you feel when you have to do your military training and salute Il Duce every day?" my mother asked. "You're almost eighteen now, aren't you?"

"I shall run away or kill myself. I haven't decided," Dolfi replied.

"If I were you, I'd run away," my father muttered. "I could not serve these Fascists."

Frau Brunner did not ask me where I had found Dolfi. She seemed to think that I had pulled him out of the American woman's bed at the Hotel des Palmes and she was tearfully grateful.

"He is all I have in this world," she sobbed and gave me two lengths of flowered crêpe de Chine. "If I keep them any longer they'll rot," she said. "I'm sure that Rosalia will be able to make you something from them."

Rosalia held the fabric to the light and measured it against her arm.

"Just enough for two simple dresses," she said and I begged her to make them before Bessie came.

"You could wear your blue frock again." She smiled. "It was admired at the opera."

"How did you know that?"

"I was told you were the beauty of the Politeama. But you must not let praise like that go to your head. Remember that your greatest treasure is your honour. Without that the most beautiful woman in creation is like filth in the street." She put her head on one side and smirked in the looking-glass on the dresser shelf. "Not a line in my face and that is Our Lady's blessed sign of approval."

"Skulls have no lines or wrinkles either," I said, roughly, because I could not bear to think that Rosalia had been discussing me with anyone. The only person who could have spoken to her was the Barone.

She seemed to know what I was thinking and her smile disappeared.

"The Barone di Marineo is the head of our family."

"Oh rubbish!" I said and then remembered that I desperately wanted to wear something new when Bessie arrived. "You must remember, Rosalia, that I am not Sicilian. I am English."

Rosalia smiled again and folded the crêpe de Chine.

"I shall cut this tonight for you, Gina."

I did not correct her.

Oh Bessie, those last few days were always a torment of excitement and joy for me. I could see you before you arrived, hear your voice threaded through all the sounds that filled my ears and there were times when I found myself about to tell you something and suddenly realized that you were not there. Once I walked into the card room at the Villa and screamed your name aloud, but it was only a maid with red hair dusting. Every night I swore that I would stay awake because I knew that I could never sleep with such a pulsing and tingling in my veins, such tides of anticipation rushing through my whole body. Just before a chrysalis begins to stir to life you can see the shiny carapace tremble, movements so small that you have to watch very closely or you will miss the instant when it suddenly cracks open and the butterfly shakes its crumpled wings in the sun. It was as though I were waiting for the moment when I would break out of my old buried shell, stretch out my arms and fly to my Persephone. My excitement seemed to spread out across the country: the flowers sparkled in the sunlight, every puddle on the road became a flashing aureole and the cathedral bells rang out like jubilant voices across the town. Even Benno was caught up in my frenzy and told me that he had bought three new ostrich feathers to decorate the pony's harness and Rosalia promised to make a special cake filled with fruit and poppy seed for your arrival.

We were in each other's arms before I saw her parents or the stranger who was with them. First, we hugged and kissed and then we danced around each other, amazed at the changes a year had made in us. Bessie had been allowed to have her hair cut and shingled and now she looked just like her mother.

"It's a grey Axminster with a blue border and bunches of flowers in each corner."

"I don't understand," I said bemusedly.

"Your carpet, silly! Uncle Bob said I could have anything I wanted for my birthday, so I told him I wanted a carpet for your room. It's absolutely gorgeous. Mother says she's afraid to step on it, but it's for you, Demeter."

Mrs Chambers was laughing and shaking her head.

"I don't know what to make of you two. Sometimes I think I must have had twins and the midwife took one home by mistake."

She was kissing me then and Mr Chambers gave me a bear hug with his good arm. I couldn't see them after that because I was crying so much.

"I haven't the faintest idea how we're going to live when you come to us, Gwen. Probably bread and scrape seven days a week."

"Oh, we'll manage, Betty, with a little bit of luck."

Mr Chambers did seem much happier and Bessie whispered to me that she was sure they were going to be all right now.

"Of course we will, darling." Mrs Chambers shook her copper hair at Mr Chambers and stuck out her bottom lip defiantly. "I've given up worrying. Let tomorrow take care of itself, that's what I say now."

Another person was standing nearby but I still had not seen him because Bessie and I had our arms around each other and were laughing at each other's tears. Mr Chambers swung about and pulled the stranger forward.

"Good Lord, Roger, you must think we all go mad when we arrive in Trapani. This is our adopted daughter, Gwendolyn Harcourt di Marineo."

Roger Whitlow was very tall and bore no resemblance to his uncle, but he bowed slightly and shook my hand, saying that he didn't think a formal introduction was necessary because Bessie had told him so much about me.

"I gather it's really Demeter and Persephone, isn't it?"

I felt myself blushing and muttered something about a childish joke and in the next instant Colonel Whitlow had arrived and hurried him off.

"Nice young chap," Mr Chambers said. "He's here to persuade his uncle to sell up and return to England before the old boy gets into any more mischief."

Bessie pulled me aside and whispered urgently, "Is he here? Where's Dolfi?"

"Bessie *bellissima! Carissima!* I am here!"

Dolfi was leaning over the terrace above us with a long rose between his teeth.

"You stupid idiot!" I shouted.

He ignored me and vaulted down to Bessie, fell on one knee and gave her the rose.

"Ask him if he stole it," I said.

"I stole it because you stole my heart, Bessie," he moaned.

"Dolfi! You said that last year!" I screamed.

"Thank you very much for the rose, Dolfi. I'll put it in water in my room," Bessie replied quietly.

"I am so happy that you will be able to watch it die, Bessie," Dolfi jeered, and laughed to see her flinch as though he'd struck her.

He was gone, leaping up the terraces, and I stared at Bessie, amazed. "How? How can you possibly even like that little horror?"

Bessie shook her head and held the rose to her lips.

"He's a monster, and Bessie, he's not even a clever monster. Dolfi is the most stupid and the laziest boy I have ever met. I was supposed to teach him Latin but all he's done is read four Dickens novels. He doesn't even read them properly. He stops all the time to play the parts and jump over the furniture."

"I still love him," Bessie said simply.

It was my hope that in the space of a year she would have got over him but she seemed just the same. Sighing, I knew that I would have to protect her and wait until she saw Dolfi with my eyes. After all, we were sixteen and perhaps she needed another year to recover from her infatuation. I thought of the old fairy story about the princess who kissed a frog and he turned into a prince; if Bessie once kissed Dolfi I was sure he would change into a hideous, croaking, slimy toad with filmy eyes and a stinking breath. I consoled myself with that thought.

In the next instant my despair vanished.

"Don't you think that Roger Whitlow is awfully handsome?" Bessie whispered conspiratorially.

It was beginning—she had seen someone else and I did not imagine for a moment that Bessie could love two men at the same time. I tried to remember Roger Whitlow, but I had an awkward habit of staring at the ground when strangers were introduced to me. Besides, Colonel Whitlow had rushed him away so that I had scarcely seen him.

"My father thinks he's ripping—Roger is a captain in the army and he's been given extended leave to take his uncle back to England before he tries to fight the Italian army singlehanded. Roger's commanding officer served under Colonel Whitlow in the Boer War. He is a little old—twenty-four—but everyone says you look much older than sixteen."

"Bessie, you didn't—"

"I simply told him about you. Well, I didn't have to tell him much because my parents were raving about you."

"I hate people talking about me."

"You shouldn't be so self-conscious. I thought you'd be over all that by now. We're almost grown-up."

"I don't like him," I said flatly.

"You've only just met him," Bessie said triumphantly. "Oh, it's heavenly—we'll be able to play tennis—the four of us."

"Not Dolfi!"

I knew my Persephone's way of making neat patterns of people and I groaned. This was the summer I had longed for and now it was going to be ruined by Dolfi and someone else as well. The following afternoon I was showing Bessie my little office at the Villa and how I kept the books.

"You are a genius," Bessie gasped.

I flushed with pleasure because I already knew that her typing was better than mine, and I did not expect such praise.

"We don't start bookkeeping until next year," Bessie said. "Oh, Miss Frobisher is panting for you to come. I've told everyone at school about you. I can see the future," she went on dreamily. "I'll marry Dolfi and you can teach me how to run the Villa. Every year, you'll come back from India with Roger and we'll spend the summers together, only then I shall be waiting here for you to arrive. But we mustn't look too far ahead. First, you'll be returning with us to Manchester."

"I—my mother may—"

"My mother is going to speak to your mother," Bessie said firmly. "There won't be any problems this time."

"I'll really be going back to England with you this year?"

"I—I'm not sure. Mother says it will be best if we send for you when—"

"What does Mother say?"

Mrs Chambers was at the door and pretending to look fierce. She was so pretty, with a rose silk bandeau around her head, that I wanted to tell her how much I admired her and how two Fascist officers had asked me her name that morning.

"What am I supposed to be saying and doing?" she said.

"I was telling Gwen that she would be coming back with us this year."

"I'm going to discuss it all with Mrs di Marineo. Is your mother any better, Gwen? Well, that's a stupid question. Nobody ever recovers from a stroke. Bessie, would you tell your father that we're going up to the Whitlows' for cocktails. You're invited too." Mrs Chambers nodded and smiled at me, her blue eyes glinting under the bandeau, which almost covered her brow. She was wearing a different perfume that smelt of roses and lily of the valley.

Bessie left and Mrs Chambers leaned forward over my desk and whispered, "Can you keep a deep dark secret?"

"I think so," I replied slowly.

"It's more of a favour to me than a secret," Mrs Chambers said.

"You know I'd do anything for you."

"There will be a letter arriving here at the Villa addressed to you. The envelope will be typewritten and I want you to give it to me without telling a soul. There will be a message in it for me."

I was so puzzled that I stared at her in silence.

"Gwen, I can tell you about it but I daren't breathe a word to my husband and it wouldn't be fair to ask Bessie to keep a secret from her father."

I nodded.

"We have been having the grimmest time financially." She pouted and her face seemed to darken for an instant. "Well, I needn't burden you with the gruesome details. I'm sure Bessie has told you about it. Mr Chambers is within inches of bankruptcy."

"If things are so bad how can I possibly help?"

"My brother Travis is making money—heaps and heaps of money and he's helping out."

"That's wonderful," I breathed.

"Mr Chambers doesn't know it, he's such a fool with money, but Travis is paying for our summer here in Trapani and he's arranging to have something done to help the business."

"Bessie always said he was her favourite uncle, Mrs Chambers."

"The letter will be from him and I would like you to hand it to me very discreetly. If my husband ever found out that my brother was his financial salvation I think he would die of humiliation."

"I always sort the guests' mail," I said. "I'll make sure nobody finds out."

Mrs Chambers was giving me her confidence in a way that my own mother had never done and I felt such gratitude that I could barely speak: I loved her so much and my own mother meant so little to me. Whenever I told myself that, I felt a wrenching guilt because I desperately wanted to return with Bessie to Manchester but I also knew why Mrs Chambers wanted me to wait. She did not think I should leave before my mother died. That was the implacable circumstance I dreaded to contemplate: the price of my release to paradise in Manchester with Bessie and her parents was my mother's death. The sense of selfish shame that choked me was all the more painful because I could not love her, but then I was never loved by anyone except Bessie.

A prehistoric painting had just been discovered in a cave near Palermo that showed three curious figures in a ritual ceremony. One figure was being sacrificed: his back was arched with a noose around his neck attached to a rope lashed to his ankles. I could not understand what it was until my father traced his fingers around the bound figure on the page. "The more the man tries to ease the agony of his back the tighter the noose is drawn around his neck. If he moves, if he seeks to escape, he strangles himself. It is a horrifying torture." I thought now of the bound man being sacrificed to his own pain and I felt my mother like the rope around my neck and tied to my ankles. Shivering, I resolved to push every consideration from my mind and live for the day like Mrs Chambers.

We were all invited to Colonel Whitlow's and I was able to sit over to one side of the terrace with Bessie and examine Roger carefully.

"He is good-looking," Bessie whispered urgently.

I shrugged, but I had to admit that Roger was rather like a number of film stars that I had seen in the magazines Bessie sent me. He was tall with dark hair and a tan acquired in India. When he puffed on his pipe he had a rakish mannerism of half closing one eye so that you were greeted with a quizzical grey wink. Colonel Whitlow brought him over to us.

"I'm counting on you two gels to show my nephew around. Can't expect him to spend all his time with an old duffer like me."

Roger laughed easily. "Your problem is you've got too much dander in you, uncle. I wouldn't risk slapping some of these Fascist chaps around. They look a rough bunch to me."

"My God, you should see them on parade!" Colonel Whitlow began to whoop and wheeze. "I could do better with a bunch of Bengal belly dancers. Rough! The only rough thing about them is the way they slope arms. Most of them get the rifle stuck in their ears or up their—" He coughed and fell into a spasm of wheezing.

"I'm counting on you both for tennis tomorrow," Roger said, smiling at us. "I'm sure we can find a fourth for some mixed doubles."

That is how Dolfi came to join us the following afternoon in a white silk shirt and blue striped trousers.

Roger looked him up and down with a disgust that delighted me.

"Ever heard of tennis whites, old fellow?" he asked Dolfi coolly.

Dolfi shrugged and said that when in Sicily you did as the Sicilians did.

"None of us here is a Sicilian," Roger said evenly. "I hope your tennis is an improvement on your manners."

It was a splendid match and Roger and I won easily. Dolfi tried to rush the net, pushing Bessie to one side so that once he almost knocked her over, but Roger and I cooperated and while I covered the net he took the base line. Even Frau Brunner came out to watch the match and only once called out when Dolfi shoved Bessie out of the way and a man shouted, "Bad show!"

"He cannot help it." Frau Brunner appealed to the little crowd.

As we came off the court an old Hungarian lady who had been a famous actress before the Great War stood up and applauded, then clasped her hands under her chin.

"The angels have come down from heaven! I have never seen four such beautiful young people," she cried ecstatically.

"That Captain Whitlow is a charming friend for Bessie," Frau Brunner said to me afterwards. "He is an English gentleman so he will not break her heart."

Roger said he had argued with his uncle for three hours without taking breath but at last he had persuaded the Whitlows to compile an inventory of their villa's furniture and even discuss the sale of the house.

"It won't be difficult to find a buyer," Roger told us. "Uncle's kept everything in good repair and now the Fascists are in charge, Sicilian properties are becoming quite fashionable again."

Not with the English. That was something we all recognized as the beach echoed with Italian and German voices throughout the summer and even Bessie's father sighed and said he was beginning to feel like a stranger in Trapani. The first letter addressed to me had arrived at the Villa in a plain white envelope and I gave it to Mrs Chambers, but she did not seem very happy when I saw her later that day. I knew immediately that it must have contained some disappointing news about money.

I was waiting for Bessie on the terrace when I felt a warm and familiar arm around my shoulders.

"How's my third best girl?" Mr Chambers said.

"Happy—very happy," I replied.

"I thought you'd forgotten all about me."

I laughed and he said he felt as though he'd been jilted.

"Not that I blame you—Roger's not bad-looking, provided you like a young fellow with prospects and two arms. Colonel Whitlow says he's slated to be an aide to the Viceroy in Delhi."

"Roger's not even a friend," I scoffed.

"The four of you have been spending a lot of time together."

"That's because there's no one else here for him. Besides, he does keep Dolfi in order."

Mr Chambers was silent and I saw him squinting off to the left where the salt pans were like furnaces of white fire in the sunlight.

"We may not be staying in Manchester for long, Gwen."

"But that's—" I almost said, "Our home."

"It may be time to pack up and go to Kenya—or Australia. There are plenty of opportunities there. How do you feel about emigrating?"

"I don't mind—so long as we all stay together."

"Like fleas on a puppy dog's tail." He chuckled and after a few moments he said almost to himself, "Betty's been marvellous about it lately. She's given me—I don't know—the kind of boost I needed. When I get back I'm going to see if I can pull the business round and if I can't—then it's off to a new world for all of us."

I would have enjoyed it more if Dolfi had disappeared on one of his mysterious adventures in Palermo or wherever he chose to go, but he always tagged along after us. Roger was driving his uncle's car and we made trips down the coast to Marsala and Selinunte where Roger said I was better than any guide and a lot more interesting. It had always been impossible for me to curb Dolfi's revolting manners but when one morning he proceeded to urinate at the side of the road in front of us, Roger took hold of him by the scruff of his shirt and shook him. To my amazement, Dolfi actually looked shamefaced and apologized to us.

"Oh, you could see it all," Bessie said to me that night. "Dolfi needs a man's discipline and Roger must remind him of his own father."

"But his father was Sicilian," I said.

Bessie coloured with anger and told me that anyone with an ounce of common sense could see that Dolfi was English.

"He looks much more English than you! He doesn't have black hair like you."

"Everyone knows my father's Sicilian," I said.

"Frau Brunner couldn't marry Dolfi's father because his family wouldn't accept the daughter of hotel-keepers."

We squabbled about it and next day when we climbed around the rocks the argument was still fretting us.

At high tide the sea covered the inlet and left tresses of seaweed. We discovered it one afternoon and made it our own private beach. Dolfi sprawled on his back, his face to the sun, and I saw Bessie staring at him as though she was transfixed. Her straw hat had a gauze veil attached to it because she burned so easily, and her arms and shoulders were covered with tiny freckles. I said that Bessie looked like Danaë, who had been locked up in a brazen tower where Zeus visited her as a golden shower and became her lover.

Dolfi rolled over sideways and stared at Bessie. "Gold? I think she looks as though she's run through a dirty puddle."

"Put a sock in it!" Roger said irritably. "Everyone knows Bessie is a knockout."

I could have leaned over and hugged him. Instead I asked him to tell us about India.

"Well, I'm hoping to see more of it this time. And if I can pull the right strings I may be able to join an expedition to Tibet that's being organized by some friends of mine."

"Take me with you," Dolfi said suddenly.

Roger laughed and I said, "Oh, please take him, Roger. It would be such a blessing for everyone if you could take him to Tibet and leave him there."

"My cousin loves me passionately." Dolfi sighed.

"She doesn't at all," Bessie retorted sharply.

Dolfi rested on his elbow and beamed at Bessie.

"Would you like me to marry you, Bessie?"

Bessie turned away, mumbling something we couldn't hear, and I told Dolfi not to behave like a Sicilian. The argument began again.

"Dolfi's father is English," Bessie said.

He listened for a moment and then he began to crow and hoot with laughter.

"My mother! Did she tell you that story about Randolph Achurch? Did you believe her? Don't you know what the servants call her?"

We sat dumbfounded as Dolfi hugged his knees in delight, rocking back and forth in the black sand.

"The mattress. *Signora Materasso—*"

"That's enough, Dolfi!" Roger said.

"She always sleeps with the chef. Don't you remember that Swiss chef? Bertrand something or other—I've forgotten his name, but I shall never forget seeing them at it together on one of the sofas in the garden room. She used to take him to bed and discuss menus with him while they fucked. I think half the local aristocracy has had it on with her, and every able-bodied servant."

"Dolfi!"

Roger had dropped his pipe and was standing over Dolfi, blazing with anger.

"You filthy little exhibitionist! Your mother! You're talking about your mother!"

"She's a fat whore!" Dolfi shouted, and Roger slapped him across the face with such force that Dolfi spun backwards and fell over. Roger pounced on him, picked him up by the seat of his bathing suit, carried him down to the water and flung him in.

"I hope you drown!" Roger shouted.

Dolfi twisted over on to his knees and swam out past the rocks. We saw him floating on his back, arms outstretched.

"I—I'm sorry about that," Roger said.

As I handed him his pipe, I noticed that his hand was trembling.

"I completely lost my block. Absolutely no excuse for behaving like that. Made a damn fool of myself."

"I think it's Dolfi who should apologize," I said and realized that we still didn't know anything more about his father.

Dolfi changed after that incident and whenever Roger was with us he was less boisterous and seemed content to let Roger take charge of the conversation. It was becoming a summer of wonders with every day more perfect than the next. Bessie's parents had found a group of Americans and they spent most of the day at the pool drinking pink gins, discussing photography and going on trips. I was trying hard to fall in love and there were times when Roger and I walked together through the winding mossy streets of Erice with Bessie and Dolfi behind us that I could almost believe I had. We stood looking down at Trapani from the ancient Elymian wall along the parapet and Roger sighed.

"Funny sort of feeling—when you can stand in a place and look down and see where you were the day before."

Dolfi craned forward, making seagull noises and flapping his arms, but at one glance from Roger he subsided.

"I think that's why I really want to go to Tibet: stand on one of those peaks and look back—at myself."

"You don't have to climb a mountain to do that," I said.

"Oh, now we are going to be lectured by the Professoressa," Dolfi moaned.

"That's enough, Dolfi. What were you going to say, Gwen?"

"I think there's an archaeology of the self. It's—" and when I had begun I didn't know how to conclude. "It's—a way of standing in yourself and looking back at all you've been."

"I prefer to do it on a mountain," Roger said quietly. "It's less disturbing—not so many peaks and precipices."

Dolfi yawned and I saw Bessie take his hand sympathetically.

It was a glorious summer and a perfect love affair for Bessie and me: they did nothing and we imagined everything.

Nine

If Colonel Whitlow had not insisted on supervising the packing himself, it would all have been completed within the month, but he examined every cup and counted each spoon and delivered little reminiscences about everything. We were all helping until the afternoon when the shell boxes appeared and after that Roger said it would be best if we left the Colonel and Mrs Whitlow to finish packing on their own. Roger and Dolfi had just carried some nailed trunks into the spare room while Bessie and I sorted china for Mrs Whitlow. She then produced the shell boxes. I had often seen one or two of them in the drawing room but now they were ranged in ranks across the dining-room table and along the sideboard. There were seventy-six of them and Mrs Whitlow stood in front of them, her eyes misting.

"I know where I found every shell. These are from Cape Town and these little star-shaped ones are from the beach near Colombo—"

"My God, Beverly, I hope you don't think I'm going to pay good money to have all that junk crated back to England, do you?"

Colonel Whitlow was glaring at the boxes, his face mottling.

"They're my hobby, dear. I've spent years collecting the shells and making these boxes. I'm sure that some of them are very valuable."

She held one up by a handle of two dried sea-horses standing on their tails with their noses touching. Shells were arranged like roses and fans, another sagged under the weight of a cathedral of cowries surrounded by a forest of branched coral.

"Looks like fifty bloody wasted years to me," the Colonel shouted and then Roger had him by the arm and was leading him out to the balcony.

"You can't possibly leave those garden statues," Roger said. "Some of them are antiques, aren't they?"

"Antiques!" Colonel Whitlow roared. "If you can't tell a Graeco-Roman marble when you see it you should go round to the Burnsides'. He's got everything but gnomes in his garden."

"I can't part with them," Mrs Whitlow whispered. "Not my shell boxes."

Colonel Whitlow reluctantly agreed to let her take six back to England but Roger spirited the rest of them to the museum and there we packed them in a separate container and wrote "kitchen utensils" on the outside.

"The old boy will never realize he has one more crate when they're taken down to the ship." Roger chuckled.

My mother was watching us from her reclining chair as we wrapped each box in paper and when we were finished she told Roger that he was a remarkably thoughtful and astute young man. It was so unexpected to hear her praise anyone except my father that I sat back on my heels and stared at her. Something had happened to her voice in the last few weeks and she seemed to be struggling to articulate. She always spoke with a peculiar emphasis, but the words came more slowly now with a muffled intonation of the vowels. When I asked her if anything was wrong she told me she had caught a chill and I believed her.

My parents went upstairs to the drawing room and the four of us sat in the *bagghiu* admiring Roger's handiwork.

"It was a brilliant idea," Bessie said.

Roger shrugged. "I think I have the makings of a decent staff officer given the chance."

Rosalia served supper and I noticed that she was hovering over the roses, pretending to pull off dead flowers, but really listening to us.

"If you like," I said, "Rosalia will tell our fortunes. Won't you, Rosalia?"

Bessie said she already knew hers and it was going to be a life full of love. Dolfi announced that he was cursed and he was glad of it because being cursed made him intelligent and good-looking like the devil.

"I don't believe you're cursed," Bessie said consolingly.

"Roger?"

Rosalia came slowly towards us and stood in front of him without smiling. Roger regarded her quizzically and when she did not speak he said, "Can you tell my future just by looking at me?"

"You will bring grief to all who know you."

Before any of us could answer Rosalia was gone and we heard her clattering pots in the kitchen.

Roger seemed nonplussed and I told him that Rosalia's fortunes were never very pleasant.

"Unnerving sort of thing to say to a chap," Roger said, lighting his pipe.

"Oh, she wanted to frighten you off, that's all." Bessie's voice was sharp and decided. "She can't bear it when Gwen mixes with her own sort of people."

"Ah, I see—" and Roger's laugh lost its edge.

"She's probably breaking her heart that Gwen will be leaving here this year and going home."

"I don't believe in fortune-telling. Nothing I saw in India impressed me. It's just a parlour game like finding sixpences in the Christmas pudding," Roger said firmly. "Fortune is what you make yourself."

"Don't say that to Rosalia. She believes in *destino*," I replied.

"Yes? Well, that's where the Anglo-Saxon temperament wins out over these Mediterranean types. We put our faith in gumption, hard work and determination. That's why we have an Empire."

"Let's play wishing," Bessie said suddenly. "What do you want to be and what do you most want to do in all the world?"

"I want to go to Tibet with Roger."

We thought Dolfi was asleep—he often dozed when he was not the centre of attention—but he was wide awake and gazing at Roger. Stretching out his arms on either side he then said that if he couldn't go to Tibet he wanted everyone in the world to love and admire him.

Roger and I laughed but Bessie said in a small voice that she admired him and Dolfi poked out his tongue at her. Dreamily, Roger watched a spiral of smoke coil up through the vine and murmured, "I would like to join an expedition to Mount Everest after I've been to Tibet. What do I want to be most? Chief of the General Staff. What do I really want to do? Be the first man to reach the summit of Everest."

"Don't you ever want to get married, Roger?" Bessie sounded reproachful.

"I can't afford to get married, Bessie. Well, I suppose if I met some excessively rich heiress—"

"Gwen is a Harcourt from Russell Morton in Shropshire," Bessie said triumphantly.

"Well now, I think we should elope on the spot, Miss Harcourt," and they all began to laugh while I writhed with embarrassment.

I was still raging at Bessie that night when it was time to go to bed. My mother no longer complained that I was spending most of my nights with Bessie at the Villa or that I did not come back to the museum for days at a time. She seemed happy to be left alone with my father. Now I was pounding my fists against the pillow and moaning that I could never see Roger again or face anybody after such a humiliation.

"It was a joke." Bessie tried to placate me. "Everyone laughed except you."

"You made it sound as though I was fishing for a proposal."

"Oh, don't be so stupid, Gwen. We're both too young to get married. But he does like you very much. I can tell by the way he looks at you."

"He doesn't love me."

"How do you know? He can't possibly say anything when you're still so young. But I just know he'll ask you to wait for him."

I really began to believe I was in love with Roger, especially when I gave Mrs Chambers a letter the next day and she smiled roguishly at me and said that everyone was jealous of me.

"After all, you have the most attractive young man in Trapani following you around like a lap dog."

She read the letter in my office and I saw her frown and almost stamp her foot. Obviously, Travis was not being as generous with money as she expected.

Bessie and I spent hours at night discussing the nature of love and whether I had all the right symptoms. Did I tremble when Roger came near? Was he in my mind every minute of the day and night? Would I sooner be with him than anyone else in the world?

"I'd sooner be with you, Bessie," I told her and she sighed.

"Oh, I hope you don't take after your mother. I hope you're not going to wait until you're old before you fall in love."

"I don't care for him the way you—the way you seem to feel about Dolfi."

She was silent in the dark and then I heard a gulping sob from her bed. The bedclothes rustled and instantly she was alongside me, her arms around me, clutching me so tightly that I was in pain. Her body felt feverish and she shook as though some nightmarish beast had seized her in its jaws and was worrying her. Suddenly she put her face to mine and kissed me with a passion that frightened me. I struggled to free myself and took her by the shoulders, holding her away from me.

"I love him so much," she moaned. "I'll do anything he wants. I don't care. I want him to love me. Oh Dolfi, please love me."

I took her by the wrists, telling her that I was not Dolfi, and gradually her sobbing ceased. If this was love, I told myself, I wanted no part of it.

Roger was so gay and whimsical the next morning that all my embarrassment with him was swept aside in laughter.

"Miss Harcourt di Marineo, I take it we are now formally engaged and contemplating elopement with the understanding that the moment you sign the registry I appropriate all your worldly goods and abandon you at the church door. Please understand, Miss Harcourt di Marineo, that I couldn't contemplate marriage with you under any other circumstances."

Delighted, I agreed to this engagement and Bessie was content.

"You see, it may seem like a joke now," she said darkly. "But one day it will be serious."

Imagination had taken hold of us and we planned weddings and honeymoons and discussed our futures at night holding hands across the space between our beds. For us the future was like an empty palace that we could fill with fountains and tapestries and people who were kind and clever and beautiful. Roger had never kissed me but this made no difference: I was in love in a warm and comforting way that did not torment me like Bessie's passion for Dolfi. Only once did Roger talk to me about love and that was in the evening when the four of us were sitting on the terrace watching the darting lanterns of the fishing boats as they followed the channel between the islands out to the open sea.

"I have the best fortune of all," Bessie said quietly. "To be surrounded with love. Are you in love, Dolfi?" she asked quickly and he replied as though her words were linked to his.

"Yes, I'm in love."

"With yourself," Roger said, and we all laughed but I felt the thrill of joy that swept through Bessie.

"I've only seen perfect love once in my life," Roger added quietly. "Your parents, Gwen. I was amazed when Aunt Beverly told me about them but it's true. They are still in love with each other. Even now, when your mother is so ill, you can see—not just affection in your father's eyes when he looks at her, but adoring, passionate love."

"Yes," I said dully and hung my head and stared at my shoes.

"You see that sort of thing in soppy films but you never expect to find it in real life. If it does happen you can't imagine it lasting beyond the honeymoon. Perhaps it's our fault because we think the girl must always be a Juliet and the Romeo a young and handsome fellow. Perhaps—the lesson of your parents is that a love like that can happen between two people who are old and sick, or two people who—who just don't fit the pattern of romantic fiction."

Bessie had hold of my hand in the darkness and squeezed it because she could sense my chagrin.

"I think it's peculiar when people are so old," she said tersely.

"It's like watching a miracle," Roger replied. "Can you imagine the blank terror people must have felt when they saw a dead man raised to life, the blind given sight or a dry twig burst into flower? Everything we know about life is proof that love doesn't endure—and yet, there are your parents, Gwen. Unsettling but pretty remarkable," he concluded lamely.

"I love like that," Dolfi cried. "That is what is in my heart."

"Come off it, Dolfi." Roger laughed. "Chaps don't discuss their feelings in public. Rather like telling people about your underwear, you know."

Bessie's hand in mine was trembling.

Day followed day in sunny splendour and there were moments when I felt as if I could reach the sky with shining hands and scatter light across the world. Roger, Dolfi, Bessie and me: as if we had come from the four corners of the earth to greet each other like legendary beings blowing the winds in a medieval map, or the elements blending in the alchemist's crucible and becoming gold.

I always tried to spend an hour in the early morning or in the evening before dinner with the books, writing up the accounts, because I regarded this as my special duty at the Villa. Two weeks before Bessie was to return home, when I was in the little office, Mrs Chambers looked round the door and asked me if a letter had arrived for her. I handed her the white envelope reluctantly because I remembered how annoyed she had been when she read the last one. She opened it slowly, grimacing slightly as the paper tore unevenly. I was about to offer her a paper knife when I saw her whole expression change. It was like a heavy curtain drawn back and instantly a dark room was flooded with sunlight. She laughed and spun on her heel, pirouetting, flourishing the letter over her head.

"I knew! I knew he'd agree!"

"Travis?" I said tentatively.

"Everything is perfect, absolutely, smashingly, wonderfully perfect, Gwen!"

She sat down and read the letter again slowly. I could see her lips moving as though she wanted to taste each word.

"Well, no more worries now," she said sighing and smiled at me. "Thank you for your help, Gwen dear."

I found myself sharing her joy because I knew that the home in Manchester was now saved for Bessie—and for me too. Mr Chambers would not have to think about emigrating to Kenya or Australia and everything would be just as Bessie had planned.

"When are you going to tell Bessie?" I said anxiously.

"Not yet," she replied with a little frown. "Diplomacy is still the order of the day. I can't let Mr Chambers know who has saved him."

"I see," I replied.

"I hate to say this to you so bluntly, Gwen, but you'll be with us by Christmas."

"Christmas?"

"I didn't talk to your mother. It wasn't necessary. She's very, very sick. You know that, don't you?"

I could feel the cord tightening around my throat as I tried to escape from the pain.

"You must let me take charge of everything, dear. I really think I've managed this rather well," she said gleefully, and gave me a theatrical wink as Bessie came in to say that Roger had offered to teach us billiards.

Colonel Whitlow had still not finished packing by the time Bessie and her parents were due to leave. Even Roger, who was usually so calm, seemed distracted.

"Just when I think everything's ready to go down to the port and be shipped, he decides to check one of the boxes again. He almost opened up 'Kitchen Utensils' yesterday."

We were in Benno's cart because Colonel Whitlow had sold his motor the day before to a banker in Marsala.

Bessie said she was glad because everyone would be at the Villa to see her off. It was just the same. Whenever she spoke about leaving a lurching wave of grief swept over me and tears stung my eyes.

"Mother told me that everything will be all right now in Manchester. No more money troubles," she whispered.

I could only try to smile.

"I doubt if I'll ever get back to India." Roger sighed. "I wouldn't be surprised if they don't cashier me over this. I've written and explained about uncle, but I can't take indefinite leave while he decides that he should have packed his books in extra oilskin."

We passed the Burnsides on the road to the Villa and Canon Burnside explained that Maud had been wandering again.

"It's time for us to go too," he said and Mrs Burnside waved and smiled and said she hoped to see us all at the bazaar.

"You won't be the last to leave here," Roger said to me. "I think the Burnsides will be off before the year's out. This place is finished," he added and looked around him.

"It was lovely once but everything's changed now," Bessie said firmly. "Even my father says he doesn't want to come back here and look at all those fat Germans on the beach. It's not English any longer."

Roger and Dolfi were with me when Bessie left. Mr Chambers had hired a car to drive them to Messina.

"Leaving in style," he said, and helped Mrs Chambers in with a bow.

She turned and smiled knowingly at me and I tried to return her smile.

"Dolfi!" Roger's voice was firm. "Bessie deserves a kiss goodbye."

"If it's really goodbye," Dolfi muttered but I don't think Bessie heard him. He was about to kiss her cheek when she twisted suddenly and her mouth was on his.

"Dolfi, you won't forget me, will you?"

He shrugged and was about to walk away when Roger called him back.

Bessie was hugging me then and promising to write as soon as she was home.

"Your home," she said.

They were gone.

Roger patted me on the shoulder consolingly and I was glad that he was there.

That afternoon Frau Brunner came to the office where I was trying to read the figures through a blur of tears.

"So sad for Bessie to say goodbye to her English friend. The romance of a summer is very sweet but it can't last. India is a cruel place as I should know. Roger is a perfect gentleman and such a good influence on Dolfi, don't you agree? He is speaking better."

I scarcely heard her because all I had in my mind and my heart was Bessie. Before she left I had made her a silver cord like the one I had worn to the opera and she said that we would wear them at the family Christmas party. I did not need to close my eyes to see the Chamberses' living room with its Christmas tree and the three poems pinned to the mantelpiece. Every year they wrote some verses about the past year on Christmas Eve and left them for everyone to read. This year, Bessie said to me, there would be four poems and she knew mine would be the cleverest and funniest of them all.

The Whitlows did not leave for another month and even when all the boxes and crates had been shipped, the Colonel kept running back to the house to make sure that nothing had been left behind. At the very last Mrs Whitlow gave me a shell box.

"I kept it especially for you, Gwen. You can put hairpins in it—all sorts of useful things."

It felt sharp and unfriendly in my hands, with spikes and prickles jutting out at odd angles, but I still have it and when I gingerly pick it up I remember the Whitlows at the station. Even then the Colonel was scanning the sky and predicting bad weather.

"Everything will be lost—that boat wasn't seaworthy. Any fool could see that."

"It's too late now, uncle," Roger said firmly and almost lifted the old man on to the bus.

"See you in England," Mrs Whitlow called to me and they were gone too.

Every day I went to the Villa and helped Frau Brunner with her letters and I wondered what she would say when I told her that I was going home to England. She was oblivious to any ideas except her own and no matter what I said to her, she remained convinced that Dolfi and I would marry and that Roger was infatuated with Bessie.

"Ah, a summer romance, and now little Bessie is in Manchester and Roger will be in India. It is very sad but it is like my own story."

She sighed gustily and placed another pile of accounts in front of me.

"I have spoken to friends in Palermo and in spite of my tears they insist that Dolfi must register for his military training next month. The Fascists say that boys like Dolfi must set an example."

I could not imagine Dolfi taking orders or wearing a uniform but I said nothing to Frau Brunner and sorted the bills from the receipts.

"It might be an excellent thing if you marry before my little Dolfi begins his training, Gwen."

My shock must have shown in my face.

"It is for my sake. What if some sickness should strike me down? What if I were killed? What would happen to the Villa?"

I stared at her, unable to speak, but I could feel the blood rushing to my face.

"Property. Property is what endures. Can you imagine what Dolfi would do with the Villa if I died tomorrow?" She paused. "You are quite right. It is unthinkable. He would lose everything in a month—a week."

"I shall never marry Dolfi, Frau Brunner. I loathe and detest him. Besides, Bessie loves him."

Frau Brunner was laughing, her great chest rocking like a boat in a storm and her corset stays creaking.

"Your parents will decide for you, Gwen. I'll call at the museum and speak to them. I know you're only sixteen, but Dolfi is eighteen and he will be away for two years, so when he gets back from his training, he will be twenty and you will be eighteen. That is a perfect age to begin marriage and if anything happens to me in between, I'll know that my Villa is safe. I've taught you well, but I saw that you had a clever head on your shoulders and that you were old for your years."

The whole idea was so ludicrous that I began to laugh.

"Dolfi will refuse and so shall I."

Frau Brunner sat back and smiled pleasantly at me.

"My dear child, do you really imagine that you can please yourself in this life? Or that you have free will?"

"I am not going to marry Dolfi," I said quietly.

"Gwen, you will do as you must, because you have no choice. And it is better this way."

I could only shake my head. If she had told me that I was going to grow wings and fly between the Villa and the museum it could not have seemed more absurd to me.

"I was weak with Dolfi's father," Frau Brunner said grimly, "and I cannot tell you what that fiend did to my poor heart. It will be different with you. Begin with hate—and after some time you may find Dolfi quite amusing."

I saw very little of Roger that week because there was another complication over the sale of his uncle's villa and he had to consult a lawyer in Palermo. When he returned, he took Dolfi with him to help supervise the cleaning of the house because he could not speak Sicilian and the new owners were coming at the end of the month.

Bessie's first letter disturbed me for it contained news of a terrible row at home. Her mother had made her stay in her bedroom so that she only heard scraps of what her parents were arguing about downstairs but she was sure it concerned money. I sighed when I read that because I knew that Mr Chambers must have found out that Travis had saved him from bankruptcy. There was very little else in the letter because Bessie was obviously upset but she begged me to ask Dolfi to write to her. "I shall never forget that kiss he gave me when we said goodbye and how he said he loved me with all his heart." It was then I first came to understand that imagination and desire are stronger than experience and reality.

It was late afternoon and I was about to leave the Villa when Roger and Dolfi said they were going back to town with Benno so they could walk along the beach and would I like to join them. For three days it had been oppressively humid with lowering skies and thunder but no rain to break the sultry heat. I was glad of Roger's company because I had seen very little of him since the Whitlows left. His handsome brown face was lined with fatigue and there were deep shadows under his eyes. Usually his hair was combed back smoothly but today a strand wavered across his forehead and even his shoulders were slumped. Benno left us near the station where he was picking up some bags and we walked down across the esplanade to the sand.

Dolfi was silent and Roger said very little except when he helped me over the seaweed that was ridged in terraces after a particularly high tide. All the summer visitors had left and at the end of the beach the painted eyes of the fishing boats were glimmering in the dusk as they watched for the passage through the shallows to the open sea.

"I'd like to walk ahead a little and think," Roger said sombrely.

I knew all the moods of parting and saying goodbye and I let him go in silence. Occasionally a heavy drop of rain fell, pocking the smooth sand, and the air smelt sourly of rotting weed and jellyfish. The beach could have been at the end of the world and we were to be the last to leave it. Roger's head was bent as he strode ahead and although his shape was blurring in the half light I could still catch the drifting aroma of his pipe. Dolfi was miserable, I knew, because he would soon be in uniform and learning to be a soldier.

"You are my cousin," he said abruptly.

"I've never understood the relationship, Dolfi," I said. "Nobody ever wants to tell me about your father."

"My grandmother and your grandmother were sisters."

"If we are descended from Adam and Eve then we're all cousins of a sort," I said lightly.

He was standing in front of me, preventing me from walking forward. I tried to step round him but he put his hand on my arm.

"Because you're my cousin, you will help me."

"What have you done?"

"I am going to run away."

"Oh Dolfi, you're always running away." I laughed. "Everyone's used to your mysterious disappearances now."

"This time I shall never come back."

"I'm sure you've said that before too."

Suddenly I knew that Dolfi was going to propose to me. He had been ordered to marry me by his mother and for once he was doing what she wanted. I tried to forestall him but Dolfi held up his hand to stop me.

"Listen to me, cousin. You will understand because we have the same blood. I am in love."

"Dolfi, I am not interested in your little performances. They're childish and stupid."

"I am in love with Roger and we are going to run away together."

I was about to laugh at him but in the same instant I felt a terrible recognition.

"We have been lovers all summer and we cannot live apart."

Thoughts and pictures rushed through my brain at such speed that I almost felt dizzy: times at the beach when Dolfi and Roger would slip off behind the rocks to change and we never noticed how long they took. Bessie and I had been content to wait and talk about them, and when we talked about them we never noticed their absence: it was as if they were sitting alongside us. Our imagination had made them present even when they were . . . Where had they gone and what had they been doing when Bessie and I sat planning weddings and honeymoons?

"We couldn't let people know about us. Roger said we had to be discreet."

Bessie and I had been their protection. Two young couples like angels from heaven playing tennis, exploring the ruins, swimming from the beach of black sand.

"We're going to India. I shall be Roger's secretary."

At that I tried to laugh but the sound that came from my mouth was a ragged cry.

"You! A secretary! You can't even spell the simplest words."

"Roger will teach me."

I covered my ears because I did not want to hear any more.

"You will help me, cousin."

"No."

"You must tell my mother."

"Dolfi! I hate you with all my heart and soul!" I shouted at the top of my voice.

Roger turned back and I saw him walking slowly towards us.

"Is it true, Roger? Or is he lying to me as he always does?"

Anger was buffeting my head and I felt my temples were about to burst.

Roger stood next to Dolfi and even in the gathering dark I could see that he was shaking spasmodically.

"I didn't expect anything like this to happen, Gwen. I thought it was an attraction—I won't deny that there have been others in my life, but this possessed me. Dolfi is my life."

"And you are mine, Roger."

To my horror, I saw in their faces the same glowing fire that burned in my parents' eyes.

Roger put his arms around Dolfi and began to stroke his hair.

"You can't go to India," I said finally.

"I have my posting there," Roger replied.

"Do you think you can take him with you?"

"Yes."

"As your secretary?"

"Yes."

"You are mad, Roger."

"I admit that too, but I can't live without Dolfi."

"What will your commanding officer say? What will everyone say?"

"We shall be discreet."

"Dolfi—discreet?" I laughed incredulously.

"Nothing will dissuade us," Roger said brokenly. "We're leaving tonight. Everything's arranged. We hope you can explain what has happened to Dolfi's mother."

"You expect me to tell her that you have eloped with her son?"

"My mother will listen to you," Dolfi said.

"You'll ruin your career."

"Dolfi is more important."

As he said that Dolfi looked at me over his shoulder and said pityingly, "It is impossible for her to understand. She can't love, Roger. She could not even love me."

Ten

Some actors, I am told, feel a sense of loss amounting to anguish when the play ends and they close the dressing-room door, step out of their costumes and remove their make-up. The self created by greasepaint and a circle of light reluctantly yields to another more drab and mundane that worries about the landlord and unpaid bills as it shrugs on a raincoat and goes out to a cold street swept with rain. Last week I read about a theatre in Liverpool that was haunted, not by ghosts, but by their absence. A touring company was just ending its season with *Much Ado About Nothing* and at the final curtain even that dour audience stood and applauded the two young actors playing Beatrice and Benedick. They took their last bow and hand in hand walked from the stage, through the wings and down to the stage door. Still in costume they opened the door, stepped out into the street and vanished. They were never seen again.

When I heard that story I saw myself with Rosalia stumbling down from the gallery at the *opera di pupei* and I remembered the sensation of suddenly falling into a world of shadows and phantasms. Reality was not the sauntering passers-by or the dusty, ragged mule dragging a cart laden with house tiles; even the stones under my feet were the substance of dream for I was still in a world of jousting knights and Bradamante in her cave. What I saw around me in the street was unreal: a tattered deception of life; what I had left behind in the theatre was reality with its terrible passions and bloody conflicts. I almost felt my mind physically adjusting to this new order as the daze of the theatre left me and I became aware of familiar sights and smells. That night as I sat in the *bagghiu* listening to the measured voice of the fountain it seemed as though I had woken from sleep and a long summer spent dreaming in a mysterious and wonderful play. The loss of it did not anger me, rather I was amazed that I had been enchanted for so long.

Bessie and I had been wooden dolls like Marfisa and Bradamante talking of love in the falsetto notes of the puppet master, moving as an unseen hand adjusted the wires. And yet it was the happiest time of my life for it was never necessary that Roger should love me, simply that I should imagine it to be so. If imagination could give so much joy, if it was possible to be as happy as Bessie and I were that summer, what value could reality possibly have?

Nothing of this was very clear to me at the time but it was the reason why I did not sit that night in a storm of tears over Roger's betrayal. He had done nothing to deceive me. My grief was for Bessie because I knew how much she loved Dolfi. As the shadows slowly mantled me I wondered what letter I must write to make her forget him. Mr Chambers used to do an imitation of George Robey's Fairy Queen with a shrill little voice and a flapping hand that made everyone guffaw, and we knew about Oscar Wilde and the German baron who lived in Taormina and chased boys. Bessie would never believe that Dolfi was queer and Roger had always seemed the perfect English gentleman. I almost laughed then for it was marvellous how they had deceived everyone! They had written a play and we were not simply an audience for them; they had given us parts and, unwittingly, we had played them so successfully that everyone applauded our performances. Mrs Chambers had said that all the women were jealous of me because Roger was like my lap dog and Bessie still imagined that Dolfi was in love with her. Now Roger and Dolfi were on their way to Marsala where they were picking up a coastal boat that would take them to Naples. From Naples they were going by P&O to India.

If I had reluctantly fallen down into the world of known things, Roger and Dolfi had taken up residence in a brilliant world of their own imagining. They had left the theatre in their costumes, but could they vanish like that Beatrice and Benedick in Liverpool? Colonel Whitlow always said that Roger would have a military career as distinguished as that of his father and his grandfather before him, General Harrison Whitlow, who first saw active service as a young lieutenant at the Crimea. While we were walking back to the museum Roger had spoken of his ancestors and of his determination to have his own regiment by the time he was forty. "With Dolfi?" I asked him and Roger would not answer me directly but kept speaking about mountains and climbing across glaciers and up sheer rock walls to reach the peak.

"I shall get everything I want and have Dolfi too."

Those were his last words to me.

Dolfi tried to kiss me goodbye but I pulled away from him and he told me that I would never see him again in this world.

I closed the door of the museum against them and almost felt a sense of relief as I walked through to the *bagghiu*.

I decided that nothing I could write would make Bessie understand what had happened. It would be best if I waited until I was in Manchester where I could explain slowly—and even then I knew I was rationalizing my cowardice.

There was a darker shadow in front of me and I realized that Rosalia must have been standing there, watching me.

"Have they gone?" she asked.

I did not answer but I heard the glint of amusement in her voice.

"*Finocchi*—I watched them all summer."

Rosalia had seen the wires and the patches on the puppets' clothes.

"They are both cursed and what they think will bring them joy will be a misery."

I heard her sigh with satisfaction.

"Tomorrow morning I must tell Frau Brunner what has happened," I said.

"She will have to find another husband for you, won't she?" Rosalia was mocking me but I was too tired to answer.

"I only care about Bessie. I don't want anything to eat. I'm going to bed."

If my sleep had been a riot of nightmares it would have seemed the natural consequence of that day, but I had only one dream and I woke from it laughing. Bessie and I were dancing in a magnificent ballroom, twisting and bending with such grace that we heard bursts of applause from an unseen audience. Dolfi and Roger joined us and we changed partners, but Roger kept stumbling over my feet and Dolfi spun around Bessie and sprawled on the floor. Roger tried to dance on his own but he tripped and fell and Bessie and I stood there laughing at them as they struggled to help each other up.

It was a dream that left me feeling strangely buoyant and as I walked up to the Villa I wondered without any particular anxiety how I should explain what had happened to Dolfi.

Frau Brunner was standing at the top of the terrace steps with her legs apart as though braced against the wind and as soon as she saw me, she began to scream.

"He's gone! My little Dolfi has gone."

Not only had she found out that he had run away but she knew something I did not. Dolfi had opened the safe in her bedroom where she kept foreign currency and stolen what she described as a small fortune.

"He's in love with Roger," I told her. "They've gone to India together."

"In love?"

She bellowed her derision. "He does not want to do his military service so he has made use of that kind young Englishman. Ah, Roger Whitlow has a good heart. Look how he managed to save poor Beverly's shell boxes. A heart of pure gold. And that little fiend who is just like his father has persuaded Roger to take him to India."

There was nothing I could say, I knew that Frau Brunner's rage would yield its own explanations.

"And he did not want to marry you, Gwen. Dolfi wanted nothing that was for his own good and would have pleased me. I have poured out my heart's blood for that little devil, but he has treated me like his father."

She went off wailing and I made my way down to the office.

It was a tiny room at the back of the house, no larger than a cupboard, with a desk, two chairs, the filing cabinets and a barred window that looked out on to the stairs. None of the servants ever came to it. But that morning I had a visitor who walked in after a perfunctory knock. The tall fair militia captain who had searched the museum was standing there, smiling at me.

"I've often wondered where you hid yourself in the Villa."

"If you'd asked, anyone would have told you."

"Ah, but this office is like a secret hiding place. Down a corridor, a flight of steps, another passage and—Beauty in her magic cave."

"It's Captain Prosimo, isn't it?"

"Ah, you have discovered my name."

"I know everyone who comes to the hotel."

"But I did not know that you were Doctor di Marineo's daughter."

"Really?"

I turned a page of the ledger and ran my pencil down a column of figures. This man generated a prickling atmosphere of fear: people said he was not in the regular militia but was really an officer in OVRA, the secret police.

He sat there smiling at me but I did not raise my eyes or speak. I turned the page and concentrated on the figures.

"We've never seen you at any of the rallies."

"No."

"A great many young people attend them. There are splendid opportunities for politically conscious people these days."

"I'm sure there are."

"But you are not interested in politics?"

"No—politics are for men."

"Your father—is he interested in politics?"

This was why he had found his way down to the office. This was the question I had to answer. I turned another page of the ledger and looked at him.

"Yes, my father is very interested in politics."

I could feel the slight sharpening of his attention but his smile remained the same.

"My father has made it his lifelong study."

"Doctor di Marineo is a great scholar. I would like to know his conclusions."

"The real problem"—I leaned forward and concentrated—"is the extent to which the Phoenicians made allies of the Elymians or whether the two races intermarried and became indistinguishable. Some scholars believe that the Phoenicians drove the Elymians back to the hills by force of arms, others maintain that there was an amicable settlement between the two."

I could see a small spot of colour on his cheekbones but I did not laugh.

"I was not speaking of ancient history, Signorina, but of current politics."

"Oh, my father is not interested in anything after the birth of Christ. He is an archaeologist, not a journalist."

"Archaeologists dig up rubbish and then talk about it!"

Captain Prosimo left, jamming his chair back against the wall with such force that the files clattered. I felt extraordinarily pleased with myself.

After her fury at being robbed subsided, Frau Brunner began to grieve for Dolfi, but she never doubted that he would be back very soon. He had run away so many times in the past that she did not seem greatly concerned.

"Once he escaped from his boarding school in Switzerland and he was gone for six weeks. Six weeks! I thought I was going mad with worry, but he wrote to me from Rome. I had to leave in the middle of the season and arrange another school for him."

I wanted to believe her but what I could not forget was Roger's passion on the beach that night as he spoke of climbing mountains with Dolfi at his side. Even as I thought of that I felt like laughing because Dolfi could not walk more than a few yards without stopping to imitate something or mimic someone passing. I tried and failed to imagine him trudging through the snow with a heavy pack on his shoulders or suffering frostbite and dying of cold like Captain Scott in the Antarctic. Dolfi could not bear the slightest pain and once when he tripped on the rocks and grazed his shin he sat and howled like a child. What malicious god had decided to make Roger and Dolfi lovers?

Bessie was back at school and she only referred once more to her parents' argument. She had asked both of them about it but neither of them would tell her and she assumed it was money as usual. I was certain that Mr Chambers was humiliated and furious when he discovered that it was Travis who had provided the funds to save his business. Her next letter was full of school news and came with a bundle of magazines. She carefully made notes against the fashions and told me what she thought would suit me and what she intended to have made for the spring. She begged me to tell her about Dolfi. I wrote and said that he had run away to escape his military training and no one knew where he was.

This was the truth because as the weeks passed and Frau Brunner's gloom spread through every room of the Villa like an oppressive fog, not one word had come from him, or from Roger either. Frau Brunner's mood changed again and one day she told me that she had reported his absence to the militia. Dolfi's eighteenth birthday had passed and he should have been in uniform and beginning his training. Three weeks later she went to the English consul in Palermo and told him that her son had run away to India and she despatched a cable to the Viceroy's office in Delhi. Again, there was a long delay and then she placed a letter in front of me.

"Tibet?" she said. "Captain Roger Whitlow and his companion, William Smith, have joined an expedition to Tibet."

Tibet could have been Arcady or El Dorado—it sounded unimaginably distant and strange and yet Roger had often spoken of it. Was this where their dreams had taken them? And who was William Smith but Dolfi Brunner, though for a moment I wondered that he had chosen such an ordinary name.

Frau Brunner sat there repeating "Tibet" over and over again as though she could make it familiar by repetition.

"When will he come back?" she cried to me through her tears. "When will I see my little Dolfi again?"

I think the only bright moment of the day was when I walked from the museum to the Villa, or when Benno let me ride in his painted cart. I sat in the back among suitcases and boxes from the station and Benno would look at me over his shoulder and sing a love song so heartbreakingly dolorous that it made me laugh. At first I had been fascinated by the Villa's account books but now they irritated me. On the work table in the curator's room at the museum there was a pile of journals that I knew my father had not even opened and two trays of potsherds remained unsorted. I told myself that I was living for Bessie's next letter, but the truth was so horrible that I could not bear to hold it in my mind for more than a second. What I know now is that I was waiting for my mother to die, and I was impatient.

She no longer came down to the *bagghiu* and her reclining chair, but remained in her room. My father seldom left her side. I tried to speak to her but the left side of her face seemed to be paralysed so that her mouth drooped and a thread of saliva trickled down her chin. Very gently, and murmuring loving words, my father would take a handkerchief and wipe it away for her.

I was in the office, reading a letter from Bessie that ended, "How is your mother?" with each word underlined when Frau Brunner threw herself down in the chair.

"Tibet—I have been reading about Tibet. It is a land of shamans and devil worshippers, and sometimes the mountains fall down on travellers and crush them. The people are savage and believe that strangers who have white skins are ghosts to be stoned. Oh, my Dolfi! My little child!"

"I'm sure you'll hear from him when the expedition gets back to India, Frau Brunner."

"I think he is dead."

"No—" I was about to mention bad pennies but decided against it.

She rocked back and forth with her stays cracking and complaining and suddenly she said that she wanted me to sleep at the Villa for the next week or two.

I was puzzled and when I asked her why she said that my parents were concerned about my travelling back and forth between the museum and the Villa, and she wanted extra work done.

"It doesn't take me long to type the letters and—"

"I know it's not the high season but this is a good time to take an inventory."

"Are you going to sell the Villa and leave like the Whitlows?"

"An inventory is necessary for the insurance. Ah—" she sighed gustily. "I could never bring myself to sell my home. But if my little Dolfi is dead—"

"I'm sure you'll hear from him when Roger gets back from this expedition."

"To Tibet."

When Benno brought me home to the museum that evening it seemed that Frau Brunner had already spoken to my parents about the inventory and everything was arranged for me. Rosalia was waiting at the door as usual with her shawl over her head and Benno surreptitiously made the *mano cornuta* at her.

"Is my mother very ill?"

"That is for God to say."

By the fret of lines around her mouth I knew that she was angry, but not with me.

"You can take a suitcase with you to the Villa. Miki will drive you tomorrow morning."

I trailed upstairs and knocked on my parents' door. My mother was propped up against the pillows, my father beside her, holding her hand in both of his.

I began awkwardly. "If you're very ill, Mother, I think I should be here to help you."

She shook her head.

"I would much sooner stay."

This time she moved her hand dismissively.

"It is best," my father said quietly. "Your mother needs quiet now."

"I'm not a child! I don't run up and down stairs or—"

My mother turned her head slightly and I knew that I was upsetting her. At the door she suddenly spoke and I waited as the syllables came clogged and rough.

"The Nonsuch chest—Eleanor—mine—yours now."

I went downstairs with my teeth clenched so tightly that I felt a sudden rasping pain in my jaw.

"It's no use. I tried to speak to her."

Rosalia was holding a cup of coffee and I took it from her automatically.

"Why? Why does she hate me so much?"

"There is no place in her heart for anyone except your father."

"I'm her daughter."

"She cannot bear to look at you."

"What have I done to make her hate me?"

"You will be alive when she is dead and you do not love your father as she does."

"But she knows I love my father."

"Would you give your life for him? Is he in your mind and heart every moment of the day and night?"

"Of course not."

"That is what she expects."

"I can't love like that."

"Drink your coffee and I'll help you pack your clothes."

She paused and gazed up the staircase to my parents' door. "If she were not mad she would want you to be with her. A mother's hand reaches out for her daughter when death stands at the foot of her bed."

"My father is the same," I said bitterly.

"They are mad together," Rosalia said firmly. "They should have lived on a desert island where there are only birds and trees."

Their door was open next morning and I paused to say goodbye to my mother. Neither of them saw me, for my father's head was against her shoulder and her arms were round him. I did not hear what she was saying to him but I saw her right hand fluttering against his back as with the other she stroked his white hair. I turned away without speaking and walked down to the car.

Frau Brunner's moods swung from vindictive threats and predictions to a raging grief that reduced her to broken sobbing. One day she told me that she had spoken to the *comandante* of the militia and the moment Dolfi returned he would be arrested and imprisoned.

"There are severe punishments for boys who evade military service," she said grimly.

The next day she was convinced that Dolfi had simply run away in a fit of high spirits and now he was dead in a Tibetan avalanche. Following her around the Villa with a notebook and a pencil, I had to pause at regular intervals while she threw herself on to the nearest chair to sob and mop her eyes.

My father came twice to the Villa and said that my mother was still very weak, but a little improved, he thought. When I asked if I could see her, he said that the doctor had ordered absolute quiet for her. I wrote to Bessie and told her that my mother was dying and I think my letter must have crossed with hers because in it I found a loop of red wool and read that she was knitting me a scarf. It was, she said, to be my Christmas present.

The inventory began with the suites upstairs and Frau Brunner examined every cushion and vase while I made a note of it. The maids were scurrying up and down the halls with rags and mops, because Frau Brunner pulled furniture from the walls, tested the webbing under the chairs and stripped every bed to check the mattresses. Usually, the staff was given a holiday at I Morti, the four days of mourning that begin with All Saints' Day on the first of November, but this year she insisted that everyone must help with the inventory. The grumbling of the servants became a subterranean roar as she went from room to room with me in her wake ordering curtains to be taken down and mirrors silvered.

From one of the side windows I saw a straggling crowd of brightly dressed people laden with picnic baskets and bunches of flowers winding their way along the road from Trapani towards the cemetery where they would sit among the rows of tombs and celebrate the dead. I faintly heard children laughing and a snatch of song as the people went past to that other town of glistening white marble and painted sepulchres on the side of the hill. A corpse is never buried in the earth in Sicily and even the poorest can hope to find a place in a charity mortuary. There the dead sleep more comfortably than they ever did in life. As I watched, a group of nuns went by with a retinue of children from the orphanage dressed in brown capes and carrying little bouquets of flowers. They were going to beg alms from the living who were eating and drinking in the cemetery.

I wondered if I would soon be walking up that hill behind my mother's hearse and where among all those marble tombs she would be buried. Even as the thought entered my head I felt my eyes full of tears and I stumbled. I could not tell at first who was holding me but I smelt the cologne and felt the stiff whalebones.

"You must go home now," Frau Brunner said. "Miki is downstairs with the car."

I did not have to ask why he had come for me.

"You must be a brave girl, Gwen, but remember that your mother was not a young woman and while she lived she was very happy. Ah, how we all envied your parents! Such a romantic love! They were like sweethearts to the end, devoted to each other. Rosalia said she died in your father's arms and now he is like a lost soul. Poor man. My love for Randolph was like that. I should have followed him to India and died there with him, then I would not have married a fiend in my grief and lived the rest of my life in misery."

Was that supposed to console me? I thought bitterly.

Miki drove slowly because people were still making their way up the hill, some of the women carrying baskets on their heads while the men sauntered ahead smoking. Children ran about and between them, laughing, and two tried to jump on the running board of the car. Miki blew the horn and they screamed with delight and pretended to shoot him.

My mother's coffin lay on the table in the *bagghiu*. Beside it sat my father, his head on his chest, one hand on the polished wood. He did not look up when I came in or even seem aware that I was standing in front of him. This was my moment of release, for the coffin had replaced a wall of living flesh dividing Sicily from Manchester; it was a wooden fence no higher than a step. With one stride I could pass over it and find Bessie waiting for me on the other side, and yet, in that same instant, it was not joy or grief that I felt but a spasm of blind anger. I wanted to pound on my mother's coffin and demand to know why she had always hated me. No, not hate, for hate was a passion I could have understood. I had endured something much worse from her and that was indifference and occasional irritation. My rage was compounded with guilt because I had been waiting for her death, waiting for the time when I could decently leave her house and Sicily and go to my real home in Manchester where there were people who loved me. Rosalia was guiding me upstairs to my bedroom without my even being aware that she had taken me by the arm.

She closed the bedroom door and I saw that she was shaking.

"Your father is a lunatic!"

I sat on the edge of the bed and wondered where I had placed my notepad. My letter to Bessie would be in the morning post.

"He is going to drown your mother!"

Her words jolted me and I looked at her in amazement.

"Yes! Yes, I have spoken to him but he does not hear anyone."

"You can't drown someone who is dead."

"It is the same. God blessed her and took her at this sacred time when to die is a sign of grace, but she is not to be laid in the Marineo crypt. No, your father wrote many weeks ago to your mother's family in England because it was her wish to be buried at her old home. Last week a cable came from lawyers saying that her family did not know of any Evelyn di Marineo, that for this family Evelyn Harcourt did not exist."

"I don't think it matters now. She's dead."

"What is this family in England? Are they animals that do not recognize their own blood?"

I shrugged and recalled that my notepad was in my desk drawer.

"Now, he is going to give her to the sea. I tell you, his head is in the moon."

"Buried at sea?"

"This evening, and that pagan priest Signor Burnside will say the prayers for her."

Turiddu and two of his men came at dusk and carried the coffin out to a cart on their shoulders. I walked behind it with Rosalia, Miki, my father and Canon Burnside.

"It is a trifle unusual," Canon Burnside said cheerfully, "but I can appreciate your father's feelings. You must respect the wishes of the dead and Evelyn expressly said that she didn't want to be buried in Sicily. She mentioned it once or twice to me, as a matter of fact, and I think that was what she was trying to say to me when I was giving her the last rites yesterday. If she can't be buried in England and your father won't have her laid to rest in the Protestant section of the burial ground in Palermo, then the sea is a reasonable alternative. She was always fond of the sea, wasn't she? I mean —in the old days—I remember her bathing with Maud before the foreigners came and occupied the beach. We're leaving at the end of the month," he added confidentially. "Maud's finding life very difficult here. She'll be much happier in Brighton. My son has found us a charming little bungalow overlooking the beach. Maud won't know she isn't in Trapani once she's settled in there."

The town was almost deserted, for everyone had gone up the hill to visit their dead. We were taking a coffin to the sea.

Miki shuffled at my father's elbow making plaintive little sounds of consolation and sorrow as he glanced sideways at my father's bent head. I walked with Canon Burnside and behind me I heard the chinking of Rosalia's rosary and her muttered prayers. Somewhere a dog howled but the only other sounds in the town were the rattling of the cart and the echo of our footsteps through the quiet streets. The darkness spread and I saw a thousand little points of light from the cemetery as people lit their lamps and candles.

Turiddu's men carried the coffin on board the boat as though it were a cask of fresh water and I saw them wedge it against the mast. Two of them came back and helped my father up the side and another put out a hand for Canon Burnside.

"You mustn't worry, my dear," he said. "I've done more than my fair share of burials at sea. Sometimes, it really seemed as though the Indian Ocean were a graveyard and—" He paused abruptly, then laughed. "Dear me, for a moment I thought I'd forgotten the good book, but it's here. Should know it by heart now, but the old memory's not what it used to be."

I stepped forward to climb up after him but Rosalia pulled me back and I saw Turiddu shake his head as his men pushed the boat from the beach. Miki ran to the stern and waved his cap to me in great circular sweeps.

"They will not take you," Rosalia whispered.

"But why—"

"It brings bad luck to have a woman on board."

"They have my mother!"

"They complained about that but the dead are different. Besides, at I Morti there is a special blessing for those who give honour to the dead."

The boat was in deep water now and through the dusk I saw Canon Burnside turn and wave to me.

"Say the prayers with us," he called. "I shall be singing hymn 132. You know it, don't you, dear, 'Rock of Ages.' It was one of your mother's favourites. I think there was another she always enjoyed but I can't remember . . ."

His voice vanished with the boat into the darkness and all I could see was the lantern at the stern rising and falling as though swung by a human hand.

"Blessed Madonna, forgive this sin," Rosalia cried.

Perhaps there were tears on my face, or the fine spray that blows across the water in the evening. I touched my cheek and it was wet to my fingers but I did not feel as though I were crying.

"There are no flowers," I said abruptly.

"She will not rest. She will return to haunt the house and bring a curse upon all those who did not bury her."

There was a glow of phosphorescence on the waves that left scrolls of light across the sand and a shimmer of light on my shoe where the water had touched it. We did not wait there on the beach for the boat to return but made our way back to the museum.

Rosalia opened the door slowly and said "*Buona sera*" to the spirits she believed must be greeted when you returned to an empty house.

"I can feel your mother here," she said.

"Here?" I scoffed. "She's with my father—she'll always be with him."

I saw the flowers first—a garish wreath of white lilies tinted pink with pallid stiff chrysanthemums. There was a card from the Barone di Marineo. It did not puzzle me that the flowers were on the kitchen table while the door to the street had been locked. I remembered how when I was a child the shutters were taken down while we slept and there was a yawning hole where the front door had been.

"Ah, he remembered! His heart beats with the love of family."

"My mother hated flowers like this."

"We must take them to the sea."

I was restless and we carried the wreath down to the rocks at the end of the beach where the current swept around in a great arc. The movement of the tide was igniting myriads of tiny jellyfish so that the phosphorescence glowed in a flood of white fire to the horizon. I threw the wreath towards the light and it floated away like a shadow. I thought of my mother's coffin gliding down into that shining sea to rest among the wrecks of Phoenician argosies and Greek galleys, Roman triremes and Spanish galleons. I reached out, cupping the water, and it seemed as though the candles of the dead were burning in my hands.

"You should say a prayer," Rosalia said, and I heard the sound of her rosary again.

I shrugged. "My mother was not religious."

"Would you like to see something very strange—something you have never seen before?"

Rosalia's voice was mysteriously seductive and I glanced quickly at her.

"I know everything here."

"You have never seen the grotto," she said softly.

Eleven

I know every inch of this shore," I said, but Rosalia replied softly that I had never seen the grotto.

"We've explored all the caves here," I said sharply. "I hardly think there's a Blue Grotto that we've missed."

"Come with me."

I wanted to go back to the museum and write my letter to Bessie, but it would not be possible to post it for another three days while people celebrated I Morti. A nervous restlessness had taken hold of me and I knew I would not be able to sleep so I agreed to follow Rosalia without seeming interested or impressed by her air of mystery. The sky was clouded now but the air was reflecting a pale phosphorescent glow from the water and a traceried sheen on the wet sand.

Rosalia walked across the rocks and I saw that she was making for our secret beach, where the four of us had spent so many summer days talking about love and destiny. The tide was ebbing, the sand crunched hard under my feet and although there was no moon the sea continued to burn with light as if all the stars were drowning. Rosalia went across to the rocks and pulled herself up between them and on to a ledge. We crept along it for a few yards and then slipped behind a boulder, climbed a few rough steps and saw a hole in the cliff less than three feet high. She went down on her hands and knees and disappeared. I hesitated for a moment, then followed her into a grotto where I was able to stand. Rosalia lit a candle and in front of me I saw a little shrine with a shabby gilt statue of the Virgin Mary. I was about to tell Rosalia that I had seen dozens of shrines like this when Rosalia turned and faced me and in that flickering light her voice seemed to come from a skull.

"This is where a good mother brings her daughter," she said.

I realized the grotto was black with candle grease and there were little pools of wax in front of the Madonna.

"I am not a Roman Catholic," I said firmly. "This is all superstition."

"Ah, but you need not pray to the Madonna. A woman's honour is the same whether she is Catholic, Jew or pagan Moor. What I want you to see is this."

Just to the side of the shrine was an aperture in the rock.

"Put your ear to it," Rosalia said.

I bent down and heard a moaning that I knew must be the echo of the sea or the wind through a rock cleft.

"It is her spirit."

"My mother's?" I scoffed.

"No, the spirit of the last girl who was buried alive in there. This is not an ordinary grotto where people come to pray to the Holy Virgin, it is sacred to women and their honour. No man has ever come here. If he did he would die before the next full moon because the moon is sacred to Our Lady."

I remembered my mother telling me the legend of Diana the huntress and her bow, the crescent moon, but Rosalia had taken hold of my arm.

"Listen and I shall tell you what happens to a girl who has lost her honour. She is not simply *disgraziata*, an outcast like a stray cat to be starved and beaten, a *puttana* who can be used by all men because she has given herself in sin to one man, she is brought here and thrust down that hole. You don't believe me? Put your head into it and you will see that it is possible to force a body into the crevice. A girl who has lost her honour is given a potion that makes her drowsy and then the women of her family carry her here. I remember the last was Rita Cusumani, a girl of great beauty and with a pride that made her walk to Mass on Sunday carrying a white silk handkerchief as though she were a queen. Her father had planned a fine marriage for her to a young man in Marsala but Rita fell in love with a carter here in Trapani. Guido used to follow her to Mass and stand outside her house and one day she came down to him. He took her by the hand and they ran away to a village in the mountains and there Guido took his pleasure from her. But he could not marry her because he was betrothed to his cousin, so one day he told Rita that she must return to her family. Her father and brothers were going to kill her on the spot, but her mother said that Rita must be allowed to save her soul. That night her mother came to her and with kind words gave her a cup of soup that had a potion in it. She fell asleep and as she slept her mother and three women carried her here. They took hold of her like this and pushed her headfirst into the crevice. See what it is like to have your head in there—"

Whether it was because her story had captivated me or from curiosity, I bent down and put my head into the hole. It was impenetrably dark, as though I had been swallowed and now I was being crushed in a stomach of stone. The moaning was louder and seemed to be inside my head. Such a horror filled me that I fell backwards and crouched trembling on the ground.

"Can you imagine what it was like to wake in such a place with such unbearable pain? Her head was far below her feet and there was a sharp stone cutting into her shoulder and another into her side. She tried to move but her arms were pinned and she could see nothing and feel only the agony of the stone. A drop of water fell on to the side of her face and it was that water that kept her alive for ten days until her screams grew faint and the breath had gone from her body. Listen! Listen! You can still hear her spirit begging for help, pleading to be forgiven. But there is no forgiveness for a woman who sacrifices her honour. What is sacred to God must be returned to God or given under the sacrament of marriage to her husband. There is only the grotto for those who are disgraced. Down there are the bones of many girls who were *disgraziata*."

She reached down into the hole and slowly drew back her arm with her hand closed.

"A bone from her foot where she tried to kick against the stone."

She opened my hand and placed a small straight bone in it.

"It's a bird—it's not human."

"It is a relic of Rita Cusumani. Keep it always and remember what happens to a girl who loses her honour."

I wanted to shout that all this was stupid superstition like her dream book and prophecies but terror was choking me. Never in my life had I been so afraid. Sweat was trickling down my face and into my eyes and I began to shake convulsively.

"Now," Rosalia said with great satisfaction, "we must go home and wait for your father to return."

Rosalia had done this deliberately to frighten me and I was quite certain that the bone in my hand was from a dead gull on the beach, but the terror kept twisting inside me so that I was bent double from the pain.

"This is all superstition," I gasped, almost choking from the smoky air inside the grotto. "My mother never tried to frighten me. Not once! She didn't believe in spirits. My mother would never have brought me to a place like this. Or if she did I would have learned about myths and legends, not some stupid story that is supposed to be true."

Rosalia's face was without emotion and seemed transparent in that strange milky light.

"Your honour is your jewel."

"You are a witch—and nobody believes in witches any more!"

"The jewel is for your husband or for God."

"You're a wicked old woman and I hope you fall and break your neck," I shouted, and plunged for the entrance.

Outside the air glistened and I took deep breaths but I could not throw the bone away. Reason told me it was a bird but my emotions shrieked that I had a relic of Rita Cusumani in my hand. Without looking back I stumbled along the ledge until I found the steps down to the secret beach. The water was lapping my ankles when I stepped on to the sand and I took off my shoes and waded back to the rocks. Not once did I look back to see where Rosalia was.

I went straight up to my room when I was safely inside the museum and tried to sleep but I kept drifting into a terrible nightmare that still haunts me. Just as I was falling asleep I felt myself being carried to the grotto and forced down into the crevice and I woke screaming from that twilight horror into a pit of darkness. Rosalia had closed my shutters and pulled the curtains while I was sleeping. I flung them open and as the morning light flooded my room I heard footsteps downstairs and the sound of voices: Canon Burnside's short snorting laugh, the sound of cups rattling and the aroma of coffee.

"It was a miracle," Canon Burnside said to me later and Turiddu nodded in agreement.

"Our good captain here intended to return as soon as the service was finished. You did sing with us, didn't you, Gwen? I remembered that your mother's other favourite hymn was 'Silent Night,' so we sang that too. Well, everything had gone splendidly, quite splendidly."

He lowered his voice.

"Just one distressing moment when we had to hold your father back. I think he wanted to follow your dear mother into the deep. As I was saying, it had all gone remarkably well and our good captain was at the helm when suddenly the sea around the boat began to thrash like a whirlpool and we realized we were in the middle of a school of tunny. Astounding sight! The men put out the nets and then the fish were gaffed and pulled up on to the deck. I tell you, the hold was so laden that I thought we would sink."

He yawned. "Great sport, but too much excitement for a pair of old codgers like us, eh, Enrico?"

My father sat with his hands clasped in front of him and did not answer. Rosalia set out the coffee and bread and made the sign of the cross.

"It was a sign of grace," she said. "You buried the Signora and God rewarded you."

Turiddu laughed and crammed the bread into his coffee.

"We should bury someone every night if we get such good fortune from the sea."

My father remained silent, staring at the floor as though all life had left his body. I spoke twice to him but he did not answer. Canon Burnside whispered that I should be patient and soon my father would be his old self again. There was no need to whisper—he would not have heard a shout at his ear. Turiddu said he had to get back to the *tonnara*, and I went upstairs and wrote my letter to Bessie.

My mother was dead and yet I could not find any words of grief as I told Bessie about the burial at sea and Rosalia's grotto. When I was sealing the envelope I remembered that Frau Brunner had sent a cable to Delhi and I decided to cable a message to Bessie's parents. A letter would take at least three weeks to get to England but a cable would reach Mr and Mrs Chambers in days and then I could begin to pack.

At the Villa, I typed lists of bed linen and lamps, chairs and china, and there were separate lists of all the furniture that had to be repaired or replaced. It was almost Christmas and I had not received any word from Manchester.

"Manchester is not Tibet." Frau Brunner shrugged. "Perhaps your cable went astray or was lost. Send another."

I did, and waited while Christmas came and went. Frau Brunner's new Dutch chef cooked a special dinner but there were very few guests at the Villa and no one seemed particularly merry because Frau Brunner spoke of nothing except Dolfi and the dangers of Tibet. At the museum my father drifted from one room to another, or I would find him staring at the roses, or holding a piece of pottery in his hand. One afternoon I discovered him in the *bagghiu* sitting beside my mother's old reclining chair and for one moment I saw her there, her tousled short grey hair against the cushion. My father looked up and smiled at me.

"You felt it, didn't you, Gwen? She's here with us."

I wanted to tell him that I thought I had received the image of his longing, but I did not know how to express it so I kept silent.

My father had always been a slight man but now he was like a dry twig in a hedge that has caught a thread of white fur from some straying animal. It was not that he was thin and old and his clothes hung from his bent shoulders as though they had never belonged to him, it was the inhumanity of his appearance. He was living, but not in this world, and certainly not with me. Suddenly he put out his hand to me.

"Gwen, you're suffering too. And you're so young that you will have much longer to grieve for her than—" His voice trailed away.

Again I did not know how to answer him because I realized that what I felt was as far removed from his feelings as Manchester from Trapani.

"I think I should go home to England," I said abruptly.

"Yes, yes, of course. Eleanor wants you."

"I would like to go to Manchester and live with Bessie."

"Ah yes, your mother was very fond of Bessie."

"Would you mind very much if I left you here, Father?" I almost heard my mother reproaching me as I spoke the words but I plunged on. "I'd always come back to see you here and you could come to England."

"No—I must take you to Russell Morton and then—"

He shook himself, lifting his head with a physical effort that seemed to strain him. I felt that he was forcing himself away from some other place and back into a body that irritated him.

"There is much I have to do here. Turiddu came to see me yesterday."

"Not politics, Father. Captain Prosimo was asking about that."

"I must not spend the little time that is left me selfishly. There is work to be done."

The letter came next morning.

Oh Bessie, there were a thousand times when I wanted to tear it up or burn it, but I have kept it, reading it over and over although I know it by heart. It has become a talisman for me that does not ward off evil like the coral *corno* around my neck, but serves to remind me that no matter how wretched and miserable I may be feeling, there was a time when I felt much worse. There is still so much I don't understand but one day I'll give it to you and you can tell me what the letter really meant. I try to decipher it as though it were an ancient sherd marked with a fragment of design, and from that piece of clay I have to create a cup or a beaker and then decide its use and who first held it. Your letter said so much, but nothing that I really wanted to know.

The first thing I noticed was that it was addressed from the Connaught Hotel in London and I remember feeling an enormous wave of relief because this seemed to explain the silence of the last weeks. You must have been travelling and now you were in London and I would hear about trips to the theatre and to cinemas.

My dearest Demeter,
I have been ill so that is why I could not write before.

Ill? Poor Bessie must have had influenza or some horrible disease that kept her in sick bay at school—

I have cried so much that I do not think I have any tears left in me. Mother has left father and he has gone to Kenya where he has a married sister and he is going to help on the farm there. Mother is

> going to marry Nancy's father and tonight we will be on our way to Canada by boat.

I read this calmly as though it were a passage in a book, feeling that in the next lines Bessie would tell me it was a joke.

> Mother says she fell in love with HIM (I cannot give him a name and I shall never call him Uncle Bob) at the wedding and he wrote to her all through the summer.

Mrs Chambers had lied to me? I was her second daughter, she always said that and put her arms around me and hugged me. I could see a way she had of standing on one toe with arms outstretched and suddenly pirouetting when something pleased her. I had often tried to copy her but it always seemed clumsy and affected when I did it.

> He proposed at the end of summer and when we came back mother told father and he broke down. Mother said she was sick of being poor and never having enough money for trips and nice things and father said he trusted her. They came and told me all this at school and I said I would go to Africa with my father and we could send for you because I hated HER for what she had done.

I was ready to go anywhere with Bessie. Mr Chambers had spoken to me about making a new life in the colonies and I had told him I didn't mind if we couldn't live in Manchester.

> Mother was so cruel that I shall never forgive her. She said that father was not my real father and he had no claim on me because my real father was dead. Oh, Demeter, I held on to him and he was crying and said he loved me but it was no use. There was a settlement and he left for Africa before the business went bankrupt. Mother says that Uncle Bob is my father now and he can do far more for me than my own father did. She is lying. But I know now she is a liar and I hate her and as soon as I am grown up I shall run away and never talk to her again. Uncle Bob gave me a gold wristwatch and I flushed it down the toilet and she got histirical and slapped my face and I shall never forgive her for that either. She is a BITCH. I hate her! HATE HER! HATE HER! She says we are going to make a new life for ourselves in Canada and I am not to write to you again because she does not want any ties from the past. I think my heart is going to break and I shall

probably die. I wish I could die. She says that if I write to you she will send me to a reform school because HE is already being very good about taking me and you will be with your rich family at Russell Morton anyway. My father took me when I was a baby and I think a baby is a lot more trouble than a girl of my age. If I were brave I would run away but I am so afraid of what she will do to me. SHE is not my mother. SHE IS NOT WHAT SHE WAS. I told her she was different and she said she was in love. As soon as I am older I shall write to you no matter what she says. Is Dolfi all right? Has he written to his mother and mentioned me? I do love him so much and I know he will never forget me.

I still had no sensation as I read this because I knew it was not meant for me even though the letter ended like the hundreds of other letters she had sent me over the years.

Your ever best and dearest friend,
Bessie Persephone Chambers.

At first I could not think of Bessie but only of her mother and I saw myself handing her the letters when she came down to my office, and the scent of her perfume that remained when she had gone. To this day lily of the valley is a perfume that nauseates me and if I find myself standing next to a woman who is wearing it I have to move. Mrs Chambers had betrayed my love. Oh, I can look back now and realize how gullible I was to believe her story about Travis and the money that would save the business, but how despicable she was to lie to me. And she had made me keep her love letters a secret from Bessie, who might have known what to do. Instead, I had helped her, and in so doing I had separated Bessie from me and from her father. She had made me the agent of my own misery.

Could I believe everything Bessie had written? Was her suffering real or was some of it pretended because she knew that Nancy's father was a millionaire and had chauffeurs and yachts? Had she decided to leave her father because he had only poverty on his side and Uncle Bob had money? When Nancy married Travis, Bessie had said that Mr Fletcher was rolling in money. She had repeated that phrase with a particular emphasis on the vowels until I saw him like King Midas turning everything he touched to gold. Had he touched Bessie and made her a golden image of herself? Could Bessie be lying to me as her mother had done? I questioned everything. Yes, even you, Bessie, because there were silences between your words that remained a mystery to me. Somehow, I sensed that the truth was not in what you said but in what you could not tell me. I am still tormented by what the letter did not reveal. I despised myself for doubting you, but I no longer felt that I could trust or believe anything.

It is painful for me to write this now because I still cannot think about that time without physical pain. Of course, it is not difficult to understand how easily I had been deceived, and how eager I had been to deceive myself. Why had Mrs Chambers not written to me? Was she ashamed of having lied to me? And why did this new life require that I should be dismissed as Frau Brunner did an unsatisfactory servant? Had Bessie written to me before and had the letter been stolen by her mother? I could not understand why Bessie sounded so afraid in her letter. These, however, were all questions I asked later, for immediately after I read the letter I began to cry and I couldn't stop. Rosalia thought I was weeping for my mother and tried to quiet me. I gave her the letter and she looked bewildered because she could not read English. I don't know how it was done, but finally she understood that Bessie was gone and I would never have a home with her in Manchester.

"What did you expect?" she said, and her voice mirrored her astonishment. "Why did you think they would care for you or want you with them?"

"I loved them!" I cried.

"They are not your family."

"I must find Bessie."

That was my only thought. I remembered the tall glowering man who had not smiled in any of the wedding photographs. If Bessie was in Canada then I would go there, anywhere to find her. And at that moment the futile absurdity of all I had hoped for crashed down on me like a house in an earthquake.

I believe I was blind for three days but I scarcely recall what I felt or did until I found myself pushing away a cup that Rosalia was holding to my mouth.

"You're not going to drug me and and take me to the grotto!" I screamed.

"It's only pomegranate juice," she said.

Grief was not something I felt as an emotion; it was a physical pain that made it difficult for me to breathe and blurred my sight. I remembered the phrase in the Bible about scales falling from a person's eyes. I had always imagined a mask being removed to reveal a vision of dazzling light and colour. It's not like that at all: if the scales are ripped away, your eyes become bleeding wounds that leave you blind and in agony. The scales give beauty and reason to life, without them there is only darkness. When I tried to get out of bed I stumbled and almost fell. I began to retch and my mouth was full of a bile so bitter that it burned me.

"Listen to me," Rosalia said, and that was the voice I had heard in the grotto. "Bessie was your friend but she is not your sister and she must go with her family wherever they choose to take her."

"What is her family?" I cried in anguish. "Her father loves her but he's gone away to Africa and she hates this man her mother loves."

"Family is blood."

"It's not. Family is love and trust—" and I remembered how Mrs Chambers had used and abandoned me. If I had been her real daughter would she have treated me like that? Or was what she had done to Bessie much, much worse? Because I knew Bessie had loved her father and I remembered how many times I would sit and watch enviously when he pulled her on to his knee and called her his second best girl. My whole life was memories of Bessie and her parents and now I knew what my grief was: it was as if I had woken one morning and looked down to find that my legs had been cut off and what I had were two pink stubs like the scars at the end of Mr Chambers' lost arm that we pretended to bury in the sand. I was not whole any longer. Part of me was gone and to this day I mourn its loss.

It was a house of the dead. My father chose to interpret my grief as sorrow for my mother, and when we talked it was as if we were speaking from different worlds.

"I'm a very selfish man," he often said to me. "I think that I am the only person who misses her, who finds it hard to live without her, but I forget you're her daughter."

I tried to remember my mother but all I could see was Bessie. During that time I relived every moment of our lives together and I wished that I had a time machine like the one in H. G. Wells's story. I would go back to the day when I first met Bessie on the beach at Trapani. She had been playing alone and Assunta took me by the hand and introduced me to her. Here was another little English girl for me to play with, and Bessie was not cold and unfriendly as children often are when confronted with a stranger. She smiled at me and told me I could help her build a castle. Joyfully we had spent our summers together doing that. I would recall every summer and then I would come to the last . . . This time I would not sit trustingly while Mrs Chambers prattled on about Travis making loads of money, I would take the letter and give it to Bessie's father and tell him that Mrs Chambers was in love with Robert Fletcher. Then I would suggest that he take Bessie and me to Kenya. The ending never satisfied me because I knew that Mr Chambers loved his wife, and if they were reconciled after he had seen the letter would they blame me for interfering? What could I have done had I known? Or was my folly born that day I first met Bessie and we built a castle together? People often pitied me because I had such old parents but I never really thought of them as my mother and father: the Chamberses were my real parents and Bessie was my sister. Afterwards, we became closer than sisters for we were Demeter and Persephone.

Grief became rage and I remember once standing on the roof and cursing Bessie's parents: her mother because she had betrayed my love, her father because he had been so weak instead of fighting for Bessie as I would have done. My eyes were spent with weeping; my soul was in tumult; my heart was poured out in grief and all I had left was the power to curse. With arms outstretched, I cursed the town and everyone in it, I called for blights and famines on the island of Sicily. I wanted plants to rot and decay in the winter cold and shrivel and die when the sirocco blew. Let all the land be a waste of death.

"You can spare this country your curses." Rosalia was at the window. "It has been cursed enough to give every soul in it a life of misery without any need of your *maledizioni*."

That evening my father said gently that anger would not bring her back.

"I want them to be punished for taking her from me."

"The fates are never moved by human passion."

"I want her back. We belong together."

"My dear, I think it's time we made other plans for you."

"Somebody must know where she is—"

He was not listening to me and I knew he was preoccupied with a more important matter.

"It is time we went to England. Eleanor is expecting you."

"At Russell Morton?"

"Your mother's home. Ah, she was right, they would not even take her dead body because they felt she had disgraced them. Yes, I was her disgrace and she gave up so much for me. But you are Eleanor's niece."

Before he had finished speaking I had flown up to my room and pulled out my old English atlas.

My mother had often shown me where Russell Morton was. The house and the village were less than a mile from Much Wenlock and less than a finger's length to the north on the map was Manchester. From Russell Morton I could go to Manchester and speak to the people who were living in the Chamberses' house. I could call at the business and find out Mr Chambers' address in Kenya. He, I knew, would tell me where Bessie was. I closed the atlas and felt the first stirring of hope. Nothing would keep me from Bessie.

I was a creature obsessed. At the Villa I followed Frau Brunner impatiently as she finished in the kitchen, counting every saucepan and fork while the Dutch chef sat smiling vacantly at her. The inventory was finished at last and Frau Brunner held the tabulated sheets in her hand. It was like a book and for a moment I could see her responding to the weight of it.

"My parents left me the Villa, and it was to be yours, Gwen."

"I could never have married Dolfi," I said.

"Ah, I had such hopes and now I can discover nothing of my poor little Dolfi. I dream of him in the snow or buried under mountains of ice."

"I'm sure you'll hear from him eventually."

"My heart will break before then."

"I shall write to you from Russell Morton."

"Yes, you should go back to England. You never really belonged here. None of us did. The Burnsides are going next week."

"I shall be the last to go, then."

"Perhaps I should sell the Villa and go to America. How can Dolfi return here when the militia are waiting for him? They will make him serve in a penal company."

"I'm sure Dolfi will be all right."

"The Fascists are making life very difficult. New taxes, and now they are talking about banning all gambling. They claim to be more virtuous and honourable than the saints, but they are just clever at finding other ways to rob us."

I wanted to pack and leave within the week but my father seemed incapable of doing anything quickly. There were changes in the house I could not understand. He sold my mother's piano and some paintings, and finally the car.

"Why do I need a car?" he said to me when I asked him. "I am not a young man and everything I have to do I can do on foot. I shall not be making any more trips."

"You'll be coming to England to see me, father."

"Will I need a car for that?"

Miki was distraught when two men came and drove away the Austin. He clung weeping to the wheel and my father almost had to pull him from the front seat. He appealed to me, making strange fluting noises as though he was in pain, and all I could do was shake my head. It seemed unnecessarily cruel of my father to sell the one thing that meant so much to Miki but I was impatient to leave. Week followed week and I began to despair of my father ever being ready.

I shook hands with Rosalia when I said goodbye because I had a horror of her touching me with that bone-smooth face of hers but Miki and I held each other, crying. He pointed to the *corno* at my neck and I nodded. I had no fear of any evil now. It would take me less than a day to travel from Russell Morton to Manchester and I knew my aunt would understand when I told her why I had to make the journey.

Twelve

Every stone of the grey Georgian house was familiar to me although I had never seen it. I sat opposite my father in the wide hall that I knew from my mother's descriptions: she often told me how her grandmother used to examine the linen fold panelling for dust by standing on a special set of library steps, running her white-gloved fingers down the grooves while a maid held her ankles firm. On either side of the hall were the Flemish tapestries from the seventeenth century, of the Massacre of the Innocents and the Beheading of John the Baptist, and at the end, below the Turner seascape, the Nonsuch chest. Above it all, the ceiling was carved in lozenges with vine leaves and bunches of grapes and I realized why, when my mother sat in the *bagghiu* and looked up into the grapevine, she used to say that it reminded her of Russell Morton. Carved oak doors opened on either side, one to the formal dining room where people sat at a leaved Jacobean table that had come into the family when my great-grandfather married one of the Shropshire Maws, the other into a drawing room that overlooked the knot garden and the rose trellises.

"She gave up all this for me."

My father murmured the words as he spread out his hands and gazed around him.

"Why hasn't anyone sent for us?"

I had asked that question at the hotel in London and again at the public house in Much Wenlock where we spent the night. My father had telephoned my aunt but I gathered that she would not speak to him and so he had hired a taxi from the local garage and we were driven out to Russell Morton in the early morning.

It was autumn, with frost crackling on the road, and the trees and the hedgerows looked as though they were on fire. Everything was familiar to me and yet it was the first time I had ever seen an English countryside: poetry and passages from novels I had read flooded my mind in a jumble of associations, and pictures came to life as a farmer smoked a clay pipe and shook the reins over a fat white Clydesdale pulling a cart piled high with scarlet apples. This was Housman country and I almost expected the Shropshire Lad to saunter past us with his cap pulled down over his eyes.

> His folly has not fellow
> Beneath the blue of day
> That gives to man or woman
> His heart and soul away.

The feeling of having been here before, of having travelled this road many times, took hold of me, and yet with the familiarity there was a prickle of doubt. My mother often told the story of the Indian scholar of English Romantic poetry who stepped out of the train at Oxford and stood enraptured in front of a railway embankment covered with dandelions. "All at once I saw a crowd, A host of golden daffodils," he cried. I looked back twice to make sure there were apples in the cart and not turnips.

There was no possible way I could fail to translate my mother's home correctly for my vision changed.

When we turned into the gates of Russell Morton and the house was in front of me, I suddenly felt I had my mother's eyes, as everything around me summoned up a memory that was not mine, but hers. This was the source of her calm assurance, this house impervious to change, every angle demonstrating the authority of settled incomes and moral rectitude. Grey stone weathered to gold in the morning sun, a circle of grass so smoothly green that it looked polished, and a sundial where my mother first learned to tell the time. No pestilence, famine or war had ever troubled this place except when the telegrams came to tell my grandmother that her two sons had died during the War within weeks of each other. Later, when she received the letter announcing that her daughter was marrying an Italian, my grandmother declared her to be dead and forbade anyone in the family to mention her name. With great ceremony, she took the family Bible and crossed out my mother's name.

The grandfather clock inside the door chimed ten and still we waited.

"They rise late in a great house like this," my father said.

My mother always said that promptly at eight the family and servants gathered for morning prayers in the breakfast room and my grandfather would open the Bible and give the text for the day. After his death my grandmother continued the custom but added a short homily.

At half past ten the door of the drawing room was opened by a maid who seemed flustered and nervous. She coughed twice before she blurted out, "Madam will see you now."

My father got up slowly and smiled at me.

"This is your family and your home, Gwen. They will never recognize me but you must not complain of this."

I would endure anything, I thought, because directly north of Much Wenlock was Manchester and there I would discover where Bessie was.

My mother had described the drawing room furnished in damask rose satin; now the portly chairs were covered in chintz, but I recognized the fireplace with the logs ready to be lit when the morning sun left that side of the house. The faint perfume of cloves and bergamot was in the air and I knew immediately that it came from the pot-pourri in the blue and white china bowl on the mantelpiece. In the middle of the room, seated by a small table, was my Aunt Eleanor. She had changed from the photographs my mother had shown me of her. This was a heavy-set woman with faded brown hair pulled tightly into a knot at the back of her neck. She did not speak and stared out of the window as we came in.

The maid bobbed and said haltingly, "Mr—" She stumbled over the name and said, "The Italian gentleman and his daughter, madam."

"You shouldn't be here," she said. "You had no right to come."

"I have brought you your niece," my father said simply. "I could not permit her to travel alone."

"I told the solicitors to write to you," she said abruptly.

"Mrs Wigram, I know with my heart how you regard me. I am unwanted in this family and I respect your family."

"Respect!" She half rose from her chair and her forehead seemed divided by one deep line. "What respect did Evelyn have for her family and her faith when she married an Italian Roman Catholic?"

The three words came out almost in a shout and she began to tug at a long rope of pearls.

"It is true that I was baptized a Roman Catholic but I have not practised that religion for many, many years and Gwen has been brought up in the Church of England."

"It killed my mother!"

"Mrs Harcourt died many years after the marriage. It is important to be correct with dates—"

"My mother devoted her life to charitable works and she had a right to expect Evelyn to do the same. She had never shown the slightest interest in getting married. It was her duty to remain here and care for Mother. It was all very well when she went grubbing around the countryside looking for Roman ruins, taking courses in London. We were all prepared to tolerate a few eccentricities in her. But she took herself off to Italy—one would have thought the ruins here weren't good enough for her."

She twisted the pearls as though they were alive.

"My mother was a councillor of the Royal Society for the Prevention of Cruelty to Children, the Royal Society for the Prevention of Cruelty to Animals, and a dozen other worthy causes. Do you have any idea how much money my mother helped to raise for the helpless and the poor in the course of her life? And there was a time when my sister was of invaluable help to her—before she became obsessed with old ruins. Self-indulgent, heartless and irresponsible! That was my clever sister! No sense of the word duty. We are not born into this vale of tears to indulge our animal senses, my mother told her, but she wouldn't listen to the word of God or man. I had to bring my husband and family back here in order to care for Mother. My husband always preferred the climate in Australia but he understood the meaning of duty and family responsibility. He was prepared to sacrifice his own health so that I could look after my mother. Flaunting herself around Italy, amusing herself, no regard for anyone except herself. Then we hear that she has married a—Lothario."

Through all of this tirade I had the curious sensation that I was watching puppets in a play as remote from my own life as Ruggiero and his paladins. The idea of my father, standing now with his white head thrust forward like a bird, as Lothario almost made me laugh. His eyes had been closed and he polished his spectacles while Mrs Wigram's voice buffeted around the room. I heard him speaking with difficulty and there was an Italian inflection to his words.

"Mrs Wigram, I know that your sister displeased her family when she did me the honour of marrying me. Now, all I ask is that you give her daughter a place in your family."

Nobody had written for me. Nobody wanted me here. They would not receive my mother's dead body and they would not receive me. I looked at my father in amazement that he should ever have imagined I could find a home here. The absurdity of it overwhelmed me and I quickly covered my mouth with my hand. We had all listened to my mother, and we had all believed her when she said that Eleanor would keep me here in order to punish her. Why was it that we found it so easy to believe each other's fictions, just as Bessie and I had accepted Roger and Dolfi's stories, or the promises that Mrs Chambers had made to me? In London I had asked my father if Eleanor had ever written and he had said quite simply that she would never communicate with him in any way.

"I told the solicitors to write to you. They did. I know. I received a copy of the letter they sent."

"Mrs Wigram, I knew they could not mean that you would refuse your own niece. This is your sister's child. This is your family."

"Evelyn chose to divorce herself from her family and the break was irrevocable."

"Gwen is not Italian, she is not Roman Catholic."

"I am not aware she exists."

"Are you blind? She is here—" My father tried to push me forward but I would not move.

"Her blood is yours."

"My sister is dead."

"She lives in her daughter."

I did not see her come into the room. A fat, tall girl was standing at the back of Mrs Wigram's chair.

"She looks like a Harcourt, Mother."

"Edith! I told you not to come in here."

The girl ignored this remark and stared at me. I met her gaze. Bessie would have known how to describe her appearance better than I: scragged fair hair over a blotched complexion and a dress that looked as if it needed washing. There was something unkempt and bedraggled about her, as though she was more contemptuous of herself than the opinion of others.

"I thought you might need some help, Mother."

"I can't make this stupid man understand that he—he is not wanted here and neither is his child."

"Frankly, I can't imagine why anyone would want to come back here. It's a place any sane person would want to leave."

"Mrs Wigram, may I speak to your husband?"

The woman bridled as if unused to being challenged with an appeal to her husband.

"Mr Wigram is grievously ill."

"He's dying," Edith said calmly.

"If you imagine that I would burden him with this sordid episode from my family history you—"

"I ask only that you recognize your family!"

My father's voice was beginning to falter and I knew he was on the verge of lapsing into Italian.

"You think that girl has a claim to this estate. Well, if the solicitors didn't explain it to you, I shall in plain words that even you can understand. Evelyn's income dies with her. Any dependents of hers have no claim on the estate. My mother saw to that when she rewrote her will. This is the Harcourt family now: my daughter, and my son who will marry one day and provide a new generation of Harcourts for Russell Morton."

"We must go," my father said brokenly to me in Italian. "These are a strange and inhuman people."

Mrs Wigram laughed shortly.

"Your English daughter! Did she understand a word of what we were discussing?"

"She understood very well," I said. "But no discourse is possible with a fool. If you were Italian I would tell you of an old proverb that says to deny your family is to challenge fortune."

Edith gave a snorting laugh and leaned over her mother's shoulder.

"You see! I'm not the only one who notices your stupidity."

Mrs Wigram tore at her pearls and the string broke, scattering the beads across the carpet.

"Pick them up!" she shouted at her daughter.

"Put them where the monkey put the nuts," Edith retorted and slouched out of the room.

My father and I walked slowly through the gardens and down to the wrought-iron gates with the Harcourt griffin on either side. Nobody had asked us how we were to find our way back to Much Wenlock; we had not even been offered a cup of water in that house and I was hungry. It was cold with a thin damp wind and my father stumbled. At first he refused my arm when I told him to lean on me, later he seemed grateful for it. I should have been distraught and belabouring him with reproaches, instead I was in a mood of frozen tranquillity. Why should I feel hurt at being rejected here when I had been denied Bessie's love and her home in Manchester? Everything in life goes by comparisons, and for someone who had just lost everything, it did not mean much to be turned away from Russell Morton. Is the man dying of cancer troubled when he is told he has a hangnail? Still, even in this remote disinterested mood I wondered why my father had been so certain that I would be made welcome here.

"It's all right, Father. I didn't want to come here anyway."

"Your family—" he repeated over and over again.

Every ten minutes or so he stopped and polished his spectacles as if rubbing would reveal a different, kindly landscape where people gladly acknowledged the bonds of family. I knew now why he had sold the car and some of the paintings. If my mother's income ceased with her death I could not imagine how we were going to live. My father received a pittance to run the museum and maintain the dig and it would be impossible to support four people on his income.

"What am I to do with you?" he suddenly cried in anguish.

"We shall have to manage, Father."

"I have no money."

"I'll work."

"No, no, you don't understand. There is no money for your fare. Nothing.

All I have are my tickets back to Sicily. I spent everything to bring you here."

Like a mocking flourish, the last lines of the poem I remembered that morning returned to me.

Here by the labouring highway
With empty hands I stroll:
Sea-deep, till doomsday morning,
Lie lost my heart and soul.

I could have upbraided my father then and demanded to know why he had taken so much for granted, but when I looked down at his confused, hurt eyes, all I could feel was pity for his unworldliness. At that moment he ceased to be my parent and became my child that I would have to care for until his death. He was a tiny, frail man, and I could have lifted him easily in my arms, but I felt him now like a heavy burden across my shoulders. He had brought me all the way from Trapani because he could not imagine people ever refusing to help a child of their blood, and he had never thought for one instant that they would turn me away. We stood there on that isolated Shropshire road with a fine rain starting to fall and it was as if we had been cast ashore on a barren rock in a vast sea.

"What am I to do with you?" he cried again.

This time I could not answer because I knew I should have to apologize for my birth and for casting a shadow across that great love.

"I cannot buy you a ticket on the train. I have only a few shillings left."

Reproaches were on my tongue but I did not utter them.

"I have no friends in this country."

Neither of us heard the car. It pulled up alongside us and Edith wound down the window.

"Are you going to stand there in the rain communing with nature?"

"Please, you must not trouble yourself with us," my father said awkwardly, with a stiff bow. "Your mother has expressed her wishes."

"Oh, stuff my mother. Get in."

She drove erratically and said that she had only had a licence for ten days. A jolting stop brought us to the pub.

"I would like to thank you for your assistance and invite you to lunch but—"

"You're broke. Don't worry, it's on me."

My father ate very little and said that he was in need of a rest because he was feeling dizzy.

Edith stared greedily after him as he left, wiping the cream from the edge of her plate with her finger and licking it.

"My God, so that's Lothario. I always wondered about him. What was he like when he was young? Was he very handsome?"

"I never knew him when he was young."

"It's all excruciatingly funny, really. I mean—I expected to see something like a head waiter crossed with Valentino."

I shook my head and stared at my plate.

"The sun's out again," she said. "Let's go for a walk. I know a place where we won't be disturbed."

She called for the bill, challenged two items on it, and paid, grumbling.

"You have to do that," she said *sotto voce*. "Otherwise the yokels try and pop one over you. They think they have a feudal right to rob the lady of the manor. Oh, don't worry about your lodging here. I'll pay for that too."

"You don't look like a fairy godmother," I said.

"That will get you into trouble, Gwen."

I was puzzled.

"Your sense of humour. You like to make fun of people, don't you?"

I shrugged.

"And that's a very un-English gesture. No, you seem to think you're invisible, but all the time you're staring at the floor, you're watching people, aren't you?"

"I didn't know you were observing me so closely."

"My dear, I was enthralled! After all, I'd heard about the child of lust for years."

I wished I had gone upstairs with my father.

Edith drove along a rutted road, swearing as the car jolted, gears clashing in a way that would have produced screams of protest from Miki.

"If we walk up here we'll have a splendid view and see the coloured counties spread out or whatever. I hope you don't want to recite Housman or anything soppy like that."

We sat down on tussocks of gorse that were warm from the sun.

"I don't believe all that stuff about damp ground giving you piles, do you?"

My mother must have been here many times. She told me that she first became interested in archaeology when a barrow was excavated near three dolmens close to Much Wenlock.

"I've thought about you ever since I was a little girl."

I must have looked surprised because she continued, "And how I envied you. I used to spend hours imagining what you were like and what you were doing. Someone—a friend of mine—said he met you years ago and that you were a cross between a sibyl and a Minoan princess. Oh, I used to dream about you and see you walking through groves of orange blossom with men of indescribable beauty begging you to smile at them."

Dolfi and Roger? I hardly think they belonged in her raptures.

"I used to be very romantic—my defence against my mother's Bible bashing."

"Can you give me some money, Edith?"

"You're very direct."

"My father sold paintings and our car to bring me here because he was certain I would be welcomed."

"He must have known what my mother was like. Everything has to be saved for my brother and me. I wish you could meet my brother. I think you'd like him. He's at Cambridge now. He's going to be a journalist."

"Can you help me?"

"Yes, of course."

She groped around in her purse and produced a small leather bag.

"There's a hundred gold sovereigns in there and if you want to know where they came from, they certainly didn't come from my bank account. No, I raced upstairs and spoke to my father. He's pretty decent really. I told him about you and he gave me the money. He's always believed in carrying gold. When he was roaming around the Australian bush he used to wear a money belt with sovereigns. I'll be sorry when he goes—"

"Will you thank him for me?"

"Mother will have a fit when she finds out."

"Must you tell her?"

Edith laughed raucously.

"My dear, one must promote the cause of justice in the world: we can't leave it all to the League of Nations. She and my grandmother used to make my life miserable when I was a child. I loathe the Bible and I detest God, if you can really hate something that doesn't exist except in people's nasty diseased minds. They were so afraid that I would turn out like your mother. When they were beating texts into me I used to dream of your parents making love on satin sheets in a silver pavilion surrounded by a perfumed Sicilian garden, and then I dreamed of you. I'm three years older than you so I used to imagine you as old for your age."

I opened the bag and the gold sovereigns spilled into my lap, shining in the sunlight. My mother had watched them dig into the barrow and she was there when a man handed out a gold scabbard. It was over a thousand years old but when they brushed the earth from it, the metal became alive in the summer air and gleamed. Perhaps some of that Danish gold had been melted down and was in these coins, or they held flecks from the gold of

Egypt and Mycenae. I would not be able to use them to make rings and coronets; as soon as I found out their value I would have to spend them on tickets to take me back to Sicily and then my life would be spent caring for my father, just as my mother had wished. Had she cast a spell over Mrs Chambers and taken Bessie from me, was she responsible for her sister's animosity towards me? Was it any wonder I had felt her presence at Russell Morton and here on the side of the hill? Her jubilance was everywhere around me on that quiet unmolested hill.

Edith rolled on to her side and was scrutinizing me with her hard blue eyes.

"I really feel I'm doing a service to society by making my mother's life as miserable as possible. Of course, when I'm twenty-one I come into oodles of cash and then I shall do what I like. Meanwhile, she's terrified of upsetting me because I may die again."

"Again?"

"I have died twice. Oh, there's a special term for it—aphasia or something or other. The first time I was seven and I had flu and I don't remember anything until I woke up to find the whole family round the bed praying and Grandmother screaming that God had performed a miracle. I was out cold for two days and if it hadn't been the middle of winter they would probably have buried me. The next time I was sixteen and I was out for three days but they knew what to expect then so they just sat round praying, and, sure enough, I revived. Everyone says that I had no pulse, no heartbeat—I was dead. I must say, I only have to tell Mother now that I'm feeling a little faint and she comes to heel immediately."

She went on talking while the sun moved across the sky and I played with the sovereigns in my lap.

"Ask me a question," she demanded abruptly. "I'm bored with this Sphinx role of yours."

"Why are you so—dirty?"

"I wash occasionally but my mother hates to see me like this. She'd like me to play tennis with the local squires and rush round setting traps for a husband."

"Don't you want to get married?"

"I'm not sure. Have you slept with a man?"

I felt the colour rush to my face and I shook my head.

"I have. It wasn't so much. I did it first with one of the gardeners. I thought of myself as Lady Chatterley, but it wasn't so marvellous. Uncomfortable and sweaty, really. So then I let David Maybrick serve me. He was Frederick's tutor at Cambridge. It wasn't quite so sweaty with him but it wasn't earth-shaking either."

I slowly put the sovereigns back into the bag and decided not to tell her that once, long ago, David Maybrick had said that he loved me.

"Your parents—it must have been . . . Tell me, what was it like for them?"

"I don't know."

"Tell me," she said urgently. "I've been absolutely honest with you. God, I've talked for hours and told you everything about myself."

"I could never understand it," I replied slowly. "It was a mystery to me."

"But they were in love."

"They lived for each other. I think they shared the same heart and the same bloodstream. My father's only half alive now." I wanted to add that I thought he was a little mad.

"I want to love like that. I want to feel!"

There was a note of urgency in her voice that startled me.

"My brother thinks you can get it from books, but it's not there. I wasn't the dimmest student and I had two years at Girton, but it wasn't there either."

"I would have given anything to go to school in England. I've never been in a school of any kind."

"That's why you can live through your senses. You can feel."

"I'm very grateful for this money," I said, "but there's something I want much more. I have a friend—Bessie Chambers—" I told her about Bessie while her expression changed to one of wry derision.

"Were you lovers?"

"Yes, we loved each other."

"Did you sleep together? Oh, it's all right, I had a lover at school and I know some who are still lesbians."

"We were more like sisters," I replied stiffly.

"I only had a brother, so I wouldn't know about that."

"I think you only feel passionately after pain," I said slowly. "I know I love her much more now that I've lost her."

Oh, the folly of giving heart and soul to any man or woman.

"You'd like me to find her for you?"

"Oh please—" I found myself crying and I fumbled for a handkerchief.

She looked at me greedily, as though envious of my emotions.

"I have a pencil and paper in the car. Give me all the details and I'll do what I can."

"Could you go to Manchester?"

"If I have to."

"Edith, I can't tell you how grateful I am! If I can just find out where she is and write to her—"

"It all sounds frightfully prepubescent to me. But—I envy your passion."

"You'll find someone to love one day."

"Please, don't comfort me with clichés, you sound like a favour in a Christmas cracker. No," she paused and frowned, "I want to feel with every part of me. Everyone says you get it from sex. Marie Stopes says so, but it wasn't like that for me. I just thought David was taking too long at something that seemed very animal and ordinary to me."

The side of the hill was striped now with purple shadows and I said I must go back and look after my father. We walked down the hill and even though we had spent some hours together I still felt uneasy with my cousin. There was a barbed watchfulness about her, a restless disquiet that affected me like the dripping of a tap or a creaking window.

In the car I wrote down every address I thought would help her find Bessie.

"I've never done any detective work. This sounds fun."

She wrapped up the paper carefully and put it in the glove compartment.

"Ah, I almost forgot," she said, and handed me a necklace. "It belonged to your mother."

On a heavy gold linked chain there were eight lockets and in each one a miniature.

"Nobody would want to wear it but I thought you could look at it at every now and then and remind yourself of your charming relations."

She left me at the public house and said she didn't want to see my father again because he'd been a frightful disappointment to her. But she pulled my face to hers and kissed me on the mouth and said that she would be my Bessie.

Her kiss, the smell of her body, affronted me and the idea of her replacing Bessie was like blasphemy. I muttered my thanks for the money and the necklace and hurried into the pub. My father was sitting in his room, gazing out of the window.

"Edith has come to the rescue," I said brightly. "We can leave tomorrow morning. I don't want to spent any more time here, do you?"

"I—I thought when you didn't come back after lunch, that your aunt's heart had softened and she was going to accept you."

"I'm afraid not, Father. We can't expect miracles every day."

I held the bag over the bed and let the sovereigns fall out across the counterpane.

"Edith, the fairy godmother, came to the rescue."

He looked at the money in amazement and then turned to me, his face glowing.

"Do you know where I went this afternoon? I went to the church and there I found the graves of the Harcourt family, and I read the plaques in the church that go back to the fourteenth century."

He began to gather up the sovereigns, his hands trembling with excitement.

"I can believe now that this English God answers prayers. I stood in that church and I prayed that I might be able to see your mother's name among her family. There is a space for a marble plaque and on it I shall have your mother's name, the dates of her birth and death, and then those lines she loved:

'Good night. Ensured release,
Imperishable peace,
   Have these for yours.
While sky and sea and land
And earth's foundations stand
   And heaven endures.'

"I shall order a memorial for your mother," he went on briskly. "I saw a stonecutter's shop at the end of the main street. She will have her name honoured among her ancestors in the church."

"No, the money was given to me."

I took hold of his wrist, his fingers opened and the sovereigns fell on to the bed.

"Gwen! Have you taken leave of your senses? I am your father. I shall say how this money will be spent."

"No, Father, it is mine. I've learned how to manage money and I shall use it to get us back safely to Trapani. No sooner do you see a few sovereigns than you're thinking about Mother."

"This is what she would want. It would only take a portion of all that money."

"No."

"If you have no respect for me—then respect the memory of your mother. Her body is in the sea—what resting place is that?"

"My mother is dead."

"Not for me—never in my heart," he cried.

"You have her memorial, Father."

He looked at me, white with anger and grief.

"You have me."

Thirteen

Memory always comes to me with voices, and a sound will recall the past more easily than an object. Often, when I am alone, especially in the early morning between sleep and waking, it is like a murmuring, a confusion of whispers in my head, and if I concentrate I can hear the voices of the past and presently they will become figures moving in a landscape more real than my shadowy room. I've often wondered why this should be so: I think it comes from my childhood when I used to play in the *bagghiu* and listen to my parents in the curator's room, or to Assunta and Miki in the kitchen. If I listened carefully I could find out what was happening all over the house without moving from my hiding place under the vines.

I shall never forget Russell Morton, more, I think, because I saw it through my mother's voice and her words defined everything there. Sometimes, it is difficult to know what is my own memory and what is someone else's but I can still hear the chirping tones of the woman who addressed me in the train to Rome.

"Going south for the winter, dear?"

When I told her I was going home, she seemed surprised. Nobody, it seemed, lived in Sicily any more and it was no longer fashionable for holidays. The question was the same from other travellers: "Going south for the winter?" Finally, I just looked away and heard a woman say to her husband, "Sullen piece of goods, isn't she?" And her husband replied, "Can't blame her with that doddering old chap on her hands." Everyone thought he was my grandfather and asked me if he were ill.

My father never mentioned the sovereigns to me again. He barely spoke to me on the long journey back to Trapani but I could tell from his eyes that he was stricken by what I had done, and now he was a little afraid of me. If I had really loved my father I would have given him all the money and told him to commission a memorial plaque for my mother with every penny we possessed; if I had been a good Sicilian daughter I would have done the same and begged my way back to Trapani. Instead I kept the sovereigns and changed them for English pounds to buy my tickets and pay for our lodging and skimpy meals. My father had already bought his train fare, but he had forgotten the necessity of food and hotels; when he emptied his pockets in the pub at Much Wenlock he had less than thirty shillings. I mentioned this to him, and he told me that he had been hungry before, and he could endure hunger again.

Rosalia was standing at the door waiting for us; she bowed to my father when he gave her his case. She did not speak or seem surprised to see me although I had not sent her a cable to let her know I was coming back. Miki, however, laughed and danced and carried my bag on his head up to my room. I had never thought to see that room again and now I felt nothing except a frozen calm as I looked around. The vine was in full leaf and the clustering sour green of the grapes promised a good harvest. My father's footsteps were very slow as he came up the stairs and when he opened his door I heard him cry out something unintelligible. I could not bear to stand there listening to him weep so I went down to the kitchen.

"You did not like your English family, Gina? Weren't they rich enough for you?" Rosalia said drily, handing me a cup of coffee.

"They did not want me."

"Ah, you were too proud to be treated like the poor relation, so you came back."

"They didn't want my mother and they don't want me. There they are —all of them."

I passed her the gold necklace with its miniatures. She opened each one in turn and I told her who they were. When she came to the picture of my mother she kissed it and said an Ave.

"They are all there. My grandparents, my uncles who died in the war, my aunt and my mother, and my two cousins. I am not there because I don't exist."

"Tell me about this strange thing."

At first Rosalia scoffed and said I was telling her a story, making a frog into an elephant—I was *furiosa* like my father with my wits in the moon. Gradually, she stopped jeering and hunched over the lockets, touching each one in turn with her finger, darting quick glances at me from her black eyes.

"Bring me the bucket!" she said.

I knew what she meant but I could not believe that she wanted it here in the kitchen. The bucket was a mystery that came to my room for a few days every month smelling of disinfectant. When I was having a period I dropped the cloths in the bucket, covered it tightly with a lid, and every day it would disappear, returning half full of fresh water and disinfectant. Where Rosalia washed and dried the cloths I never discovered, but I knew she had several lines outside her room on the roof. My mother always forbade laundry to be hung from the windows, but she made an exception for a part of the roof where it was impossible for our washing to be seen from the street.

"Bring it to me!" Rosalia shouted.

"It's almost full," I whispered. "I had some with me."

"Then there will be blood," she replied.

She placed the bucket on the kitchen table, took off the cover and held the necklace over the crimson contents.

"*Sangu lava sangu*," she muttered, "blood washes blood," and reached down into her dress for her crucifix.

I stood there appalled with embarrassment and shock as Rosalia held out each locket to me in turn.

"*Morto*?" she asked, and I would nod, but when I shook my head, she plunged the locket into the red water and began to pray. She removed the locket and the crucifix followed headfirst as she demanded justice from Christ and the curse of death on the unnatural family. Three times she cursed a locket in this way: my aunt and my two cousins, Edith and Frederick.

"You will have a necklace of the dead to wear soon, Gina."

I snatched the necklace from her and ran to wash it clean.

"They will die," Rosalia cried triumphantly. "A family that casts out a child is damned by God, by His son and by His blessed mother and all the holy saints!"

I told Rosalia she was a stupid superstitious old woman and curses were nothing but empty air like ghosts and yet, even as I spoke, my mother's presence was there in the house and I could hear her voice wherever I turned. She had contrived to bring me back here and I would have to care for my father until he died. Her will was stronger than Rosalia's spells and incantations and all the brilliant plans I had made for my life. I sat by the little fountain with my head in my hands: a Boadicea without a kingdom or any place to call my own, a Boadicea without hope. I heard Rosalia in the kitchen and Miki sweeping and when I looked up I saw my mother's roses in bloom: the Horace Vernets, the yellow tea and the Madame Meilland. I was among them in one stride, tearing at them, trampling them. Not until I had torn up every rose and stamped on them all did I stop and realized my hands were bleeding.

Rosalia was watching me, her arms folded under her shawl.

"If you want blood, take this!" I cried and held out my hands to her.

The expression on my father's face was like a blow and I became calm.

Slowly, he picked his way across the tangle of bushes gathering the bruised flowers, trying to smooth the petals.

"We can plant vegetables here," Rosalia said comfortably. "There is enough room for *pomodori* and *insalata*."

"Yes," I said. "We'll have a vegetable garden, and after dinner I want to draw up a budget for the house."

When I explained what I intended, Rosalia was shocked and told me that my father, as *capo di famiglia*, must have charge of all the money.

"My father does not understand money. I do."

She shook her head and told me I was *ingrata* and *rebella*, but I knew that only an ingrate and a rebel would save us from starving.

I explained to my father why it was necessary to watch every lira and he said he cared nothing for money. He had work to do for the Party.

"Somebody has to look after the museum. I won't be able to help you as much as I did, father," I said, and he turned away impatiently.

"Please, father," I went on, "I beg you, don't get involved with the Communists again. You know it's illegal to belong to them. Captain Prosimo warned me."

"I shall not let a daughter govern my soul," he cried and went up to his room.

Miki put his head on the table and Rosalia watched me intently.

"Rosalia, I shall have to rely on you."

She smiled.

"We cannot live on the money my father receives from the Burgoyne estate. I must work. Tomorrow I shall go to the Villa and make Frau Brunner pay me a weekly wage."

She put out her hands deprecatingly, as though tolerant of my folly, for Frau Brunner was notorious for her meanness.

"No, I shall persuade her and every Thursday the museum must be open to the public and I shall teach you how to show people around. If anyone offers you a *mancia*, take it."

How scornful I had been in the past when people tried to press a few coins into my hands. The estimated cost of running the museum and feeding four people was on one side of my exercise book, all income on the other, and I did not see how I could make them meet unless Frau Brunner paid me at the same rate as the other staff at the hotel. Certainly, I worked as hard as any of them, but she had never offered me a penny before. Nonetheless, I was now the head of the family and I would have to provide for it. Rosalia, I knew, made a little from telling fortunes and interpreting dreams; poor Miki, I discovered, had never received a wage since he was employed by Leonard Burgoyne. He worked for his keep, and was, Rosalia assured me, very fortunate, for why should a mute who could neither read nor write expect anyone to care for him? I had seventeen pounds left from the money Edith had given me and I made Miki take one of the sovereigns. When he was not working, he spent his time looking mournfully at the space where the Austin had been and once I found him assiduously polishing an invisible car.

Walking up to the Villa next morning with my head down, I heard someone shouting behind me and Benno rattled alongside me, his cart glittering, the ostrich feathers dancing on the pony's harness. He jumped down and kissed my hands, telling me with tears in his eyes that he was sure he had lost me forever, and when he saw me, he thought at first I was a phantom on the road ahead of him and he prayed to San Domenico to save him and then—the prayers of his heart were answered.

He nodded approvingly when I told him that I did not like my English family and I was staying to care for my father as my mother had wished.

"Ah, you have a Sicilian heart," he said and handed me out in front of the Villa as though I were a rich guest.

Frau Brunner and the Dutch chef were drinking tea in her apartment when I arrived and I sat with them while she told me that there had been no word from India.

"I feel in my heart that my Dolfi is dead," she wailed.

The chef told her she must be hopeful and pressed another iced *kuchen* on her.

"I write, write all the time to the Viceroy and I get nothing but polite little notes that say the expedition is in the mountains and my messages have been sent to Dolfi—William Smith as he calls himself."

"Are you quite sure it is Dolfi?" I asked.

"But of course I am certain. Ah, he has never been away for so long. Every week I get a letter from the militia demanding to know where he is and when I tell them he is in Tibet they do not believe me."

The Dutch chef gathered up the plates and left us with a list of menus.

"That man is a jewel," Frau Brunner sighed as he left.

In as few words as possible, I told Frau Brunner what had happened in England.

"Ah, people can be very cruel," she said. "But there is work here to occupy you. I must tell you that this Fascist government is trying to be more moral than the Pope. They want separate accounts for the card room, and the takings of each table must be itemized. Before these black saints I used to pay taxes, but not like this. And it is very difficult when so many of them stay here, and some of them question the staff."

Frau Brunner listened to my request with a heavy breathing silence that I knew preceded a series of shrieks.

"Money! You want money from me? I who trained you, who gave you a profession? Does the pupil expect the teacher to pay him? Does the world walk on its head?"

"I am very grateful for all you have done for me, Frau Brunner, but I am eighteen now and I can manage the books and do anything you want in the hotel."

"Scrub and polish?" She sneered.

"If I have to, but that would be a waste of all you've taught me. You've said you'd never trust anyone but me with the books, and I can understand why."

"I shall never permit you in my home again! I shall have you turned away at the gates! I shall—"

She paused then and looked pensive.

"I am enduring a torture of suffering and pain and now you afflict me with this."

"I understand the books better than anyone."

"I cannot afford to pay an extra salary."

"I must have the money, Frau Brunner."

"You have always been trustworthy but—"

"Yes, I've watched every lira that came into the Villa and checked every lira that went out."

"Yes." She sighed deeply and I knew we understood each other.

"You would have made such a good wife for my Dolfi. With you to manage him he would have been such a good boy."

I thought at first she was laughing at me but she seemed serious enough.

"I shall, of course, expect more than simple bookkeeping from you. You can come early in the morning and Benno can take you home in the evening. You will be in charge of the laundry and the second-floor rooms. I have been losing sheets and this will give me the opportunity to get rid of Calogera."

I nodded in response to everything she said and then I asked for a week's wages in advance. Again, there were shrieks of protest but in the end there was agreement between us.

That evening I told Rosalia what to order for the house and I looked for my father to give him my good news. He was not in the museum and Miki made me understand that he had gone out in the late afternoon.

"Did he go to the Pepoli?"

Rosalia said that one of Turiddu's men had called for him and they had gone off together.

I did not see him for several days because I left in the morning before he came home, and I was never sure what time he went out in the afternoon. Sometimes he was away for days at a time and he arrived home hoarse and exhausted, as though he had been lecturing for hours.

"What is he doing?" I asked Rosalia.

"Speaking to peasants." She shrugged.

"What can he possibly tell them that will help them?"

"Oh, he speaks of the Kingdom of Heaven in Russia."

"Do they listen to him?"

"Who can say? Do stones have ears? They would prefer the marionettes, but your father has a golden tongue and what he says makes a pretty story."

"But everyone seems satisfied with the Fascists."

"He is mad," Rosalia said finally.

Misery was my companion that summer and whatever Frau Brunner demanded, I did, whether it was bookkeeping or even making beds when one of the maids was ill. I never complained because, for some reason I cannot understand, I wanted to punish myself, and the more I suffered, the more I rejoiced in my fatigue and my grief. If fate had afflicted me, I would show that I had the power to hurt myself even more. I became the scourge of the hotel staff, padding the corridors silently, spying and pouncing on cobwebs or a fleck of dust. The young Fascist officers flirted with all the maids but they avoided me because I glowered at them like a Fury when they spoke pleasantly to me. I took a grim satisfaction in their dislike and indifference. Every night I came home to the museum so tired I could barely climb the stairs to my room, but I always found the time to write a letter to Edith or to any of the addresses where I thought I might garner some information about Bessie.

I slipped a photograph of Bessie and myself into the frame of my looking-glass. Roger had taken it on the terrace during that magic summer. Our arms were round each other's waist and we were both laughing into the sun. Nobody replied to my letters; nevertheless, I wrote each night, though more often than not I did not even bother to post the letter. Occasionally, some came back with "Address Unknown" scrawled across the envelope. I used up all my own notepaper and began to use discarded stationery from the Villa; I even used a collection of headed papers from the hotels Frau Brunner had visited on her European tours and which she never left without a few souvenirs in her valise.

There were no English guests at the Villa that summer, only Germans and Italians and a few Americans. I passed among them, politely answering their questions, taking refuge in the office or the laundry room where I counted towels and pillowcases and screamed at the laundresses who tore a tablecloth in the mangle or left a wrinkle or a slanting fold when they ironed.

In months I do not think I saw my father more than three times, and only once did he talk to me. He seemed confused by my questions and it was only when I said that the Fascists were helping people that his eyes blazed and he trembled with anger.

"Have you seen the peasants? Do you know how they live?"

"Yes, I walk up the hill early in the morning when they're going to the fields."

"You walk less than a mile to the Villa, but they tramp six, seven miles to the vineyards and the farms, and the same when they drag their way home. I know. I often walk with them."

"Yes, I realize how poor they are and how hard they work, but what can you do for them?"

"They must take the land for themselves."

"By what means, father?"

"With the strength that generations of suffering have given them. If they unite, if they strike against the landowners, change must come. It is the peasants who will lead the revolution."

"Father, if the Fascists knew what you were doing—"

"I must strike a blow for the Party. I know my people. My father was one of them."

"What will happen if you're arrested?"

"I shall defy them."

The winter rains arrived early and there were only Fascist officials left at the Villa, and so few of them that Frau Brunner told most of the staff that she would not need their help until the spring. She did not tell me to go because I was doing the work of four people and whenever I went down to the kitchen or the laundry I was met with muttered curses or black looks. Sometimes, I thought bitterly of my father trying to help the workers while I oppressed them. The letters came back more regularly now and all had "Address Unknown" written across the envelope. There was no reply from Edith, but none of my letters to her was returned so I knew someone had received them. I had really thought that she was the one who would discover Bessie when she spoke so gaily in her brusque, offhand voice of finding it amusing to play the detective. When I heard nothing, my depression became a despair that left me like one of the puppets I once saw hanging from a peg behind the stage: if I moved, talked and worked it was without conscious effort. My only moment of respite came when I wrote to Bessie. Those were the letters I never posted, but I scrawled my pain across the page, sometimes writing her name over and over again, sometimes linking her name with mine, often Demeter and Persephone, and occasionally Demeter alone.

As the country filmed with green, so slight and delicate that you could not really call it spring grass, my despair became a torment. This was the time when I had always felt a thrill of excitement as the time approached for Bessie to arrive and every day dragged endlessly before we fell into each other's arms. I would be searching through my clothes for something new to wear and wondering if I should use some of my mother's cologne. This year there had been no box of clothes from Swan and Edgar's and one evening I found Rosalia sorting through my mother's dresses.

"Some of these can be cut to fit you, Gina," she said, holding up a blue serge skirt.

"I shall never wear any of my mother's clothes," I retorted, but of course, Rosalia was right and Miki managed to stretch some of her shoes for me so that they were not too uncomfortable.

Benno had bought new feathers for his horse and he was anxiously watching the sky for rain when I saw Frau Brunner waving something from the terrace.

"He is alive! My little Dolfi is alive!" she shouted.

Would I be expected to marry Dolfi if he came home? I wondered grimly.

"I have a letter from Roger Whitlow," she said and pushed it into my hand.

It was still barely light as I opened it.

My dear Frau Brunner,

Upon my return from Tibet I was able to elucidate the baffling messages that my friend Bill Smith kept receiving by courier when we were at the base camp. At first he was certain he was being pursued by some old flame but then the name rang a bell with me and I remembered you and your son, Dolfi. I am sure that wherever he is, Dolfi is flourishing. He accompanied me as far as Bombay and then found some friends and went off to cruise around the Pacific with them. I am sure as I write this that he is enjoying himself on a coral atoll and entertaining everyone with his brilliant imitations.

I can appreciate your anxiety about him but Dolfi is a regular scamp and I doubt if he'll set foot in Italy while there's the chance of his being drafted into the military. He really was in a positive funk whenever he saw a uniform.

You may have heard the dismal outcome of the expedition. We did not reach the top, and on the way down we were hit by a succession of blizzards. Poor Bill was lost and my two other chums were swept away in an avalanche. I managed to struggle out with a couple of porters—we were the only survivors. It must be regarded as one of the worst mountaineering disasters of recent times. However, I am bearing up, and have received a promotion that will keep me at a desk for some time to come.

How well I remember that super holiday in Sicily. My uncle and aunt have settled down remarkably well in England. I hear from them regularly . . .

"Such wonderful, wonderful news! My heart is bursting with joy," Frau Brunner gasped.

I folded the letter and handed it back to her.

"To have been blind for so long! *Lieber Gott*, I thought of everything but not what was in front of my nose. How can Dolfi return when the militia is waiting here to arrest him?"

There was something so repellent in the jaunty tone of Roger's letter that I felt it like an acrid taste in my mouth. I was also sure that he was lying. Did it really only occur to him when he was back in India that Bill Smith's correspondent was Dolfi's mother? It seemed as though all his friends had died on the expedition but he had been promoted, and how had it been possible for Dolfi to find friends so suddenly in a place like Bombay?

"I shall sell the Villa."

I could not answer.

"It is what I should have done as soon as he left. Ah, and I will not deny it was in the back of my mind when I made the inventory. Now, everything is ready and I shall get in touch with some prospective buyers."

"But where will you go, Frau Brunner?"

"To America. I have friends there, important people in Palermo with connections in America have often told me I should buy property there."

"How will Dolfi find you in America?"

"I shall advertise—someone will send word to him. And he will know then that it is safe to return to his mother—in a country where there is no compulsory military training."

"I shall still be able to work here, won't I?"

Frau Brunner grimaced. "Not everyone is as generous as I, my dear child."

That night I was silent in the back of the cart as Benno sang to me. If I could not work at the Villa, there was no possibility of my finding a job in Trapani. If it were Palermo it might be possible to give English lessons but there was nothing in Trapani where I had to stay and care for my father as my mother had wished.

Frau Brunner was in an ecstasy of excitement as she sent off volleys of cables and drafted advertisements.

"If only my dear parents had bought a hotel in Taormina—that is the only fashionable place in Sicily these days. But I shall find a buyer."

She had American maps and magazines everywhere and one day she pointed to a town in Florida and said she intended to buy a new hotel in Miami.

"I have friends there and they tell me it is so beautiful and land is very cheap. It is all very well for Mussolini to talk about building a new Italy and this little German, Hitler, who has such big ideas for his country. Europe is finished and it is time for America. Dolfi will be very happy there and he will be a good boy and help me run the hotel. You see how important it is to be prepared for all emergencies in life, Gwen? What foresight I had when I made an inventory of the hotel." She paused and frowned at me. "An inventory must be complete. Why didn't you include the typewriter?"

For a moment I was confused.

"The typewriter I lent you when Dolfi was studying with your father."

Instead of being hurt and angry, I was proud that I felt nothing and said simply that I would not be able to carry it back to the Villa myself and I would have to ask Benno to bring it in his cart for me.

Rosalia had overheard my father discussing the plans for a vineyard strike with two other Party members and she told me that they were planning to call out all the peasants when the landowners were most vulnerable—at the time of harvest. The next day Captain Prosimo passed me on the stairs down to my office and commended some dish on the menu, then said almost as an afterthought, "Is your father still interested in politics, Signorina?"

He was not at the museum and Rosalia told me that my father had been away for two days.

"I know he's being watched," I said.

"Ah." Rosalia looked up to heaven and made the sign of the cross. "He is *pazzo* and all he really wants is to die and be with your mother."

"What about us?" I shouted.

I wrote a note to him, telling him what Captain Prosimo had said, and left it on his pillow.

Towards the end of summer, Frau Brunner told me she had sold the Villa to a Swiss family who intended to run it as a TB and rejuvenation clinic.

"There were some difficulties about the treatment they used. The treatment is based on monkey organs and some patients died, so the Henschels could not continue their work in Switzerland, although everyone says they've discovered the fountain of youth. This will be perfect for them. They will have cages for the monkeys and beautiful rooms for the patients."

"They will not want me."

"No, but perhaps when they have finished all the necessary alterations there will be something for you to do. The family consists of three brothers and their wives so I am sure they run the clinic themselves. Perhaps some of the staff will continue working here—who knows? I shall, of course, take my chef with me to America. You cannot run a good hotel without a good chef and this one knows my ways."

Three more letters arrived back with "Address Unknown" written across them, but there was nothing from Russell Morton.

Frau Brunner was arranging to sell most of the furnishings from the Villa and every day there were agents and dealers going from room to room with notebooks and pencils in their hands, looking like hungry chickens pecking for grain, darting into corners and appearing suddenly from behind pieces of furniture. It was like watching the sack of a great city. All that would be left for the Swiss would be the remains of the *albergo* that had once been a *palazzo*, another ruin like all the rest in Sicily.

Fourteen

Benno was waiting for me at the foot of the stairs that evening and I was grateful because I felt stupid with fatigue. He put out his hand and, without thinking, I climbed up and sat beside him instead of in the back of the cart. Whenever I was with Benno I heard Bessie giggling and for a moment I closed my eyes so that I could stop the memory fading. The sound of the wheels, the snuffling whinny of the horse and the warmth of someone alongside me brought back other summer memories in a flood: Bessie holding my hand or resting her head on my shoulder as we planned our future in Manchester together, singing with Roger and Dolfi as we came home to the Villa in the dusk with swallows fluting over our heads. My hand was being kissed and when I opened my eyes, I was surprised to see Benno's face and not Bessie's shining blue eyes close to mine.

He told me that he had always loved me, that I was the queen of his heart and for my sake he was prepared to leave his wife and his children and live only for the beauty of my grey eyes that were like the sea in early morning or the autumn mist that embraced the mountains like a lover. I should have laughed then and climbed into the back of the cart. Instead, I let him open my hand and kiss the palm while he spoke of the years that his heart had ached for me. It was not the kisses or the sound of his voice that moved me but the warmth of his body. I leaned against him and it was as if all the pain of memory was gently drifting from me as I slipped into a mood that had neither thought nor reason, only feeling. Gently he turned my face to his and kissed me on the mouth. I do not know whether I responded but now the warmth was like a drug and I almost felt that I could fall asleep while his lips were on mine.

Love, he spoke of love that was like a fire, love that would burn away every obstacle between us, love that would endure forever, and I cared nothing for what he said, so long as I could feel his body next to mine. The air was heavy with the perfume of orange blossom and I knew we were not on the road because there were trees all around us.

He lifted me down from the cart and when his arms were round me, I wanted him to carry me out of this world, beyond memory and reason to a place where I could rest and sleep without dreaming. The sharp scent of grass cut through the perfume of the orange blossom like a note of music and I felt him leaning over me, opening the front of my blouse and fondling my breasts with his fingers and his lips. I looked up through heavy lids to a tracery of branches that were the bones and veins of my own body. I was in myself but my body was the tree and the soft earth being turned by a gentle hand.

Did I love Benno Sciafa? Not at all, yet my senses were receiving him as the sand does water. When he entered me, I felt a sudden pain that died in the tide of joy as his body enfolded me and I sank more deeply into the sensation of my flesh, as if I were being drawn back into a womb that would never thrust me from this comforting darkness into a glaring tumult of separation and grief. There was nothing except feeling, mindless sensation, universal flesh, as primal and innocent as the coupling of animals.

"Tell no one," he whispered urgently when he helped me into the cart. "We can come here again and make love and one day we shall run away to Australia where I have brothers who will help me, for you are my soul and I have no life without you, *carissima*."

I think I was asleep when the cart stopped at the corner of the street.

"I cannot take you to the door," he whispered. "She is waiting there for you."

"Your father has not been home today," Rosalia said nervously when she saw me.

I told her I was very tired and wanted to sleep and I scarcely remember washing and getting into bed. Next morning I saw that my drawers and petticoat were stained with blood, so I carefully washed them and put them at the back of the wardrobe where Rosalia would not find them. Of course, I should have realized then the seriousness of what I had done and been stricken with remorse, but all I wanted was the warmth of Benno's body again and the soft pressure of his mouth on my skin. Tradition has it that the passage from virginity to womanhood is fraught with symbols and rites dictated by custom and religion; for me, it was as simple as stepping across one of the little streams that coursed across the mountain road in spring, or taking off my old clothes and putting on fresh. I had no feeling of sin nor any sense of loss, for all I had experienced was a dreaming pleasure and relief from pain. Nothing seemed to have any reality now except my desire; I remember that I stumbled twice when I came down the stairs.

"He has not returned," Rosalia whispered.

"Send Miki to find out what he can," I replied and wondered to hear my own voice speaking calmly in that place when my body was a mile away, lying under the orange trees with Benno pressing me into the warm earth.

"You think like a man, a true *capo di famiglia*. You should have been a son," Rosalia said and I almost laughed.

Frau Brunner sent off thirty crates of furniture that day and I think I packed all of them. Twice, she complained that I was not listening when she spoke, but I merely shrugged because I was forcing myself not to wonder what would become of me when the Swiss doctors arrived to make the Villa a clinic where the old and the sick would be rejuvenated with organs from monkeys. Smiling, I thought they should all be taken to the orange grove to be reborn.

Benno was waiting for me that evening at the bottom of the terraces and I sat beside him while he shook the reins and made the horse gallop.

"I cannot wait to hold you in my arms," he said passionately. "You have changed my life. Last night I could not look at my wife and when she asked me what was wrong I told her that I had a migraine. You are my only love, you are the love of my life. Ah, this is *destino* and I was always *fortunato*. I have loved many of the foreign women who come to the Villa, some of them have pursued me and even offered me money. But none of them meant anything to me, no one was in my heart except you. My brothers wanted me to go with them to Australia but I told them that I would find my fortune in Sicily, and now I have you."

His voice became one with the wheels and the calling of the gulls as they swept in from the beach before they settled for the night. I knew he expected no answer to his rapturous nonsense, and indeed, I do not think I spoke at all when he was making love to me. Words have memories embedded in them and I had slipped into a warm tide beyond the reach of meaning and time. To this day, the perfume of orange blossom will make me drowsy and if I want to sleep I only have to place a few sprays beside my bed and I begin to feel a languor in every vein and nerve. It was dark when he turned into the orange grove and he sprang from the cart and caught me in his arms.

We must have been there for a long time because I saw the moon rise between the branches over my head and once Benno gave the horse a sack of grain.

"I shall write to my brothers and they will find a place for us in Australia," he whispered. "For you, I shall cast aside my wife and children as though they were leaves that had blown into my cart. I love you because you are silent," he said. "My wife never stops talking; even when I am making love to her she talks until I have to hit her to make her quiet and then she cries."

This was being said to someone else, for I was lapped in the speechless warmth of feeling and if his words had meaning it was not for me.

"*Domani*," he murmured to me as we came to the corner and I heard Rosalia calling.

"He has been taken! They have him at the police station," she cried and suddenly I returned to myself.

Miki was in the kitchen whimpering and beating his ears with his hands.

"How long has he been there?"

"Miki doesn't know, but he was arrested at one of the vineyards."

The little man stood on a chair and began to wave his arms and open and shut his mouth as if he were addressing a crowd.

"I must go and see him," I said.

"No, wait. If we are lucky they will just question him and he will be back this evening."

Miki put his head in his hands and began to cry.

Less than half an hour before I had been with Benno and now the world was rushing back on a tide of pain.

"If he is not back here by midnight we must go and demand his release."

"Demand?" Rosalia laughed shortly. "You do not demand anything from the Opera Vigilanza Repressione Antifascismo. Comandante Prosimo is like the Duce here, and even the militia officers have to do whatever he says."

Some of this was correct, I knew, for I had seen officers of much higher rank defer to Captain Prosimo at the Villa.

"Let us pray that they see how crazy your father is." Rosalia sighed, and mumbled Aves as she told her rosary.

We sat in the kitchen even though it was stiflingly hot and the sound of the fountain was pleasantly cool in the *bagghiu*. Without anyone speaking of it, we knew it was because in some way we wanted to share my father's discomfort. And that was too mild a word because I had heard stories of what happened to prisoners of the OVRA.

Rosalia was crocheting and I picked up some threads of ribbon and began to work with her.

"Your hands are faster than mine now, Gina," she said, and smiled.

My mother's presence was like a physical weight in the house that night, for it was not simply the heat oppressing us but the sense of her anxiety.

We did not have to wait until midnight. A little after ten we heard a car pull up outside the museum. I ran to open the door and saw Captain Prosimo.

"*Buona sera*," he said pleasantly to me, touching his cap.

Then I saw my father.

A soldier had him by the scruff of the neck and he lifted him like a rag from the back of the car and dropped him on the museum step. Miki rushed down and put his arms around him.

"His health will be much improved," Captain Prosimo said, wagging his finger and laughing. "We have prescribed medicine to purge the Communism from his system."

He was still laughing when he drove off and I bent over my father. The front of his shirt seemed to be covered with oil and I smelt something grossly familiar.

Miki and I carried him through to the kitchen and placed him in a chair. He fell forward across the table and I saw that the side of his face was bruised. Had they beaten him and then used oil to try and cover the marks of their fists?

Rosalia was lighting the stove and filling every pot with water.

"Go to your room," she said to me sharply. "You must not see your father."

"What right do you have—"

I was stunned by her words and about to lean forward to comfort my father when Rosalia pushed me back.

"They have made him drink castor oil—God knows how much. Soon he will be screaming. If you must do something, fetch Dr Polcari, although I do not think he can do much to help. Miki and I will get your father into a bath of hot water. Only that will help ease the pain."

I ran through the streets and left a message for the doctor. When I came back the stench filled the house. It was like a latrine in midsummer. My father was uttering gasping screams and when I walked into the middle of the *bagghiu* I glimpsed him in a tub with Rosalia pouring steaming water into it while Miki spooned something white into his mouth. I turned and went up to my room where I lay awake all night, listening to him moan. A little after midnight the doctor came and I heard his voice but I did not go down.

Just before dawn, Rosalia and Miki carried my father up to his bed and I rose and went into his room. His eyes were closed and the bruises looked as if patches of purple had been stitched to his skin.

"What did Dr Polcari say?"

Rosalia was kneeling beside my father's bed praying. She did not look up as the beads tumbled through her fingers.

"Your father must rest."

"That is not what I asked, Rosalia."

"What hope is there for an old man who was sick before they took him and beat him and poured castor oil down his throat until he choked?"

"He's dying?"

"God decides that, Gina."

"Let me be alone with him."

Slowly, Rosalia got up from her knees and I sat beside my father. He seemed to be asleep but his breath came in shallow gasps and every now and then he winced in pain.

I wanted to beg his forgiveness, but I was not sure what crimes I had committed except that the burden of them was like a stone upon my back. Strangely, I could think of a dozen ways in which I had failed or hurt my father but Benno was not among them. His hands were cold and damp and I held them in mine, trying to warm them. All my arrogance and pride came back to torment me, reminding me of the way I had treated him in Shropshire when he had asked for money to honour my mother and how eager I had been to wrench his authority from him. I should have given him a part of the money to buy a memorial for my mother, and at the very least I could have been gentler and more understanding. Why had I been so harsh? I asked the same question over and over but the answer was always the same: I was my mother's Boadicea, never happy unless I could lead and take command. I had made every servant in the hotel hate me, all our English friends had gone home, and now I was here alone. Swinging between self-pity and hatred of myself, I tried to comfort my father.

While he was doing his best to help the peasants I had been making love in an orange grove with Benno Sciafa and even though the enormity of what I had done now overwhelmed me with disgust and fear, my body was still rejoicing. In those few moments with Benno I had found a refuge from pain and loss, I had been able to slip out of the world and become triumphantly animal, without conscience or memory. Whispering, I tried to explain this to my father, although I knew he could not hear me. I held his hand to my cheek and it felt like a piece of the algae that washes in after storms; Bessie and I used to festoon ourselves with seaweed when we were little children, pretending we were mermaids or pirate queens. The weed was always dank and smelt of decay. My father's hand was cold and it smelt of death.

I stayed with my father that day and the next, but there was no change. Sometimes he frowned and mumbled a few words of Latin but none made any sense to me; once he opened his eyes and smiled and said distinctly, "Death's herd are we, and all the world a sty." He swallowed automatically what Rosalia gave him and seemed comforted when she wrapped blankets round him. Miki was convinced my father was improving; he nodded vigorously and grinned whenever he came into the room.

Frau Brunner sent word that she needed me at the Villa and I knew I must go. I had often heard my father speak about the terms of Leonard Burgoyne's will: he was to remain as curator until his death, then the contents of the museum and the house itself would become the property of the government. When my father died . . . Dr Polcari had told me that he was in God's hands. What would happen to me then?

"I am going to give you something very important, most valuable," Frau Brunner announced after she had perfunctorily observed that my father was an old fool to try and swim with the Communists. "They say everybody should have the same. Well, I tell you what would happen if I gave all the staff here an equal share in the hotel. By the end of the year I would have it all back in my hands because they are stupid and I am clever. Now, what I have for you here will open doors for you."

She had a letter in front of her which she signed "Brunner," with a flourish.

"The Villa d'Athena is known internationally and in this reference I have said that you are capable of managing every aspect of a hotel of this quality. I have praised your industry and above all—your discretion. Naturally, you will be asked what that means and you must invent something about private detectives and a duchess. You can imagine what people like to hear. There—with my blessing."

She folded the letter and handed it to me.

"If this were not a business letter I would have written that I wanted nothing more in this world than to see you marry my little Dolfi. Ah, what a wife you would have made for him! Do you know that every day one of the servants brings me a complaint about you?"

"Will I be able to get a position in a hotel here in Sicily?" I asked.

"The world is out there," she said.

"But I have Miki and Rosalia to look after."

"Like your father, they are very old, and they will die."

I shook my head because everything was confusion and despair.

"Now, we must work very hard because I have found a buyer for all the crystal. There is no need to leave fine stemware for these Swiss monkeys—pressed glass is good enough for them."

I knew that Frau Brunner had included the crystal in the terms of sale but I did not mention this. She was busily substituting everything she could, selling off the Persian carpets and Limoges china, replacing them with Belgian rugs and Johnson's kitchenware.

That evening Benno was waiting for me and before I had reached the bottom of the terraces he was telling me that his heart was broken, he had not closed his eyes since he was last with me; three days without me and he was a lost soul crying for the heaven of my body.

"My father is dying," I said coldly. "Go away. I don't want to speak to you."

"Let me take you home," he begged, but I was already walking down the dark hill.

It became a game for Frau Brunner to see how dexterously she could cheat the Swiss brothers. Four fine tapestries in the card room were rolled up and sent off to a dealer in London while she bought four gaudy imitations at an auction in Palermo. The best silver went into a case and was despatched to her friends in Miami while she replaced it with sets of Britannia metal that she bought as a job lot from the sale of a restaurant in Naples. The Villa had always been known for its elegance; even my mother used to say that Frau Brunner had taste. Now it looked tawdry, with colours that jarred: two immense Chinese vases in the foyer went to Rome and in their place a pair of hideous Majolica urns argued for the right of ugliness against the Belgian carpet in shades of purple and rose.

"Do you think," she said gaily, "that monkeys will worry about the weight of the silver?"

I think I mentioned that the Henschels might imagine they were being cheated because they had bought the Villa with most of its furnishings.

"Ah," Frau Brunner chortled, "but I specified the *seasonal* furnishings. Now, what we have here are the winter furnishings. The summer was not mentioned."

Every night I sat with my father, but he did not regain consciousness. Dr Polcari said he must have had a heart attack at the police station because he barely had a pulse now, and what there was fluttered irregularly. For a while Benno waited at the bottom of the steps for me but I refused to speak to him and at the end of a month he seemed to have forgotten me. One afternoon I went out to the garages behind the Villa and heard a girl's rippling laughter and Benno's voice. I was glad that he had taken me to the orange grove.

Turiddu came often, sometimes alone, sometimes with one of his men, and they would sit beside my father, staring at him.

"Don't let the filthy priests get him," Turiddu said.

"I won't," I promised.

"He is a martyr, but not to the cursed Church."

"Will there be a strike in the vineyards?" I asked.

"The peasants are always afraid—but there—in your father, they have a martyr. They will never forget what he told them. Every time he spoke of the revolution he knew there was a sentence of death on his head. He was not like these Fascist bullies preaching freedom while they load you with chains and fill you with castor oil."

"I—I have not been a good daughter," I said abruptly, and felt foolish as soon as I had spoken.

Turiddu put his calloused, bent hand on my arm. "You will not stay here in Sicily, Signorina. There is nothing for you here. Go, go where you can find freedom and friends."

I wanted to explain to him how I had been turned away by my family in Russell Morton and would have to remain in Sicily, but he was bending over my father, kissing him on the forehead.

"He was a king among us when we were children," he said.

Everything in that house had suddenly become precious to me for I realized that when my father died it would no longer be my home. Every crack in the paving of the *bagghiu* was familiar to me and my earliest memories were of sitting under the vine watching the light fall through the leaves. Now I was going to lose it, as I had lost Bessie and Russell Morton and everything else I had ever loved. No matter how I tried to think of a way to live and support myself, a bleak fury sat inside my head saying that I was being punished for my wickedness and worse was to come.

One evening I came down and sat in my mother's chair by the fountain, wondering what would happen to me when my father died. Rosalia was picking tomatoes from my mother's garden and, on impulse, I spoke to her.

"What was my fortune, Rosalia? What did you see in the cards for me?"

She straightened up slowly and stood in front of me, her mouth puckered.

"It was not fortunate."

"I didn't expect luck," I said wryly.

"There was a hanged man which is misfortune and many graves."

"Am I going to die?"

She shook her head slowly. "Many graves and a journey through death, but at the end, if you can reach it, a paradise."

"In this world or the next?"

"I do not know. Sometimes the card predicts great fortune, love and riches, but it can mean the riches of heaven."

"Well, at least I end well."

I closed my eyes and thought how little I believed in heaven and hell and the prayers Canon Burnside taught me when he confirmed me. It was easier to believe in gods who quarrelled and lusted and persecuted people for whims than in a god who was all-perfect and loved mankind. I could see no evidence in my own life or in the world around me that there was a deity who had any special love for humanity. When I opened my eyes, Rosalia was gone, and there was a stray cat by the fountain, glaring at me with eyes so crazed that it did not seem to belong to the natural world. Its fur was matted with dirt: I realised that it was a female and must have given birth very recently, for its stomach dragged in a lank pouch. The cat did not move and I thought it had come to drink, but in that same instant I saw that its jaws were stained with blood.

I ran into the kitchen and swept the scraps from our supper on to a plate; however, when I looked for the cat, it had gone.

Frenzied, I called for it, running out to the street, but the animal had vanished and two stray dogs slunk towards me, watching me from a distance, their yellow eyes fixed on the plate. I threw the scraps at them and heard them yelp with excitement as they fell upon the food.

Rosalia was tapping her forehead as I returned to the kitchen but I did not try to explain. Whenever I mentioned my worries to her and and my dread of the future, she told me to pray to the Blessed Virgin for help.

After my father died, where would I live? I had no friends or relations in Trapani. Would I die of hunger if I could not find work? I loved my father but there were times when I sat beside his bed and felt like shouting in anger at him. I knew that he cared for me but why had he done so little to provide for me? The answer was always bitterly the same: had anyone ever possessed the right to trespass in the domain of my parents' great love? Had either of them ever had a thought for anyone except the other?

I knew that the bucket had been placed behind the screen in my bedroom for over a week by the faint trace of disinfectant in the air. I had no need of it and Rosalia spoke sharply to me about it every evening when I came back from the Villa.

"I don't know what's wrong with me," I told her.

Three days later I woke in the morning so nauseous that I could barely struggle from my bed to the bathroom. When I lifted my head from the basin, Rosalia was standing at the door, her face like a wedge of bone.

She took hold of my hair as I was rinsing my mouth with water and twisted my head around.

"Who is he? What is his name?"

"I don't know what you mean!"

"The man who has given you a child!"

"I won't tell you! I—"

"His name or I shall kill you!"

"The grotto! Is that where you want to take me?"

"Tell me who he is!"

"God—believe it is God—and I am the Blessed Virgin you're always praying to," I shouted.

She shook me by the hair until I screamed and wrenched free from her.

"Benno Sciafa—it was Benno, wasn't it?"

I would not answer.

"*Disgraziata*! You have lost your honour!"
She began to wail and tore her face with her fingernails.
"Ah! I swore to protect you, and I have failed. I have betrayed my trust."

Fifteen

Baffled and in despair, I sank into a numb apathy, ignoring Rosalia's lamentations and going each day to the Villa where I worked until the last box of furniture had been carried out to the waiting carts. I did not see Benno again at the hotel. Frau Brunner departed quietly with her Dutch chef a few hours before the Henschel family arrived in three Daimler limousines. Within minutes I heard them stamping and shouting as they went from one room to another and discovered what was meant by "seasonal furnishings." All the staff was dismissed and I too was told that my services would not be needed at the hotel. I was at the foot of the terraces as a flock of lawyers arrived and the Henschel brothers settled down to make statements and issue writs to try to recover their money.

Every morning I had been vomiting, but I still could not believe that something had taken possession of my body. When I placed my hands across my stomach I felt nothing there. Bessie had often told me of girls at her school who got into the family way and how one left in the senior year to be married, and another tried to fix herself up with blue pills and boiling hot baths. Eventually, her parents came and took her away and when she came back she told everyone that it had been nothing more than a gastric upset and she wasn't pregnant at all. Nobody, Bessie assured me, had believed her.

Terror began to shake me from my apathy and I lay awake in my bed trembling. If I slept, would Rosalia and some of her friends come and carry me to the grotto? My reason told me that she had tried to frighten me with a horror story but I could not rid myself of the dread of that frightful place. I turned the bone she had given me over and over in my hand until it snapped between my fingers. As I had always suspected, it was part of a bird's skeleton, but I still felt it was from the body of Rita Cusumani who had been buried in that terrible stone hole.

When I was walking home from the Villa for the last time, I kept hearing Mr Chambers' voice that afternoon on the beach when he picked up a bent stick and sang for me Harry Lauder's "Keep Right on to the End of the Road." The song kept running through my head and I provided a bitter refrain. This was the end of the road for me, all my plans and hopes had come to this: I was pregnant, with no money and two old people to support. What would happen to me when I had a baby and how could I possibly work?

As I turned the corner where Benno had always stopped the cart and let me down I saw a priest and two white-robed altar boys swinging censers leaving the museum. Grey smoke drifted in perfumed coils through the air as they went off in the opposite direction.

Furious, I flung open the front door and raced up the stairs to my father's room. Outside his room on the landing there was a candle and a square of bread on a straight-backed chair. He was lying as I had left him, his eyes closed, his lips barely parted, but there was a trace of oil on his forehead and the room smelt of incense. Rosalia was at my shoulder when I turned.

"He made a good act of contrition and he has received the blessed sacrament," she said.

"How dare you bring a priest here!" I cried. "You know how my father feels about the Church. He always said he hated the Pope and Rome!"

"He has been received back and his sins have been forgiven."

"That's impossible!" I shouted. "He's unconscious. How could you do this to him?"

"Don't raise your voice," Rosalia hissed. "There is someone in the *bagghiu* who will speak to you."

The scars were not healed on her face where she had scratched herself and her eyes were puffy and swollen like a toad's. I looked back at my father and I almost envied him because he was beyond everyone's reach.

We all of us write our own stories, inventing roles for other people, sometimes mutilating the actors we select, occasionally embellishing them, so that they fit our plots. My stories had all come to an end but I would not permit Rosalia to cast my father as a penitent Christian. I knew him too well for that.

I followed Rosalia downstairs. At first I thought the triton was casting a darker shadow than usual in the *bagghiu*. Rosalia placed a lamp beside the shadow and I saw the long satin-lined cape and black pointed shoes, the wrinkled white hands on the snarling monkey. The Barone raised his head and I knew that he had been crying.

"Kneel to him," Rosalia hissed.

I did not move, even though I felt her plucking at my elbow.

"This is a house of sorrow," the Barone said slowly, "and now you have brought shame to it."

I stared at the ground and did not answer.

"Your father, that foolish man, is close to death, but he has made his peace with the Church and he will rest in the Marineo crypt until God calls him to judgement."

Rosalia was on her knees, sobbing her gratitude for the Barone's goodness, his noble heart and the love he had shown his family.

Anger was colouring my face but I could not speak.

"Ah, you are blushing, my child, and that is a sign of repentance. Would that it were as easy for you to seek forgiveness as it is for your father. His life will be counted in hours now, but you must repent every day as you look at the child of your sin."

Rosalia cried that Benno was a man of notorious reputation with women and that he had taken me by force. I had come home from the Villa one evening with my clothes torn, screaming hysterically.

"Did Benno Sciafa rape you?" the Barone asked quietly.

"No."

"She is afraid to denounce him. He swore that if she told anyone he would come with his friends in the night and kill her!"

I shook my head.

"A girl who has been brought up in a house like this can have little regard for her honour. That woman—your mother—"

Passion silenced the Barone for a moment and he thumped the ground twice with his cane.

"Ah, if you had known your father when he was young—when he was a child. His father had been a fisherman, but his leg was broken one *mattanza*, so he worked in the tunny factory, a poor man of no education and little intelligence. The mother was just a *contadina* who gave birth regularly to dead babies. Only one child, your father, came in her middle age and survived. How they loved Enrico! I remember when they brought the baby to my father for his blessing.

"They were poor, but they lived on dry crusts so they could send the child to the convent school instead of letting the streets educate him. He was very small for his age and at first the nuns did not want him because he was so frail and he did not speak. The good sisters hesitated and then, because they had kind hearts and because he was a Marineo, they took the little boy. Ah, God in His mercy stretched out His hand and touched that child. One day, two of the nuns came screaming to the priest's house and when he managed to calm them, they told him that a miracle had taken place. The priest, a wise man, was sceptical, but he followed them back to the convent and there he found a little boy, not yet five, sitting in a corner reading a Latin grammar. I tell you, the priest began to tremble, for this was a prodigy, a miracle. The child had seemed barely able to speak but when the priest took the book from his hands and pointed to a sentence in Latin, the child translated it. How could this have happened?"

I wanted to cry out, to stop his words with my own, because I knew that every syllable was like the brick of a prison he was building around me. The prison was my family and I would never be able to escape from it.

"It was clear to everyone that Enrico di Marineo had a vocation because he was not like other boys of his age. At the *liceo*, he was interested only in his studies and never looked at the girls. Our family has had five cardinals in its history, and here, my father said, will be the sixth to bring glory to the name of di Marineo. Of course, the priests wanted him to enter the seminary, but my father would not permit this. He did not want his prodigy being snatched away by a religious order, or condemned to preach to goats and stones in the Abruzzi because some envious cleric had accused him of the pride of learning. Priests can be as jealous as other men when a marvel like your father appears among them. No, my father sent his prodigy to the *liceo* and then to the University of Milano. When he had finished his degrees and was a *Dottore* he would then permit him to enter the Church and take his vows. As a doctor of philosophy, he would be made secretary to a cardinal, and it is often the secretary who inherits the cardinal's hat."

The thought of my father in scarlet was as absurd as my dreams of a home in Manchester with Bessie or at Russell Morton with my aunt. I shifted slightly and Rosalia hissed at me to be still. The Barone frowned as if he were contesting the power of memory and time.

"Was this an idle dream? By no means. My father, of blessed memory, was a shrewd man and a politician of great vision. Enrico di Marineo was the idol of his teachers, and all said the same thing. This boy does not possess the ordinary carnal passions. If he has passion, it is only for learning. When he was twelve, he had five languages and I still have the letters of gratitude he sent my father: the first in Italian, then Latin, and Greek—a fourth in Hebrew, and the fifth in Aramaic. My father was as proud of those five letters as if the boy had sent him a box of gold coins.

"Who could have foreseen that the University of Milano cherished vipers? Professors had taken refuge there who included among their numbers the damned Illuminati, Freemasons and Marxists. The boy was seduced and, before his studies were complete, he wrote and told my father that he could not enter the Church because he was an atheist and a Marxist. My father argued with him, your grandmother pleaded with him on her knees, but the boy was obdurate. Starvation is the most effective teacher, and he would have come to his senses before long, but he was befriended by a lunatic Englishman, Leonard Burgoyne, who made your father his secretary."

There was silence for a moment and all I could hear was the sound of Rosalia's rosary and the slow splashing of the fountain.

"Was this man *effeminato*? No, like your father, he had no passions and the two lived together like a pair of mules. A secretary? A drudging assistant to a mad Englishman, and your father could have worn scarlet and been a prince of the Church. Who knows? With such learning and control of the flesh he might have aspired to the papal throne and gripped St Peter's keys. What a loss for the family! Honours snatched away from us and the child my father had cherished digging like a *contadino* in the ground for the garbage of the past. It was the greatest disappointment of my father's life for he had cherished this dream for over twenty years. I tell you, it broke his heart! When he was an old man, my father wept whenever he saw a cardinal."

The Barone bent over his stick and his lips moved inaudibly. Rosalia began to cry again and curse Benno Sciafa. With the slightest gesture, the Barone silenced her.

"When Leonard Burgoyne died, your father remained in authority here, a solitary mule, and I resolved to put him out of my mind. Then, one day, as if God were mocking us all, the mule took a wife. What a wife! A woman so old and ugly that little children would scream in terror when she passed by them. I can hear her voice now, rasping and clapping like a broken shutter. Of course, your father was only interested in her money and she did bring him a good dowry. God laughed again and from this union came a child of incomparable beauty. When I first saw her, I was amazed that two old frogs could give birth to an angel. The ways of God—more mysterious than we can ever comprehend. I watched over that child, afraid that two lunatic old people would not guide her in virtue and good behaviour. To provide some proper guidance in this house I sent for my dear Rosalia who was happy caring for my two sisters. When she was with my sisters, Rosalia was treated like one of the family, respected and loved. It was purgatory for her to be here."

Rosalia sobbed loudly.

"The child was in your care, Rosalia, and you have failed."

"Forgive me, Signore, I did everything in my power but I could not be her parents. And Gina has a will of her own."

Gina has nothing now, I thought, and she can do nothing except listen to this old man who is writing her life.

"Now, as *capo di famiglia*, I must do what I can to see that justice is done. For you, Gina, there will be a marriage, though not the marriage I would have chosen for you. Benno Sciafa has three brothers in Australia; one of them, Giacopo, has just become a widower and he will accept you as his wife and be a father to your child to preserve the honour of this family. All he has now is a daughter and he will be content if you bring him a son."

"Thank the Barone," Rosalia hissed.

I remained silent.

"You will be married here by proxy tomorrow morning and take the ship from Naples for Australia in three days' time. Everything has been arranged for you."

This was my end then. I could feel the strings that were jerking me into motion. The Barone stretched out his hand and I knew that if he had suddenly commanded me to dance I would have been forced to stand on my toes or turn and bow.

"There is one small gift I have kept for you."

He held out a box.

"Open it, my child."

A pair of gold earrings in a satin case.

"Thank the Barone, thank him," Rosalia said.

"No, her shame will not let her speak," the Barone said gently. He got up slowly.

Only when he was gone could I find words.

"Have you lost your voice as well as your honour?" Rosalia cried. "You should have knelt to the Barone and begged his forgiveness and thanked him for his goodness. He is the head of our family; he has cared for you ever since you were born."

"Who is this man I am to marry?"

"Instead, you stood there like a stick, like a marionette on a peg."

"Tell me about him."

It was not as though I were angry or afraid, because I had long passed beyond ordinary feeling. All I felt now was a flicker of curiosity, and I asked as if I were enquiring about the weather.

Rosalia began to chew on her lips and her head moved nervously from side to side.

"He is Benno's brother."

"I know that."

"He is older than Benno—perhaps forty, forty-one."

"His wife has died?"

"Yes—he was married before."

"Here in Sicily?"

"Yes. There is no point talking about this. You will be a married woman and your honour will be saved. Who am I to say what marriage is like? I never chose it and I shall be a virgin until they carry me to the cemetery in my white coffin. A wife must obey her husband as if he were God, and he has the right to beat her if he chooses and command her to do whatever he pleases. Ah, they say there are joys for a married woman but I could never see them and I remained a virgin; every night I thank the God who has saved my honour for Himself."

"What sort of man is this Giacopo Sciafa?"

"There is no need for you to ask. Early, very early in the morning, we shall go to the church and Benno Sciafa will marry you in the name of his brother."

I was patiently persistent, asking the same question over and over again.

"A woman cannot expect to marry a saint! She must accept her lot and pay the price of Eve's transgression."

"He has had two wives?"

Suddenly Rosalia began to cry. "I would not have wished this man for you! But it is for the best and perhaps you can make him gentle. He wants a son, and if you give him one, he may change."

"Why did his wives die?"

"He is a man with a violent temper and—Oh, people say many foolish things, and none of them are ever true."

"Tell me, Rosalia."

"They say his first wife died when he beat her and he left Sicily before the police came to arrest him."

"And the second?"

"I don't know. Oh Gina, the Barone would have made a fine match for you but you cast aside your honour—for what? A Benno Sciafa who makes love to all the foreign women at the Villa and chases after every *puttana* in Trapani."

I could question her calmly because none of it had any meaning for me; her words rattled around in my head like dried peas on a plate. My plan was decided and I had no fear of Giacopo Sciafa. I knew what lay at the end of the road.

"Will Miki be all right?" I asked suddenly.

"Something will be done for him." She shrugged.

Rosalia told me to go up to my room and at two o'clock in the morning we would go to the church. The priest had reluctantly agreed to conduct the ceremony, but he insisted that it be done secretly without scandal.

It was very quiet in my room. Occasionally, I heard Rosalia's voice in the kitchen and twice she crossed the *bagghiu*. There was nothing to fear now because I knew exactly what must be done. I sat there and contemplated everything I had just heard as if it were a story told about strangers: a snatch of conversation from a nearby table on the terrace of the Villa. Bessie and I often used to eavesdrop as enigmatic messages were passed between guests at adjoining tables and later we would spend hours trying to interpret those strange exchanges: "She was a fool to have told her." "Well, perhaps, but she could never have seen the consequences." "Pamela did the same thing." "Pamela was experienced." "It was an accident really." "Not when you consider the Talleyfords." Everything I had just been told by the Barone and Rosalia was as mysterious and remote as coded messages between strangers. Whatever was said had no meaning for me because I knew the end of my story and it would be as disappointing for the Barone as my father's refusal to become the sixth di Marineo cardinal. That thought was very satisfying to me.

Rosalia was at the door holding a long black shawl.

"This, you must wear this," she said.

"No, I always wear a hat in church."

"Your face must not be seen. You are *disgraziata*. The priest had to be persuaded by the Barone himself."

I reached into my wardrobe, took out a grey felt hat that had belonged to my mother, and pulled it down hard over my ears.

"Well, I'm ready for this superstitious nonsense," I said and heard my mother's voice.

My composure at this point astounds me now. I only know that I felt like the stand-in who reads lines at rehearsal for the leading actor who is giving a performance somewhere else. This Gina, dressed for her wedding, was not Gwen Harcourt di Marineo who had decided to play a very different part in another play altogether. The church was several streets away and we walked quickly, with Rosalia trotting at my side, trying to place the shawl over my head. I pushed her away roughly and told her I would throw it into the gutter if she put it near me. Every time she reproached me I held my head higher and strode out like my mother. We went round to the side of the church and when Rosalia knocked at a little door, it was opened by Miki. He had a small bouquet of wild flowers that he pushed into my hands.

If the streets had been dark, the church was gloomier and it took a moment before I saw where I was. A lobby opened into a corridor, at the end of which heavy leather-covered doors led us into the church itself. The perspective was strange, for the cupola disappeared into a sombre cloud above my head and the cavernous expanse of the church loomed in front of me: I suddenly realised that we were standing behind the altar. At the side of a baroque column, a priest was rising slowly up and down on his toes, as though he were planning to fly up through that darkness and escape to the light of the sky. A little in front of him, the Barone leaned on his cane, gazing at the floor. I concentrated my vision and saw a third figure against the wall. At first, I could not recognise Benno Sciafa in the bedraggled, wan figure who scowled at me. I had never seen Benno without a brilliant jacket sewn with tiny mirrors and sparkling beads, a scarlet sash and white trousers with braid down the sides. This man could have been wearing clothes cut from old sacks and his hair was as dusty as though he had just come from the brickfield.

The priest refused to look at me, brusquely motioning for me to stand in front of him, and then the marriage ceremony began with Benno Sciafa speaking for his brother Giacopo. I answered mechanically as if I were playing the part meant for someone else. Only once did I falter, when I suddenly remembered how Bessie and I used to rehearse our weddings and count our bridesmaids.

We signed our names and it was over.

"You will both repent of this sin," the Barone said solemnly, and the priest cleared his throat because there was much he must have wanted to say but could not in the Barone's presence.

I saw the measure of Benno's repentance outside the church. The painted cart had vanished and in its place was a handcart.

"If you work diligently, you may one day recover what you have lost, Benno," the Barone said.

Benno took hold of the shafts and dragged the creaking cart off into the darkness without a backward glance.

"Your honour has been saved," Rosalia said triumphantly when we closed the museum door behind us. "In three days' time you will be on your way to this new country as a married woman."

I went silently up to my room and carefully took off the grey felt hat and placed it in my wardrobe. The house was quiet at last and I crept down to the museum and opened the locked cupboard. The key creaked against the bolt because I do not think anyone had used it since that time, years before, when I found Dolfi examining the Phlyax vases. A flood of moonlight poured across the cases and spilled into the drawer that held the long Elymian strigil with the squat figure at its base. For a few moments I held it in both hands, running my fingers down its length, and I seemed to know instinctively what it was and how it must be used. Now the Barone's story was finished, and I would write my own.

The moon was at the full and every grain and seam in the rocks was etched ink-black in the white clarity of a light so brilliant that even the stars had become a milky haze over my head. Against the rocks the rising tide was breathing like a heavy sleeper and when I came to the secret beach it was already brimming with water. I dragged off my shoes and stockings and waded across to the far side.

Crouching, I climbed into the grotto and found myself on my knees in front of the little Virgin with her cracked gilt crown. That night she was not the queen of heaven, but Persephone's winter self, Hecate, who reigned over the world of the dead and witches, mistress of the Furies. She knew what I must do inside that stone womb. All my hopes were gone and when I closed my eyes, I could no longer see your face clearly, Bessie. We used to play our death game on the beach when we were little children, making wreaths of seaweed and driftwood, burying each other in the sand and reciting long prayers over the grave. There would be no grave for me except the one where my mother lay. Perhaps in death, in that wasteland of the sea, she would put out her hand and draw me to her.

I knelt in the circle of light, holding the strigil between my legs. It would not be the Barone's story: there would be no son for Giacopo Sciafa. Slowly I raised myself up and then forced myself down, with all my weight, on the clawed point of the strigil. The stone seemed to be exploding around me and I realized it was my own scream buffeting back from the walls.

It was as if molten fire had been poured into me; I rolled to one side, moaning, and pulled out the strigil. It broke; the two pieces were in my hands, sticky with blood. Something alive was dying inside me, screaming in protest as it beat against the walls of my body.

"Leave me! Go!" I shrieked and again the sound hammered my ears in booming waves.

"Hecate—take it!"

The statue seemed to be staring at me as I felt something being torn from my body in convulsive waves of pain. When I looked down, I saw the dark stain spreading out from between my legs. Dragging myself through the mouth of the grotto I fell into the moonlight and crawled across the rocks to the secret beach, now flooded by the tide. For a moment I knelt there, hurling the broken strigil as far as I could into the deep water, and then I threw myself down from the rocks.

My arms were over my head and the tide lifted and carried me past the opening of the beach to roll in the open surge. I told myself to swim towards the light and I tried to strike out for the horizon but I was caught in something that moved faster than I. Again and again I tried to swim across the current but it held me and swung me along at its will. Something was being ripped from my body and I screamed and screamed as it was torn away. The water filled my mouth and I began to choke. If I could force myself out of the current, if I could only dive until the air was emptied from my lungs, I would be free of pain, but it was as if I were being carried on the back of a great horse lunging through the sea.

Something was swimming beside me, something that was more terrifying than death, because it was my own flesh. I swam frantically, trying to escape it, but the shape was taking hold of me and dragging me into itself. It was not death I was afraid of then, but of a life that was bent on swallowing me in its fearful small mouth.

Thrashing and kicking, I fought to be free of it, while the water rushed me towards the moon and the vacancy of death. The agony was over at last and I was empty, with only the current holding me in its arms, rocking me into sleep and the absence of all things.

Irritably, I tried to sleep again but there was a harsh obstruction under me and when I reached out I felt sand. In the same instant there were hands at my shoulder and when I opened my eyes, I saw I was floating in a sea of blood.

"This will not save your father," a voice said.

Dazed, I tried to turn my head and saw Giuseppe. The other fisherman they called Alfio was standing in the bloody water from the boat and making the sign of the cross.

Turiddu climbed up from the sand like a crab and put a blanket around me.

I remember that I was crying and someone said to run to the museum and fetch Miki and Rosalia. The current had swept me round past the rocks and into the beach and already the first light of morning was glinting on the sea. Turiddu brought me hot wine and water in a cup and I drank it slowly while my tears turned to something like laughter.

The Barone's story was to be mine after all, for I had not been able to write the one I planned. Or was it that Demeter could never die in Poseidon's kingdom? When Poseidon once sought Demeter's love, she changed herself into a mare to escape him, but he miraculously took on the form of a stallion and from that union came a great winged horse.

"Never disparage the ancient myths," my mother always said. "However fanciful, there is always an element of truth in them. More than you'll find in these barbarous Catholic perversions."

"Your father is a great hero," Turiddu was saying. "And the peasants will not forget him."

Two old women were carefully washing a withered little child in the bloody water.

"This is not what he would have wished—not for you—a young lady of good education. This is superstition."

"I know."

"Your father will die as a Communist martyr, but he will not be unavenged."

Turiddu began to chuckle and he leaned closer so that I felt his beard brushing my face.

"A certain captain has a pretty *puttana* in the town that he visits every night. Ah, a girl like that has many suitors and one day the captain will be found at the side of the road with his throat cut. It is a dangerous business, courting pretty women."

He began to laugh and slap his knees.

"Do it soon," I said, and marvelled at the coldness of my voice.

I heard Rosalia calling to me and stood up slowly, for I could feel nothing in my body.

She was talking to the fishermen and my father's name was mentioned several times. They were speaking about my devotion, and the duties of a daughter and my distress. I let her take my arm and lead me across the beach towards the town.

The way back to the museum seemed to be up a cliff face where it took all my strength to save myself from falling at every step. I needed Rosalia's help to wash the blood from my hair and afterwards I told her to throw the clothes away. She was asking me a thousand questions but I would not answer. I was very tired.

"Your father is standing at the gate of heaven," she cried. "Why do you want to call him back?"

So weak that I could no longer stand, I fell on to my bed.

"What is wrong with you?" Rosalia asked, suddenly suspicious.

"I'm tired. Let me sleep."

"Did you try to wash in the red water for your father or— What has happened?"

"Fetch the bucket for me, Rosalia. I shall need it."

Rosalia became hysterical, asking me if I had lost the child.

"There is no child," I said, and fell asleep.

It seemed as though I had only slept for a few moments when I woke, because the light seemed the same as when I'd fallen on my bed. There was blood on the sheets but I had no pain. It was only when I tried to get out of bed that I felt the blood pulsing from me.

"When did it happen?" Rosalia asked.

"That's the wrong question," I replied flippantly.

"Giacopo Sciafa is expecting a son," she said nervously.

"Expecting?" I began to laugh. "Who has the right to expect anything? Even God was disappointed when the Serpent spoilt His plans for humankind."

Perhaps it was the loss of so much blood, but I was beginning to feel lightheaded.

"You must rest until it's time to leave for the station," Rosalia said. "I shall pack for you."

"Yes, do that for me," I said and went slowly to sit by my father while she changed the bed and began removing clothes from my wardrobe.

She told me that my passage to Australia and a little extra money was the price that had been received from the sale of Benno's cart and white pony. If sometimes I felt as though I had been cursed at birth, I now wondered if I had the power to curse others. Benno had not forced me to love him. I had gone willingly into the orange grove with him and yet for this, he had lost everything.

I do not know how many times the bucket was brought up to my room and taken downstairs, while I felt myself growing weaker by the hour. Perhaps, I thought, it would still be my story and not the Barone's that would record my life. Nothing seemed of any relevance until, on the second morning, I held my hand against the window and saw every bone and vein like a forest of trees against the light. I became fascinated by that forest and walked among the quiet trees where everything was silent and safe from the world. If Rosalia spoke to me, I held my hand in front of my face and disappeared into the forest where nobody could reach me.

On the day of my departure, I woke to find that my bags had already been carried downstairs and Rosalia was helping me out of bed. There was a confusion of noise outside in the street that made me wonder if a crowd had come to jeer as I left Sicily. It was no more than a momentary thought, for nothing really troubled me at that time or dispelled the drowsiness that had taken hold of me.

Very slowly, because any jarring movement made me bleed again, I walked into my father's room. He lay there so still that I could not see a flicker of breath and I wondered if he were dead.

"Father, I'm going away now," I said, more to myself than to him.

"I don't know what is going to happen to me, but it doesn't matter—I can't struggle any more. Someone else will have to write the story."

His hand was so light and cold in mine that it felt like a scrap of old paper.

"Nothing turned out as I expected."

His eyes were opening and I saw that he was trying to say something to me.

"Father—help me, please," I cried.

"Evelina," he murmured and I knew he was dead.

2

Griffith

Sixteen

If bitterness could kill, I think I should have died then with my father. His eyes were open, but sightless with the scale of opaque whiteness that comes with death and he was smiling. For one moment I wanted to scream and pound his head with my fists, dragging him back into life and some awareness of me. My hand was in front of me, but suddenly I was no longer in that room: I was in a forest of trees, running softly, passing between the trunks like a shaft of light, knowing that you were there, just beyond my reach, Bessie. We were laughing as we ran silently through the pale forest with the trees slipping past us, no sound anywhere in the muffled quiet.

Someone had taken hold of me by the arm and was pulling me to my feet. It was a man who kept saying that I must leave; he could not get through the crowd in front of the museum so he had taken the cart round to the back, but he was afraid that soon the people would be trying to get in there too. I shook my head and walked slowly because I could feel a thread of blood trickling down my leg, trying to find its way to the earth. The shouting and screams grew louder outside and I wondered if the crowd was going to kill me before I found my executioner, Giacopo. Was this the fate of the *disgraziata*, to be stoned and torn apart by a mob?

In the *bagghiu* I heard the pounding at the front door of the museum and then I saw Rosalia and Miki. He was crouched against the wall holding a canvas sack crammed with bank notes while Rosalia watched him with her arms folded across her chest.

"The old fool," she said. "He's won the lottery."

The voices grew louder outside as Miki put the bag between his knees and began to drive an imaginary car, his body swaying as he turned a sharp corner, honking to warn oncoming traffic.

"You gave him a sovereign, Gina, and he asked me to give him the numbers for his dreams. Such dreams! The book almost fell apart in my hands. But early this morning they told him that he had won and now all the world is out there clamouring to see him, to photograph him for the newspapers, begging him for a share of the money."

"Miki, I'm so glad—" I said, but he did not hear me as he swerved to avoid something on the road.

"Will he be all right?" I asked, for the man was pulling at my arm and telling me he could not wait.

"Ah." Rosalia sighed deeply and stared at Miki. "I shall have to marry him to save him from all those leeches."

I almost stumbled in my shock.

"Do you imagine he can look after that money on his own? No, it will be gone like a drop of water in the desert. He won't be left with enough to buy the smell of a car once that crowd takes hold of him. Half of them out there are claiming to be his cousins, his children, his beloved relations, and only a wife can protect a man from hungry relations."

When he heard Rosalia speak about the car, Miki looked up at her and laughed.

"It will be a great sacrifice for me"—Rosalia sighed and clasped her hands—"to surrender the virginity that I had promised our blessed Lord, but it must be done for the honour of the family. Don't be afraid, I shall be a good wife to the old fool and not a lira will be stolen. We will have a car and a little apartment in Naples and I shall pray every day to the Madonna for her forgiveness."

I wanted to sit and laugh at the capricious effrontery of fate but I was too weak and the man was urging me to leave.

"This is her blessing upon you too, Gina. When you are a married woman with a family of your own in Australia, you will not have to spare a moment worrying about Miki and me."

"And my father?"

"He has made his peace with the Church."

"He's dead. Someone should close his eyes."

"I shall do everything necessary and then I shall call the undertaker. Come, Miki—"

She pulled the old man to his feet.

"We must go upstairs together now."

Rosalia and Miki were taken from my life as though they had been lifted from the stage to be kept for another play in which I had no role, not even the mention of my name in the prologue. Dimly, something of what we'd said had been understood by Miki and he was scrambling up, still clutching the sack to his chest. For a moment, he looked at me and I saw he was crying.

"I shall always wear it," I said, and touched the coral *corno* he had given me so many years ago.

Very slowly, Miki reached into the sack and reluctantly, as if he were peeling off a piece of his own skin, he handed me a hundred-lira note.

The man was pushing me towards the door and I felt the blood again, reaching down towards the earth like a messenger warning Hecate and the underworld that I would soon be with them. A rush of people came around the corner, pushing and jostling, just as the man was helping me into the cart, but not one of them was interested in the *disgraziata*. Some of the younger men were climbing on each other's shoulders, trying to reach the roof as the police arrived and began to beat them down with sticks. I sat on my bags in a state of numb calm and considered, without any anxiety, how I would get to the ship in Naples. In Australia, I knew that there was only death waiting for me and I watched the blood run down to my feet and wondered if Hecate would claim me before Giacopo killed me as he had his other two wives.

The underworld was the hold of the ship where the steerage passengers were jammed into cabins that stank of sweat and vomit and where only children or dwarves could stand upright. In a shed at the wharf a doctor had placed a stethoscope on my back and said I was clear of TB. He motioned for me to open my mouth, grasping my chin and poking around my teeth as though I were a donkey for sale in the market. Somebody pinned a piece of paper with a number on it to the front of my dress and I was pushed up the steps and on to the ship. Great bales were swinging overhead but I hardly saw them and even the noise of the wharf was like a droning roar in my ears. There were stewards at regular intervals who read the numbers and pushed me down stairs and along corridors that grew darker and more narrow. Nobody had spoken to me except to ask my name, and when I nodded, that was sufficient to move me along in the queue. The doctor and the Australian immigration officer had assumed that no one could speak English and they were right. Most of the steerage passengers even found it difficult to understand Italian, for they came from the Abruzzi or Calabria and spoke dialect, but all of them were convinced that they were on their way to El Dorado or some promised land where no one was hungry and everybody could become rich.

I was in the care of the Graziola family, a married couple with two young children and a baby called Francesco who was a little over a year old. The parents clearly expected me to mind the baby and watch the children for them and when I told them I could not leave the cabin, they shouted at me and called me the *cretina*. It was all I could do to reach the stinking toilet that fifty people were sharing. Although I was no longer able to eat, the blood, a fine thread like a hair, continued to run the length of my leg as if it were a vein. Once, the woman, Lucia, saw it and told me to get some clean rags for myself but I had no strength to leave my place on the end of the bunk that I shared with the little girl. She often brought me a cup of water and I drank that and once she gave me a plate of bread and meat, but I could no longer swallow. I knew I was dying and in the few moments when I left the forest and considered this, all I could feel was a sense of triumph that it would not be the Barone's story, but my own. No matter what he had planned for me, I would never be Giacopo's wife and the son he desired had died in the grotto. Everyone was at the mercy of the puppet masters who attached their strings to our arms and legs and set us dancing to their own stories. It was this that angered me: I had no story of my own except the freedom of the forest I found in my hand. My anguish was that whenever I tried to escape, to tear off the strings that bound me, I paid for my freedom with death. Was this what Rosalia had seen for me? No matter how I had struggled to escape from my mother, she had controlled me to the very end and I had remained with my father until he died with her name on his lips. The burden of that great love had been placed across my back and it left me despairing and without hope.

I leaned my head against the burning metal of the ship and felt nothing, because I seldom left the forest now. It was enough for me to raise my hand to the light of the porthole to find myself among the trees, moving through them like mist with you at my side, Bessie. The child distracted me when the parents placed him on my lap and told me to nurse him while they went up on deck to get some air. Faintly, I gathered that we were passing through the Suez Canal—and the little girl was shrilling with excitement because she had seen camels and pyramids.

All I wanted was to be left in the forest, but the baby was dragging at my hair and screaming. I held my hand against the porthole but in that instant there was another hand, a fist, between my own and the light. The father was shouting at me and the woman shrieking that the baby's head was broken. I saw the fist in front of my face and then someone pulled it back.

"That's enough of that. Bunch of bloody savages."

Another voice. "What's the trouble here?"

The Graziolas were shouting again and I dimly heard them accusing me of throwing their child to the floor.

"There's nothing wrong with him," one voice said.

"I think you should examine the girl, Doctor," the other responded.

"Commy stay, Signora? Malady?" the older man said.

"No, please—go away," I said fretfully. "Please, let me die. I mustn't lose my friend again."

"For Christ's sake, she's English."

I tried to push them away but I could not raise my hands. The man in the white uniform was holding me and carrying me like the angel of death and then the forest surrounded me with its silence.

There was a whiteness around me and at first I thought it was the forest, but the sheet over me was stiff and smelt faintly of disinfectant. My head was so heavy that I could scarcely turn it and yet there was something beside me that made me think I must be in a strange garden. It resembled a sunflower, with a mottled red centre and a fringe of yellow petals moving in odd little jerks as if it were being shaken. The flower toppled sideways and I saw a man rubbing his bald head and yawning. He looked at me and gaped.

"My Gawd, you're alive."

I tried to speak but my lips were so dry that he fetched a damp cloth and placed it over my mouth.

"The doctor said you wouldn't make it, but I had a feeling the old bugger wasn't ready for you. I can't stand it when anybody young croaks. There's time enough for dying and it's never late enough, I always say. Do you know what my old man wanted written on his gravestone? 'Unfinished', and those are my sentiments precisely. We've been feeding you with a tube the way they did with those raving old suffragettes in Brixton Prison."

"This is the ship?"

"The SS *Rangitiki*, P & O Line, bound for Aden, Bombay, Singapore and Sydney."

I knew then that I would have to play my part for the Barone until I found Giacopo.

"Come on, ducks, you're not giving up now, are you? Here, have something to drink."

He raised my head and I swallowed a liquid so sweet that I almost retched.

"Pure glucose. You've got to get some energy. When Dr Bowles carried you up here I don't think you had a teaspoon of blood left in you. I told some of me mates we must have shipped on a few vampires with them Dagos. How long were you haemorrhaging?"

"I don't know."

"Was it a mis? Or—well, it's time for your wash and brush-up and the best way is if I place a sheet over your head so you can't see. What you can't see never embarrasses you. No wonder most people like to make love in the dark."

I felt him washing me and saying I'd had septicaemia and it was a miracle I'd survived, but it was as if he were touching and talking about someone I'd only met once and never really known.

"Now, I think I can find you a dab of cologne somewhere and when you're feeling better, I'll get some shampoo and wash your hair. You're lucky to have it. Dr Bowles kept telling me to cut it, but I could never bring myself to find the scissors and when you looked as if you were at death's door, he didn't bother reminding me again. I'm very sensitive about hair, having so little of it myself."

It was then I began to cry.

"Did I hurt you, dearie? I'm sorry, but you have to be clean. We don't want you smelling like one of them dirty Dagos. Remember Florence Nightingale and her germs."

He was patting my hand and I tried to pull it to my face. He understood immediately.

"Ah, we all need a bit of affection, don't we?"

I did not have the strength to cry for very long, but I clung to his hand.

"Mind you, we're all waiting to hear your story. I thought Dr Bowles was going to—he was knocked for a sixer when you answered him in English. I mean, it's like trying to make sense of a cage of monkeys down there in steerage."

"I'm—" For the first time in my life I could not say that I was English for I was not really sure who I was.

"I'm Taps—hospital orderly and general dogsbody for Dr Bowles."

"I'm in hospital?"

"In sick bay. We've got you screened off from the hoi polloi."

My senses were returning to me and I could hear sounds behind the dark green screens to the right and at the foot of my bed. When I turned my head to the left I glimpsed a porthole and through it a blue that must have been the sky.

"We're on the portside, so you won't have the sun beating in on you. Half of Italy's camping out there on deck—you should see them! Worse than a pack of gypsies."

"Where are we now?"

"In the Indian Ocean, docking at Bombay in eleven days' time."

When Dr Bowles came that afternoon he asked me point-blank if I'd aborted and I told him a little of what had happened. He stared at me and tapped his nose with his stethoscope. I was surprised that he did not upbraid me.

"And you consider yourself married?"

"Yes."

"But you're not an RC?"

"No, but I had to get married, there was nothing else I could do, and nowhere to go."

"I had an aunt once who married a foreigner—came to a sticky end."

"I was married by proxy to Giacopo Sciafa."

"You don't seem too cheerful about it. You nearly did yourself in with whatever you used to get rid of the baby."

Far from reproaching me with what I'd done, Dr Bowles seemed gratified and told me I was very brave even if I had almost killed myself. He regarded me as a tribute to his medical skill, although I meant much more than that to him: I was a soul that had been snatched from the jaws of Rome. For Dr Bowles, I was proof of all his prejudices about Roman Catholics and corroboration of everything he had been told about an aunt who ran off with a Greek and died in childbirth.

"I'm going to give you the address in Sydney of a hostel for—well, girls who've found themselves in trouble like you. There's a fine bunch of women running it and they do a good job of getting places for their girls in domestic service."

He was a kind man at heart and it was by his insistence that I was kept in the sick bay for the remainder of the voyage. When I was able to stand, he asked me to translate when any of the migrant Italians needed him and Taps wryly told me that I would soon be taking his job.

"Dr Bowles came from the Royal Navy so he doesn't have the best bedside manner in the world," Taps said as he made me swallow a spoonful of minced raw liver. "But he's a fine doctor and if he says offal and iron will fix you, then it's liver and tacks for you until you stop looking like Hamlet's ghost."

It was another two weeks before I could move around and then I used to sit beside Dr Bowles while the migrants paraded before him and I tried to understand Calabrian and Tuscan. He never really understood when I explained to him about the dialects and he attributed my inability to understand many of them to my being more English than Italian.

"Your late mother has a lot to answer for," he would say, and shake his head at me. "Leaving you to the mercy of a pack of Romish devils. I wonder they didn't pack you off to a convent."

One day he placed a Bible beside my bed.

"Have you see this before?"

"Yes."

"Ah, but have you read it?"

"Not—not very much."

"You see!" he exclaimed triumphantly to Taps. "Knows the Bible but not permitted to read it. That's the papists for you."

Taps explained to me that Dr Bowles was an Irish Presbyterian and had strong views about race and religion. Much of his kindness to me was the result of his conviction that I was a Protestant victim of the Roman Catholics.

"You wouldn't want a child of mixed blood, would you?" he said to me once. "Now what you have to do is take the next step and become a hundred per cent English. These fine women in Sydney will look after you and they may even be able to find you a position in a shop or an office. When we get to Bombay, I'll send them a cable."

I could never really talk to Dr Bowles but Taps became my friend, as he still is. He found a little spot between the lifeboats and tackle on deck just wide enough to take a deck chair for me to sit in during the day. Dr Bowles said I could walk around the second-class passengers' deck at dusk and if anyone spoke to me I was to be careful to say that I had been ill and that I was not Italian. Sometimes Taps joined me there and we held hands, watching the sun blaze down across the horizon like a city put to the torch. I am sure that if anyone had seen us, they would have thought we were lovers, although I realized from the very beginning that Taps was not like Benno.

"I never cared when they called me a pansy," he used to say. "Pansies are for thoughts, I told them, and you've never had a thought in your life. I've always known I was a deep thinker so pansy is the right name for me."

He asked me about you, Bessie, and I tried to explain that you were more than my friend, you were—the other half of my life.

"I know exactly how you feel, Gwen. I had a friend like that once but—"

"Did you lose him, Taps?"

"He got married. Don't ask me what it was all about. A fit of conscience or maybe she had some money, anyhow we had this row and the next thing he was hitched."

He told me that he planned to make four more trips and then he was going to find a job ashore.

"I fancy myself as a gentleman's gentleman and I've picked up some very nice references on board. I've worked in the pantry and on cabin duty, and if it weren't for Dr Bowles insisting on my being in the sick bay, I'd be serving in the first-class lounge. Appearance is a lot and although I don't have the looks of some I try to make up for that by being pleasant."

Often I nodded off to sleep like an old lady when he was talking, for I seemed to be tired all the time and even walking up to the deck made me breathless, but I was no longer bleeding. Dr Bowles had almost convinced me that immediately the ship berthed in Sydney I should go straight to the Presbyterian Women's Hostel, when something made me realize that I must find Giacopo Sciafa. It is not easy for me now to understand why I had this driving urgency to stand in front of the man who had married me in the person of his brother. Certainly, it had nothing to do with any sense of loyalty to the Barone or to the words I had spoken behind the altar in Trapani. Even Taps told me that a proxy wedding didn't bind me to anything and when Dr Bowles found out that I had not been baptized as a Roman Catholic, he said the marriage wasn't worth a cup of candle grease. No, it happened one evening when Taps left me on deck and I held my hand up against the light of a sunset that was more disturbing than beautiful, for the boat seemed drenched in fire and blood as if we were steaming through Armageddon to the mouth of hell. I was tired and I wanted to rest in the forest, but when I raised my hand it was gone. Straining, I stared and tried to recall it, but I saw nothing except the shape of my palm and my fingers against the fire of the sky. Then the horror shook me to my soul.

I knew you were dead, Bessie. There is no explanation for my recognition of this. I wish I could understand it now myself. All I knew was that you had been with me when I was among the trees and I had felt your presence then, close to me as when we slept together with our arms around each other. I also knew that I was dying when I ran through that forest with you at my side. This, I felt sure, was why Edith had not written to me. Who would care to tell a person that her dearest friend, someone closer to her than a sister, was dead? What little reason I had left shaped and confirmed my conviction and I knew that if you were dead, then I wanted to be with you. Since I had neither the courage nor the strength to try and kill myself a second time, I had to find Giacopo Sciafa.

Was this madness? Sometimes I think I was deranged on that ship because I have so many strange impressions that may have been the result of what I saw or what I dreamed. Taps has told me that I talked incessantly when I was asleep, and you were always the one I spoke of most. He said I often shouted at Dolfi, but I always came back to you, Bessie.

I did not have the energy to argue with Dr Bowles, who was providing me with a very different future from the one the Barone had planned. When he found out I could type and do bookkeeping, he saw a splendid career for me in an office and said I should wait a few years until I'd saved a little nest egg and then marry an Australian Protestant.

"Mrs Bowles and I waited fifteen years before we could afford to get married and I sometimes think that time was the happiest I've ever known. It's not the getting but the hoping that sometimes gives you the most pleasure in life."

He never expected me to answer him and I seldom tried.

"Ah, Australia's a fine country," he often said. "But they're ruining it with all this immigration. You can't mix races."

I thought of Sicily and once I said that England had seen a great many invaders.

"Ah!" He pounced because this was his favourite subject and he was never so happy as when he was discussing race. "Ah, but they were all the same racial stock—Nordics, the lot of them. Vikings, Normans, Saxons—fine stock. But look at that—that detritus down there."

The Italians were on the lower deck making up their beds for the night, taking in the washing from a hundred different lines that spiderwebbed above their heads.

"They try very hard to be clean," I said.

"Clean!" Dr Bowles guffawed. "Have you forgotten what it smells like down there in steerage?"

Taps nudged me quietly and I was silent.

"Misplaced charity, my dear," Dr Bowles said. "There—down there—will be the ruin of Australia. You should see the difference when we bring out English migrants. They may come from the slums of Liverpool but they have the right breeding."

I heard a snigger from Taps that became a cough and later he said that the English migrants were so filthy they had to fumigate their cabins whenever the ship was in port.

One afternoon I asked Taps if he had a looking-glass because I could not remember what my face was like. He brought me one reluctantly and I tried to recognize the strange, gaunt mask that hardly seemed human to me. There were two eyes so large and rimmed with purple shadows that they looked as if they belonged to some peculiar animal. The cheeks were hollow and there was a pallor to the skin that was more like the wax images of saints in the cathedral of San Lorenzo at Trapani than living flesh.

"Aren't you glad now I didn't cut your hair?" Taps said consolingly. "Without your hair, you wouldn't have a feather to fly with."

"How can I get to Griffith when we reach Sydney?" I asked, putting down the looking-glass.

Taps squinted at me and grinned. "You don't fancy the Presbyterian ladies?"

"I saw a map and Griffith is to the south of Sydney. It's an irrigation area."

"I've got a much better idea. My friend—the one I told you about—is Henry Frock. He's running a pub in Woollahra and that's near the middle of the city. If he can't find you something, he may be able to put you on to someone who can. Everything in life depends on who you know, Gwen. I always made a point of doing some little service for any passenger in First Class who had a title and, in consequence, I now have a collection of references that includes five baronets and a marquis."

As he spoke, he laboriously wrote a name and address on a slip of paper.

"You tell Henry that you're my friend. Say that Taps—oh, just wish him all the best from me, but if his wife is around you better not say anything."

I took the address, folded it and promised I would get in touch with his friend.

The purser, as well as Dr Bowles, called for my assistance as the *Rangitiki* approached Sydney. There were migrants wanting to change money, asking how to reach country towns if their relatives could not meet the boat. I suddenly realized that Giacopo would probably be on the wharf waiting to see what kind of wife the Barone had sent him and I found myself shivering.

He had never been a person to me. I had never imagined someone who was tall or short, bearded or bald: he was simply my death. Everyone was talking about the Harbour and how it was more beautiful than Naples, with *palazzi* on every point and fish for the taking that you could see in shoals below the surface of the water. This was what I heard while I was in a dining room with a Chinese steward, trying to interpret for a crowd of migrants all clamouring to be heard. Taps came down with a conspiratorial wink and rescued me.

"Have you made up your mind what you want to do, Gwen?"

"Oh yes—"

"Right you are, then. I've got your bags sorted out and they'll be taken through customs by Fong over there. He'll hold them until you get a taxi. There'll be dozens of them round looking for a fare."

As soon as I set foot on the wharf, my head started to spin and I thought my legs had turned to rags. Somebody laughed and said I hadn't got my land-legs yet and then I saw other people staggering. For a moment I stood awkwardly, trying to balance myself, while the crowd surged around me.

The two women were standing over to one side, peering up at the ship, holding a placard with my name written on it. "Miss Gwen Harcourt," it read, and nothing else. If they had looked like pillars of righteousness in serge suits it would not be difficult to understand why I stumbled off through a group of Tuscans weeping and laughing at once, waving to the family they had just seen waiting for them behind the gates. But they were two middle-aged, eager and cheery-looking women in floral dresses and straw hats who would probably have welcomed me like a daughter. Instead, I found my boxes and bags with the Chinese steward and asked him to get me a taxi.

The driver wanted to charge half a crown to take me to Central Railway

Station but I haggled for two shillings and sat back, exulting that I had deceived those who had befriended me. Taps expected me to go to his friend Henry, and Dr Bowles had cabled the ladies from the Presbyterian Hostel to meet me. The name of every migrant who was being met by relatives was on a list in the shed and my name was not on it—neither Harcourt, di Marineo or Sciafa. I knew then I would have to travel to Griffith alone and when the grumbling taxi driver dumped my luggage in front of a porter at the station I rejoiced that no kindness, no single thought of gratitude had deflected me from my purpose. Dr Bowles and Taps had saved my life and if I had been rational I would have thanked them on my knees for all they did for me. Instead, I fled the wharf like a prisoner escaping from her tormentors.

I know that Taps understood, but Dr Bowles was convinced that I had been kidnapped by the priests he always suspected were travelling in disguise, mingling with the Italian migrants like ordinary men. Taps told me that it took all his efforts to dissuade him from calling the police and demanding that the local convents be searched for a young Protestant captive. In many ways he was a bigoted, stupid man and I only helped confirm his prejudices. Six years ago I met him again at a rally of the New Guard and he turned and walked away when I spoke to him. I don't blame him. Sometimes I think the worst, the most inhuman crime is not murder but ingratitude, because it destroys friendship and denies love. Yet my ingratitude was not the vice of cowards as Themistocles said, and only in the strangest and most perverted way was it the result of selfishness. If I was a marble-hearted fiend at that time it was because I resented those who had saved the life I did not want.

I was used to the crowds at European railway stations and the orderly, friendly people here amazed me. The ticket seller told me I needed the Yanco Griffith line and showed me where to leave my bags while I rested in the Ladies' Waiting Room for the train.

"You won't be bothered here," he said, and I found a corner and nodded off to sleep.

The train left at four in the afternoon and when I handed my third-class ticket to the guard he told me it was going to be a long journey. I nodded, expecting nothing else, but I knew that at the end I would find Giacopo Sciafa. He would be standing at the gate and when I passed him I would be running free in the pale forest again with Bessie at my side.

Seventeen

"Are you going home too?"

A woman was leaning towards me, her knees almost touching mine.

"I had six weeks with my family in Coogee, lovely it was." She sighed. "Good things never last, do they?"

I nodded and she smiled.

"Now it's back to the grind and I hate to think what Len and the kids will be like when I get there. It'll be a month of washing, that's for sure."

She asked me if I'd had my tea before I left and when I shook my head she said I must be famished and reached up for a bag.

"They don't give you much room in third class, do they? You should see what first class is like! Lovely velvet seats and places to rest your feet and waiters coming in with trays of tea and biscuits. That's the life."

I thought she was strangely unconcerned for someone on her way to the forest and she must have read something in my face because she paused and put her hand on my arm.

"I'm sorry, love. I thought you were just naturally pale but you've been ill, haven't you?"

"Yes."

"I was pretty bad myself. I went up to Sydney to have the baby because I almost lost Patricia, she's my third, and Len said I had to have proper care this time. It didn't make any difference. He was born dead. A pretty little baby. They washed him and let me see him before they—he couldn't have a proper burial because he wasn't baptized and the minister said he'd been with God from the very beginning, but I felt him kicking right up to when the pains started."

She began to cry soundlessly, with tears running down two creased furrows on her face. When she first spoke to me I thought it was odd that she had wrinkles that went from her eyes to her chin, now I saw that they were the paths for her tears. Of course she wanted to reach the forest too and I placed my hand on hers.

"I think we're going to the same place," I said.

"Griffith?"

"Yes."

"Then we'll be able to keep each other company, won't we? I reckon that's what gets me down most at Yenda. Len's growing rice and that's a new crop for the area so there aren't any neighbours close. The kids go off for the day and I'm alone. The work doesn't bother me but sometimes I start magging to myself."

"I'm used to being alone."

"But you're just a kid."

"I'm nineteen."

"Wish I was nineteen again. I don't think I would have got married—not as soon as I did, but it was the War and Len was my favourite and I didn't know then that he wanted to be a farmer. He had a job in a bank before he signed up."

She passed me a package of sandwiches and I opened the hot, greasy paper.

"Cheese and tomato, love. You daren't trust meat in this weather. On the farm we have a drip safe and you can't even rely on that to keep stuff cool."

Not until the bread was in my mouth did I realize how hungry I was and I ate ravenously. The woman was staring at me and I could see she was puzzled.

"Were you in hospital?"

"Yes."

"You better have something to drink with that or you'll choke."

The tea from her thermos was so rank that I felt my eyes watering.

"Thank you. I didn't understand when the ticket agent told me it was a long journey."

"If it were daylight you wouldn't see anything out there but wheat country and scrub for hundreds of miles."

The food had made me sleepy and I began to nod.

"You've really been ill—I can see that. Look, why don't you make yourself up a bed and try to get some sleep? I'll show you what to do."

She opened my case, pulled out a coat and placed it on the wooden slatted seat, rolled up one of my mother's skirts for a pillow and told me to lie down. I obediently did as she told me and was asleep before I could thank her. Through the night I woke fitfully, wondering if the ship had run aground before I realized that the train was shunting back and forth at some small station. It was dawn when I sat up and saw fields stretching to the horizon like a tawny sea. The woman, smiling at me, told me I didn't look like death warmed over any more.

"We didn't even introduce ourselves last night. I'm Norma Reynolds," she said, putting out her hand.

"Gwen," I replied. "My name is Gwen Sciafa."

Suddenly her expression changed and she asked me sharply to spell my second name.

"That's Italian, isn't it?"

"Yes."

"But you're not a Dago—"

"I was born in Sicily."

"My God—and I sat here, talking to you as if—"

I sat silently, watching her.

"You might have told me. I mean—"

She was shifting irritably in her seat and her glance swerved away from me as if she could not bear to look at me.

"I'm sorry if I've offended you—"

"But you speak proper English. I thought you were a Pom."

"My mother was English, she was a Harcourt from Russell Morton in Shropshire."

"I don't care where she came from, I just can't believe you—you're not married to one of the Sciafas, are you?"

"Yes."

"Are you sure you're married? You're not wearing a ring."

"The priest took back the ring after the ceremony."

"My God Almighty."

It seemed too much for her. She stood up and opened the window. A rush of hot air filled the stifling compartment and she slammed it shut.

"I was married by proxy in Sicily."

"Bloody Dagos—filthy, money-grubbing vermin, driving decent Australians off their farms. The Murrumbidgee Irrigation Area was supposed to be for soldier settlers like Len, but they came creeping in and next thing the Aussies are gone and they're buying up every bankrupt farm they can lay their hands on."

Angry now, she sat opening and closing her hands.

"I'm sorry I ever spoke to you!" she said finally.

At a place called Temora, everyone left the train and I trailed after Norma. As she stepped down on to the station she suddenly turned and looked at me hopefully.

"You were joking, weren't you?"

"No."

"It doesn't make sense. No Dago ever marries outside his own lot. They stick together like fleas. Do you really know what you're doing?"

"Yes, I'm going to meet my death," I said simply.

She gaped at me and then her expression changed.

"I'm sorry, love. I didn't realize. Now, you just come along with me. They shouldn't let someone like you travel on her own."

I heard her telling the waitress in the Railway Refreshment Room that I was soft in the head and suffering from fancies. The waitress smiled sympathetically at me and put a mound of sausages and eggs in front of me.

"You eat all that up," Norma said kindly to me. "I hope there's going to be someone to meet you at Griffith."

"Oh yes," I said.

"I'll be getting off at Yenda, otherwise I'd keep an eye on you."

The food was greasy but nothing seemed to satisfy my hunger and I scraped my plate and wolfed down a pile of bread and jam.

"I don't know where you put it," Norma said admiringly. "And in this weather! Mind you, my Len expects a hot dinner and pudding when it's 110 in the shade."

For the rest of the day she addressed me like a child, pointing to kangaroos bounding alongside the train as if they were trying to race us, explaining the difference between kangaroos and wallabies, telling me about her children and how Len was planning to build a kitchen on to the veranda.

"It's in a corrugated-iron shed a few yards from the house now and in the summer it's like standing in a fiery furnace. Daniel only had to do it once, I always say, but sometimes I get six weeks at a stretch. The kids wet branches of leaves and put them on the roof but they don't make much difference and you have to get that hot meal on the table every night."

I listened to her wonderingly for it was as if she were speaking from a different world than mine. Every now and then I closed my eyes and tried to see the pale trees of the forest but the light outside the window was too bright. Mile upon mile of wheat shimmering in the noon sun and patches of dull green trees like shadows with hardly a house to be seen. I could never have imagined a country with so much land and so few people. Every corner of ground in Sicily was cultivated and even on the bare slopes of Enna you found goatherds and their flocks. This was like a great fertile desert.

The change was so sudden that I thought I must be in a different country. The wheat was gone, the tawny gold and dusty green had changed to emerald squares of orchards. Peaches and apricots were ripening and I saw acres of vines growing in earth that was like dark chocolate. Between the orchards, the muddy canals were bordered with wild flowers and tall grass.

"It's a miracle, isn't it?" Norma sighed. "It's a hard life, no mistake about that, but it beats raising sheep in a drought. All we have to do every evening is turn the wheel and the water pours in from the main canal."

Apricots and almonds, acres of orange and lemon trees and then the flat paddocks of rice. This was not what I expected. In my mind I had been sure that the wheat land would end in a place of stones.

Yenda was nothing but a signpost at the side of the road. As the train came to a jolting halt I saw a man and three children waiting by a sulky. The horse was stamping the flies away and when the children saw their mother they began to scream and the two eldest unrolled a piece of canvas with "Welcome Home Mum" painted across it. Norma asked me once more if there would be someone to meet me at Griffith and then her husband had flung open the carriage door and was lifting her down. I watched them drive off through the chessboard of green until they vanished from my sight.

The landscape disturbed me because, although I had never imagined Giacopo, I had often pictured the place where I was going to die. It would be a grotto like the cave where Bradamante's soul had been taken up to heaven by an angel, or that other grotto where I had killed Benno's child. When I stood in front of Giacopo, that was what I planned to say to him first.

"Giacopo, I killed the son you wanted."

His anger would be so great when he heard this that he would kill me, for a man who had already murdered two women would not hesitate at a third. My soul would then escape to the forest I had lost and find Bessie waiting for me there.

The guard was shouting "Griffith! End of the line!" Slowly I climbed down on to the platform and waited until my bags were taken from the box carriage. It was twilight and I heard men laughing and shouting from a hotel across from the station. People were being greeted by friends or family but no one was looking for me. An elderly couple stopped and asked me if someone was picking me up and I nodded. A few lights came from the scattered houses and the railway guard wanted to know if I needed a lift.

"I have to find Giacopo Sciafa's farm," I said.

"I wouldn't know where that is," he said abruptly and walked away.

If I found myself in such a plight now I think I would be panic-stricken, but my mood then was so strange and so unrelated to the world around me that I was not even concerned. I looked about me calmly and wondered if the driver of one of the lorries parked by the station could take me to the farm.

An old Indian with a dusty turban carried a box out of the railway shed and I asked him if he would drive me to Giacopo Sciafa's farm.

"Giacopo?" He poked a finger under the turban and scratched his head. "I know plenty Sciafas."

"There are three brothers, Giacopo is the eldest."

"Ah, him! He's not a good man. He get very drunk and fight. You don't want to go near him, missy. Once he try to kick me."

"Can you take me there? I'll pay you."

I held out three florins and he looked at them for a moment and nodded.

"Soon it getting proper night—I don't like to be on the track after dark."

"There's still some light in the sky," I replied.

Vanda was a hawker and his cart was laden with pots and pans, rolls of cloth, old magazines, tools and horseshoes. I sat beside him and we set off through the dusk. He did not ask me who I was or why I was going to Giacopo's. When it was almost dark the moon came up so quickly that it was as if someone had switched on a huge electric globe and instantly we were travelling along a silver road between ebony trees. The sounds of Vanda's cart were like the contents of a whole house being shaken together; chinks of metal, the regular thud of wood striking wood, the clatter of tins, the creaking of ropes.

"That's his house."

Vanda was pointing to a small weatherboard cottage that shone lividly in the moonlight.

"Maybe no one home," he said, for there were no lights in the windows. "I put your bags on the veranda and go. Maybe he's asleep in there."

"Yes, thank you."

We saw the flickering light of a candle at the same time and I knew there was someone inside the house. Had Giacopo already lit the candle for my death?

Vanda was creaking and chiming off down the road, the lantern on the back of his cart cutting yellow arcs through the white moonlight. It was not Charon who ferried people across the Styx but this old man and his shuffling horse who did not care to stay long in the land of the dead. I saw the candle flutter and I knew it was time for me to meet Giacopo.

For some moments I stood on the veranda, listening to the stillness of the night. I could hear myself breathing as I stared at a moon so bright that it dazzled my eyes. It was a small house and my knock echoed through it as if I had struck a drum.

There was no response. I knocked again and waited. Somewhere close by a chorus of frogs answered but the house was silent. He was waiting for me inside. Slowly I pushed against the door and found it was not locked.

It was a room I had seen a hundred times when Bessie and I peered through windows in Trapani. A square table with an embroidered cloth, straight chairs and a dresser. Over in one corner, a gilded altar to the Virgin Mary decorated with paper flowers and a candle that sputtered into a puddle of wax as I watched it.

"Giacopo!" I called.

There was no sound. I walked through to the next room, which must have been a bedroom. The cotton counterpane was white and over the bed was another small altar, to St Rosalia. A rosary encircled the place on the pillows where someone's head had rested. Beside it was a crucifix. The coloured congoleum on the floor was waxed and reflected the moonlight like water: everything was shining as if someone had just cleaned it in readiness for me, but the house was empty.

The kitchen was a shed opening out of the main room and there by the sink I found a kerosene lamp and matches. I lit the lamp and placed it in the middle of the table. Bread and a pot of jam were under a cotton cover in the kitchen and I cut myself half of the loaf, covered it with apricot jam and ate it slowly. Someone had been in the house less than an hour ago and lit the candle so I knew that I was expected. Next to the kitchen was another little shed with a bucket of water on the floor and soap on the shelf. I took off my grimy clothes and washed myself and when I opened the door I saw that the water came from a cistern at the side of the house.

I could not bear to lie down on that bed with its rosary and crucifix so I made myself a bed on the table with the counterpane and my coat. My nightgown smelt faintly of the *bagghiu* and though I tried to summon the forest to my mind, I kept returning to the triton and the vine over my head. When I opened the window a coolness was rising from the earth and I lay down to sleep. Soon he would come and when I woke, Bessie would be with me.

He was standing at the end of the table.

"*Chi é lei? Lei é la mia morte?*" I asked. I could see he did not understand me. I repeated it in Sicilian, "*Ma chi é vossia? Vossia moriri mia . . . Fà?*" I said.

"Non—non parler Italian," he replied slowly.

"Who are you?"

This was not Giacopo Sciafa—this tall young man with sandy hair in an open-neck shirt, staring at me as if I were a genie or a jinn. He was not even Italian.

"You can speak English?"

"Yes, of course." The sunlight was flooding the room and I blinked.

"I'm Alan Gilchrist, law officer of the MIA. Vanda told me he'd dropped a girl off here last night who seemed—well, he said I should investigate."

"My name is Gwen Harcourt—I married Giacopo Sciafa by proxy in Sicily."

"Giacopo Sciafa is dead. He got blind drunk some time ago and fell into one of the irrigation ditches on his way back from the pub. They found him face down in the morning. It doesn't pay to wander round these parts at night if you're drunk."

If I had been mad, or living in another world, I returned to sanity at that moment as Alan Gilchrist pushed his spectacles up into his hair. I felt as I had that afternoon when Rosalia and I left the puppet theatre and I found myself in a street with ordinary people engaged in everyday affairs. The puppets were still somewhere in my mind but I knew they were imaginary and that what I saw around me was reality. The forest will always be somewhere at the back of my mind—I know that is where I shall go when I finally leave the world of the living—but that morning when I climbed down from my bed on the table I knew I was in a world that was more exciting than any I could ever imagine. People speak about miraculous conversions, of being changed irrevocably in the twinkling of an eye, and when Alan said those four words, "Giacopo Sciafa is dead," I became myself: not the Gwen who maundered on about forests and finding death, but a young woman who was filled with an insatiable curiosity about her surroundings and how she was going to live. I should have known that my extraordinary appetite was a sign that I was returning to life. It was as if I had been held in thrall to the Barone's story as I had been to my mother's, and now, for the first time, I was free. This freedom was all the more intoxicating because I did not know where it would lead me or what would become of me. I raised my arms over my head and stretched and there were no strings tied to my wrists; I felt like clapping for joy.

The young man seemed as bewildered as I was and this served to put me at my ease. Slowly, I explained to him about the death of my parents and the marriage to Giacopo.

"He died sometime late last year," Alan said frowning.

"I was married in November."

He seemed to understand that I was hungry and went out to the kitchen, lit the stove and cut some bread. It was obvious he knew the house because he found some tins of fruit in a cupboard and soon we were having breakfast together.

"You look very young to be a widow."

I knew he was asking my age and I smiled but did not answer.

"When Giacopo died, his two brothers immediately tried to buy the farm together, but property can't be subdivided in the MIA, not in a Home Maintenance Area like this, so they've been fighting like Kilkenny cats over who should have it. They appealed to the Board and I've been out here a few times trying to get them to agree to a settlement, but they were at each other's throats in minutes. They're awaiting a decision from the Board now to determine the heir, but if they can't agree then who gets the farm, it will be put up for sale. Sciafa had a fine orchard here and there'll be other bids. Whatever people say about the Sciafas, they're bloody good farmers. The livestock has all been tallied and that's divided between the two of them at the moment. There are still a few chickens clucking round out there."

"Somebody lit a candle here last night."

"That would be one of the Sciafas. The women come over here to clean and the men take turns pumping up the water from the main canal. I think they like to keep an eye on the property and on each other."

"Can I stay here if I am Giacopo's widow?"

"Do you—do you really want to? You'd probably be entitled to something, but I doubt if you'd be allowed to take on the lease."

"I've been very ill. I think I'd like to stay here for a while."

And because, as I know now, I am more Sicilian at heart than English, I was looking around the house and wondering what I could sell. Such was my euphoria that I could see myself running the orchard, picking fruit and selling it for huge profits while my second self was selling the contents of the house and going to Sydney. I walked out to the back where the trees were heavy with apricots and peaches.

Alan followed me, saying, "He was a rough man but he was one of the best farmers in the area."

"Would you help me carry in my bags? They're still out there on the veranda."

While he stacked my boxes against the wall of the living room, I changed in the bedroom and combed my hair in the square of mirror on the wall. For the first time there was a little colour in my face and even though I could see the bones of my cheeks I no longer resembled some strange animal.

I knew he was staring at me, but whenever I caught his eye he put his head down and frowned, or turned away. He was not as handsome as Roger Whitlow and his manner was abrupt and awkward, but he stayed for over an hour with me and when he left, he said he would try to call again that evening and bring me some supplies. He asked for my marriage-lines and I gave him the square of paper with the Barone's signature and seal in the right-hand corner.

"I suppose a proxy marriage is valid," he said cautiously, adding, "I've heard that it's quite common for the Italians here to send for wives and marry them, sight unseen."

"It was not a marriage of love," I said.

He looked at me quickly. "You weren't forced, were you?"

"There was nothing else I could do."

He was driving a little Singer roadster that started with a series of small explosions, almost throwing the car into the air. At the turn of the road he leaned out of the car and waved to me before he disappeared in a column of dust.

The air was cool in the early morning and I walked out to the back and down into the orchard. Ditches ran between the trees and I saw where a larger canal had been cut at the edge of the property. I reached up and picked an apricot, rubbing off the soft down against my breast. It was tart, but I could taste the promise of sweetness. For so long I had lived in the forest of death. Now as I walked through that orchard I felt as if all the strength of summer were rushing through my veins. There were chickens roosting under the house and I found three eggs and boiled them for my lunch. No food has ever tasted better.

A little after three in the afternoon, I saw the Sciafas arriving. The men walked in front, followed by two youths and two women in black shawls; behind them were a little boy and girl holding hands. I stood on the veranda and watched them approach. They stood at the bottom of the steps and looked up at me, expressionless. One of the women broke the silence. Shrilly, she told me to go away. The taller man motioned to her with his hand and she fell back with her head down.

"Giacopo is dead," the smaller man said.

"I know."

"Go away!" the woman shrilled. "No one wants you here. You have no right."

"I am his widow. The Barone di Marineo was my sponsor."

"Barone!" The taller man spat. "Barones count for nothing in Australia."

"I have spoken to Mr Gilchrist, the MIA lawyer, and he will determine who owns this property."

"It is our land!" The brothers both shouted together and the women shook their fists at me.

"Giacopo's daughter must be fed."

The woman dragged the little girl forward and the child stood there barefoot with a finger in her mouth and began to cry. I suddenly remembered Margaret Moglen with tear-stained cheeks, waiting for us all day by the fountain. This child had dusty brown hair, so she must have resembled her mother since both the Sciafa men were as swarthy as Arabs. The boy inched forward and tried to wipe away the girl's tears with a piece of rag.

"Let her stay with me," I said.

"Never!" The woman screamed and I shrugged.

The girl began to cry loudly and the boy put his arms around her, trying to comfort her. She buried her head against his chest and he patted her on the back as if she were a puppy, whispering to her. Petulantly, she threw away the rag and sobbed so he pulled out the tail of his shirt and tried to wipe her eyes with that.

"We will get the police," the taller man announced.

"I have already spoken to Alan Gilchrist," I said again.

They began talking together and suddenly they left, walking away without a backward glance, disappearing in the tunnel of dust that swallowed everything that moved on the road, for although the land around was green and moist, the road was parched with drought.

Nothing could shake my mood of optimism and hope as I walked out into the orchard again, with a haze of heat over the trees and the branches so heavy with fruit they were touching the ground. Rosalia had been wrong. If I was married to death, it was not my own death. The Barone's story was finished and I could now begin my own. In Sicily, the mention of his name produced silence and respect; here, it apparently counted for nothing. I was in a different play now and the puppet called Gina Sciafa had become a human being.

Alan Gilchrist arrived at seven, saying he could not come earlier because he had to wait for a copy of Giacopo's death certificate. He placed two papers in front of me: one was the death certificate, the other, the marriage licence. Giacopo had died on November the eighteenth, I was married on November the twenty-second.

"Even accounting for the dateline, it could not have been a marriage."

"The Sciafas will be delighted," I said.

"At least you've managed to settle their differences. Lucio, the younger, is going to lend his brother the money to buy the farm for his oldest son. It will be Sciafa land from here to the river."

"I had visions of running this place myself."

"The MIA would never transfer the lease to a widow. If you had a son of legal age, it might be considered."

Alan had brought out a hamper of food and as we talked, we spread the table with cold chicken and salad, bread and fruit. I found some bottles of wine in the kitchen.

"It used to be a criminal offence to have alcohol anywhere in the Murrumbidgee Irrigation Area, and it's still against the law to make your own, but nothing can stop the Italians producing pinkie," Alan said. "So I'll pretend I brought this with me and lost the label."

I found two glasses and we talked over the wine.

"Have you any friends or family in Australia?" Alan asked me.

"No one."

"You don't want to go back, do you?"

"Go back to what? I think I can find something here. I can do a lot of things."

"Nobody pays much for housework."

"Housework!" It was impossible to keep the scorn and my mother out of my voice and he looked at me, surprised. "I can type and do bookkeeping. I could teach Latin and Greek."

If I had said that I was able to levitate he could not have been more surprised. I went over to the heaviest of my boxes and asked him to open it for me. Alan has told me many times that when I assured him I was a classical scholar, he thought a lunatic had wandered into his life. He prised open the tea chest and lifted out a Loeb Virgil.

"That isn't much test of anyone's Latin," I said, still echoing my mother. "Every schoolboy should be able to translate that at sight."

Dolfi always said I was arrogant and pompous and with my newfound optimism, I rather think I surpassed myself that evening. I opened the Aeneid at random and it fell open at Book VI: "*His demum exactis, perfecto munere divae, devenere locos laetos et amoena virecta Fortunatorum Nemorum sedesque beatas*."

I read the Latin first slowly and then translated: "This at length performed and the task of the goddess fulfilled, they came to a land of joy, the green pastures and happy domains of the Blessed Groves."

Slowly, he took the book from my hand and continued.

We argued over the meaning of *miratur*, and he said he needed a drink. He gulped down the wine and stared at me.

"You are the most amazing person I've ever met," he said wonderingly.

"You see—I can do much more than sweep floors and cook like some *contadina*."

"You should be in Sydney. There are good schools there that could use a teacher, and law offices where someone who knows Latin as you do would be invaluable."

"I had hoped you'd come out to tell me that I was the owner of an orchard and this house, Mr Gilchrist."

He shook his head and asked me to call him Alan. My excitement was so intense that I found myself trembling. I knew I could never live like a *contadina* on an orchard or a farm, content to watch the seasons change. My

Blessed Groves were not here but—I tried to remember Sydney, the city I had passed through on my way to Central Railway Station. In those days when I was *capo di famiglia* in Trapani, I had often thought what I could accomplish if only I were in Palermo. Now, I had no ties and Rosalia's prophecy that I would marry death was not a sentence of execution but a declaration of freedom.

When I lost the forest, something of my anguished longing for you vanished with it, Bessie. I have never forgotten you and I often flinch when I remember the pain of losing you, but you were no longer the fixed pole around which my life revolved. If there was one person who concentrated all my attention, it was myself and I examined this new creature with fascination and delight.

Alan told me about the schools in Sydney and the university where he had studied Classics and Law.

"One day—one day I'm going back and I'll be admitted to the bar as a barrister and teach Roman law and when I've written my great work on real property, I'll be a judge."

"I shall be a professor of Greek and Latin at that university."

"No women professors," he said glumly.

"I shall disguise myself as a man."

If I could not be a professor, I was prepared to settle for a job in a solicitor's office. It was at that moment I realized I had exactly three pounds and fifteen shillings to my name.

"There may be something for you in Griffith," Alan said portentously.

We were both a little drunk, and why not? I was celebrating my birth. How long did we talk that evening? I've forgotten, but the sky was paling when he left and I threw myself on the bed and slept without dreaming.

Eighteen

"Did you really think you were a *contadina*?"

The woman was holding a cup of coffee just as Rosalia used to do and I sat up in bed, took it from her and drank slowly, trying to remember where I was. The wine had given me a headache and I could barely see who was standing against the light.

"Yesterday, when I saw you at the top of the steps with white hands, looking down your nose like a *bella signora*, I could tell you were not one of us."

"You are—"

"I'm Rafaella, Paulo's wife."

I sat on the edge of the bed and such a sensation of lightness and buoyancy took hold of me that I felt as if I were on a hill top, with a brilliant landscape and a dozen shining roads stretched out in front of me.

"My sister died in this bed. Whenever she had a miscarriage, Giacopo used to get drunk and beat her. Nina was as strong as me once and she could work like ten men! Ah, *Madonna mia*! No matter what she did for Giacopo, whether she broke stones or dragged the plough like an ox, it was never enough because what he wanted from her was a son. I have a son, Aldo and Martina have two boys and now she is pregnant again and she knows it is a boy because she has a craving for vinegar. All Giacopo wanted was boys of his own to help him with the farm. He was a hard man, but look what he made here, look what he gave her!"

"Giacopo was dead when I married him."

"The Holy Mother has protected you."

I washed slowly and saw that Rafaella had already cleaned away the remains of the supper Alan Gilchrist and I had shared.

"This young man—perhaps he is interested in you?"

My first reaction was to scoff and then I thought of the way we had talked until it was almost dawn.

"Yes, yes I think he's more than interested in me. He may almost be in love with me."

"Ah, then you should marry him. A girl of your age should have a husband. And you could never be a wife for a farmer. Mr Gilchrist is a good man."

"I don't think he'd beat me."

"He's an Australian, and everyone knows that Australian men are like wax in the hands of women. Not all men are like Giacopo. My Paulo is not like that. He knows I work as hard as he does and he respects that."

She held out her hands to me.

"I often tell him—these hands do the work of two men."

Rafaella must have been thirty, but her wrinkled brown face made her seem fifty and when she smiled, her broken teeth made her look like a friendly old dog.

"Aldo is going to sign a lawyer's paper and give us all the profits from this farm until his son is old enough to marry and bring a wife here. We will then have enough to buy more land for ourselves. Ah, life is very good here."

She walked out to the first row of trees and touched the leaves reverently.

"Everything grows here and this earth—"

She bent down and picked up a handful of soil, crushing it in her palm.

"Feel it! Smell it! It is so rich and good you could eat it. Here, it is not like Sicily. Here, '*lavoriamo per conto nostro*.' "

In Australia, they worked for themselves—that was the phrase I heard again and again from the Italians.

"Your coming was a blessing. Ah yes, this very morning, Paulo said I should not come here and speak to you, but I told him that you had been sent by the Blessed Mother herself. Aldo and Paulo were at each other's throats over this farm and I think they would have killed each other if you had not come. Now, there is peace between them and in a few years' time, when he is a man, we will have enough money to buy Rocco a farm. I have already written to my family in Messina asking them to keep an eye on a likely bride for him. There is no one here among the Italians—they are not good people. Too many Calabresi have come here and they are all thieves and the rest are from the Veneto and their women are all immoral. You cannot begin too early and if my family in Sicily watches over a girl, they will know her character, whether she is a good worker and virtuous."

People often say I have a suspicious nature and it is true that I seldom give my trust to anyone. Rafaella's black eyes met mine without flinching and her smile was wide, yet there was a doubt in my mind that I could not define or voice. I began to probe tentatively, more with statements than questions.

"There was a little girl—"

"Angelica is my sister's child. When Nina was dying, I swore that I would care for her."

Perhaps Rafaella's only concern had been that I might want to keep her niece. I assured her that since I was not Giacopo's widow, I had no claim to the child. She grinned at me as we walked back into the house and then she said plaintively that Rocco loved Angelica as a sister and the little girl was like her own daughter. Hunkered in a corner of my mind, the suspicion still warned me to be on my guard even as I was lifted up on a surge of sparkling optimism. All my fetters were broken and I was free. I told Rafaella about Miki and Rosalia and she rocked with laughter and told me a joke about an old man who kept his wife happy with a carrot.

"It helps"—she winked—"if the carrot is made of gold."

Rafaella cut some bread she had baked that morning and we dipped it in olive oil and salt.

"You eat like a *contadino*!" Rafaella said admiringly.

"I never cared very much for food, but now I'm always hungry."

"You're not—"

Instantly her face was dark and she glowered at me.

Was this the suspicion? I knew immediately that if Giacopo had told the family that Benno was marrying me by proxy, he had not informed them that I was carrying his brother's child. And I knew there must be a reason why none of them had sent word of Giacopo's death to Sicily. Rafaella was leaning back in her chair, frowning, because it was clear that she expected me to be a virgin.

"I'm not pregnant," I said.

"It's because you're so thin," she said and seemed relieved. "No Italian would look at you, but Australian men are not so particular. When Giacopo told us he was bringing out a Marineo for his wife, we were delighted. It is a good family and related to the Sciafas, as mine is. We never thought he was fool enough to want a *bella signora* for a wife."

My hip bones jutted out through my dress, my stomach was a hollow and my arms were sticks. Perhaps Alan Gilchrist had been sorry for me as I once was for the starving kitten that wandered into the *bagghiu*. There had been a warmth in his clasp when we shook hands very formally on the veranda with the dawn about to colour the sky, but that could have been the wine and nothing else.

Rafaella nudged me and laughed. "Mr Gilchrist spoke about you to Paulo and Aldo. He said he wanted you to stay here until the weekend."

"Yes, I'm going to Sydney to find work," I said defiantly, with three pounds and fifteen shillings in my purse.

"Work! You should get married."

"I want to earn money."

"It is for the man to make money and the wife to save it."

"I like to have money in my own hands."

It was so slight that I scarcely noticed the flicker of attention as she gave me some more bread.

"Giacopo was a miser. He never let my sister have sixpence to spend and when she begged on her knees for a little money to buy candles for the Blessed Mother, he counted out the pennies. Nina died on the eighth day of September, the day all women hold sacred because it is the birth of the Blessed Virgin. He complained that it would cost too much to bury her in the cemetery in Griffith and in that room, standing by the bed where my dead sister was lying with a rosary in her hands, he argued with the priest because he wanted the cheapest service. I tell you before God, I am ashamed now to look that young priest in the face! A fine young Australian priest who speaks Italian to us and who comes out before the doctor when anyone is dying. Giacopo—" She bent sideways and made as if to spit. "That piece of devil's shit would have buried my sister like a dog out there in the orchard and stood on her grave to pick his fruit."

I did not answer and she carefully brushed crumbs from the table with the side of her hand.

"The Blessed Mother protected you."

"Yes, I am very grateful," I replied guardedly.

"All he cared about was money and he did not trust the banks. He bought sovereigns—gold sovereigns. If you had his money you could light a thousand candles to the Blessed Mother."

"Perhaps he used the money to build this house and improve the farm."

"Aldo and Paulo know what money he made. Giacopo came here first and his was the first crop of apricots in the area. Everything he touched was gold—everybody wanted to grow one kind of peach but Giacopo said he would try the clingstone—Pullars, they call them—and now everyone has torn out the old varieties and they grow Pullars like Giacopo. We pick fruit from our trees—Giacopo picked gold."

She shifted slightly, turned a little away from me and then smiled archly with her head on one side.

"Perhaps you have found his gold?"

I wanted to burst out laughing but I managed to keep a straight face because now I understood why nobody had sent word to Sicily: they wanted time to search for Giacopo's fortune. This was the old dream of the *contadini*

—one day, digging in the field, the spade strikes something that does not ring like a stone. Feverishly, the peasant begins to dig with his hands and there is an earthenware pot spilling gold coins and jewellery across the earth. Because he is not a fool, the peasant covers the spot and returns at night with a sack. After that, he tells stories of inheriting from a rich uncle in America, packs his few rags together and leaves the village forever. My mother used to laugh when Assunta told her that some poor old woman had a bag of money hidden in her chimney or that the relatives had dug up the earth floor of a wretched beggar's hovel and found gold. The poor, as my father said, always dream of lotteries and buried treasure and occasionally fate showers riches on someone like Miki and all the dreams become reality. Rafaella was leaning across the table, staring at me, and I could now give a shape to my suspicion.

"I have not found any gold, Rafaella, but I shall look for it."

"Giacopo always had ideas of being the *padrone* and I think he may have wanted a *bella signora* for a wife to show everyone what a grand *signore* he had become. A *bella signora* like you does not leave her home and family to come all this way for a husband unless he promises her family that she will be cared for like a princess."

"I have no family, Rafaella."

"No family? You have the Barone di Marineo!"

She leaned across the table until her face was almost touching mine.

"Come, let us talk like sisters. You can trust me. I am not like that bitch Martina. She is Aldo's second wife and she does not come from a good family like us. Now, perhaps because you are young, the Barone did not discuss these matters of money with you so I shall explain everything to you. I am sure that Giacopo wrote to the Barone and told him where he kept the money and the Barone—perhaps he may have mentioned this to you?"

Her greed was like a child's and I smiled.

"Is this what you all believe?"

"We have been to this house every day. We have looked everywhere."

"Perhaps there is no money."

"There must be!"

She slapped her hands on the table.

"Giacopo was a rich man and a miser. He boasted about his money to Aldo and Paulo. He said that both of them together would never be as rich as him."

"If there is money it belongs to his daughter."

"Ah—you are indeed a *bella signora*! And would you have the heart to steal from a child? Not a *bella signora*!"

"If I find anything in this house, I shall tell you."

"You swear?"

"By any oath you like."

"On my dead sister's grave?"

"On her grave."

"If you break such an oath she will haunt you."

"Of course."

Bessie, I suddenly remembered the death game we played on the beach in Trapani and I thought that to be haunted by a stranger would hardly bother me, but to be haunted by someone you loved would be a joy, not a terror. There are some ghosts I would be happy to live with and it would delight me if they floated through the wall and said they wanted to share my house. If only memories could appear before us like pictures of substance, not those faint shifting images in our heads that vanish when you try to concentrate them. Rafaella was satisfied by my silence and told me she would come the next morning with some fresh bread but if I found Giacopo's money I must send word to her immediately. She led me out on to the front veranda and pointed in the direction of her farm.

Whenever I walked down through the orchard and touched the trunks of the trees it was as if the sap was entering my fingers and pouring through my veins; the very earth under my feet seemed to give me energy. Perhaps it was as rich as Rafaella had told me. And yet I could laugh when I remembered how only a few hours before I had seen myself as a farmer, making mountains of gold from a few acres of fruit trees. In my own way, I knew I could imagine fabulous inventions to match any of Rafaella's and perhaps to dream of love at this time was a fantasy as absurd as any story of the paladins of Carlo Magno; even so, despite my cautious demurring, no matter where I turned my mind it was like a magnet drawn to a fixed object and that object was Alan Gilchrist. I told Rafaella that I was going to Sydney to make my fortune like Dick Whittington on his way to London but what I really wanted was to see Alan again.

Bessie, I longed to be able to talk to you as we did when we imagined that Roger and Dolfi were in love with us. We examined our feelings then and I remember you asking me a thousand questions to determine whether I was really in love with Roger or just keen on him. If only you had been with me, we would have been giggling and whispering and threading our emotions through the finest scrutable needles to embroider the pattern of our love.

These were my thoughts as I walked back through the orchard, reaching up to pick an apricot that was already dusted with a flush of yellow. My mouth puckered at the sourness but again there was the promise of sweetness in the fruit. At the steps I glimpsed something move just behind my left shoulder, and when I swung round, a little figure darted off behind a shed. I caught a tangle of brown hair and knew it was Angelica. Over by the fence I saw the boy, Rocco, shifting nervously from one bare foot to another. I called to her but she would not come near me and I went into the house. Twice I saw her peering through a window at me, but when I smiled and called her name she vanished as though terrified of me.

It was dusk when I heard Alan's car coughing its way up the road in a series of small explosions. I waved to him and he came up to me, laughing.

"I used to have an old cob that sat down in the traces whenever it was tired, and since it needed a rest every three miles, it took me quite a while to get around the area. Everyone assured me that a car would never let me down. The only trouble is that they were right! I think the Singer's first cousin to a kangaroo. I spend more time in the air than on the road."

We talked awkwardly and I thanked Alan for the bag of food he'd brought with him.

"I don't suppose you'd care to have dinner with me again," he said.

"If you don't stay, I'll have to eat alone," I replied and because I was nervous, the peremptory curtness of my mother's voice chose the words and their inflection.

He had brought ham and cheese with him and together we picked tomatoes and lettuce from the vegetable garden at the side of the house. I told him to be careful where he walked because he might be standing on Giacopo's pot of gold.

"Is that what Paulo's wife told you? I think I know what Giacopo was worth and every penny he possessed was ploughed back into the farm. It's no wonder he was so successful. He worked twenty-six hours a day and he knew what he was doing. Not like some of the soldier settlers who thought they could make a go of it here. Giacopo had worked with stone fruit in his own country and he remembered everything he knew and used it here. Besides, he was one of the first to get started. He told me once that he'd gone to Broken Hill to work in the mine, made a few bob there and then bought a lease in the MIA."

"Rafaella said he was a miser with a bag of sovereigns hidden in the house."

"Do they really believe that? No wonder they were all spending so much time out here. I thought they were just keeping an eye on the property, but they were really watching each other."

We laughed about hidden treasure and bags of gold and I found myself telling him about the Sicilian peasants and how occasionally one of them found a hoard of Greek or Roman coins.

"You've actually seen the temples at Segesta and Agrigento?"

"Yes, of course."

"I'd give anything to go there."

Drily, I told Alan that everyone I had known wanted to leave Sicily. Even Rosalia was going to take Miki and his lottery off to an apartment in Naples.

"But the temples, the Greek theatres—"

"I think it must be a pleasant enough country for tourists," I said. "It's not so easy to live there if you're poor, though, and almost everyone is poor. Every Sicilian dreams of America or Australia."

"There's a lot of feeling against the Italians in the MIA—envy, most of it. A Giacopo Sciafa arrives here ten years ago and achieves all this while the Aussie farmers around him go broke."

We were talking easily now as we made a salad and spread the table.

"Thank you for asking the Sciafas to let me stay here until the weekend," I said.

He had a mannerism of shaking his head and then running his hand through his hair. Sometimes he forgot that his spectacles were in his hair and he accidentally flung them off.

"I was thinking—" he said slowly.

He was, I thought, much better-looking than Roger Whitlow with his polished hair and smooth manners. Alan seemed to move in jerks and starts and yet there was an intelligence in his grey eyes that I had never seen in Roger, and certainly not in Dolfi.

"You may be able to find a job here in Griffith, Gwen."

"Teaching Greek and Latin?"

"Not much scope for that yet, I'm afraid, but you said you could type and do bookkeeping."

"I have a very good reference from Frau Brunner who owned the Hotel d'Athena."

"Do you think you could look after a law office—a small law office?"

"Of course."

My confidence was boundless. If he had asked me whether I could follow Blondin across Niagara in a barrel, I would have airily agreed.

"Well—this may not be what you're looking for. Certainly, I don't think it's what you should be doing. You know I'm attached to the Shire of Wade as a registrar of properties and general legal dogsbody. It's my job to see that none of the terms of the Home Maintenance Area are violated. That's why I spend most of my time on the track, making sure that boundaries are where they should be, no subdividing or anything of that sort."

I nodded without paying much attention to what he was saying. It was despair that had led me into the grove with Benno, it was excitement and hope that trembled in me as I smiled at Alan.

"It's a good job and I suppose I'm lucky to have it. God knows there are plenty of briefless barristers hanging around Macquarie Street and any number of solicitors who are barely making a crust. But—"

Something was disturbing him, yet even though I knew that I was the source of his unease, I sensed there was something else.

"Tell me what you really want, Alan."

I knew I was speaking provocatively and I was overjoyed when I saw the power I had to affect him.

He was flushing scarlet as he told me that he wanted to be a barrister himself one day.

"I'm sure you will be."

"You don't know what an egotist I am. Some day I want to wear silk and be a king's counsel—" He paused awkwardly and concluded hurriedly. "A KC like my father, although, I have thought occasionally . . . No, law's enough for anyone."

"Are you interested in politics?"

"I'd like to sit on the bench and make law," he replied firmly. "If I can't become a judge one day, I wouldn't mind lecturing at the Law School."

"If you taught Roman law I could help you, but I wouldn't know about torts and contracts and all the other things lawyers study."

Did I really think I could make him propose to me that evening? I know he wanted to, but Alan was circumspect, if not subtle, and I was jubilant when I saw how clumsily he evaded what he really wished to express.

"I have an office in Griffith that I keep for private clients. It's not much, just the front room of a cottage in Banna Avenue, but it's a good position and I work there at night and on Saturdays. I'm beginning to build up a small clientele. I look after everything myself."

He coughed and I waited for him to continue.

"What I really need is a clerk. It's not easy to find a secretary out here and I couldn't afford to pay much. Three pounds a week and she could live in the back of the cottage."

It was not what he really wanted to ask me and he knew I was aware of this. The very thought of someone being in love with me was so intoxicating I felt my head begin to swim.

"I wish I could offer you more," he said.

"Oh no, I think it's very generous."

Three pounds would almost double my whole fortune.

"It would help you—find your feet before you leave for Sydney. I could give you a reference and I know some lawyers there."

"Thank you, Alan."

I reached out across the table and touched his hand. Quickly, he turned the palm towards me and pretended that I was shaking hands with him to seal our agreement.

"A gentleman's agreement?" he said rather too heartily.

"No—it can't be that," I said. "Let's make it a pledge between friends."

This seemed to relieve him a little and he began to relax.

"I never had a girl as a friend," he said.

"Why not? Were they all dowdy and ugly?"

"Oh, I'm not talking about looks. It's talking—a friend must be someone you can talk to, someone who doesn't think you're mad when you want to read Homer instead of the *Sentimental Bloke*."

That was the first time I had heard about Bill and Doreen and I laughed until I was crying when Alan recited:

> "'I wish't yeh meant it, Bill.' O, 'ow me 'eart
> Went out to 'er that ev'nin' on the beach.
> I knoo she wern't no ordinary tart,
> My little peach.
> I tell yeh, square 'n all, me 'eart stood still
> To 'ear 'er say, 'I wish't yeh meant it, Bill.'"

"I don't know what's worse," he said ruefully. "A girl who thinks that the only poetry you should read is the *Sentimental Bloke* or a girl who's heard it for the first time."

"I think it's very funny," I said. "Is that what Australians are like when they're in love?"

"I—no, I don't think so. Australians find it difficult to discuss their emotions."

"Not like Italians."

"Definitely not like Italians."

"So what does an Australian do or say when he's in love?"

"Nothing—probably nothing at all."

"Then how does a girl know when a man's in love with her?"

He stared at me fixedly and suddenly moved the lamp to the side of the table so that I could not see his face.

"She always knows."

He stood up abruptly and said he had to make an early start the next morning to discuss a development with the surveyor at Mirrool. It was almost midnight but neither of us had noticed. He shook hands again with me on the veranda and told me he would be able to borrow a small lorry next Saturday to carry my bags.

"Yes, the books are heavy."

He looked back at me with a sudden expression of amazement.

"Oh, we'll take great care of the books. I'll see you have your own shelves at the cottage."

I heard his car chug explosively down the road and then I waltzed around the living room, feeling a rushing tide of excitement take hold of me. He was in love with me and that was what I wanted more than anything else in the world—somebody who would look at me with such a passion of desire in his eyes that it would draw me out of the dark grotto into the sunlight, where I could feel and smell the life of the world all around me. I lay awake in bed, recalling every gesture, every intonation of every word Alan had spoken that night. I knew he was in love with me and I was also certain that he had fallen in love with me when he first saw me.

Love at first sight always had a special significance for us, didn't it, Bessie? It was the way every proper love affair began and I remember how you assured me that Roger had fallen in love with me at the bottom of the steps at the Hotel d'Athena. Of course, it was not me he had seen then, but Dolfi. One glance and your soul, your life becomes another's. Did Alan belong to me like that? Had he surrendered his life to me? I had thought he was my murderer, instead, he had seen me, and loved me. It was the way—the thought of my parents was like a momentary chill and I flinched. Whatever happened to me, it would not be like that, and I was irritated that I should think of them. All I wanted was to be loved by Alan Gilchrist: it did not seem important that I should love him.

Rafaella came out the next day and again on Friday with bread and strawberries from her own vegetable garden.

"This is the Garden of Eden," she would say and then ask if I had found Giacopo's money.

She wanted to know where I had been looking and offered to help me search. This gave her an excuse to go through all my bags and boxes when I decided I wanted to find what Rosalia and Miki had packed for me. At the bottom of one bag I found the painting of Russell Morton and Rafaella gazed at it admiringly.

"Ah, you come from a very rich family."

"Oh yes, the Harcourts are very wealthy."

"So, of course, Giacopo would have needed a lot of money to bring you here."

Everything came back to the bag of gold and I noticed how Rafaella was examining my clothes under the pretence of shaking out the creases. She seemed puzzled that I did not have a multicoloured trousseau like a Sicilian bride. Rosalia had packed the best of my mother's clothes—all sensible linens and serges in dismal shades.

Rafaella left in the middle of the morning and immediately Angelica then arrived, to dart around the house and peer through the windows at me until it was dark. As before, I called to her and invited her to come in, but the sound of her own name seemed to frighten her and the moment she saw that I had seen her, a cotton skirt fluttered and she was gone. Always in the background, hiding behind a tree or by the fence, was the boy, Rocco, scuffing his bare feet in the ground.

On the Saturday morning I was waiting when Rafaella appeared, dressed more formally than usual, with a shawl over her head. Imploringly, she clasped her hands and knelt in front of me.

"You would not take bread from the mouth of an orphan, would you?"

"I have not found Giacopo's money, Rafaella. He must have buried it somewhere in the orchard."

"Ah—" She began to rock back and forth, moaning.

"I saw a stretch of ground behind the orchard with rows of new trees planted. Perhaps it's there."

She looked up at me hopefully.

"You are sure it's there?"

I was becoming irritated and I heard the sound of a motor chugging up the road.

"No, I'm not sure, but if there is any gold, I think it's all in your imagination."

I ran out to greet Alan as he backed a lorry up to the front steps.

Nineteen

When people said that Griffith was a town I could always think of a dozen different objections to the use of that word. In the first place, it was impossible for me to imagine a town being new. Towns were ancient settlements like old timbers encrusted with layers of barnacles and weeds that grow upon each other after the original wood has decayed and disappeared. When you walked through a Sicilian town you knew there was more buried beneath the landscape than you could ever see above it. The history of the past lay beneath your feet and sometimes, if you had a guide like my father, he could evoke the past so vividly that you saw the Phoenician traders in their striped cloaks bartering copper pots for cattle with Elymian farmers, the Greeks arriving in painted ships and the Romans after them. I do not think anything unsettled me more than to be in a country without history and eventually, nothing gave me a greater sense of freedom. Once Alan and I had been swimming near Finley's Beach at Mirrool Creek and afterwards we walked along the bank until we came to a place where there seemed to be a natural bridge across the water.

"What is that called?" I asked, pointing to the sandy spit.

"I don't think it has a name," Alan replied.

"Every place has a name."

He laughed and told me there were more places than names in Australia and that there were still unexplored parts of the Northern Territory and Tasmania.

"It must have a name," I said stubbornly.

"What if no one ever bothered to christen it?"

Every rock, every turn of the road in Sicily was sacred to a god or a saint, or served as a memorial for some dignitary or an event in history. For Sicilians, the landscape was not made simply of earth and sea; it was the immanence of the past that shaped everything we saw and did and sometimes it seemed as though we all lived in a charnel house where we made our beds and lay down among bones. Bessie always said that being raised by old parents had made me different and perhaps there was some truth in this; yet it was not my parents, but my knowledge of my past that set me apart from everyone else. My hands had held pots that Elymians used to drink from and I once repaired a cup that the lips of an ancient Greek had touched. When my father said he was the last of the Elymians I could feel the wave of history that carried him across the surges of time to my own life. If I am never able to decipher my name and who I am, I often have the sense of what I am, compounded as my nature is of Sicily and England.

Imperceptibly, as I pointed across the creek, I felt myself being drawn back into myself: history was not the perception of things around me but my possession of a vast reservoir of time and people. Archaeology had always meant studying the ground beneath my feet: now I began to sense that the past was within me. There were times when I was to feel that past like a physical weight, and sometimes I wondered if people would throw up their hands in horror when they recognized me as an errant ghost from the past masquerading as a woman of the twentieth century.

"Can I give this place a name?"

"If you want to."

"Yes, but I don't want it to have a secret name like the games we play when we're children. I want everyone to recognize it."

"In that case, we'll have to see it's added to the local shire maps and persuade everyone to use the name."

Alan told me it took him more trouble and conniving than anything he had ever done, but when the next maps for the Shire of Wade were issued, the sandy spit across Mirrool Creek was called Gwen's Bridge. It is still there and I wonder if anyone knows that the name was given because Alan Gilchrist was in love with me.

Not that he spoke of love that day when he gave the little bridge my name. Everything was as new as though we had just discovered it.

Indeed, when he drove me into Griffith and I saw what passed for a town I was dumbfounded by a scattering of buildings along Banna Avenue and rows of small dark trees they said were kurrajongs that in time would grow so tall that the whole street would be shaded by them. Alan's office was in a fibro cottage, with an office in front and a bedroom and kitchen in the back where recently a clerk at the court house had been boarding until he was transferred to Wagga. Alan apologized for the dingy furniture but I was more interested in where I was going to work than in where I was expected to live.

There were law books lining the front room that gave it the effect of a library; a desk, a table and four chairs.

"How many clients do you have?"

"About a dozen—I only recently moved in here."

"Will I be working over there?"

"Yes, at the table."

"Good. I'd like to see the office books and I'll need a typewriter."

The cottage was almost identical to Giacopo's house and as we unpacked together I told Alan that I would soon make myself at home. He was amazed by my own books, especially when I told him that I had left ten times as many at the museum in Trapani. I often wonder what happened to my father's library. Perhaps the director of the Pepoli took the books, or did Rosalia give them to some of her friends who used them, page by page, to light their stoves?

When we had finished unpacking the books, Alan offered to show me the town, and we walked around the dusty circular streets and up to Scenic Hill.

"There are no ancient ruins here," he said apologetically. "Griffith used to be called Bagtown when it was nothing but a collection of shanties. Now, you can almost see the town growing as you look at it."

I told him it was a change from living in a country where every town was decaying.

"Mussolini's changing all that, isn't he?" Alan said casually.

Anger almost made me stumble and I felt the blood rushing to my face.

"What do you know about Italy? Are you going to tell me that Mussolini is a great man because he makes the trains run on time? Do you know what he greases the tracks with? Castor oil, and what's left over is poured down the throats of those who disagree with him!"

"I'm sorry. I didn't understand. People aren't very interested in politics here." He apologized lamely.

"Then you should count yourself fortunate. It's a sign they don't have any real problems."

I could see that almost everything I said intrigued him, although I was sensing a change in his manner that puzzled me. There was a certain formality about Alan that Saturday, as if we had never spent two evenings talking across the table at Giacopo's farm. Now, whenever he mentioned himself, there would be an abrupt turn in the conversation and suddenly he was giving me details and statistics about the town and the Irrigation Area. He told me that Griffith as a town was younger than either of us, which astonished me.

When we were walking down Banna Avenue I asked him where he lived and he seemed to hesitate for a moment.

"I live with my mother," he said slowly. "It's a largish house on Wyangan Avenue."

"Can I see it?"

"Of course, but it's getting late now."

"I'd like to meet your mother too."

"Well, she's—"

"She's an ogre?"

"No, no—nothing like that."

We were back at the office and he took my hand and shook it so vigorously that I felt my whole body being jerked up and down.

"Gwen—I want to make something clear now."

I smiled at him sympathetically because it was like watching someone being tortured.

"We have to keep everything on the level."

"I don't understand. You've just walked me up and down a hill, Alan."

"What I mean is that people are going to talk."

"Isn't that what distinguishes humans from animals?"

"Please, Gwen, this is serious."

I immediately looked solemn and folded my hands as if in prayer.

"You'll be working here for me and you're young and very—good-looking. People are going to think—"

"That we may be—?"

"Exactly."

I shrugged.

"You have your reputation, Gwen—I should have had enough common sense to consider that when I offered you the position here, but if we keep everything—"

He gestured and I could see him measuring our relationship with a set square. I thanked him for being so considerate and watched him walk away with his head down in the direction of Wyangan Avenue, almost feeling his pain as he forced himself not to look back. I was hanging up my clothes when I heard him cough at the door.

"I'd like to see you tomorrow and take you to church. You—you're C of E aren't you?"

Religion was far from my mind the following morning as I wondered what in my meagre wardrobe I could find to wear. There had been a wedding just before the Sunday service and we stood and watched the bride and groom leave the church in a shower of confetti and rice.

"You'll be bringing in your own crop soon, Archie!" a man shouted.

The bridegroom laughed and gave a thumbs-up sign. I heard a startled breath behind me and when I turned, Norma Reynolds was gazing at me.

"It is you! I would never have believed it. Are you feeling better, love?"

She introduced me to her husband who was hunching his shoulders awkwardly in a blue suit that was too tight for him. They recognized Alan and when he told them that I was working as his clerk they exchanged quick glances.

"And you are feeling all right now, love?"

"Miss Harcourt is going to take over the office in Banna Avenue."

Again the astonished glances between them and Len said that he hoped Alan would be able to arrange an extension of his government loan because the rice was coming up spottily and he wasn't counting on a good harvest.

"He's a good chap," Alan said later. "But he doesn't know much about rice farming. Put an Italian on that land and he'd be out there in the mud with the whole family and bringing in bumper harvests in a couple of years."

There were very few people in the church and the sermon was short and so full of platitudes that I felt even Colonel Whitlow would have approved of it. I asked Alan if his mother attended church and he said abruptly that she had other interests. I wondered if she had deliberately chosen to stay away that Sunday because of me. Not once did Alan show any sign of affection for her and I began to imagine a woman like my Aunt Eleanor sitting straight-backed in an uncomfortable chair and making life as miserable for everyone as she possibly could.

It was when Alan was walking me back to the office after the service that I saw the Italians spilling out of the Catholic church and shepherding their children along to the waiting buggies and sulkies. Some of them even had motor cars with coloured ribbons tied to the horns and St Christopher statues as mascots on the bonnets. They all looked prosperous.

"Who takes care of their legal problems?" I asked Alan quickly.

"Generally, they talk things over with Father Mulcahy; he speaks Italian and then they come round to the council offices and try to make us understand what they want."

"Do they ever come to you?"

"Sometimes, and I do my best to make head or tail of what they're saying. It's pretty difficult. Most of them don't have any English yet, and what they do have is unintelligible. That's what makes the Aussies think they're stupid. You should see them repay their loans though. On the dot. And some of them actually come in with their cash in hand. Giacopo Sciafa was like that. Mostly, when there's a legal problem, it has to do with land, like the Sciafas. They can't subdivide here in a Home Maintenance Area and this upsets them if they want to leave one farm to two sons."

"I could translate for you."

We were outside a large sprawling house surrounded with gauzed-in verandas.

"Let's talk about it over dinner."

The dining room at Mirrool House remined me of the London railway hotel, where my father and I had stayed on our way back to Sicily: squat tinny cruets on uneven feet that seemed to resent the load of bottles they were carrying and thick china that Frau Brunner would have used for the dogs or the servants. Alan introduced me to several of the people there and I could hear the buzz of whispered conversation as we chewed our way through mutton that tasted rank and tough in spite of an ooze of mint and vinegar.

At first Alan seemed unimpressed with my idea, and told me that it would probably drive away his Australian clients. He reminded me that he had a government position and had to be careful of any conflict of interest.

"You've already opened an office."

"Yes—"

"And that was permitted?"

"I insisted on it when I took the job. I couldn't support myself and my mother on what I'm paid."

"I'm sure the Italians would pay you."

"It would take too much time, Gwen. I can only spend Saturdays and some evenings at the office."

"I could talk to them first and find out what they want, that would save you time."

"How would you expect to get in touch with them?"

"I'd put up a sign outside in Italian and ask the shopkeepers to place a card in their windows. I saw a jeweller's shop at the corner—"

"George Speirs, yes, I know him."

"It would help the Italians and build up your clientele."

"My God—"

Alan leaned back in his chair and stared at me.

"I feel as if a whirlwind has caught me up. A few days ago I was in charge of my life and now you—you're like a wind at my back. I had a five-year programme set out for myself. In three years, I planned to have a large enough practice to be able to leave my government job and then spend another two years drumming up enough business so that I could sell the practice and go to Sydney and try my luck at the bar."

Was it the confidence that came from being well again? I know that as we sat in the cool of the veranda, aware that everyone was staring at us, and drinking a coffee that Rosalia would have thrown on to the garden, I felt a tide of energy rushing through me that was supernal. If there had been a time when I longed for death and the pale forest, I could scarcely imagine or remember it, and if anyone had spoken of it to me then, I would have thought they were relating a fable.

"I think I can make you rich, Alan."

"I think you could make me anything you want, Gwen."

It would have been easy for me at that moment to reach across and tell him that what I wanted him to be was my lover, but I smiled and was silent. Every nerve in my body was trembling, I felt my breath coming short, and still I forced myself to smile and say nothing.

Two tall fair girls, obviously sisters, came over to our table and the prettier of the two reminded Alan that he was expected for dinner next Saturday.

"I may be tied up, Ellie," he said curtly and swept off his spectacles.

"Oh, aren't you going to introduce me to your friend?" she asked icily when Alan had retrieved his spectacles from under the table.

The girl, Ellie Sanderson, glared stonily at me and did not take my proffered hand.

"Is she your fiancée?" I asked Alan when the two girls were gone.

"I'm not engaged to anyone," he said curtly, and told me he had promised to drive his mother to some friends for bridge.

At least she has one social vice, I thought.

On Monday morning I went to all the shops and left cards in Italian. Mrs Heffernan in the draper's refused at first because she did not think her best customers would like to see any Italian writing in her shop window.

"It's a very small card," I said.

"And you're not Italian, are you?"

"What do I sound like?" I said, laughing.

"Oh, I picked you for a Pom as soon as you opened your mouth."

The first of the Italians arrived on Wednesday and there were three more on Thursday. I listened carefully to them, copied out their requests and made appointments for them the following week. Some of them had problems with their land but most wanted help in bringing out relatives before the Development and Migration Commission was abolished and the costs of travel would no longer be subsidized by the Australian government. Their relations had to take out papers before the new legislation was introduced. At first, they were reluctant to discuss their business with me, but when I spoke Italian to them and not dialect, they began to trust me. Every one of them asked me the legal fee and offered to pay in advance. At the end of the week, Alan looked at the money in the cash box and told me that I had earned more money for him in a week than he had made in a month.

"They are shrewd people and they are all doing well," I told him. "The important thing to remember is that they hate each other more than the Australians dislike them. The Calabresi don't care for the Venetians and they both detest the Sicilians so I have arranged that none of them meet here at the same time."

We had Calabresi nights and Venetian nights and another time set aside for the Sicilians. At the end of the month Alan told me that he was making more money than he earned from his position with the council and he might have to hire another lawyer. He increased my wages to five pounds and every Sunday he took me to church and then to lunch at Mirrool House, until it became so hot that neither of us could endure the sweat and platitudes any longer and we spent our Sundays swimming instead. It was obvious that people were talking just as he had said they would, and one morning I met Norma Reynolds again in Mrs Heffernan's shop. She enquired about my health as earnestly as ever and then, prompted by a series of winks from Mrs Heffernan, asked me if Alan Gilchrist and I had any plans.

"Oh yes," I replied. "But we can't announce anything yet."

"I daresay it's his mother," Mrs Heffernan blurted.

I sighed and looked at my shoes.

"She didn't care much for Ellie Sanderson," Norma said, and I gathered that at one time the whole town had expected to hear of an engagement between Ellie and Alan.

Norma was buying wool, and before she left the whole shop had seen the camisole top in shaded feather and fan that she was going to enter in the local Country Women's Association fair.

"Two-ply wool that was so fine I thought my eyes were going to fall out. Do you knit, love?" she asked, smiling at me.

"A little."

"If you ever need any help, come to me first," Mrs Heffernan said. "And if I can't manage it, Mrs Reynolds will fix it for you," she added, smiling at her friend. "I wonder you don't sell some of the things you make, Mrs Reynolds. You're a real professional knitter and as for your sewing . . . I'm sure some of my customers would be interested."

"I may have to if things don't look up on the farm. It breaks my heart to see the way Len works and nothing goes right for him." Norma sighed and folded up the camisole in a piece of tissue paper. "I may ask around for a few orders at the fair." She turned to me. "You haven't named the day yet, have you?"

"Not yet—" I smiled.

"Oh yes, his mother." Mrs Heffernan shook her head dolefully.

If I had been destined to marry death, as Rosalia once predicted, that particular prophecy had already been fulfilled and I was now free to chart my own fate. I would make Alan love me and afterwards we would get married, knowing that it was in my power to help him make a fortune in this dusty little place. In my imagination there was a natural progression from love to marriage and the whole town seemed to be of one mind with me: I was certain that his mates were already chaffing him about wanting to get hitched. Whenever I went into one of the shops there was a knowing silence and the odd, half-phrased question that let me understand that Alan and I were regarded as unofficially engaged. Of course, I did all I could to give life to the rumour. Occasionally, I saw Ellie Sanderson and her sister and they both cut me dead and began whispering furiously as I walked past them.

In this fashion, I was beginning to write my own play, fastening the wires to Alan's arms and legs, and using the people I met in Griffith as an approving chorus. The character I could not fit into my story was his mother, and I began to think of her as an implacable opponent like my Aunt Eleanor at Russell Morton. However, if I could make Alan love me enough, his mother would be swept aside and when his arms were around me and we slept together there would not be a corner left in his heart for her. I was almost twenty and my desire for love was like a constant fever that throbbed through my body when I lay awake at night, leaving me trembling and sweating for minutes after I woke. Often the pain in my groin was so intense that I pushed a hard pillow between my legs to try to still the ache. I knew Alan was suffering the same torment, but I could not make him speak. The figure of the paladin was moving and making all the gestures of love—to my stifled rage, the gestures were without words. *Lui chè parla* was silent.

That summer was so hot that only the flies seemed to be stirring and there was a constant droning hum from them as they beat against the screened windows. I kept a rag to wipe the sweat from my hands when I was writing, but even so, the pages were blotched. It was impossible to sleep one Sunday morning and, after an hour of tossing, I climbed out of my clammy bed and tried to read while I waited for Alan. We were going to Finley's Beach to swim and I sat idly turning the pages of *The Waste Land* by a new English poet and remembering the days when the sirocco threw a rusty shroud over Trapani and everyone huddled indoors, choking with dust. This heat was different because it seemed to draw moisture from the marrow of your bones. I drank water incessantly and still I was thirsty. I tried to concentrate on the poetry Alan had lent me, but the pages kept blurring.

The noise came from the office and I thought it must be Alan, but when I opened the door, I saw two boys looking around them with their thumbs in their belts.

"The office is closed on Sunday," I said.

The older boy stared at me and I recognized Aldo's eldest son.

"You're Giovanni Sciafa, aren't you?" I said.

Both of them staring at me.

"If you can't think of anything to say, please go."

"The name's John," the larger of the two said. "He's Mike." He nodded at his brother without shifting his gaze.

"How much do you charge?" Mike grinned.

"That depends on the kind of service you want."

This seemed to convulse them and they rocked with laughter.

"How about—" John leered "—if you bent over the desk there and we took you from behind. That wouldn't knock you up, would it?"

"Get out of here before I call the police!"

"Uncle Benno wrote to our dad. He said you took him for a ride and robbed him blind. By the way, where did you hide Uncle Jack's cash? I bet you've got it stashed away somewhere here."

"You got all of Uncle Benno's money. Wasn't that enough for you?" Mike shook his fist at me.

"Benno's coming out here at the end of the year. Dad's sending for him and his family."

"He's going to work Uncle Jack's farm until he can get started on his own. You have no right to that money. You're just a thief and a tart."

John came over to me and took hold of my hair. I pushed him away and he laughed.

"Benno said you were real easy with everyone. It's a bit late now to play the virgin, isn't it?"

John was getting excited and Mike was sweating, with a dark stain down the front of his shirt.

"Why don't we do it now, like we said?" Mike's voice almost breaking in his frenzy.

"If you touch me, I'll kill you and your family and your name will be dust in the devil's shit hole!" I shouted, and they laughed again.

"I bet that's a curse from the old country." They guffawed. "You're in Australia now."

John was beginning to loosen his belt and I swung round and was reaching for a paperweight when Alan appeared in the office door.

"What the hell's going on here?" he said and stood between the two Sciafas.

"Just—just a family call, Mr Gilchrist," John said, and edged past him.

"We were only talking," Mike squeaked as they shoved their way through the door.

"*Puttana*!" John shouted over his shoulder.

I heard them clattering across the wooden veranda as Alan looked at me anxiously.

"What did he call you?" he asked. "Pot—something?"

"Oh, they're still looking for the pot of gold that Giacopo buried in his farm."

Alan relaxed and began to laugh and I found my straw hat and went out to the car. Perhaps I should have told Alan then what the Sciafas had said to me and how they had threatened me, but I was secretive by nature and I wanted to keep their threats to myself. Besides, I already knew there were shadows in my life that I did not think Alan would understand. We read Latin and Greek together, but we came from different worlds and mine was more savage than his.

After we had swum at Finley's Beach, Alan said he thought he could remember another place down the creek where the water was deep enough for swimming. Tree ferns had their roots in the water, with occasional clumps of pink Christmas bush where the sun broke through to bracken fern, and there was nothing anywhere that reminded me of Sicily. I told Alan that even in Trapani you could smell the spring flowers when the wind blew across the hills and in summer the orange blossom was like a drug in the air—here there was no perfume, only a peculiar sharp tang that reminded me of leather and citron. Crumbling a spray of eucalypt leaves in my hand I suddenly remembered you, Bessie, and how your mother sprinkled eucalyptus oil on our handkerchiefs when we both had colds one summer in Trapani.

Alan whispered to me to be quiet and we watched a brolga fishing for yabbies, its dark head on one side and brilliant eyes fixed on the water. Gently, it stirred the sand with its foot and almost in the same instant, the beak cut through the water and we saw a crayfish slide down its long throat. I had seen brolgas fishing in the irrigation ditches before but this one was within arm's reach. The creek had become a series of linked puddles and we walked on dry sand that was a palimpsest of bird and animal prints. A little later, Alan told me a liquid spill of notes was a bower bird that must have a nest somewhere near, decorated with blue pebbles and scraps of blue paper. He added that I should be careful hanging out blue clothes on the washing line because bower birds would try to carry them off. Solemnly, he said that Griffith people still told the story of having seen a frantic bower bird trying to drag away the baggy blue knickers of the minister's wife.

"Everyone said she came out and told the minister he should do likewise but he declined."

We walked for half a mile through the heavy stillness of the afternoon, laughing and talking, until we came to Gwen's Bridge and I stepped out into the middle of the sandy spit and claimed it for myself.

There had been many times when I thought of reaching out to Alan and kissing him until the kisses became caresses and we were lost in each other. This was not such a moment and I remember that I was laughing and shouting to the world that Gwen's Bridge was famous and beautiful and when I was dead a thousand years, people would come from all over the world to see it. Suddenly, I felt him by me and he was holding me and kissing me until we fell to the sand, unable to stand because we were locked together as if no power on earth could ever separate our bodies. He lifted me up in his arms even as I was struggling to kiss him and carried me over to the bank under the tree ferns. I dragged off my bathing suit and he began to kiss my body while I screamed for him to take me. When Benno made love to me it was like dreaming of being loved; now I was awake and every part of me was clamouring for his touch. Holding me so tightly that I could feel my flesh melting into his, he rocked me back and forth in his arms and it was as if I were a moth or a butterfly breaking free of a carapace of steel. I know now that I needed comfort more than love, and I found it with Alan. We made love many times that afternoon until at last we fell back exhausted and I watched the sky turn crimson through a trellis of leaves over my head.

Alan leaned over me and he was crying. I held his head between my hands and looked at him as if I were seeing him for the first time. Everything pleased me: the grey eyes meshed with fine wrinkles, the four lines across his forehead that were creased now as he tried to push away my hands and reach for his towel.

"Why? Why are you crying?" I asked him.

"Because I swore this would never happen. I lost control of myself. Gwen, I love you and now—what if something should happen?"

"Getting pregnant? Is that what you're afraid of, Alan?"

"Yes and—"

He did not understand why I was laughing and leaned over me, searching my face.

"It can happen, you know. A man has to take—certain precautions."

Did Alan imagine I was a virgin? It would have been easy to deceive him as we crushed the ferns to a tangled mat in our lovemaking. Instead, I shook my head, but I could not bring myself to tell him about the grotto.

"Nothing will happen, Alan. You haven't got me in the family way. I don't think anybody could do that. I was very ill on the boat coming out and I lost so much blood that it's left me with anaemia. I still take the iron pills that Dr Bowles prescribed for me. Since that illness I have never had a period. You can't make a baby without blood."

Twenty

I should never have asked you to work for me. I've trained myself not to act on impulse but—"

He sat, hunched over his knees, staring across at Gwen's Bridge. Two wallabies came down to the opposite bank and stood with their paws against their chests, black muzzles twitching, sniffing the air uneasily. They took turns drinking, one watching while the other stretched out and took the water. Neither of us spoke or stirred while they were there and yet, in an instant, their heads were up and they bounded off through the ferns.

"Even a bloody kangaroo shows more sense than I have—"

"Are you angry because you made love to me?"

His face was anguished and I had a sudden vision of a sherd I once held in my hands that showed the ceremony of a man strangling himself as he tried to relieve his pain.

"I'm angry because of what I've done to you, Gwen."

"Are you saying that you don't love me?"

"I've never felt like this about anyone or anything in my life. When I first saw you—it was like walking into a dream. I saw a girl in a white dress asleep on a table with her black hair spread out and shadowing her face. At first I thought she was dead because she looked so pale. Some people are romantic by nature, Gwen, I'm not. There are plenty of good reasons why I should distrust emotion and yet, seeing you that morning was like opening the door on another world. I remembered La Fontaine's story about Sleeping Beauty and the picture of her in one of the first books I ever read." His voice was almost breaking. "You don't bloody well expect to find Sleeping Beauty on a fruit farm in the Murrumbidgee Irrigation Area."

"You haven't taken a vow of celibacy, have you?" I said gently and he began to laugh.

"Don't be—it's just that I have responsibilities."

I was silent, but he knew I expected an explanation.

"Responsibilities to you and to myself."

"Talk about mine first."

"You're nineteen."

"Almost twenty."

"You shouldn't be thinking about getting married—at least, not to the first Australian who falls in love with you."

"In Sicily I'd be considered an old maid."

"Even so—"

"Alan, why don't you tell me about your mother?"

It was almost as if I had struck him. He twisted away from me and when he looked back the lines in his forehead were deeper than ever.

"What do you know about her?" he asked.

"Very little. Did she prevent you marrying Ellie Sanderson?"

"Ellie and I were never engaged."

"But she wanted to marry you."

"I—she may have."

"And your mother interfered?"

"You missed your vocation, Gwen. You would have made a bloody good barrister. I feel as though I'm being cross-examined."

"Alan, if you don't want to marry a Sicilian migrant, you shouldn't be ashamed to say so. I'm sure most Australians would feel the same way."

"Of course I want to marry you."

"Then how can your mother prevent you? Is she very rich?"

"She hasn't got a penny of her own. Never did."

"You look after her?"

"Oh yes, I have to look after her."

The bitterness in his voice startled me and I waited for him to continue.

"You may have heard about my father—"

I shook my head.

"Gordon Gilchrist was a KC before he was forty and he was a member of the New South Wales parliament when he died. If I tell you that he was admired and respected, that is an understatement. The influence of a man like my father extends long after he's dead—that's how I got this job with the MIA, but I owe him more than a livelihood. Thanks to my father's political beliefs, I'm alive today and not buried in a French war cemetery with a lot of my mates. Dad was opposed to conscription and he fought it to the end. I remember once when a crowd of militant women broke our windows and pushed handfuls of white feathers into the letterbox, then stood outside, shouting abuse. But nothing made Dad waver and even his enemies never questioned his sincerity. At election time his supporters turned out in droves and he was sent back for another term. He was a

Labour man but he called Billy Hughes, the prime minister, a Pommy gravedigger to his face. I'm thirty-two now, so I was almost old enough to be conscripted in 1916, and I think I would have gone if it hadn't been for him. A lot of my friends were jumping the gun and enlisting as soon as they were sixteen and the recruiting sergeants always managed to turn a blind eye when some kid who was big for his age came up before them. But when it was a question of being loyal to my father or loyal to Great Britain, I chose my father. I've never regretted it, especially when I see two of my schoolmates who were gassed."

His eyes were wide and shining as he spoke about his father and then I watched his expression change.

"Dad was fifty when he married my mother. It was in London and he was appearing before the Privy Council in a big case for the Australian Workers' Union. I don't know why he married her, I don't even think he really knew himself. She was a singer—of sorts."

"Did he ask you to look after her before he died?"

"How did you know that?"

I almost laughed at his surprise.

"Oh, I understand perfectly what happened. As soon as my mother knew she was dying, she begged me to care for my father."

"And you did?"

"Yes."

"Then you realize why—why I can't get married yet."

"No, I don't. Surely a man can have a wife and look after his mother too."

"She's not—an easy woman."

"Was she opposed to your marrying Ellie Sanderson?"

"Opposed? We had scenes that made the *Götterdämmerung* sound like *Chu Chin Chow* and Ellie and I had never gone so far as to discuss marriage."

"Does she expect you to remain a bachelor all your life?"

"She says that she couldn't bear to share me with another woman."

"Is she your lover?"

For a moment I thought he was going to strike me, his anger was so violent his hands were opening and closing convulsively.

"That's—obscene!"

"What other conclusion can I draw from what you've just said?"

"I don't even like her! But I promised my father that I would look after her."

"Did your father forbid you to get married?"

"No—no, he didn't," Alan replied slowly and I knew he was mine.

"You want to be a barrister and a judge, don't you, Alan?"

"Yes—I remember telling you all that out at the farm. I must have drunk too much of Sciafa's pinkie that night."

"I think I'd make a good wife for a lawyer."

He put his arms around me and pulled me to him and again I felt the comfort of his body.

"I love you more than reason or sanity. There is nothing in my head except you. At work, they all twit me about being in love and I've given up trying to deny it."

"When will I meet your mother, Alan?"

It was his turn to be silent as he held me and stroked my hair.

"I couldn't bear to lose you, Gwen."

"Marriage shouldn't make you think of loss."

He gave a laugh that sounded more like pain than mirth.

"When you meet my mother, you may not want to marry me. You must understand, Gwen, I can't just dump her."

"I understand. No matter how hard you struggled to break free, you would never really succeed. I tried once and I failed. The dead always manage to hold us to their will. Sometimes I think we are the real ghosts, not those phantoms in limp sheets that wander round clanking chains on stormy nights. We are ghosts because the dead live inside us and direct our will in spite of all our desires to the contrary. There are times when I can hear myself speaking with my mother's voice and when I'm reading, I'm suddenly aware that I'm seeing the page with my father's eyes. And there is one person who is always with me."

I told him about Bessie and he looked wonderingly at me.

"I never had a friend like that. Perhaps boys tend to hang round in groups."

"She's gone now and I don't have any idea where she is, or even whether she's alive. I wrote dozens of letters and most of them were returned to me. It was almost as if I were enquiring about someone who was dead. All I wanted was to be with her, but my mother had her way despite all my plans to return to England."

"I'll break it to my mother this evening and we'll buy a ring from George Speirs tomorrow afternoon."

"I'd like that very much, Alan."

"This will be our year, Gwen. We'll never forget 1929."

It was almost dark when we stumbled back to Finley's Beach and found the car—we would have walked much faster if Alan had not kept his arm around me all the time. I was loved. To me, it felt as if I had reached an oasis of trees and flowing water after travelling for years across a desert of stones. "Comfort" seems such a plain and trite word to describe the warmth and security I felt with Alan, and I think it may need another starving person to appreciate the sensation when she is suddenly given a plate of food. Comfort for me was compounded with gratitude and hope, with rest and security, peace and warmth. I knew I had made a clumsy beginning to my life, but I was Gwen Harcourt now and soon I would be Mrs Alan Gilchrist. There was no reason why Alan should talk to the Sciafas, or why he would believe them if they ever told him about Benno and the child. For the first time, as he drove me back to Banna Avenue, I began to think about what I had done in the grotto. What if I were never able to have a child? Bessie and I often used to discuss the number of children we would have and whether it was more important to have a boy or a girl first.

"You're not getting cold feet, are you?" Alan asked me, reading my silence as doubt.

I told him I was trying to draw a mental picture of his mother and he said drily that I should wait until I had seen her for myself.

"She makes quite an impression on people," he added.

Again, there was a vacant place on my stage, for I realized that I could not use Aunt Eleanor for Alan's mother after the fashion of the puppet master who would sometimes take Orlando's head and fix it to the body of another paladin. When we got back to the office I took Alan by the hand and led him through to my bedroom.

"Can't you spend a little time here, with me?" I pleaded.

We made love on my narrow bed with the same urgency of the afternoon and afterwards not even the shower was able to cool us.

"There seems to be a fire in you, Gwen. I've read of women who want to make love but—"

He was spreading my damp hair across his knees.

"I have to be loved, Alan. Promise me that you'll always love me."

It was a childish demand and he smiled.

"If I can't love you as I do now I'll let you go to someone who can."

We were half asleep and our conversation had dwindled to an exchange of playful threats when Alan suddenly sat up and said he had to go home before his mother had a seizure. I was asleep before he had gone and yet I clearly remember holding my left hand up to the moonlight and imagining not a pale forest but the shining band of a ring on my finger. Not only did I have the comfort of Alan's love, I no longer felt abandoned and left to stray in a waste land. Tomorrow I would be officially engaged and receiving congratulations in all the shops and at Mirrool House. I would be just like all the other young women who made marriage the goal of their lives.

Business was so flourishing that Alan had hired another lawyer, a dismal young man called Fred Dangler, and many were the jokes made in town about his name! He boarded at the Victoria, a new hotel near the railway station, and he complained continually about the heat and the flies. At first, Fred irritated me because he muttered while he worked but I told myself that if I had been able to tolerate Dolfi fidgeting opposite me when he was supposed to be learning Latin, I could certainly endure Fred's mutters and snuffles. At first, I expected him to resent me, but instead he told me that I should become a lawyer myself.

"You've got the vote now so there's no reason why you shouldn't become lawyers and doctors. Men are finished, this is going to be the age of women."

After that, we became friends and if I had enjoyed law as much as Fred did I might have taken him seriously. Alan often spoke of the law as the formal expression of society's quest for order and right reason, but I always saw it as a complicated and boring game, like snakes and ladders across an enormous board with forfeits and losses at every throw.

The ring was so beautiful that I found myself constantly admiring it, walking down Banna Avenue with my hand in front of me, as if I were about to bestow a blessing on everyone who passed us. Four tiny diamonds glittering in the sunlight. I could feel Alan's tension and I thought it was because he had spent thirty pounds for it and then I realized he must have spoken to his mother.

"Did you tell her about us, Alan?"

"Yes, you're invited to tea on Saturday afternoon. We'll leave Fred in charge and go round at five. With a little bit of luck we should be back by six-thirty."

"I gather she's not happy."

He stopped suddenly and stared at me.

"My father must have been drunk or mad when he married her."

It was only when we were making love that I felt the strain leave Alan's body and he lay with his arms around me, his face buried in my hair. The night before I was to be introduced to his mother he abruptly said that he had had a nightmare that was haunting him.

"I started up last night, shouting my head off. I even woke my mother. Not that it takes much to do that. She's always wandering around the house at night like Lady Macbeth."

"We had a servant in Trapani who used to interpret dreams."

"This dream—I can't get it out of my head."

"Tell me, Alan."

"We had just made love."

"Was that a nightmare?"

"No—no—wait, Gwen. I felt this enormous sense of joy and fulfilment and I threw my arm out like this—in that same instant I felt something alongside me in the bed. I looked across and saw my father. He was lying there with his eyes closed."

"Usually the dead are inside us, Alan, and they live for us in memory. Sleep sometimes sets them outside of us."

"Do you ever have nightmares like that?"

"Oh yes, quite often." However, I knew that mine were not dreams, but memories of what I had lived.

The house in Wyangan Avenue was no different from any of the others with its dusty flower garden in the front and red gravel path to a wide veranda. I had steamed my straw hat so that the brim was stiff and had pinned a spray of miniature roses to the collar of my white cotton dress. My wardrobe was scant and I was planning to find a dressmaker who could cut my mother's clothes to fit me. For this occasion I had tried on one of her linen dresses but it fell from my shoulders like a tent, so I had made do with a white cotton of my own that was so plain it could have been a school tunic. When I looked in the mirror before we left I knew I was not smart, but the reflection that stared back at me was neat, serious and respectable.

Alan opened the front door and I was engulfed in a cacophonous stench. It seemed a thousand tiny dogs were yelping and barking around my ankles and the smell would have made the night-soil carter blanch. Beady little eyes were fixed on me and rows of flashing teeth surrounded with tan fur were gnashing furiously. Some of the dogs had ribbons on their heads and they bobbed and weaved like demented powder puffs as they threw themselves in the air with the force of their barking. I was so busy trying to extricate myself from the jaws of a dozen of them that I did not see the owner of the voice. It was pitched to a *parlando*, a peculiar head tone that reminded me of Mrs Byng Patterson who used to come to my mother's musical afternoons. I was very small when the Pattersons left Trapani, but I remember sitting on the very edge of my chair, transfixed by the tone affected by Mrs Patterson before she sang "The Lost Chord" or "I Dreamt I Dwelt in Marble Halls."

"Mum, you said you'd keep the dogs locked up!"

"Dearest, they get out! You know how they always get out! Besides, you can't expect me to keep them locked up all the time. That would be cruel and heartless."

"They're biting Gwen!"

"Don't open the front door! If they go out in this heat they'll get sun stroke."

Alan was picking up handfuls of the dogs and throwing them into the back of the house while the voice chimed at him. I climbed up on a chair. My new lisle stockings were laddered and there were flecks of blood on my instep.

"What are they?" I cried because all I could see was a fuzzy horde trying to fight its way back into the hall.

"I'll manage them! Din dins!"

The voice vanished down the hall and the dogs scuttled after it, their claws scraping and scuffling on the linoleum. They were gone and Alan helped me down from the chair.

"I'm sorry."

"So am I," I retorted angrily as I realized my stockings were ruined beyond all hope of repair.

"They are"—the voice had returned—"in response to your question—Yorkshire terriers. Champion Yorkshire terriers. I breed and show them and I do consider, Alan, that the hallmark of a gentleman should be his love of animals."

The voice became a woman for me as I tried to blot the stains from my stockings with a handkerchief. It was difficult at first to discern a shape in the flowing shawls and canopy of lilac tulle swathed around her head. A straggle of brilliant henna curls had escaped from under a velvet toque and she looked as if she were made up for a sideshow, with circular patches of rouge on her cheeks and kohl on her eyelids. I was feeling dizzy from the smell and I walked gingerly because the dogs, in their excitement, had left little puddles on the floor.

"All the dogs, Mum!" Alan was pointing to a fat, sharp-eyed ball of fur in his mother's arms.

"Not Siegfried!" she said resonantly. "You know how he pines for me."

She motioned with a free hand covered in rings and we picked our way into the living room.

"If you will both sit quietly, I shall bring the tea. It's quite ready. Help!"

I jumped and then realized she was still speaking.

"It is quite impossible to get domestic help in this wilderness of the spirit."

"She can't get anyone to work for her," Alan murmured and I nodded sympathetically.

There were often interludes in the puppet opera when the *buffo* comedians clattered on to the stage and began to knock each other down and that afternoon in Mrs Gilchrist's cluttered, smelly room, I felt as though I were watching one of those scenes. I had cast Mrs Gilchrist as a tragedy queen;

at the very least, a formidable antagonist like my Aunt Eleanor. Instead, it was a zany who sat pouring tea for us with her little fingers extended as if they wanted nothing to do with her hands, and a fat ball of fur snoring wheezily in her lap.

I took the cup she proffered me and was thanking her when she held up her hand.

"No!" she intoned.

Again I jumped and some of the tea splashed on my skirt.

"No! I detest being called by that name. I prefer always to use my stage name—Valmai Vitale. Vitale—it means life, in Italian."

"Not really," I murmured, dabbing at the stain.

"Oh yes, but of course, you are Italian, aren't you?"

"Yes," I said bluntly.

"Ah—" she sighed melodiously with a dying fall and drank slowly, putting her head to one side and dropping scone crumbs in front of the dog's nose. It growled irritably and she brushed the crumbs on to the floor. Alan's expression puzzled me, because he was not laughing as I expected; instead, he was glaring at his plate.

"I should have known you were Italian because your hair is so dark, but you have a pale skin and Italians are usually so dark."

"You're not dark, Signora Vitale," I said.

"No, I've always had a remarkably good complexion, but then I never go out into this cruel sunshine. People will tell you that I never venture outside the house unless it's raining or until the sun has set. There are—I gather—some very romantic stories told about me. Mrs Fletcher Stevens, my neighbour but one, and a devoted friend, told me that I'm called the lady of the twilight. Rumour and gossip are always the fate of artists. We are the toys of the vulgar populace."

"Mum, you know that Gwen and I are going to be married," Alan said abruptly.

She stood up as if she had not heard him and smiled archly at me.

"I think we should have a little music, don't you? Music to soothe the savage breast, music that mends the frazzled sleeve of care."

Siegfried was tucked under her arm like a handbag as she selected a record and placed it on the gramophone. The needle scratched and she bent over, leaning on her elbow, with one hand under her chin and the forefinger to her cheek.

There was a whispery scraping and then a voice of such ethereal beauty filled the room that I felt my skin turn cold and prickle.

"There is a voice!" Mrs Gilchrist sighed gustily.

It was the Bell Song from *Lakmé* and I sat back overwhelmed by the range and sweetness of the tone. As the last notes faded I looked at Mrs Gilchrist in amazement.

"Mrs—Signora Vitale—you had a wonderful voice."

She simpered and bobbed her head as if acknowledging applause.

"Oh, for Christ's sake, Gwen," Alan shouted. "Can't you recognize Nellie Melba when you hear her?"

"Australia's crowning glory, I always call her," his mother said and sat down.

"Mother, we don't want to hear any more records. We just wanted you to understand that we're getting married."

"I really think it's time for me to feed the doggies," she said, smiling gently. "It was very wrong of me to tell them it was din dins and then not feed them. Our four-footed friends are very sensitive to ingratitude, you know, and they feel things more acutely than people."

"Congratulations might be in order."

Mrs Gilchrist swept past us without speaking and we heard her open the door to the back of the house where she was greeted with a shrill cacophony.

"I think we should go," I said and Alan followed me out of the rankly smelling house.

Before we reached the corner I began to laugh and I had to lean against a fence because I could barely stand. Alan did not move to help me. Instead he stood there, grimly watching me, his hands in his pockets. There was no mirth in his voice when he finally spoke.

"She's as good as a circus turn, isn't she?"

I tried to imitate her voice and bent double, howling with laughter.

"Can you imagine what it's like having that as your mother?"

I was still mopping the tears from my eyes and looked mistily at him.

"I'm sorry, Alan. I couldn't help it."

"No one can. She has that effect on everyone. Only I live with her and she's my responsibility."

"I understand—"

"No, you don't. No one does. She's not certifiable. Can you say someone's mad because she's vain, egotistical and keeps dogs? Besides, even if she were, I doubt if I could bring myself to sign the papers that would put my mother away as a lunatic."

"She didn't protest when you told her you were getting married."

"No, silence will be the first response. Afterwards there'll be hysterics and lamentations."

"She only seemed concerned about the dogs."

"Can you imagine what it's like living in a kennel?"

"No, I can't. Do they go into your room?"

"Never, my door is always closed. My mother observes only two rules I've set down: one, my room is private and two, she never comes near the office. I may rent the house next to the office and stay there. We need extra room."

As we walked down to Banna Avenue I saw a straggle of people waiting on the veranda outside the office.

"Business is good," Alan said.

"When can we be married?" I asked abruptly.

"I get a vacation in May. There's no need to wait for June, is there?"

There was an announcement in the *Griffith Gazette* and afterwards even people I hardly knew were stopping me on the street and congratulating me. I had no fear of the Sciafas now. Whatever Benno may have chosen to tell them would be kept in the family. If they denounced me publicly, the shame would fall on the family as well as on me and not one of them would risk that. I saw the two Sciafa boys one evening as I took a bundle of letters up to the post office and they spat as I walked past, but neither of them spoke to me. Alan was my lover and my fiancé and his ring was the pledge of our future marriage.

The aroma of sulphur and ripe fruit filled the town as lorries and drays brought cases of apricots, peaches and grapes to the long sheds where the fruit was pitted and placed on wooden trays. The sulphur was lit under them and the doors closed. As soon as the fruit began to weep, the trays were carried outside and left to dry in the sun.

The end of the season was always celebrated with a ball at Mirrool House and Mrs Heffernan was in a frenzy of excitement as she ordered dresses from Melbourne and Sydney for her customers. One morning, panting and scattering hair pins, she beamed at me across the counter.

"What are you wearing, dear? Bubble skirts are the rage, and shot taffeta for the evening."

"I need a dressmaker who won't charge me very much," I replied cautiously.

"Everyone's busy," she said.

"I may need to have something made over."

"Oh—" Her contempt inspired a fresh shower of pins and then she told me that everybody wore something new to the harvest ball.

"It will be new—in a way. Do you think Mrs Reynolds would help me?"

"I really couldn't say. You'd have to go out and talk to her."

Mrs Heffernan lost all interest in me as two women came in to pick up their packages from Sydney.

I had enough money to buy a new dress like all the other women in town, but the truth was that I couldn't bear to spend my savings. Alan had offered to open an account for me at the bank and when I told him what I was doing with my wages, he said I was worse than the Sciafas. Every week, I bought a gold sovereign and hid the coins in a corner of my mattress. Was I a Sicilian *contadina* at heart, or was it because I remembered Frau Brunner who once confessed that she put all her faith in little gold bars?

Longingly, I remembered the blue cotton with the handkerchief-pointed skirt Bessie had given me, but that had been reduced to shreds long ago. Besides, this was a formal occasion. My mother's violet taffeta and satin was so old that the fabric split in my hands and her long black crêpe de Chine beaded with jet and steel was green when I held it to the light. There was nothing except the petticoat—a black shot taffeta. When I shook it out the fabric rustled and the colour was deep and lustrous. I would use this, I decided, and next day I asked Fred if I could borrow his bicycle and rode out to the Reynoldses' rice farm.

Twenty-One

Lorries and carts laden with fruit went past me on the road and I waved to some of the drivers I had come to know. If I were ever asked to describe Arcady, only one picture would come to my mind—the day in late summer when I rode out on Fred Dangler's bicycle to see Norma Reynolds, with the perfume of peaches and apricots in the air and a burnished haze across the orchards. The image of Alan's mother was still in my mind and every time I thought of her I began to laugh. All Sicilian girls are warned about their prospective mother-in-law and how the older woman will try to turn her son against his wife. The condition between the two women was generally one of war, at best an armed truce. Nothing in life was more important than a son, and no prize on earth more valuable than an only son. I had often listened to Assunta, who thanked the Madonna with tears in her eyes that her fiancé's mother was dead and the only unmarried sister had decided to take a position as cook for a Swiss family in Lucerne. I also knew that the war between a wife and a mother always ended with victory being won in bed.

"Look behind these modern superstitions and you will always find the old religion," my mother said, and I thought of the *Oresteia* and Apollo's defence of Orestes before Athena. It was an evil thing for a son to kill his mother, but there could be no expiation for a woman who murdered her husband. The bond of blood between mother and son was strong, but the bed bond between a man and his wife was sacred and whoever violated it merited being thrown to the Furies. "The mounter, the male's the only true parent. She harbours the bloodshoot, unless some god blasts it. The womb of the woman's a convenient transit." Giacopo Sciafa would have taken me for his wife in the hope that I was carrying a son for him and every Sicilian woman who held a son in her arms knew that she was reflecting the glory of the Madonna who let her womb be used as a cradle for God. Orestes murdered his mother to avenge the honour of his father, and Athena, who was born of Father Zeus alone, forgave him, but there was no mercy for the woman who violated the bed bond. When Alan and I made love we were one flesh and there was no place in our bed for anything except our passion. If I had been musical I would have sung as I bicycled through the orchards and out into the rice country where the road was built up to a ridge and it seemed as though I were riding along a narrow causeway between the muddy paddocks.

Norma Reynolds was astounded when I propped the bike against the steps of the veranda and called her name. Flustered and wiping her hands, she came out and immediately enquired about my health.

"You're all right, dear? You're not having one of those turns, are you?"

"I've never felt better." I laughed.

This was true. When I looked in the mirror to brush my hair every morning I could no longer see a chalk mask staring at me.

The Reynoldses' house was exactly the same as Sciafa's, with an extra room tacked on to one side, but the lack of prosperity was evident everywhere. The congoleum in Giacopo's kitchen was new and glistened; here, there were patches concealing holes and places where the pattern had vanished altogether.

Over a cup of tea, Norma told me that they were on the verge of selling out.

"It'll break Len's heart to leave the land but we can't live on debts and what I can scratch out of the vegetable garden. Thank God, the chickens are laying well and there's fruit enough for the kids. They're over at the Binnses' place now. Poor buggers, they're in the same boat."

"Alan tells me that rice is a difficult crop."

"I wouldn't know what it is. Perhaps we flooded the fields too early or for too long. I don't know, but there wasn't enough of a crop to make a decent rice pudding. Only the Dagos seem to have the knack of growing it. There's a family of them about three miles away and we went out when they were harvesting. It made Len weep to see it."

"Perhaps he could talk to them and find out what went wrong with his own crop."

"I suggested that, but Len could never bring himself to ask them for advice—even if they could speak English, which they can't." She paused and frowned. "You're not having any more of those fancies, are you? I mean, you really upset me on the train. Mum's old auntie Millie had spells when she thought she was Queen Victoria and behaved like it—expected people to curtsey to her when they came into the room. Tried to knight my father once with the carving knife. He was frightened out of his wits—thought she was trying to cut his head off. Eventually, they had to put her in a home where everyone was potty. I remember going out to see her once and there were kings and generals everywhere and archbishops walking round with mitres made of newspaper on their heads. I've heard of people imagining they were famous, but I never heard of anyone imagining she was a Dago. I mean—that's like getting a craving for dirt, isn't it?"

"My only fancy at the moment is wondering what I can wear to the ball. I'm beginning to feel like Cinderella without a fairy godmother."

"Oh yes, Len and I went last year, but I doubt if we'll make it this year. You don't have much heart to go dancing when all you can think about is having to walk away from your property and leave four years of hard work behind you. I told Len, he'll just have to get his job back at the bank. I'm sure they'd be glad to have him."

"I can't afford a new dress and Mrs Heffernan told me every dressmaker in Griffith is busy. I wondered if you could help me."

I spread out the taffeta petticoat and Norma examined it doubtfully.

"It must be a hundred years old by the cut," she said finally.

"It was my mother's, but the material's still good, isn't it?"

"Oh yes, that heavy silk lasts forever."

"I know exactly what I want but I can't sew and Mrs Heffernan said you could do anything with a needle."

"Yes, I always had good hands. Mum apprenticed me to Madame Gerard in Sydney when I was fifteen. She was French and all the society women came to her. Of course, I never worked after I was married. Len would never allow that."

It always seemed to me that to exchange work for slavery was not very sensible, but then I hated housework and after a week at the office I had told Alan he would have to get a cleaner to scrub and polish. Twice a week an old deaf pensioner came in and I made sure she did the washing as well. I could see now that I would need all my tact to persuade Norma to help me.

"I cut this picture out of the *Illustrated London News*."

"My—"

"It's cut to the side with leaves on one shoulder and on the opposite side of the skirt."

"It is very smart—"

"Could you make it for me?"

"I've not made anything like that in years. Mind you, Madame Gerard did some gorgeous evening gowns."

"I want to pay you. I can't afford very much, but I'd like to give you three pounds."

"Oh no, I couldn't accept money from you. Len would kill me."

"He won't kill you if he doesn't know. Surely there's something you need for the children."

She laughed shortly. "Start with shoes—"

"Tell him that you're doing it as a special favour to help me out."

"I suppose—"

I placed three one-pound notes on the table and she stared at them.

"I'll have to measure you," she said.

"My mother was tall, a big woman, and I think there'll be enough material."

"Oh yes, dressmakers always get told that when the client's skimped the material. Still—we'll do our best."

She held the picture to the light.

"The Princess de Villiers, eh? A charity ball for the poor of Paris. I think the poor would be better off if she'd given them the price of that dress. Well, I don't know whether we can make you look like a princess but we'll try. What are you going to trim it with? Look, every one of those leaves is edged with something like braid."

"I'll bring you out some braid next time. I can make that myself."

On the way back to town in the heavy, golden dusk I heard a chinking, clattering rattle of sounds ahead of me and I rode up alongside Vanda's cart. He told me to tie my bike to the back if I wanted a lift.

"You look plenty different now, missy," he said to me, grinning. "I think when I take you out to that Sciafa place you were like someone dead."

"Oh no, I'm very much alive."

I told him about my dress and he nodded over the reins.

"What I need now is some gold thread."

He winked at me and said that Vanda had everything for a pretty girl, for a price.

"Gold thread?"

"Gold for saris—Indian women make patterns and I bring them what they want."

"Can I see it?"

He told me to climb into the back of the cart and look in a cardboard box that was under some tool cases and bolts of canvas. The thread was in looped tresses, and there was every brilliant shade in that box, from vermilion to a blue that seemed electric even in the half light. I found three tresses of the gold thread and carried them back to the front seat where they shone in my lap like Rapunzel's hair.

"They cost plenty money," Vanda said sorrowfully, and I haggled with him until we reached the station. I could tell he was enjoying himself by the way he chucked the reins and spoke to the horse in his own language.

"You got a good head for money," he said to me later. "You make a good wife. Make your husband rich and everyone else poor."

That night I began to knot the ribbon and it was as if Rosalia were in the room with me, smiling as she told me there was Saracen blood in the Marineos.

Two days later I went out to have a fitting and I took the braid with me, or what I had managed to complete. Even when I was talking to some of the Calabresi in the office, I kept knotting. One of the men told me that he had seen his mother do something like that when she sat outside the house in the street with her face to the wall. Benito Ruffano was a shrewd old man who had often asked if his youngest son, Tommy, could help in the office because the boy talked of nothing except becoming a lawyer. Alan said we could easily pay him a few shillings and so the boy now came every afternoon after school, with his hair wet and combed and wearing a clean shirt and tie.

The dress was beginning to take shape, and even Norma seemed pleased when I turned around in front of her.

"I tell you straight, there were times when I thought I'd forgotten everything I'd ever learned from Madame—how to faggot and mitre corners and all those little touches you never bother about when you're making kids' clothes. And best of all, Len didn't mind a bit when I told him it was a favour to you. I hate having to lie to him but he'd make me give the money back if I told him the truth, and I couldn't do that because the money is already on the kids' feet."

The gold braid astounded her, and I watched her bridle as she examined it.

"I know every crochet and knitting stitch invented and I've even made up a few myself, but I've never seen anything like this."

She tried to copy me and began to curse under her breath when the knots unravelled.

"It looks so simple when you do it."

"That's what I said when I first tried. It took me months to learn how to do it."

Eventually she gave up and said she couldn't be expected to learn new tricks at her age. However, I knew that she would be practising as soon as I was gone because it infuriated her to have me watch her blundering with the thread.

Reluctantly, I ordered a pair of black satin pumps from Mrs Heffernan for thirty-seven and sixpence and decided not to wear gloves because the Princess de Villiers had bare hands in the picture. I wore the pumps for my last fitting and Norma sat on the floor and stared up at me in amazement.

"I wish Madame Gerard could see this. She'd be that proud of me."

I had seen women dressed in great finery at the Hotel d'Athena but this, I knew, looked as if it had just arrived from Paris.

"Oh, and there's something else I'd like you to see."

With enormous pride, Norma showed me that she had mastered Rosalia's knotting stitch and I hugged her.

"You must have Saracen blood in you too," I told her.

"I beg your pardon, there's no mixed blood in the Willoughbys," she replied huffily and I apologized for my joke.

"One other thing I'd like to ask you, Gwen. If anybody asks who made your dress, don't mention my name. Len wouldn't appreciate that. Just say you ordered it from Melbourne—or Paris. That's where the idea for it came from in the first place."

I left all my mother's old clothes with Norma and she told me that she would take them apart, turn the fabric if it was worn and make whatever she could from them. In two weeks I had a wardrobe of skirts that fitted me and two dresses that were smart and plain. As I dressed for the harvest ball I thought about the Princess de Villiers and wondered if she had felt such rapturous pleasure when she saw herself in the mirror. All I wanted then was to have Bessie there to admire me and tell me that I really had made something of myself.

Alan arrived promptly at eight with the green Singer freshly washed and polished. He stood for several moments transfixed and then he could barely speak.

"Don't you know how beautiful you look, Gwen?"

"It's the dress."

"No, the dress is just a trimming."

"It's because you love me."

"I'm glad we're going to be married, that's all."

"What do you mean?"

"If you weren't spoken for and I took you to the harvest ball looking like that, you'd have every bachelor in the area proposing to you."

I gave a mock sigh. "And they'd all have mothers, wouldn't they?"

"No. No—" he said slowly. "I don't think anyone has a mother like mine."

"Has she been difficult?"

"Well, we've run the gamut of shrieks and fainting fits. I've reached the point where I just let her pick herself up off the floor when she decides to collapse."

By the time we arrived at Mirrool House I had managed to get Alan to laugh, although ruefully, about her.

"She can't prevent us from getting married."

"That she can't—and won't," Alan said firmly and we walked up the steps through sparkling lights and into a room decorated with baskets of fruit and coloured lanterns.

I saw immediately that I was dressed differently from all the other women there who were rustling up and down in pastel taffetas and satins. Mine was the only black dress and when the first foxtrot was announced and we went out on the floor, I knew that everyone was admiring what Norma Reynolds had made out of my mother's old petticoat.

It would have been better if, when the music began, I had not taken Alan firmly round the waist and stepped forward. We burst out laughing together.

"I'm sorry. I'm so sorry," I said. "I always used to dance the boy with Bessie because she was short and I was so tall."

"Let's try it this way," Alan said chuckling, and we found ourselves dancing. "And don't worry. If anyone saw you, they'll simply think you learned to dance at an expensive girls' boarding school."

A dozen different men asked me to dance or tried to cut in when Alan and I were on the floor and he delivered a short, set speech to all of them.

"Push off, mate. This is not my girl, this is my fiancée and she's booked for this evening and the rest of her life."

I met Ellie Sanderson in the ladies' room. As she patted a curl in place on her forehead with a dab of spit, she asked me how I was getting along with Alan's mother.

"Quite well, thank you."

She laughed sardonically and said she had dropped Alan like a hot brick after she met his mother. "Can you imagine living with her?"

"I don't intend to live with her," I replied.

"No? She'll never let him go," she said thinly. "And don't think she's just another crazy old coot. Underneath all the carryings on, she's a crafty devil. I should know."

Ellie put her shoulders back as if she deserved a medal for having survived a painful ordeal and gave me what was clearly meant to be a withering smile.

There was a spidery little man with a notebook and a camera waiting outside the ladies' room.

"Miss—Miss—I'm the Busy Bee from the *Gazette* and I've been following you round for the last half hour. I don't want to spoil the excitement for you, but a little bird has just told me that you are going to be made belle of the ball and I need a photograph and a few notes about that delicious gown for the social page."

Alan came across and winked at me over the little man's head.

"Well, I can tell you where the dress came from," he said expansively. "It's a Paris model, imported at vast expense for this occasion from the most exclusive couturier in Gay Paree."

"Really?" The pencil was flying across the page. "Of course, I knew it was French when I saw it. Whom did you say the couturier was?"

Alan looked at me helplessly and I said quickly, "Chanel."

"Ah, well, who else? Those braided *paillettes* are inspired. And now, perhaps a photo of the two of you."

Alan backed away, laughing.

"No, the honours of the evening are for my fiancée."

The globe on his camera flared and I blinked and almost immediately I was looking around me hazily as I heard the band conductor call my name.

The prize I won that night was a silver pin of a basket filled with enamelled fruit in different colours. It has a place now in Mrs Whitlow's shell box where I keep my special treasures.

"Wish I'd known you were going to pick up jewellery like that," Alan said afterwards. "I could have saved on the engagement ring."

Whenever I wear the brooch now I remember stumbling up to the platform and looking out on a hundred smiling faces in a room fragrant with fruit and bowls of waratahs and chrysanthemums. The *disgraziata* was being praised and in the shouts of approval and the applause I felt that I was no longer a Sicilian or the English lady my mother had wanted, but an Australian who could bring a new world to life in this great garden. Oh, but there's a serpent in every garden and as my hand was being shaken by a dozen different members of the Griffith Council I suddenly recalled a girl in the ladies' room, moaning that she had the curse and did anyone have a spare pad she could use.

It had meant nothing to me when she spoke and yet now, as I thought of the garden where I was going to make my home, I knew that I was barren, and did not belong in a place of fruit and flowers. I was an interloper, someone who was trespassing under false pretences. The pain of this recognition brought tears to my eyes and I was glad when people touched me on the shoulder, assuming that I was overcome and crying for joy.

That night, after we made love, I lay across Alan's arm and wondered if I could ever tell him about the grotto and what I had done there.

"I feel as though I've just made love to a movie star," he kept saying over and over.

"Alan, would it matter very much if we didn't have children?"

"Oh, I think we could put up with a couple of kids in a few years' time."

"What if I could never have any?"

"Of course you'll have children, if you want them."

"Haven't you noticed that we can always make love? That there's never a time when—when it isn't possible for me?"

"Well—yes—" he said slowly.

"I haven't had a period in seven months," I cried.

"That's nothing to get alarmed about. If it continues, we'll see a specialist, although I've heard that plenty of girls have anaemia. It's nothing serious. And—even if it were, it wouldn't matter to me if we didn't have a family. I said I'd like kids, but that doesn't mean that I'd love you any the less if you couldn't. It's you I want to marry, not a bunch of future Aussies."

Gratitude was always part of the love I felt for Alan and never more so than that night. After he went home, just before dawn, I lay awake for a time, gazing at the dress that was hanging in front of the wardrobe. It seemed to have a life of its own and the braided leaves rustled as a breeze from the window stirred them. I saw myself dancing again and heard the voices congratulating Alan on having picked a winner. There were no Italians invited to the harvest ball and I wondered what the committee would have done if my name had been given as di Marineo.

The next day was Sunday and Alan drove me out to see the Burrinjuck Dam that controlled the water from the Snowy Mountains and gave life to the Irrigation Area. As we ate our lunch in the shadow of the mantling concrete cliff, Alan said how much at home a few Roman engineers would have been there.

"I don't think they cared much for scenery, Gwen. Not like the Abos—for them every rock and tree was sacred. I sometimes wonder how many of their ancestral gods we uprooted when we built that."

"Does it matter? They're not our kin."

"Some people study their beliefs, Gwen."

"If we don't share their blood they can never be part of us."

"That's a pretty bleak outlook."

"I'm a Sicilian—so I know what Phoenicians, Saracens, Romans, Greeks and Normans felt because they are my ancestors. But don't ask me to understand an Aborigine."

"What about me? Can you understand me?"

"Oh yes, I'm half English."

We spoke about Roman and Greek temples and, even as we talked, I remembered the hills stretching out before me from the temple at Segesta where my mother and father had fallen in love. That was a question I refused to put to myself even though it was always coiled like a serpent on my tongue: Did I—could I—possibly love Alan as much as my mother had loved my father?

I closed my mind to the thought as Alan told me stories about the miners and navvies who had come from all over Australia to help build the dam they once called Barren Jack. It had been officially opened the year before and Alan had been invited to represent his father at the celebrations because of all Gordon Gilchrist had done for the area.

We were making our way home in the late afternoon when we saw a crowd of about twenty men in a paddock down below the road. Above them, a group of Italians stood smoking and watching whatever was going on. I could read contempt and disgust from their gestures and in the same instant, over the rattle of the motor, I heard a gasping scream that sounded almost human. Alan brought the car to a jolting halt.

"Wait here!" he shouted to me and ran down towards the men.

I followed him and asked the Italians what was going on.

"*Ammazzano i cavalli*, they are killing horses," one of them said and they all spat in unison.

"It is for gambling, Signora. They tie a horse to each end of a rope and see which one is strong enough to drag the other over a line. This is a great sport for them, even though it breaks the horses' hearts."

I could see the Australian men gathered around two Clydesdale horses, the huge broad-backed animals they used for digging ditches. The men looked like gangers and they were urging the two horses to pull while one flogged the head of the larger horse with a whip. The smaller one, a grey, was on its knees, its neck stretched out, screaming for air as it dragged on the rope.

"Stop that!" Alan shouted and pushed his way through the crowd. The gangers must have been drinking because I saw some of them swaying as they turned on him. He was in front of the winner now, pushing at its shoulder. Obediently, the great horse moved back and the grey stumbled and fell sideways as the rope sagged.

Furious, one of the men swung a punch at Alan. Instantly two others were trying to do the same. I screamed but no one could hear me through the shouting. I turned to the Italians. "Are you going to let them kill a man as well as horses?" I cried, and they spilled down from the road and began kicking and punching their way through the gangers. It was impossible to see what was happening. The two horses had made their way to the side and were standing together, gasping for air. The small grey had its head across the larger horse's neck.

I followed the Italians and when one man punched wildly and almost hit me, I screamed that I would tear his eyes out if he touched me. Alan was on his knees and I pulled him up and dragged him from the mêlée.

"You idiot," he said. "You've started a riot."

It was all over in minutes and the Italians left victorious, sauntering down the road, slapping each other on the back and looking back over their shoulders and jeering at the gangers who were trying to stand upright. Three had given up the struggle and were lying on their backs, snoring.

Alan walked over and examined the horses.

"Who's in charge here?"

A middle-aged man shuffled forward and said they had just been having a little fun.

"Not with council property, you don't! Get these horses back to your camp and see they're not worked for at least a week."

"We've got a contract for a quarter-mile channel," the man complained.

"You will also be getting a visit from the police because I'm going to press charges against you. Don't worry, I know most of you by sight."

He turned to me.

"The law will deal with this."

I handed his broken spectacles to him and forbore saying that I thought a few Italian *contadini* had really settled the matter and had probably saved his life.

Twenty-Two

We argued all the way back in the car as Alan tried to focus on the dark road through his broken spectacles; no matter what subject came to mind, we managed to disagree. Alan asked me what I thought of *The Waste Land*.

"I wasn't impressed with it," I said dismissively. "It's too dry and unfeeling for my taste. It will probably be forgotten in a few years' time."

"Dry? It's a masterpiece of irony."

"Let me tell you what irony means for a Sicilian," I replied. "It's when a man finds his wife has been unfaithful to him, so he lies in wait for her lover and by mistake, he kills his own brother. That is irony."

He shook his head in dismay.

Whatever we said, neither of us could understand the other's attitude towards the brawl between the gangers and the Italians. To me, it had seemed a natural, human gesture to go to Alan's assistance and ask the Italians to help me.

"It's only aggravated the whole situation, Gwen."

"Oh, don't sound so pompous, Alan."

"You know there's bad blood between the Italians and the gangers. The police are always breaking up scuffles at the pub when they start slinging off at each other. Don't you think it's possible now that the gangers will want a return match?"

"Those were Calabresi. They know how to fight."

"For pity's sake! Whose side were you on?"

"Yours, of course."

"I can appreciate what you did, but there was no need to involve the Italians."

"I hardly think they would have stood there and watched me fight for you."

"I would have got out of it somehow."

"Don't you remember what happened? They had you down and they were kicking you."

He rubbed his side and winced.

"Yes, I recall that—"

"And you still want to talk about the law?"

"If you don't invoke the law, what do you have left, Gwen? A mob of drunks punching each other up."

"Maybe I am a Sicilian after all," I said tersely and we didn't talk again until we were back in Griffith.

At the office, Alan put his arms around me and kissed me.

"I'm just getting used to loving a celebrated beauty, now I find she's Joan of Arc in disguise. Give me a chance."

I watched him drive off towards Wyangan Avenue and again the serpent voice asked me if my feeling for Alan was like the great love that had taken possession of my parents and transformed them. Sometimes, memory can be a consolation, which is probably why old people live so comfortably with the companions of their past; occasionally, it remains in the system like a poison ready to erupt and infect every action of the present. The whole scale of our being had seemed changed as Alan and I were sitting in the shadow of the towering wall of the Burrinjuck Dam. Often when we were alone together in the bush we made love with an exquisite perception that we were not only part of each other but sharing the warm blur of life around us; that wall had humbled and diminished us. While we were speaking there, our voices were unnaturally hushed, with long silences between sentences. We talked artificially and pretentiously about aqueducts and Roman engineers because we were crushed by the oppressive weight of that concrete cliff. In Chinese paintings, the figure of a man is dwarfed by the landscape above and around him and that is how I felt when I considered my love for Alan and then remembered my parents' love. If what they had known was love, then I was unworthy even to speak that word.

The following day, Alan told me grimly that his mother had taken to her bed with what she insisted was a heart attack and when the doctor told her it was hysteria, she had threatened to commit suicide.

"Do you think that's likely?" I asked, trying to repress a hopeful inflection.

"He doesn't think so. She has a couple of her admirers in looking after her. Oh yes, she has a few. Of course, there's so little to do in Griffith that someone like my mother becomes a fascinating hobby for these lonely old ducks—the last war left a lot of widows. They even believe Mum was a great prima donna in London before she married Dad. Eighteen months in the chorus of the Carl Rosa Opera company was about the most she ever managed."

The following Thursday the *Griffith Gazette* published Busy Bee's account of the harvest ball over double pages with photographs surrounded by decorative scrolls. In the middle was an oval picture of me looking startled and curiously named, "Gwen d'Harcourt of the old Shropshire family." There was a brief notice of my forthcoming marriage to Alan Gilchrist, son of the late Hon. Gordon Gilchrist, KC and Mrs Valmai Gilchrist of Wyangan Avenue, and a much longer description of my dress.

"Shall we guess at a price of a thousand guineas for this captivating creation from the House of Chanel in Paris where the royalty and aristocracy of Europe purchase their ball gowns?" I knew that Norma Reynolds must get the paper and I hoped she was laughing as much as I was when I had finished Busy Bee's rapturous description, borne aloft on wings of fractured French: *"Tout chic," "ravissement de beauté," "élégance et charme en tissu de moiré."* In an especially convoluted passage Busy Bee mentioned the price of a thousand guineas again, intimating that the harvest ball at Griffith was not unworthy of such an expense for a ball gown and what a great pity it was that some of the women present were wearing hand-me-downs and had not seemed to appreciate (from Busy Bee's clear recollection of last year's gowns) that the harvest ball warranted a lady presenting herself in the very finest raiment that her purse would permit.

I saw Norma Reynolds and her husband coming out of the bank that afternoon. Len had his head down and was walking ahead, while she trailed behind. He did not see me but when I passed them, Norma smiled at me, and her smile was followed by a wink. Immediately, she seemed almost ashamed of having been deflected from partnership in her husband's misery and bustled up alongside him and said something to him. He did not hear her or even seem aware that she was there.

It was a little after dawn when I heard sounds outside the wall of my bedroom and at first I thought it must be a stray dog. I went out to the back, but could see nothing at first through the film of autumn mist that was silvering the bushes. Then, wrapped in black shawls, they were before me.

Rafaella shook her fist at me and Martina's hands were extended like claws.

"Where is the money?" Martina screamed.

"You have spent the gold of an orphan on a dress!"

"There was no money in Giacopo's house. Go away before I call the police."

Rafaella began to wail, rocking back and forth.

Martina's belly was swollen and she lurched towards me, raking the space of air between us.

"A thousand guineas! A thousand guineas!" she shrieked over and over again.

"Listen to me, both of you!" I shouted. "There was no money in that house and the dress was made from an old petticoat!"

Martina threw back her head, wailing. "It was in the newspaper. Giovanni and Michaelo read it to us. A thousand guineas for a dress from Paris."

"Do you always believe the lies they print in newspapers? Who would be mad enough to pay a thousand guineas for a dress? I could tell you who made it for me here in Griffith."

"The child saw you!" Rafaella pointed at me. "She looked through the window and saw you at the table counting the gold sovereigns."

"This is nonsense. Angelica is making up fairy stories."

"Give us back the money!" Martina wailed.

"Go home and forget this rubbish," I retorted.

"Gold in your hands. Angelica saw the coins."

Martina was writhing with anger, clutching her belly with one hand and tearing at her hair with the other.

"You will die for this! We will kill you!"

I turned and slammed the door on them, closing my ears to their threats and curses. The absurdity of an old petticoat causing such fury was like a farce but there was nothing comic in the women's rage. A faint prickle of fear made me shiver and I put on a cardigan and made myself some coffee.

How could I convince the Sciafas that Giacopo had not been a miser with a bag of gold hidden in his house? He had probably lied to his family, boasting of his wealth, using it like a bludgeon to cow his brothers. It is not always reality that determines people's actions, but what they believe to be reality, and often that belief is shaped by desire. If a man charges you with killing his pet dragon, how can you defend yourself? Can you say that dragons do not exist while he insists that he followed a trail of dragon's blood to your doorstep? The passage in the *Griffith Gazette* said that my dress cost a thousand guineas in Paris and the Sciafas accepted it because they wanted to believe that I had stolen Giacopo's money.

Half dozing in my chair I tried to push all thought of the Sciafas from my mind and soon I must have been asleep. If what happened next was a dream, it had all the power of a vision because although I struggled to wake, my limbs had no strength and my lids were so heavy I could see only a thread of light. They had come for me, the women in black, and they were carrying me on their shoulders to the grotto. The rock was pressing against my head as they forced me down into the crevice and already the pain was like a vise twisting my body.

I woke suddenly and found my head between the edge of the chair and the table with my whole body contorted, but even as I recognized familiar shapes, the horror remained with me. Absurd as it may have been, I knew as I rubbed my aching neck that the Sciafas had been sitting together as a family and planning my death. Not only had I disgraced them, they now believed that I had robbed Benno and Giacopo. The honour of the family would have kept them silent until they read about the thousand guineas in the newspaper and then honour would demand revenge even if they all stood convicted of murder. For weeks I had felt that Rosalia's prophecy was nothing more than a shadow in my past, now I saw it looming before me.

Fred Dangler arrived early that morning with a note from Alan saying that he had to go to Canberra for a hearing of the Water Conservation and Irrigation Commission and would not be back until Friday.

"Don't assume I'm in charge," Fred said. "I tell everyone that a woman's the boss here."

At noon I happened to look up from my typewriter and saw Aldo Sciafa across the street staring at me, and in the afternoon Paulo was there in the same spot. I said nothing to Fred but when Tommy arrived after school he announced that I must have an admirer.

"One of the Sciafas." He grinned. "But he's married."

I shrugged and told him I had no time to waste looking out of the window at every lounger. One moment, I felt like running to Paulo and screaming that there was no money, that he was crazy with greed and the child was lying. The next, I decided to take the dress and throw it at his feet. The result was that I remained silent until a message came from Alan's house.

Mrs Gilchrist insisted that I see her at once and reluctantly I walked round to Wyangan Avenue, aware that now Giovanni Sciafa was following me.

There were only three dogs on her bed but they all jumped up and barked furiously at me when I sat down. I recognized a fourth as Siegfried, who had appropriated one of the pillows and was snoring next to her head. The frowsty little woman who had shown me in solicitously plumped Mrs Gilchrist's pillows, without disturbing Siegfried, before she reluctantly left us alone together, closing the door with an ostentatious flourish.

Mrs Gilchrist's hair was parted in the middle of her head, held back from her face by a broad blue ribbon that made her look like an old doll masquerading as a child.

"My heart—" she said musically.

"Why do you want to speak to me?" I asked bluntly.

"My daughter-in-law—my future daughter-in-law." She sighed. "I was overcome with passion when I spoke to you last and my words were harsh. Now, I beg your forgiveness."

"I'm glad you can accept our engagement, Mrs Gilchrist."

"Oh, I must accept the inevitable. When you're young, you're full of hope, but at my age—what am I but a poor sick old woman, unloved and uncared for?"

"You have friends and your son, Mrs Gilchrist."

I should also have said that she had me, but I could not bring myself to say that.

"Now I'm dying and when I'm dead you will be able to get married without a worry in the world. Why should a young man have to carry the burden of his mother? You're right. Everyone is right and I have been weak and selfish." She began to cry and one of the dogs whimpered in sympathy. "These are my only true friends." She hugged each dog in turn. "You will not have to wait long."

"Mrs Gilchrist, are you saying that you don't want Alan to marry me until you're dead?"

"Such a little time—a year at the most."

"The doctor says you're a healthy woman and there's nothing wrong with your heart."

"Heart? Heart? He is referring to a mechanical pump. I am speaking of the HEART that is breaking."

It began to sound like the refrain of a popular song and I repressed a smile.

"You are a bitterly sour and cynical young woman who will not make Alan happy. That boy has been my whole existence."

The tables on either side of her bed were covered with photos of Alan at various ages and with a sweeping gesture she laid claim to his whole life.

"I love him—he is all I have left. You mustn't take him from me—not so abruptly."

It was a conversation I could envisage stretching down through the years, with Mrs Gilchrist begging for time and Alan asking me to be understanding.

"No. We are not going to wait. Alan and I are planning to be married in May."

She half rose from her pillows and pointed dramatically.

"An unlucky month! There is no good fortune found in May!"

"Mrs Gilchrist, there is no reason why we should discuss this any further. Our minds are made up and you must reconcile yourself."

"To being alone? To living without a man in the house? I can't endure it! I won't! It's inhuman and savage of you to ask this. I love him! I love my son!"

"No, you don't," I shouted and the frowsty little woman almost fell into the room. "If you loved him you'd want nothing more than his happiness, but you're only concerned with your own comfort."

"I can't see why you should be in such a hurry to get married," the frowsty little woman said. "You're not in the pudding club, are you?"

All the dogs yapped in unison when I left but even through their clamour I could hear Mrs Gilchrist screaming and wailing like a mad Lucia through a dozen different octaves.

The footsteps were behind me and at the corner I swung round and faced Giovanni.

"Leave me alone!" I said. "I shall go to the police and complain that you're following me."

"You do that," he said. "Maybe the police ought to know about the money you stole."

Michaelo stepped out of the shadows and was at my shoulder.

"I reckon someone should tell Mr Gilchrist that he's marrying a *puttana* and a thief."

"Tell him what you like," I shouted and tried to push past them. I think it was Michaelo who tripped me, but when I fell, Giovanni forced my face into the road and kicked me. I clambered to my feet and ran towards the light at the end of the street. They followed me, jeering and catcalling, and I saw a straggle of clients waiting on the veranda.

"Don't worry. The harvest is over. We've plenty of time on our hands. We'll get you. That's just a taste of what we have in mind for you," Giovanni said.

"Come on, there's too many people around," Michaelo whined. "I want to go home. Christ, I'm feeling crook."

The side of my face was bruised and pocked with gravel, and I hurried around the back of the house to my room where I washed the dirt from my face and hair. When Fred asked me what had happened I told him that I'd been knocked down by a passing sulky. That night I locked and bolted every door, but twice I woke, shaking with fright, because I was certain that someone was outside and next time, I knew, they would kill me.

Fear alone did not keep me awake: my head was burning and the grazes on my knee and ankle felt as if they were infected, yet all this was nothing when I considered how the truth would affect Alan. When he returned, I would have to tell him about the grotto and what I had done there and I knew it would be like taking him by the hand into a world of nightmare and death. He did not have the blood to understand my life. Yet I was resolved to marry him, if only because I yearned for the security of the commonplace and the chance to lead a life shared by thousands of young women my age. For too long I had been a reluctant rebel, driven off from settled places and made to find my way through wild and isolated passages. This was my chance to return to ordinary and accepted paths where women found partners and walked comfortably in the state of marriage. The four little diamonds were the promise of protection and acceptance and I wanted that promise fulfilled. Mrs Gilchrist would oppose the marriage but Alan was my lover before he was her son. He spoke about law and duty when we argued, as we often did, but when we were in each other's arms and I felt his flesh throbbing in my body as though it wanted to possess every part of me, I knew he was mine. The Sciafas, however, were a different threat, driven by madness and greed.

As I lay there thinking, Rosalia returned to me. When I turned my head, I almost expected to see her standing there, watching me, her hands folded under her black shawl. I remembered walking across Trapani with her and how people stepped aside, nodding nervously to her, and how, after she had passed, they surreptitiously made the *mano cornuta*. When I crawled across the roof of our house and looked down into the street, I saw how the women bowed to her and the men took off their caps and spoke deferentially because they feared her power as a *jettatora*, a *strega* possessed of the *malocchio* who could command the powers of darkness. Unconsciously, my hand was holding the coral *corno* that Miki had given me when I was a child and, in that same instant, my resolution was formed and I determined to make the Sciafas quail before me as I had seen the *contadini* tremble when Rosalia spoke to them.

The following day at dusk I borrowed Fred's bike, hung a lantern from the back seat and rode out to Aldo's farm, almost a mile past Giacopo's property. There were lights in the house and after I propped the bike against a post and crept up to the veranda I saw them all at one table: Aldo and Martina, the two boys between them, and, with their backs to me, Paulo, Rafaella, their son and the little girl, Angelica. Martina was shrilling and I heard my name, for who else could the *puttana* be? A dog growled somewhere near and then I heard a chain rattle as the growls changed to a frenzied barking. I took the lantern from the bike and held it in front of me.

Aldo was first to the door and the rest followed him. I stood in front of the steps and spoke:

"By Saints Zita *verfine*, Abbondio *vescovo*, Avia *martire*, Filippo e Giacomo, Pellegrino *martire*, by Mattia *apostolo*, Medardo *verscovo* and Saint Vito *martire*, I curse this house and those within it. I drink blood as I drink gold and it is not money that I need to quench my thirst now but blood. The saints of heaven witness this curse and the fiends of hell confirm it. Though my soul burn eternally in the fires of hell I call upon the power to blight this house as I shall blight your trees."

Aldo began to bluster and was about to walk down the steps towards me, jabbing the air with his fist, when Paulo pulled him back. I cursed them through the litany of saints and the demons of the inferno who tear the flesh of sinners with red-hot pincers and flaming knives and when I was finished, the two women were on their knees praying and Aldo and Paulo were making the *mano cornuta* at me. I spat three times on the ground and rode off into the darkness.

Would the two boys follow me? I kept looking back over my shoulder but there was no sound behind me and when I arrived back at the office I began to feel safe. However, there was a curse to be fulfilled: next day I went to the produce store and bought three salt-licks, the kind that farmers left in a corner of their paddocks for their cattle. They were heavy and I decided that the only way I could get them out to the farm was to load them in a sack and carry them on my back.

When Alan returned from Canberra, he said he had just been home and he said his mother was hysterical. The doctor had called again and given her a sedative.

"She wants us to wait until next year to get married," he said drearily.

"Oh yes, she told me the same thing. I said we were getting married next month."

Alan sat with his hands clasped around his knees, his brow creased.

"Does it make so much difference if we wait?"

"Yes, it does!" I cried. "Of course, it's more convenient for you like this. After all, you get what you want every time you come here and you don't have to give me a home. I'm like a prostitute you've hired on a long-term lease. It was quite common in Sicily for a man to make his selection from the bordello and pay to have one woman kept for his services alone. She was no longer a common *puttana* then but a *mantenuta*—I didn't know that was the custom here in Australia too."

"You have a filthy mind, Gwen, and a tongue to match it!"

"The filth is what you're doing to me! Everyone knows we sleep together, that you spend part of every night here with me. Some of the men must be congratulating you on being able to get a woman who'll work for you and service you so cheaply."

I thought he was going to strike me. His hand was raised and I watched him lower it slowly with his eyes closed as though he could not bear to look at me.

"Gwen—why, why are you talking like this?"

"I want you to swear that we'll be married next month."

For a moment, he seemed to be wrestling with himself and again I had the vision of the man who was strangling himself to relieve his pain.

"We'll be married whenever you want, Gwen."

Involuntarily, I cried out as he pulled me to him and kissed me.

"I'm sorry," he said. "I didn't mean to hurt you."

He touched my bruised face with his finger.

"It doesn't hurt any longer," I said and led him towards the bed. There would be no doubts left when I opened the front of my blouse and placed his hands over my breasts.

Later, when Alan was about to leave, he asked me diffidently if I would like him to order a table for us at Mirrool House the following night and I generously said that he should sit with his mother. Our lovemaking that night had been passionate and I had held him in me until he was exhausted and fell back gasping. Yet as we lay there, my hand gently stroking his thigh, I had flinched with a spasm of shame because I thought this must be what a whore did when she feigned more passion than she felt and used lust to control a man. Neither of us was experienced in the ways of love but I sensed that I had become part of Alan's being; he could no more live without me than he could exist without air.

As soon as Alan left the following evening to have dinner with his mother, I packed the salt-licks into an old sack and bicycled out towards Aldo Sciafa's farm. The channels to the orchards were opened every evening by Dethbridge wheels that measured the amount of water released and I would have to leave the bike by the road and carry the salt down to the channel. Twice I had to stop and rest because my back was like a rod of fire; I was bending so far over the handle bars that I almost fell.

My father had told me once how the *contadini* punished a *padrone* who ill-treated them and skimped their wages. When the time came to weed the vineyard, they went out with pockets full of salt and dug a handful into the roots of each vine. The withering was always gradual but eventually the vines turned black and died. The Romans had salted the fields of Carthage after the city was conquered and now I would do the same to Aldo's fruit trees. When they were blighted and dying the Sciafas would know I had the *malocchio* and the power to curse them.

I left the bike under some dusty bushes at the side of the dirt track and carried one of the salt-licks through the trees and down to the canal. There was no one about—Sciafa's house was in darkness and the dog barked with the peremptory unease a watchdog has when it knows it is alone and nobody can come to its aid. I soon found the Dethbridge wheel. The channels were already trickling with water. Quickly, I dropped the salt-lick into a channel leading to a paddock of young trees. It dissolved in minutes. Demeter could blast the fields or give life as she chose, and a surge of triumph rushed through me as I watched the salted water trickling off through the trees.

Two more would make their destruction certain and I crept back swiftly to the road. My bike was there but the sack was gone and I looked round feverishly for it.

"If you want the salt, it's in the car," Alan said.

"Why did you follow me?"

"Because I was worried about you. Tommy saw what direction you'd taken."

He strapped the bike on to the back of the car and told me to get in.

"What were you planning to do?" he asked me.

"I was going to salt Aldo Sciafa's new paddock."

"You realize that's a federal offence?"

"I don't care what it is. His two boys pushed me down the other night and I wanted to punish them."

"By salting their orchard!"

"Yes—it's an old Sicilian custom."

"Damn you, Gwen! I'm sick of hearing about these Sicilian barbarisms. This is Australia and if you can't live here like a decent, civilized human being you should bloody well go back where you came from."

"Let me out of the car!" I screamed.

"Not until we have this out!"

"There is nothing I can say to you—nothing that you would ever understand! I had to curse them!"

How could I go back to the beginning and explain the *mano cornuta* to him and what it meant to have been threatened with the grotto? There was no way to express what I felt and all I feared, and if I could have struggled to make myself understood in Italian, I knew Alan had less than a dozen words in that language. At least, he did not know that I had already dropped one of the salt-licks into the channel, that death was already finding its way to the roots of the young trees.

"If the Sciafas had seen you doing this, they would have been justified in trying to kill you. As it is, they're all in town."

"Looking for me?"

"No, they're at the hospital. Mike Sciafa has come down with polio. If he lives he could well be a cripple. Are you going to claim that as a result of your curse?"

There was nothing I could say and I remained silent, staring at the dark road. Alan stopped the car near Scenic Park and asked me to promise never to speak to the Sciafas again unless he was with me. It was not a difficult promise to give because I no longer had any fear of them. One night I had stood in front of their house and cursed them and the next their son had a disease that almost always crippled when it did not kill.

"Would you like me to have the other brother charged with assault?"

I shook my head and he stroked my hair.

"God knows I try to understand you, Gwen, but there are times when I feel as though I'm talking to someone from another planet."

"Never try to find out where that planet is," I said and heard my voice thick with tears. "You don't belong in such a savage place."

A week later I was working at my desk when I looked up and saw Martina and Rafaella.

They sat down awkwardly and I did not ask them what they wanted.

"Spare him. Spare my nephew," Rafaella said brokenly.

"Lift the curse from him," Martina cried and placed her hands on her belly.

"Do not harm this child."

"The curse has run its full measure," I said and the women looked at each other in relief.

"She is not all devil," Rafaella said and helped Martina to her feet. At the edge of the veranda they both turned and surreptitiously made the *mano cornuta* at me and I pretended not to see them.

Twenty-Three

Mrs Heffernan had just finished telling me that the Reynoldses were leaving their farm at the end of the week when Norma came in and placed three single pound notes and a handful of silver on the counter.

"That should settle the account, Mrs Heffernan. I've been the rounds and paid up everything we owe at the shops. I wish I could have done the same at the bank—but they won't lose. They'll soon find a Dago to buy the farm."

"You'll be back one day, Mrs Reynolds," Mrs Heffernan said cheerfully, picking up the money with obvious relief, scattering half a dozen hairpins as she closed the till.

Norma and I walked back down the street together and I told her that I wished she could win a lottery or inherit a fortune and stay in Griffith.

"No such luck!" She laughed shortly. "I'll give you my address in Sydney—just in case you need another Paris ballgown. You know, Gwen, that gave me the only decent laugh I've had this year. I sat at the kitchen table where I'd cut out that dress and I laughed until my ribs were fit to bust. Len thought I was hysterical and wanted to throw a bucket of water over me. I couldn't tell him about it—not about the old petticoat."

Carefully, I folded the slip of paper she gave me and placed it in my notebook.

"You should really set up a business of your own, Norma. You have golden hands."

"Len would never permit it, love. You're not married yet so you don't understand that when your husband says no, you do as he says."

"I don't see why."

"Because it's right and the Bible says you should."

"When I'm married to Alan I'll go on working at the office."

"Maybe you will and maybe you won't. That'll be for him to say. No proper man likes his wife to work. He's the breadwinner—it's a sort of slur against his ability to support a family if the wife is working." She paused and gave me a sidelong glance. "It's all right, is it? With his mother, I mean."

"Yes," I replied shortly.

"I did hear she was carrying on a treat."

"Alan and I are getting married very quietly in May. There won't be a reception or anything like that."

"Well, I can understand that, love. What with prices down for fruit again and the whole state tied up with this coal strike. Len says we're in for another depression like the 1890s—that's when his father had to walk away from his property in the Riverina."

"We may go to Melbourne for a few days as a honeymoon."

"Sounds like heaven to me. My parents are going to put us all up. There's not much room in their house but Len will get his job back at the bank and the kids will have to sleep on the veranda until we can afford to rent a place of our own. They'll miss the life here—" She seemed to lose the thread of her words and began to cry quietly. "Len always dreamed of going back on the land. He hated city life—it's so hard on him and he's a real battler, no one can say he didn't work."

Everyone was complaining about falling prices and the Reynoldses were not the only family who had to leave their farms; only the Italians were prospering and by now they were the greater part of our clients. Everyone said that business was bad but our law office was flourishing; one day Alan showed me the blueprint of offices he planned to build near the main row of shops in Banna Avenue.

"I've bought the land and we could start building in July."

"Where are we going to live, Alan?"

"Why—upstairs, over the offices. We'll have a modern flat there."

I liked the idea of this, possibly because it reminded me of my home in Trapani with the museum downstairs and the living rooms above it. There was a bubbling excitement when we stood on the land together and Alan walked the length of the future walls and told me he was planning offices for at least three lawyers.

"One of them will have to be Italian," I said. "You should make Tommy an articled clerk."

"I've already spoken to his father," Alan replied.

My future was spread out on that bare ground where nothing was buried, no ruins of ancient settlements or the broken pots and crumbling bronzes that revealed the people who had drunk wine and cut meat without a thought for those who would come to build where they had spent their daily lives. We were the first builders and it would be for other generations to examine our remains and wonder how we had lived.

I heard that Michaelo Sciafa recovered at the hospital and that the polio had only left him with a twisted leg. There was an outbreak of the disease in the area that autumn and others were not so fortunate. Every week in the *Griffith Gazette* we read of another child who had died or was left paralysed, and no one had any idea what caused it or how to cure it except, of course, the Sciafas who knew that I had cursed their son and then saved him from death. They did not bother me again and once when I saw Paulo and Rafaella at the post office, they looked askance at me and fled.

Three weeks before our marriage, Fred and I were working at our desks in the front office.

"Women—there's no stopping them," Fred said. "Look at this Irene Longman—she's been elected to the Queensland parliament. It's the beginning—soon you won't be eligible to stand for office unless you're female."

It was late afternoon and I was trying to make sense of a complaint that Nicolo Briaggi had brought us about a new allotment that was being proposed near his farm when Alan came in carrying Siegfried.

"That's a nice-looking dog," Fred said.

Alan dropped the dog on the floor and Siegfried waddled over to Fred and wagged his tail.

"Would you—Fred, would you mind taking him for a walk—or something," Alan said hoarsely.

"Not in the least. I should have dropped these files off at the council offices this morning."

He whistled and Siegfried waddled after him, keeping an exact three paces behind Fred as though he were a trained Queensland heeler.

Alan slumped in Fred's chair and put his head in his hands. I waited for him to speak.

"They're dead," he said finally, then stared at me. "Can't you say anything?"

"I thought you might explain what you meant if I waited."

"God knows, you have the tongue of a viper at times, Gwen, but sometimes I think it's worse when you're silent."

"If you want to argue with me, at least let's have a subject, Alan."

"They're dead," he said dully and I realized he hadn't heard me. He wanted the sound of a voice, any sound, to intrude between himself and what he knew he must tell me.

"I came home—about an hour ago. They were in the hall, everywhere—little bloody heaps of fur. She's killed the dogs."

"Except Siegfried."

"He was asleep in a wardrobe. I had to bring him here."

"Where is your mother now?"

"The doctor's with her and two of the neighbours. I cleaned up what I could—buried the dogs in the back yard. Mrs James said she'd finish inside the house."

"It was a mad thing to do. She must have been crazy."

"She screamed at me—said that she'd kill herself next."

I waited for him to finish but he stared at me with anguish in his eyes. The coldness was spreading from my heart through my whole body and I thought if I had to move suddenly I would stumble and fall. I was numb with dread.

"She doesn't want you to marry me, Alan."

"No—no, she's not asking that, Gwen. All she wants is a little time."

"What is a little time? Last time I saw her it was a year."

"That's all, Gwen. A year isn't so long."

"And what will she want next May—another year—and another year after that? I tell you, Alan, I can see the future as if it were a blueprint in front of me on that desk. She's still there between us, older and crazier, and we are older too."

"Gwen, we can live together. We'll have the apartment—"

"I want to be married. I'm sick of being your mistress."

"She's my mother, Gwen, and I promised my father that I'd care for her."

"At my expense?"

"I can't let her commit suicide."

"Oh, she won't harm herself, Alan."

"Those dogs were her life and yet she took a knife and butchered them."

"No, they were not her life. Every one of them was a child, a child that never grew up and wanted to leave her. A child that she could kill when it annoyed her. Those dogs were you, Alan, the child she wants you to remain."

"Gwen, I have—for my father's sake! God, I love you but what—"

"No, you don't love me enough."

I wanted to tell him that I knew my father would have sacrificed the world if my mother had asked him, that there was nothing, not my life or any other thing, that would have prevented him doing what my mother wanted.

"Please, Gwen, I'm not asking for so much. I just need a year to get her used to the idea. I swear, if in a year's time she still won't agree, we'll get married at her funeral if that's the way it turns out."

He was kissing me and I could feel his tears on my skin but it was as if I were frozen.

"For God's sake, answer me, Gwen!"

"Either we get married now or I shall leave you."

"You can't give me an ultimatum like that!"

"Why not? Hasn't your mother given us one?"

"A year is not so very long, Gwen—"

It was his reasonableness that enraged me. In love, the kind of love that I wanted, there can be only a passion that reason cannot deflect from its object.

"Obviously your feeling for me is like an old coat that you can put on and take off at your convenience, Alan."

I would goad and torment him until he gave me his life and his soul for I would settle for nothing less than the love my mother had been given by my father. Moments passed as he stared at me and I could feel him struggling against a tide of anger that was visibly shaking him.

"The game's always yours, isn't it, Gwen? Always demanding to know how much I love you, setting terms and times as if I'm being examined in a court of love where you're the judge, the jury and the prosecuting attorney. Isn't it enough that I've told you in a thousand ways and shown you in as many more how much you mean to me? I'm—I'm terrified at times at the power you have over me, especially because I know I can't trust you."

"Trust!" I screamed. "Love is all trust."

"I don't trust you because I don't understand you. Is it rational to salt a man's orchard, to blight his trees because you have a grudge against him? Tell me what you're afraid of, why you can't appeal to the law for redress. I'm a lawyer, I can help you."

Should I have told Alan then about the grotto and what I had killed there?

"My love for you is as strong as my life, but I'm always the defendant and the verdict against me is guilty, or at the best, not proven."

Because I knew he was right I became angrier and I scarcely heard what he was saying to me. I remember shouting that he would come to me on his knees—

"You're the lodestar of my life, Gwen, but I'm not going to become your bloody slave."

"You don't love me enough!" I cried over and over.

What was I crying for? Not Alan and not myself, but my parents and all the grief of Sicily. It was not rational and perhaps I was as mad then as I was when I ran through the pale forest with Bessie, but I expected Alan to compensate me for what I had lost.

"Have I ever asked you how much you love me?" he challenged me.

"No, you took it for granted that I worshipped you."

"Never worship, Gwen. I'd lay down my life for you but I won't grovel at your feet and call you God, if that's what you want."

I remembered my father taking my mother's hands across the table and kissing each in turn.

"You will always be part of my life, but not the whole of it. I'm not going to sacrifice duty and obligation to satisfy this ravening romantic hunger of yours. Nothing I could do or say would ever be enough, Gwen. Don't you think I have dreams and ambitions of my own? I don't want to spend the rest of my life here in Griffith. There's a world out there I've never seen and should see if I'm ever going to do anything for this country. Yes, I'm ambitious to accomplish more than my father, but first I have to make something of myself. My father left very little, and what he did leave, my mother went through in a couple of years. I've had to work to establish myself. A poor man has no freedom in politics—and that's what I want to become eventually: member for this electorate, cabinet minister, prime minister. I talk about the bench and becoming a judge, but that's not what I really want. The chance to carry on my father's work—this is a bloody great country and I want to help it grow. Gwen, you could share that life with me. Christ! I sound like a pompous idiot."

He was shocked by the passion of his eloquence and mumbled something about soapbox oratory.

"Ah, now you at least appreciate my value as a clerk."

He had revealed himself to me and I struck at his confession as if it were an open wound. His face darkened and he raised his hand as if he were going to strike me, opening and closing his fist and deliberately looking away from me.

"My father used to read Shelley—there were two lines—'In many mortal forms I rashly sought/The shadow of that idol of my thought.' I don't know who is the greater romantic—you, Gwen, because you want something that I doubt even exists—"

Oh, but it did, I thought, and I lived with it for all the years of my childhood.

"Or me, for imagining that I had found a woman whose love equalled mine."

"You'll beg me to return to you, Alan."

"Romantics are always prophets—and they're generally wrong. I've told you, I won't beg and I won't put on chains for you."

Perhaps I should have spoken about my parents then, and how a great love never equivocates or seeks delay; it is a seamless web that excludes universes of concern. Instead, I was silent and when Fred came back with Siegfried at his heels, we were sitting opposite each other staring at emptiness.

"That's a really nice dog," Fred said. "He's taken to me."

"He's yours."

"Your mother doesn't want him?"

"No."

"He'll be company for me at the hotel. They won't object to a dog that size. I can keep him in my room and he can sit here under the desk when I'm working."

Alan did not believe me when I said I was leaving but that night I began to pack with a dry anger that made my fingers clumsy, as though I were an old woman with rheumatism in my knuckles. Alan's mother had spilled blood and the sacrifice of that blood had been answered.

3

Sydney

Twenty-Four

A little before dawn I walked down to the railway station and found Vanda waiting for the milk train. I told him I needed a carter for some boxes and we haggled for half an hour over the price. At eight o'clock I was sitting beside him on the seat of his clattering, jingling cart with my boxes and bags behind me. On the way, we passed Fred, walking towards the office with Siegfried at his heels, but he was so engrossed in a conversation with the dog that he did not see me. As the train lurched out from the station like a late-night drunk leaving a pub, I wondered if Alan would come round to the office in the morning or wait until the afternoon. I had left my letter to him on the narrow bed where we had so often made love; in a corner of the envelope I had placed the ring with its four little diamonds.

It was not possible to keep the bitterness and anger from the words I wrote—I was at pains to remind him that a good part of the success of his law firm had been due to me and all the Italians who had become his clients. If he kept Tommy Ruffano, the business would continue to prosper and he would undoubtedly remain the most eligible bachelor in Griffith. Perhaps Ellie Sanderson might be persuaded to take my place in his life and he could then marry her in a year's time. There were other things I said to him that I'm ashamed to remember: imperious demands and accusations so cruel that I wince now when I think of them, but as I wrote I saw Valmai Vitale in my mind and insensibly she became my own mother. I was going to Sydney and there was no point in his trying to follow me or find me because I never wanted to see him again. It was not easy to write those lines because the well-trodden phrases that a thousand disappointed angry lovers had used still managed to burn with my anger and grief. If I really had possessed the power to curse, I would have called down the plagues of hell on Alan's mother. I could imagine her, propped up against her pillows, singing her new role as bereaved parent who must console her wayward son for the loss of a most undesirable daughter-in-law.

Yes, I did love Alan then, even if my love was not the passion that had fired my parents. And losing him, I knew that I had forfeited my place in that ordinary world where girls waited for husbands and planned their future lives as wives and mothers. Marriage was respectable and customary and for me at that time it had all the savour of fresh bread and cheese when you are starving. Now, I was alone again and far from the settled places where people found their comfort. Yet, not once, even as I grieved, did I think of turning back.

The green outside the window was changing to the dusty gold of stubbled wheat fields and the burnished haze continued for miles. I had not slept for over thirty hours and, exhausted, I stretched out in the empty compartment with my head on a rolled cardigan and felt the pain of anger fade like a breath on glass. It was early afternoon when I woke; the guard put his head in the door and told me that I'd slept clear through lunch at Cootamundra. I told him I was very hungry and he said he thought he could snatch a few sandwiches from first class for me.

In my purse I found the two Sydney addresses: I kept one in my hand and folded the slip of paper from Norma and carefully put it back. There would be no room for me in her parents' house in Coogee. Possibly I was still muddled with sleep and famished but I suddenly realized that someone was sitting opposite me. She was looking out of the window and the sunlight made her red hair incandescent. I must have cried out for she slowly turned her head and smiled conspiratorially as she always did when there was a secret she was about to share with me. It was Bessie—not the Bessie who said goodbye to me that last summer in Trapani, but Bessie when she was twelve, wearing a pink sprigged muslin and a necklace of seed pearls. She leaned forward as if to whisper to me—and she was gone.

When the guard came back with a bag of sandwiches I had my head in my hands and I was crying. He told me I'd feel better when I'd had something to eat as I tried to make sense of what had happened. It was an omen, I was sure of that; if Rosalia had been there she would have interpreted it for me. Even so, I was certain that Bessie had come to me as a sign of good fortune. When the train arrived in Sydney the following morning I felt an ease of spirit that I had not known for years. Besides, in my heart I was certain of Alan's love and I knew that he would follow me.

Only a stray cat seemed as interested in the Rutledge Arms as I was; when no one answered my knock at the front door I looked for a side entrance. The cat miaowed silently and slipped under a gate in a paling fence with its tabby striped tail pointed like an arrow for me to follow.

Two people were arguing in a kitchen at the back as I walked down the narrow passage and soon I could make out the drift.

"A poofter! A poofter and a ponce! That's what you are and don't try to say the contrary because I remember you and that rotten little piece of muck and garbage. I remember—"

That was a woman's voice like chalk on a blackboard. A man's voice responded, deep and timbred like a bell.

"Florrie dear, be reasonable—"

"Taps still means more to you than I ever will!"

"Florrie—"

Neither of them heard my knock so I opened the door and walked in just as a pound of butter landed with a thud and stuck to the icebox. From the direction, I suspected that the thrower was Florrie.

Both of them stood gaping at me: Henry Frock, a slender, diminutive man with suspiciously black hair vaselined across a bulging forehead and Florrie, tall and spare with a curdled complexion and netted curls. I explained that I was a good friend of Taps and he had said I should come to the Rutledge Arms if I ever needed a room.

"A friend of Taps Desmond?" Florrie said incredulously and raked me up and down.

"You heard her," Henry said. "A very good friend was what she said."

"I would never have believed it," Florrie said finally. "A nice-looking girl like you and that nasty little piece of you know what. Well, the War took the best men and only the riff-raff were left for us women."

After Florrie had casually scraped the butter from the icebox as though it was the usual place to keep it cool, she made tea and we sat and talked.

"We can let you have a room providing you don't want anything fancy and Henry here will get your stuff from the station. But as for a job—"

"Times are very bad—very bad indeed," Henry intoned.

"There's thousands and thousands out of work. Some say it's as high as twenty per cent and rising. We've felt it here in the pub, I can tell you. Takings are down, way down."

"I'll find work but perhaps I could help out here until I get what I want. I'm used to hotels."

Florrie sniffed. "We've got a regular barmaid and Henry does most of the heavy work."

"At least, if I worked, it would pay for the cost of my room until I found a position."

Florrie insisted that I pay her a week's rent in advance and I gave her two pounds ten. All I had in cash was eleven pounds, but there were twenty-seven gold sovereigns sewn into the lining of an old jacket.

"You sound as though you can just walk into something," Florrie jeered.

"Tell me the best hotel in Sydney and that's where I shall start."

"The Australia Hotel—you'd walk into the Australia and ask for a job? You must be mad!"

The Frocks let me have a small room with a veranda that was little more than a ledge for birds, but when I stood there, I saw the whole of Sydney stretched out beneath me like the heavenly kingdom. It was July, with a crackling sparkle to the light, a blaze of poinsettias by a wall at the corner, wattle trees that seemed to float like yellow powder puffs along the road at the bottom of Cascade Street. Beyond them, descending ranks of terracotta roofs set among trees and, at the heart of the city, the turquoise lustre of the Harbour. The two spans of the Bridge, with a wide gap between them, hung in space like hands waiting to grasp each other and over my head a flight of seagulls spiralled on an eddy of wind. Everywhere I looked there was a shining, as if I were contemplating an icon of precious enamels fretted with gold leaf. I could not believe that I had seen nothing of this exuberant lacquered beauty when the *Rangitiki* docked and I made my way to Central Station. A seagull flew so close to me that its wing almost brushed my face and the startled shriek it gave made me remember Dolfi leaning out across the parapet at Erice, flapping his arms, pretending to be a bird.

They were all of them gone now, Roger, Dolfi and Bessie, my parents, Rosalia and Miki, and I added Alan's name to that list. Oh, not without pain, and yet I arrogantly told myself that his love had been tested and he had failed. The failure was mine but I did not understand that then. It did occur to me that he would grieve when he read my letter and I shrugged irritably when I thought of him suffering. Alan, I told myself, had already written the story of his life and it would take him from Griffith to a place on the bench as a judge or into politics: he had chosen to make me a part of his life but what I wanted was my own story. I knew that I would miss him, that I would be tempted to write and tell him where I was even as I put my hands out in front of me and smiled to see them bare. There was a certain intoxication in finding myself alone on that ledge looking across Woollahra to the tall buildings of Sydney with all the scents and smells of a city in my nostrils.

"He's gone to get your stuff from the station," Florrie said behind me, and I stepped back out of the sunlight.

"There's a shed out the back if it won't all fit in here."

"You're very kind, Florrie, thank you."

She had a way of standing with her hip stuck out at one angle and her shoulder at another that made her seem belligerently ambivalent. I knew she had dressed for this interrogation with her hair combed into dozens of little curls and a marcel wave across her pencilled eyebrows.

"I still can't get over it—you and Taps."

I shrugged and smiled.

She drew in her lips as if she were going to swallow them and reversed her shoulder and hip.

"He was—all right—was he?"

"Oh yes."

"They do say that little men sometimes have ones the size of donkeys and they're not as clumsy as some big men are, if you get my drift."

I smiled and she chewed her lips again.

"How would you say he was—in bed?"

"Indescribable."

"My—"

Her surprise made her sit down abruptly on the bed and the springs squeaked in protest.

"He didn't talk about getting married?"

"No—"

"No," she said bitterly. "They have to be dragged to the altar these days. It's all the fault of the War, and if we do have a depression as everyone says, they'll make that an excuse for not wanting to provide for a wife. Not that Henry supports me—the Rutledge Arms belonged to my Geoffrey who was killed at Gallipoli. Every Anzac Day I wear black in memory of him."

"I want to work—I don't want to get married."

"That's easy to say, dear, but there's already hundreds and hundreds looking for jobs. They advertised for a counter hand in the pastry shop around the corner and when I looked out the front door the other morning I thought there must be a riot in the street."

Only youth and inexperience could explain my confidence that morning.

"I shall end up being a very important person in this city," I said calmly.

Florrie swallowed and then managed a smile.

"I see—and how do you propose to manage that?"

"I shall make a mountain of money."

"A girl your age? My dear, even if you're planning to swing a handbag round King's Cross, and if you do have anything like that in mind you can find yourself another place to stay, you won't find it easy to make money in Sydney. I tell you straight, everyone says if the prices of wheat and wool go any lower we'll have a slump that will make the 1890s look like a picnic."

"I need a day to get ready and then I'll have an interview with the manager of the Australia Hotel."

Florrie told me afterwards that she was convinced then that I was an escaped lunatic from Parramatta, but she was also insatiably curious.

The sounds of the public bar downstairs seemed to be over my head instead of under my feet, but nothing disturbed me as I sorted through my old notepads and placed two small bottles of ink I had just bought on the table in front of me.

I found a sheet of paper from the Dorchester, another from the Ritz and the reference Frau Brunner had written for me. First, I drafted a reference on a scrap of paper and then, in a sloping backward hand, I wrote a fulsome letter of praise for my services from the manager of the Dorchester on the cream and gold headed sheet and another in French, with different ink and another style, from the manager of the Ritz.

Two days later I stood at the top of Martin Place and felt like Alaric before Rome—all I had to do was stretch out my hand and the city would be mine. A fleeting prickle of compassion touched me when I saw that all these jostling well-dressed people were oblivious of my intentions. I was the Elymian who had been conquered by the Phoenicians and driven into the mountains, the Phoenician who had coined money while calling the Greeks his master, the Greek who swore allegiance to Rome and never relinquished his language or his gods, the Roman who was forced to kneel to the Vandals and the Vandal who became the slave of the Saracens. I was the Saracen who lived under Norman rule and the Norman who took an oath to the French kings and still kept to his own ways. I was the French landlord who escaped from the Sicilian Vespers and watched his fellow countrymen burned by the Spanish Inquisition before the cathedral in Palermo. I was the Spaniard who learned English so he could serve his English master and the Bourbon loyalist who put on a red shirt and marched with Garibaldi to Rome. Through every persecution and calamity I had survived and nothing could withstand my enduring cunning. I was a Sicilian.

The entrance to the Australia Hotel had squat granite columns and reminded me of the Hotel des Palmes in Palermo although this foyer lacked the ornate gilding and frescoes of the Palmes or the chandeliered brilliance of the Hotel d'Athena. I became aware that a pallid uniformed clerk behind the reception desk was coughing enquiringly. For a few moments I stared at him bleakly as Frau Brunner always did before she spoke to one of the staff. This was a game I had learned when I was very young indeed and it was the pallid young gentleman who spoke first in a minced affectation of vowels.

"May I be of help, madam?"

"The manager, thank you."

Not a please, because this was a statement, not a request.

"Perhaps if you could inform me of your business—"

An older man in a frock coat had joined him and I stared at him so coldly that he flushed slightly.

"Miss Harcourt from the Dorchester."

"Ah—"

The two withdrew and I saw the older man go to a phone.

Mr Gresham was obviously puzzled that I should have invaded his private office but I did not intend to enlighten him until he first asked me, a little awkwardly, why I wished to see him. He was a sleekly plump man in his early fifties wearing a frock coat and a red carnation in his buttonhole. I was dressed plainly but well in a serge suit of my mother's that Norma had turned and cut to fit me. By his glance I knew that he was trying to price my clothes and my accent. Without answering him directly I handed him the three letters.

"You come well recommended, Miss Harcourt."

I nodded and allowed myself the slightest smile.

"You are looking for employment?"

"I was advised to see you first. Mr Devereaux of the Dorchester wishes to be remembered to you. We always suggested that our Australia-bound visitors should come here."

"I wish I could be of help but we are fully staffed and trade is very slack in Sydney at this time."

"Mr Gresham," I said with an edge of sharpness in my voice, "I think I can be of help to you. It is always possible to suggest improvements in the best-run hotel. Let me see any one of your rooms and I will show you what I mean."

He seemed a little bewildered and read the letters again, then stared at me.

"You're very young to have had so much experience, Miss Harcourt."

"Mr Gresham, I'm thirty years old."

"Thirty?"

"Of course, I did not live and work in Paris for nothing. There are ways to keep oneself looking youthful."

Almost instinctively he smoothed his silver hair and adjusted his spectacles.

"Special creams, I daresay?"

I smiled enigmatically.

"Such products are generally unobtainable in the Antipodes."

"I carry my own."

Frowning, he returned to the letters. I watched his lips move over a phrase. For one terrifying moment I felt sure that he had discovered my forgery. All my aplomb began to collapse; I shivered involuntarily. He leaned across his desk, holding the Dorchester letter to the side.

"The matter of discretion mentioned here—was it—a divorce?"

"It could have led to a divorce but we acted quickly and very discreetly. The Duchess was grateful."

There was the faintest pink flush in Mr Gresham's cheeks and he nodded approvingly.

"I understand perfectly, my dear Miss Harcourt. It was the Duchess of—"

"We denied that a Duchess had ever been in the room."

"Very wise."

I smiled and felt a trickle of sweat run down my spine.

"Now, my dear Miss Harcourt, I don't think there is anything here at the Australia, but I do have connections in this city and I may know the very place for you—much smaller than this, I'm afraid, and not what you're accustomed to, but times are difficult and if you're willing to lower your standards a little you'll find Glenarches a very pleasant hotel."

Twenty-Five

"The cheek! The hide of her! I tell you, Henry, that's the sauciest bitch I've ever met! She's got more push than Jessie the elephant!"

"Indeed she has—she has indeed most surely."

Henry enjoyed his own voice: whatever he said was always accompanied by a short refrain as he savoured the rich tone with his head to one side like someone who continues to chew reminiscently when the last mouthful of a good dinner has been swallowed. It was almost midnight and they were still talking in the room next to mine.

"I told you what else she did at the Australia, didn't I? Marched Mr Gresham into one of the nearest bedrooms and told him what was wrong with it. First, she found dust along the window ledge and said the arrangement of the furniture was up your arse, and then she pulled back the bedcovers. Christ, I'd love to have seen his face when she did that! He must have thought she was trying to put the hard word on him! She points to the creases on the bottom sheet and says that no discriminating guest would want to cut her ladylike backside on edges like that and he ought to inform the laundry how to press and fold sheets correctly. Jesus! Can you imagine?"

"A remarkable scene, my love—quite remarkable."

Only someone who has walked a tightrope or gone over Niagara in a barrel can appreciate the kind of fatigue that follows a day spent spinning from one lie to the next, knowing that you are balanced on a razor's edge of credibility, watching every syllable, noting every nuance of gesture like a poker player in a game where the stakes are for life itself. When I remembered what I had done that day I began to shiver at my effrontery and duplicity and yet I knew I had not lied about my ability to run a fine hotel. Frau Brunner had taught me well.

I went up to my room and moved the bed so that it faced the window. From my pillow I could look up at a sky that was the colour of the wine-dark sea you sometimes saw a little after dawn or at dusk in Trapani. The Southern Cross dipped and glimmered like the lamps of a fishing boat anchored by the islands and I knew that I was as far from Trapani as I was from these strange constellations.

I tried to breathe evenly for every now and then I began to gasp with panic—it was as if I had just fallen to earth after walking across endless space between the stars.

"Do you think she worked in all those posh hotels in Europe?"

"Difficult to say, my love. Very difficult—"

"Mr Gresham ended up falling all over her. You don't think she gave him a bit, do you? I mean to say, if she took on Taps Desmond, you could hardly say she's particular."

"Taps was a good friend of mine, Florrie, and it pains me when you speak of him so lightly—very painful for me."

"I reckon he was more than a good mate. Jesus, I only hope my Geoff isn't looking down from heaven at this very moment and seeing you on his side of the bed."

It was not really the letters that had made Mr Gresham my ally. He certainly appreciated that I knew how to run a hotel, but even while he was showing me the kitchens and laundry rooms of the Australia, he kept peering into my face and remarking on the quality of my skin and the absence of wrinkles. I told him that as soon as I started working at Glenarches I would send him a large jar of the cream I used.

"For pity's sake, Henry, Glenarches is where silvertail squatters stay when they're in town—"

"I know it well, my dear—very well indeed."

"Mind you, it only has a private bar, but some of the best people go there."

"Mainly elderly people from the country and those who decline domestic duties and want the comfort of a hotel—as one might say."

"I didn't even know it had been sold and that the manager was retiring."

I heard a resonant snoring and Florrie began to grumble to herself and thump the pillow irritably.

Mr Gresham gave me the address of a firm of accountants in Bligh Street and a letter of introduction to a Mr Fortescue-Bragg. It was obvious that Gresham had already phoned him before I arrived because I was met by a curt little man with darting eyes who told me that he was interviewing several people for the position. He too commented on my youth, but I did not mention magic creams to him. Instead, I stared at him coldly and said that all intelligent women managed to look younger than their years and he smiled and seemed satisfied. There were moments when I could feel the tightrope sway beneath my feet and saw the yawning depths of space all around me, but I was still contriving to keep my balance when we drove to

Macleay Street by taxi and Mr Fortescue-Bragg introduced me to the retiring manager of Glenarches.

The hotel was smaller than I imagined—an undistinguished cream building of three floors set back from Macleay Street behind a painted brick wall with four palm trees on a patch of front lawn bordered with pink begonias. Mr Lennox, the manager, bristled as the accountant showed me round and I learned that the property had recently changed hands and the new owner said he was dissatisfied with the returns on his investment.

"You won't find it easy to make a profit here, Miss—"

Mr Lennox seemed to find it difficult to recall my name as I began to make notes of what needed to be done.

"We have always had a clientele of older people here and they dislike change."

"Old people are partial to comfort," I responded tersely, testing the springs on one of the lobby sofas.

Whenever I showed Mr Lennox what needed changing and when I observed that I thought the hotel was overstaffed, the accountant gave the slightest nod of approval. His complete acceptance of me came, however, when an old lady summoned the manager to the dining room. Lunch was being served and a bewildered waitress stood by a bay-window table as the old lady shrilled that her plate was at one o'clock and she positively refused to eat from a one o'clock plate.

"I dunno what she means," the waitress babbled. "The food's all fresh. I brought it straight from the kitchen."

"One o'clock! I won't sit in front of a plate at one o'clock."

"It's almost two by the grandfather clock in the hall, Mrs Fielding," Mr Lennox said suavely.

I stepped between them and moved the old lady's plate an inch to the left so that the hotel monogram was exactly in the middle and facing her.

"Yes, that's better," the old lady said, and fell on her lunch as if she were famished.

"I shall leave at the end of the week," Mr Lennox said.

"Can you start tomorrow?" Mr Fortescue-Bragg turned to me and I nodded.

If the Frocks could not live harmoniously together, they snored melodiously with a whistling tremolo from Florrie and a baritone accompaniment from Henry. There were sounds from Cascade Street, cats squalling, an occasional car and, towards dawn, the creak and clatter of delivery carts. Possibly I slept fitfully, but I do recall lying there watching the sky change from deep plum to lilac and wondering when Alan would be with me again. I missed the warmth of his body next to mine and the way his arm always folded me to him even when he was sleeping. Of course, he would beg me to go back to Griffith, but I had a better idea. He could leave his mother in the country and come to Sydney as he had always planned and then, perhaps, we would get married. It might take him a week, or a month to come for me, but when he did arrive, he wouldn't find a miserable girl pining for him and full of apologies for running away, but a successful young woman managing a smart hotel as a result of a lot of bluff and two forged references.

Over breakfast Florrie made me promise that I would spend some of my free time with her and I agreed.

"It's important to have a woman friend, love, and I do know this wicked old town if I say so myself. Is there a fellow—someone you fancy at the moment?"

"Yes. He's in Griffith though. His mother didn't want us to get married, so I left."

"Mothers!—I lost a chap I was really keen-on before I married Geoff because his rotten old mother said I wasn't good enough for her precious son who ended up a drunk and then got himself gassed at the Somme."

Henry offered to drive me to Macleay Street and I noticed that he was wearing his Sunday-best suit.

"Must make a good impression on the Glenarches staff when I carry in your bags—very important, first impressions."

I was thinking about Alan and for one moment I closed my eyes and imagined him sitting next to me with the little green Singer vaulting through the dust of a dirt road. Of course, I could write to him but even as I thought of what to say, I determined against it. When the decision had to be made, he had chosen his mother, and that was what I proposed to say to him when he came looking for me in Sydney.

The singular malevolence of a curse is that it blinds you before it afflicts you.

Ah, if only you had been there, Bessie, I'm sure your common sense would have demolished my arrogant assumptions of the quality of love. Admittedly, the questions I had put to myself were proof that I was not passionately in love with Alan, yet I cared for him and it was his voice I wanted to hear that morning, not Henry Frock's mellifluous tones.

"How was he? When you met him? He was all right, wasn't he?"

There was a different note in his voice as we drove along Jersey Road, a timid anxiety that seemed almost childlike.

"Taps? Oh yes, he was doing quite well for himself on the boat as a sick-bay orderly and planning to take a job ashore soon as a valet."

"You didn't—you weren't—"

"No," and I smiled when I heard the relief in his voice.

"I was very grateful, most grateful indeed when you—when you let Florrie think—"

"Oh, Henry, I've seen men who loved each other before. Sometimes love is like water—it can assume any shape or form from cruelty to compassion, it can warm you or freeze you, it can drown you or give you life. It has the power to become anything and change everything."

"Yes, more often cruel than kind, I'd say." He sighed and his voice was thinner and less resonant.

"Taps and I were on the halls together just after the War. Oh, we weren't a top act and we never made any of the really big houses, but we did well enough, mainly on the piers. We had quite a following in Brighton and Blackpool. 'Taps and Henry' was the name of the act: Taps danced. Oh, he was a lovely dancer, and I did a comic imitation of him, trying to follow his steps and falling over my feet. It was very amusing. The young people used to enjoy it immensely. Then of course I sang. We were resting for over six weeks, not a booking in sight, and that tends to get you down in the long run so we bickered and argued and—Taps left me. Next thing I heard he'd gone to Australia as a steward for P & O. I followed him but he was already on his way back to England so—it's hard to say what happened then, but I was down on my luck when I met Florrie and she married me. When Taps called after his next trip I was at the Rutledge Arms. I'll never forget his face—never if I live for a thousand years."

For two days I walked around the hotel observing and making notes while the staff muttered and whispered behind my back just as they used to do at the Villa d'Athena. By Saturday, when Mr Lennox left, I had made up my mind to get rid of two maids, a laundress and a waitress. Mr Fortescue-Bragg whistled thinly when I told him what else I intended to do and said he hoped the new owner would stand for it.

"Does the new owner want to make money or not?" I said sharply.

"Oh, it's not exactly a person, Miss Harcourt. More like a private company."

"You don't communicate with a brick wall, do you? You talk to a person?"

"In a manner of speaking—"

"Good. Then inform the person that I shall dismiss four members of the staff now—and I want them off the premises before they have a chance to complain to the guests or the rest of the staff. I shall need a small amount of money to refurnish the front rooms—new curtains and slipcovers. I think I know someone who can make them for me cheaply. One room will be a cardroom—old people enjoy playing bridge and whist. And we must have a wireless set in each suite—old people dislike silent rooms."

"You have a remarkable understanding of the elderly, Miss Harcourt."

"I've lived with them all my life," I replied.

I told Mr Fortescue-Bragg the sort of chintz I required and two days later, eleven rolls arrived at the back door. A month later I decided to take Sunday afternoon off and visit Norma Reynolds. I also sent Mr Gresham a jar of cream: it was Pond's face cream that I bought at the chemist's for one and sixpence and packed into a different jar with a little orris sprinkled through it. At the end of a fortnight Mr Gresham said the change in his skin was miraculous. Everyone said it was impossible to find a job at that time, and yet I had become manager of Glenarches and any day I expected to find Alan in the lobby where he could see how successfully I was managing the hotel and making as much money in Sydney as I had for him in Griffith.

It was almost five weeks and yet I had not received any word from him. Surely, it could not have been so difficult to trace me? My father would have walked the world to search for my mother and not have rested until she was in his arms. Perhaps Mrs Gilchrist had committed suicide and he had been called upon to supervise her funeral. That was a brighter thought and I smiled bitterly to myself as the Coogee tram rattled along through red-roofed suburbs with occasional brilliant glimpses of the ocean on my left. No, I was certain that Alan was already making enquiries, and he might even have hired a private detective, and then one morning he would be there in front of my desk, pushing back his spectacles, holding out his arms to me. I was not going to be a Mariana of the Moated Grange, growing old and weary waiting for the lover who never came. I was Gwen Harcourt and if Alan loved me as much as I knew he did, I would marry him here in Sydney.

I was not to see Alan for another four years.

Norma was both apprehensive and happy when she opened the door of the tidy brick bungalow in Coogee and introduced me to her parents, her three children and Len.

"Oh, she brings back the old days, doesn't she, Len?" Norma said brightly and Len nodded brusquely.

The strain at the afternoon tea table was so intense that it was as if we were reaching for words through a mesh of taut wires.

Norma's parents seemed both beleaguered and resentful.

"Of course, any friend of my daughter's is welcome here although it is difficult entertaining with so many people in such a small house." As she spoke, Mrs Willoughby glanced pointedly at Len.

I had brought a bag of fairy cakes with me and a slab of seed cake that was left over from Saturday's afternoon tea and this helped to make the table look handsomely spread. The children were ravenous and I suggested they might like to take a plate of cakes out into the garden.

"What a good idea!" Norma said in the same bright voice. "It is a little cramped in here. Children always take up more room than grown-ups, don't they?"

"You must find it quite a change working at the bank," I said to Len and immediately saw a sharp glance from Norma's father, who appeared about to say something and then decided against it.

"Oh yes, he goes off every morning sharp at eight and we don't see him again until six," Norma said.

"Some people seem to be able to get jobs," Mrs Willoughby said thinly. "I gather you've done all right for yourself, Miss Harcourt."

"Yes, but I had several years' experience in a big hotel."

"Bloody foreigners!"

It was an explosion of vehemence that shook Len and the table. Mr Willoughby glared and held the cup and saucer to his chest as if his son-in-law was going to take them from him by force.

"Len, please—" Norma said soothingly. "Not in front of guests."

"There'd be jobs for everyone if it weren't for Lang stirring up his Bolshevik followers. The whole democratic system is rotten to the core. Look at Europe, there's progress and improvement for you. Mussolini is doing the right thing in Italy and Hitler's going to make Germany the most powerful country in Europe. What are we doing here? Making ourselves a dumping ground for the refuse of England and Europe. An Aussie can't get a job because there's a dozen Dagos in the queue ahead of him."

Mrs Willoughby nudged her husband, who was leaning across the table as though deciding whether to attack his son-in-law with his fists or the teapot.

"Arthur, I think we should let the young people discuss politics if that's what they want, and go and see what the kids are up to with all those cakes. We don't want them getting sick, now do we?"

She almost pulled her husband to his feet and the two went out muttering to each other.

"We're just staying here until we can get a place of our own," Norma said. "Only it's difficult finding a house to rent these days."

This was hardly what I had seen when I walked up from the tram stop. Every third house had a "For Rent" or "For Sale" sign in front of it.

"Colonel Campbell has the right idea—put Australia first and let some of the men who fought for this country run it," Len said.

"You've heard of the New Guard, haven't you, Gwen?"

I shook my head.

"Len goes to the meetings and rallies regularly, don't you, dear?"

"Put the politicians against a wall and shoot them—that's what the Colonel says. They're traitors to this country and they should be treated like traitors. No mercy! No mercy!"

"Have some more tea, dear?" Norma said quickly, but Len was staring at some vision of blood that excluded us. His head jerked spasmodically and then he leaned back in his chair and smiled.

"Why don't you take Gwen down to the beach, Norma? It's too cold to swim yet but you haven't seen much of Sydney, have you?"

"No, I haven't."

Norma was already scrambling to her feet and saying she'd look after the dishes when she got back.

The afternoon sun was warm and I bent down and let a handful of sand trickle through my fingers.

"It's powdered shell—that's why it's so white."

"Oh, we have wonderful beaches and it's lovely for the children."

"Norma, does Len have a good job?"

"Oh—Oh, of course he has—he goes off every morning. The neighbours say they could set their clocks by him."

She paused suddenly and squatted on the sand, huddling over her knees as if to protect herself from the pain. I had to sit down beside her because her voice was so faint.

"Every morning, he gets dressed, always particular about his shirt being just so and his shoes polished, and he goes out—"

"Yes—"

"I think he goes to one of the big libraries in the city and reads there. He doesn't eat anything all day because when he comes home at night he's white with hunger."

"But his job at the bank?"

"They had nothing for him. The manager was an old friend of his father's and even that didn't make any difference. The banks are letting staff go. Nobody's hiring these days, everyone's getting the sack."

She rocked back and forth and when she spoke again it was like a wail.

"I don't know what to do—I just can't cope any more. It's so hard on my parents, they're old and entitled to a little peace and comfort, but Dad's pension's been cut and he was an organizer for the Australian Workers' Union so you can imagine how he feels about Len's politics. If it weren't for the kids, Dad would throw us out and I can't blame him. Len's joined the New Guard and they may be able to do something for him, although I can't see how it helps to march up and down Martin Place and beat up the union workers who've been locked out. I mean—what can I do? The kids are getting scrawny and Maisie has sores all over her legs. Len wouldn't dream of asking for charity. He has his pride, Gwen. After all, they made him a captain during the War and he was decorated twice. The little money he had when his parents died, he put into the farm at Yenda. We walked off that place with nothing but the clothes on our backs. If it hadn't been for the few quid you gave me, the kids wouldn't have had shoes. What can I do?"

"You can work, Norma."

"Len wouldn't let me."

"Are you going to starve with your children and your parents because of his pride?"

"I couldn't get a job even if I tried. There's no one being taken on at any of the dressmaking establishments. Oh, don't think I haven't taken a peek at the columns in the *Sydney Morning Herald* whenever I get the chance to see a paper."

"You can work for me."

"Another Paris ballgown?"

Even though she was crying she managed to giggle.

"I am going to make Glenarches the most comfortable and best-run hotel in Sydney."

"I wouldn't put anything past you, Gwen."

"Most of the guests there now are elderly and I want more like them. They say there's going to be a depression."

"There is one now!"

"But there will always be people with money—"

Norma gave a short laugh as if I had just observed that the sea was blue.

"Old people who can't afford a houseful of servants, but who can afford a suite at Glenarches. That's my clientele."

"Len would never let me work—and that's flat, Gwen."

The decision had left her voice and what I heard now was more defiance than firm resolution.

"Old people need attention and I am going to train a staff that will make them feel that Glenarches is the most comfortable home they've ever known. Now, at their age, they can't manage sewing. I've seen some of them poring over the same piece of embroidery week after week. I want a seamstress on the premises who'll adjust hems and make alterations—and make slipcovers and curtains if they're needed."

"Len would never let me—How much can you pay?"

"Four pounds a week and you'd get lunch and I'll see to it that you take some leftovers home from the kitchen every night."

"Four pounds—"

"Would you like me to speak to Len?"

"Oh Gwen—"

She was crying and laughing at the same time, standing and stretching her arms over her head.

We strolled along at the edge of the water and I suddenly felt a twisting pain in my chest for the scrunch of sand on my bare feet reminded me of all the times Bessie and I had talked the length of the beach at Trapani.

Norma's excitement began to ebb as we climbed the hill to her parents' house so I took her hand and held it as I would a child's. She looked at me and shook her head.

"Where does it come from, Gwen? Where do you get the gumption? You're only a kid."

"I was born a thousand years old. I'm a Sicilian," I replied and she reminded me that she'd fallen for that joke once before.

Len was leaning moodily over the front fence smoking a hand-rolled cigarette that could not have had more than a pinch of tobacco in it. I watched him struggle to be pleasant to us.

"Enjoy the beach?"

"Len, I want to talk to you alone. We'll just stroll around the block, Norma."

Before he could answer, I pushed Norma through the gate and took Len by the arm. He was so dumbstruck by my action that he followed me without speaking.

At the corner I turned and faced him. He was over six feet tall but I saw him put his shoulders back as if to make himself taller still.

"I need Norma to help me at the hotel."

"My wife doesn't have to work," he said flatly.

"She has to work because you can't find a job."

"Did she tell you that?" He blanched as if I had slapped him.

"It wasn't difficult to discover such an obvious fact."

"God!" He turned and pounded the corner of a garden wall with his fist, pausing only when a woman bending over gardening, looked up enquiringly at him.

"Yes, there's no need to raise your voice," I said quietly and smiled and nodded at the woman.

"I thought there was supposed to be loyalty between a man and his wife."

"I need her."

"What are you running up there at the Cross? A sweat shop?"

"A respectable hotel for old people."

"I won't permit it."

"Are you going to let your family starve?"

"The Guard will help us."

"I'm prepared to give Norma four pounds a week."

"Four pounds! You call that a wage? Do you think I'd let my wife go out to work for a miserable four pounds a week?"

"Four pounds and food."

He was struggling with himself, anger knotting the veins in his forehead. Len must have been a handsome man at one time; now he was like a raging old tramp.

Norma began cutting the slipcovers and curtains the following Monday and after lunch in my suite, she looked seraphic.

"You've really landed on your feet here, Gwen. Haven't had a tuck-in like that for ages."

"I keep a close check on the kitchen and I'll see to it you have a packet of leftovers every evening. It won't be scrapings—that's for the dining-room and kitchen staff. At first they were shocked when I offered it to them, but now most of them have discovered cats and dogs at home that are grateful for the scraps. Nothing is wasted here."

"I can't wait to write and tell Mrs Heffernan that I'm working."

"Do you correspond regularly?"

"Every second week or so."

"Does she mention Alan?"

"Yes, and she wanted to know how you were getting along."

"I suppose he's engaged to Ellie Sanderson now."

"No, Ellie's marrying a chap on a wheat farm."

There was silence between us and Norma leaned over and touched my arm gently.

"He's not taking anyone out. Mrs Heffernan says he's been like an old man since you left. Why don't you write to him?"

I shook my head.

"Would you like me to mention your address to Mrs Heffernan? You know what a gossip she is—she'll make it her business to let Alan know where you are."

Tears were stinging my eyes as I nodded.

"Don't you worry, dear, Mrs H. and I will play Cupid between us."

Thanks to Mrs Heffernan I heard regularly about Alan but he never wrote to me or came to see me.

Again and again I told myself that he had not loved me enough and slowly I began to wonder if he had come to understand that I was fulfilling the curse of my parents' great love—demanding to be loved more than it was in my power to love in return. I went from month to month hearing of the success of his new firm and longing to be able to share my own success with him; at the very least, to feel the comfort of his body against mine, but there was no word except the scraps of news related by Mrs Heffernan. I resolved that if Alan had vanished like all the friends of my childhood, I would be like Frau Brunner and live for the gold sovereigns I was accumulating in the office safe.

Once a week, Mr Gresham called and took me to a concert at the Conservatorium or a play at the Theatre Royal and Norma insisted on calling him my beau. From the first, I suspected that he was not interested in women, and later I found that men did not appeal to him either: Ted Gresham was one of those happy souls who are contentedly in love with themselves; every day the object of his love smiled adoringly at him from the mirror. He liked me because he was convinced that my cream was making him eternally young and because I never mentioned marriage or romance to him.

Norma thought Mr Gresham was charming when she met him one evening but Florrie hooted with derision when I told her that he now took me out regularly to concerts.

"An old bird of that age! I wonder he knows the difference between his cock and his nose. Now, if you were going out with Danny Burns—"

Danny Burns was an Irish comedian who was becoming the talk of Sydney with an act he did on the Manly ferries; reluctantly I agreed to go with Florrie the following Sunday afternoon.

"Gwen, I'm not lying—Danny Burns is the sexiest, wickedest man alive. Half the women in Sydney would like him to put his shoes under their beds—and if all I hear is correct, Danny doesn't even wait to take off his shoes."

Twenty-Six

"My God, I could burst out crying when I see them," Florrie said, pointing to a straggling line of men outside a soup kitchen at Circular Quay. "Hundreds of poor bastards queuing for half a day's work or a plate of food. I bet you never saw anything like that where you came from."

"No," I replied. "There was nothing to queue for."

Everyone realized by 1930 that it was a world depression, yet Glenarches was like a small haven of well-being in the middle of a swamp of poverty. I remember Mrs Martin Havers coming to me in tears when the New South Wales Savings Bank failed and telling me that she had just lost half her income, but I knew that the income she had left would have kept a dozen families in comfort to the end of their days. Florrie was sure she was going to lose the Rutledge Arms because trade was so slack and then I had an idea that saved the day for her. A small hardware shop next door closed and we persuaded the pastry cook at the end of Cascade Street to sell pies and hot vegetables there. If you bought a pint of beer at the pub you were given a ticket and that entitled you to a pie and vegetables for twopence. There was an outcry at first that the licensing laws were being flouted since it was forbidden to sell food in a public bar, but the Frocks were able to convince the local magistrate that it was the pastry cook who sold the food, and it was just being eaten on the pavement where the men always drank their beer. After that, Florrie was convinced I could turn garbage into gold.

"I reckon they should put you in charge of the Bank of England," she always said. "Then the whole country could go back to work. Ah—" She breathed deeply as we bought our tickets for the Manly ferry. "A breath of fresh air on the Harbour and a good laugh is what we both need: seven miles from Sydney and a thousand miles from care."

Florrie was also determined to find me a lover and she appraised every passing man with an eye to my needs. "No, you don't want him. Skinny brute—probably got a matchstick in his pants." Or another, "Not bad, but you can tell he's married by the nervous way he's eyeing the sheilas. There's only one thing worse than a man who can't get it up and that's one with a watchful wife." All of them had failings except Danny Burns. Florrie had already made four previous trips on the Manly ferry to see him and now she was dabbing her lipstick in anticipation.

"Sometimes he actually kisses a woman in the audience. Oh my God, it's got to be me this time. I'll probably faint if he touches me, pass out and not remember a thing afterwards. I think I must have been unconscious when I married Henry," she added thoughtfully.

"Is Danny Burns very good-looking?"

"He should be in Hollywood making movies. Henry heard on the QT that he's just about to make a local film and parts of it are going to be shot right near us, in Paddington. He's much funnier than Charlie Chaplin. No, Danny's the sort of fellow you should go for—not that old mothball of a Gresham. And you must have got over that mother's boy of a lawyer in Griffith by now. A girl your age wants to have some fun and a few giggles on the side. Falling in love shouldn't be a tragedy."

I was beginning to enjoy myself as the entertainment began on the top deck of the *Dee Why*; the breeze tasted of brine and the sparkling effervescence of sea and salt air was making everyone feel a little tipsy. Perhaps care had indeed been left behind us in Sydney and we could pretend we were cruising to the islands of the Pacific where everyone lived in a perpetual summertime of ease. Two jugglers came on first, followed by a crooner and a team of performing dogs with frilled collars who waltzed solemnly in pairs. The applause was perfunctory and the performers bowed quickly as if they knew they were simply a prelude for the star of the show, Danny Burns. The ferry rocked as it struck the swell from the Heads and a woman screamed excitedly.

"Over here, he comes in this way—" Florrie was dragging me over to one side and across a lifeboat.

I looked down into the slide of a glass green wave and almost lost my balance.

"Now, here—"

I could feel Florrie shaking with excitement as she elbowed her way to the front and pulled me along with her.

All I could hear were women screaming and the sound of feet pounding the deck.

"Danny! Danny!" they screamed over and over again and a flock of seagulls on the rigging screeched with them.

I saw him shuffle forward in a white suit, a wide straw hat on the back of his head and a red carnation drooping dejectedly from his buttonhole. A spotted bandanna was tied loosely round his neck and a large gold hoop dangled from one ear.

Someone I couldn't see struck a few chords on the piano and the crowd began to shout, "Dino the Dago! Dino the Dago!"

It was a very simple act and I wondered why everyone around me was convulsed with laughter. Florrie was choking and gasping, holding on to my arm for support—the woman alongside her was turning purple and seemed on the verge of apoplexy.

Dino the Dago could not resist women and his nature was so lascivious that when he approached a lady he had to clap his hat over his groin to conceal his excitement. That's all it was and yet as he shuffled up to a woman in the crowd and spoke to her in something that was supposed to sound like an Italian accent, the woman shrieked and Dino would roll his eyes and tell her that he was forced to "eata his spaghetti cold because he hadda the hot feelings for the ladies." He told a string of jokes, did some animal imitations, sang a few choruses of Dino the Dago's love song, inviting the audience to join in, and then he went around again with his hat in front of him, ogling the women in the crowd.

He stood before me but my mouth was frozen and I couldn't speak. As if from a great distance I heard the laughter change to a questioning murmur and then he was holding me to him and crying.

"You bitch! You bitch!" he said over and over again. "I could never make you laugh!"

The voices grew louder. A man at my other elbow was pushing me through the crowd. A door closed behind me and Dolfi began to kiss me.

"My sister! My sister that I thought I'd lost forever."

"I'm not your sister," I managed to say finally.

I hadn't realized that Dolfi was so short, or perhaps I had grown taller since I last saw him with Roger on the beach in Trapani. He had been very beautiful then, a young satyr with a skin that looked as if it were dusted with gold. Now he was pudgy, but it was Dolfi and I too began to cry as I remembered how many years of my childhood had been spent with him and how much Bessie had loved him.

We were in a dressing room that was hardly larger than a cupboard when I suddenly realized that my knees were touching someone else's.

It was a dark-haired young man who looked from Dolfi to me with an expression of dismayed panic. He seemed unable to speak so Dolfi introduced him as his manager, Terry Mapes.

"I'm a distant cousin of Dolfi's—we grew up together," I said.

Terry began to smile then, but whenever he looked at Dolfi it was as if this young man had stolen the eyes of Roger Whitlow.

The door was being pounded against my back and I heard Florrie demanding to know if I was all right, and the voice of a man arguing with her.

"We can't really talk now, we have another show in half an hour—come round to our flat late this evening." Terry scribbled an address on a slip of paper and handed it to me.

"Why—why didn't you laugh?" Dolfi scowled at me. "Everyone else thought it was funny—why didn't you?"

"Oh Dolfi, I think I was remembering too much too quickly," I said.

Florrie was still babbling questions as we made our way to the upper deck.

"Your cousin? And he's not Irish?" Fortunately, Florrie managed to answer most of the questions herself, until it was time for the return trip.

"Didn't you recognize his picture in the newspapers?"

"No—"

"Your cousin? Not a first cousin though? Well, you could still marry him if you wanted to."

At eleven o'clock that night we walked round to the Challis Avenue address in Pott's Point Terry had given me. It was a flat in a large block overlooking the Harbour and I discovered that for over a year Dolfi and I had been living within a quarter mile of each other. I must have walked past his door a dozen times without realizing it.

"So, you're running a hotel, just like my mother." Dolfi grinned. "Not that home for bags of bones in Macleay Street. I thought it was a hospice for the dying."

"Your mother trained me well," I replied, and Terry whispered that Dolfi was always irritable after a day on the ferry.

"She must be very happy to know you're so successful," I added diplomatically.

Dolfi looked steadily at me over the rim of his glass.

"She doesn't know where I am."

"You've written to her, haven't you? She told me she was going to buy a hotel in Miami."

Dolfi sucked the rim of the glass thoughtfully, his eyes half closed.

"She must love me so much now, never knowing whether I am alive or dead and blaming herself. Yes, she will blame herself, I'm sure," he sighed.

"Dolfi, she sold everything in Trapani because she knew you wouldn't return to do your military training."

"I didn't care about the Fascists. They would never have stopped me returning to Sicily if I'd wanted to. I had a lot of friends—close to Mussolini."

"Would you like me to send a letter to Miami—it might reach your mother. Or you could telephone the American Embassy—"

Dolfi smashed his glass on the table and swore at me in Sicilian.

"You dare write to my mother and I will cut your hands off!" he said savagely.

Terry brushed up the splintered glass and whispered that Dolfi didn't mean it, he was overwrought after such a long day and difficult audiences.

"I was fed up with Sicily—I wanted to to leave."

"We all left eventually."

"I'm sorry your father died. He was a stupid little man but I liked him. He had such great hopes for me as a scholar. When he was teaching me Greek, he often said he wanted me to run the museum after his death because I was such a gifted scholar. And—" He sat up and asked excitedly, "Miki? What happened to Miki?"

When I told him about the lottery, Dolfi's whole mood changed and he began to prance up and down the room.

"He was a genius, Terry. I've told you about Miki who taught me everything he knew. Oh, he used to look at me with such pride and say that one day I would be the greatest comedian in the world."

"He was a mute, Dolfi."

"You see—listen to her! Always sour, always unpleasant. The Professoressa, we called her, because she always knew more than everyone else and couldn't wait to tell you. I give you my word, Miki spoke to *me*."

"When did you leave India?" I asked him, trying to change the subject.

Dolfi threw himself down into a chair and glowered.

"I detested India."

"Your mother had a letter from Roger—"

"Roger—"

I watched Dolfi's expression change again. He almost snarled.

"I killed him."

"Dolfi—" Terry sighed deprecatingly.

Florrie was sitting transfixed, staring at Dolfi, and as Terry filled her glass he glanced sideways at me as if to warn me that Dolfi was lying. As if I needed to be told that!

"Oh shut up, Terry! I'm talking to my sister. Gina is the only family I have in this country. I suppose you're going to be jealous of her now?"

Terry shook his head and looked out at the Harbour. There was a glint of tears in his eyes.

"I loved Roger," Dolfi said intently and I heard Florrie choking.

"But he betrayed me so I took a kris—that's a long dagger with a wavy blade—and I cut his throat—very slowly, after I had drugged him. It was only because I was a master of disguise that I managed to escape the Bombay Lancers and hide on a boat bound for Australia."

Dolfi had dozens of different stories to account for his parting from Roger but I think Terry managed to piece together what may have happened. When the two lovers arrived in India Dolfi discovered that Roger planned to introduce him as a servant—and began to treat him like one. They quarrelled and Roger threw him out. Dolfi told of roaming through bazaars with fakirs and holy men, but it was more likely that he was picked up by a sailor on a ship bound for Australia. Terry said he had found him wandering around on the docks at Darling Harbour, taken him home and discovered his talents as a comic. At first, Terry had continued working as head of the millinery department at Farmer's but soon he was devoting all his time to finding Dolfi work. When I met them, Dolfi was on the brink of real fame. He had just agreed to make a film entitled, *Dino Down and Out,* and there was talk of him appearing at the Tivoli on the same bill as Roy Rene.

The satyr had become Priapus and everyone believed that Dolfi, or Danny Burns, the name Terry had chosen for him, was lust incarnate, the living symbol of male virility. Women adored him and men guffawed whenever he walked on to the stage with his drooping carnation and his hat clamped firmly over the part of his body that rose to greet every woman in sight. What astonished me was not that people should find him so funny, but that Florrie, who had seen him with Terry, who knew they were lovers, was still convinced that Dolfi was intent on pushing every woman into a corner and forcing himself on her. Once I screamed at her because she insisted that I might get Dolfi to the altar if I played my cards right, and when I told her that Dolfi had been a homosexual for as long as I had known him, she said that Terry was just his manager and Dolfi's poofter act was almost as good as his Dino the Dago.

Very foolishly, one Sunday evening, when we were alone and Terry was washing up in the kitchen, I told Dolfi why I had left Trapani.

"You sacrificed your honour? You disgraced yourself—and me?" Dolfi was outraged and began to splutter. I stared at him in amazement.

"You, Dolfi? What are you talking about?"

"The honour of our family!" Dolfi replied with great hauteur, got up from his chair and went into the bedroom, slamming the door behind him.

A week later he arrived in my office at Glenarches with a large bunch of roses. I should have known who it was by the excited squeaks I heard in the lobby. Terry looked around the door and said that Dolfi had come to apologize, but Dolfi had found an audience and was not going to leave it so quickly. The squeaks became titters and the titters hysterical shrieks as

Dolfi assured the old ladies that he loved them all but if he stayed any longer with such beautiful women he would need a new pair of trousers.

"He's sorry he spoke so rudely to you the other night," Terry said as Dolfi blew a last kiss to his admirers.

"It's true, Gina," Dolfi said magnanimously. "I was very unkind."

"I think we're always going to argue, Dolfi. We're hardly alike."

"No. No, the fault was mine. A good-looking girl can pick and choose but you were never pretty—"

I saw Terry turn scarlet and gesture imploringly to Dolfi, but Dolfi was intent on giving his own explanation for my fall from virtue.

"Don't say a word against her, Terry. What chance did she have of making a good marriage? Look at her now—tall as a beanpole, thin as a rake! And the way she has of snapping at everything people say to her—like a starving dog. The man must have been a sexual maniac who wanted to make love to her—"

I began to laugh and Dolfi glared at me.

"You are also very stupid," he said. "When I am doing my brilliant imitations you look as solemn as a funeral, but if I tell you something for your own good, as if I were your own brother, you burst out laughing. Miki always said you were a little soft in the head, and he was right."

My chest was hurting me as I rocked in my chair. With canonical dignity Dolfi gave me his back and addressed Terry, who looked as if he were going to fall into his shoes with embarrassment.

"Terry, there was only one girl in Trapani who was as stupid as my cousin and that was her best friend, a fat, freckled little pudding with red hair who would have dropped her knickers for me in the middle of a crowd of nuns."

I was gasping between laughter and anger—

"Don't speak about Bessie. Not Bessie—"

The words came out in a rush because I could feel my rage rising to a shriek.

"Both of you, please! Please be quiet! There are two nuns out there in the lobby."

"Nuns? I mention nuns and they appear!" Dolfi said delightedly. "You see, even their vows are not proof against my charm."

He bounded past Terry and I saw him bowing to two black-robed nuns at the front desk.

"I am coming all over myself," he cried and shoved his hat against his groin. "I luvva all the ladies especially the religious ladies."

One of the nuns shrank back in horror and covered her face, but the other, older and more heavily set, grinned at Dolfi, leaned forward and with a booming laugh tweaked the hat from his hands.

"Now then, you haven't really got anything there to hide, have you, young man?"

Dolfi staggered back and almost fell through the front door, to the enraptured squeaks of the old ladies who seemed to think this was all part of an elaborate charade. Terry stumbled after him, babbling apologies, genuflecting to the older nun who gave him Dolfi's panama and boomed that hats were meant for heads not for other parts of the body. Her laughter filled the lobby and rebounded from every corner; even the pier glasses by the windows and the chandelier seemed to be chiming in response to her mirth.

She was a broad-shouldered woman, the width of her shoulders was visible beneath the black robe and shrouding veil. A wisp of grey hair had struggled from under her wimple and, still chuckling, she pushed it back. I was not sure how to address her and wondered if she had come collecting for the poor and unemployed.

"Soliciting is not permitted in the lobby of this hotel," I said quickly and the nun grinned at me. She had a strong brown face and intelligent, good-humoured eyes.

"I'm Mother George and I'm here to see my aunt, Mrs Fielding—She's been ailing. If you like, we'll go outside and come in through the tradesmen's entrance."

"Mrs Fielding—I'm so sorry—I—"

"Nuns may look like penguins, but we do have aunts and cousins and sisters and brothers." She paused and frowned at her companion who was still standing with her hands to her face, shielding her eyes.

"Oh, don't carry on like that, Sister Joseph. There was nothing worth seeing. Just a silly young man playing the fool." She shook her head and sighed. "Do you think you could give Sister a cup of tea somewhere while I talk to my aunt?"

Half an hour later, when the old ladies had stopped fluttering and giggling and were taking tea, the hotel appeared to have recovered from Dolfi's religious encounter. Most of the kitchen staff were Catholic and they had made such a fuss of Sister Joseph that she seemed mollified when it was time to leave. Mother George stood in front of my desk and looked quizzically at me.

"My aunt speaks very highly of you."

"Thank you, Mother George."

"You're a puzzling young woman. Why would someone so young and pretty want to spend her days with these old ducks?" Sister Joseph raised her eyes and her hands fluttered slightly.

"I grew up with old people," I replied and turned some papers on my desk.

"Get out into the world and live!" she said exuberantly. "When I walked into the lobby just now with all those old sick people I thought it was Lourdes. Embrace life—take it to your heart!"

I could only nod but Mother George left me unsettled and irritable. That same afternoon Norma told me she had heard that Alan was leaving his practice in Griffith and Mrs Heffernan thought he might be going into a big legal firm in Melbourne. I told her I wasn't interested in what Alan did —it was over three years since I had left Griffith and he had never tried to get in touch with me. Alan had vanished from my life like Bessie and her parents. Yet sometimes those who disappeared popped back like puppets through trapdoors on the stage. If only it had been Bessie and not Dolfi.

Norma was fitting me for a new black skirt and complaining that I never bought enough material for her.

"I can't get it out of the little scraps you buy," she said.

"Remnants are cheap," I replied.

"You must be able to afford a length of decent material," she snapped.

It was a moment when all my life seemed to be flaking and crumbling into decay around me. I was fortunate to be making money when unemployment was rising every day and people were begging for work, but everything I earned ended in that bag of gold sovereigns in the hotel safe. Once a week the sleekly silver Mr Gresham arrived and we went to a concert—Dolfi said I should ask him to marry me because nobody young and handsome would ever want me. I knew I had the gift of making money for myself and for other people: the Rutledge Arms was flourishing and Norma was getting her wages and tips from the hotel guests when she altered clothes and mended for them. After all, Demeter was the mother of Ploutos, the god of wealth, but I did not think anyone would understand that. And what was Demeter without Persephone?

"I'm sorry, love, I didn't mean to upset you," Norma said.

"No, I was just wondering what I had become."

"A success—that's what you are. If you'd just enjoy yourself a little more. You're so young."

"Then why do I feel so old—older than any of those old people out there. Why do I look at them sometimes and feel as if they were my children?"

If only I could have menstruated like Florrie and Norma or some of the maids who often whispered to me that they needed half an hour to lie down because the curse was cramping them so bad they couldn't stand up straight. I was dry and withered like a crust of old bread or a stick that had not known sap or leaf for years.

"You need to mix more with people your own age. Even Florrie and I are too old for you. It's nice you have your cousin, Danny, but—"

"My parents wanted me to be a scholar," I said mournfully.

"Oh well, I'm sure that's very nice, but I was thinking of something brighter."

Norma no longer apologized for earning money. She told me with a tilt of her chin that she had fought it out with Len and if he couldn't get work that was not going to stop her. He was spending all his time with the New Guard although he hadn't received a penny from them. They still lived with her parents but Len now had a bed on the veranda and the children slept inside, the girls in her room and the boy in another.

"I can't say I miss it," she said. "There was too much of it in the past and never any fun in it for me. If it weren't for the depression and the kids, I think he would have done a vanishing act on me ages ago. Len always hinted that he'd married out of his class when we got hitched. No, after three kids, and two born dead, you don't miss it. It's my kids' future I'm concerned about now."

Sleep had become a torment to me because I remembered Alan and the passion of his love and sometimes, when I did sleep, I woke crying with my breasts throbbing and a dull ache between my legs. Perhaps I had deliberately walked away from the settled life and into the waste land when I packed my bags and took the morning train from Griffith. If I had waited a year, Alan would have married me in spite of his mother, I was sure of that now, but I had not been prepared to wait. It had been easy for me to leave because I expected Alan to follow me and in my imagination I rehearsed the scene when he would kneel in front of me offering me his life and I would graciously forgive him. It's always possible to hold two contradictory ideas in your head at the same time and even as I was waiting for him to stand in front of me, begging me to marry him, I relished being alone, pitting my wits against a strange city. Later I remembered what I had said and written to Alan and then bitterly I told myself that he was probably glad to be rid of me.

I was in pieces and could not find myself; I was as broken as the sherds of pottery that I used to sort in the museum at Trapani. But there I could always find a pattern and slowly, fragment by fragment, a beaker or a pot would take shape in my hands. Now I did not know what I was—Sicilian or English, Australian or *la gran romantica* dreaming of passions and desires that belonged in opera, not in life. If Bessie had been there she would have shaken some sense into me, but my stupidity and my pride were both inhuman then.

Whenever I saw Dolfi, and he clearly regarded Glenarches as his second home, I found myself wondering if Bessie could now fall in love with this metamorphosed Dino the Dago. I know that I gloated over his thinning hair and spreading fat because they were like punishments for the way he had spurned Bessie: I also know that I deliberately magnified every sign of approaching age in Dolfi. Occasionally, grudgingly, I had to admit that he was still the Dolfi of Trapani, golden-haired and with eyes so deeply blue they were almost black. This was the Dolfi that Norma and Florrie saw, and this was the Dolfi that I detested and refused to recognize. Fortunately, I was always spared his company if Mother George was in the hotel visiting her aunt.

It was a little after ten one evening and most of the guests were comfortably playing cards or reading when Dolfi and Terry arrived. Terry came through to my office and said that Dolfi was outside and refused to come in if there were any nuns about. I was tempted to say that I was entertaining the whole convent.

"I never thought to see my cousin entertaining nuns," Dolfi said, making himself at home in my armchair with a large glass of Cointreau and gin, a drink he had invented himself.

"Mother George's aunt is a guest here," I replied patiently.

"She's trying to convert you."

"Rubbish."

Terry murmured that Dolfi had been very upset by Mother George.

"You saw what she did! She tried to grab my private parts!"

"Dolfi! It was your hat!"

"Please," Terry said imploringly, "please don't argue. My head is splitting."

"Your head is splitting because there's nothing in it," Dolfi jeered and Terry put a hand across his forehead and leaned back in his chair.

"That nun wants you for her convent, Gina. Mother Superior she calls herself—she's nothing but a madam."

I told him he was ridiculous and picked up a book, trying to read.

"Let me tell you about these nuns. They all smell because they like to play with dead bodies."

I turned away and closed my eyes as Dolfi began to stalk the room, his teeth bared, hands extended like claws.

"Oh please, Dolfi—please."

Terry was a Catholic and had been educated by nuns so I understood why he was so distressed.

"I was a Jesuit once so I can tell you everything about nuns," Dolfi said darkly. "You have a monastery here—over there, a convent, and in between a tunnel where they bury the babies that are strangled the moment they are born."

"Oh Dolfi, that's not true," Terry replied tearfully.

"Nuns are all depraved and lascivious vampires who wear nothing under their robes—"

"Like Scotsmen," I interjected.

"Naked, so they are always ready to jump into the confessional and oblige the priest. I tell you, I have seen these things! Did you imagine those little dark cupboards were simply places where people confessed their sins? No, it is where priests take nuns standing up. I know all their tricks. Do you think this was the first nun who tried to seduce me?"

Dolfi drank and told us at great length about the nuns who had kept him prisoner when he was a boy and made him service the whole convent; the nuns who lay in wait like white-slave traffickers for girls like me, slipping drugs into their tea and dragging them off to their bordellos. I poured Terry some fresh coffee and we talked quietly as Dolfi imitated the sounds of nuns and priests making love in fractured Latin, or recited spells to banish all religious while I wondered how I could get him out of the hotel without disturbing the guests.

"He's a genius," Terry said faintly.

"A rather odd kind of genius, Terry."

"I'd give my life for him and he knows it, but he can be so temperamental at times and very indiscreet. I sold everything to get him started. He didn't have any clothes when I met him, and now he's making money and he throws it away—horses, two-up, anything. Horses mainly—he picks out a name with a pin and bets on it. I try to save what I can for him and he accuses me of stealing from him. I don't know why I put up with him. If people found out that he—we—he makes life so difficult."

"A shark has more gratitude than Dolfi."

"He doesn't appreciate what it means to be a public figure, Gwen. When the artists on the Manly ferries were asked to donate something to help the unemployed musicians and performers in Sydney, he refused. I had to make all sorts of excuses."

"Dolfi is detestable."

"He's very fond of you, Gwen."

"No, he's not. We've always disliked each other—but we've disliked each other for so long that it's a bond of sorts. And he is my family."

My family? Was it the Barone or Rosalia who made me say that? You cannot abandon anyone of your family because he is part of your life and shares the same blood—to reject your family is to reject yourself. Every day I told myself that I would refuse to see and talk to Dolfi, and yet, whenever he came to Glenarches, I made him a grudging welcome. Dolfi was a distant cousin, but he played a leading role in all my memories of Trapani. I could see my father bending over Dolfi's shoulder at the long table in the museum and Frau Brunner crooning over him on the balcony of the Villa d'Athena. And always I saw Dolfi taking Bessie's hand and pulling her across the rocks on the way to the secret beach. I would never give up my memories and so I could not ignore Dolfi, even when it was one o'clock in the morning and the night porter and Terry had to carry him out to a taxi. This snoring corpse was more than a revenant. Dolfi was a messenger from the dead who already were holding my future in their hands.

Twenty-Seven

Terry had finally arranged for Dolfi's first stage appearance at the Tivoli after weeks of haggling and arguments about the act. Roy Rene, who played Mo as a black-jowled Jew spitting all over the stage, insisted on top billing and reluctantly Dolfi agreed to have his name appear in second place. Mo was the most famous and best-loved comedian in Australia, yet Dolfi fell into diatribes of abuse if his name was even mentioned.

"The Jews should drag him from the stage!" Dolfi screamed during rehearsals. "He's shaming all of them!"

"What about you and the Italians?" I retorted.

"That's different," Dolfi said scornfully. "I'm a comedian, Roy Rene is a bumbling clown who makes fun of his own people. Besides, everyone thinks I'm Irish."

There was very little for people to feel cheerful about in 1933—some economists said the depression was getting worse and Norma told me in terrified whispers that the New Guard was planning to march on Parliament and take control of the country. Mother George said that at least half the students at the convent school could not afford to pay fees. It was not their lack of money that distressed her, but that somehow the girls always managed to discover who the "paupers" were and then complained about having to support them. Poverty, as Australians were discovering for the first time, did not bring out the best in people. Mrs Fielding was so terrified of revolution that she insisted on her windows being locked even on the warmest summer night. I asked the doorman to check everyone who entered the hotel after the afternoon when a decently dressed gentleman was caught begging from the guests in the cardroom. The poor and the destitute came with all accents those days from the roughest working class to the most refined: the staff were taught to be on the watch for any stranger.

I had gone into town to check some of the accounts with Mr Fortescue-Bragg and to ask him about a curious incident of the previous morning. Out of the corner of my eye, I had observed him escorting an opulently dressed woman through the cardroom. She was not one of the guests and her clothes were more flamboyantly expensive than the shabby gentility I was accustomed to seeing in the hotel. A dark, plush velvet cloche hat almost concealed a pair of fine diamond earrings. What puzzled me was that the woman was bending down and appeared to be examining the curtains.

Mr Fortescue-Bragg came regularly to the hotel but he always came alone. My sudden appearance seemed to startle him and as I smiled and waited for him to introduce his companion, she passed me with a nod and walked briskly out to the front garden. Mr Fortescue-Bragg made a few desultory comments about his appointment with me the next day and followed her. I watched them leave in a waiting taxi.

It was a puzzling incident of no particular importance and yet when I asked him that morning if I had seen Mrs Fortescue-Bragg, the little man blushed to the roots of his wispy hair and said it was merely a client who had an interest in hotels. Smiling wryly to myself I thought that perhaps even this dry and elderly accountant had a mistress: I had nothing in my life except Mr Gresham.

I spent two hours with the accountant and was walking up Castlereagh Street, threading a path through black-robed lawyers on their way to court. There was another demonstration in Martin Place and four mounted policemen standing at each corner of the crowd were starting to move forward. I saw some of the placards: "Migrants Out," and "Australia for the Aussies," and another reading "Down with Dagos." No matter how unemployment figures grew, the Italians were surviving and resentment against them was rising. I decided not to stay and watch because it reminded me of that day in Trapani when Turiddu and his friends tried to join the procession with their banner.

"Are you going to walk past me like a stranger, Gwen?"

I did not recognize Alan at first in his wig and gown, and I cried out involuntarily.

His voice was the same, resonant and strong, and at the sound of it the cave of memory opened and I was standing on Gwen's Bridge with him and sleeping with his arms around me. I scarcely heard what he was saying: I was listening only to memories.

"Are we friends or foes?"

I muttered something about friendship because I could not trust myself to speak from my heart.

"Come and see my chambers, if you have time."

We said very little to each other as we climbed the stairs to his room where briefs were bundled along the shelves and across his desk.

"I knew where you were and what you were doing," he said.

"Mrs Heffernan?"

"The local Figaro."

Perhaps I shouldn't have spoken so impulsively, but there seemed no point exchanging trivialities when what I wanted to know could be said in one short sentence.

"Why didn't you write to me, Alan?"

For a moment he was silent and frowning, then he spoke slowly and deliberately.

"Were you expecting a reply in kind, Gwen? I would have needed letters of fire to match your particular combination of scorn, derision and abuse."

I forced myself not to recall what I had written in that last letter and made myself concentrate on the present moment. Alan's high white collar and black coat made him seem older but he still pushed his spectacles back into his hair, flecked with grey now.

"Nobody appreciates being given an ultimatum in quite those terms, Gwen. A spaniel might have accepted it—I'm a different breed of dog."

Then, in that instant, I should have told him about my parents and the grotto. I could have made him understand, I know that. Instead, the only words that came to me were a childish reproach.

"I really believed you loved me."

"Did you expect me to come chasing after you on a white charger?"

"Yes—yes, I did, Alan."

That was not all I wanted. Carlo Magno himself knelt before Frastrada when he beseeched her to marry him and, creaking, he did not rise until she had given him her hand. The paladins and the emperor loved as my father had, casting aside fame and empires for the sake of love. Oh, I may have been a woman in years then but my heart was the heart of a child in Trapani watching the puppets joust and die for love.

"I had already promised my mother that we'd wait a year."

"She came first then."

"Never first—"

I could see the muscles in his face twist as though from pain.

"I shall always love you, Gwen. In many ways I'm very like my father; because I love you, I can understand why he married my mother. He had a vision of a certain kind of woman in his mind and he waited year after year to find her. In London, when he was over fifty, he gave up hope and married the first woman who threw herself at him. It was as simple as that. I was more fortunate. I met and loved the woman I'd always dreamed about. She left me, but I have the memory of five months of joy that will sustain me until I die. All I have to do is remember that love and it's like turning away from the cold to warm myself at a fire that never goes out. I used to say that you were a romantic, Gwen. Perhaps I was the romantic after all."

We were silent for a time and when I spoke the words came awkwardly through a tangle of emotions.

"I waited for you, Alan."

"I hoped you'd come back to Griffith."

"No—"

Again a silence. If we loved each other, that love was not running clear and direct between us as it had with my parents, or so I told myself. What I had before me then was a man; what I wanted was a creaking paladin on strings. We struggled to make conversation—

"I'm getting into politics," he said. "And I have you to thank for that, Gwen. Somehow, I was always afraid to follow my father in that direction, probably because I thought I could never accomplish what he did, more likely because my politics are not his. He fought for peace—all I can see is an army of dictators in Europe who make the Kaiser look like a bully in short pants. I remember you telling me about the Fascists and what they did to your father."

I had told him so much about Trapani, but I had never spoken of the grotto. Looking at his briefs, I said he must have a good practice.

"Yes, I'm getting my share of work," he replied, adding that I had done remarkably well for myself.

"I've made a little money." I shrugged and asked if his mother were in Sydney.

"No, she's still in Griffith. I'm leaving for London next week and a case that should take at least two years at the Privy Council. I'm briefed as junior to Howard Denman."

Alan did not reach out and take my hand or kiss me. He sat there staring at me as we conversed awkwardly and I could not read his expression. Abruptly, he said, "Will you come with me, Gwen?"

The serpent was on my tongue because although I longed to feel his body against mine, I could not answer him directly. I hesitated and saw the pain and the anger in his eyes.

We remained seated, facing each other, both of us motionless although we felt desire like hunger between us. It was my flesh that finally answered him.

"I want you to make love to me, Alan."

"We can get married in England," he said eagerly.

"No—love me—here—now."

I felt the sudden tension in his body and his voice came strangely.

"It can't be just that, Gwen."

"I'm asking you to love me!"

"Will you come with me?"

"I—how can you expect me to answer that so quickly?"

"Yet you want to make love here."

"Alan, you're setting limits and making rules again and I don't want that."

"When you decide what it is that you want, I'll probably be able to answer you."

"Stay here with me," I said forlornly.

"No, Gwen, there are things I want to see and do in Europe. The world isn't the sum of our feelings for each other."

"It must be! It should be!" I almost shouted.

"There's talk of another war. I have to see what's going on in Europe for myself."

Drily he added, "Have you forgotten how ambitious I am? Prepared to sacrifice you and everyone else for that ambition."

He was chaffing me as if I were a child. I tried to cling to him but gently he held me away from him.

"In Griffith I told myself that I would never ask you again to be my wife. I knew what would happen and it has. I won't make that mistake again, Gwen—"

Where was my paladin? Love had been so easy when Bessie and I spoke and thought of nothing else that summer in Trapani. We had imagined love then, and a dream was all I had ever known and wanted. I could not answer Alan except with more reproaches.

"An affair was good enough for Griffith—now it has to be marriage or nothing," I shouted angrily.

"Yes—marriage or nothing. Can you understand now what I feel for you?"

Bewildered, I shook my head.

Alan made some coffee and talked desultorily as if we were casual friends.

"Next time—if there is another time—the proposal will be yours," he said lightly, but with an edge to his voice that made me wince. Those were his final words and we shook hands outside the lift with a pair of wigged barristers eyeing us curiously.

The tram rattled up to King's Cross and I knew that once again I had turned aside from a customary life to wander in solitary places. If I could only see myself clearly, as I had when I was a child. I felt as if I were being torn apart in a crowd, with pieces of myself distributed among strangers. Instead of looking back, I made myself concentrate on what I had just learned about Alan: he still owned the law practice in Griffith, although now Fred Dangler was in charge—Fred Dangler and Siegfried as Alan put it: the dog had taken on a new lease of life since he had slept through Mrs Gilchrist's massacre. Alan had not lived in Wyangan Avenue for some time. It was not easy to determine from the little he told me what actually had happened, but I gathered that one night his mother had come to his bedroom and there was a violent argument. Alan had packed a bag that same night and moved into Mirrool House.

Despairingly, I thought what my life had become—guardian to a hotel full of elderly people. Dolfi always said that if I had made a success of Glenarches, it was only because his mother had taught me so well at the Villa d'Athena, and he would follow that by sneering at me as an old maid, telling me that no man would ever want me. Yet Alan had just offered me marriage and for one instant I was about to jump off the tram and run back to his chambers. I would leave everything here and go with him. The ship's captain could marry us and at last I would have my feet in a settled path, no longer an exile. I looked out of the window of the tram—and I saw her standing on the footpath, staring at me, her finger to her lips.

It was Bessie, not the Bessie who left me in Trapani but Bessie when she was eight and we were going to Sunday service at Canon Burnside's. She was wearing a white leghorn trimmed with black satin ribbon and a voile dress speckled with a confetti of different colours. Her finger was pressed to her lips as if warning me to be silent. Suddenly the tram jolted forward and I fell back against the seat. When I craned out of the door to see her, she was gone.

"Make up your mind whether you're getting off or staying on," a woman grumbled, and I shook my head as I tried to understand what had happened.

Norma was in tears when I got back to the hotel and at first I thought that one of the old ladies had upset her.

"It's Teddy. I told Len that I wouldn't have him going to any of those New Guard rallies, but Mum phoned and said that one of Teddy's mates told her that Len had picked him up from school. I won't stand for it! The kid's not going to hang around with those hooligans while I'm his mother. Len was there on the Harbour Bridge when that fool de Groot rode up in front of the Governor and cut the ribbon himself. Now he wants Teddy to join the League and go out shouting and cursing with the rest of those damn fools."

I took her by the arm and we ran out to the pavement just as Mother George and Sister Joseph were about to get into a taxi. Hurriedly, I told her where we were going and why we needed a taxi urgently. It was not my nature to sit quietly and mourn, I said to myself; I would forget Alan in the turbulence of action. We drove off with the echo of Mother George's laughter and her parting words: "Wish I could go with you but Sister Joseph doesn't approve of violence, do you, Sister?"

Norma gave the driver an address in Paddington.

It was a small furniture factory at the corner of Ocean Avenue with "Calsano's Veneers" painted across the door. A group of men outside in faded army uniforms were unfurling a banner. "Dagos Out" it read in flaring red letters, and I watched Len handing Norma's son a placard with "Scab Workers" lettered across it. In the car, Norma told us that the owner of the factory, a Milo Calsano, had just sacked two Australians and taken on some Italian migrants who were working for half the going wage. The New Guard was there to teach him the Australian way.

A dozen Guards were shouting and beating methodically on the wooden gate as Len rushed forward and put his shoulder to the bolt.

"Drag them out and lynch the Dago bastards!" he yelled.

Norma was arguing with Teddy and a couple of men who tried to intervene when she pulled the placard from the boy's hands and pushed him towards the taxi.

"You get in there or I'll beat the living daylights out of you!" she screamed.

Len saw them and yelled at her to leave the boy alone.

The two stood facing each other, the boy thrashing and kicking between them.

"He's my son and I'll tell him what to do!" Len shouted.

"You can tell him what to do when you can feed and clothe him," Norma retorted. "You're nothing but a bludger living in my parents' home and off my money. I never want to see you again. When you can feed the kid, you can have him, but not until then. Now you—" Norma gave the boy a shove that sent him hurtling towards the taxi. "You get in that taxi and talk to the nice driver."

At that instant two Italians turned the corner and stood aghast as they saw the uniformed crowd.

"*Andate via!*" I shouted to them. "*Presto! Andatevene!*"

The men were so surprised, they stood there as if I were Medusa, and they could already feel the stone filling their bellies.

Len bellowed "Scabs!" and the Guards threw themselves against the Italians, beating them to the ground.

I saw Turiddu and his men in that crowd and Alan knocked down by the gangers and they were all calling on me to help them. Climbing on a fence, I began to scream for the police at the top of my voice and then I flung myself in among the men, cursing them in Italian because I had forgotten my English.

Almost at the same moment the police were there and I felt myself lifted up by my hair and the back of my skirt as if I were a cat and dropped on to the pavement. The side of my face was throbbing as I tried to scramble towards the taxi through the jumbled shapes of blue and khaki. Barely able to focus, I glanced up and saw Dr Bowles with a New Guard ribbon in his lapel. I was about to speak to him but he glared past me and turned away in disgust.

Norma's eyes were upraised, her lips pursed, when I finally collapsed alongside her in the taxi. I knew she was convinced that a strain of insanity ran in my family.

"You did the same thing in Griffith, didn't you?" she said tersely.

"My mother always called me Boadicea," I replied. "Let's go to Florrie's and have something to eat."

Teddy chose to eat his pie and its dobs of mashed potato and peas with the driver on the front seat while Norma kept a watchful eye on them both. Florrie and I stood on the pavement with a throng of men eating pies from the palm of one hand and swilling down beer from mugs in the other.

"God, you look a mess," Florrie said to me.

"You would be too if you decided to take on the New Guard single-handed," Norma retorted.

"You're so bloody cunning in some ways, Gwen," Florrie added and gave me a wet towel and some ice to hold against my face. "But when it comes to managing your personal life, a half-baked idiot could do better."

Behind me I could hear Henry's cathedral tones: "Three pints coming up—coming up now."

"I would have had Danny's ring on my finger by now, if I'd been you."

"I just met Alan again and I refused to go with him to England," I said miserably.

"Alan? That mother's boy from the bush? You keep your sights fixed on Danny Burns—he's going to make Mo look like an amateur when he opens at the Tivoli. His film's coming out at the same time and he'll be world famous before you know it. Mrs Danny Burns—now that's something to aim for. You want to put Alan out of your mind. Dead romances are like old fish."

I was between laughing and putting my head against the wall of the pub and weeping when Norma got out of the taxi and joined us.

"I've been looking at them," she said. "They're not all working men—I mean, there's some nicely spoken, well-dressed chaps over there."

"We've become fashionable." Florrie bridled complacently. "Having a pie and peas outside the Rutledge Arms is the in thing these days. The two Fairfax boys were here last week and just yesterday Beau Liddel came in for a pie and a beer and insisted on the horses having a beer too."

Everybody in Sydney knew about Beau Liddel who would commandeer one of Resch's brewery wagons with its six matched Clydesdales when he was drunk and drive it.

"We had to bring out a bucket of beer for each of the horses and then he tried to feed them pies. It would have made a cat laugh—there he was, Beau Liddel, roaring at the top of his voice, 'These pies aren't fit for horses!' Even the policeman was doubled up when he cautioned him."

"Oh my God!" I cried. "That taxi's still over there with the meter running!"

My jaw still ached and I lay awake most of the night thinking of Alan and Bessie. I remembered that gesture of hers so well, a warning to be silent because something extraordinary was about to happen. Bessie, my Persephone, must be dead, why otherwise would I have seen her? First in the train from Griffith and then on the kerb in William Street, and yet this afternoon she was younger, as if memory and time were taking her to a beginning and me to an end. Confused and in pain, I tossed on my pillow, trying to understand what Bessie meant. Was it true, as Dolfi always said, that I was stupid? Or had my life become a series of mysteries that I could not interpret?

When I was telling Florrie what Alan had said to me she gaped in amazement.

"You don't know what he was really saying?"

"No," I replied.

Then she said there were things you were supposed to understand without being told and that I knew nothing about men. Perhaps she was right, just as Bessie was when she tried to teach me a killing look and said that she was clever while I was wise.

Wisdom is no guide when you're travelling in the country of love.

I would have given anything to have felt Alan's arms around me that night, to have heard his breath so close to mine that it would seem we were sharing the same body. Was this what Bessie was telling me? Should I have jumped off that tram and run back to his chambers, begged him to take me with him to England? No, that wasn't right, because it had been in the very instant that I decided to go back that I had seen Bessie on the kerb pressing her finger to her lips and frowning.

The following morning the night porter woke me and said there was something I should see downstairs. Bleary with sleep I felt my way down to the lobby and tried to decipher the daubed letters on the glass front doors.

I walked outside and read, “Dago bitch. Go home!” in letters still dripping paint.

“Find some turpentine and get rid of that immediately. It must have been some drunks.”

My voice was firm and I could hear my mother’s peremptory tone as I spoke, but my stomach was twisting with fear. It was the New Guard; probably Len had daubed that warning.

“If you see your husband,” I told Norma at lunch, “tell him that I won’t stand for him or his Fascist friends damaging this property. I’ve already spoken to the police and they’re going to have a man stationed outside the front gates this evening.”

“I don’t think I’ll be seeing him again,” Norma said, and her eyes showed that she had spent the night awake and crying. “I put all his stuff in two cases and left them on the front veranda. Everything was gone this morning.”

Someone on the staff must have gossiped because one of the old ladies asked me if the unemployed were going to storm Glenarches. I went about smiling and deprecating the rumours and by afternoon everything seemed tranquil again. However, even as I was attributing the incident to some drunken larrikins, I knew that I was under siege.

Dolfi was elated when he arrived with Terry that evening and for once I did not have to listen to a monologue about nuns. Several of the stagehands at the Tivoli, where he was now in the final rehearsals, had told him he was making Mo look like a busker and he was crowing with delight.

“I am going to be the most famous comedian in the world,” he declared in ringing tones that echoed through the hotel.

“Please, Dolfi, don’t make so much noise,” I said, and told him that the guests were very nervous about the New Guard.

Dolfi sank back in my chair and glared at me across his glass, reminding me that my life was a failure and I had disgraced my family. With a solemn face he declared that his only regret was leaving Trapani when he did. If he had remained there I would still be a virgin.

When I laughed, he was furious and said that I was as stupid as I was ugly. I was the only person who was never amused by his jokes and insisted on grinning like a fool when he was giving me advice for my own good. He dragged Terry to his feet and stalked out in a huff, saying that the next thing he expected to hear was that I had become a nun in Mother George’s bordello.

It seemed that I had failed everyone—even Dr Bowles, who had saved my life on the ship and who had arranged for some Presbyterian women in Sydney to take care of me. I hadn’t really cared for the man, but I shall never forget his expression of disgust and disbelief. Why, I asked myself, was the past crowding back on me, bringing only reproaches with it? Dolfi, with his continual criticism, even Dr Bowles, and Alan. I had been given a second chance there, and I refused it.

I walked over to my bookcase and picked up a volume of Homer that my father had annotated for me when I was a child. How distressed he would have been to see me at Glenarches, hoarding gold like a *contadina*. My mother always said that I had been educated to be a classical scholar and called me Boadicea when I argued with her. I slammed the book shut and decided that I had made enough money and it was time now to become what my parents had always wanted. If I could go back and start afresh I would know how to walk safely through life. This, I assured myself, was what Bessie was trying to tell me. Alan did not love me as I desired and I was not going to remain here at the hotel like the ghost of Frau Brunner, a hostage to the bully-boys of the New Guard. The next morning I took a bus and a tram to Sydney University and walked up the hill to the Gothic buildings on the rise.

A student told me where to find the Nicholson Museum in a corner of the quadrangle, adding that he thought it was open.

The past was flooding my head with voices and images that flashed before my eyes like a demented lantern show. The museum of my home, the Pepoli in Trapani and the Museum of Antiquities in Palermo; my father holding up a sherd to the light, my mother smiling at him and murmuring something I couldn't hear, all of it coming back to me so quickly that I leaned against one of the cases to keep my balance.

There was very little to see—a collection of plaster casts and a poor selection of pottery that seemed mainly Cypriote, but it was a museum and I had spent most of my life in places like this.

"Can I be of assistance?"

A youngish, dusty man in a ragged gown was contemplating me through blurred spectacles.

"I would like to work here in the university," I said and he almost took a step backwards in surprise. I too felt my breath caught short because this was someone I had known before. The voice was the same, sharply inflected, asking Bessie if she had sore eyes—Bessie whom he once described as a fat little red-haired girl. I had refused to speak to him again after that and now he was here, squinting at me bemusedly.

"Work? You—you're a student?"

"No, I'm a classical scholar."

I saw my father's student, David Maybrick, standing in front of me, but he still had not recognized me. His mouth was quivering under a ragged moustache stained with tobacco and he spoke solemnly as if to a schoolgirl.

"I see—you have your degrees from—what university?"

"I never went to school or university. I was taught by my parents in Trapani. My father, Enrico di Marineo, was a great scholar, you know that."

"Dear Lord—you can't be—my dear girl, what a delightful surprise! You remember me, don't you?"

As I was nodding, I tried to see in this shabby scruff of a man the young archaeologist who had once given me a parcel of books.

He made me tea in the curator's room over a gas burner and I drank slowly from a cracked cup that felt greasy and looked worse.

"Employment here?"

He seemed to think I was making an elaborate joke—it was some time before he realized how serious I was.

"My dear girl, you can't teach without degrees. You have no qualification."

"I was a better scholar than you when I was twelve," I retorted and his face coloured.

"There has been a lot of water under the bridge since then, or should I say, *Mira quaedam in cognoscendo suavitas et delectatio*, but a degree helps."

There are so many stories in mythology of people who defy an oracle, like Oedipus, whose disobedience led to all his misfortunes. But there is very little about those who simply could not interpret the words of the oracle, who tried, but were unable to read the signs before them. Bessie had come to me, once to encourage me with her smile on the train from Griffith, once to warn, and yet I did not know what she was warning me against when I saw her with her finger pressed to her lips. Was it against returning to Alan, or against staying at Glenarches? I looked around me at the museum and realized that the answer was not here; knew that I could never return here, not in this way, and not to a place that smelled like a grave.

"So there is nothing for me here in the university," I said.

"Admittedly, there is nothing to prevent you from taking courses—but I forget, since you never went to school, I doubt if you could even be admitted as a student."

At that moment I felt as if I were standing in a pit of ashes and if I stayed there any longer I would be buried in it.

"You do need work, you said."

He was chewing his tattered moustache and I read the expression in his face and laughed inwardly.

"David—" Now I could not restrain my laughter. "I probably make more in a week than you earn in a month."

"I did not become a scholar to make money," he replied stiffly.

"You know, I'm trying to understand why I came here," I said ruefully. "It was a whim—I was thinking about my parents."

"Oh yes, I found a mention of your father in a footnote the other day. He had a small reputation in his field."

David Maybrick was deliberately provoking me but I would not respond.

"If you are interested in continuing your classical studies, I'm afraid that I'm far too busy to take on any additional students. However, there is an old chap who coaches in his spare time. Let me give you his card. Of course, he's not qualified in an academic sense but he's quite sound. Students he's coached speak highly of him."

He handed me a card and I dropped it in my purse without looking at it.

"You've seen your cousin, haven't you?" David said as I rose to leave.

"Oh yes, we have dinner occasionally. He's doing wonderfully well for himself too—the film is almost finished and he opens soon at the Tivoli."

David seemed bewildered.

"I meant your cousin Edith. She's back here in Sydney."

After his final battle with the Saracens, Orlando blows his horn three times and falls back dying in a lonely valley. The dead arrive to welcome him; trapdoors open in the stage and Orlando's drowned father, Milono, stretches out his hands to him; his brother springs up from another trapdoor in full armour, and the ghosts of Carlo Magno's paladins drop down from above, singing the hero's praises. At the performance I saw, the strings of the angel descending to take Orlando's soul to paradise became tangled with those of a paladin and there was some fierce tugging and muffled curses before the angel and the paladin were released and Orlando's ascension was completed. It is like the scene in *Macbeth* when eight future kings appear at the command of the witches together with visions of dead children and severed heads. For a brief space, the stage is crowded with ghosts and their ambassadors while Macbeth ponders his past actions and probable fate.

For almost half an hour I sat on the stone coping of a wall outside the university watching the traffic on Parramatta Street and the city shimmering through the summer haze. Dolfi had come back into my life as suddenly and erratically as he had first appeared on the steps of the Villa d'Athena and now, like a dingy and bedraggled Hermes, David Maybrick had brought me news that my cousin Edith was in Sydney.

There was a logic of events that made it possible for Dolfi to be in Sydney, but David Maybrick and Edith? Unconsciously, I had always thought of myself as the only exile, forgetting how many people were leaving Europe for a new life in America and Australia. Edith's father was Australian, I recalled that, and she had been born in this country, so it was reasonable enough for her to be here. David had accepted a post as tutor at Sydney University because, like other scholars in England, he knew he would have to wait for someone to die before he could get an academic place. This did not seem so extraordinary when I considered it. What was remarkable was that they should all have returned to my life at the same time. And why Dolfi? I had never cared for him and if I had been told that he was leaving for India tomorrow, it would not have disturbed me. No, I suddenly felt an imperative certainty about these events. They were like the dead crowding the stage before the angel appears: they were the heralds for Bessie.

Two passing students stopped and stared at me because my face must have revealed the passion that left me suddenly breathless. I got up slowly and stumbled past them with my head down, muttering about feeling dizzy in the sun while assuring them that I was much better now and didn't need a glass of water. Edith's address was on a scrap of paper in my purse and I was sure that she knew where Bessie was, or perhaps Bessie herself would be standing in the lobby of Glenarches when I got back.

There was no sign of Bessie as I walked through to my office and, amazed, I wondered what had made me act so impulsively, rushing off to the nearest museum like someone bewitched. As soon as I had seen those ranked cases and plaster casts I knew that I could never return to cataloguing pots and sorting sherds, nor was I inclined to spend the rest of my life deciphering ancient Greek texts. No, I had been sent to the museum to find Bessie.

Edith's address was in Darling Point, and in my mind I saw again that crowded stage with paladins jostling each other and the angel trying to ascend through a tangle of strings. Dolfi was living less than a quarter mile from me, Edith was almost as close. There was a telephone number, and when I called, an elderly woman answered and said Miss Wigram had been ill but she would be pleased to see me the following day.

Trelawney had been advertised in all the papers as the most luxurious apartment building in Sydney and while I was admiring the foyer with its fountain and coloured marble floor, I realized that Edith must now be a very wealthy woman. Not only was she a Harcourt from Russell Morton, but she would certainly have had a share of her father's estate. A uniformed concierge escorted me up in the lift to the top floor, then a brisk middle-aged housekeeper ushered me into a vestibule lined with *trompe l'oeil* woodwork. While she bustled off to see if Edith was ready to receive me, I had time to look around.

One side of the wall imitated bookshelves and when I touched it, a door opened into a real library. It was there, browsing along the shelves, that I first became acquainted with Brantôme and de Sade along with a great many similar works: *The Way of a Man with a Maid*, *The Romance of Lust* and something called *The Yellow Room* with illustrations. There was no attempt to conceal these books—they were all ranked together in a corner and some of them were marked with turned-down pages. It was a collection of erotica, and not a small one. Opposite the door was a pharmacopoeial collection and underneath it a series of books on anthropology and witchcraft. It was a curious library, without a single book of poetry or any of the usual works of literature.

The housekeeper returned and told me quietly that Miss Wigram would see me now but I must keep in mind that she had been very ill and it would not help her condition if she were excited in any way.

All I wanted from Edith was information. There was a smouldering rage inside me as I remembered how she had ignored my pleas to help me find Bessie, how all the letters I posted from Trapani went unanswered. If she told me where Bessie was I would be satisfied and leave.

The room startled me with its pallor: there was no colour anywhere. Walls, ceiling, furniture and carpets were shades of white, and long venetians obliterated all view of the sky and the Harbour. A white figure with hair so fair it was like ivory lay on a daybed.

"Why did you wear such hideously bright colours? I can't bear colour."

Was this Edith? Where was the fat and grubby young woman of Russell Morton in this wraith wrapped in lace and chiffon? I sat down on a white brocade chair beside her and tried to see if there was anything I could remember in her face. She looked old, with eyes buried deep in dark hollows and lines wedged at the side of her mouth.

"Where is Bessie?" I asked abruptly.

"Oh, charming as ever," she drawled and then I recalled her voice. "Not, 'Poor Edith, you look positively frightful. I'm so sorry you've been ill. Are you feeling better now?' "

"I wrote you dozens of letters."

"Yes, and I received and read them, Gwen dear, but there was nothing I could do at the time. My father died three weeks after you left. I helped nurse him. I was fond of my father and I wasn't going to let my mother make his last days a misery."

"My father died too."

"Then you can understand why I wasn't able to mount a search for your missing friend."

"You do know something now."

"Yes, I rather think I do—"

"Please, tell me! Edith, I beg you!"

I think I was on my knees and sobbing with relief. Only with Bessie would my life become whole again. Only she could make me understand myself and bring back that perfect summer.

Twenty-Eight

The passion of my anxiety seemed to please Edith and she smiled, pointing to a corner of the room.

"Over there in the top drawer of my desk you'll find a writing case. It should be in there."

It was a cutting from a newspaper dated 12 July 1928, announcing the marriage of Robert Fletcher of Ottawa, Canada, to Miss Beryl Morrison of New York. There was a list of guests but no mention of Bessie or her mother.

"I don't understand what this means," I said.

"Fletcher didn't marry Bessie's mother after all."

"But they left England to get married! They had an understanding."

"Something must have happened to change his mind."

"It doesn't make sense."

"Not to you, although I imagine it makes perfectly good sense to the present Mr and Mrs Fletcher."

"What happened to Bessie and her mother?"

"My dear Gwen, who gave you the right to understand everything? In life, you're lucky if you get ten per cent right."

The sudden bitterness in her voice made her sound like another person and I stared at her in surprise.

"You can spend your life trying to understand and fail, or you can try to reach something much simpler—to feel, just to feel and still end where you began."

I knew Bessie's last letter by heart and I recited part of it to Edith now.

"So—Fletcher dumped her. Serves the bitch right if what you just told me about her is true."

"What could she have done afterwards, though?"

"What can jilted women do—get over it if they have any brains, or commit suicide if they're stupid. At least I never tried to kill myself for a man. Mind you, I'm trying to persuade David Maybrick to kill himself for me, but he seems obdurately committed to life despite all his professions of undying love. Giving up the chance of a good job at the University of Cape Town to follow me here isn't enough to satisfy me."

She went on deprecating the quality of David's love, but I didn't hear her. At the very worst, I told myself, Edith would say that she hadn't bothered to make enquiries about Bessie, that she had been too busy with whatever occupied her, yet here she was, bored at last with David Maybrick as a subject, and telling me that she had written to a number of friends in Manchester and they informed her that Fletcher had indeed left with Mrs Chambers and Bessie and there was a great scandal about it all. What no one knew was when—or if—they were married. The newspaper cutting showed him marrying an American woman who was neither young nor good-looking, so what could have happened to Mrs Chambers and Bessie? Was Bessie dead as I sometimes believed? Was that why I saw her from the tram?

Mrs McGregor, the housekeeper, brought in a tray of tea and left us after warning me that Miss Wigram must not be fatigued. I drank the tea automatically, scarcely listening to Edith, who smoked long white cigarettes in an even longer holder of bleached bone.

"The treatment almost killed me. The doctors said I would be scampering around in the sunshine by summer, but they were wrong. I did everything and I failed."

"I'm sorry, Edith. I wasn't listening."

"You haven't changed. Nothing means anything to you except this Bessie."

"She was half my life."

"Do you think she spends all her time worrying about you, Gwen?"

"I don't even know if she's alive."

"Oh, she's probably married with a mob of kids now."

I shook my head because I didn't know, and not knowing was more painful than any tragedy Edith might have told me.

She was leaning forward and staring at me with the same hungry intensity I remembered when we were sitting on the hillside.

"That bruise on the side of your face, Gwen—did someone strike you?"

Briefly, I told her about the riot of the Italians and the New Guard.

"What did you feel when you were fighting?" she asked urgently.

"Nothing—nothing except anger," I replied.

"Ah, but I saw it in your expression just now. You looked possessed—as if you were alive in a way I can only imagine. If only I could have been you!"

"You wouldn't really want my life, Edith."

"You understand yourself—"

The absurdity of that made me laugh, and I told her that I did not particularly like the little I knew about myself.

"I'm imprisoned outside of myself," she moaned.

I must have looked at her enquiringly because she took hold of my hand and pressed it to her breast.

"It's here—inside me—but I can't reach it."

"You said once you wanted to feel and just now—"

"Oh yes, and I've done a great many things since we had our little chat in Shropshire. It's the outside that presses in on me—that's why the room is white. White doesn't disturb me as colours do."

"Most people are afraid of what's inside them."

"Freud and all that nonsense." She scoffed. "I've been psychoanalysed. It didn't help. De Sade glimpsed the truth when he said you found it through outrageous pain, but no matter what I did to myself and to others, I could never break through to my own being. He was the greatest philosopher who ever lived, and I know that if anyone held the secret, it was he. To be a powerful being is to live like nature—her only laws are the bloodstreams of her own vitality: Vesuvius swallowing Pompeii, a lion tearing open the gut of a freshly killed deer. I tried to follow him—to lead a boiling life and destroy as wantonly as Nero. Nothing—"

"I have no idea what you're talking about, Edith."

"Promise me you'll read him—there must be something I missed."

"I don't know what it is you want."

"It's here—in me—I just told you—and when it's released I'll feel—"

"Feel what?"

"Myself like nature."

I sat there staring at the picture of Robert Fletcher, unsmiling even on his wedding day.

Mrs McGregor was clearing her throat behind me and I realized that Edith was lying back with her eyes closed.

"You'll come back, won't you?"

"Yes, of course," I replied automatically.

"Take de Sade with you—all his works are in the library."

As I was leaving, I asked Mrs McGregor what was wrong with my cousin.

"She had a severe illness that required treatment," she said flatly.

Nothing made any sense to me as I walked back across the park and up the hill to Glenarches. The unemployed were camping under the trees in humpies made of sacking and some of them were already lighting camp fires. Two policemen went round ordering the fires out but they could do nothing against such a crowd.

Robert Fletcher and Bessie's mother must have quarrelled—or was that another story I was fabricating in order to make a pattern of what I couldn't understand? I was convinced that Edith was deranged and I determined not see her again—and yet I knew that I would because she was my cousin.

As soon as I got back to Glenarches, I phoned the Canadian consulate and asked if they could help me find Robert Fletcher of Ottawa. A secretary gave me the address of Fletcher Enterprises. I wrote the same evening and six months later I received a reply signed by a secretary: Mr Fletcher had no knowledge of any woman by the name of Betty Chambers or of her daughter Elizabeth, and did not wish to hold any further communication with me. Nothing else. I crumpled the letter in despair. If Bessie was dead, I no longer had the strength to question or struggle. Almost insensibly, I felt that I must wait for her to come to me, just as Edith and Dolfi had come back into my life.

Edith was with me when the letter arrived and I recall that she picked it up, smoothing out the creases with her white fingers. At least once a week her chauffeur drove her to the hotel and she had dinner with me in my suite. She was still the same Edith because I don't remember her once inviting me to a restaurant.

"You can eat so cheaply when you're managing a hotel, can't you?" she always said.

Even though I was now paying for a guard to patrol the outside of the hotel at night, there were more harassing incidents. I had no doubt that the New Guard was responsible, and no matter how I threatened the staff with instant dismissal if they gossiped, word of these incidents always reached the guests. For days the tranquillity of Glenarches would be undisturbed and then, inexplicably, something would happen. One morning the cook told me that a case of lettuces from the market was spoiled. The lettuces looked as if someone had poured acid on them because when the box was opened in the kitchen it was full of brown slime.

Just a coincidence, I assured everyone, and fortunately people were prepared to blame some unemployed workers who had been caught stealing fruit and vegetables in Paddy's Market. I sighed and shook my head with everyone else, but that morning I received a scrawled note in the post: a single sheet and across it, "Go home you Dago bitch."

I decided to behave as if nothing untoward had occurred, but Mrs Fielding was now insisting that the nurse sleep in the bed next to hers, and it needed several visits from Mother George and all her good humour to calm the old lady's fears.

Once I tried to discuss my troubles with Edith, but she had no interest in anything except herself. Her obsession went beyond narcissism: Dolfi, for all his failings, enjoyed himself even if no one else existed for him except as an audience. By comparison with Edith, he was the soul of innocence.

Edith spoke ceaselessly about being shut in outside herself and wanting to be free—and I could never comprehend what she meant. "Free to do what?" I asked her, and she always replied: to be herself. She had some idea that only by means of this release could she feel, and for my cousin, feeling was the totality of being. She had tried everything from drugs to experiences in Berlin that made the circles of Hell seem like Glenarches on a summer afternoon. The stories she told were not like Dolfi's fabulous atrocities. Laconically, almost as an afterthought, she spoke about trials of pain where a man was tortured and children ritually mutilated, of orgies where animals and freaks copulated in frenzies of lust. At the last, she had tried heroin and cocaine and only when she was dying did she realize that the drugs were suffocating her, not releasing her. She had spent six months in a Swiss sanatorium trying to recover her health. What the doctors found incomprehensible, she said, was that she had no difficulty giving up the addiction once she knew that drugs could not release her.

Sometimes, I would come back to Glenarches and find her asleep on my bed, or smoking in a chair, and occasionally all I saw from the door was a spiral of smoke ascending to the ceiling. Like Dolfi, she regarded the hotel as her second home, yet I could never bring myself to tell her to leave. Wearily, I tried to listen as she complained about the noise from the street or the shape of my lampshade. Everything was either a recounting of horrors or a catalogue of complaints so trivial that Mrs Fielding seemed an angel of tolerance by comparison.

She had just thrown my father's copy of Herodotus aside and was saying, "Never read history. Historians are the most dangerous liars of all because they believe in narratives. Narratives imply order and order is death in life."

"Leave my books alone," I screamed at her, but two days later I found her dozing in my chair with another of my books on the floor beside her.

Even Dolfi had been startled by some of her stories and the casual way she recounted these horrors, holding them out at arm's length from herself like drowned kittens. Edith had believed that the only way to be fully alive was to deliver herself up to the most monstrous impulses. She had attempted this and found what I did when I read de Sade—a boredom that was stupefying.

One evening Dolfi and Edith were both delivering monologues from opposite sides of the room while Terry and I chatted quietly between them. At least Terry listened to me when I wondered if Alan would ever write to me.

"You did send him away," Terry said.

"If he loved me, he would have come back to me," I retorted.

"What? Give up a big case in London? You really couldn't expect that, Gwen."

But of course I did, because that was what my father would have done.

As if on cue, Dolfi and Edith turned on us and told us to pay attention, berating us for our rudeness and selfishness.

Once, I foolishly asked Edith if she had ever been in love and that reduced her to gasps of laughter.

"I actually married once and filed for divorce three weeks later. There is nothing above love I don't know and haven't experienced."

Often she asked about my parents and I must have told her a dozen times how they met and how they lived each other's life.

"I believe I could love like that if I could find myself," she said.

"Perhaps you're like the Princess in *Turandot* and you need someone to love you."

"Love? I once made a man die for me, and I could make David Maybrick do the same if I didn't know it would bore me going to his funeral. If suicide were a release, I'd kill myself now, but that would be like taking heroin. Death is a denial and the feeling would be stillborn. I had another of my 'turns' in the sanatorium and the clever doctors thought I was dead. Nothing ever happens then—it's like waking from sleep into the same boredom."

There was an affinity between Edith and me that I did not choose to recognize at that time: she wanted some inexplicable kind of release to find herself, I wanted Bessie to feel myself whole again. Perhaps Edith sensed this before I did and it was the reason she insisted on calling me her only friend.

There were two more incidents at the hotel before Dolfi's opening at the Tivoli, both of them trifling, but the atmosphere was becoming charged with little currents of alarm. I called all the staff together and told them that they would have to be more watchful than ever and said that some of the unemployed must be resentful of old people living so comfortably at Glenarches. When I received another letter, this time without a postmark, I hired a private detective as a porter and told him to keep an eye on the staff.

Dolfi's picture, *Dino Down and Out*, was released a week before the opening night at the Tivoli; next day all the papers said that the young Irish comedian was a natural film actor and a sequel would be in production shortly. It was difficult to resist the excitement and when I left for the theatre with Mr Gresham, even Mrs Fielding insisted that she be brought downstairs to see us off.

Terry was in a state of subdued hysteria because Dolfi had vanished for almost two days when the show was in its last week of rehearsals and the management had threatened to cancel the act. Dolfi had been unconcerned by all this and calmly said that he required a rest and stars did not need to rehearse like amateur performers. He insisted that Roy Rene was a vindictive old man who had written to his Jewish friend, Charlie Chaplin, and successfully prevented Dolfi from receiving a fabulous Hollywood contract. The newspapers, particularly the Sunday rag, *Truth*, all declared that there was open war between Roy Rene and Danny Burns. However, Terry told me that Roy Rene had intervened to stop the producer sacking Dolfi on the spot when he disappeared; still, for Dolfi, any rival was an enemy conspiring to destroy him. "The Contest of the Comics" was how the opening night was being described and bets were taken on who would get the most laughs.

Edith, to my astonishment, accepted Dolfi's invitation to attend, saying that she admired his selfishness, and that she regarded this as his greatest talent. I saw her briefly in the foyer on the arm of a beaming David Maybrick.

Dolfi was greeted with the familiar roar of "Dino the Dago!" when he pranced on stage and found himself in the middle of six stately showgirls wearing little but feathers and a few spangles. For one wrenching moment, the lights and his make-up made me remember the golden satyr of Trapani and I realized that every woman was looking at him with Bessie's eyes. What happened to Dolfi's straw hat convulsed the audience and Mr Gresham murmured to me between titters, "Frightfully risqué—much too blue for my taste—didn't really want to let him have a reception room at the Australia for his party. He's only a second cousin of yours, isn't he?"

"Much more distant than that," I replied, and as Dolfi capered and swooned in front of the showgirls, I saw the Phlyax vases and their jaunty little men with enormous organs, and Dolfi holding a vase from the locked cabinet in one hand while he used the other to scratch his head with the Elymian strigil.

What amazed me was that there were groups of Italians in the audience and when Danny appeared for his curtain call, they stood, screaming ecstatically, and the ushers had to stop some of them climbing through the orchestra and on to the stage with bouquets of flowers. The Jews in the audience were more restrained for Mo's performance, yet they too cheered as Roy Rene spluttered and spat across the footlights.

For the finale of his act Dolfi must have had a spring in his trousers because he left the stage waving his hands and blowing kisses to the audience, his hat perched on some contraption below his waist. People were weeping with laughter and called him back a dozen times for an encore. Dolfi was a star.

If there was a competition between Mo and Danny, it was a draw because

Roy Rene received an equally uproarious response from the crowd and, at the party after the show, Dolfi was so angry he could barely speak.

"He should be banned! Driven from the stage!" Dolfi screamed. "The man is a lewd immoral monster! That whip and the showgirl holding the banana—it was obscene!"

Only one person seemed to dislike the show as much as I had, and that was David Maybrick, who sat sourly at the party while Edith flattered and praised Dolfi. Whether she was really amused or was simply enjoying herself making David miserable was difficult to say. "Dolfi has found himself," she said to me more than once.

"Would you like to have what he's found?" I replied and she accused me of deliberately misunderstanding her.

When everyone milled around congratulating him, and the newspapers came out the following morning acclaiming his genius, Dolfi was mollified, but he said he would never appear on the same bill again with such a filthy comedian as Roy Rene.

The following night Dolfi and Terry burst into my office with the news that 2FC had offered them a radio show.

"In America," Terry said, "they're producing plays on phonograph records and selling the records all over the country to radio stations like 2FC. Of course, you need a cast of actors and a recording studio—"

"Actors?" Dolfi sneered. "I could play every part."

"Dolfi's going to do three different characters in his 2FC skits," Terry said excitedly.

"Tell her about Miss Snapper." Dolfi giggled.

"Well—" Terry began lamely and Dolfi continued.

"Dino is in love with an ugly schoolteacher who has a long nose and speaks like this . . ."

I heard my mother's clipped accent and I realized that Dolfi was imitating me.

"The teacher's name is Miss Gwenadalina Snapper and Dino is mad with love for her—except when there are other women around and then he's mad for them too."

"It sounds funnier than your levitating hat at the Tivoli," I said tersely.

"Nobody will associate it with you, Gwen," Terry assured me.

"Not unless Dolfi tells every journalist in Sydney who it is—and I'm sure he will."

"I only mentioned it to Billy Garvin—" Dolfi said.

"Garvin lives in sewers and wants everyone to be his neighbour," I shouted. "It's not enough that I'm being driven out of Glenarches by the New Guard, now you have to make fun of me on radio, Dolfi!"

"It's all your fault, Gina," Dolfi sneered. "You treat the staff at Glenarches as though you were my mother and so naturally everyone hates you."

"I'll write to your mother in Miami and tell her about her famous son!"

"Do that and I'll tell Billy Garvin you sleep with dogs and poison your guests."

"Please—I can't bear it when you both scream at each other," Terry wailed.

"Has no one any consideration for others? I would appreciate a little quiet when I'm resting. You all seem to forget how ill I've been," Edith said and we suddenly realized that she had been asleep in the armchair by the window.

The following Saturday night the Tivoli was packed with Italians who greeted Dino the Dago with delirious applause and cheering. Terry told me that Dolfi now had such a following that the same groups came back, night after night. One prosperous-looking family of seven, two stout women with a little bald-headed man who threw flowers at the stage, and four men in tight suits waving and applauding, had been there on the opening night and they were there again on Saturday.

I remembered that in Sicily everybody had relations in America; more chose to emigrate to the United States than to Australia. Surely Dino would be as popular there as he was with this Tivoli audience. His priapic capering offended me, but if everyone else, and particularly the Italians, believed him to be a comic genius, it didn't matter that I thought his act was dismally absurd.

After the show, Terry and Dolfi took me to supper, Dolfi driving his latest acquisition, a red Bugatti sports car that looked like something left behind by Martians. Because the sequel to *Dino Down and Out* was already being planned and Dolfi's radio show was booked for six weeks, they were renting a Spanish villa on the waterfront at Darling Point near Trelawney, with a staff of servants that would have been enough for a small hotel.

"I intend to give brilliant parties with only entertaining and brilliant people like myself," Dolfi said expansively.

"Can you afford all this?" I asked Terry quietly.

"We could—if only he'd stop gambling," Terry replied.

"I was thinking about what you told me the other day—making records of plays and selling them to radio stations."

"It could become quite a business here, too, as more people buy wireless sets."

It was less than an idea at that moment but, as Florrie always said, I had a talent for making money.

"No, I was thinking, perhaps—we could sell to America."

As I spoke, Dolfi was warbling with his head thrown back and steering the car down the wrong side of the street. Terry and I both grabbed the wheel at the same time and I thought that only a lunatic would ever invest money in somebody who called himself Dino the Dago.

A week had passed at Glenarches without any incidents, but when I arrived back that evening a dead rat had just been found on one of the card tables and several old ladies were having hysterics, then inexplicably the lights failed just before midnight and when the police arrived, they found that the main electric cable to the hotel had been cut. The detective was certain that someone on the staff was responsible and so was I, especially when I no longer received threatening messages in the post. Instead, I would go up to my suite and find an unstamped letter pushed under my door.

"Len's written to me from Melbourne," Norma said tearfully. "He wants Teddy to join him there. Perhaps if I let him go, these terrible things will stop."

"Tell him to go to hell," I replied, wondering how long I would be able to continue running Glenarches.

I had just opened another of these unstamped letters when I looked up and saw Mother George. There was such grief in her face that I barely troubled to read the latest threatening scrawl.

"What is it? Is anything wrong?" I asked her.

"I was sitting with my aunt, reading to her. She always enjoyed that."

"Yes, I know."

I did not say any more for I could see what had happened in Mother George's face.

"I reached the end of the chapter and I asked her if she wanted to sleep. Oh, my dear, she was dead."

Twenty-Nine

Most of the guests at Glenarches were Anglican and a number of them were bigoted anti-Catholics, but they all put aside their prejudices when they spoke about Mother George. "After all, she was Betty Trevanion of Rutherglen before she became a nun," they told me. A few had suspected that Mother George was hoping for a death-bed inheritance from Mrs Fielding until they heard from some of the Irish kitchen staff (who always entertained Sister Joseph as if she were the Holy Father himself) that it was Mother George who paid for Mrs Fielding's suite and her private nurses. "Trust a Trevanion not to let the Church take all her money," the older guests murmured sagely then. And yet I think it was Mother George's laughter they all looked forward to and enjoyed when she was upstairs with her aunt, booming and gusting down the stairs "like one of the blessed Lord's cannon," as the cook said. Certainly, it was her laughter that always unsettled me, not by its noise, but with the echoes it carried of a life beyond my reach, as if I were living in a cave and listening to the muffled sounds of a world outside the darkness.

When I asked her if I could do anything to help, she said, with a glint of humour, that Sister Joseph had taken charge.

"She enjoys occasions like this," Mother George said wryly. "The priest and the doctor will soon be here and Sister will see to it that none of the guests are disturbed. My aunt has been dying for over a year now, so I ought to thank God that He took her without suffering. It was a good death, but I shall miss her."

Her rough brown hands were clasped around a rosary and I thought she might be praying but then I realized she was talking more to herself than to God.

"She was the only one of my family who understood. The only one who didn't call me a wicked fool—she knew that I was in love."

I don't know why I chose to speak about my parents at that moment. She listened intently as I told her how they met and how their love had endured to their death—and how bitterly I had always resented that love.

"Love is jealous, it always separates you from someone," she said sadly.

"They never wanted me." I sounded like a child.

"Can you forgive them?"

"No."

She reached out and took both my hands in hers.

"You will never be able to love until you learn how to forgive."

"I want so much to be loved," I said, and I could not believe that this petulant demand was mine except that I was hearing my own voice.

"So that you can punish your parents by refusing love when it's offered?"

I put my head on my knees and began to cry. Her hand was on my head.

"Let me tell you what only my aunt knew. I did not speak of it—not the whole of it—even to my confessor and perhaps that was a sin. I told him I had a vision and I was called to serve Jesus Christ. He believed I had found my vocation, for those were words he must have heard many times before, and with his blessing I entered the convent where I had been taught as a girl." She paused. "He never really asked me about my vision."

There was a whisper of laughter and I felt the warmth of her hand.

"Do you remember what St Paul wrote to the Corinthians: 'How is it then brethren, when ye come together every one of you hath a revelation?' Poor St Paul. Every ecclesiastic should be leery like that when his flock become visionaries. My sympathies are all with Bishop Butler when he was being plagued by John Wesley's insistence on privileged communications with God. 'Sir, the pretending to extraordinary revelations and gifts of the Holy Ghost is a horrid thing, a very horrid thing.' My aunt understood when I told her. 'If you are in love with God then you must forsake everything and everyone for that love,' she said. I know my father did not speak to her for over a year when he discovered that she had encouraged me. She wasn't a very clever woman, not particularly devout, and we both know how difficult she could be at times and yet, when I needed her then, she had a special grace that gave me strength. What I experienced that day by the lake was not a horrid thing."

Her hand was burning and I shifted slightly as she spoke.

"There was a little jetty by the lake where Tom and I used to leave the boat when we came back from the island—that was where we made love. It was wrong of us, but we were engaged and he was leaving for the Middle East the next day and—there were hundreds like us. He left at noon and I went down to the jetty at dusk to remember and to cry because Tom and I had grown up together and there wasn't a day when I didn't think about him and mention him in my prayers. Such a stillness across the lake and the ghostgums on the island so white they were luminous and floating against the sky like the fingers of God. First the stillness, as though the whole world had come to an end and even my breath was an invasion of that quiet. Suddenly, I felt the warmth here in my heart and it was flooding out through every nerve and cell of my body—I could feel myself in every minute particle of flesh and bone and all of it was in a fire of ecstasy. 'Jesus, take me!' I called, and it was as if I were being ravished by a fire of love that seized my earthly body and consumed it utterly."

The heat from her hand was so intense that I took her wrist and moved it away from my head.

"He was there within me and without—Jesus had claimed me for His bride. Do you think I could have spoken of that to a priest—told him what I felt? He would have thought me a neurotic or laughed; oh, kindly enough, I imagine, and told me I was too old for adolescent hysteria. They say it's the beatific vision, but those words are like shadows of the truth. I was ravished by God—it was beatific coitus and the fire of that love still burns in my heart: God is my father, my lover and my child. My aunt understood —she was the only one. Tom tried but he couldn't . . . he married and both his daughters are at our school now—Rutherglen has a manager. My father always expected me to run it with Tom. There was no one else to inherit after my brothers were killed in France." Again she paused. "So many people were hurt when God called me."

"My parents weren't gods."

"They believed they were."

"I should never have been born," I cried.

"You were born to love, Gwen, and one day you will."

Sister Joseph was coughing peremptorily at the door and we both went across to Mrs Fielding's suite. The doctor was there and a robed priest at the bedside—the room smelt of incense and I clenched my fists because I remembered my father's death. However, Sister Joseph managed everything decorously and discreetly and nobody saw Mrs Fielding's body carried from the hotel late that night. Mother George was right—Sister Joseph was at her best and obviously enjoyed presiding over funeral rites.

The whole affair would have passed without disturbing any of the guests at Glenarches if someone had not spread the rumour that Mrs Fielding had died of food poisoning. The Benton-Smythes, an old married couple who had been at Glenarches when I first arrived, told me that they were leaving the following week. I knew that soon I would have vacant rooms and suites at the hotel.

"Scandal has to be avoided at all costs," Mr Gresham said when I spoke to him that evening. "It may be time to find another place—perhaps Brisbane or Adelaide."

"If I could only find out who is responsible," I cried angrily.

"You should not have engaged in a political dispute." Mr Gresham frowned. "Politics and hotels do not go together."

Only Frau Brunner had managed that, I thought sardonically.

Dolfi crowed when he heard that Mrs Fielding was dead, and said everyone knew that nuns always murdered their old relations for the sake of a legacy. Immediately he began playing various death-bed scenes until he was so drunk he collapsed on my sofa and Terry was about to call for the porter.

"No, let him sleep there," I said. "I want to know how much it would cost to make these recordings you were speaking about. Everyone here listens to Dolfi on 2FC and they love him."

"The cost—" Terry seemed confused so I explained that I wanted to know how much money we would need to set up a recording studio.

"You'd need an agent, shipping, distribution—the studio, of course, and a contract with someone like His Master's Voice to make the records. Oh, at least two thousand pounds," he sighed.

"Would Dolfi really work?"

He was snoring now with his head lolling to one side and looking so dissolute that I almost lost my nerve.

"A chance to play a dozen different parts? Ask him tomorrow morning when he's sober."

I did, and when I returned to my office, I locked the door and opened the safe. There was enough there in gold sovereigns to get us started.

Next morning I announced to the staff that I intended to give in my notice at the end of the month and there were no more incidents while Mr Fortescue-Bragg was bringing prospective managers to the hotel. Like most of the guests, Norma assumed I was getting married; when I told her I was going into the broadcasting business, she looked at me as if I were mad.

"What do you know about broadcasting?" she asked.

When I mentioned what I was planning to Edith she said that she wouldn't lend me a penny and there was no point asking her. She seemed more abstracted than usual and announced she was going to take a health cure.

"I won't be able to spend so much time with you," she said, then added, "I have plans of my own."

Everyone except Mr Fortescue-Bragg thought I was crazy to invest all my money in a recording studio. He listened quietly to me and then gave his qualified approval.

"I've watched you over the years here at Glenarches and you have a marked commercial gift. This hotel was always regarded as something of a white elephant until you turned it into an old—a refined residential establishment for older people."

I remember his coughing to conceal his astonishment when I opened the safe and began filling a leather bag with the sovereigns.

"A curious way to keep your money, Miss Harcourt."

"I don't trust banks," I replied.

"Please, you will find that Mr Henderson conducts a most reputable business. The Australian Mutual Trust never failed even when that anarchist Lang was running New South Wales and telling people they didn't have to pay their bills."

Dolfi became restive when Mr Fortescue-Bragg explained the terms of our agreement to him.

"Why—why does she have fifty-one per cent of this company? I am the star."

"Because she is providing the capital," Mr Fortescue-Bragg said gently.

"And providing you with the opportunity to play more parts than any actor in history," Terry added.

"It must be written into this contract that I am to play all the parts I want—the casting is to be mine," Dolfi pouted but he was satisfied.

On stage, Dolfi was still the golden satyr of the Villa d'Athena but that morning I could see him disappearing in fat and wrinkles. In the Chiesa del Purgatorio in Trapani there was a baroque altar to St Catherine with plaster *putti* holding back a sculptured curtain of red marble. Even when the sculptor put them in place they must have had a particularly lewd appearance, with suggestive gestures and smirking smiles, but time had blotched and faded them so that they looked like depraved *homunculi* acquainted with every perversion of the flesh. The golden satyr was becoming the gilt *putto*.

Terry was going to take charge of the productions, I was to be the business manager and Dolfi was the whole acting company. We discovered the floor of an office building near the State Theatre that we could convert, and while Terry hired scriptwriters, I saw HMV and negotiated a contract between them and our new company, "The Danny Burns Radio Theatre."

Just when I was busiest Edith decided to take up tennis and every day she insisted that I play with her or go to a class on Swedish drill.

"Is this going to help you feel whatever it is you want to feel?" I complained in exasperation.

"It's a step—a necessary step. I must be physically strong for what I intend to do."

I never asked her what it was she was planning. It would not have surprised me had she told me that she was going to walk across Australia barefoot or swim to New Zealand. She grumbled when I told her that I needed every moment to get the studio ready for production and told me that my selfishness was inhuman. I suggested she use David Maybrick as a partner and immediately her mood changed. When I next saw David he was togged out in tennis whites and said that Edith was a different person and that they were hiking and swimming together.

"I rather think we'll be discussing marriage very seriously soon." He smiled complacently and I thought wryly what a splendid couple they would make. He continued talking at length but I didn't listen, for Terry and I were creating a radio serial for Dolfi.

Dolfi had his own ideas and insisted we have a Dickens novel adapted for radio.

"I would like to play Quilp in *The Old Curiosity Shop*," he said.

"But who can we get for Little Nell? We can't afford to pay actors," I replied.

"I shall play Little Nell too," Dolfi said expansively. "And when she dies I'll have the whole world crying. Dickens is a very good writer, but he needs me to bring his characters to life."

The Old Curiosity Shop and *Dino the Dago* were our first productions and Dolfi played every character, marking his script with different coloured pencils so he would not lose his place, darting from one side of the microphone to the other, bending and crouching, and at one point when Quilp torments the dog, imitating the dog as well.

We needed someone to introduce the show and although Dolfi wanted to do that as well, we explained that it would not sound well to have him introducing himself. There were announcers we could have hired if we had had the money, but all my capital was in the studio. It was Terry who suggested Henry Frock and so it was his cathedral tones that announced the Danny Burns Radio Theatre to the world and even Dolfi agreed that Henry had the right voice.

"He sounds important," Dolfi said. "And this is going to be the most important event in the history of entertainment."

When I heard the first recordings, I had to admit that Dolfi did have a kind of genius. He howled and snarled as Quilp and his little Nell was a fluting whisper that sounded more affecting than a real child's voice. The voices blended and were credible because they were all Dolfi, just as Dickens' characters were all his own creations. Terry did the sound effects, although nothing could match Dolfi's ability to recreate galloping horses and cats fighting, and I sat at the controls with the engineer watching the time and the sound levels as the wax record was cut. At the end of the month we had a pile of records—and not a single sale. Even Florrie referred to Henry's radio performances as his little hobby because we told him we couldn't pay him until the shows sold. I was in despair: my bag of gold was gone and yet I was determined not to borrow or sell any part of my share in the company. That's if anyone as lunatic as myself could be found to invest in Dolfi.

"I haven't a penny," Terry said mournfully.

"Then we must give a party," I replied.

"A party? My God, Gwen—we can't afford to pay the rent. We owe the record company and—"

"I'll ask Mr Gresham to let us have a room at the Australia and we'll invite everyone. Oh yes, make sure all the press is there, even that reptile, Billy Garvin."

"But why a party?"

"To celebrate the success of the Danny Burns Radio Theatre," I replied and wondered if I could persuade Mr Gresham to let me have credit at the Australia. Ah well, I shrugged, it would not be the first time I'd bluffed him.

Norma refused to make any of my clothes over when I told her that I needed a new gown for the party and reluctantly I agreed to get some material.

"Not another remnant, please, Gwen," she said.

I opened my purse to see how much loose change I had—all the gold was gone—and I found the card that David Maybrick had given me when he suggested a tutor in Classics. My first reaction had been to throw it away but something on it had caught my eye: "Joel Aaron—remnants, ribbons and fabric ends." There was an address in Randwick and I decided to go there after lunch.

Ashby Lane was not easy to locate and I walked up and down for half an hour before I found myself in an alley, and yet the address on the card read, "Off Ashby Lane." I would never have discovered it if two shabby women had not walked purposefully past me and through what looked like an old carriageway set in a wall. The shop was almost invisible but following them, I saw the two pick their way across a yard full of broken boxes and bales and disappear through a grimy door.

The shop was a jumble of bins spilling over with rags and ribbon ends. Several women rummaged through them, holding up lengths of fabric and arguing with a grizzled old man behind a cluttered table.

"Not sixpence for this—it's got a hole in it. Thieving old Jew!"

"Sixpence or nothing, Missus."

"Christ! You'd steal a baby's rattle, wouldn't yer, Joel."

"And sell it to you for sixpence, Missus."

It was a game and the women badgered and haggled until they beat him down by a penny. The old man then pretended to tear his hair and weep and the women left laughing.

At the bottom of one of the barrels I found a length of blue silk and I was about to measure it against myself when the old man raised his hands and spoke in Greek. They were lines I'd often heard my father recite when Assunta had been clattering the pots in the kitchen all morning or shrieking at Miki. He always added a line of his own invention— "With one exception to this rule, your mother."

"Dire is the violence of ocean waves," the old man solemnly intoned, "And dire the blast of rivers and hot fire—"

"And dire is want, and dire are countless things; But nothing is so dire and dread as woman." Laughing, I finished the lines for him and watched him drop his hands and stare at me as if I were an apparition.

"If a god made woman, And fashioned her, he was for men the artist Of woes unnumbered, and their deadly foe."

He gave me a flourishing bow but I could not add my father's last line because I suddenly heard his voice in the *bagghiu*.

"Greek? She speaks Greek and not with the accent of England."

"My father taught me."

"And why has this miraculous young woman come to the old *shmatters* man?"

"David Maybrick gave me your card. I'm really here to find some material for a dress to wear to a theatre party."

"Come into my office. The shop is closed now."

A burly woman was about to step across the threshold when the old man slammed the door and said that he was closed for lunch. We heard her protesting angrily while we made ourselves comfortable behind the shop in the room that he called his office.

Here everything was order, with ledgers and piles of newspapers on shelves and a sheet of paper on the table covered with rows of numbers.

"I have a little interest on the side." He touched his nose and winked.

Every paper was open at the racing page and there were marked calendars on the wall.

"I do the weights."

I was puzzled and shook my head.

"A field of horses is handicapped in terms of the relative weight carried by the starters. There is no certain way to tell what horse will win a race, but if you keep a record of the weights carried and the results, then it is possible for a bookmaker to set the odds from those calculations."

"And this is your real work."

"My dear, I am a *shmatters* man. This is just a little hobby."

We sat there talking about Euripides and lost plays. My father always said his dream was to excavate a site and find a sealed jar filled with scrolls of papyrus—or several jars in an ancient library. He did not want the pot of gold that every *contadino* dreamed about or even a hoard of precious jewels. When we walked down to the beach to buy our fish in the early morning he sometimes told me what lost plays of the Greek dramatists he longed to discover—those of Aeschylus most of all, Sophocles and then the comedies of Euripides.

An hour passed in a moment as Joel Aaron and I talked and suddenly we heard not one voice but several outside the door clamouring to be let in.

"You must go out through the back, my dear, otherwise all those harpies will think I am entertaining a young lady and say even worse things about the old Jew than they do now."

Both of us laughed because we were already friends and when he asked me to come back and read with him I was delighted. It was not until I was walking down Pine Street that I realized I had forgotten the silk. I hurried back and came in through the front entrance to find Joel haggling with half a dozen women. One of them had the blue silk in her hands. As soon as he saw me gesturing helplessly at him, Joel said *my* fabric was already wrapped and I owed him four and sixpence.

"Don't let him overcharge you, love," one of the women said. "Bloody old thief, he is."

Norma opened the parcel at the hotel and sighed contentedly.

"For once, you've got enough for a proper outfit. And you must have paid a fortune for silver brocade. I haven't seen a quality like that since I was at Madame's."

The party was a glorious affair even though I felt it was more of a *danse macabre* than a festive occasion. My gown was admired and photographed and when Billy Garvin insinuated himself under my elbow and asked what we were actually celebrating I told him to wait until next week when we would be announcing the sponsors and stations that had bought our serials. By now, I was not only poor, I was in debt. Even in Trapani after my father had died, I had never been in such a financial plight. At least I had not owed money to anyone there.

"Investing in your cousin is like throwing all your money into a lottery," Joel said. "Danny Burns has helped to make some of my bookmaking clients rich men."

I had been staying at Glenarches to show the new managers, a jovial couple from Adelaide, how the place was run, but spending most of every day and half the night at the studio. A week passed and suddenly we made a sale, and another—two in Victoria, and one in New South Wales. Whether it was the result of the publicity from the party, or the recognition of Dolfi's genius as he insisted, I can't say, but soon, all over the country, five times a week at seven o'clock you could turn on the radio and hear the theme song of *Dino the Dago*. Gwenadalina Snapper was an immediate hit and I winced as I heard her patronizing everyone and powdering her long nose with a sound like sandpaper.

"Am I really like that?" I once asked Terry miserably.

"Dolfi sees everyone as extensions of himself," Terry replied and I knew he was right.

What I could never deny was his ability to entertain people and I can still see the old people at Glenarches crowded around the radio, rocking with laughter as Dino blundered from one escapade to the next. If we were not showing a profit yet, we could at least pay our outstanding bills. With the first cheque we received, I paid Mr Gresham.

"There was no hurry, my dear," he said pleasantly. "Twenty-eight days is the general rule."

Another month was gone and we made three more sales and I suddenly wondered where I was going to live when I left Glenarches. Terry and Dolfi said I could stay with them and Florrie offered me my old room back at the Rutledge Arms, provided I could stand the noise; Joel and Minna, his wife, wanted me to live with them until I could afford a place of my own. Reluctantly, I agreed to go to Dolfi's Spanish mansion because I wanted to keep an eye on my investment—a task that Hera of the thousand eyes would have found daunting.

I remember sitting on the edge of their swimming pool late one afternoon while Dolfi shrieked at Terry somewhere in that ugly pink house with its mirrored walls and palm trees. Servants left in a continuous stream because working for Dolfi was, as one frazzled maid said to me, like working for Beelzebub and the Emperor Nero rolled into one. His parties were notorious and so noisy that he was once served with an eviction notice. I used to spend most evenings with Joel and Minna but no matter what time it was when I came back to the Chateau Miramar, Dolfi would be screaming and dancing for a group of his admiring fans.

Not all were admirers. Billy Garvin sidled up to me one evening when I was trying to creep quietly upstairs. Dolfi had brought home what seemed to be the entire Tivoli cast and there were statuesque showgirls reclining decoratively on every sofa and a performing seal on top of the bar being fed sardines.

"The famous Gwenadalina Snapper," Billy grinned.

I shrugged and tried to get past him but he was on the stair above me, blocking my path.

"Danny Burns is your cousin, isn't he?"

"Everyone knows that," I replied and added that I was tired.

"And now you're quite the queen of broadcasting."

"Hardly." I laughed.

"It's a long way from Sicily for you both, isn't it?"

"If you're asking me about our family background, my mother was English, my father, Sicilian. Dolfi—"

"Yes, I notice that all his friends call him Dolfi."

"Dolfi's mother was Bavarian and his father—"

"What about his father?"

"I never met him."

"Wasn't his name Carmelo Rossi?"

"Possibly—he used a number of stage names. His real name was Daniel Patrick O'Banion."

I pushed past the grubby little ferret and went to bed. The following Sunday there was a large photo of me in *Truth* and an article by Billy Garvin on Danny Burns' Italian cousin under the heading, "Miss Snapper Better in the Flesh." I felt as though I had been stripped naked in public and if I could have left Sydney under an assumed name I would have been gone by Monday morning, but I had barely four pounds left in cash. Every penny I had made since I came to Australia was invested in Dolfi and as I listened to him shouting and heard the shattering of glass above me I realized why Joel thought I had taken leave of my senses.

It was a grey afternoon with streamers of mist across the Harbour that reminded me of the day when my father and I left England. My misery was made worse because I had just received a letter from Alan. He said that he had not seen the sun for six weeks in London and made a joke about growing moss instead of hair. The letter was full of news and yet strangely impersonal with its account of the great victory he had won before the Privy Council: for the senior counsel, Howard Denman, had been taken ill and it was Alan who had presented the case. There was no mention of his returning to Australia—instead he wrote of being admitted to Gray's Inn and gave every indication of staying in London. The only hint he gave of his feeling for me was to end his letter, "Yours, as ever," and when I read that my bitterness almost choked me.

I could have agreed to marry Alan that day in his chambers and been living in London now, not featured in *Truth* among the lurid divorces and murders, the notorious appendage to the famous Danny Burns. This was not what my parents had wanted for me, and Joel and Minna, who treated me as if I were their daughter, were shocked when I showed them the article.

Dolfi sounded as though he were presiding over a six o'clock pub fight and as I leaned forward, covering my ears, I saw Edith waving to me from the pool in front of Trelawney. She looked brown and healthier than I had ever seen her when I walked across the rocks to her.

"How can you bear that zoo?" she asked me, laughing.

"I can't afford to rent a flat of my own," I said miserably.

"You can have mine, if you want it."

"Yours?"

"Yes, I'm leaving."

"Are you going home to Russell Morton?"

"No, I've been taking instruction. I'm a Roman Catholic."

Thirty

I lit a cigarette, but Edith shook her head when I offered her one.

"No, I've given that up."

"You're not serious about this, are you, Edith?"

She stretched out her arms as though embracing her new vocation and smiled.

"People are denied so much when they're raised as Protestants. I was always taught that the Roman Catholic Church was the source of every iniquity on earth and yet what we really want and need is always what is forbidden to us."

"You were preaching de Sade to me a few weeks ago—"

"Months—you've lost track of time."

"You actually want to be a Roman Catholic?"

"I am a Roman Catholic."

"Your mother—"

"I wrote to my mother last night and I have no doubt that she will be very upset. Of course, she'll blame you, Gwen."

"Mc?"

"She always referred to you as a papist."

"I'm an Anglican."

"Not with an Italian father and living in Sicily: you don't find a fish swimming in the desert. My mother is quite simple-minded about these things."

The streamers of mist across the Harbour were meshing into fog and the booming wail of a ship's siren and the shrill response from a tug made it seem within hand's reach. I could believe that Edith was capable of any aberration and yet in some ways this confession shocked me more than if she had told me that she had just committed a murder, because it was so out of character.

"When I was growing up, I always wanted to be you, Gwen. I used to lie awake and imagine you in gardens of mysterious flowers and among Greek temples with lovers who were like gods. When you came to Russell Morton I thought I was going to fall in love with you and for years I imagined us in each other's arms, kissing as only women can kiss. How stupid I was then and yet—you were the key, you held the secret."

"The secret of what?" I cried in exasperation.

"Of feeling."

"Edith, if you worked, if you didn't have so much money, you wouldn't be so introspective. I thought you were going to marry David Maybrick."

"David Maybrick!" She hooted with laughter and the tug siren echoed her. Still laughing, she told me to come up to the flat with her.

"David was my exerciser—yes, that's the best way to describe it. Of course, he wanted to exercise in bed, but I told him to wait."

"He thought you meant marriage."

"I meant until I was fit enough to enter the convent."

I stumbled as we got in the lift and, chortling, Edith took hold of my arm to steady me.

"Yes, I'm going to be a religious."

Her white room astounded me—for the first time all the blinds were up and the great bay of windows was open to the Harbour and the sky. Only that evening the mist was pressing against the glass and with a shudder I felt as if I were in the pale forest with Edith at my side instead of Bessie.

"Now, let me tell you what I have planned for you, Gwen. You simply can't go on living with that obscene little beast of a cousin of yours. Dear heaven, at night I can hear the noise of his orgies up here."

There was a frisson of excitement about Edith as she paced to and fro, sitting down for a moment, then jumping up to finger an ornament or smooth her hair.

"You, Gwen, are going to have this flat."

"Edith, at this moment, I have less than four pounds to my name."

"Well, don't ask me to lend you any more money. You never returned what I gave you at Russell Morton."

There was a note of the old Edith Wigram in her voice and I began to relax and lit another cigarette.

"I paid for a five-year lease on this place, and there are two left. The agent reminded me that there was a clause in the lease against subletting, so you may as well live here for the next two years. It won't cost me anything and I'm not going to let him have the satisfaction of imagining that his property will be free of the usual wear and tear. McGregor has a contract and I have to pay her for the same length of time or else she'll sue me, and I can't afford any scandal now. I've already sold the Rolls and sacked the chauffeur so that's settled." She frowned for a moment, then said querulously, "I think I'm entitled to a small expression of gratitude for my generosity, don't you?"

"It is very kind of you, Edith. I never imagined I'd be living anywhere so luxurious as this."

Edith was never generous. Whenever I had visited her in the past McGregor had brought in a tray of tea but Edith preferred to come to Glenarches and always expected Dolfi and Terry to pay for her when we went out together. Now, I had the feeling that she was not giving me anything, but, in some way, was bribing me. I could understand the lease but not a contract with McGregor. Was she too being paid to keep quiet?

"What do you expect from me, Edith?"

"Expect? Nothing except a thanks awfully, you really are very kind, Edith—or is that too much?"

"You know that I'm grateful."

"Then everything is settled."

"Edith, I don't want to offend you but—is it possible for you to become a Catholic after—some of the things you've done?"

Her smile was glowing, as if I had just paid her an unexpected compliment.

"My dear, the worst sinners make the greatest saints. It's because I've walked through Hell that I shall reach Heaven."

"Where were you taking instruction?"

"From Bishop Donovan. I wasn't going to waste my time with the local parish priest. I'm Edith Wigram—and the Wigrams count for as much in this country as the Trevanions. Bishop Donovan's only concern was my health, but you can see how fit I am now. He said he envied my willpower in being able to give up smoking. Of course, I shall be bringing a very handsome dowry to the convent."

I still did not see any connection and blundered on as if I had lost my hearing and my sight.

"Where is this convent?"

"Mount of Angels—I shall be very useful there. After all, I studied for two years at Cambridge before I dropped out and I know I'll make an excellent teacher."

I remember scrambling back across the rocks to the Chateau Miramar in that turbid fog and wondering if I were on a strange planet beyond all reach of time and logic. More by feel than sight I made my way up to the house and found Dolfi and Terry reading scripts.

"We're introducing an American character into the Dino skits—that should make them easier to sell in the States," Terry said and looked anxiously at me. "Are you sick?"

"Old maids always have that pinched look." Dolfi smirked.

"Edith has become a Roman Catholic. She's going to enter a convent," I blurted out to them.

It was as if someone had just twisted a knife in Dolfi's ribs.

"Mother George!" he shrieked. "That old bitch! It's not enough that she tried to rape me at Glenarches—dragging my trousers off in the foyer, tearing at my private parts, now she's procuring women for her bordello."

Memories began to take shape in my mind as I said slowly, "I doubt if Edith spoke to her more than once or twice when she was at Glenarches."

"That was enough time to drug her! To poison her mind! Call the police!"

Terry and I tried to calm Dolfi but he was frantic with rage and insisted that we all go to Trelawney and see Edith at once.

When Edith laughed at Dolfi's explosions of obscenity and anger, he suddenly turned on me.

"You—you will be the next," he shouted.

I shook my head. "No, Dolfi, I'm not very religious. If I am, I believe in the gods of Homer and Aeschylus."

"You must get married at once. I shall speak to Mr Gresham this evening. Once you have a husband the Church won't be able to kidnap you for the convent."

As Dolfi was dragging me through the door I turned to Edith.

"Were you there in my suite when Mrs Fielding died?"

Edith only smiled but I knew what had happened.

Fortunately, when we arrived at the Australia, Mr Gresham had left on a business trip to Melbourne and so, in the foyer of the largest hotel in Sydney, Dolfi stood and addressed whoever was present.

"I have neglected my duty to you, Gina. I should have found you a husband. You won't be safe from those filthy nuns until you're married."

Some of the people there recognized Dolfi and laughed and applauded as if we were all rehearsing another skit from Dino the Dago and Miss Gwenadalina. Oh, how I loathed those creatures and the way they seemed to be more real than any of us.

Terry and I managed to hustle Dolfi out to the car but he was still fuming late that night and, at one point, insisted that Terry marry me.

"A man can't have two wives!" I shouted, and Dolfi slapped my face.

If Terry had not rushed down to the edge of the Harbour, screaming that he was going to drown himself unless we stopped fighting, I think Dolfi and I would have ended tearing each other apart.

"Terry can't swim," I cried.

"You've murdered my lover!" Dolfi bellowed and we both ran down just as Terry, holding his nose, was about to fling himself into the water.

I moved into Edith's apartment next day and McGregor greeted me as if I were her daughter. I explained to her that I had no money at the moment but soon we hoped to hear that the Danny Burns Radio Theatre had sold in America.

"He may be the noisiest, wickedest scamp alive," McGregor said slyly, "but when I listen to that Dino the Dago on the radio I laugh so much it hurts. You'll get your money, Miss Harcourt."

Edith was gone. Three weeks later Mother George sent me a note saying that she would like to see me and the following Saturday afternoon she arrived with Sister Joseph.

"Have you come to tell me that Edith is leaving the convent?" I asked Mother George.

"On the contrary," Mother George said slowly. "She seems very happy in our order. Of course, she's only a novice."

"A most promising novice," Sister Joseph added.

"You were very close to your cousin, weren't you, Gwen?"

"No, I was not."

"I gather her family is not Catholic."

That morning I had received a letter from Edith's mother and I handed it now to Mother George. She read it aloud, frowning, while Sister Joseph gasped and raised her hands at regular intervals to murmur, "Heretics."

Miss di Marineo.

No greeting?

My daughter has just informed me that it is her intention to become a Roman Catholic and enter a religious order against every tradition of her father's family and in spite of the Harcourts' long service in the Protestant cause both here and in foreign lands.

Can you have any understanding of the pain and the grief that this has caused me, especially now, when my son is in Europe and unable to be at my side although I have written to him and told him it is his duty to go out to Australia and bring his sister to her senses? Of course, it is the money the papists want and unfortunately Edith has an income of her own, but you should tell these Catholic conspirators and friends of yours that Edith won't get a penny when I die. It is the curse of your mother all over again on our family, but this time I know who is responsible for my daughter's insane wickedness. Like father, like daughter!

I have written to Edith and told her that in my eyes and in my heart and before the Heavenly Father who made her, she is dead and I shall never have any further communication with her in this life. In the next I pray to God that we shall not be in the same place and we have the assurance in the Bible (Revelations, 13) that the Beast that is Rome will not reign forever. May God punish you for what you have done to my daughter.

Eleanor Harcourt Wigram.

"Blasphemy! Blasphemy!" Sister Joseph cried and began telling her rosary.

"Why did your cousin choose our order?" Mother George asked evenly, her eyes holding mine.

Sister Joseph interrupted as I was about to speak.

"Sister Catherine's sacrifice will be rewarded," she said and that was when I first heard Edith's new name.

"I am very uneasy about her vocation. There is something too fervent—"

"You can't be too fervent in the service of Christ," Sister Joseph said reprovingly.

"Perhaps not. Suspicion and lack of faith are not becoming in anyone, least of all a Mother Superior. Sometimes there is an excess of religious zeal at the beginning."

Mother George stood up and walked across to the bay window.

"You can just glimpse the light reflecting on the chapel roof," she said smiling. "And there—a path of gold across the Harbour. God has given us so much beauty in this world that I wonder why we can't all live as saints."

When they were gone I knew I should have told Mother George what I suspected, and I often wonder now what motives of selfishness made me keep silent. Was it because I enjoyed living in Edith's flat with McGregor as housekeeper, or did I want to punish my aunt who blamed me for Edith's conversion? Reading my aunt's letter again I remembered my mother's burial and how my father had stood, losing his English in front of Aunt Eleanor at Russell Morton, apologizing for his presence in her house, unable to believe that she could refuse a home to her own niece. Edith was only giving me now the home that her mother had denied me. Did I want vendetta? Was it all or part of that, or simply that I did not really know if Edith had been in my suite that afternoon when Mother George spoke of her vision?

McGregor and I cleaned out the library and I put my own books on the shelves. There were some works that I hadn't seen before, *The Cloud of*

Unknowing, Julian of Norwich's *Revelations of Divine Love* and Richard Rolle's *Divine Love.* At first, McGregor wanted to burn the de Sades and the rest of the pornography but I took a few of them to a second-hand book shop in George Street and offered them as samples of a collection. The bookseller's eyes glistened when I handed them to him and he quickly told me that it was a criminal offence to own such works in Australia.

"That is why I expect an excellent price for the whole lot," I said coolly.

The following Sunday morning Dolfi, Terry and I had a meeting with our scriptwriters, Athol Tench and Murray Crashaw, to plan the new productions.

"What we need," Terry said, "are shows that will sell here and in America, so classic historical works are our best bet."

"I want a monster part," Dolfi said. "Something that will make people shiver and love me at the same time."

"The Hunchback of Notre Dame," Athol suggested.

Murray's head was on the table and he kept muttering that he needed a drink.

"You'll get a drink when we get an idea from you and not before," Dolfi said savagely.

"The Phantom of the Opera," Murray groaned and Dolfi poured him a shot of whisky.

"I also think we should record the Dino skits in a theatre with an audience now that the Tivoli contract has run out," Terry suggested.

"That is very intelligent," Dolfi said and kissed Terry on the cheek. "People want to see me as well as hear me. It is not just my voice that they admire—it is me."

Dolfi leaned back in his chair, prodding himself in the chest with a fat forefinger, smiling as he contemplated his reflection in the eyes of an adoring audience.

We agreed that Dolfi would not be able to play every part in these new productions, and once he was sure that we were only talking about maids, butlers and voices in the crowd, he assented with great magnanimity. Henry developed a second line as butlers and family doctors, provided they didn't have more than a few dozen words, and I was called on to play maids. This was the beginning of my acting career: I announced characters, opened doors, took hats and said, "Oh sir, you jest," at frequent intervals. Every word I uttered came out as a squeak after moments of harrowing fright, with my throat rigid and my lips like lead weights. Once, my script was shaking so much as I sweated in terror that Dolfi, who was playing Scaramouche, improvised and said there was a wind stirring the trees of the forest and they must hurry back to the castle before the storm overtook them.

Dolfi always complained about my lack of talent but he also enjoyed acting with someone as inept and untalented as myself.

Murray and Athol were sent off to write and I inadvertently said that I was going to see Edith that afternoon.

"What?" Dolfi screeched. "You are going to the convent? I forbid it."

I saw Terry cower down in his chair and put his hands to his ears.

"I am going to see my cousin, Dolfi."

"Your cousin is dead! What you have now for a cousin is a *puttana* in nun's robes."

"Mount of Angels is a respectable school for girls—"

"A school!" Dolfi cried. "Is that what they call bordellos these days?"

"Nonetheless, I haven't seen Edith since she entered the convent and I am going to call on her this afternoon."

"Then we will go with you," Dolfi said. "Terry, get the car."

"You're not going to follow me into the convent and make a scene," I said.

"We will wait outside and if you do not return in half an hour I shall call the police and we will go in and rescue you."

At least I was driven across the Bridge to the other side of the Harbour and when I pointed to groups of girls and their parents walking around the gardens, playing tennis and vigaro with hardly a nun in sight, Dolfi grumbled, but he did not try to follow me through the gates with their finial of sleeping angels. There were gardens and playing fields and over to one side of the main building, almost out of sight, rows of plain little stones where the nuns of the order were buried. I expected lowering walls and grim passageways, but instead a plump little nun showed me into a sunny parlour with stained-glass windows intent on changing the room into a gaudy jeweller's shop.

Edith was wearing a plain brown habit with a white veil over her head and as she spoke her hands fingered the beads of a rosary. Sister Joseph sat on a stiff-backed chair by the door.

"You shouldn't have bothered to come," Edith said and I saw Sister Joseph nod approvingly.

"I wanted to see how you were, Edith."

"I have never been so happy in all my life. And please remember that Edith no longer exists. I am Sister Catherine."

Again the faintest nod from Sister Joseph.

She was thinner and all the tan had left her skin, but she seemed consumed with an excitement that I couldn't understand.

"Is there anything I can bring you?" I asked awkwardly, because she showed no indication of being pleased that I had come, or even that she wanted to talk to me. I felt as though I had called her away from something important and it was only courtesy that made her speak to me.

"Everything I want is here," Edith replied.

"We're adapting *David Copperfield* now as a serial. You should hear Dolfi as Micawber. He—"

I stopped because I saw she was not listening.

"I have no interest in such worldly things."

"Would you like me to go?" I asked abruptly.

"I prefer to spend my few leisure hours in prayer," Edith replied and we both rose at the same time.

As I was walking down through the gardens to the main gate I caught sight of Mother George scoring for the vigaro and when she saw me, she gave the book to a girl and walked across to me.

"Well, what do you think of your cousin?" she asked.

"She seems very happy here."

"Some of the nuns think she has the makings of a saint. What do you think?"

"I never liked her, Mother George, and I like her even less now."

Her laughter shook the air around us and she said that my honesty was like a cold shower. Did anyone appreciate such candour, she asked me, and I shook my head.

"It's probably the first raptures of the religious life. They'll wear off in time." Suddenly Mother George became serious. "I wouldn't be surprised if she isn't asking to leave us by the end of the year."

Some of the girls had recognized Dolfi and were crowding round the Bugatti asking for his autograph while a nun tried to shoo them back inside the gate.

"They haven't all been corrupted by that old Mother George. They gave her the wrong name—she's the Dragon," Dolfi said complacently as Terry drove us back to Darling Point.

Some of their friends had already arrived at the Chateau Miramar when Terry pulled into the driveway and I slipped off to Trelawney. I went across to the windows and looked across the Harbour to Mount of Angels where Edith had chosen to discover her feelings, or whatever she hoped to find there. Of course, Mother George was right. When she failed to achieve some ecstatic experience or vision, she would be back and searching for something else.

The seventy-six pounds the bookseller had given me for Edith's library paid some outstanding bills and kept the flat running, but I knew we were never going to make real money out of the Australian sales. Joel told me that I had thrown my money away and when I said that Dolfi was becoming as popular as Mo, he said that he had never found anything entertaining in the parody of a Jew or the imitation of an Italian. I agreed with him, although the rest of Australia clearly did not.

It was Tuesday morning when we received a phone call from the manager of His Master's Voice saying that their American agent had sold the Danny Burns Radio Theatre to over three hundred stations, and the following afternoon, Terry rushed in to say that we had a sponsor in Australia: Lifebuoy Soap was now going to be our national sponsor. We had made almost eight hundred per cent profit on the cost of our first production with more to come from replays.

After screaming and dancing with delight around the microphone, we all went to Florrie's and had pies and champagne while Henry proposed toasts to the comic genius of the age, Danny Burns. Dolfi sang for the pub crowd and kissed a burly wharf labourer who looked for an instant as if he were going to punch him until Dolfi suddenly rolled his eyes and said, "I ama so sorry. You are so gooda-looking I thoughta you were my beloved Miss Gwenadalina."

"If you knew anything about men you'd have got him to name the day, Gwen," Florrie whispered to me.

"That's a man?" I retorted and burst out laughing.

It was winter and difficult to find flowers, but I went to a florist in King's Cross and bought a bunch of hothouse roses and found I had just enough money left to catch the tram to Bellevue Hill.

When Minna opened the door I was sure she must have heard the news already because her dark eyes were sparkling and before I could speak, her arms were around me and she was hugging me.

"The show's sold," I managed to gasp.

Joel had me in his arms then and we all spoke at once.

"I'm going to be rich!" I cried.

"He has come," Joel shouted.

"We did not expect him—I opened the door and thought it was some poor man looking for work and it was him," Minna said. Suddenly she saw the flowers. "Flowers? You knew?" she cried and she smelt the crushed roses.

"He's upstairs getting changed. Such a fine young man." Joel beamed.

It was impossible to make sense of anything so we all went into the dining room and Minna poured glasses of Madeira. I told them about the American sale and they congratulated me, but not as warmly as I expected.

"Maybe it's a flash in the pan, maybe not," Joel said cautiously, glancing continually at the door as if expecting someone to come in.

"Go and fetch him," Minna urged Joel and he leapt from his chair and was gone.

I was beginning to feel a little lightheaded because Minna kept filling my glass.

"Who is this man?"

"This man?" Minna seemed shocked by my question. "This man is Kurt Stern, Joel's nephew from Austria. He is the first of the family to arrive here in Australia. Soon, you wait and see, they will all come: Joel's little sister and her husband and the two married daughters and their families. All my relations are in America and when will I ever get to see them except in photographs, so now we will have a family here."

I do not know why I should suddenly have felt resentful and yet my eyes filled with tears. Joel sometimes called me his daughter and I was beginning to feel as if the Aarons were my parents. Now, I was learning of a real family that was on its way to fill Joel and Minna's life. I had come with news that would be in all the papers the next morning: the first Australian radio show to sell in America, and all they could think about was their nephew. Why did I always give myself so many opportunities to dislike and despise myself? Perhaps when Dolfi said I was ugly, it was not my appearance, but my nature that he was describing.

"Gwen, what is it?"

I turned to Minna and she held me and stroked my hair.

"I'm just tired and I drank too much champagne at Florrie's and now the wine here—"

"Dry your eyes quickly, they are coming downstairs."

If Kurt Stern had resembled Joel I think I would have fallen in love with him straightaway, but he was disappointingly different. Joel was like a shaggy old eagle contemplating the world with a sardonic gaze between hunched shoulders; Kurt was dark, almost effeminate in appearance, with lustrous eyes and an olive skin. He could have been a handsome young Sicilian until he spoke and then it was not his accented English that caught my attention, but the precision of his speech and the formality with which he kissed my hand.

"To the first arrival," was Joel's toast at dinner.

"When are they coming? Why didn't the rest of the family come with you?"

Minna and Joel asked these questions over and over and Kurt was laconic and brief in his answers. He couldn't speak for his mother. She changed her mind a dozen times a day. As for his father, he did whatever his mother wanted.

Joel nodded at that and told us that Erika had been the youngest and the petted child of the family.

"Can you imagine—my mother was forty-six when Erika was born?" Joel smiled. "She was such a blessing, a *mazenka*, this little child."

"She's fifty now and fat," Kurt said.

"I was the eldest son and after my father had cradled her, I held her in my arms."

The whole conversation was a succession of family reminiscences punctuated with prayers of thanks in Hebrew from Joel, and throughout the dinner I sensed that Kurt knew as little Hebrew as I did. Whenever he spoke to me there was a note of reserve in his voice that seemed to be setting me apart from the family. I was silent and finally Joel leaned across the table and clasped my hand.

"Why is our daughter so serious?"

"I'm not really your daughter," I replied sadly.

"You are the daughter of our hearts," Joel said and I began to cry.

Kurt shifted irritably in his chair and Minna immediately asked him if he were tired.

"No, but I'd like to walk. I'm tired of sitting for so long."

"Good." Minna smiled. "Gwen will walk with you."

"I prefer to be on my own."

"Why does he behave like that?" Joel said helplessly when Kurt was gone.

"*Dummkopf*! His wife is dead and he is here at table with a young woman and so he begins to remember. Do you wonder that he is upset?" Minna retorted.

"Ah—of course."

"Kurt was married to a most beautiful and rich girl from one of the best families in Vienna, the Laufers, who own a bank with branches in Italy and Switzerland. Very powerful—very rich. Kurt heard she was dead just before he left Austria," Minna said breathlessly.

"Heard?"

"Renée was in Germany," Joel said sombrely. "She went to help organize resistance against the Nazis. They caught her and they killed her just as they will kill every Jew in Germany. Hitler has said he will cut out the Jewish cancer, he will make Germany a Jewish Gehenna and—"

"Tonight is for rejoicing," Minna said soothingly. "Come, let us sit and talk about Gwen's great success. Do you remember saying that she would lose every penny in this foolishness? What are you going to say to her now, *du alter Yold*?"

It was not the moon flooding my room that woke me, but the uproar from Chateau Miramar where Dolfi was holding another of his parties. I went to close the windows, doubting whether he would be able to work the next morning. The moon had cut a broad highway across the Harbour and I looked towards Mount of Angels. I found myself thinking about Kurt and from Kurt I began to wonder what Alan was doing in London. I had replied to his letter; however, there had been no answer from him and I shrugged irritably. It was easier to think about Kurt.

I understood his chagrin at finding me in his uncle's home, sitting there at the dinner table like a presumptive daughter. In future, whenever I saw him, I would make it quite clear to him that I was not trying to take his place in the family. Once that was settled between us, I thought, we might even become friends.

Thirty-One

In Griffith I had given Alan an ultimatum: unless he married me at once I would leave him and yet, when he asked me to be his wife in Sydney, I temporized. He was gone now and I doubted if I would ever see him again. Norma still maintained that he must love me because he hadn't married anyone else, but I knew that for a man like Alan, love was not the all-consuming passion that had controlled my parents' lives and that Mother George felt for God. Gloomily, I wondered if I were capable of loving anyone and when David Maybrick asked me to have dinner with him one evening, I listened impatiently while he moaned about the way Edith had treated him.

"She led me on," he said.

"Only if you were willing to be led."

"For pity's sake, Gwen! Edith and I had an off and on affair for years. I was Frederick's tutor, her mother liked me and—"

"Yes, yes, I know how you met, David."

"Now she refuses to see me. I actually went over to the convent to talk to her. After all, she's gone through phases like this before—Gurdjieff was all the rage for about six months, then Theosophy and heaven knows what else after that." He was crumbling the bread into pellets like grapeshot and scattering them across the table. "A terrible drag by bus," he went on, "and then some snippy old nun telling me that Sister Catherine had no desire to see me."

"Edith wants to be a saint."

"That's absurd."

"Perhaps, but you must admit it's an original ambition."

He mumbled something in response to this and finally accepted one of my cigarettes. "We had such plans. I want to take up archaeology professionally and get into a dig of my own at Paestum, and I thought Edith would help me. After all, she's rolling in money and my work would have given her such an interest in life. Now—"

"Find another rich woman," I said laughing. "Rosalia always said that among the *contadini* the widow would accept her next husband across her dead husband's coffin. For a man it was much quicker. He would already have made an offer to another woman when his wife was on her sickbed."

"Damn you, Gwen! I think I'm entitled to a little sympathy."

I was thinking drearily about myself and the cautionary warnings about never getting rid of a lover until you had another in hand. Those prudent economies of the heart were as foreign to me as impulse and squandering were to my business life. It should have been Alan sitting opposite me, not this young-old man with his calculating eyes.

"Why should I sympathize with you?" I said abruptly.

"Because I—I'm pretty cut up about this. I was very fond of Edith."

"I can't imagine what you found in her to like. She may be my cousin, but sometimes I think I could find more in common with a complete stranger on a bus than with Edith."

"Well, she isn't a great beauty like you—"

I looked over David's shoulder at the reflection in the mirror behind him and tried to see myself as a stranger would. A young woman looked back at me guardedly, a woman with black hair knotted at the nape of her neck, a thin pale face with grey eyes and a mouth that was too wide to conform with any standard rule of beauty. Without my realizing it, David had taken my hand and was pressing it fondly.

"She was always second best, Gwen. I fell for you when I was studying with your father in Trapani. My God, that was years ago, wasn't it? And now you're a successful businesswoman."

"Successful?" I drew my hands back. "I'm Miss Gwenadalina and if I'm making a fortune, I sometimes think I became an old woman before I was young enough to enjoy my money."

"We could make a go of it, don't you think?"

"No, David, not here or at Paestum or anywhere," and I told him I had to go home and read scripts that evening.

There were any number of men like David Maybrick and none of them interested me. Mr Gresham was always warning me about fortune hunters and I knew he was right: I was a withered stick encrusted with gold. When Norma sighed and said she was getting hot flushes and the curse was coming at all different times, I shook my head in disbelief.

"Why was it ever called a curse? It's the river of life for a woman," I said to her.

Norma had set herself up as a dressmaker in George Street and I often went and had a cup of coffee with her when we finished recording.

"I took a leaf out of your book," she said to me when I first saw the elegant fitting room with its silk wallpaper and gilt chairs. "Old Mrs Bennington at Glenarches took quite a fancy to me and she lent me the money. So, it's not Norma Reynolds any more, it's Madame Reynaud and if anyone wants me to speak French I've learnt half a dozen phrases from Maisie's French grammar book."

There was always a stream of clients but one afternoon, Norma showed me her masterpiece, a cloche of shaded blue ribbon and a bag to match.

"You remember that stitch you showed me all those years ago in Griffith? Well, I sat down with some ribbon I got from your friend Mr Aaron and made this."

"Rosalia would have been proud of you, Norma."

"No, wait, this is the good part. I was talking to Terry about it the other day and he asked to see what I was making. After all, he was head of the millinery department at Farmer's before he became Danny Burns' manager and he's interested in hats. He said I shouldn't tell a soul that I'd made it, just say it was a Paris import."

"Like my mother's old petticoat."

"And if I made a few of them he'd take them over to Farmer's for me and sell them to the buyer."

"You should make a good profit."

"I run them up in my spare time, and Maisie's faster than I am. I'd say they cost me three pounds—Terry says that Farmer's will sell them for two hundred guineas."

"But what will you make?"

"One hundred pounds a set."

Norma began to mop her face and said she didn't know whether it was the flushes or the excitement.

As I was leaving she swallowed hard and said she had something else to tell me.

"I've taken him back. Oh, I know how you feel about him, Gwen, but he is my husband."

"Damn him!" I exploded. "He forced me out of Glenarches."

"Not just him—a whole bunch of the New Guards were involved. They're finished now. Len still says Colonel Campbell is the greatest man in Australia, but he's dead in the water, just like Lang."

"I'm surprised Len is allowing you to have a business of your own," I said bitterly.

"That's all different now. He does odd jobs for me—delivers dresses, picks up fabrics when I need them. We've rented a house two doors down from my parents and he looks after that as well—"

"Cooks dinner for you?"

"Yes, he does as a matter of fact. Oh Gwen, he was starving in Melbourne. He tried to get work cutting timber and then he managed to make a few bob shovelling grit to sell to people who kept chooks. Len's not a young man and he was sick when he wrote to me. Some people managed to survive the depression—you and me, we did all right—but not Len. He'll never get over it."

"You're a fool, Norma. If you wanted a man, you should have looked around for someone better than Len."

"I'm not a raving beauty like you, Gwen, and I'm almost fifty. The kids were glad to have him back—Teddy especially. I can make enough money here for the lot of them: Maisie's working with me, Pat wants to go into nursing and Teddy has ideas about engineering. I can manage to look after Len and the kids, and the clients like it when he delivers their outfits. He's nicely spoken and very polite."

Was it Norma's control of her life that irritated me or the fact that she was prepared to take back a man who had been swaggering around with Campbell's Fascist army and probably painting slogans on the wall outside Glenarches? For Len Reynolds and his mates I was a Dago bitch and yet Norma, my friend, had taken him back. When I was walking up George Street to catch my bus home, I saw him, a bowed grey-haired man who stepped aside and doffed his hat to me as I walked past him without speaking.

That night I was marking up Dolfi's scripts for the following day and still feeling that in some way Norma had disappointed me. Was love really a matter of daily compromise like learning to live with a creaking door, or was it the inflexible passion of my parents and Mother George? Was Edith, in her own way, pursuing love when she spoke to me about wanting to feel with all her being? And was I more like my cousin than I could ever bear to admit when I accepted the reality of my parents and Mother George and knew that I would never experience this great love? If love was a mystery as the popular song said, then it was a mystery that was beyond my power to unravel. I could have talked to Bessie, and she would have understood my sense of watching others joyfully playing a game to rules that I had never learned, just as other children used to watch us enviously on the beach at Trapani when we whispered and went off together to play.

I latched the veranda doors because Dolfi and some of his friends were screaming and throwing bottles at each other across the pool. The day before he was to be evicted Dolfi had bought Chateau Miramar, to the dismay of the neighbours, and against the advice of Terry, who wanted to invest the American royalties that were pouring into our bank accounts. McGregor had left early to see a film and it was some time before I realized that there was someone ringing at the front door. When I opened it, I saw

Kurt Stern standing there with a bouquet of primroses and violets in his hand.

"The doorman said you were at home and I bribed him into letting me come up unannounced."

"Did Joel and Minna send you?" I asked awkwardly.

"No, and that is why I'm here." He went down on one knee with his hand on his heart and said theatrically, "Forgive me, for I have wronged you, gracious lady." And then he kissed my hand.

"Oh please, get up." I laughed. "You sound like Dolfi playing Scaramouche."

"Am I as good as all that?" Kurt smiled. "I heard your cousin on the radio yesterday and he's very clever."

"Oh yes, wonderfully clever. That's Dolfi out there now."

A babble of voices and a piercing shriek from Dolfi were followed by silence. When I opened the doors to the veranda, I could just glimpse a crowd of people carrying someone up to the house from the pool.

"It sounds like a fine party," Kurt said.

"They'd be delighted to have you there. Dolfi keeps open house for half of Sydney."

"I would much sooner talk to you and receive your forgiveness."

"For what?"

"My rudeness when I first met you."

"Oh, I've forgotten all about that," I lied.

"You see, I thought that Minna was matchmaking. The first dinner with my Australian family and I find a beautiful girl sitting opposite me."

"Was that really what you were thinking, Kurt?"

"You obviously have no experience of Jewish aunts, who are sometimes much worse than Jewish mothers. When my uncle told me about you and I realized you were not Jewish, I knew that Minna was not matchmaking."

I was confused in a way that made me stumble over my words and I offered to get him a drink. Instead, he asked me if I would like to walk with him.

"We could find a little coffee shop and have supper."

I laughed and told him that there was no such place in Sydney.

"Where do people go to talk?" he said incredulously.

"In their homes—or there are at least two good restaurants."

"Two?" He sounded incredulous.

We decided to walk and have coffee with Joel and Minna afterwards and soon we were strolling down to Double Bay and towards Bellevue Hill, with Kurt stopping at every turn to marvel at the view.

"This Harbour makes Naples look like a puddle—there should be painters here by the thousand. And if there were, they would probably all kill themselves because they could never hope to equal what nature has created. Is that why the people here are so dull? I've been to the city and everyone is either despondent or drunk. In Vienna, the depression is much worse, people are starving and yet you hear laughter and the perfume of coffee and chocolate fills the streets."

He was homesick and I asked him if his family planned to follow him.

"Who knows what my mother will decide to do? If you have money, you can still live such a good life in Austria."

"Was it because Vienna reminded you of your wife? Is that why you emigrated?"

Kurt evaded my question. Instead, he told me about his work as a chemist making cosmetics.

"Is that what you're going to do here?" I cried. "Oh please, you can help me. Every three months I have to make up a pot of cream for an old friend, but if you begin making cosmetics—"

We were still laughing about my miraculous wrinkle remover when we found ourselves at the Aarons' house.

"I am so glad that I am not expected to marry you," Kurt said gleefully, and although I tried to share his laughter the sound caught in my throat.

It was Kurt and Henry Frock who taught me how to drive when I bought my first car, a cream Franklin, and the car was an excuse for me to practise driving and to show Kurt parts of Sydney that I had not even seen myself.

"If it were not for you, Gwen," he often said, "I would die of boredom in this country. All these girls with long ballerina legs and red peeling noses who gape like fish when you speak to them and the men, wiping away a beer moustache so they can talk about racing and football. This is a paradise without conversation and that is a description of limbo."

He refused to join the little group that studied with Joel, saying that all he could remember of his Latin was the *Gallic Wars* and Caesar continually going into winter quarters. I would join Joel's students in the library while in the next room Kurt played Strauss waltzes on the piano. Only when we had coffee at ten would he join us and even then, if the conversation turned to politics, as it generally did, Kurt would sigh and say that we reminded him of a group of gravediggers. How could there be another war, he said, when Europe had not recovered from the last? In every village there was a memorial listing the men who had been killed. Nobody was prepared to make that sacrifice again. When Joel said the war was not over, that these were not years of peace but simply a time of respite while nations waited for a new generation to man the armies, Kurt replied that his uncle had been away from Europe for too long. As for Hitler, everyone in Austria made jokes about the little paperhanger who couldn't make a living in Vienna, so he worked very hard and became the Führer of the Germans.

Although I told Kurt a great deal about Trapani and my parents, he deftly changed the subject whenever I mentioned his wife. Of course, I always told myself, even to hear her name must have pained him. Joel had given him the money to begin making cosmetics in a little factory in Surrey Hills and one evening we discussed what he should call his new face cream.

"I think the best name for a cosmetic is 'Hope,' " he said, laughing, while I argued that he needed something less obvious to make Mr Gresham and women want to buy it.

Kurt first met Dolfi and Terry at the studio and for a moment I thought he must be homosexual. Dolfi was playing six different parts in an episode of "Michael Marvel—Ace Detective," and when he saw Kurt in the control room, he ogled him and poked out his tongue. As soon as Henry began reading the concluding announcements, Dolfi dropped his script and rushed into the control room, falling across the engineer and almost ruining the wax record. He reached over me and kissed Kurt on the mouth. Instead of pushing him away, Kurt laughed and said that he wished Dolfi were a pretty girl, because he would have returned the kiss. Pleasantly, he said that he had given up boys when he was fourteen under strict instruction from a talented Hungarian parlour maid. Dolfi asked him if he didn't want to be young again and when Kurt assured him that he was enjoying being grown up too much, they both laughed and afterwards we all went and had dinner together.

"I like him," Dolfi said to me later. "He's intelligent and very handsome and he appreciates my genius. If you weren't so plain and gawky, Gina, I think he might fall in love with you and ask you to marry him."

Kurt's gaiety made everything turn on a joke or a song and when I told him one evening that he had lipstick on his collar, he laughed and said that if Australian girls persisted in throwing themselves at him, he was enough of a gentleman to catch them. He never seemed interested in making love to me, however, even though we saw each other three or four times a week, and at weekends we took a picnic to the beach or swam in the pool at Trelawney. Kurt exasperated me. I did not want another friend like Terry or David, I wanted a lover who would make me forget Alan.

The sound of the surf was like a muffled gong as we lay in the shade of a pine tree at Whale Beach while the water beyond the breakers changed from green to sapphire and a lapis blue. The surf droned hypnotically, the waves rising up like crystal walls to splinter in a dazzling spectrum of light on the white sand. There was so much colour and light and warmth that it was, as Kurt said, as intoxicating as the wine we had drunk with our lunch.

We spread our rug on a patch of springy grass in front of a private garden planted with orange trees: the perfume of the orange flowers, the wine and the tang of salt were making me drowsy and I thought that by now any other man but Kurt would have leaned over me and kissed me as I lay back, waiting to be loved. Instead of a lover, I had a friend at my side, and I felt irritably betrayed by the orange trees and the languor that was turning my body into sound and perfume and light.

"My uncle says you have the best business head of any woman he has ever known, and Minna agrees with him, which is rare."

"Oh yes, I'm the mother of Ploutos—nothing else," I said, and felt tears prickling my eyes.

Expecting sympathy from Kurt, I thought, was rather like asking for logic from a butterfly. He avoided the sad and serious as a butterfly does the shade. I expected him to tell me a funny story at that moment; instead I heard the droning boom of the surf for some time before he spoke.

"You can't have a child. Is that what you mean?" he said gently and I sensed that his face was close to mine.

Almost as if I were repeating a story about someone else, I told him about Benno and the two nights I spent with him in the orange grove and everything that followed after, from my midnight marriage to the morning when I woke and thought Alan Gilchrist was my death. My voice seemed muffled as if I were speaking inside a cave.

"Do you still want this lawyer?" Kurt asked quietly.

"Ask me if I will be hungry tomorrow. I don't know—perhaps that's a shopgirl's answer and yet it's the truth. It's almost two years since I saw him last. If I could be certain that I loved him—"

"Why must we always talk about love? Why can't we be satisfied with pleasure?"

"Because love is—" and I faltered.

"You see? There is no answer except a string of clichés like flyblown paper angels on a cord at Christmas. Tell me, why can't we be satisfied with this?"

He was kissing me then and at the same moment he slipped down the straps of my bathing suit and caressed my breasts.

"I wanted you that first night but I did not wish you to be given to me."

My need to be loved was so anguished that I was trying to kick out of my suit and give my body to him when the shrill voices of children pulled us apart. Looking down, we saw three little boys below us, arguing over the plan of a fort.

"Will the gracious lady invite me home to her flat where we can make love in a comfortable bed without being observed?" Kurt murmured. I nodded frantically and began to gather up the rug and our plates.

"Leave it—leave everything," Kurt said. "Let's go quickly."

He drove back to Darling Point at speeds that had me clinging to the dashboard, but not once did I tell him to slow down or point to the needle trembling at sixty as we crossed the Harbour Bridge.

I wanted love as a drowning person clutches at a raft but Kurt would not let me satisfy my passion immediately. Gently, he calmed me and soothed me like a child, stroking my back, whispering in my ear, kissing me so delicately that it was like being touched by a soft tongue of fire.

Making love, as Kurt told me, was an art as distinct from fornication as a Bach fugue was from a barnyard gallop. In that one afternoon, as the light outside my bedroom window changed from gold to red and then to the velvet indigo of an Australian summer night, I must have reached a point of mindless ecstasy a dozen times. Alan was always a considerate lover but Kurt seemed more intent on pleasing me than with anything I could give him.

"When I was sitting opposite you that night at dinner, I had to look away very often, because I kept seeing you like this," Kurt said to me as he stroked me from my neck to my thigh.

I turned my head towards him and saw his face profiled against the light like a young emperor on a Roman coin. Kurt was twenty-nine but there was an imprint of time in his eyes that often made me think he was Sicilian. Impulsively, I reached up to him and he held my wrists and smiled.

"No. Don't say now that you love me. Simply that we have given each other much joy."

"Why can't I say that I love you, Kurt?"

"Because I'm a chemist and I dislike words and things that have no meaning. Pleasure and pain I understand. Love is nothing and everything."

"People have died for it."

"You are a beautiful woman, perhaps the most beautiful I have ever loved, and for me love is a verb, not a noun. You have delighted my senses and I want to love you again and again until I know you. I'm like the young violinist who has a Stradivarius placed in his hands—he prides himself on his musicianship but this instrument tests and challenges him as nothing else has. He finds himself playing miraculously across tonal harmonies that he never even knew existed. You have that power over me, Gwen, and I am in awe of you."

"Did you love your wife like this?" I asked him, and even as I spoke I wished I had choked on the words.

He was silent for some time and we both heard that precise moment when the tide turned and the water plashed irregularly against the wall at the end of the garden.

"I'm sorry, I shouldn't have asked you about her," I blurted as he turned and faced me, his dark eyes shadowed in the moonlit room.

"I hated my wife and I rejoiced when they told me she was dead. Is that what you wanted to hear?"

I was so shocked by the suppressed fury in his voice that I pulled the sheet over myself as though trying to hide from him.

"You know," he said lightly, "I am going to make us some coffee. I shall make it because you brew something that tastes like thin mud. I do not think you are a very good cook."

"I can't cook at all," I replied involuntarily.

He bent down and kissed my nose.

"Then no man will ever want to make you his wife and you will have to be content to remain a beautiful old maid," and he walked out to the kitchen.

Kurt rented a flat at Pott's Point and it was there one afternoon that we decided to call his new creams, "Paris Rose." Mr Gresham received the first test jar long before it reached the shops and after a week my old friend told me that he could see a vast improvement in his skin.

If Joel and Minna knew we were lovers, neither of them gave us the slightest indication that they were aware of it. We had dinner with them at least three times a week and afterwards Kurt played the piano while Joel lectured the students and sometimes a member of the Classics department from the university. Kurt never spoke about his wife and I never asked him about her again. I knew that he was seeing other women but even though I raged with jealousy I forced myself not to taunt or reproach him. There was an agreement between us: we loved each other and yet what we did was not love. I suppose there is a certain pleasure in the parody that mocks reality; there is also a fretful despair underneath the sweetness of recognition like the worm-rotten wood that an artful decorator conceals with a lacquer of glossy paint. Perhaps all I could expect was the semblance of love since I was the imitation of a woman.

This was my mood when McGregor told me, with a pleated frown of disapproval, that there was a foreign woman and a little girl who wanted to see me. Saturday morning was when I liked to rest and I was about to tell her to send them away when McGregor said she thought the name was Scarfer.

Thirty-Two

"Scarfer?"

I was about to add that I knew no one by that name and then suddenly Benno's painted cart rattled into my head trailing all the sounds and the rich fruit aromas of Griffith when the drays and trucks came laden into town.

Rafaella was wearing a grey serge suit that was too tight for her and she sat down with obvious relief, easing her heels out of her black-laced shoes. Angelica looked quickly at me and then stared around her with quick, darting glances. I remembered two children with dusty bare feet, holding hands when the Sciafas confronted me in front of Giacopo's house. Angelica had seemed about six or seven to me at the time, but now I could see she must have been much older, even though she was still tiny.

Rafaella sat down and priced everything with her eyes.

"You've done real good for yourself," she said in English.

"I hope you've been successful too," I replied.

She shrugged as if moving a weight from her shoulders.

"I have two sons now, so Paulo is very happy. Two sons in four years and another on the way for which I thank the blessed Mother of God. Martina had a daughter, but what could she expect when you had cursed her? It was like Giacopo's new orchard—nothing really thrives there. Twisted little trees and small fruit."

I did not answer and McGregor brought in a tray of coffee and biscuits.

"Is that real silver?" Angelica asked, pointing to the coffee pot.

When I nodded, I saw Rafaella smile as if confirming a suspicion.

"Yes, you did real good with Giacopo's money. I told Paulo you were too clever to spend it all on a fancy dress."

"There was no gold, Rafaella."

"I never saw a place like this except at the flicks—such a big flat and your picture in the papers all the time."

"Rafaella, why are you here?"

"Because it is time you did something for your family. You have a duty to your family."

"My family? What family?"

"Your stepdaughter."

Angelica sniffed, but she continued to cram biscuits into her mouth.

I was so astounded that I felt the cup slipping from my hands, and then reacted so quickly that the coffee splashed across my dressing gown. I asked them to excuse me for a moment while I changed.

When I was closing the door of my wardrobe I saw Angelica staring at me from the door.

"Are all those clothes yours?" she asked incredulously.

I beckoned her to me and she ran her finger across the silk nightgowns and gasped.

"Angelica, why has your aunt come to see me?"

"She wants to get rid of me."

"Why?"

"Because she caught me nicking off to take dancing lessons with my best friend, Sheila Smithers. I can stand on my toes—look!"

She pulled off her canvas sandals and took four steps across the room, balancing on her stubby little toes.

"They're very cruel to me," she whimpered, and when she rubbed the tears from her face, there was a grimy smudge across her cheek.

At that moment I saw Margaret Moglen standing by the fountain, waiting for Bessie and me.

"Uncle Paulo said dancers were all *puttane* and he got a block of ice and shoved it—here. Then he tied my knees and ankles together. I told my teacher what he'd done and the police sergeant came and roused on him and Uncle Paulo said he wouldn't have me under his roof again. There's no one else but you, Auntie Gina. You won't send me away, will you?"

I looked from Angelica to her aunt sitting straight-backed and drinking coffee in little sips. Rafaella was gazing out at the Harbour, holding her coffee cup with one hand, while the other made a *mano cornuta*.

Norma and Florrie both warned me I was mad to take Angelica. A half-grown girl would never give me anything but trouble, Florrie said, but I knew why I had agreed to look after her and pay for her education. It wasn't that she reminded me of Bessie. Angelica was tiny, with fine bones and a pointed face that made her look like a ten-year-old when she was almost sixteen and, as I soon discovered, she lied with a facility and lack of intelligence that meant she was always being found out. It was not as though I imagined that Bessie was returning to me as Angelica. Bessie was always a glowing memory, her red hair and brilliant blue eyes lighting a corner of warmth in my mind where I could always find comfort. No, Angelica reminded me of Margaret Moglen, and I remembered too the anguish of being turned away from the home where I thought I was going to live with my cousin Edith. Perhaps I am a Sicilian at heart, and when Rafaella reminded me of the duties of family it was as if she were pulling me to her with a rope of blood. What finally made me agree was when Angelica told me about her best friend, Sheila Smithers, who had left Griffith with her family and was now a boarder at Mount of Angels.

I spent a day buying Angelica new clothes and after we came back to the flat and the boxes and tissue paper were strewn across the floor, she threw her arms around my neck and told me that she'd loved me ever since she first saw me. At first, I felt a surge of happiness and I hugged her, then another, colder current cut across my emotion.

"If you love me as you say, why did you tell your Aunt Rafaella that you saw me stealing Giacopo's gold?"

"I never ever meant such a wicked thing," she wailed. "They made me say it so you could be blamed, but I know you're good and kind. Everyone's hated me ever since I was born and I wasn't a boy. Dad used to belt me and my stepmother hated me because if I'd been a boy Dad wouldn't have been so rough on her. No one's wanted me ever," she wailed.

It was difficult for me to sleep that night and I wondered wryly if the iron tablets I regularly took had affected my mind more than my body. There was a sour caution in my nature that made me question and doubt even when I was happiest. I tried to tell myself that I now had a lover who gave me more physical pleasure than anything I had ever experienced, and yet I was chagrined because I suspected that Kurt was probably giving any number of different women the same kind of satisfaction.

Minna had spoken to me about Kurt the night before when I went to her bedroom to comb my hair. She began diffidently, first thanking me for making Kurt feel at home in Sydney, then abruptly taking hold of me by the elbow so that I was facing her directly.

"Kurt is like our son and yet—I must say this to you because it is something Joel cannot see. And if he did, he would not admit it. Kurt does not have a good character with women. I can see this, and I wonder if it is why Renée took such an interest in politics and left him. Sometimes, when people blame a wife because she has run away from her husband, it is because he has forced her to leave. You too, Gwen, you are like our daughter and I could not bear it if Kurt made you unhappy. I'm afraid he is the kind of man who enjoys playing with women but who does not want to live with any one of them. Ah, Kurt is from Vienna, and you know what they say about Viennese men. They kiss your hand and give you flowers, but they are gone in the morning—generally with the housekeeping money."

Kurt was never serious. I could see how this irritated his uncle whenever the discussion was of politics, and those days Joel spoke of little else with Hitler threatening to occupy the Rhineland and the threat of civil war in Spain. Kurt had a talent for deflecting a subject so that it became a joke or an anecdote and once at dinner Joel pounded his fist on the table so violently that the soup flew from his plate as he shouted that Kurt was the grasshopper shrilling of spring when the snow was already falling. Only once had I heard anger in Kurt's voice and that was when he told me of his hatred for Renée. I often wondered about it and tried to imagine what she had done to make him hate her. It was an unusual word for him to use. Had she loved him too much and asked more of him than he could ever give?

When we made love our game always had an edge of peril to it, as if we were dancing on the edge of a cliff where to lose one's balance would mean plunging into a chasm of passionate oblivion. I sensed, too, that Kurt was challenging me not to trip, and even though I yearned to hear him say that he loved me with all his heart and soul and I writhed in anguish when I discovered there were other women besides myself, I did not break the rules he had set for the game of love. The pleasure was all, I told myself, and we treated each other's bodies as if we were daemonic musicians with all the instruments of a great orchestra at our command. Sleep came to me fitfully that night and I drowsily watched the film of morning thread its way across the room, listening to the harbour tugs and, faintly, the roar of the lions across the Harbour at Taronga Park.

Angelica was at my dressing table before I realized there was someone else in the room, and in that remote mood between sleep and waking when you seem to be indifferently aware of yourself and everything else, I watched her open my jewel case, fitting rings on her fingers and admiring them, then carefully opening the lockets of the necklace Edith had given me in Russell Morton.

"They're all dead—except my two cousins and my aunt. It's a necklace of the dead." She gave a squeaking shriek and immediately began to cry.

"It's all right," I said. "I would have been curious too."

"I didn't mean it—I don't know what come over me."

I got up slowly and took the necklace from her.

"I don't think this is a very lucky piece. I've never worn it myself."

As soon as she saw that I was not angry, Angelica began to examine the rest of the case and opened the little satin box that the Barone had first given me when I was a child.

"Oh, they're lovely earrings," Angelica said. "They're much nicer than mine."

"Take them," I said.

"Oh, I love you!" she cried over and over again, her arms around my neck. "I love you more than anything in the whole world, Auntie Gina. I'd die for you, honest I would."

I laughed as she held the earrings to the light.

"You should save that sort of love for a handsome young man."

She said she hated boys and the conversation between us was as light and unimportant as scraps of paper tossed in spirals by the wind, but I remember her saying that if she did fall in love it would be forever.

"You can fall in love many times," I told her and she shook her head vehemently.

"Only once—if it's really love it never happens again."

I watched her slip the rings from the lobes of her ears and replace them with the Barone's gift. I'm not sure why it is, but pierced ears, the sight of wires being pushed through fleshy holes, has always disturbed me and I brusquely told Angelica to go back to her room because I wanted to sleep.

We drove across the Bridge to Mount of Angels and Angelica was jumping with excitement at being in a car and the prospect of seeing her friend Sheila at the convent.

"Her family lives in Homebush. I will be able to stay with Sheila for the hols, won't I, Auntie Gwen?"

Yes, that was what had made me decide to take her. If only there had been a rich and kind aunt in my life who could have kept Bessie and me together. Angelica begged permission to change her name so she could be enrolled as Angela Scarf, and I agreed to this too.

"I don't want them to know I'm a Dago at school," she said. "I had enough of that in Griffith. Angela Scarf sounds nice and I can use it when I become a dancer."

Sheila, a plump girl with pigtails, was waiting for Angelica, and the two of them embraced and squealed and ran off together while I spoke to Mother George.

"It's very generous of you to pay for this child," she said as I filled out the cheque for twice the usual amount, but I knew about Mother George's flexible fees.

"I daresay there are other parents who are charged much more," I replied tersely.

"Oh, my dear, there's a brewer's daughter here who's paying for at least six other girls. When I do the rounds of the convents I always remind the superiors that it's their duty to rob the rich." She chuckled and gave me a shrewd sideways glance. "If you like children so much, you should get married and have a family of your own."

"Mother George, I'm barren."

"Rubbish! See a good doctor."

"I've been to three of the best gynaecologists in Macquarie Street. They all told me the same thing. I'm anaemic and I'm neurotic."

"For heaven's sake, don't talk like that, you sound like your cousin. Such asceticism! I swear if all the novices took after her we'd have an infirmary, not a teaching order. I told her I thought an order like the Carmelites might suit her better—" She sighed irritably and handed me a receipt. "Gwen, my dear girl, God will decide whether you're going to be a mother."

"I'm not sure I believe in your God, Mother."

The great laugh boomed out then and I thought that not even my doubts could stand against it.

"Just so long as He believes in you, Gwen." She paused and gave me one of her quizzical glances. "Why's the aunt so anxious to get rid of this little girl? Italians are generally devoted to children—their own and everyone else's so far as I can see."

I spoke about dancing and the lack of opportunity in Griffith and knew that I was dissembling. Angelica had told me about the block of ice and afterwards Rafaella let slip that Paulo had accused Angelica of being a *puttana*. Where else should the *disgraziata* go but to the house of another *puttana*?

Mother George suggested that I see my cousin before I left and half an hour later I was sitting opposite Edith with Sister Joseph guarding the door and beaming at the cadaverous creature that was now Sister Catherine. Sometimes in the Easter processions the *penitenti* were accompanied by the figures of famine and disease that pranced and capered into the crowd, terrifying the children with their painted skeletal faces. What I saw in front of me that day could have been the gaunt shape of hunger that every Sicilian knew.

"Are you teaching?" I asked Edith after telling her that a distant relative of mine was now a pupil. It was not simply Edith's appearance that appalled me. No matter what I said, she seemed to be straining to hear someone else and when she replied, it was with a faint edge of irritation as though I had selfishly called her away from some important task.

"I do whatever Reverend Mother asks," Edith said, and I gathered from this that she was indeed taking classes.

"Even eating when it is an agony for her to put the food between her lips." Sister Joseph was leaning forward, her cheeks flushed. "Sister Catherine would like to live on the host alone."

"What is it you want?" I cried in exasperation.

Slowly Edith turned her face to me and there was such hunger in her face that I dropped my eyes from hers.

"God," she said simply.

I heard Sister Joseph sigh rapturously and I stood up, clattering my chair on the polished floor.

"I'm glad I was raised a Protestant," I said, and they both exchanged a quick glance as though my shortcomings were so obvious that they did not merit comment.

"We shall pray for you," Sister Joseph said thinly.

"I pray for the world," Edith murmured.

"And for your mother, I hope," I added acidly.

"Oh yes, she needs my prayers now that Frederick is in Spain. Family friends write and tell me that she is quite alone, but no one is alone who has Our Lord as friend and comforter."

Suddenly her tone of abstraction changed and sharply she called after me, "The lease will soon be up. Don't imagine that I'm going to pay the rent for you. You'll have to leave Trelawney."

"Don't disturb yourself, Edith," I replied angrily. "I've been thinking of buying Trelawney as an investment. You've just decided me."

Every time I saw Edith she seemed a different person and I could not discover the dishevelled young woman of Russell Morton or the languid dissolute of Trelawney in this gaunt creature with feverish eyes. Mother George told me that she was now Mother Superior of her whole order in Australia and spent a great deal of time travelling from one convent to another, and whenever she returned to Mount of Angels she was surprised to find that Edith had not been blown away by the Southerly Buster. She chuckled as she spoke although I heard the vexation in her voice.

As I was leaving, Angelica scampered up to me with her friend and threw her arms around my neck.

"If I could die for you, I would, Auntie Gwen," she said.

They were an odd little pair, I thought, as I drove back to Darling Point and perhaps, I told myself, Bessie and I had seemed equally as ill-matched to other people. Sheila was much taller than Angelica and she bulged from her uniform, whereas Angelica looked like a ten-year-old who had wandered over from the junior school.

The following week, McGregor cooked dinner for Terry and Dolfi, Kurt, Norma and myself, and as we sat with our coffee, Norma opened her hat boxes and showed us the cloches and bags she had knotted of different coloured ribbons.

"That's how you should advertise your creams," Terry said.

"A jar of cream with every hat?" Kurt laughed.

"No, I like the product name of Paris Rose."

Dolfi began to wriggle seductively around the room and leaned over Kurt's shoulder, nibbling his ear.

"You need a beauty to advertise it. Someone who is the embodiment of the Paris Rose," Terry added.

"Me! Me!" Dolfi swooned.

"You'll have to hire a model—Yes, a beautiful girl wearing that pink cloche with the rose on one side. Make her the Paris Rose. Hire a billboard at the top of William Street with her face on it and—Paris Rose—creams for ageless beauty."

"We already have the model—the most beautiful girl in Sydney." Kurt smiled at me.

"You'll do it, won't you, love?" Norma was sweating as though she were drunk, mopping her face with a large handkerchief. "You can't imagine what those hats mean to me—Maisie says they're works of art, and they are to me, you know. Imagine, a black crêpe dress, pale pink shoes and that hat with the bag to match."

"I'm not a model," I said flatly.

"*Du bist mein Röslein von Paris*," Kurt sang liltingly.

Dolfi was standing in front of the bay windows, his fat legs splayed, his face like an astonished moon.

"You're all mad! Oh, I see—" He began to giggle. "You're making fun of her. I don't think I approve of that. Gina may be old and ugly but I refuse to stand here while you mock her. She is my cousin and it is a disgrace to have an old maid in the family. I shall speak to Mr Gresham again—he must marry her."

They were all laughing at him then and I thought Dolfi was going to throw his glass through my window.

"I've always told you—Gwen's a knockout," Terry said.

"You've no call to be ashamed of her," Norma added and then Dolfi shouted at them and told them they were all blind fools and it was cruel to praise me for what I so obviously lacked.

"What are you trying to do to me?" I shouted. "First, I'm Miss Gwenadalina Snapper, a character in Dolfi's story. Now you want me to be the Paris Rose and become part of Kurt's story. When can I be myself?"

"I create a whole world, you stupid old hag!" Dolfi screamed at me. "You should be grateful to me. I have made you a personality! All of you are like little stars revolving around my great sun."

"Create? All you do is shit, Dolfi, and give names to the turds!"

Dolfi tried to slap me with a wide swinging blow and Kurt stepped between us and sprayed a soda siphon on his face. He fell back spluttering while Terry walked around in circles, covering his ears.

"Please! Please! I can't bear all the shouting."

"Now, Dolfi, *du kleiner Scheisskopf*, if you don't behave yourself, I'm going to pull your trousers off and the next blast of soda will be up your arse," Kurt said pleasantly.

Giggling, Dolfi collapsed in a chair and said he'd like that very much. I was shaking with rage and then I began to laugh as I looked from Terry treading his circles to Norma, who was carefully packing away her hats and murmuring to each one as if it were alive, "You're going to a blonde and she'll have to be very careful to pull you down so you just touch her eyebrows." Obviously Norma had pulled an invisible helmet over her own head so that she was oblivious to everything except the silk ribbon cloches in her hands.

Dolfi's good humour was restored and he told us about the horse he'd just bought and named Dino.

"I'm going to race it and it will make millions for me," he shouted and proceeded to ride an imaginary horse around the room, whinnying and neighing.

Terry leaned forward and I thought for a moment he was crying.

"You must be discreet, Dolfi. You must be discreet," he said over and over in a low mumble.

Whenever I drive to the top of William Street and see that woman in the pale pink hat, smiling mysteriously as if she alone knows where to find the fountain of youth, I have difficulty recognizing myself. It took at least forty different poses and two hours of being prodded and pulled into position by the photographer until Terry was satisfied and Paris Rose was born. Wearily, I agreed to wear the hat to the Randwick Races on the day that Dolfi planned to race Dino, a tall black gelding with unpleasant eyes. Because he was now an owner, Dolfi was given a lady's pass to the members' enclosure and I agreed to display the pink hat, knowing that every newspaper would carry my photograph the following day and Kurt's face creams and Norma's hats would get a free advertisement.

Dolfi was a sensation in the saddling enclosure after his horse had come in first. Lady Anderson, the wife of the governor of New South Wales, presented him with a silver plate and he promptly fell into his Dino the Dago act to the wild applause of the crowd, clamping his hat to his groin and pretending not to know what hand to use to accept the plate. Lady Anderson was flustered and while Dino was ogling her and the crowd roared, she stepped back and dropped the plate. The laughter was like thunder, but several members of the racing committee and a police sergeant were watching Dino with stony faces. Disgustedly, I thought this was what had become of me: a character in my priapic cousin's skits and a walking billboard for cosmetics.

My parents always despised people who had nothing but money to commend them, and yet what else did I have to show for my life? Besides, what I had accomplished was not so remarkable: I never heard of a Sicilian who failed to prosper in Australia. The Sicilians fell on this country like a pack of starlings and with their sharp eyes they saw plenty where Australians saw only poverty, they scratched the dirt and discovered gold where the Australians found stones, even in the worst years of the depression they survived and flourished. It was no wonder that the Australians were refusing to admit them as migrants and had sent a shipload of them back on the *Otranto* in 1930. Their fruit shops were all over Sydney and if a construction lorry went past me on the road it was sure to have an Italian name painted on the back.

My success had been spectacular: Trelawney was now my own property and people spoke in awe of my wealth, but I had neither husband nor child and my lover was probably in bed with another woman at that very moment. Sometimes I think it is better to be given nothing in life than to be given one thing and denied all else. If you live in a dark cave you cannot imagine the light, but if one ray of light enters, then the darkness is unendurable. Also, I chafed at the indignity of being made a part of someone else's story, and if Paris Rose was a more appealing character than Dolfi's Miss Gwenadalina, I still wanted to write my own story without feeling that I was being jerked and pulled by wires. Even in love, I was playing according to the rules that Kurt had set and when my body responded ecstatically to his tongue and his touch, my mind raged that I was nothing but his puppet.

Billy Garvin was following me as I walked away from the fence and wherever I looked I saw his pocky face and smelt the odour of stale cigarettes and beer.

"He's a great star, your cousin. And what a natural comedian! What did you think of him just now—making the governor's wife look a real idiot?"

I pretended not to hear him and frowned at my card.

"I'd like to have seen this act his father did, when he was called Carmelo Rossi. There's no Italian blood in him, is there? Not like you, Miss Harcourt."

"You know all about me, Billy," I snapped.

"You're in the public eye yourself, Miss Harcourt. Everybody wants to know about the Paris Rose."

"Look at the billboards," I retorted and slipped out of the members' and past the bookmakers against the rail shouting the odds. In that crowd I lost him and stood watching Ned Morecombe josh the punters milling around his brilliant-striped umbrella. Nobody there was interested in my hat or how much it had cost in Paris. Everyone was goggling as the clerk chalked up fresh odds on the blackboard and Morecombe shouted that he was losing a fortune, a whole bloody fortune on the day.

The sun was directly in my face and I was holding up my hand to shade my eyes when everything tilted and I fell headlong into a dream. A bunch of purple grapes swung in front of my face, grapes so ripe that the skin was cracking with sweetness and a fragrance like that of the summer vine in the *bagghiu* filled my nostrils. The air tasted of wine. I turned my head slowly for it was as though I were waking from a long sleep and dimly I saw a blaze of tawny hair crowned with vine leaves and bright blue eyes in a flushed face.

"Have a grape," the man said and belched.

Thirty-Three

There was another voice that I recognized instantly, for it was the first I heard when I left the pale forest on the ship bound for Australia, and what I had thought then was a tattered orange chrysanthemum was the bobbing fuzz of hair on Taps's head. Taps, who had fed and washed me, was trying to steady a swaying giant.

"Now, that's enough, Mr Liddel, you've had enough and—"

"Taps, don't you know me?" I cried.

"Oh my God—it is you! I saw you from a distance and I thought and then I thought it couldn't be—"

"If you two know each other, have a grape to celebrate."

Again, the swinging bunch of purple grapes in front of my eyes.

"It was shocking," Taps whispered. "Up in the committee dining room there was this big epergne of fruit and flowers and Mr Liddel reached into the middle of it and grabbed that bunch of grapes and the next thing there were oranges and apples, a regular orchard flying around the room."

"I saw this beautiful lady and I decided she should have some grapes."

"Take them from him, please, Gwen. I'll phone and talk to you later. I must get him out of here."

"Oh no you don't, Taps. This lady is mine. Do you believe in love at first sight?"

I looked up into Beau Liddel's face and answered slowly.

"Yes, I do, Mr Liddel, but not for me, it will never happen to me."

"It just has and that's the proof."

He pointed to the grapes in my hand as Taps tugged at his arm.

"Please, sir, there's a couple of stewards coming this way. We don't want any more trouble, do we?"

Taps was nodding frantically at me and I stepped back and tried to vanish in the crowd.

"Where's she gone? Where's my rose?" I heard him call after me.

It would be easy to say that I had been accosted by a drunk and since no one had ever seen Beau Liddel sober, that would have been true enough, but I felt as though I had been struck by a lightning bolt. Ariadne, abandoned on Naxos, staring at the sea that carried Theseus from her, must have felt as I did when she looked up and saw the god Dionysus riding through the air to her on a chariot hung with vines, a goblet spilling wine from his hand, his face flushed with long carousing. I kept shaking my head and yet I had taken the grapes from him and they were stickily sweet in my hands. Meditatively, I swallowed one and felt the liquid honey on my tongue and suddenly I was a child again watching the wasps spinning around the drops of sugar falling from the *zibbibbu* grapes in the *bagghiu*.

Taps phoned that evening and said he would be round to see me on Sunday morning and like everyone else, when he stood in front of the windows and gazed out at the Harbour freckled with white sails, he told me that I had done very well for myself.

"I must have seen your picture a dozen times in the papers, but I never associated it with you."

"Oh yes, I'm well known as one thing or another," I replied drily and again felt like a puppet on which different heads were screwed as the plot demanded.

"Mr Liddel did nothing but talk about you, Gwen."

"I'd sooner hear about you, Taps."

"Well, as you can see, I've done all right too. A gentleman's gentleman, and in spite of the booze, Mr Liddel's a real gentleman and most considerate."

"Have you seen Henry?"

"I heard him before I went to see him. Funny, when he was on the boards together, I used to laugh at that voice of his. Like a foghorn dipped in treacle, I used to tell him. Now look at him—a star of radio."

"He's still the same old Henry."

"Is he? To you, he may be, but—success changes people. It was always Taps and Henry in the old days. Now, I'm a valet and he's a star."

"You've seen him, haven't you?"

"Oh yes, I called round to the Rutledge Arms for a beer and there he was, surrounded by his fans. Mind you, he recognized me and I think he was glad to see me again, but it's gone, Gwen—it's finished."

"You loved each other—"

"Once we did, not any longer. You can't pretend to love someone. We're just mates now."

"I'm sorry," I said awkwardly.

"Time does it—she's a fair bitch and no mistake. People remain the same in your head but time's busy doing her worst and when you do find the person you once loved—he's different. Time digs her claws into him and he's not yours any longer."

He paused and blew his nose.

"Did you ever find that friend of yours?"

"No—I've given up looking now, Taps. Sometimes I have the feeling that Bessie will find me one day."

"Half your luck. I'm warning you though, if you do see each other again, she'll probably be a stranger." He sniffed. "Life's a bitch—who would have thought that Henry, poor little Henry that I used to make room for in me act, that Henry is now the star. Beats all. Life's a tragedy, isn't it?" he said mournfully.

"A tragedy? No, it's a farce that often makes you cry."

Sometimes we are prophets of our own lives and what we say will resonate in the future as though we had second sight. There were many times when I recalled what I said unthinkingly to Taps that Sunday morning.

The next day there was a box of roses at my door and a note from Beau Liddel inviting me to dinner. I called and when Taps answered in a suitably gentleman's-gentleman voice, I said that I appreciated the flowers but I was far too busy to have dinner the following night or any other in the near future. Even as I was speaking I tasted the sweetness of the grape in my mouth, but I put the receiver down firmly and told myself that I was not going to exchange an unfaithful lover for one who was never sober. Besides, I was speaking the truth when I said that I was busy. We were now producing so many serials that not even Dolfi could play every part and we finally decided to hold auditions for actors. Not only was Dolfi the star of the Danny Burns Radio Theatre, he was also making another Dino film and the Tivoli was offering him a thousand pounds a week to appear in a new variety show.

The auditions were under way when I arrived at the studio, tired and irritable after negotiating a new contract with His Master's Voice. Everyone acclaimed my business sense and marvelled that a woman could have done so much and yet I always felt that I was being manipulated by others. I did not have my own story. Often I felt like the actors who arrived at the studio never knowing what part they would be asked to play that day, and sometimes were expected to take half a dozen roles in a single morning. As I found a chair in the control room and listened to Henry read with the actors I remembered what the manager at the record company had said to me when I was leaving: "Miss Harcourt, I wish I could say that I enjoyed doing business with you but I sometimes think you'd skin a louse for its tallow." Was this what I had become? Boadicea with a cash register for a heart?

Dolfi's reaction to the actors was predictable. He enjoyed hearing some of them fall over their lines and when an elderly woman lost her place in the script and began to cry, Dolfi wanted to hire her on the spot. However, when one young actor displayed a remarkable range of voices, Dolfi stood up and shouted that he wouldn't have him in the studio. The only way to placate and circumvent Dolfi was to shower the inept with praise, which immediately made him jealous, and jeer at the talented.

"Absolutely hopeless—a voice like a kookaburra with a cold." Terry sneered at a fine actor from the West End.

"Oh, frightful, appalling accent," I added and Dolfi immediately insisted that we give him a contract.

Henry was enjoying himself, reading with all the acting aspirants, but towards the end of the afternoon he began to slur his lines and was holding the scripts at arm's length and squinting to focus. Perhaps I was dozing because we had hired everyone we needed and, although the stragglers were dismal enough to satisfy Dolfi, even he was half asleep. The name jerked me awake.

"My name is Valmai Vitale and I have had years of experience in drama and operetta with the Carl Rosa Company in London. I am now going to render Portia in the quality of mercy and Lady Macbeth's dagger scene. Thank you, but I do not require anyone to read with me. Mine is a solo performance."

My eyes were closed and I did not realize that I was hammering the edge of the chair with my fist as that appalling voice filled the control room with vowels like rotten plums and the hirrient head tone of a swarm of wasps. When Mrs Gilchrist finished, Terry and Dolfi were both leaning forward, their faces pressed to the glass screen. Dolfi grabbed the microphone and told her to speak to Henry, he wanted to hear them together. The two engaged in a little stiff conversation, and it was apparent that they were trying to upstage each other.

"Get Athol—I want them both for Dino—" Dolfi shouted. "I'll give him a plot line now—she's the rich widow determined to marry Henry who's the local minister. Yes, Henry will be the Reverend Whiffle and she—she will be Mrs Cholmondley—only nobody can pronounce her name correctly. She's going to use Dino as a go-between."

I told them that Valmai Vitale was the worst actress I had ever heard and they both looked at me as if I were the village idiot.

"Of course she's absurd, and so's Henry whenever he tries to act. That's why they'll make a great comic team," Terry said.

Valmai was radiant when they told her she was hired and I stood back, watching her shake her hennaed ringlets and pose with a lacquered finger to her cheek like the little girl in the Pears' Soap advertisement. When she saw me, she tripped forward and kissed me.

"My dear Gwen—I did hope you'd be here."

"How's Alan?" I asked awkwardly.

"My son? Yes, of course," she trilled. "You knew him in Griffith, didn't you? Oh, Alan's still in England. Quite the Englishman now from his letters. I was expecting him to send for me, but he didn't, so I had to make my own life. The moment I heard the Danny Burns Radio Theatre I knew where my destiny lay and I left Griffith. What can we expect from men? Nothing but heartache. We poor women have to learn to live with disappointments, don't we?"

Only Henry seemed to share my dislike of Alan's mother.

"Dear heaven, the woman's a freak—a freak, I say. To think that I'll be performing with her. I'd sooner do a skin part and play donkey in Christmas panto."

Dolfi and Terry came back to Trelawney and Athol Tench was locked in the library and told to write a script for Valmai and Henry before they would give him a drink. Another box of roses had been delivered that morning and there were bowls of flowers on every table. Whenever my attention wandered the musky scent of the roses made me feel as though I were standing in front of the Villa d'Athena with Frau Brunner's terraced roses fainting in the summer heat.

Kurt joined us and found Beau Liddel's second card among the roses. He read it aloud.

"Beau Liddel—now there's a catch," Terry said. "He must own half of New South Wales and a fair-sized wedge of Victoria."

"He's a drunk," I said.

"Yes, Beau Liddel, I've heard of him. He rides around the city in a brewery wagon." Kurt nodded.

"Only when he's very drunk," Terry assured him.

Kurt was still holding Beau Liddel's card and smiling at me with an expression I could not read.

"My congratulations to you, Gwen," he said at last, then he shouted, "Oh, I can't keep it to myself any longer. I adore you."

Dolfi had been amusing himself imitating Valmai and Henry, inventing scenes and dialogue for them, chortling at his reflection in my Florentine mirror, when he saw Kurt pull me to him and kiss me.

"How dare you take such a liberty with my cousin!" he shrieked.

"Oh, I've done much more than kiss her," Kurt replied.

"Then you must marry her! I will not permit my cousin to be treated like a common *puttana*."

"I would be honoured to—with your permission," Kurt said easily and bowed gallantly to Dolfi.

I thought at first they were joking because I was accustomed to Dolfi's curious assumption that he was my guardian, but Kurt held my face in his hands so that his eyes held mine.

"Now, are you going to be my wife as your cousin says?"

"Why? Why are you asking me now?" I asked incredulously.

"Because I love you, Gwen."

"You said—"

"Oh, I may have said a dozen different things then and meant them all, but when I saw that I had a rival who could buy you a garden of roses, I knew I must have you."

"You sound like a child."

"No, I'm Count Bobbie."

"Tell us a Count Bobbie story. I like them," Dolfi cried.

"Well, this is my story and it is why I am going to marry your cousin, Dolfi."

"There are witnesses, Kurt, so don't think I'll let you wriggle out of it. Gwen is in my care and I've spent years and years trying to find a husband for her." Dolfi frowned.

"Count Bobbie was engaged to the most beautiful young girl in Vienna. Everyone congratulated him but then the engagement dragged on and on, and eventually Bobbie announced that it was all over, the engagement was broken. 'Why? Why? What happened?' all his friends asked. 'Here you had the most beautiful, faithful girl in all Vienna and you decided you didn't want to marry her! Why?' 'Well,' Count Bobbie replied, 'I discovered she was a virgin and I thought if no one else wanted her, I didn't either.' "

Dolfi spluttered and choked and rolled on the sofa, laughing, repeating the story over and over to himself in different voices while I stood dumbfounded.

"You." I stared at Kurt in disbelief. "You'd never be faithful."

"Ah, but I would if I knew that someone else wanted you."

That night, after we made love and lay back exhausted with the sound of the turning tide echoing strangely in the room, I propped myself on my elbow and looked wonderingly at Kurt.

"It was all a joke, wasn't it?"

"Why are you such a literal-minded young woman? It's as though a goddess suddenly appeared on earth in a blaze of glory and as everyone waited to hear what jewelled words were going to fall from her lips, she politely asked if someone could lend her a cup of sugar."

"Kurt, I don't want to hear any more jokes or funny anecdotes, I—"

"You want me to be serious. I am now. I've only asked a woman to be my wife once before and that was such a calamity I've tried to make a joke about it ever since. Some people are stoical in grief, I'm Viennese and if I make jokes it's because I don't want to embarrass people with my tears."

"Why did you hate your wife?"

"Because I should never have married her, but everyone said that the Laufers were such a fine Jewish banking family and it was such a good connection, and her father would be able to do so much for me. Renée was pretty, very svelte and sophisticated, and we enjoyed making love. When she discussed politics I didn't listen and my parents said she'd forget all that nonsense once she was married. I thought she was reacting against her parents—particularly her father who counted money in his sleep. As it was, she refused the very generous allowance he wanted to make us and we scraped along on what I could earn. With enough money, anything can work. Champagne will make a dinner of bread and sausage seem a feast, but to eat it with water is misery."

He rolled on to his back and lay with his hands behind his head, and I wondered what he was seeing in the milky shadows on the ceiling.

"If she hadn't been so anxious to marry me, I would not be here in Australia now. Renée was a Communist, a member of the Party, and when I would not give up my job in a cosmetics firm to become a serious chemist, whatever that meant, and when I told her I'd sooner spend my nights in a coffee shop than at Party rallies, we really began to quarrel. She said I was frivolous and irresponsible, and perhaps I am, but I don't consider it a crime to use my talents as a chemist to make women look and feel more attractive. That was the trouble, my talents never equalled her ambitions for me. Night after night of listening to her harangue me as a bourgeois dilettante, the enemy of the working class, reading me long articles from the *Rote Fahne* while I played the piano. She wanted to sell our apartment on the Arenberg Ring and rent a couple of rooms in Favoriten where my father has his factory. Eventually, she left and went to Germany to join the KPD and help organize the Communist attack against the Nazis. Of course, the Germans are always so methodical and bureaucratic, not like the Austrians, and the KPD kept Party archives and carried carbon copies of letters in suitcases. The Nazis rounded them up and butchered the Communists by the hundred. I heard Renée was arrested and then there was no word for several weeks. Finally, her father, who had friends among the Nazis—oh yes, there is a confederation of money—they told him that Renée had died in prison. She was probably beaten to death. That's what they did to the Communist leaders who were taken alive."

Neither of us spoke. Liquid shadows from the Harbour floated against the wall and the tide echoed as if we were locked in a sounding shell.

"Was that enough to make you hate her?" I asked him quietly.

"I hated her because she made me seem worthless. Because she made me despise myself. I don't deserve to feel so contemptible."

"Is that why you made love a game between us?"

"I was not going to let another woman crush my soul! That is what Renée did to me. And now I shall always feel responsible for her death. Sometimes I imagine what happened to her before she died—we heard so many stories in Austria about the Nazis. My uncle is right—they are trolls from the pit of hell."

He was knuckling his eyes with his fists as if he could rub out memories and sights.

We were silent together for a long time.

"Am I making the same mistake again?" he said at last. "Asking you to be my wife?"

"You know I can't have children," I said dully.

"Do you think I want a replica of myself? Children are the immortality of the poor. Perhaps I am a grasshopper, as my uncle says, but I am a good little Kurt at heart and I know how to amuse myself. If only this country had more to offer and I had more money. All these women with divine bodies and faces like scrubbed potatoes who think a jar of cream is a prodigal indulgence. Let me tell you what Australia is like. Once I managed to get into the bedroom of the most beautiful actress in Vienna. On stage, she was all grace—a sylph who barely seemed to touch the ground, she was so delicate in all her movements. I offered to help her undress but she told me to get into bed and wait for her. I did, and first she put a finger in her mouth, poking out some fragment of supper from between her teeth and chewing it thoughtfully, then she scratched and stretched and farted and when she threw herself down beside me I was no better than a eunuch. Sydney is like my Viennese actress—such beauty and all abandoned or cast aside like a whore's clothes. There should be pleasure boats and music on that harbour, kiosks and places along the shore where people can flirt and dance. Why don't these Australians take pleasure in their beauty?"

"Am I like your actress?"

"You, Gwen—no! In you there is a silence that sometimes terrifies me. Even when we make love I feel as if I'm on the border of a mysterious continent where I could lose my life."

"You're a romantic." I laughed, remembering when someone else had called me an arch romantic.

"I believe in Freud and sex," he responded.

"What will Joel and Minna say when we tell them we plan to marry?"

"Ah—that will be very interesting—"

"I'm not related to them but they're like my parents. I know they want you to marry a Jewish girl."

"They are realists. In life you never get everything you want and you should never ask for the same thing twice. I've already had a Jewish wife."

When Kurt was asleep, I walked into the next room and stood in front of the bay windows with the Harbour spread out in front of me and three islands glimmering in a moonlight so incandescent it was as if a sheet of lightning had been frozen across the water. I remembered when I used to stand with Bessie on the terrace of the Villa d'Athena, watching the fishing boats pass between the islands and making plans for our lives as though we were cutting out patterns for cardboard dolls: I was going to marry Roger and Bessie would marry Dolfi and manage the hotel. Now, I was going to be Kurt's wife and I was sure that I loved him if only because I felt the surging triumph of having overcome all the rules that Kurt had set for the game of loving, the verb that must never become a subject noun, the play that must never be resolved. The victory was mine now and Kurt was to be my husband. This time, I told myself, there would be no conflict over the way we should live. If there were shadows in my disposition, they would disappear before Kurt's gaiety and perhaps, in time, I might become the Paris Rose smiling under her pink silk cloche. Why then at that moment did I suddenly think of Alan and in the next instant taste the sweetness of a grape in my mouth?

"Are you sorry you accepted me?"

I did not realize that Kurt was standing behind me and I jumped in surprise as he put his arms around me and held my breasts.

"You're not angry because I don't want to change the world?"

"No—"

"And you'll be a good wife and learn to make coffee?"

"No!" I laughed and we went back to bed and made love.

The following morning we opened the front door on to a forest of rose bushes in full bloom.

"I like this Beau Liddel more and more!" Kurt exclaimed, and read the card. "Listen to this, *liebling*. 'The roses didn't do any good so I'm sending you the bloody trees.' "

"This time I can get rid of him," I said firmly. "I shall tell him that I'm engaged to another man."

"Don't be too harsh with him." Kurt smiled. "I like to know I have a rich rival who can buy you such flowers."

The gardener planted the roses in front of Trelawney and I sent a formal note to Beau. A reply came back with four words on it. "You're not married yet."

That night we told Joel and Minna.

I expected them to be disappointed because I was not Jewish. Instead, they both sat glaring at Kurt.

"Are you going to behave like a married man?" Minna asked coldly.

"I shall try," Kurt said, and reached out and took my hand. "If Gwen doesn't forget to remind me."

"You are not what I hoped for her!" Joel growled. "You are a philanderer."

"I can change."

"We shall see," Minna said dubiously.

Later, Joel brought out a French champagne and drank our health and Minna insisted that I have one of her diamonds set as an engagement ring.

Joel was almost jigging in his excitement and kept trying to get Kurt to join him. "This will convince your parents and the rest of the family that they must leave Austria at once. Your mother will insist on being present when her eldest son is married. That is one occasion she would never miss."

"I'm not Jewish," I said faintly.

"You're Jewish enough." Joel beamed.

"And I can't have children," I added.

Minna winked at me. "Any woman can have children if she knows the right prayers to say at the proper time."

"They will all come—tomorrow I shall send Erika a bank draft for ten thousand pounds to bring out the whole family. Cousins, every one of them—this country will be a haven when Hitler is killing the Jews in Europe."

"Ten thousand pounds!" Minna gasped.

"I would find twenty thousand and send that if I thought I could save some more of our people. If I had to sell everything I own and go back to pushing a barrow of *shmatters*, I would do it to save them from Hitler. What do you think, Kurt?"

"Yes, for a wedding and ten thousand pounds, they'll come." He sighed. "My poor Gwen, you do not know what is happening to you this evening. My parents—my two sisters and their husbands who both work for my father. You will have such a family."

"That's what I've always wanted," I said.

"Wait till you meet my mother," he replied.

Three weeks after Kurt's proposal, Dolfi and Terry insisted on giving us an engagement party at the Chateau Miramar with at least a hundred of Dolfi's more intimate friends. Some of the musicians from the Tivoli played on the lawn and Kurt tried to teach me how to dance.

"Why are you so clumsy?" he cried.

"Because I always danced as a man."

"If you lead me once more—no, drag is a better word—I shall slap you."

I was in love and Kurt's gaiety was infectious and yet there were moments that evening when I felt as if I were watching someone else dance in Kurt's arms. The woman he held was the Paris Rose and I was standing to one side, mournfully watching the person who was masquerading as me. Somehow, the puppet invented by Terry and Kurt had managed to snatch my soul.

Dolfi's parties always ended in brawls, and this was no exception. He insisted on making a speech and said tearfully that he was overwhelmed with joy and gratitude that he had at last found a husband for me, and he didn't mind that it was a Jew, because the only Jew he could not tolerate was Roy Rene, undoubtedly the worst and most obscene person ever to call himself a comedian and a disgrace to Jews everywhere. There were a few boos and catcalls from the crowd but Dolfi continued to denounce Mo until some of his friends threatened to pull him from the table and throw him in the pool. Suddenly he saw Henry trying to evade Valmai who was swaying amorously after him and that led him to toast another couple. Valmai pursued Henry and it all ended with Florrie pushing her in the pool and everyone screaming and throwing bottles.

Wearily Kurt said that it reminded him of his family and we walked back across the waterfront to Trelawney.

"I think we should get married before they all arrive."

Joel still took his classes twice a week, but no matter what text we agreed to read we always ended discussing politics. Hitler had invaded the Rhineland and General Franco was in arms against the Republican government in Spain and yet for most people in Australia the news seemed like rumours of war on another planet. When I spoke about it to Terry he said he thought we should work some Nazi spies into our new crime serial, and Dolfi immediately gave us a variety of German accents. The police had tried to stop a performance of the anti-Nazi play *Till the Day I Die* at the Savoy Theatre, and it was clear from the crowd that a great many people there were sympathetic to Adolf Hitler. My cousin Frederick was now writing regularly for the *Economist* and Joel read approvingly from his articles.

"He says it is only a matter of time before the war spreads across Europe. Your cousin is right, Gwen. This is not a little skirmish—it is 1914 all over again. That war began in the Balkans, this time it has started in Spain."

Some European Jews shared Joel's fears because slowly small groups of them began to arrive in Australia and Kurt was jubilant when the first Viennese coffee shop opened in Market Street.

I was sitting there one afternoon waiting for him, tired after a day of working out a recording schedule so that Dolfi could make his film at the weekends and appear at the Tivoli in the evening.

There was a vibrant hum of conversation around me and I leaned back contentedly, listening to the lilt of voices and smelling the fragrance of coffee and chocolate. The young Austrian couple who ran the café had just placed a large slice of *Sachertorte* in front of me and the coffee was foaming and dusted with cinnamon. The day before I had been to the convent with Kurt for the school concert and watched Angelica dance a solo in a white crinoline covered with large blue roses. Even Sister Joseph, who told me she was a worldly child, had to admit that Angelica was a talented dancer. She was not a scholar and her reports came back with warnings and complaints in every subject, but she always managed to win a prize for dancing.

Florrie and Norma were convinced that she would bring me nothing but grief and neither of them liked her when they met her at Trelawney, yet Angelica had hardly required me to look after her. Every holiday she went to stay with her friend in Homebush and when I asked her if she had heard from her Aunt Rafaella she shook her head and said she didn't care what happened to any of that crowd in the bush. I wrote to Rafaella and told her about Angelica but there was never any reply so after the third note I didn't bother to send any more news.

"Don't you miss them?" I asked Angelica one evening when I'd taken her to the Theatre Royal to see *The Maid of the Mountains* with Gladys Moncrieff.

"Why should I?" she retorted. "I hate Dagos."

"You're Italian. We both are."

"Nobody at school knows."

"You liked Rocco, didn't you? He was your friend."

"I hate him worse than all the others. You're the only one of my family I love, Auntie Gwen. I'd die for you, honest I would," she replied with the gushing phrases that were her greatest expression of affection.

Angelica seemed such an ordinary little mouse, interested in clothes and make-up and determined to become a soubrette in the theatre. There was no harm in her. She lied constantly, but children who lie are often afraid to tell the truth, and I could imagine the kind of life she had led with the Sciafas.

It puzzled me that both Kurt and Dolfi should dislike her—especially Dolfi, who appreciated anyone who flattered him: Angelica was very proud of her famous uncle.

"She's a *puttana*," Dolfi said.

"You're unspeakable," I retorted.

"Gina, you fool, a little girl who rubs herself against your legs when she speaks is either a reincarnated cat or a *puttana*. She's probably being trained at the convent by that filthy old nun with the big laugh."

"You imagine all these things," I told him.

"Your little angel wants me to speak to the manager of the Theatre Royal for her now that she's ready to leave school—and she's prepared to do anything, anything at all for a place in the chorus. Don't you think I know what she means?"

"She's young, she's trying to be a vamp."

I remembered what Bessie and I were like when we used to walk home together from the Villa d'Athena.

Kurt grinned when he saw her dance at the concert and said he thought she would do well—on stage and off.

"You men are all the same!" I hissed.

"It's known as collective common sense."

I was so angry with him that I felt vindicated when I introduced him to Edith after the concert and she snubbed him.

What trouble had Angelica given me? Nothing but the cost of her schooling and her clothes, and I could well afford that. When she threw her arms around me and told me she loved me I felt that I had been able to repay one debt in my life. Or was that just a sentimental sop to my conscience? Angelica was not Margaret Moglen and the debts of the spirit must be repaid in kind and never in cheap currency. She would die for me, Angelica always said, and I thought those words were nothing more than schoolgirl gush, as trite and well-worn as the coins I used to bribe memory into silence.

Thirty-Four

"Gwen, that poster doesn't do you justice."

At first I did not recognize the measured English voice and when I looked up in surprise it was a moment before I saw Alan Gilchrist in the man who had just spoken. He did not seem older, but there was a gravity about him that I had never seen before.

He sat down and gazed at me as if he were trying to create me with his eyes—I shifted nervously and tried to smile as the blood rushed to my face.

"The first thing I saw when I arrived yesterday was your poster and then my mother told me about your success."

"I didn't know—I thought you were still in London."

We tried to make conversation, asking the obvious questions and answering in clichés, and then we sat silently, staring at each other.

"What do you see, Gwen?" he asked quietly.

"I'm not sure. At first, I felt as though it was only yesterday when we said goodbye in your chambers and now I can see how different we are. You were always serious, now it's as if you were a judge and I—" I could not finish.

"Gwen, please—" He put his head in his hands and laughed ruefully. With that one gesture he pushed his spectacles up into his hair and I recognized the Alan Gilchrist I had loved.

"I meant it as a compliment."

"Think of another."

"You're a King's Counsel now, aren't you?"

"Oh yes, I wear silk in court."

"And you're going to practise here?"

"If you need a barrister, tell your solicitor to brief me."

"You know your mother is acting for our company now—will she be living with you?"

"My mother has a flat in Pott's Point and I am presently staying at my club. No, Gwen, thanks to this new career of hers I don't feel I have to look after her. She did tell me that she was known in Sydney by her stage name and she'd be grateful if I didn't inform people that she was my mother—it was so ageing to have a son of my years."

We were both laughing when I realized that Kurt was standing at my shoulder.

"I hope I've discovered a secret tryst."

Kurt leaned over and kissed me and I introduced Alan to him.

"You were once Gwen's suitor, weren't you?" Kurt said gaily.

"Yes—"

I could see Alan scrutinizing Kurt, but his expression did not change when Kurt told him that I was his fiancée. Either he no longer cared for me or he was able to control his feelings as I could not.

Why did I suddenly feel guilty as the two began to speak about London and Alan pushed back his chair to leave? We shook hands and he said he hoped that we'd see each other again soon and I wanted to ask him if Gwen's Bridge was still there, but I didn't ask him that either.

"This was the lawyer who wanted you to be his wife?" Kurt said when he was gone.

"I would have married him if it hadn't been for his mother, and now she's working for me. Our new comedy team—Valmai and Henry."

"This man has presence. When he sits down he occupies the whole room. Did you notice that? I don't think there would be space in his life for a woman like you. Perhaps a nicely decorated little doormat might suit him. Your admirer will go into politics—and if he does, I'll vote for him."

"There was space for me once."

"Ah, I see I have another rival."

"Kurt, love isn't always a game—"

"My dear Gwen, it's too dangerous to be anything else. Now, let me tell you the worst possible news."

He paused theatrically, with an appearance of such grief that I began to laugh involuntarily.

"You will not be laughing when they are here. Uncle Joel has just informed me that the bank draft has been cashed in Vienna which means that my family is on its way. Also, I have received a letter from the German consul who tells me that enquiries are being made in Berlin and the death certificate of Frau Renée Stern will be sent to me. That is all we need for a marriage licence and if we are sensible, as soon as it arrives, we will get married and leave Sydney before my parents and the rest of the family arrive."

My feet were now on a settled path again and I was not going to be led away from it by memories of a bridge of sand or the vision of a bunch of grapes before my eyes. Kurt and I were to be married and I would no longer have the feeling of being set apart from other women, a solitary with friends. I kissed him across the table and quietly he told me that he was the most fortunate of men. Over the hum of conversation a Strauss waltz was playing and I told myself that this was the measure and the meaning of love, this was love for the Paris Rose.

There once had been a little girl in the town of Trapani who was always told by her parents to look behind the surface of things and there she would discover reality. Truth was always hidden and had to be dug out with a spade which, because it could not speak, was incapable of lying. But that little girl had become Paris Rose and for her there was only surface and shining and behind the picture of the painted smile there was nothing. She was, she continually told herself, very happy.

Paris Rose wore a large square-cut diamond ring and because her clothes were designed by Madame Reynaud, the society and fashion pages described her as one of the best-dressed women in Australia. At social occasions she was always seen on the arm of her handsome fiancé, Kurt Stern, and everyone admired and envied her. In the autumn of 1937 Kurt and Paris Rose went to the Sydney Easter Show with Angelica and Sheila who was, if it were possible, plumper than ever. Sheila was going to work in the Department of Roads thanks to her uncle who was a supervisor and Angelica had been promised an audition at the Theatre Royal by Tally Winters, who was one of Dolfi's cronies. The two girls planned to share a little flat in Macleay Street not far from Glenarches where, in another life, Paris Rose had once been the manager.

If Paris Rose had not dispossessed me there are two incidents I would have observed and pondered on that day. When we were passing the pens of the prize pigs, Angelica poked Sheila in the ribs and began to giggle.

"Why don't you jump in and join your brothers and sisters?" she sniggered, and Sheila began to cry.

"Sheila looks just like a pig in a pinny, doesn't she, Uncle Kurt?"

"No, *poppoli*, the real pig is the person who behaves like one—and that is you."

I fancy that Paris Rose chided Angelica and promptly thought of something else more entertaining than pigs and adolescent girls.

In another pavilion Angelica and Sheila both gasped in admiration at the exhibition of iced cakes designed to resemble rustic cottages. Nothing less edible could be imagined than the spun-sugar shingles, hollyhocks and frilled curtains blowing from barley-sugar windows, winding paths of chocolate cobblestones and marzipan ducks walking across a lawn where every blade of grass was a filament of sugar. Paris Rose was marvelling at these triumphs of preposterous frivolity when Angelica said they were the most beautiful things she'd ever seen and Sheila agreed with her.

"Be very careful of houses like that," Kurt said darkly.

"Oh, but you could eat them—if you wanted to—" Sheila said, licking her lips.

"Pretty, charming little houses and inside every one of them there is something so evil it barely has a shape."

The two girls stared at him and he lowered his voice to a whisper.

"A black toad that is really a witch lying in wait for her victims that she will fatten for roasting in her oven. Whenever you see anything as pretty as that look for the wickedness at its heart."

They giggled and said that Hansel and Gretel were for little children, that they were much too old for fairy stories.

Sheila and Kurt were ahead of us and I felt Angelica's hand in mine.

"I wish you'd write a letter to Aunt Rafaella."

"I thought you never wanted to see her again."

"I'd like her to know that I have a boyfriend."

"Who is he?"

"Sheila's cousin—he's studying to be a teacher at Sydney University. I like him."

"Well—if you want her to know—"

"She said I'd never find anyone to marry me. Jack is potty about me."

"If you want me to write—but she never answered any of my letters before."

"Just tell her that I'm unofficially engaged."

"Are you?"

"As good as," Angelica said, looking up at me with a sideways glance.

I asked her if she was in love and she wriggled irritably and said she wasn't going to hang around waiting for Clark Gable.

"So you don't expect to fall in love and never again." I smiled.

"Maybe I'm copying you," she said and I felt a sudden apprehension and could not have explained why.

Every week a silver-wrapped box arrived at Trelawney for Paris Rose, and inside it, nestling in layers of soft tissue paper, a bunch of purple grapes. There was never any card but Kurt and I knew who had sent it.

"You have intelligent, charming admirers," Kurt would say, eating the grapes with considerable relish. "Grapes are my favourite fruit. This is what Eve really gave Adam; he would never have sacrificed Paradise for an apple, but for grapes like these . . ."

I saw Beau Liddel once in the saddling ring at Randwick when Dolfi was racing another of his horses. His back was turned to me but I was sure he knew I was there.

"You should discard David Maybrick and keep Beau Liddel and Alan Gilchrist—they are both remarkable men," Kurt often told me.

"David has never meant anything to me. He was in love with Edith once."

"Your catatonic schizophrenic cousin—yes, she's very suitable for him. No, I like having three rivals, but what does David Maybrick do for my ego? He is such a miserable fellow."

"People say he's a fine archaeologist. Besides, he's going back soon to England."

"You already have one scholar in Alan Gilchrist, you don't need two. No, you have a famous lawyer, a playboy and the third should be an actor or an industrial magnate. I can't decide which I want. An industrial magnate would be compensation for the fact that my little cosmetics firm is doing well but not making millions. A Krupp would be most satisfactory but then, an actor would be gratifying since I am not as good-looking as I should like to be."

Even though Kurt had abandoned the game of lovemaking and declared his love for me, Gwen had been cast aside at the same time and Paris Rose had taken her place. Paris Rose delighted in endless flirtation, for as Kurt told her, if you were not being unfaithful to your lover in the bedroom, it was your duty to be unfaithful to him in your mind. Like one of Schnitzler's plays or a gin sling, the sweetness was always accentuated with a dash of bitters.

Paris Rose died on the 10th of June at five-thirty in the afternoon.

Dolfi had just finished a six-week season at the Tivoli to standing room audiences and the film was to be released that night at the State Theatre. At the same time, the recordings had been going on regularly, with the studio booked from eight in the morning until six at night. Most people would have collapsed, but Dolfi was possessed of a daemonic energy and while we all groaned with fatigue he rushed from the studio to the Tivoli and out to the film at weekends, dragging us behind him. People said that Dolfi would stand up in his grave to acknowledge an audience and I think they were right.

When we first began recording Henry and I had read small parts and Dolfi had played the rest; now we had actors, and among those actors was the monstrous Valmai Vitale. Every time I heard her voice I flinched, but there was no denying that she was a comic sensation, especially when she played opposite Henry, who loathed her with a passion that was almost as great as mine. One morning she billowed up to me and whispered that she would be grateful if I did not tell anyone that she had a son. Alan was looking so middle-aged, she told me, and she had her career to consider.

Dolfi encouraged her belief that she was a Mata Hari who was irresistible to men and he deliberately pushed her towards Mr Gresham one evening. My old friend was retiring as manager of the Australia and after he had managed to elude Valmai he told me in a quiet corner that he was returning to England.

"I don't care for the way things are shaping up in Europe," he said, "and I'd like to be in England if there is any trouble. I'm too old to serve the King, but I'm a loyal subject and if England needs me, I shall be there."

Valmai discovered us and flounced towards us, beads and bangles rattling in demented counterpoint to that vibrating voice.

"My dear Mr Gresham—did I hear you mention England? Did I tell you I was born in Devon?—" and she burst into song. "'In Devon! In Devon, glorious Devon! Where the cider apples grow!' Or was that Somerset?"

"Someone should strangle that woman," Mr Gresham said and vanished with astonishing alacrity for a man of his age.

He left Sydney a month later and I really think his departure was hastened because of Valmai Vitale. We said goodbye at the wharf and I remembered the Whitlows and the Burnsides, and all the other English residents who had left Sicily and returned to England. This was different.

"If there's a war, wouldn't you be safer here in Australia?" I asked him.

"My dear girl, if England goes to war, a Gresham must be there."

The only person who seemed completely unconcerned about the threat of war was Morton Silberstein, the vice-president of Metro Goldwyn Mayer, who had arrived in Sydney for the opening night of *Dino on the Town.* We expected a loud-spoken American in a plaid suit; instead the only informality about Morton was his insistence that we use his first name. In a dark-grey suit and a spotted silk tie he looked like a cousin of Mr Henderson at the Australian Mutual Trust.

"He's going to make Dolfi an offer," Terry said ecstatically to me.

"What will happen to the Danny Burns Radio Theatre?"

"We'll sell you our interest in it—perhaps Kurt would like to come in with you. He has a flair for show business."

"It wouldn't amount to much without Dolfi."

"You'd have his name and you could use actors. Some of them can double up parts. They've all learned from Dolfi. Oh, Gwen, this is what I've worked for ever since I met Dolfi. He's a star here in Australia, but in Hollywood, he'll become a greater comedian than Charlie Chaplin."

"I think you're probably right. In the meantime, you'd better keep Dolfi sober while Morton's here."

"Morton's going to spend six months in Australia. He's announced his visit as a talent quest, but I know that he really wants Dolfi."

"Could you sell him Valmai too?"

"She's marvellous, Gwen. You've seen the rushes of the film—those scenes with Henry trying to climb up the belfry to get away from her are wonderful."

It was to be a gala opening for the film with every celebrity in town present. Dolfi wanted Roman candles and Catherine wheels, but had to settle for searchlights when the police refused permission for a fireworks display. Kurt was to arrive for me at six and McGregor told me that the cold asparagus and salmon was ready under a cover for us.

"I can't leave until I see you in that gown, Miss Harcourt," she said.

The dress was a lilac chiffon draped in the Grecian mode and beaded with seed pearls. When McGregor hooked me into it and I stood in front of the cheval-glass I knew I had never worn anything that suited me so well, except for the blue handkerchief lawn that Bessie had once stolen for me.

"You're the Paris Rose and no mistake," McGregor said admiringly.

The phone rang at that instant and as I lifted the receiver I glanced at the clock and saw that it was five-thirty.

I heard Minna's voice and even before she had said three words I knew there was something wrong. She told me to come at once. I asked her if Kurt was all right and she assured me that he was, but I must come, come at once.

It took me less than fifteen minutes to drive the Franklin to Bellevue Hill and in that time I tried to imagine what had happened. Was it Joel? Yes, of course it must be Joel, and I expected to see an ambulance outside the house when I parked the car in the driveway. Everything was quiet but as I pushed open the front door, Minna ran from the living room and threw her arms around me.

"Gwen! Gwen! We didn't know—we expected the family."

"What is it?" I cried. "Where's Joel?"

"He's there—with Kurt and—"

Without waiting to finish, I pushed past her and into that room I knew as well as my own home. I saw Joel first in a chair by the window, holding a sheet of paper in his hand. Kurt was at the table with letters and photographs spread out in front of him. He was bent forward as if he were praying or crying. I spoke and he looked up at me with his face twisted and eyes so dark it was as if someone had burned holes into his head. Twice he opened his mouth to say something—there was no sound. I had never seen him drunk before, but that night I could smell the brandy and saw the glass in front of him.

Minna alone seemed capable of interpreting the mysterious tableau and I turned to her.

"We were expecting Joel's family next week—instead—we received letters and—those photographs."

I took one in my hand and I saw a woman's face, or what must have been a woman. The light was stark and only a doctor could have had such an unsparing vision. Half the face was normal but the other side—I flinched and Minna gave me another. A flap of skin was pulled across the place where her eye must have been and the bones seemed to have been pushed inwards.

"Renée was discovered in a Mannheim prison by agents hired by her family and after she came back to Vienna, they wrote at once for Kurt to come back. She asks for him—"

I think Kurt laughed at that moment but it was a sound I had never heard before.

"She was captured by the Nazis and beaten. They did not get her any medical attention and it was too late to reset the bones when she arrived in Vienna. These were taken by a famous surgeon in Vienna who—"

Suddenly Joel spoke.

"I have a letter from my little sister Erika. You must hear it, Gwen. It is a letter that only my sister could write."

He held the letter out from him and as he spoke I could hear him translating and trying to imitate a fluting girlish voice.

Mein lieber good and kind brother.

You cannot imagine what surprise your letter and kind gift gave us. We sat around the fireplace and first we all cried a little and then we laughed and cried again just as if we were children. Ah, if you could only see me now with my wrinkles and fat bottom, you would not recognize your little sister. Now, I shall tell you what we have all decided and you must remember that we did not make up our minds quickly or easily. Who could do such a thing in this family when everybody has a different opinion about everything from noodles to Mozart? No, we sat and talked and first we realized that you must be hearing all sorts of terrible things about Austria that simply do not exist. Of course the Nazis are disgusting people, but what can you expect from Germans? Never happy unless they are in uniform and giving orders. If only the good old emperor were on the throne here they would not be so noisy—the Emperor Franz Josef would have put this little paperhanging Adolf in his place. As it is, we have a very

> good pact with Germany and there will not be war between us. People have always hated Jews, but we have never made a show of our religion, and *we have never had any trouble.*

He laughed and for a moment I thought he was going to tear the letter across, but he recovered and read on in that fluting imitation of a woman's voice.

> Now, Richard's partner, that silly man, Paul Frommer, has decided that he wants to go to America and it was a perfect opportunity to buy his share of the business cheaply. Richard made him an offer, and Paul jumped at it, so now Stern and Frommer, Gas Oven and Stove Manufactory belongs to our family and I cannot tell you what a wonderful future this makes for our two sons-in-law, who are both working for us, as you know.
>
> Not only have you made it possible to bring the whole business into the family, but we decided that it would be so pleasant for us all to have a little place of our own to go to on holidays. So, we have bought the most charming little chalet at the foot of the Rax on the Semmering Plateau. Whenever we go there it will be like taking the cure in some expensive resort, the air is so good and pure and Richard does suffer so badly from bronchitis. Because you have always been so good and generous, we decided it was time for a new car and with what was left from your generous gift we bought a Steyr 220—ah, you should see the beauty—dark green with a beige trim and leather upholstery so soft it is like sitting on velvet.
>
> I think you will agree that we have managed very well with your money and we hope that our beloved Kurt will come home and spend the holidays with us. Ah my dear brother, it is you who will bring the whole family together! Can you imagine the pain of my breaking heart when I know that my little Kurtzi is thousands and thousands of miles away with kangaroos and other wild animals? It is a pity that Kurt has met this *shiksa* in Australia, but then our little Kurtzi will find pretty girls anywhere. He must come home now and sort things out with poor Renée. Poor thing, I cannot bear to look at her she is so disfigured, but I know my Kurtzi and he is such a clever boy that he will be able to decide what is best for everyone. Frankly I do not think that poor little Renée will live very long but then what woman would want to live looking like that? It is a pity in a way that he met someone

> in Australia when Vienna is full of pretty girls, but life is like that and every day I thank God I have such a kind generous brother who still thinks of the little sister who used to drop beetles in his soup and sing when he was trying to study. If I could only lose ten kilo I would be in heaven and you might recognize your little Erika, but you would not know this fat old Frau who signs her letter with kisses.

Joel crumpled the letter and beat his forehead with it.

"I shall make us all some tea," Minna said helplessly.

"I must go," I said and Kurt shouted that he would not permit me to leave him.

"It's the opening night of Dolfi's film—"

"And I am going with you."

"I think you should stay here, Kurt. I'd prefer to be alone."

I was speaking, but it was my mother's voice I heard at that moment, peremptory and concise.

"Do you think this—" and he pointed to the stark photographs, "this makes any difference to us?"

"Please—you must not talk in this way—not now." Minna was between us, almost pushing us apart with her hands. "We must be silent for a little while. There will be time to discuss all of this tomorrow when we are not so upset."

"Upset! Is that the word you use when your family is dead!" Joel cried.

I turned to the door and I thought for a moment that Kurt was going to follow me, but he was too drunk and fell across the table, sobbing.

Minna hurried me through the door saying over and over, "This needs sleep—we must all sleep and in the morning it will be easier to talk."

She closed the door behind me and I stood looking out across the Harbour where electric lights were contending with the last glimmering of the day.

All I remember is the calm that I felt and the odd incidents that irritated me on the way back to Trelawney. A woman was backing out of her driveway as I turned into New South Head Road; I recall blowing the horn and she almost crashed into a tree. The gardener of the neighbouring block of flats was hosing the lawn and the water spilled across the pavement so that I had to walk out on to the road to avoid spotting my satin evening shoes. I was extraordinarily annoyed by that and glared at him. When I was upstairs in my bedroom, I called Terry and told him that Kurt would not be able to attend the opening. Dolfi came on to the phone then and began to scream at me, shouting that he would not have a vacant seat in the middle of the stalls, it was like a missing front tooth, and I heard Terry soothing him and saying that he would find someone for me.

I walked out on to the veranda and lit a cigarette, waiting for my escort, and still I was incapable of recognizing myself as part of what I had just experienced. The emotions were too stark, the horror as Joel read his sister's letter and Kurt's charred eyes did not belong in the rational order of life. Nothing like this should ever happen to Paris Rose. These were the scenes that Athol Tench and Murray Crashaw described in their serials, when I sat in the control room as Dolfi wailed and beat his breast at the microphone so that listeners around the world could pull out their handkerchiefs and weep vicariously. I had no tears that night and when Billy Garvin arrived at the door in a crumpled dinner suit and tie with a frayed edge, I did not show any sign of dismay.

"You're quieter than usual." Billy snuffled in my ear. "You haven't broken up with your fiancé, have you?"

"You have a malicious mind," I replied.

"Just a reporter, Miss Harcourt, just doing a reporter's job."

"Kurt is ill—it happened very suddenly."

We walked into the theatre with flashlights exploding on every side and I saw them illuminate that broken face in the photograph.

"Are you all right yourself?"

"Oh yes, nothing has happened to me, Billy."

"Thought you were feeling faint for a second. Don't blame you—never seen a mob like this turn out for a comedian. That's all he is really, just a comedian."

The searchlights swung and dipped across the road and Dolfi was greeted with frenzied screams as he pranced into the theatre, pausing in front of one girl in the crowd with a declaration of undying love and his hat clamped to his groin.

"I don't know how that will go in the States," Morton said at my elbow.

"He's getting too big—" Bill muttered.

"He's a fairy, isn't he?" Morton whispered.

"Oh no, he's a god," I replied and Morton paused for some moments before he laughed.

"Yeah, yeah, bigger than life. I get you." He chortled.

"Is he really going to the States?" Billy murmured as Morton moved away to join the film's producers.

"Oh, I think it's very likely," I replied.

"The public needs a change—they don't want to see someone going up and up all the time. The real fun is when somebody comes crashing down like a plane. Makes for real human interest, that does."

The film was a triumph and all Dino's Italian fans were there to cheer and throw flowers at him when he made his progress out of the theatre. I am sure that Valmai thought the applause was for her because she stood in front of the theatre, curtseying and blowing kisses until two ushers pushed her into a waiting car.

"Bloody old fool," Henry muttered.

"Where's your feller?" Florrie asked brightly. "He must be dead or dying to miss a show like this."

"No, he's not dead. He just received word from Austria that his wife is alive," I replied and wondered why Florrie should suddenly clamp a hand to her mouth as if she were about to have hysterics.

The fireworks were at Chateau Miramar that evening with bursting suns and twisting wheels of light exploding over our heads and falling into the water, fuming and hissing like pantomime dragons. Lanterns swayed between the palm trees and torches lit the water's edge. There were lights all around me. The diamond Minna had given me as an engagement ring caught every sparkle and glittered with all the colours of the spectrum.

"Oh God, Gwen, I just heard from Florrie." Terry had his arm around me and pulled me to him.

"I'm sure everyone knows now," I replied.

"No—no, she told me because I'm your friend. Come over here where it's quiet—quieter."

"It happened, but I can't believe it, Terry."

"That's shock. It'll hit you in the morning—right between the eyes. You're going to stay here with us tonight."

"No, I think I'll go home now. I can walk back across the lawn."

"You mustn't be alone—not tonight. Oh Gwen, Kurt loves you. If this is true, it won't make any difference to the two of you. He'll get a divorce. You may have to wait a little longer before you can get married, but you haven't lost him."

Terry told me to take a sleeping pill when I refused to stay at Miramar and went home to Trelawney, but I was asleep as soon as my head touched the pillow.

Rosalia was in front of me as we carried the bundle across the rocks to the grotto. My mother strode out ahead of us carrying a lantern and telling us to hurry. The body was very light and I felt no strain as I held one end of it in my arms. I heard the sound of water against the rocks to my left and a rising wind while we climbed up that narrow twisting path to the opening in the cliff. We pushed through the straggle of weeds and shrubs that covered the entrance and then we were in the grotto. Rosalia lit a candle in front of the Madonna and the little pink-faced doll rocked through the smoke and smiled at us. We bent down and unwrapped the cloth that was wound around our burden. The last fold fell back and I saw Renée lying there with one eye open and staring at me. I wanted to scream but Rosalia put a hand on my wrist and pointed to the cleft in the stone. My mother and I lifted Renée up and pushed her feet-first into the crack and there was no strain as first her feet went into the hole and then her body. Rosalia stood there, hands folded in front of her, but I pointed to the cleft and began to scream, for there was an eye glaring at us from the darkness.

Thirty-Five

I woke screaming, hearing the water battering against the sea wall. Staggering, I slammed the window shut and switched on the lamp at my bedside. It was almost dawn and I lay shivering as the rain hammered against the windows, shaking the frames. The sirens wailed from the Harbour and I heard the foghorns sounding through the cracks of thunder like voices trying to calm the storm.

It was still barely light when a key turned in the front door and I knew it was Kurt. He stood at the end of my bed and I could see that he had not slept.

"Is there any coffee?" he asked.

"Yes, in a thermos flask."

"I'm hungry," he said and we sat down to the supper that McGregor had left for us the night before.

I tasted nothing, swallowing automatically as Kurt ate voraciously.

"Was the film a success?" he asked.

"Oh yes, everyone says it's the best yet. Henry and Valmai were very funny." My voice trailed. "I cannot believe we are sitting here—" I said and Kurt looked at me and laughed.

"It's either this charade or madness. Minna called the doctor last night and he gave everyone a sedative. Passed them out like bonbons at a children's party. Everyone except me. I'm a chemist and if I need a sedative it will be one from which I never wake."

"Your wife wants you to return to Austria."

"Renée? Oh yes, it's quite remarkable. For the first time since I knew her she now declares in passionate prose that she loves me, that I am all she has in life and she must see me before she dies. You know, I think she prefers me to Karl Marx."

He tried to laugh but he gagged on the sound and poured himself some more coffee.

"You really should learn to cook, Gwen. Coffee does not improve with age."

I was silent as Kurt poured himself another cup, then with one gesture swept it from the table.

"My family—her family, the fine, upstanding, rich and respectable Laufers, they all implore me to come home to Renée. My parents know that I detest her, they know that my marriage was finished. Her father sympathized with me when she ran off to Germany to fight the Nazis. Everyone understood why I came here to Australia. My God in heaven, do you think anybody would have left Austria for this country if he had not been driven out?"

He stopped and abruptly kicked the broken fragments of cup across the floor.

"They are all having such a wonderful time in Vienna, my mother is enjoying her new car and my father feels so proud when he takes the wheel and they drive up to the mountains. It's spring there now and the mountains are covered with flowers. The goatherds are moving their flocks up to the high meadows and larks are nesting in the churches. Here, it's almost winter and everything is strange and unnatural."

The wind was still rising and the sirens and foghorns were so close that I had to strain to hear him.

"Everybody having such a good time and looking forward to summer. Why should they have to bother about a cripple with a freakish face? Did you see the other photos? It's not just her face, the Nazis broke her hip as well, so that she walks with a limp and she is in constant pain. Who wants to sit at the table with something that reminds you of boots and prison camps and days and nights of being beaten in a bloody cell? Let Kurt come home and look after her."

"Kurt—"

All I could say was his name, but it seemed enough and the next instant he was holding me and kissing me with a passion that took my breath away.

"I want to love you now, Gwen. Now, because you are my wife. You are my life and everything I love in this world. I have no existence without you."

Oh, the passion was still there, but we were like children playing in a graveyard. The reality of what had happened fell in upon me when we lay back, spent, listening to the wind and the blare and moan of the tugs from the Harbour.

"I could wish every member of my family dead for this," Kurt said over and over.

We were silent, knowing that Renée was there with us, watching and noting what we said.

"Can't the doctors help her?" I asked abruptly.

"Nothing. Her parents took her to the best specialists in Vienna. The bones have set. Of course, they could open the socket—the one that's covered with the skin of her eyelid now—and give her a glass eye. That would make her look very attractive, don't you agree?"

"Kurt, she can't be pushed aside like garbage."

"No? Why not? If I had been responsible for this, if I had beaten and abused her, I would feel differently perhaps; but this is what she did to herself."

"She didn't mutilate her own face."

"When she went to Germany and joined the Communist Party there she knew what the consequences might be. She chose to risk her life and it's a great pity that she didn't die in prison. Who would want to live like that?"

"She's alive, nonetheless—"

His head was between my breasts and I could barely hear his voice. "You are my life, my soul is in your hands! I cannot even bear to look at those photos. My God, I've always had a horror of ugliness and death. Why do you think I'm happy inventing face creams and perfumes that will make women prettier? I'm not an intellectual and if I have any talent, it's the ability to amuse myself and other people. It's true: I'm shallow, glib and always a little dishonest with myself and everyone else, but Renée knew all this. Those were the words she used to describe me before she left to save the world for Karl Marx, and now Karl has failed her and Kurt doesn't seem so bad after all. If you can't be the Empress Maria Theresa and lead your people, then you must settle for a husband like me, particularly when you only have half a face."

"I think Minna was right last night. It won't help us to talk about her like this, Kurt."

"How do you want me to speak of her—as my dear, captivating little blonde Renée?"

"No, I think we should be silent for a while and—"

"Ah! That is what I'm afraid of in you, Gwen—your silence, when you sit and stare at me with those great eyes like clouds. I have to talk. I must know that you love me and this will not change us."

"We've already changed," I said drearily and Kurt put his hands in my hair and kissed my face again and again.

"We are the same—we love each other and we will be married as soon as I can divorce this—this dybbuk. There must be institutions that will care for people like her."

"Kurt, if she loves you—"

"I don't want her love!" he shrieked. "I'd sooner she spat on me and cursed me. I couldn't bear to be in the same room as her. If she were a leper I would feel the same way."

"Kurt, what if she still wants—if she refuses to divorce you—?"

"Refuse? *She* left me, are you forgetting that? If I were not a coward, a failing I share with all my other shortcomings, I would pray for her death, or sue the Nazis for not doing a better job."

"This is what Minna warned us about, Kurt! We're using ugly, savage words and those words have the power to make us over in their own image."

"Now you're being metaphysical like Uncle Joel. All right, listen to me with attention because I want you to remember what I am going to say: if she tries to prevent our marriage, I shall return and kill her with my bare hands and then you will have two deaths on your conscience."

"On my conscience!"

"Yes, Gwen, everything depends on you. If you love me as much as you say, then Renée will be nothing more than an aggravating interlude, but if your love is not strong enough, then you will be able to teach Adolf Hitler a new way of killing Jews."

Afterwards, as I was getting dressed, I thought how unfair Kurt had been. He was distraught, but why was the burden of decision left to me, as though in some mysterious way I was responsible for Renée's resurrection and now it was the quality of my love that would resolve the crisis. Why had I been cast as the maiden in a folk tale whose character is the subject of a series of trials to discover if she is worthy of the prince?

Terry called and I told him that Kurt and I were discussing what must be done. "Divorce—he can get a divorce, since she walked out on him," was Terry's reassuring comment. Of course that was the solution. Kurt had not shown me her letters. He told me that he threw them away unopened and yet, why was it that throughout Kurt's tirade I heard a voice that came from my first memories when Bessie and I sat on the beach at Trapani playing the game of measuring each other's love. "Would you still love me if I . . ." "I love you as much as . . ." and now it was my love that was to be weighed in the balance. Of course, if I loved Kurt as my mother had my father, then it wouldn't matter if Renée and a horde of Renée's little children had claimed him; nothing would ever part us. I loved Kurt now, I told myself over and over again, but how much and at what cost?

A little before lunch Angelica arrived with a gangling, freckled young man doing his best to hide in the hallway as she pulled him forwards. This was Jack Smithers who blushed and cowered when Angelica informed me that she had known him for almost a year now and when he graduated they would be thinking about marriage.

"There's no hurry," she said, shaking a mop of freshly peroxided golden curls, "because Jack has years to go before he gets his certificate and I'm an understudy for the chorus now."

I don't recollect Jack saying a single word and when I offered to take them both to lunch and he was about to accept, Angelica said quickly that they had to get back to the city or they would miss the matinée.

"Mr Winters says I'm one of the most promising dancers he's ever auditioned and if I practise hard, I'll be in the chorus by the end of the year."

As they were leaving, she suddenly ran back to me and whispered, "You did write to Auntie Rafaella, didn't you?"

"Yes, yes, I think so."

"Well, write to her again, please, and tell her that I'm officially engaged."

"Are you?"

"As good as—she always said I'd end up on the shelf. Well, this will be one in the eye for her and Rocco. Oh, can you let me have a tenner? I've run short this month."

I winced as she spoke but I wrote a letter that afternoon, describing Jack as a pleasant young Australian with good prospects. At least, I told myself bitterly, I hadn't failed with Angelica. I had never tried to make her over into an image of myself or what I imagined a girl of her age should be. When she wanted to become a blonde and have her hair shingled, I didn't argue with her and gave her the money to have it done professionally. She always longed to be a dancer and now she was going to join the chorus of the Theatre Royal. At least she had been able to reach her chosen goal in life. I posted the letter that afternoon and for one moment I felt I had accomplished something that had not withered or turned to ashes. Angelica was a simple little creature at heart and I had made her happy.

After the dazzling success of his film, Dolfi was querulous and bad-tempered. If he could have had a triumph like that every night, he would have been at peace with the world, but the following day was like every other and there were no fireworks and searchlights illuminating his glory. He insisted on seeing me as soon as he heard about Kurt's wife.

"This is all I could expect from you, Gina. A scandal just when Morton Silberstein is here. Billy Garvin will pick it up and it will be in next Sunday's *Truth*. 'Paris Rose jilted by fiancé's foreign wife'—I can see the headlines now."

"Why don't you write them for Billy yourself? He's such a friend of yours."

"Dolfi, Gwen isn't to blame—" Terry said quietly.

"She's to blame because she's nearly thirty and she's not married."

I sat back and stared out at the Harbour while Dolfi railed about my damaging his reputation and his chances of signing a contract with Metro Goldwyn Mayer.

"Americans are very sensitive about moral issues like this."

"Dolfi, I'm such a distant cousin of yours that I don't really think it will affect your chances in Hollywood."

"I wanted everyone to be talking about my film and me—now, Billy will have something else to write about and my name will simply be a part of your messy love life."

"Kurt thought his wife was dead. There was no deception on his part," Terry said. "In a few months, he'll get a divorce and marry Gwen. People get divorced all the time these days. It's almost the American way of marriage."

"Is that a fact?" Dolfi said sourly. "And what is he going to do with this particular wife if he can't get a divorce? Tie a brick to her neck and drown her in the Danube like a mongrel dog?"

"I think I'll leave tomorrow," I said abruptly. "Someone has to negotiate our sales in Melbourne and Adelaide."

"Yes, give yourself time to sort all this out in your mind, Gwen," Terry said soothingly and offered to help me pack, but I told them I would arrange everything myself. A silver box was delivered as we were speaking and I opened it and handed the bunch of grapes to Dolfi.

"Does Kurt think you're sick?" he asked and gulped the fruit in handfuls.

Just before I left, I phoned Minna and gave her a message for Kurt. I needed some time to be alone and he must try to get everything settled while I was away. As soon as I returned I would see him. There is always time to think on trains and in hotel rooms.

Radio seemed to have been invented for the Danny Burns Radio Theatre. The first recordings we made had been sold and sold again and wherever I went I heard Dolfi's thousand voices as he played Musketeers and detectives, David Copperfield and Little Nell. Sometimes it seemed that I was walking from station to station and on to advertising agencies and accountants with an open satchel that everyone wanted to fill with money.

I was in Adelaide when I saw an old copy of the Sydney *Truth* with a feature story about my engagement and the discovery of Kurt's wife in Vienna. It was written in heartrending paragraphs with photos of Kurt and myself, but there was no picture of Renée. If Billy had found out that she was disfigured he would have been able to give an even more lachrymose tone to his spasmodic prose. Kurt made a statement in which he said that he had been estranged from his wife before she left him and now he was proceeding to take action for a divorce. I crumpled the paper and threw it away. What was it Terry used to say about publicity? Ever tried to find yesterday's newspaper?

Very sensibly, Kurt was taking the only possible action and seeing lawyers about a divorce. This was what must be done, I told myself. After all, she had chosen to leave Kurt and now she must live with the results of that decision. As I signed contracts, I began to see Kurt's marriage as another contract in which Renée had broken the terms of agreement and lost everything. There was no reason for me to consider her. I hadn't played the role of predator bent on stealing the man who rightfully belonged to another. And yet, how I raged at being trapped in such a tritely ambivalent situation.

I saw as many films as I could when I was away and whenever Robert Donat came on the screen I found myself thinking of Kurt. In modern life it seemed there were always complications of this kind, and if I had wanted a man without luggage, I should have married a boy like Jack Smithers when I was sixteen. Renée had destroyed her own life, but I was not going to be made part of her tragedy. This was the conviction I held in my mind. I would choose, just as Kurt told me I must, and my choice was to love him and wait until we could get married. I sent him a telegram and he was at the station for me when I arrived.

"You still love me?" he asked immediately.

"Oh yes, the only other man I could ever love is Robert Donat, and that's because he reminds me of you."

I think we could have made love in the car, but we managed to wait until we reached Trelawney. As soon as I walked in I smelt the brown boronia and in the next instant we were tearing off each other's clothes, gasping and crying in our need for each other's body.

"I was in torment when you left but I knew what you wanted me to do," he said finally.

"Have you settled everything?" I asked.

"Everything—" He stretched out his arms like an athlete acknowledging the cheers of the crowd.

"Even Renée Laufer can be reasonable when faced with the inevitable."

"When can we get married?"

"As soon as all the legal formalities are over—"

"When?"

"Gwen, you sound like Alan."

"Alan Gilchrist?"

"Everyone says that he's the best lawyer in Sydney so I went to see him. He refused to speak to me because of this curious rule about barristers and solicitors, but he gave me the name of a law firm, Crashaw, Milford and

Tennyson—doesn't that sound impressive? Afterwards, he took pity on me and we had dinner once or twice at his club. I was being very good while you were away and I did not look at another woman even though I was tempted once or twice."

This was the Kurt I knew and loved and yet there was a different note in his voice like an orchestra playing with a missing instrument.

"They must have given you a date?"

"When do lawyers ever speak in certainties? It's always wherefore and whereas and on the other hand."

"Renée has agreed?"

"What else can she do? She knows precisely how I feel about her. My hand aches from writing her abusive letters."

Everything had been arranged while I was away and I could lie back in bed and contemplate my future with Kurt.

He brought me in a bunch of grapes and we ate them together.

"The bloom is off them—they arrived three days ago and I was tempted to eat them, but McGregor insisted on putting them in the refrigerator for you."

The perfume of the boronia was cloying and I got up and opened the windows to the Harbour. A race of skiffs spanned out like flying geese across the point, mainsails almost grazing the water. Two went over as I watched and Kurt said gleefully at my elbow, "We are not like those poor fellows, Gwen. We are going to finish and win the prize."

"When?" I said on a breath, but I don't think Kurt heard me.

The house in Bellevue Hill was very still when I went there the following day. Minna whispered to me in the hall that Joel had been ill and he had not been able to go into his shop for two weeks. He was sitting in his favourite chair looking out across the serried red roofs to the Harbour and the sky.

"If I had only thought to send them pictures of this—if they could have seen the beauty of Sydney, they would have come, don't you think?" he said dully.

For a moment I could not speak because it seemed as though he had shrivelled into a shard of his former self.

"There now, aren't you glad that your daughter has come back to you?" Minna said brightly.

"My daughter?" He lifted his head and stared at me, then put out his hand.

I took hold of it and pressed it to my cheek and began to cry.

"Why? Why must we cry all the time in this house?" Minna complained fretfully.

"We cry because my family is dead," Joel said harshly.

"You read your sister's last letter, *du alter Narr*. She was so happy in the mountains and the business is doing well now that they have got rid of that Frommer *putz*."

"My sister is walking into Gehenna!"

"Ah, you believe all the worst that you read in the newspapers. The Austrians have a pact with Germany—they will be like the Swiss and if there is a war, they'll make money out of it, you will see."

"That I should have lived all these years with such a stupid old woman!"

Minna flounced out in apparent rage but I could tell that she was pleased to have roused Joel from his grief. We sat then and talked about events in Europe and he showed me several fresh articles written by my cousin, Frederick.

"This young man has seen the Nazis and Fascists in Spain—the Republicans will be slaughtered."

"A lot of people have gone to fight against them, even some Australians."

"They will end like that poor creature of Kurt's—if they're lucky."

"Joel, you promised not to mention her name!" Minna was at the door with a tray of coffee. She put it down with a clatter and shook her fist at the old man. "Why couldn't you hold your tongue? Why did you have to mention Renée?"

"Why shouldn't I hear about her?" I replied easily. "Kurt and I spoke about Renée yesterday."

"She was always a difficult girl from what I hear," Minna replied. "It comes of having so much money and being given everything when she was a child. The Laufers made a great fuss of her."

"She's agreed to the divorce, hasn't she?" I asked quietly.

They looked at each other and Joel shifted irritably in his chair.

"You see, I warned you that Kurt wouldn't tell her the truth."

Minna began awkwardly when no one spoke. "It is not Kurt's fault and you mustn't blame him."

"I don't blame him for anything. He believed his wife was dead when he proposed to me."

"That—that is what you must tell yourself always," Minna said, patting my arm.

The three of us sat in silence and I understood everything.

"I see, she still wants him to go back to Vienna. Renée won't agree to a divorce."

"Kurt detests her," Minna said. "And I can't blame him even if she is such a poor thing."

"He did not tell you the truth!" Joel said and smashed his fist against the side of his chair. "He is Viennese through and through—full of pretty words and charming compliments that mean nothing—nothing!"

"I'll speak to him later—we—I may have misunderstood what he meant. I'm sure he spoke to a friend of mine—a lawyer—"

"Alan Gilchrist. A good man. He made a speech the other night at the Trades Hall saying that this country must be prepared to defend itself. In the next war, distance will not save us. Do you know, that is why I came here—it was the most distant country in the world from Europe."

"She knows that. You've told Gwen that a thousand times," Minna snapped.

"Where—what was I saying?"

"Nothing of importance," Minna retorted quickly.

Joel tugged his grizzled hair, now more white than grey, and shook his head.

"Nothing sits properly in my brain. I—" His chin jerked up and he stared at me. "Kurt should have been honest with you."

"She'll agree in time," Minna said soothingly. "At the moment she thinks that Kurt is all she has left in life, but she can't expect him to be a husband to her with thousands of miles between them."

Before either of them told me any more, I knew I must say something to divert their attention.

"Joel, when I was in Melbourne I spoke to some people who were talking of forming an agency, to try and bring out refugees from Europe."

"No—no, not another penny will I give them! They will take the money and spend it on new motor cars like my sister."

"Perhaps you could organize something like that in Sydney. There must be hundreds of Jews in Europe who know that Hitler is planning to destroy them. If they could be told that they'd be welcome here . . ."

When I left, he was arguing over the idea of an agency with Minna and Renée's name was not mentioned again. Kurt had lied to me, because he believed what he wanted to believe and not what the lawyers had told him. From Trelawney, I phoned Alan and told him that I wanted to see him for dinner that evening.

The food was not particularly good and the music was too loud at Prince's but everyone was extravagantly dressed and bending and diving on the floor as if they had just come from an expensive dancing school.

Alan was sombre and I assumed it was from sympathy for me. He spoke about the political battle he was waging, trying to make Australians recognize the danger of another war, but I scarcely heard him and interrupted.

"What I want to know now is the likelihood of Kurt being able to divorce Renée if she opposes it."

"I'm sorry," he said drily. "Divorce must take precedence over a world war. Have you spoken to Kurt about this?"

"Yes, and I'm sure he lied to me."

"Perhaps because he's very much in love with you, Gwen."

"Are you going to send me to a solicitor? I'm putting a very general question to you."

"There's a contested divorce going through the courts now. You may have read about it: Wilkinson versus Wilkinson. She left her husband eleven years ago after a number of complaints of physical abuse to live with another man by whom she now has three children. Ten years ago she filed a petition for divorce from her husband. He is living with another woman but he refuses to divorce his wife on religious grounds."

"But surely it's obvious—"

"There are no obvious solutions in law, particularly in the area of divorce and especially when one party to the marriage is in a different country. If the action is opposed, it must go to trial, and that verdict, when it's heard, is subject to appeal."

"Do you remember we once argued about irony, Alan?"

"I don't remember our arguments, Gwen."

"Well, this is a fine example of Sicilian irony. I was not prepared to wait a year to marry you, now you're telling me that I may have to wait a dozen or more years to marry Kurt."

"That is not what I said at all."

He had flushed suddenly with anger but as he patiently repeated what he had just said, his voice was measured.

"If Aesop had told that fable about the Wilkinsons, the moral could not have been clearer," I retorted.

Everything around me seemed tawdry and noisy like a cheap carnival, the gaiety was offensive and I stood up and said I wanted to leave.

Outside I took a deep breath of the chilly August air but nothing cleared my head. Alan was asking the doorman to call a taxi, but I told him I wanted to walk.

"Where?"

"Oh, across the park, anywhere—"

"Gwen, I'm sorry this should have happened."

If Alan had only reproached me then I think I would have understood him, but I thought his smouldering calm was the same irritation that Joel felt when Kurt interrupted his talk of politics.

"No—" I turned and stood facing him. "No, what I really want to say is unspeakable. We're sorry that Renée Stern wasn't kicked to death in a Nazi prison camp so that her husband could now be free to marry me."

"If she agrees to a divorce—"

"I gather that a number of people have already spoken to her in Vienna and she's refused."

"If you—"

"Yes!" I almost screamed. "It must be me. Does everyone expect me to go to Vienna and beg that poor broken-faced woman to give me her husband?"

Alan shrugged helplessly and we walked on silently for a moment.

"Ah, it would be so pleasant if life were made up of little ironies, those polite evasions and minor griefs that you see in English plays, but I am a Sicilian and life comes to me in bloody thunderclaps. My old friend Mr Gresham took me to see a Jacobean tragedy at the Conservatorium some years ago. I think it was *The Duchess of Malfi*. Everyone left the theatre with pursed lips, saying how far-fetched and melodramatic it was, but for me it was like the story of any noble Sicilian family."

"You're only half Sicilian, Gwen."

"Yes, and that's why I can't accept what happens to me. Part of me wants to sit on a chintz sofa, drinking tea and refusing to complain about my troubles, while the rest of me is being dragged through calamities of grief."

I did not realize that I was standing by the fountain in Hyde Park with its calmly smiling Theseus pulling back the Minotaur's head, his sword raised.

"Gods! Gods and heroes! Is that what the stupid artist imagined they are like?" I screamed. "They should be standing in a cauldron of blood with faces so terrible that we could not bear to look at them."

"Let me take you home," Alan said quietly.

"I'll go alone—get me a taxi," I replied and Alan did not try to argue with me.

My rage was subsiding a little when I slammed the door behind me and heard the sound echo through the building. A contested divorce could take years, Alan had said, and what would I be during those years except a mistress? Not a *puttana*, I was far too rich for that and not promiscuous enough, but a *mantenuta* known politely as a fiancée. I took off the diamond engagement ring and threw it across the room.

Perhaps Renée had written to me while I was away. McGregor had left all the letters in neat bundles on my desk and I began to read through them methodically. Social invitations—they were there by the dozen; people obviously didn't know that Paris Rose had died some time ago. Begging letters—I pushed those aside—and fan letters that Terry's secretary would answer.

The envelope had almost slipped under a pile of crumpled letters when I noticed the black border. Without knowing why I began to tremble when I saw by the seal that it was from Mount of Angels. Opening it slowly, I turned the stiff, engraved card in my hand and at first the words blurred before my eyes. "Pray for the soul of our beloved sister in Christ—"

Edith was dead. The date of her burial was on the card—three days before.

Thirty-Six

Rosalia used to tell a story about an old woman who spilled the contents of her basket as she was fleeing from Mount Etna's tide of burning ash. She stopped to pick up her trinkets, scrabbling them into the basket; the fiery ash swept down and buried her. Wondering why I should suddenly think of Rosalia and the moral fables she had for every occasion, I realized the card was still in my hand. McGregor had rearranged some of the furniture while I was away and I did not care for the way she had two chairs facing each other as if they were deep in conversation, and the boronia was wilted and had an acrid smell. So my cousin Edith was dead, I thought, and if anyone had . . . The horror came over me like a wave as I staggered back against a little table and knocked it over. I heard glass breaking but my eyes did not follow the sound, for I was seeing something in my mind that was so terrible that my tongue clamped against my palate and if I was screaming there was no sound.

I felt her hands beating against the coffin and my breath came short as I reached for the phone. My hand was trembling so violently that I could not hold the receiver. I took it in my left hand and smashed it across my wrist so that this pain would drive back the horror in my head. Who could help me? I dialled the number of Mount of Angels and heard a ringing that seemed to echo down a cavern. There was no response. It was a quarter to eleven—someone must have been awake there. I slammed down the phone, trying to make myself think logically. Kurt—Kurt would help me, but when I phoned there was no answering voice. I thumbed through my address book and found Alan's number. He must have had his hand on the phone because he answered immediately.

"Alan, I'm going to Mount of Angels—meet me there, please."

"Is it Angelica? Is she ill?"

"No—no, Angelica left school six months ago. It's my cousin, she's dead, but she's not dead. They've buried her."

"Yes—"

Impossible to read any comment from that single word.

"Alan, she's alive! I know she's alive and we have to open the grave."

Instead of arguing with me, Alan said quietly that he would call a taxi and meet me at the convent, then told me to drive carefully.

He must, they would all imagine I was mad, I thought as I drove across the city to the Bridge, but I would make them listen to me. In my head I could hear Edith screaming like Rita Cusumani who was pushed down that narrow cleft in the grotto and woke to find herself wedged into a stone grave with the sound of water under her and stone above and around her. Why hadn't I looked at the piles of letters when I arrived home instead of thinking about Kurt and Renée? I would have seen the black-edged envelope immediately and that would have meant a day saved. How long would it take for someone to suffocate in a coffin?

The iron gates at the convent were locked when I brought the car to a screeching halt, the angels of the finial rested comfortably on their harps, wings folded across their bodies like sleeping birds, and there was not a light anywhere. I found a bell by the door post and dragged at it. The clanging fractured the silence but nothing stirred. Over in the moonlight I could see the gravestones of the nuns' burial ground; I knew that somewhere in that place, Edith was struggling to reach the surface. I began to scream her name, pulling the bell until it was spinning in circles.

An old man, I think he was the caretaker or the gardener, came down the path carrying a lantern.

"Buzz off or I'll call the police," he shouted.

"I must see Mother George, it's an emergency!" I shrieked.

"Mother George has just come back. If you want to see her you'll have to wait until proper visiting hours. The girls are away, it's the holidays and—"

"If you don't let me in I'll tear this gate down with my hands," I shouted.

I felt Alan at my shoulder. He spoke calmly to the old man and said I was related to a nun who had just died.

No, no, I wanted to correct him—she's alive—over there. They've buried Edith alive.

Lights came on in the convent and I saw a nun carrying a lantern, hurrying towards us.

"Tell them to go away, Pat," she said shrilly. "If they want a priest they can go to the end of the street to the presbytery at St Jude's and ask for—"

It was Sister Joseph and I told her that I must talk to Mother George.

"Mother George is asleep. She only got back from Brisbane an hour ago. The poor soul is exhausted."

"You must open my cousin's grave."

Sister Joseph fell back and began to mutter Aves under her breath.

"I think it would be best to let your superior deal with this matter," Alan said and Sister Joseph nodded immediately and told the old man to open the gate. I could have pleaded and screamed there until dawn and she would not have paid any attention to me, but when a man spoke in tones of quiet authority, she obeyed instantly.

After we had waited, it seemed for hours, in the visitors' parlour, Mother George came in knuckling her eyes like a child and yawning.

"Now what appears to be the trouble?" she said heartily, then gaped when she saw me.

I took a deep breath and tried to speak slowly and lucidly.

"You must open Edith's grave now, Mother George. I know she's alive."

"Blasphemy and sacrilege," Sister Joseph muttered. "But what can you expect from a heretic?"

"And who are you?" Mother George turned to Alan.

"Alan Gilchrist—"

"Gilchrist—you're the lawyer, aren't you? Yes, I knew your father well."

"My cousin is alive and you've buried her!" I screamed.

"My dear girl, I appreciate that the news must have come as a shock to you but you must believe—"

"I believe nothing!" I shouted. "I know that she suffered from bouts of amnesia—I don't know the medical term for it—my fiancé said she was a catatonic schizophrenic. He studied psychology in Vienna—"

"Psychology! A cursed heresy," Sister Joseph shrilled.

"She told me herself that she had died, that was the word she used, died twice when she was a child and she said it had happened again when she was in Germany. I don't know, I can't remember it in detail now, but she was very sick when she came here."

Mother George's hands were folded under her sleeves and for a moment she did not speak.

"Did she overhear a conversation between us after my aunt died?"

"Yes—yes, I'm sure she did—"

"Why did you never mention any of this to me, Gwen?"

"I don't know. Perhaps because I wanted her dead or out of the way. It doesn't matter what my motives and intentions were. You must save her now—Oh God! I can hear her screaming."

"This young woman is mad!" Sister Joseph said sharply. "I'll call for an ambulance and the police."

"No, send for Dr Curnow immediately."

"Our physician?"

"He signed the death certificate, didn't he, Sister?"

"Of course."

"Call him now!"

Grumbling, I heard Sister Joseph at the phone in the hall.

"You need an exhumation order before you can open a grave," Alan said.

"No! No, there isn't time for that. We must go now. I'll get her out myself!"

I ran past them through the door and towards the burial ground. The small white headstones were like teeth and then I saw the mound of earth covered with faded wreaths. I fell on it because I could hear her now, beating against the coffin lid, shrieking with the last breath of air.

"Get back, the men can do this. Alan, can you handle a spade?"

The old caretaker handed Alan a long-handled spade and the two began to dig. The earth was soft, turning easily on the blade. Sister Joseph joined us with another lantern.

"Some of the sisters are awake," she said to Mother George.

"Go and tell them that no one must stir from her cell until I say so. At once, Sister—"

Someone else joined us and I heard an Irish voice—

"This is very irregular, isn't it, Mother George?"

"It is indeed, Doctor. That's why you're needed here now."

"I'm generally called to attend to the living. It's the priest who must pray for the soul of the dead."

A scattering of lights from the convent were extinguished almost in unison and Sister Joseph was with us again.

"Some of the novices are terrified," she said, her voice rising. "Mother George, I shall have to report this to the bishop. It's sacrilege—"

The spades rang on wood and the old man threaded two pieces of webbed cloth under each end of the coffin.

"Don't worry—I remember this was a very light one," he said cheerfully.

Alan and the caretaker on either side of the grave were already lifting the coffin. Before it was on the ground I was trying to prise up the lid with my fingers.

"You won't get it open like that," the old man said, and produced a chisel.

Two taps and the lid was up. Mother George walked slowly to the foot of the coffin and held out the lantern.

I fell to my knees sobbing with relief. I had expected to hear Edith screaming, imploring to be released as the coffin was raised; what I saw was a body wrapped in a black shroud like the wax statue of a saint in the Chiesa di Santa Maria di Gesu. At first I could not recognize Edith because she was smiling with the cross of a rosary pressed to her lips. I had never seen such an expression of calm on her face. Sister Joseph was uttering stifled cries behind me and I suddenly realized what I had done.

"I'm so sorry. I didn't—I felt she was alive."

Dr Curnow was bending over the body.

"Stiff as a board—no sign of morbid decay yet," he said as he tried to pull her fingers apart. He stood up slowly, his joints creaking. "Now, would someone like to explain to me what's going on here? I don't object to being turned out of bed for an emergency, but this—this ghoulish little exercise is beyond me."

Sister Joseph was screaming with her head thrown back, turning round and round as though she were being spun at the end of a rope, flailing the air with her arms.

"Will you be silent, Sister Joseph!"

Sister Joseph seemed about to speak but her mouth was twisting in different directions.

"You will go up to the house, Sister, and you will say nothing—nothing, do you hear me? By your vow of obedience, I order you not to speak of this to any of the sisters."

Sister Joseph ran off whimpering.

"She seems mortally distressed," Dr Curnow said, and suggested a sedative.

"Thank you, Dr Curnow, you will not be needed again this evening. Close the coffin, Pat."

My shame was such that for an instant I would gladly have changed places with Edith and been buried. Perhaps I was mad as Sister Joseph said and I would end my days in another kind of grave, locked away from the light of sanity and reason. I sat with earth-stained hands to my head listening to the dirt fall back upon the coffin. It was Mother George who took hold of me by the elbow and pulled me to my feet.

"Come up to the house. I'll make us some cocoa."

"No—no, I should go—I've caused too much trouble," I mumbled.

"First, you'll both have something to drink."

I tried to turn my face to the wall in the parlour because I could not bear to look at Mother George or Alan. He had said nothing but I knew he must believe me to be insane.

The cocoa had brandy in it and I coughed as I drank.

"Yes, I knew your father well," Mother George was saying to Alan. "He made himself very unpopular during the War, arguing against conscription."

"I hope he'd agree with what I'm trying to do now. I made several trips to Europe when I was at the bar in London and I could see that war was inevitable. Our danger is going to come from the north—"

Their discussion of politics was an attempt to gloss my madness with normality, as if their reasonable words could calm my insane terrors.

"It's very good of you both to talk as though this was just a social occasion," I interjected. "I'm more embarrassed than I can say, Mother George. I can understand Sister Joseph getting hysterical. I—I simply don't know how to apologize to you both."

"This time I will take you home," Alan said firmly.

For some moments Mother George was silent and sat staring at me, then she spoke slowly with a rasp to her voice.

"Do you think a sister is buried kissing a crucifix? Her hands are always folded on her breast in prayer. As she lived, so she is laid to rest."

I am not certain if I fainted, but Mother George had her hand on the back of my neck and my head was between my knees.

"I don't understand—" I heard myself saying over and over.

"Do you think I have some special insight?" she said as I lifted my head, finding it difficult to get my eyes to focus. Alan reached out and took my hands in his.

"They're dirty," I said childishly.

"So are mine," he said.

"Insight? Understanding?" Mother George groaned and began to finger her rosary. "I should have sent her away. I was convinced in my own mind that she did not have a true vocation, but whenever I spoke about her I was met with a chorus of approval for her zeal, her passionate ardour and yet I knew there was no humility in her love of God. No, it was greed for herself, a hunger that was fired when she heard me speak—This is my sin. *Mea culpa*!"

"No, it wasn't your fault, Mother George. I should have told you—I suspected that she'd overheard you."

"What was it she wanted?" Mother George cried.

"God."

"She was alive in that coffin. She woke and—oh, Gwen, it's too terrible to think about and yet I must—"

"Why did she seem so calm?" Alan said quickly.

"Because—" Mother George faltered and frowned.

"If she had woken in a coffin she would have been demented with fright. That is a normal reaction. The fear of being buried alive is primordial, but her body wasn't contorted in any way."

"Yes, the shroud was folded over her feet. I noticed that. All she did was place the crucifix to her lips."

The room kept shifting before me and I felt Alan's arm around my shoulders.

"Come—I'll drive you home."

"Her mother—she must never know about this," I said suddenly.

"My dear, Sister Joseph told me that she sent a cable to Mrs Wigram. The reply came yesterday: 'I have no daughter.' "

Edith on the hillside beside me, promising that she would find Bessie for me, the counties spread out before us like the poem my mother loved. Others could say that I had done no wrong, but if I had told Mother George the truth when Edith entered the convent, then she would not be lying dead in a nun's shroud. I leaned forward sobbing and Alan said quickly: "*Me liceat casus misereri insontis amici*?" Almost without thinking, I replied as I would have to my father or Joel, "*Me, me, adsum qui feci, in me convertite ferrum*."

"I haven't a sword handy at the moment, Gwen. But don't compound your grief by imagining that you can trace the links between cause and event. That's an arrogance that I'm always aware of when I'm in court, making plausible patterns of the evidence to please the judge. I think your cousin buried herself."

"With my help," I said bitterly.

The moonlight was flooding across the Harbour and through the bay windows when we returned to Trelawney; everything in the room was bleached of colour as it was when I first saw Edith. Then Alan found the lights and I saw my own furniture and realized how cleverly I had taken over her home and made it my own.

"I can never live here again!" I cried in anguish.

"Why don't you go and have a bath. You look pretty grubby," Alan said evenly. "I'll make a couple of phone calls."

"When I asked you to meet me at Mount of Angels, you didn't question me, Alan. Did you think I was mad?"

"A little—that's why I wasn't going to waste time arguing with you."

"When—was it last night we were at Prince's?"

"Yes, and you said goodnight after strenuously criticizing the artistic merits of the Archibald Memorial Fountain. Now, go and get washed."

My hair was full of earth; as I showered a gritty stream of brown water fell from me. The horror of what had happened was still like an open wound in my mind and I forced myself not to probe it.

When I came out of the bathroom, Kurt was standing next to Alan. He ran towards me and put his arms around me, kissing my damp hair.

"I told Kurt he ought to be here with you," Alan said. "You shouldn't be alone tonight."

"If I'd only known I would have gone there with you," Kurt replied.

I heard Alan leave, the door close behind him, and I wanted to call him back, to tell him that I wanted him near me, but he was gone and Kurt was lifting me in his arms and carrying me into the bedroom.

"You will not have any bad dreams this evening, because I shall make love to you all night."

"No—no, I can't—" I tried to push Kurt away from me for I wanted to call Alan back, but it was too late. His tone of laconic reserve had set barriers between us but in that instant I wanted to speak from my heart and not with words that were as dry and brittle as dead leaves. Once he had been my lover, now he was my friend and that was unendurable.

"Lie here in my arms, Gwen. There is nothing to be afraid of now. I'm here and I'll never leave you."

I could not open my eyes but I felt the warmth of Kurt's body against mine and his hand stroking me like a child. It was true that no dreams disturbed my sleep. Perhaps I was exhausted, but when I woke I smelt coffee and Kurt was at my side.

"Before you speak, drink this very slowly. The excellent McGregor has arrived and is making you an omelette to my instructions."

"I must phone Mother George and—"

"I am sure that Mother George and her nuns have already been to confession and are at peace with the world and God."

"What peace can there be—"

"My dear, I have never been on intimate terms with a nun so I cannot be certain of the conventual state of mind; however, if you were to mention soubrettes, opera singers, models and ballet dancers, it would be a different story."

He was just the same, his dark eyes glinting as he poured the coffee.

"I tried to call you but you weren't at your flat—"

"No," he said carefully. "*Abbitte tun*—I was eating what you call humble cake. Minna cooks it very well and my uncle served me such large quantities that I almost choked."

The sequence was now becoming clear to me and I remembered why I had been in such a passion of rage the night before.

"Yes, I spoke to Alan about the divorce."

"Renée will agree to it. This is just momentary spite."

"Are you sure?"

"Of course—"

He pulled out a bundle of unopened letters.

"These are all from my family and from my lawyer, and yes—there are two here from Renée. My sister, Trudi, who is the only member of my family with a spoonful of brains in her head, assures me that Renée will let me go and probably say good riddance. I have faith in Trudi and she is talking to Renée every day. When we've had breakfast I'll translate them all for you."

I was scarcely listening to him because whatever I tried to say, Edith's face was in my head. Shuddering, I told Kurt that I had killed my cousin.

"*Liebling*, your cousin was a schizophrenic and when I heard about her bouts of amnesia, it was clear that she needed a psychiatrist, not some old doctor who probably took the nuns' pulses with his eyes averted."

"What if Renée continues to refuse? Alan must have told you that some contested divorces can go on for years—"

"In my case, that is an impossibility."

He took the omelette from McGregor and proceeded to cut it and feed me.

"Remember," he said glowering, "I am only doing this because you have had a great shock. When we are married I shall beat you with a broom if you do not get up at dawn every morning and cook my breakfast."

We laughed together but still I felt myself blinking away the sight of Edith smiling in her coffin. I forced myself to think about Renée, only Renée and Edith had a way of becoming one in my mind.

"If you can't get a divorce—"

"*Liebling*, dearest love, everything seems hopeless now but you will see—Renée will change her mind like that!" He snapped his fingers. "And tomorrow she will hate me as much as she professes to love me today."

"I'm only trying to foresee—"

"My darling, you are not a sibyl and you're much too beautiful to be Cassandra. Besides, remember what happened to her."

"Alan spoke of ten years—"

"Then we live together."

"How?"

"As man and wife."

"But we wouldn't be married."

"What is marriage but a scrap of paper these days?"

"It seems to be a paper that can endure to death if somebody decides to contest the divorce."

"Listen, Gwen, what is important is our love and our loving. The first night I saw you I had such a desire that I could have taken you there among the dinner plates, and at the same time I was angry because I thought Minna had arranged a match for me. You are in my blood, you are part of my flesh. I could not live if I were told I could never love you again."

His hands were touching me to arousal and then he was on top of me, his legs wound round me, and I was content to have him love me.

"Do you think either of us could give this up?" he breathed.

Three days later, Mother George told me that the bishop had come to the convent and ordered a second exhumation of the coffin in order for the circumstances of the burial to be verified. Dr Curnow was adamant that Edith was dead when he signed the certificate, and it was true that she had lain in an open coffin in the chapel for twenty-four hours before she was buried. All the nuns of the convent were ready to swear that she was dead when they said farewell to their sister. It was, Mother George said drily, a problem that might even reach the desk of the cardinal and eventually find its way to Rome.

Business pressed in on me while Dolfi was more fractious and querulous than ever. He had been asked to make another Dino film since the last was breaking box-office records in Australia, and the promoters were steadily plumping up their offer to him as if he were a greedy child with an insatiable appetite for sweets. Dolfi, however, did not want to sign a new contract until he had received word from Morton Silberstein who, when last heard of, was meeting some other MGM executives in Brisbane where a story by Zane Grey about deep-sea fishing was to be made.

"Why did he come out here?" Dolfi said peevishly. "If it was fish he wanted, he could find plenty of dead fish in Hollywood. I was the reason he came here—so why isn't he here, talking to me?"

Whenever he was irritated, Dolfi delighted in setting everyone around him at odds, and the studio was like a bearhouse with the actors snarling and fluffing their lines. It was difficult to say who was funnier, Valmai being herself or Dolfi imitating Valmai, but the comedy was becoming very ragged as Dolfi incited her from one absurdity to the next. He encouraged her to give a series of interviews on her love life to Billy Garvin, and the following Sunday there was a long account of her passionate romances when she was with the Carl Rosa Opera Company before her marriage to Gordon Gilchrist, KC, MP. I knew how that would hurt Alan. He was already being vilified by several papers for his "militarism." The *Bulletin* had just published a cartoon showing his father as a spectral figure holding a dove and an olive branch and, in the foreground, a caricature of Alan with a rifle in his hands and grenades sticking out of his pockets.

I threw the paper across the bedroom, cursing Billy and his filthy rag, and then decided to phone him.

"I have to accept that my mother is now a celebrity in her own right," he said flatly.

"Success has made her crazy, Alan. She really believes she's the greatest *femme fatale* since Cleopatra."

"It will pass—"

"I'm very sorry."

"You shouldn't apologize, there's no reason."

We chatted together as old friends do and Kurt leaned across me to speak.

"Tell him that sometimes it is as hard to live with a mother as it is to put up with a wife."

For some reason his words stung me and I told him I was going down to swim.

"It's still too cold," he complained.

"That's when I enjoy it most," I retorted.

"Masochist!" I heard him calling after me.

Terry saw me swimming and ran over the lawns to my pool.

"He's gone, but he's coming back!" he shouted.

I shrugged and climbed out of the water, shivering in the thin October sun.

"Morton Silberstein. He's going back to Hollywood to settle the contract. He's wild about Dolfi."

"When did this happen?"

"Last night. We spoke for over an hour on the phone. Oh, I can't tell you what a difference it has made to Dolfi. He's his old self again. He can't bear being ignored or rejected. Now, he's laughing and singing—"

"So, we'll see the end of the Danny Burns Radio Theatre."

"Oh no, it's too soon to talk about that. The contract will specify three feature films in the first year with star billing for Dolfi."

"And the money?"

"One million dollars in the first year."

"No wonder they were taking their time working out the contract."

"Mr Silberstein's going by boat to Honolulu then plane to Los Angeles. He'll come back the same way and in the meantime they'll be getting out the publicity on Dolfi."

"I wonder what they'll invent for him? Gods and heroes have adaptable lineages."

"Oh Gwen, you know how I've worked for this—"

He sat there beside me, his thin hands clasped around his knees, his eyes as wide as if he had just seen the Kingdom of Heaven.

Kurt joined us in a towelling robe, grumbling as he found a warm spot on the stone.

"I called you from the balcony—"

“We were talking about Dolfi,” I said and even Kurt whistled eloquently when he heard about the contract.

“I think this is the happiest, most wonderful moment of my life,” Terry said. “I could never have been or done anything important myself, but I have helped create the greatest comic actor in the world.”

“Better than Pygmalion.” Kurt grinned. “He was like the rest of us—he just wanted a pretty girl for himself.” He paused and turned to me. “I think I am the messenger who brings good news. When you were down here swimming I read my letters from home and I am delighted to inform you that my little Cyclops has agreed to the divorce.”

Thirty-Seven

The dead are always with us, slipping in and out of our thoughts during the day, emerging at night to take clamorous possession of our bodies. In my dreams I have followed Rosalia a thousand times to the grotto, but after Edith's death, I often woke screaming and dripping with sweat. Rigid, unable to move, I was being carried by Edith and Renée, one at my head, the other at my feet, and going before, swinging lanterns, were Rosalia and my mother. Every few steps they looked back at me over their shoulders and smiled, murmuring words that I could scarcely hear and could not understand. They carried me as lightly as if I were made of air and set me down in front of the little Madonna. My mother raised the lantern and watched them push me into the cleft that opened to receive my body. I was buried inside the rock.

If Kurt was beside me, the terror vanished quickly, but if I was alone I would often find myself still awake and trembling as the light of morning filled the room. I made myself think about business, about Renée and Kurt and other problems that must be resolved. It was true that Renée had agreed to a divorce but on her terms: Kurt must return to Vienna; only when he was in Austria would she sign an order of separation. She expected me to accompany him.

Nothing of this made sense to me. I felt as if I were in a radio script that was written by Lewis Carroll for an audience of idiots.

"She's Viennese. What more can I say?" Kurt said when I asked him to explain. "She is also spoilt and rich and accustomed to doing whatever she wants."

"But does she love you?" I asked.

"With all of her heart."

"But she left you!"

"Ah, she admits that was a mistake but only because at the time she was a great idealist and thought Communism would save Germany from the Nazis. I gather that she was arrested two weeks after she arrived, and do you know who the person was who gave her name and that of her comrades to the Gestapo? The Soviet agent—their contact in Berlin. She has now concluded that politics is madness and all that is left for good in the world is the family. My little Cyclops believes that if we base a new society on the family then there's hope for the world."

"I don't understand—you tell me this and then say that she'll agree to the divorce if you return to Vienna?"

"Ah, now we have the metamorphosis of Marx to a little Metternich. She believes that I am a very popular fellow and everyone likes me. Once I am in Vienna I will have a thousand interests and you will be one among many women in my life. Because of this, she is prepared to gamble that she will remain my wife and you will be another of Casanova's conquests. Ah, if only she knew how I love you—"

"And if you remain in Australia," I said slowly.

"Then she will never agree to a divorce and she requests me to tell you that she is a very rich woman and for every shilling you can put on the table she can cover it with a pound."

I was silent and Kurt began to sing, "*A gu'ts Glas'l Wein und a Schinken dazur, Gitarr und Harmonika, das war schon g'nur.*"

The Harbour was a blue shield that morning. I watched two small skiffs that were as motionless as flies frozen in amber.

"I'll drive you along the Ringstrasse and then we'll go to a little inn I know in the Vienna Woods set in a vineyard where the May wine is sweeter than honey from heaven."

Joel was so angry when I told him about Renée's terms that I thought he was going to smash a hole in the dinner table with his fist.

"I tell you now what is not written in the Torah—when Moses led his people out of slavery across the Red Sea and into the promised land, some of them complained and said they missed the apricot dumplings in Egypt and the little coffee shops and the good conversation you could have when you were not making bricks, so a great many of them went back and they were all killed by Pharaoh."

"I did not know the Egyptians made dumplings," Minna said.

"You stupid old woman, you know what I mean!"

"I would know if you didn't tell such stupid stories to confuse people."

Joel leaned across to me. "Make Kurt stay here."

"Knowing that we can never be married?"

"So?—" He shrugged helplessly.

"It's odd," I replied. "Once I lost my chance of being married because of a mother. Now, it's a wife who's defeated me."

Only one poet described the Harbour as I saw it every day and that was

Ken Slessor. Alan had sent me some of his poems which I had read with cries of recognition, as if they were lines I had written myself and forgotten:

> Deep and dissolving verticals of light
> Ferry the falls of moonshine down. Five bells
> Coldly rung out in a machine's voice. Night and water
> Pour to one rip of darkness, the Harbour floats
> In air, the Cross hangs upside-down in water.

That evening the water was oppressively dark and without reflection, like a cavern in space so deep that even the stars had been extinguished in it. For once there was no blare of voices from Chateau Miramar: it was one of those moments of absolute stillness in a crowded building that make one feel as though time has come to an end and if one could only prevent the silence breaking, a new world would come into being. When Kurt carried a bottle of champagne and two glasses out to the balcony I felt as if he had clumsily destroyed something that was unique and precious.

"First we are going to drink—" he said, popping the cork so that it flew out in an arc towards the Harbour.

I held the glass in my hand and thought I could hear each bubble reaching the surface.

"I shall propose the toast. We shall drink to love."

I drank in silence.

"To Vienna!" He laughed.

He kissed me with such tenderness that I could feel myself responding with a passion that equalled his. I knew that I must choose every word with extraordinary care and replied slowly.

"I think Renée is mistaken, Kurt. It's not that you would leave me in Vienna but that I might leave you."

"You make it sound like a game—"

"Oh yes, a game of forfeits where no one wins."

"Please, I do not understand this."

"I am not going to Vienna with you—"

"Darling, this is our chance to be married! Renée has given her word."

"I believe what everyone is saying—the whole of Europe will be at war within months. The German Stukas are in Spain now and Hitler has occupied the Rhineland."

"Not Austria—"

"That is wishful thinking carried to madness!"

"You don't understand European politics as I do."

"Have you forgotten that I'm Italian? My father was killed by the Fascists.

Mussolini has won his victories in Africa and Hitler will follow suit in Europe."

"Of course he will. Who would deny that? But Austria has a privileged relationship with Germany."

"You're a Jew, Kurt."

"I need someone like you to remind me of that fact. I can assure you, nobody at home ever found it a problem. I did not walk around with a Star of David pinned to my lapel."

"Jews are being arrested in Germany."

"Of course they are—and they are being resettled. What is so unusual about that?"

"No—I've decided. I won't leave Australia. I think I've become part of this country."

"Then I shall stay with you in the wilderness. Like des Grieux I shall follow my beloved wicked Manon to the desert of New Orleans and we shall die singing in each other's arms."

"I could not be happy as your mistress."

"You are making so much fuss about something that is really very simple. If you want to get married then come back to Vienna. If you don't like it there, I swear we'll get on the next boat and go anywhere you want."

"No—"

"Ah, this is only because you are now playing a woman's game against Renée. You cannot permit yourself to agree to anything she wants. Because it was her idea, you automatically resist."

"Why didn't you tell me that your parents are writing to you every day, begging you to return?"

"Is that so unexpected? After all, I am their only son. And I cannot describe to you how primitive this city is because you have never seen Vienna. We'll have such a good life there full of music and laughter, restaurants and theatres—*liebling*, we'll get an apartment in—yes, I know exactly the building for us in the ninth district, Alsergrund, not too expensive and—"

"No, Kurt, if you want to go—then you should. I didn't realize how homesick you were here. Australia was very strange for me at first, but now I feel as though I'm living in El Dorado or Arcady. All I have to do is put out my hand and riches fall into it. If there are ghosts in this country, they are in me, not in the landscape. I enjoy that. I'm sorry you've been so unhappy—"

"I'm never unhappy when I'm loving you, Gwen. I could make love to you forever. When I see you, I ache for you like a dog."

"That was Dante's punishment for guilty lovers, to be frozen in the act of love, joined together for eternity."

"It is the thought of Renée that is making you say these things. You are always so rational—"

"Kurt, I am not going to Vienna with you and I won't live here with you as your mistress."

"Ah, now I understand—"

He leaned out across the edge of the balcony as if he were going to fling himself down into the darkness.

"You don't love me enough."

"I'm sure that's a part of it."

"Well, I can't exist without you!" He swung round and faced me, his face contorted with anger. "I must have you!"

His voice echoed and, as if in response to himself, he stared out across the Harbour saying, "I want so much to go home. Only you have kept me here making creams for women with peeling noses and freckles. My God! These Australian women! Their voices are always off-key and the best of them sound as if they had head colds. Their braying laughter like mating donkeys! A man could enjoy making love to them if there were a trapdoor on the other side of the bed. Finish—whoof! If it were not for you, my darling, I would have fled this country at the end of a month."

Fatigue was creeping through my bones and all I suddenly wanted was to be able to sleep without dreaming. Kurt pulled me to my feet and kissed me—

"We cannot live without each other!"

"Kurt, there's no choice—"

"We can die together!" he shouted and pushed me towards the edge of the balcony.

The voice came in a shriek from Miramar and I heard my name called over and over. Startled, Kurt released me as I turned and bent over the railing. The windows of Miramar were sending yellow streamers into the darkness; Terry was screaming and waving to me from the lawn.

"Wait, I'll come over to you," I called.

"We must talk more about this," Kurt said lamely.

"Talk?" I jeered. "I thought you were going to kill me."

Swiftly, I ran down the back stairs of Trelawney and across the lawns to Miramar. Terry was standing, hands clasped in front of him, and his hair, usually as sleek as an otter's, was in straggled spikes.

"The contract's come for Dolfi!" I shouted. "Tell me, are they sending the money by cheque or in gold bars?"

"Gwen—"

"Don't tell me Dolfi wants more."

"Dolfi's been arrested."

"Arrested? For what?"

"Gwen, it was a set-up. He was trapped. Oh, I know how indiscreet he can be, but Dolfi's been on top of the world since he heard about the contract."

"Tell me slowly what happened, Terry."

"We were all having a few drinks at the Australia, some of our own set. Dolfi vanished and I thought he'd gone to relieve himself. Well, he went to Martin Place and they've accused him of an indecent act and it could mean prison."

"What did he do, Terry? Relieve himself against the Cenotaph?"

I had a sudden vision of that morning when Bessie and I first saw Dolfi and he was piddling into a fountain at the Villa d'Athena.

"He went into the public convenience and there was a young man there who says that Dolfi touched him."

"Dolfi must have been drunk."

"I'm sure he was. He says the fellow enticed him and—it happened and the next thing a policeman came out of one of the lavatories and the young man said he was a police officer in plain clothes. They arrested Dolfi on the spot and—oh, this is why I know it was a set-up. When they came out into Martin Place, Billy Garvin was there with a photographer from *Truth*. It will be in all the papers."

This would finish Dolfi's career, I suddenly realized.

"We were all waiting at the bar for Dolfi when Billy Garvin phoned me and told me he was at the station. I went round and paid Dolfi's bail. He's going to be charged tomorrow morning and then there'll be a trial."

"Garvin's going to destroy him if he can."

"He said to me last week that he didn't like the idea of Dolfi leaving Australia and going to Hollywood. He didn't think his readers would care for it either. I thought he was just being his usual venomous little self. Gwen, I can't understand why he'd do this. After all, he's like us—like Dolfi and me."

"Is Dolfi still at the station?"

"No, he's over there—" Terry pointed to Miramar. "He's locked himself in a wardrobe and he won't come out."

"I'll talk to him."

"I think he may listen to you. Gwen, he's always been so fond of you—as though you were his sister."

"He hates me but I'm his family," I said savagely and ran towards the house.

Dolfi's bedroom was cluttered with elephants and brass vases like an Indian bazaar. Terry pointed to a built-in wardrobe in the corner. I hammered on the door, ordering Dolfi to come out.

"Never!" was the muffled response.

"Good! I'll break this down with an axe and then I'll use the same axe on you!"

"Go away, Gina!"

"You can't hide like a child."

"I want to die," he wailed.

"Good. Let me help you. I'll block up all the cracks and you can suffocate slowly."

There was a pause and I heard him scuffling inside and suddenly a frantic hammering against the wood.

"Gina, help me! I've locked myself in and I can't get out!"

"Cretin!" I screamed and Terry and I prised open the door and Dolfi fell out at our feet. He had been crying and his face was swollen and tear-stained.

"I need a brandy," he moaned.

"Get him one while I try to make some sense out of all this."

"Gina, I'd never seen him before but he was young and he looked like Roger and I—I—know he wanted me to touch him—"

"So you took hold of a policeman's private parts with another policeman watching."

Terry handed him a balloon of brandy and Dolfi swallowed it in a gulp.

"You'll help me, won't you, Gina?"

He was blubbering gustily, his fat cheeks distended, and I wondered what had happened to the golden boy with the deep blue eyes that Bessie had loved so passionately.

"We'll need a good lawyer to defend you, Dolfi."

"That friend of yours, Alan Gilchrist. I want him, Gina!"

"No! Even if he offers to help we're not going to have him involved in this."

"They'll put me in prison! I thought it was a joke, but it's a criminal offence. They're all jealous of my genius—"

"There are others like us in gaol now, Gwen," Terry said.

"I'll do whatever I can for you but not with Alan's help. He's been embarrassed enough by us."

"But he's the lawyer I want," Dolfi screamed.

"You'll do as I tell you," I shouted. "Who left me to explain to your mother when you ran off with Roger? Who—"

We exchanged recriminations and insults until we were both breathless and Terry was huddled in a chair, his hands over his ears, moaning.

"I'll ask our solicitors to get us a good barrister. Someone who'll know how to handle this mess."

Billy had timed the affair so that he made the front page of *Truth* before the daily papers could print their accounts of Dolfi's arrest. When they did, the jackals came in to feast and suddenly Danny Burns, the best-loved, the most famous comedian in Australia, was a pervert who solicited young men in public toilets. The salivating relish with which they described the incident was revolting but the papers all reported increased sales.

By Monday afternoon, three sponsors had cancelled their contracts; I knew that others would follow. Dolfi was charged on Tuesday morning and a trial date was set for the following month. Alan had phoned me on Sunday and offered to defend Dolfi, but I could hear the relief in his voice when I told him we had never considered him. He then suggested that we hire Dennis Malone, a KC who had a large sporting clientele and was as well known on the race course as he was in court. Terry, Dolfi and I were taken to his chambers by Martin Triggs, our solicitor, who had reduced Dolfi to near-hysteria on the way by reciting the sentences that had been recently meted out to sodomites caught in similar circumstances.

"You see," he intoned, "Australian judges regard homosexuality as a very serious offence and they are not inclined to consider mitigating circumstances. Prison is felt to be the only adequate penalty for such a crime against nature."

Dennis Malone's chambers were a distracting combination of sporting trophies, paintings of race horses and law books, but Triggs assured us that he was indeed the best man for the case.

Malone sat back with his feet on the desk while Dolfi gave at least four different versions of what had happened.

"Come now, Mr Burns, you pulled his dick, didn't you?" he finally snapped.

"I—I'm not sure—" Dolfi murmured and began to snivel.

"Christ!" Malone said. "There's only one defence."

"I can't go to prison! Please—somebody must help me!" Dolfi turned to me. "Gina, this isn't the right lawyer. I want your friend."

"You shut up and listen to me, young feller!" Malone had a ruler on his desk and he jabbed Dolfi with it.

"There is only one defence—you were blind drunk and you don't remember anything after you staggered into the convenience. Now, under cross-examination, you may admit to having fallen against someone, but that is all. Yes, a charge of being drunk and disorderly won't do you any harm. May even help you. No Aussie's going to condemn a man for getting drunk. I'm sure we can produce witnesses to the fact that you're often inebriated, can't we?"

"Hundreds," Terry said, beaming.

"But you're not exactly my kind of client, Mr Burns. You're going to have to learn your lines and no improvisation. I don't want you mistaking a courtroom for a stage, and if it is a stage, then you're going to play second fiddle there to Dennis Malone."

Dolfi stood up and bowed. "I am your humble servant, Mr Malone."

"Servant? I wouldn't let you polish my boots," Malone muttered. "Now, I'll be making a few statements to the press and we'll see if we can't knock some of the shine off that little bastard Garvin."

Dennis Malone's command of righteous indignation rivalled Isaiah's and when he stood on the pavement outside his chambers in Macquarie Street, thumbs in his waistcoat, bottom lip protruding, gown billowing, he provided a picture for every newspaper in Australia. Danny Burns was innocent, he thundered. If his client had been arrested for womanizing, or on even more serious charges against the female sex, he could understand it, but if anybody in his right mind could believe that Danny Burns was a poofter then pigs could fly and kangaroos yodel. It was fine larrikin stuff and made front-page news the next day in all the papers. The following Sunday, *Truth* published a series of photos showing Dolfi with some of his male friends where it was obvious that Billy had been preparing his story for a long time. Malone issued another tirade against filthy reporting and police connivance while we began to receive floods of mail supporting Danny and another stream of letters so disgusting they reminded me of some of the books in Edith's library. Privately, Malone told us that Dolfi could well be charged and might be given five years with time off for good behaviour.

Congruence is a quality of art; like harmony and order, it is what we impose on the anarchic madness of life. Those weeks between Dolfi's arrest and his trial were like being followed by a killer through one of the fun houses at Luna Park, or suddenly discovering that I had cancer in the middle of a New Year's Eve party with people blowing whistles in my ear and dancing in grotesque masks. Everyone was telling jokes about Dolfi: one comedian imitated his Dino, mincing around the stage with his hat held fast below his waist, only when the time came to lift his hat to acknowledge the applause of the audience there was a bunch of pansies pinned to his trousers. It was gallows humour because at the same time as everyone rocked with laughter, the likelihood of a long gaol sentence was being discussed. Some wag in the *Telegraph* suggested that Danny's new film should be entitled *Dino in the Clink.*

Dolfi was on the verge of insanity during that period. Some days he ran through his parts as though nothing had happened, then suddenly he would throw the script against the studio wall and begin wailing like a child. Terry and I were with him constantly, so when Angelica told me she was going to be dancing for the first time in the chorus, we took Dolfi to the theatre with us. Everyone at the Royal recognized him as we were being seated and Dolfi stood up and waved in response to the acclamation. Suddenly, someone began blowing noisy kisses at him and the mood of the crowd changed in an instant; there was a scattering of boos as Dolfi fell into his seat and began to weep. I did not know how we would ever be able to get him into court.

Morton Silberstein cabled from Los Angeles saying that he was returning to Sydney immediately. We knew how sensitive Americans were about moral issues and it seemed likely that even if Dolfi were acquitted, he would never have a Hollywood career.

Kurt was at Trelawney when I came home the following day and he kissed me as though we were still the lovers we had been before we learned that Renée was alive. "This is Australia!" He laughed. "Only in this puritanical little village would a man be charged as a criminal because he behaved like a schoolboy."

"I'm tired. I don't want to talk about Dolfi. I've been with him all day."

"But he is the reason why you must come to Vienna with me and lead a normal life. This place is barbaric and uncivilized—"

"No!" I shouted. "I'm going to stay here."

"Then I'll share the same room in the madhouse with you, *liebling*."

"Kurt, please give me the key—"

He looked at me bewildered for a moment.

"The key to this flat."

"No—this is where I belong just as you do."

"We are not going to be lovers any longer, Kurt."

"I told you, I'm prepared to stay here with you if that is what you want!"

"I want the things that other women seem to have naturally—a husband and children."

"You're barren—you've told me that a thousand times. So why do you want so much to be married?"

"Just because I'm barren, I'm not going to live as a *puttana* or a mistress. Go away now, Kurt. I can't bear to talk to you any more."

Nothing I had said to him expressed what I felt in my heart. We must have sounded like a couple of lovers arguing about residences—country or city, cottage or flat—when the truth was that I did not love him enough to abandon everything and follow him.

He left cursing me and the following morning I had the locks changed and told the doorman not to admit him. Later I heard that the perfumery was up for sale but I did not bother finding out who had bought it. Every time I drove to the top of William Street I saw Paris Rose smiling mysteriously down on the city but it was the face of a stranger.

I could not avoid Kurt and yet every time we met it was as if the passion of our love had changed to a determination to wound each other in every possible way. And we knew our vulnerable points so well. There were nights when I lay in bed, aching for him, and yet feeling such a revulsion in my mind that I would as soon have lain down with a corpse. How could I have changed, I asked myself as I twisted in grief, feeling as though every part of me was bruised. Was it because of Renée or was there a serpent in my heart poised ready to strike when I was most in love?

Kurt asked me to coffee at the Old Vienna and I agreed, knowing that we would not be likely to scream at each other there.

"This is to say *auf Wiedersehen*," he said jauntily.

"You're leaving so soon?"

"Yes, there is a very pleasant French cruise ship that will take me to Marseilles and from there I'll travel by train to Vienna."

"Kurt, the news from Europe is terrible."

"Nothing could be worse than this place. I'm sorry I won't be here to find out what happened to Dolfi. If he goes to prison I'll send him a *kugelhupf* from a special pastry shop I know in Vienna."

I never saw Kurt again. He left on the 10th of December 1937.

Thirty-Eight

Grief and anger cannot sleep in the same bed: that was one of Assunta's sayings and I remembered it as I alternately wept and raged after Kurt had gone, staring at the curtains floating in the breeze from the Harbour, waiting for the tide to turn against the sea wall. I rehearsed all the ways in which Kurt had failed and disappointed me, yet my body shrieked for him and I felt as if the flesh were being torn from my bones. Every day I worked to keep our radio theatre in business, soothing sponsors, travelling to Melbourne on the new *Spirit of Progress*, assuring station managers that Dolfi's trial would vindicate him and make him more popular than ever—and all the time feeling that I was nothing but an antic skeleton, talking, arguing, capering, for my flesh was with Kurt.

Whenever I saw Joel I was shrivelled by his despair. He was trying to organize a committee to help bring out refugees from Europe, but, he told me grimly, it wasn't easy convincing some of his friends when his nephew had just returned to Austria.

"I don't blame you for Kurt leaving," he said to me, yet when he absolved me I knew that in his heart he held me responsible for Kurt's departure. If I had agreed to remain his mistress, Kurt would never have left Sydney. Those days, Minna was the only consolation I had in that house. I would be in tears after I'd spoken to Joel and she would take me into the kitchen and put some cake or biscuits into my hand as if I were a child.

"It is not your fault. Whatever the old fool says, you couldn't have lived with Kurt under those conditions. What does he think? That you were going to be Kurt's second-best wife?"

"He wants Kurt to live."

"Kurt made up his own mind. From Adam and Eve in the Garden of Eden, men have said it was a woman's fault—she did, she did not—and we are blamed no matter what we do."

She scrubbed the same spot on the shining stove and glanced quickly at me.

"Kurt told you about the money, didn't he?"

I shook my head.

"The Laufers, Renée's father, promised Kurt half a million marks in his own name if he returned to Vienna."

Alan phoned me every day and I think it was his voice that saved me from falling into the pit of insanity with Dolfi. *Truth* and Billy Garvin made every Sunday an ordeal of torment with one fleering article after another. Terry and I tried to keep the paper from Dolfi but he always managed to find it and read it and then he would go berserk, breaking furniture, smashing mirrors, trying to kill himself. One night he threw himself over the sea wall into the Harbour and said he was going to swim until he drowned.

"I can't reach him," Terry screamed. "I can barely keep afloat."

So I dived into the water and swam after him. He shrieked at me to keep away from him, that he wanted to die, and every time he opened his mouth to shout he swallowed water and choked. We must have been three hundred yards from the shore when I finally grabbed him by the hair and tried to drag him after me. He kicked and plunged wildly until I thought he was going to pull me under with him, and for a moment that seemed a fitting end for both of us.

"Dolfi—there are sharks in the Harbour! They'll get you long before you drown."

At that, with a piercing howl, he almost lifted himself into the air and headed back for shore, leaving me treading water, too exhausted to paddle after him.

Every day brought the same procession of grotesque horrors and, looking at Terry, gaunt and red-eyed, I saw a mirror image of myself.

When the silver box arrived that week, I found a card beside the grapes. It said simply, "If you need me, call me." My hand was almost on the phone when it rang and I heard Alan's voice. He was worried about me and wanted to see me before he left for Canberra. Alan was campaigning for the Labour Party and had made a number of public speeches appealing for an increased defence budget, warning the public against the danger of an attack from Japan. The unions supported him but in the *Bulletin* he was described as a rabble-rousing warmonger. I told him that we had survived another day with Dolfi and I would let him know immediately we went to court.

Morton Silberstein arrived in Sydney and we sat and listened while he told us that MGM was disturbed, seriously disturbed by any hint of Dolfi's being a homosexual. Dennis Malone assured him that he was hoping for a verdict of drunkenness and disorderly conduct and Morton seemed slightly mollified and began to relax.

"Hell—to be called a boozer and a brawler is nothing," he said. "That just makes Danny Burns part of the democratic majority in Hollywood."

There were two adjournments for the trial date but when the day finally came, Dolfi told us that he could not appear because he knew he was going to be found guilty. We comforted him and Terry dressed him in a dark suit with a white shirt that made him look like a plump undertaker, but even as we spoke about acquittal and vindication, we remembered what Malone had said to us privately the day before: "I wouldn't bet on the outcome. It's London to a brick he'll go down."

Malone was magnificent in court, disposing of the evidence of the two police officers with derisive scorn, striding up and down as though he were in riding breeches, slapping his leg with an invisible riding crop, the living presence of a sporting Australian. His examination of Dolfi was masterly, consisting largely of a hectoring series of accusations about his known drunkenness and womanizing, all of which Dolfi strenuously denied. But the badgering continued with Malone's face inches from Dolfi's.

"You deny that you drink to excess?"

"Haven't you been arrested on eleven different occasions for being drunk and disorderly?"

Dolfi could not deny that and began to tremble.

"Aren't you in need of a drink now?"

At first Dolfi said no and then looked piteously around the court and asked if he couldn't have a small brandy.

Malone was on his toes, his finger outstretched, and he bellowed, "Mr Burns, are you not an incorrigible, incapable and incontrovertible dipsomaniac?"

Dolfi collapsed blubbering, blowing his nose and admitting that he was everything Malone had said and more. It was obvious from some uneasy shifting that a few members of the jury thought he was not being well served by his defence. At lunch we were all convinced that Dolfi would get off scot free but when he began to brandish a knife and shout about what he had in mind for Billy Garvin, Malone leaned across the table and warned him that he still had to face the Crown prosecutor, Justin Neville.

It was inconceivable that Dolfi had anything to fear from the softly spoken, diffident little man who shuffled up to the witness box clutching a handful of notes like a schoolboy facing an oral examination. Even Morton Silberstein seemed at ease and I saw him fumbling for his cigar case before he realized with a start that he was in a courtroom. At the end of the first hour Dolfi was writhing as Neville pressed the same question: wasn't it a fact that he had homosexual friends, wasn't homosexuality a feature of theatrical life, wasn't it true that Danny Burns was a homosexual himself? If Malone hadn't continually objected, I think Dolfi would have admitted everything. The jubilation at lunch was equalled by the despair of the afternoon.

We went back to Miramar followed by reporters and the Movietone news crew and locked the gates to the street, but some of them managed to get across the lawns and were peering through the windows, so we went upstairs and sat in Dolfi's Indian bedroom with all the blinds down.

"I'm finished and I may as well be dead. I'm not going back there tomorrow. They can sentence me in my absence."

Nothing we said made any difference and he threw himself down on the bed and sobbed.

"It's the end," Terry said quietly to me. "He can't endure any more. Dolfi has to be loved."

I was about to respond with some bitter remark but I said instead that I would go downstairs and get us some coffee. None of Dolfi's entourage of servants ever seemed capable of providing a glass of water unless bullied and threatened.

I was crossing the hall when Lupe, the chauffeur, said that there were three people demanding to see Dolfi.

"Only three?" I retorted. "I thought the press of the world was out there trying to fight its way in."

"These aren't journalists, miss. One says he's Mr Burns' father."

I paused and for a moment I could see the gods rocking with laughter.

"He gave me this card, miss."

I held the slip of cardboard in my hand and read, "Carmelo Rossi Esq. Accountant, 37 Birch Road, Homebush" and a phone number.

Frau Brunner's voice was ringing through my head—the fiend who had robbed her family, the monster who had betrayed and reviled her, the reprobate husband who was cast out by her father.

"There are two ladies with him," Lupe added.

"Bring them upstairs—get them past the reporters somehow," I said, adding, "Oh yes, Lupe, and tell the kitchen staff that perhaps if they all work together and use the same recipe they might be able to arrange a tray of coffee and sandwiches for us."

Dolfi was still sobbing on the bed, Terry stroking his hair and telling him that if he were sentenced, they would disguise themselves and escape from the country together.

"Get up, Dolfi," I said sharply.

Dolfi began to scream, pounding the pillow with his fists, and I bent down and shook him. "Pull yourself together. Your father is here, Dolfi. Do you want him to see you like this?"

There was silence for a moment and then he rolled over and stared at me.

"You are a bitch from hell, Gina. Only you would mock me when I'm going to prison where—"

"Lupe is bringing your father up now. I gather there are two ladies with him."

The door opened and Lupe announced Mr Rossi and his two sisters.

If the suspense had not been so acute I would have fallen to my knees on the floor, laughing hysterically, because only the malicious gods who delight in tormenting humankind could have arranged this meeting.

Carmelo Rossi was a portly little man with balding hair and pince-nez spectacles; a gold watch chain hung with medals and seals strained across his chest and he emitted a strong aroma of pomade. His two sisters were replicas of him, cast in female form. Where he was wearing a dark suit with a high waistcoat they had on mottled dark dresses with white lace collars and wore squashed black hats covered with flowers that looked as though they had been stolen from a faded funeral wreath. They could have been on the Via Roma in Palermo on their way to Sunday Mass at the Cattedrale, but I remembered seeing them at the Tivoli and at the Savoy Theatre when we recorded *Dino the Dago*. Carmelo Rossi walked to the centre of the room and placed his hand on his heart.

"I was in court today and although I have never intruded on my famous son's life, I knew I must come forward and state publicly that it is not possible for a Rossi to be—not a complete man."

Dolfi was sitting on the edge of the bed, gaping.

"My sisters are of the same opinion as myself," and the two old women bobbed their heads in unison.

I huddled in a chair, knuckles against my teeth, because I knew I was about to explode with laughter.

"Papa," Dolfi said in a voice I couldn't recognize.

"*Mio figlio*!" Carmelo Rossi exclaimed, and in the next instant they were all weeping together.

Terry stared at me in amazement and I reached out and took his hand. "Quickly," I said, "let's go and find what they've done with the coffee I ordered."

The maid was busy arguing with Lupe over the kitchen table when I stormed in, threatening instant dismissal and docked pay, just as Frau Brunner used to do. The coffee was prepared in minutes and Terry and I waited in the living room for Dolfi to introduce his family.

Mr Rossi came down first, followed by Dolfi and his two aunts behind him. They sat down and watched me while I poured the coffee. If it is possible for a grub to become a butterfly, then the change in Dolfi might be explained. We had left a sodden, hysterical animal that could scarcely be called human on the bed, this man before us sat upright in his chair with an expression of indomitable courage in his face.

"My son," Mr Rossi said emphatically, "has been the unfortunate victim of depraved and parasitic friends who have destroyed his good name and wasted his fortune. He will return with us this evening to my own home—"

I was about to speak when he raised his hand and the sisters clucked at my audacious interruption.

"He will be in court tomorrow morning."

"But Dennis Malone will want to speak to him—"

"I have given you my card. My phone number is on it. Mr Malone may speak to my son when he wishes."

Terry and I watched them leave, pushing their way through the horde of reporters to a waiting taxi.

"I think I'm going to be sick. The fish paste in that sandwich was off," Terry said and put a hand over his mouth.

"No, it's Dolfi. He always has that effect on people who try to help him."

I doubt if he heard me as he stumbled for the bathroom.

Misery and I were spending a sleepless night when a little before dawn I remembered that I had not eaten since lunch the day before and went out to the kitchen. The bunch of purple grapes was on a crystal dish and I ate them slowly, feeling the sweetness on my tongue and in my throat. The whole apartment was full of shadows. I thought I could see Edith on her white chaise-longue, my mother bent over a table opposite my father, and Rosalia standing by the door, hands folded under her shawl. Frau Brunner was examining the furniture and behind me I knew that Miki was crouched in the corner making faces. I shook my head and they were gone but the sweetness remained on my tongue as I went back to bed and slept fitfully.

Even Dennis Malone was amazed by the difference in Dolfi when we arrived at the court the next morning while Terry had obviously been busy: every showgirl from the Tivoli was there in court and when Dolfi appeared they all cooed and threw kisses. As soon as the judge sat down, Dennis Malone thundered indignantly that he was appalled by his client's behaviour in bringing so many of his intimate friends to the trial, turning it into—and modesty prevented him using the only word that came readily to his mind.

Justin Neville continued his cross-examination, but this was not the witness he had interrogated the day before. It was clear that he was put off stride by this resolute young man who announced publicly that he abhorred effeminacy in every form, and, when confronted with certain photos, said with considerable scorn that he had been rehearsing a new character called Percy the Poofter.

Foolishly, Neville asked Dolfi if he did not have a sexual preference for men; before he could answer, the showgirls burst into shrill laughter and the judge threatened to have the court cleared. Dolfi joined in the general mirth, clutching his sides in the witness box and winking at the jury.

At lunch he strode out to the assembled reporters with a pair of tall showgirls towering over his head and posed for photographs while the rest of the Tivoli chorus gave the journalists their personal reminiscences of Dolfi.

Angelica, who was there with some of her friends from the Theatre Royal, sidled up to me and said that Terry had promised them all parts in Dolfi's next film if they showed up for him and could I lend her a tenner because she'd run short again. Standing over to one side with a sister on each arm was Carmelo Rossi, watching his son vanquish his enemies and confound the critics.

The judge had clearly been impressed by the evidence of the two police officers and in his summing up he asked the jury to ignore the histrionic episodes of the second day and concentrate upon the sworn statements of two honourable members of the New South Wales constabulary. It was impossible to locate the source of the guffaw but it came from somewhere at the back of the court and soon everyone was tittering in response. One member of the jury, a stolid man with a bald head, dug his neighbour in the ribs and the two had to be reprimanded by the judge for unwarranted levity. The jury retired to consider their verdict and we all went to the Australia for dinner. Dolfi insisted on the place next to his father and sat throughout the meal looking like an altar boy who had just discovered his true vocation. Terry leaned over to me.

"I don't understand, Gwen. Dolfi's been ignoring me. He'll hardly speak to me."

"Don't upset yourself," I replied. "It's a new part for Dolfi. When he's tired of it, he'll find another."

I spoke to Dolfi's father while we were waiting for the verdict and asked him why he had come out to Australia.

"My wife and I were very happy together," he said primly, "but her father did not approve of Hilda marrying a Sicilian. He said he would disown Hilda if I did not leave."

We all of us create each other and the villain of one person's story is the hero of another's. My memories were of Frau Brunner standing with her bosom heaving and denouncing Sicilians because of what this man had done to her.

"Herr Brunner was a very powerful man and he said he would destroy my father and my whole family if I did not emigrate. When I heard about my son I wanted so much to return, but he would not let me."

Carmelo Rossi had a small pursed mouth like a fish and every time he spoke it was as if he were swallowing something from the air.

"I sent Hilda an allowance for my son—every month. I have all the receipts. Two pounds for each week until he was eighteen years of age. It was not easy to find the money when I was first trying to get work in Australia. My sisters did fine sewing and made lace and I did whatever I could during the depression until I made myself an accountant. Sometimes we lived on vegetables and a little bread and sometimes we had nothing, but I never failed to send the money for my son."

It was exactly nine o'clock when we were summoned back to court and the judge called upon the foreman of the jury to give his verdict. On all counts, the verdict was not guilty, Danny Burns was a free man and Australia's favourite comedian again. We all went back to the Australia to celebrate followed by a crowd of Dolfi's devoted fans. Dennis Malone made speech after speech but Dolfi would not respond, sitting beside his father and smiling like a fat cherub.

Terry and Morton Silberstein were talking in a corner; I could see Terry shaking his head and Morton jabbing the air with his cigar. I went over to them and Terry pulled me down beside him.

"The contract will go through," Terry said.

"Does Dolfi know yet?"

"He will when we can get him away from his father."

"There is a special requirement." Morton spoke through a cloud of smoke like a silver-haired Jove. "MGM will sign provided that Danny is married."

"Married?"

"Well, no one can say he's a fairy if he's married."

"I think you'd better break the news to Dolfi very gently," I said and Terry nodded glumly.

"A nice wedding and we'll be on our way to the States," Morton said, his face almost disappearing in the cloud.

The following week, Carmelo Rossi and his two sisters moved into the Chateau Miramar and all the servants were dismissed, with the exception of Lupe who was needed because Carmelo could not drive and Dolfi had been refused a licence when he applied for one. Lupe told me that everything had been changed in the house and he was thinking of looking for another job.

I was working at my desk in the library, setting out different ways in which the Danny Burns Radio Theatre could be run without Dolfi, when I heard the doorbell. Terry was standing there with two suitcases.

"I've been thrown out," he said and began to sob uncontrollably.

He told me that Carmelo and his sisters had taken over the house and Dolfi would do nothing without speaking first to his father.

"When I'm there, they speak Italian and I don't understand what they're saying, but I know it's about me because of the way they look at me."

"You can stay here with me, Terry."

"I didn't have anywhere else to go."

We sat together, holding each other like hurt children.

"It's the change in Dolfi. He's like a different person."

"You invented Danny Burns, Terry. Never forget that—"

"Mr Rossi says I've exploited Dolfi."

"And you also prevented his son getting married?" I said drily.

"Yes—that too. He says he's going to find a good wife for Dolfi. He's talking to Morton Silberstein all the time and he's been to the solicitors. Yesterday he asked Mr Fortescue-Bragg for the books. I said he should speak to you but Dolfi insisted—"

"Stay here with me and tomorrow I'll sort everything out. After all, I'll have to run the Danny Burns Theatre on my own when you're in Hollywood with Dolfi."

"What—what if he doesn't want me now?"

"He needs you, Terry. You're his alter ego."

"I can't lose Dolfi—not like this," he cried and put his head on his knees, weeping.

"Terry, Dolfi is unspeakable. I knew him when we were growing up and he doesn't deserve anybody's love."

"I loved him when I first met him and I shall go on loving him until I die."

The next morning at the studio, Carmelo Rossi announced that he was inviting me to dinner at Chateau Miramar where we would discuss his son's future, and then remained in the control room for the rest of the day while we recorded. When Terry spoke to him, Mr Rossi said he would only discuss matters with him if a solicitor were present. I took Dolfi aside outside the studio, demanding to know what was happening to Terry. Dolfi simpered and said he was following his father's instructions.

"Did you permit your father to kick Terry out of his own home last night?"

"Chateau Miramar is in my name. My father checked the lease."

"But Terry paid for half of it."

"All Terry's money came from me and when he didn't have enough, he stole from me. That is what my father says."

"Dolfi, I never expected anything decent or fair from you. I always knew that you had the principles of a dungworm, but Terry is your friend."

"He corrupted me. I would never have had to endure that trial if it hadn't been for him."

My hands were raised and I was about to throw myself at him and beat him with my fists, but I managed to control my anger.

"Good, I'll be at dinner tonight and I'm bringing Terry with me. And never forget, I'm a Sicilian too."

I could still recognize the house but now there were silk shawls over the chairs and lithographs of saints and smug Madonnas on every wall. Over the mantelpiece, where there had once been a painting of some delirious flamingos engaged in a mating ritual, a bovine St Sebastian skewered with arrows stared up to heaven. We sat down to a table with Carmelo at one end and Dolfi at the other and, instead of going to the bar and pouring a dash from every liqueur bottle into a glass and gulping it, Dolfi accepted a small glass of wine when his father offered it to him and sipped it as though he had never tasted alcohol before.

"I did not invite Terry to my son's house," Mr Rossi said, glaring at me as his sister piled our plates with pasta. He spoke in Italian and I replied in English.

"If you have forgotten how to speak the language of this country then you are more of a fool than I thought, Mr Rossi."

For a moment I thought he was going to choke, but it was Dolfi who reprimanded me.

"Please, you are speaking to my father, Gina."

"Ah, but he's such a new father and such a stranger to all of us, you must forgive my speaking so bluntly."

"You have the major share of the Danny Burns Radio Theatre," Mr Rossi said.

"Yes, and the other forty-nine per cent is owned jointly by Terry and Dolfi."

"No!" He struck his plate triumphantly with the fork. "No! There you are wrong. It is in my son's name."

"What are you suggesting, Mr Rossi? I gather that you not only want to drive Terry out of the house which he helped to buy, but now you want to rob him of his share of the business."

"I have seen the contracts and the terms of agreement. It is quite clear."

I turned to Terry who nodded helplessly.

"It was—was like a marriage between us, Gwen. We used the name Danny Burns because Danny Burns was both of us."

I wanted to round on Terry then and call him a trusting idiot, but instead I faced Mr Rossi.

"Dolfi owes everything to Terry. From the beginning, Terry supported him, managed his act when he was on the Manly ferries."

"What—what has this pervert done for my son since he first met him except corrupt his moral character?"

"Terry Mapes created Danny Burns."

"My son has simply fulfilled a theatrical talent which he inherited from my great-uncle who was a famous opera singer. You must have heard of Nicolo Rossi, the bass baritone who sang at La Scala and—"

"I have never heard of this man but I know what Terry has done for Dolfi."

"There would never have been these lewd and terrible charges brought against my son if it had not been for this sodomite!"

"I have known Dolfi longer than anyone here—"

"Do not say a word about him in my house. What are you but—"

"If you say the word that is on your lips, Mr Rossi, I shall curse you and your family until you rot in your coffins. Sister Agata and Sister Antonietta will have white coffins because they are virgins, but you will be thrown to the dogs of the gutter, Carmelo Rossi."

The two sisters were screaming. Mr Rossi was standing, making the *mano cornuta*.

"You are a *jettatora*," he cried.

"Yes, and my curse will remain with you!" I shouted and dragged Terry from his place at the table.

The following day I called Alan and took the documents round to his chambers.

"Are you surviving all this?" he asked.

"I am not going to let them rob Terry," I replied. "You must help me."

"Leave everything with me. I'll call you this evening."

Terry and I were trying to eat dinner when Alan phoned and said that so far as the contract for the Danny Burns Radio Theatre was concerned, Terry Mapes did not exist.

"I put everything I had into the business," Terry said mournfully. "The solicitor told us Danny Burns should be a private company with us both holding equal shares, but it all seemed unnecessary at the time, and we needed every penny to start recording. When you love and trust someone—" His voice trailed off into silence.

"Wait here—I'll go over and see Dolfi and his father."

As I walked across the lawns to Miramar I kept hearing Frau Brunner and I suddenly realized how much Carmelo Rossi resembled her. Lupe told us that he came out every morning and checked the mileage on the car and again at night, making calculations on how much petrol had been consumed; if the figures did not tally, he accused Lupe of siphoning off petrol for his own use. The sisters shopped and did all the cooking and since McGregor went to the same butcher and greengrocer, we heard about Agata examining every potato and haggling over the price of a neck of mutton.

When I reached the patio I heard voices in the living room and pushed open the sliding doors. Morton Silberstein was talking, his cigar cutting aromatic spirals in the dimly lit room.

"It's a natural—think of the publicity."

"Not for my son. I couldn't permit it, Morton."

"Now listen, Carmelo, there's a million dollars and a three-picture deal swinging on this. MGM insists on a marriage."

The two were alone and I was in the room before either of them noticed me.

"Now, that's what you Italians call *fortuna*, don't you agree, Carmelo?"

Before Rossi could answer, I sat down between them. "If any deals are being made I must be consulted," I stated. "If I'm not, I might enjoy playing a spoiler's game."

Morton laughed and for a moment I thought he was going to slap me on the back but he obviously thought better of it.

"The only deal is that we've got our tickets for the States—"

"Our tickets? How many and for whom?"

"Well, Dolfi will be taking his family."

"Not Terry."

"That is yesterday, Gwen. Tomorrow is Danny Burns arriving in Hollywood with his father and his aunts and introducing his new bride."

"Good, now what is going to happen to the forty-nine per cent of the Danny Burns Radio Theatre?"

"You'll probably want to sell your share—"

"Why should I want to do that?"

"Because I've had a great idea—what do you say to Miss Gwenadalina finally saying yes to Dino? Now there's a story that will really have people on the edge of their seats."

Without answering, I went to look for Dolfi. He was in his bedroom, sorting through scripts.

"Let me look at you," I said. "I want to see if you're completely *pazzo* or just bewitched."

"My father found me," he murmured beatifically.

"And you're going to take your new family to Hollywood with you?"

"First, we shall make a trip to Florida and there—" He raised his hands as if bestowing benediction. "I shall take my father to my mother's hotel. They will be reconciled and we will be a family for the very first time. Ah, Gina, can't you see that moment when my father takes Mother in his arms after all these years?"

Thirty-Nine

Barnum and Bailey's circus came to Sydney one Easter and Kurt and I took Angelica and Sheila to see a show that would have captivated the audience of ancient Rome with its cruelty and splendour. The aerialists were performing high above our heads, spinning from one trapeze to the next, when in an instant, the side bar of a trapeze broke and one of the men plunged to the sawdust. People were screaming in terror and covering their eyes as the rest of the troupe flew down the ladders and gathered round the broken figure. Two attendants rushed out with a stretcher and as the dead man was being carried away, the clowns came tumbling and dancing into the ring with a troupe of performing dogs and the crowd settled back and began to laugh. I doubt if many bothered to watch the stretcher and its little retinue of sequined performers pass through the entrance and vanish into the darkness.

Throughout the trial and after it, I felt like one of those mourning aerialists as I watched Carmelo Rossi and his sisters take possession of Dolfi, the house and everything they could find that was in his name. Dolfi's horses were sold, furniture was sent off to be auctioned, servants dismissed and Carmelo continued to insist that Dolfi owned forty-nine per cent of the Danny Burns Radio Theatre in his name, that Terry was nothing more than a hired hand. I argued with solicitors, I cursed the Rossis, but the fires of hell would not turn back a Sicilian if he saw money on the other side. There is an old Sicilian proverb that says it is better to sacrifice a child than money, but in his favour, I must say that if Carmelo Rossi was avaricious, he had never tried to claim his son before the trial, having been content to worship him from a distance. The story of Danny Burns having an Irish father who used an Italian stage name was part of Dolfi's legend and Carmelo Rossi would never have disturbed that illustrious fiction had it not seemed likely that his son was going to be sent to prison. In retrospect, then, Carmelo Rossi is not the monster I thought he was, but all I could see at the time was the likelihood of Terry being robbed of every penny. Carmelo was convinced that Terry was responsible for his son's unfortunate collapse into homosexuality and drunkenness and should be punished for what he had done to an innocent young Sicilian boy. And because Terry always believed that Danny Burns represented Dolfi and himself without ever having defined that relationship in a contract, the lawyers now stated that the Radio Theatre had only two owners, Dolfi and me.

After the trial, Dolfi was more popular than ever and Billy Garvin wrote fulsome accolades to his comic genius, adding an arch note that listeners would soon hear about the forthcoming nuptials of Dino and Miss Gwenadalina Snapper, who could be relied upon to keep the ebullient Dino away from bottles and public conveniences.

Alan phoned me from Canberra when this appeared, and I could hear the exasperation in his voice as he demanded to know what was happening. I assured him it was a publicity stunt—like the stories his mother gave the newspapers whenever she could drag a journalist into earshot—and he laughed shortly and mentioned some of the abuse he had been receiving because of his campaign for rearmament. Why should Australia be concerned about Europe or Japan's occupation of China? What could ever disturb this quiet continent? Alan was telling me of a series of speeches he had just made when the line crackled and dissolved into a fuzz of static.

I hung up the receiver and forced myself not to look back and remember what I had lost. Deliberately, I became the woman of business again, negotiating new contracts with our sponsors, refusing to think of Kurt and wondering what would have become of me had I followed him to Austria, or Alan to England. At least, Alan had been able to return safely to Australia. What would happen to Kurt I could not imagine. Then I laughed at my fears: Kurt now had half a million marks to spend in the coffee shops and restaurants of Vienna and a wife who condoned his infidelities. I gave all my attention to the serials and the comedies—every day was a circus with one act tumbling on the heels of the next, mirth succeeding horror. For the public, the circumstances of the trial were forgotten, fiction had vanquished reality. Dino the Dago had triumphed and I was part of the circus as Miss Gwenadalina, jigging and dancing around the ring. Yet I also felt as though I were the dead aerialist carried out unnoticed.

Nobody could understand what had happened to Dolfi because he never went anywhere without his father and whenever he saw Terry, he pouted disgustedly and looked in the opposite direction. One of the great Sunday morning sights of Sydney was to see Dolfi attending Mass at St Mary's with his father and his aunts, Dolfi walking two paces behind his father, Agata and Antonietta behind him. Terry was staying with me at Trelawney and at night he would cry for Dolfi and I would weep for Kurt.

"Dolfi can only love himself," I told Terry. "That's the greatest love of all and he never gets bored because he plays so many different roles and admires himself in all of them. Now he can play the one part that was always denied him. It won't last. Eventually he'll grow tired of this particular role and choose another. I would give anything to be there when he decides to be the ungrateful son who breaks his poor old father's heart."

"I only hope Dolfi doesn't break loose before he leaves Australia," Terry said nervously. "The police are waiting for him to slip up and next time they'll make the charge stick. There won't be one witness, there'll be half a dozen, ready to swear that Dolfi committed an indecent act."

"Good. I hope they do get him and I hope he rots in prison," I retorted.

Morton Silberstein insisted that Dolfi must get married before he would sign the contract for MGM and Dolfi's aunts had begun talking about sending to Sicily for a bride. All I did then was ostensibly to help Terry, but I knew in my heart that I wanted to punish and degrade myself because of what happened on 18 March 1938.

When I arrived at Joel's house late that afternoon I was thinking about Kurt and feeling such desire for him that I deliberately dragged my hand against the stone of the gate, grazing my knuckles. Only pain could momentarily crush the longing that I felt. I looked up and saw Rabbi Bergen coming down the steps, head down and muttering to himself. He brushed past me, apparently unaware of my presence; I thought he must be hurrying to get home before dusk, although there was still sunlight across the Harbour without a flush of scarlet to the west. Kurt had sent me three postcards, one from New Caledonia, the second from Ceylon, another from Aden, all with notes of the casual "wish you were here" variety. There was nothing from Europe. I had been recording all day and my head was swimming with the characters from our serials, their tragedies and comic manoeuvrings: Carmelo sat in the control room now and whenever Dolfi finished an episode, the perfect son would turn away from the microphone and look simperingly for a nod of approval from his father.

There was no sound in the house, but the door was open so I walked into the lobby and down to the kitchen where I knew I'd find Minna. I called her name and she came through a door that led to the back of the house.

"Gwen! Gwen! You must talk to him. You must tell him to stop. I sent for the rabbi, but he wouldn't listen to me. The rabbi was with him for over an hour, but nothing he said made any difference."

"What's wrong, Minna?"

"Joel—he's saying Kaddish for his family in Austria."

I was bewildered and she looked at me in despair—

"The prayers you say for the dead."

"Kurt—his family—"

"We heard the news early this morning. The Nazis have just entered Vienna."

In the middle of the circus, this was the terror.

"Joel cabled immediately but there's been no response."

"Kurt, where is he?"

"In Vienna. We had a postcard from him last week. He seemed very happy. Oh, why didn't he stay here? He—"

"Oh God, don't blame me for this too," I cried. "Not Edith and now Kurt!"

"Perhaps he'll listen to you," Minna said. "You're like his own daughter—"

Bitterness welled up in my throat and I tried to swallow the bile burning my mouth. I had sent Kurt back; I could have kept him here just as I could have told Mother George about Edith and she would not be lying now with the dead sisters at Mount of Angels. Rosalia once said that I would walk through graves but how many—God! How many!

Minna led me to a room at the back of the house where she used to store old boxes and furniture. In the middle, in a cleared space, Joel was sitting on a stool in a ragged shirt, bedroom slippers on his feet, his hair dishevelled. He was beating his chest with his fist, rocking back and forth.

"*Meshuga! Meshuga!*" Minna cried and tried to take him by the arm. He pushed her away.

"*Gott, du hast farfinstered meine Herz and meine Schamme!*" Joel groaned and beat his chest as though he wanted to break it with his fist.

He paused and spat on the floor, shouting, "*Ich spei auf meine Glaube!*"

"No, God will punish us all!" Minna cried. "Joel, my husband—"

I must have spoken, although I do not know what I could have said at that moment, but Joel looked at me, blinking as though he found it difficult to see anything beyond his grief.

"It is not your fault, Gwen. You are guiltless."

If he had shouted accusations at me, that would not have hurt me so much.

"How do you know what has happened to your family?" Minna cried. "Why do you think you know more than God? Perhaps they are all safe and thanking God now for their deliverance."

"No. No, I know my sister. She is saying that the Nazis will not treat Austrian Jews as though they were German Jews and she will pass around a plate of little cakes and tell everyone to behave as though the Germans aren't there."

He tore the last shreds of his shirt.

"They are dead. My family is dead," and I heard him speak their names, first his sister's, then her husband's, and next Kurt Stern.

I ran from that room and out to the kitchen where I put my head in the sink and dry retched.

"You heard him," Minna said. "It is not your fault."

"Oh, but it is, Minna. I could have made Kurt stay here and he'd be safe now."

I must have slept that night because all I can remember are dreadful nightmares of blurred and indistinct terror and when I lay half awake in the early morning the curtains were like spectral hands reaching out to me and everything in the room was strange and terrible. This, I knew, this waste of shapeless forms without meaning was the real universe that we disguise with tricks of intellect and reason when we are not sleeping. Afterwards I went out to the balcony where I found Terry asleep and shivering in a chair, with a blanket slipping from his shoulders. I tucked it round him and he woke and smiled at me.

"I couldn't sleep, so I came out here. I—I like to look at Miramar and think of him over there."

"Ah Terry—"

We sat together, staring at the ugly pink house that was now as silent as a sepulchre. Every morning one of Dolfi's aunts would come out with a basket of washing and hang clothes from two long lines that stretched across the lawn.

"It's not losing the money or the business, Gwen. It's losing Dolfi—"

The news from the ABC was full of accounts of German tanks in Vienna being greeted by a rapturous Austrian crowd. Prominent Australians were asked for their views and among them was Alan, who said that world war was inevitable and Australia must be prepared to defend itself without help from Great Britain. The attorney general, Robert Menzies, maintained that Hitler had limited objectives in Europe that would be reached when all German-speaking people were contained by the Reich.

"We should produce some new serials," Terry said. "Let's really present these Nazis as jackbooted bullies. I'll talk to Athol this morning."

He had already outlined the plot of a thriller called *The Twisted Cross* when the phone rang. It was Morton Silberstein inviting me to have lunch with him at the Australia because he had a deal that I couldn't resist.

I was surprised to find him alone at a table because Carmelo Rossi seemed to have become his constant companion.

"What I have admired about you, Gwen, is your head for business. Some people might think you're dumb because you're so good-looking."

I always enjoyed the cedar panels and potted palms of the Australia because it reminded me of my old friend, Mr Gresham.

"The marriage would be for publicity purposes only—"

I realized that I had missed a number of connecting links and asked Morton to repeat what he'd just said.

"OK, this time without varnish. We know that Dolfi is a fairy, everyone knows that, but if the public doesn't believe it, we don't give a damn, do we? Frankly, I think he's a sleazeball, but when you're used to dealing with actors, your standards drop accordingly. They've seen his films at head office and everyone's crazy about him, but there's this sex problem. However, if we had a publicity marriage, not the kind his father's talking about, the front office would be in seventh heaven." He paused and chewed thoughtfully. "Boy, can you imagine anyone wanting a hire-purchase, sight-unseen bimbo for a wife?"

"It's customary for Sicilians here to send home for brides."

"It wouldn't sell in Peoria, honey. You are the natural choice."

"Morton, you have just described Dolfi as a sleazeball. I think a turd has more appeal and a slug considerably more character than Dolfi."

I went on at some length elaborating on Dolfi's shortcomings while Morton sat back with his jaw hanging.

"You really have the guy down to a T," he said finally.

"And you're proposing marriage to me on his behalf?"

"Publicity purposes only—we'll have the press releases, some Movietone footage—and in the States we announce that his wife is arriving later."

"And I can then get an annulment."

"No problem—there won't be a wedding night. Dolfi will be leaving immediately after the ceremony."

"Well, I did something like this once before and making the same mistake twice seems to be a habit with me. However, I shall need to be compensated for the embarrassment of even appearing to be married to Dolfi."

"The Danny Burns Radio Theatre—"

"Dolfi's share made over to Terry Mapes."

"No, Rossi will agree to hand it over to you."

"Why me and not Terry?"

"Christ! You're asking me to read the mind of a Wop?"

I was suspicious, but Morton explained that Carmelo had weighed the monetary advantages of an MGM contract against forty-nine per cent of the Danny Burns Radio Theatre and decided to relinquish Dolfi's interest. What convinced me was that I did not really care what happened to me so long as I could help Terry. I had read more news of the German invasion in the papers that morning and in a small paragraph it said that Jews were already being rounded up. Kurt would be among them and if I had not—

"Yes, I'll agree to this publicity stunt," I told Morton. "But one hour before the wedding I want Dolfi's signature relinquishing his share of the company. We'll meet at Martin Triggs' before we go to the registry office. I don't imagine you'll want a cathedral wedding."

Morton sat back and lit a cigar.

"You have just made yourself a bundle." He grinned.

"You can count on Miss Gwenadalina to strike a hard bargain," I replied.

We spent the next two weeks recording Dino episodes, with Athol and Murray writing seven and eight scripts a day. When they could no longer see to type, they dictated to shorthand typists and the story continued. Miss Gwenadalina had foolishly fallen in love with Mrs Cholmondley's nephew, Percy the Poofter, who sounded like Roger with a lisp, and it was only Dino who saved her from scandal and ruin. Meanwhile, in the world which delighted to see fiction become reality, the papers were all announcing the forthcoming marriage of Miss Gwen Harcourt to Danny Burns.

Alan stood in the middle of my living room and called me a fool and an idiot. He was so angry that I thought he was going to strike me.

"What are you doing to yourself, Gwen? Why would you even think of marrying something like Danny Burns? What is happening to your life? Do you enjoy having your name bandied around like a character in a comic strip?"

"That's what I am—Miss Gwenadalina Snapper."

"You say it's for publicity purposes only, like someone diving off the Harbour Bridge. But to pretend to marry—"

"It won't be me standing there—it will be Dino the Dago and Miss Gwenadalina. People have been waiting for them to get married for years."

"Can't you see what's happening? You're turning yourself into fiction. Reality isn't Dino the Dago and his antics, it's Gwen Harcourt and—" He stopped abruptly. "You say this is a publicity stunt, but you're prepared to go through a legal form of marriage with Dolfi."

"Nothing but a form. Can you imagine Dolfi wanting to consummate the marriage?"

"Let me see the documents. I want to make quite sure you're not being ambushed."

"Alan, I have excellent legal counsel."

"You're refusing my help then—"

"No, I—this is the only way I can satisfy Rossi. He's a Sicilian and he has—*rispiettu*—he has his pride to consider. He believes that Terry seduced his son—he can never have business dealings with him."

"This is Australia, Gwen."

"Yes, but we have the past inside of us and it's not of this country."

He turned his back on me then and stared out at an ocean liner making its way slowly up the channel.

"Once I thought I knew you, Gwen. Not now—not any longer."

"Do you think I understand myself?" I cried.

"Something has changed you—Are you still in love with Kurt?"

"I can't even answer that. I don't know. What I believe is that I have the *malocchio*—the evil eye—and people who are close to me suffer and die."

"That's preposterous nonsense. Gwen, I'm not going to let you go through with this—this marriage."

"Keep away from me!" I screamed at him. "If you try to help me, you'll end like Kurt or Edith. Everyone close to me suffers or dies. You don't understand these things. It's not because I'm wicked, it's because I'm cursed."

He stepped back from me, and I saw the hurt bewilderment in his face.

"Look what I've done to you, Alan. Thanks to me, your mother is now Valmai Vitale, and I am just as much a figure of scandal as she is."

"Do you imagine I care what people say about me?"

"I do. You're going to stand for election. I've read about it in the papers. You'll either win or lose according to what people think about you. Do you imagine it will help you in politics if you're associated with Miss Gwenadalina who was recently, in another incarnation, the notorious Paris Rose?"

"If I thought—"

Roughly I pushed him away and told him that I didn't want to see him again.

There were deep lines across Alan's forehead and at the sides of his mouth and every word I said to him that afternoon seemed to set his face in anguished planes.

"Nonetheless, if you need my help, call me," he said quietly but I did not respond and walked out to the balcony, closing the doors behind me.

What astounded me was that my friends believed the fiction. I told Norma and Florrie that the marriage was a publicity stunt, but they both behaved as though I were a bride marrying the man of her choice. Henry insisted that he should be allowed to give me away even though I told him that the marriage would be at the registry office opposite Hyde Park and immediately after the ceremony Dolfi, his family and Morton Silberstein would be leaving for the United States. Angelica wanted to be a bridesmaid and when I refused, she sniffled and said she needed the publicity, so I gave her the money to have a new dress made and get her hair permed.

Florrie maintained that Dolfi would be a regular fellow when he was married.

"Look at my Henry!" she said. "He's just something to warm your feet on in bed and not much more than that, but he's a celebrity and everyone wants to meet him."

Norma had a design in mind for a spectacular wedding gown of ivory faille, but I told her that I would be married like Miss Gwenadalina in a plain grey silk.

"Every journalist and photographer in Australia will be there," Norma said plaintively. "You don't deliberately want to look dowdy, do you?"

"Miss Gwenadalina Snapper is not a fashionplate, Norma. Don't you listen to the serial?"

Late at night Terry and I would sit together watching the lights ripple across the water like tangled ribbons, both of us so tired we could barely see.

"You don't have to go through with this for me," Terry said continually.

"The Danny Burns Radio Theatre is ours, Terry. You gave Dolfi his name, you made him whatever he's become."

"No, he's a genius. It was a privilege to help him. I wonder what he's doing now," Terry murmured.

"Playing his latest part."

"The house looks so different now."

"Yes, I hear that some of the neighbours are going to complain formally about the washing on the harbourfront."

Flapping eerily on the lawn at Miramar, the sheets were held fast to lines by *chiaccu*, the loops of string and rings that I had last seen Rosalia use. There was still a faint aroma of pasta *colle sarde* on the air.

One question nagged me. "I wonder why they're insisting on signing the shares over to me as Mrs Brunner?"

"Pride, I suppose. Mr Rossi believes that I corrupted his son."

"Perhaps—"

Terry's explanation made sense but I did not find it as convincing as it had been when I used it to counter Alan's arguments. I began to wake at night and wonder what role I had been given in this particular story.

I called or went to see Joel and Minna every day. Joel told me that he had met Alan and they were trying to get government support for Jewish refugees.

"It's not easy," Joel said bitterly. "Look at this—" He threw a copy of the *Bulletin* across the table to me and I saw a cartoon of a ship passing between the Heads with a figure on the prow that was a caricature of a Jewish man with a gigantic hook nose.

"The *Bulletin* is beginning to sound like Goebbels' *Der Stürmer*," he added.

"Have you heard our new serial?" I asked.

"Wonderful," Minna sighed. "So exciting, that nice young Australian who is trying to get his Jewish wife out of Germany. I sit and listen and cry."

"We need more than words from a little box to save the Jews," Joel said. "This Alan Gilchrist is a sensible, good man and he is trying to help us. He knows there is going to be a war, but do you think he can get the politicians in Canberra to listen to him? No, they sit up there and think they are living on the moon and all they talk about is whether there's going to be another depression."

Joel, I knew, was sending cable after cable to Austria, but there was never any reply.

"I'm sure they're safe," Minna would say. "People like that float to the surface of trouble and survive it."

"You stupid old woman!" Joel shouted. "That's what they believe. 'We give no trouble and therefore the Nazis won't notice that we're Jews.' "

"I should have made Kurt stay," I whispered.

"No!" Joel's hand was over mine and holding it so tightly that I flinched. "No, you made a decision according to your conscience. They are dead, my family is dead."

"You don't know that!" Minna cried.

"I know *in mein Herz*."

"Who are you to challenge God in this way?" she cried.

They quarrelled and I sat there remembering the night when I was at that table and saw Kurt, looking like a prince from the Arabian Nights with his dark gaze.

"This crazy marriage—"

Minna was shaking her finger at me.

"It is to help a friend. She's explained that to you," Joel said.

"Even a fake marriage should be decent. Where is the ring?"

"No ring—no wedding party," I said sourly. "We sign the papers at the solicitors and then we go to the registry office. After that, Dolfi's on his way to the States and there's only one thing that would make me go with him. I would like to be there when Frau Brunner meets Carmelo Rossi and his sisters again."

As I was leaving Minna pressed something into my hand.

"Take it. You shouldn't have given it back to me. It's unlucky to return diamonds."

It was the diamond that Kurt had had set for me as an engagement ring.

"Wear it because—for a time—you loved him," Minna said.

I slipped the ring on my finger but in the darkness of the hall there was no reflecting light from the stone.

Reporters tried to push past the doorman at Trelawney and every time I went out I was followed by photographers. Terry and I managed to elude them by using a little dinghy to get around the point to a spot where we left the car. There would be another gang of them outside the studio. Dolfi posed and gave interviews incessantly in which he related the passion for me that began when we were children; the romance grew like some monstrous vine until the last vestige of truth was choked by its exuberant foliage and vivid flowers. The more abrupt and terse I was with the reporters, the more I became Miss Gwenadalina Snapper. I pushed through them, refusing to speak, and they would call gleefully after me, "Come on, Miss Snapper, just a word. We'll put an apple on your desk if you'll just give us a word or two."

We believe what we want to believe: that is the definition of faith and a dominant principle of the fiction that is more often called life. Everyone was caught up in the fiction of Dino's marriage to his beloved Miss Gwenadalina, except those who were creating the make-believe, and there were times when even Dolfi seemed to imagine that he was Dino. Terry drove me to Martin Triggs' offices and I found the room crowded with Morton, Carmelo Rossi, Dolfi and two other solicitors. The documents were spread out across the table and I checked them carefully before I spoke.

"It's clearly understood that when these are signed and witnessed, the Danny Burns Radio Theatre becomes my property."

There was a general chorus of assent, except from Carmelo Rossi, who was sitting over to one side, his plump hands on his knees, his small mouth pursed in the faintest suggestion of a smile.

Dolfi signed with a flourish and handed the documents to me, saying that it was my wedding present.

Martin Triggs then gave me another set of documents and I signed over fifty per cent of the Danny Burns Radio Theatre to Terry Mapes.

"Fifty per cent?" Terry murmured.

"We are equal partners. I can trust you," I said and Dolfi sniggered.

Dolfi and his father left then in order to arrive at the registry office first and I heard the whoops and shouts of the crowd outside.

"A regular circus," Martin Triggs said at the window.

As he spoke those three words, I felt as though I were being carried into the darkness.

Henry was waiting in the car for me, wearing a morning suit with a carnation in his buttonhole, a grey top hat on the seat beside him.

"My public," he said apologetically. "It's what they expect from the Reverend Whiffle. Merely what they expect, you know."

"Is Valmai going to be there too?"

"Oh, sure to be. You couldn't keep the old bitch out of the limelight if you threw a ton of cement over her."

I saw her on the top step of the registry office where the police had set up barricades. She had a flower bed for a hat and carried an enormous frilled parasol in case people found it difficult to recognize her. Just behind her, as close to Dolfi as she could get, Angelica was pirouetting and smiling over a bouquet of roses.

Two policemen pushed a path through the crowd and Dolfi put out a hand and pulled me alongside him.

All I could see were grinning, laughing faces stretching out into the road, a sea of gaping mouths and round eyes. I felt the wires at my wrists and ankles.

"That's the film crew over there," Dolfi pointed. "They're American—"

"Let's go in and finish this charade," I muttered.

"I always said I'd make you love me," Dolfi said.

"Love you?" I stared at him in amazement.

"Give her a kiss, Dino!" a man was shouting.

"Don't be scared of her. She won't really snap," another yelled.

"Don't you remember, Gina? You'll have to say it when you're marrying me."

"This is not a marriage, Dolfi."

He was almost hugging himself with excitement and first he giggled and placed a hand across his mouth. Then it came blurting forth.

"Oh, but it is, *carissima*. And when you're my wife, all property is shared jointly. We'll both have fifty per cent of the Radio Theatre."

"Go on, kiss her," someone was shouting, as I felt a gust of illuminating rage that almost pushed me forward on to my knees.

"It's a real marriage for me, *carissima*. Just as Mama always planned. Have you forgotten that she expected us to marry?"

All I wanted then was to put my head down and run through the crowd, but the people were like a guffawing, roaring wall in front of me.

"You lied—"

"Not really. You believed, everyone believed that the marriage was not real except Papa and me. We knew what we wanted."

It began as a sound of thunder over the noise of the crowd and I saw some of the people stirring nervously and looking down as if the pavement was collapsing under their feet. The thunder became the ringing clash of hoof beats. Once again I fell headlong into a dream.

Eight grey Clydesdales were pulling a brewery wagon laden with beer barrels and standing on the top of them, shaking the reins and laughing, was Beau Liddel.

"Out of the way!" he shouted and drove the wagon through the crowd.

The great horses towered over the people, their blinkered heads like cresting waves, the cymbal clangour of their hooves sonorous with the music of a hundred brass bells chiming along the shining black harness. If people were celebrating an everyday fiction that morning, something from vanished time came tramping over their fragile make-believe with a myth born of wine and forgetting in wild places where passions ruled and reason slept. The actors were rehearsing their play and defending themselves with wooden swords when suddenly the cardboard dragon was alive and advancing on them with glittering scales and smoking nostrils. Holiday revellers were out in the field when from the sombre woods a chariot came down upon them with a horde of wild Maenads and their little games were turned to riot by the gods. Police whistles were blowing, people falling back from the horses and Beau Liddel jumped down from his high place and threw me across his shoulder. He urged on the horses as I slid to his side and clung to his arm while the lurching, grinding wagon began to move through the crowd and out on to the street. I remember he was drunk and swaying on his feet and I was laughing as if the whole world had become a dream.

4

Avalon

Forty

The great wagon careered down the road with the cathedral on one side, the park and its frozen gods on the other, and when I looked back they had all become desultory shrunken puppets: Valmai's parasol had blown out across the crowd, Angelica was screaming and Dolfi and Carmelo Rossi were shaking their fists at me and jigging up and down as if their wires were being jerked by someone in a frenzy. Two police sidecars followed us, shouting at Beau to stop, but he shook the reins and the massive grey horses put their heads down and pounded the asphalt as though determined to crack it apart and gallop down to the underworld.

"Why did you come for me?" I asked him through my laughter.

"I ran out of grapes," he guffawed, "and I didn't think you'd fancy a bag of raisins."

He was so drunk he could barely stand, the smell of beer and wine and whisky set the Apollo of the fountain dancing on top of the cathedral like St Cosimo on the *sagrato* of Santa Maria di Gesu. One arm was outstretched in a futile demand for calm and order while everything danced and exploded in a thousand carnival shapes and all time became one in configurations without meaning. The puppets had vanished, the bells clashed as he gave the horses their heads and I wanted nothing more at that moment than to forget everything I was and share his madness.

At the corner of William Street there was a waiting Rolls-Royce with Taps at the wheel. Beau swung the cart round so that it blocked the path of the sidecars, which had to swerve to avoid hitting the barricade of horses. We jumped down and climbed into the car and Taps roared up the hill to King's Cross.

"It wasn't my idea," Taps said mournfully over his shoulder, and that made us laugh all the more. He drove down two side streets and up an alley to an open garage. As soon as we were inside, he pulled down the door and locked it, then trotted over to a Daimler that was facing into an open yard full of boxes and rusting cans. Laughing, we fell on to the back seat, while he steered the car around the debris to a passage between two houses and through another alley. Just as we reached the corner we saw the police followed by the Movietone news screeching off towards the front of the garage.

"This is a very convenient place." Beau hiccuped. "Belongs to a friend of mine, an SP bookie who occasionally likes to drive in the front door and leave by the back."

"Where are we going?" I asked him.

"Where they won't find us."

When we reached the Museum in William Street, he craned out the window and grinned as he saw the wagon being driven sedately down College Street by its driver, the great horses lifting their feet as delicately as old ladies stepping across puddles.

"Smart feller that—I told him where to wait for me."

"You rescued me," I said gleefully.

"I wasn't going to let you marry that little Burns twit."

"They're all—" I was choking with laughter. "They're all going to think it's part of the show. Miss Gwenadalina abducted, and poor Dino jilted at the registry office. Only—" I rolled sideways, laughing. "Only Dolfi and his father thought it was going to be a real marriage and they'd get half the business and I—I—" It was impossible to go on and I leaned back trying to catch my breath.

The span of the Harbour Bridge was over my head and I wondered where we were going, yet nothing seemed to matter except that I felt drunk with happiness. Beau was drinking from a silver flask which he offered to me while Taps clucked disapprovingly.

"You shouldn't—you really shouldn't, Mr Liddel. You've had more than enough and you shouldn't get Miss Harcourt started on it."

The brandy was like fire and after I'd coughed and spluttered, I stared at Beau with his russet hair and blue eyes that changed colour when you looked at them.

"I think you're a god," I said finally.

He roared and slapped his knees and then said finally that I was making him feel like one.

"Gods are terrible beings," I replied with tipsy solemnity. "They're gods because they govern the passions and when they mix with human beings they bring madness and—"

"Love," Beau said, and I shivered because never in my life had I felt such a tide of reckless, abandoned lust sweep over me. I wanted to tear off my dress and pull him down on top of me, thrusting my tongue between his lips, pushing my breasts against his chest, stretching my legs wide for him to enter me. With a gasping cry I covered my face with my hands so that I could no longer see him and tried to fight my way back to reason.

"Don't be afraid of me," he said gently. "I'd never hurt you."

Was this what my parents felt for each other? A passion of such anguish it was like pain throbbing in every nerve, an agony so intense that reason fell prostrate before it. My brain protested that I was drunk and exhausted, while my flesh shrieked derisively at its arguments and demanded the satisfaction of lust. With an effort of will that left me shuddering I forced myself to look out the window and to ask again where we were going.

"I own a lot of property," Beau said yawning. "I don't think people know about this one." He leaned back and closed his eyes.

"Don't worry, Miss Harcourt," Taps said. "He'll doze off like that for an hour or so, and then he'll be wide awake and wanting to know where I've hidden the booze. I try to keep him sober, I really do," he added plaintively.

"Who cares?" I smiled. "I hope he keeps me forever."

"Don't say that lightly, Miss Harcourt. He fell for that picture of yours first and then when he saw you at Randwick, he was like someone possessed—"

Beau was asleep and I thought I could see a lion stretched out in the sun or some great animal that seemed to be all other animals in one shape. I was drunk, I knew that, but I was also crazy—*pazzo*, as Rosalia used to say of my father. Deliberately, I tried to think about Dolfi and the wedding and that made me giggle uncontrollably. We were driving through the northern suburbs where the houses were becoming fewer; occasionally I saw the sea. I tried to think about Kurt and then I knew that something very strange was happening to my mind because suddenly everything was irrelevant and unimportant and even as I was trying to recall Kurt, he became less than a name to me. Yawning, I fell asleep in Beau's lap.

Taps was shaking me gently and I sleepily followed him down a shadowy path under flowering gums with birds calling all around me. The air was heavy with the fragrance of resin, honey and salt; scarlet and gold butterflies dipped and floated from one pool of sunlight to another. I heard the surf sounding at a distance and while something in my head told me I was near one of the beaches north of the city, another more imperative voice said this was a dream.

"Beau?" I asked Taps.

"Oh, he'll come down when he wakes up," Taps replied.

There was a garden at the back of the house where the bush surrounded a stone path and touched the windows. A creek cascaded down from a fern-covered cliff into a rock pool and as Taps led me into the house I saw a wallaby in the shadows and koalas in the high branches.

"It's a great place for animals," Taps said. "Sometimes I reckon there are more inside that garden than out in the bush. Mr Liddel seems to attract them."

It was a low wooden house that led out to a long veranda and from there you could see the surf and a scarf of white sand.

"Where am I?" I asked drowsily.

"Avalon."

It was late afternoon when I woke in that shadowy room. I was still wearing the dun-coloured silk that belonged to Miss Gwenadalina and I dragged it off and walked over it as I went to the bathroom and showered. I couldn't find any clothes so I wrapped a towel around me and looked for Taps. The house was deserted, but outside by the rock pool a bird was dancing, pluming feathers glinting bronze and gold as it moved through the shafts of sunlight. Everywhere through the trees and above my head there was a stirring, and a rustling among the bushes and ferns. I trod softly, finding steps that led to the beach. The breeze was cold and I shivered and was about to turn back to the house when I saw him striding up through the surf, throwing handfuls of torn weed to either side of him.

"Come and swim with me," he called.

This was dreaming, for he was naked and yet, as he walked up through the creaming froth of surf, it was as if the dying sun was taking new life from his body.

"Nobody wears clothes here." He smiled and took the towel from me.

I didn't protest because everything he said and did seemed as natural as the sand under my feet and the sun dazzling my eyes.

"That's the kind of surf I like." I saw the waves like dark walls crashing down in a chaos of churning spume.

"It's too dangerous," I said faintly.

"I'll bring you in on my shoulders," he said and I followed him through the torn curtains of spray.

"Dive when I tell you," he shouted and I followed him into a welter of churning sand and water where the surge tossed and beat me. Struggling, my breath almost gone, I plunged down again and found myself in a hollow between the waves.

"Dive now!" he called but even as I tried to say that I was exhausted, the wave crashed down on top of me. I was being dragged by my hair, and kicking wildly, I tried frantically to swim. Twice more he made me dive and then we were so far from the beach that I could see only a thread of white against a distant shore.

"I'll pick the wave and we'll ride in," he shouted.

I felt the heavy swell under me and suddenly I remembered that sharks came in to shore to feed at night, and we were beyond the breakers on a deserted beach. Panic was sweeping over me, my heart beating so frantically that I thought it would burst as I saw shadows in the water.

"Sharks!" I cried faintly.

"We'll race them in." Beau laughed and told me to put my hands on his shoulders.

I would have stood on top of him to escape from that glassy terrible water when suddenly he kicked under me and put his head down into the wave. I swam and felt the water rushing past me as he was lifted so high that all I could see was the green cliff below me. I knew if I let go of his shoulder I would be swept back to whatever was following us and I dug my nails into his flesh as the wave bulged and carried us up on a spreading crest.

"Now swim for your life!" I heard him shout as the wave broke around us and something clammy wound itself around my throat. Desperately, I flung myself forward and felt sand under me. Twice I was knocked down by the surf, then he was reaching out for me.

Weed was tangled in my hair and Beau laughed as I fell on to the sand and put my head on my knees.

"You're a madman," I said finally. "We could have drowned or been taken by sharks."

"I didn't see any. Sometimes a few cruise around out there but I think you saw shadows."

"Nobody swims at this time of day."

"That's why I prefer it—this and dawn. You can't just take nature when she's calm and smiling, you have to accept her in every mood if you want to know her."

We walked the length of the beach and not once did I think it strange that I should be naked and alone with this man. The breeze was cold and he pulled me to him.

"You're going to stay with me," he said and I nodded.

His body was warm and when he held me to him and kissed me I felt that same surging passion lifting me like the wave that had carried us to the beach.

"I want you to love me," I said urgently and his lips were in my hair and on my mouth and my breasts. We coupled as animals might on a mound of broken seaweed with our blood roaring against the thunder of the surf and gulls screaming into the wind. Nothing had meaning except the driving pulse of his flesh in my body and the passion exploding like stars. I fell back spent and looked up into his face. The serpent on my tongue and in my heart was dead.

There were no clothes for me in the house so I wrapped myself in one of Beau's robes as Taps set a table on the veranda.

"I went into the store at Avalon and phoned Henry," Taps said briskly. "Everyone thinks it was a publicity stunt. Mr Gilchrist was very disturbed but Henry calmed him down eventually. Danny Burns had a regular tizzy and was screaming that you'd robbed him. Nobody understood what he was talking about."

"I hope he leaves for America soon."

I wasn't clear what day it was or how long I had been in this house.

"Oh yes, a whole crowd is going down to the boat to see him off."

"Terry—"

"Henry said he'd let everyone know you're all right." He paused. "It was nice having an opportunity to talk to him."

Beau came out and kissed me as Taps looked away discreetly.

"Taps, we'll start with champagne and follow that with the white burgundy and—"

"Mr Liddel, please—"

"I need wine to celebrate."

Everything he did filled me with an exultation and we fell on the food and drink like people crazed with hunger and thirst. The moon was slipping in and out between the clouds, the breeze had dropped and only the surf sounded like a distant drum in the silence. Possums came down the vines, treading lightly along the balcony ledge and taking bread and fruit from our hands.

"I think—I may stop drinking quite so much for you, Gwen."

"Could you?" I smiled.

"I shall try," he said solemnly and belched.

I looked across the table at the empty bottles and knew I was almost as tipsy as he was.

"Who are you?" I asked him.

"Everyone knows Beau Liddel," he replied.

"You deserve to be called Beau," I said, reaching out to touch his arm hazed with bronze hair.

"The Beau is short for Beaufort—old family name. It came with money so my parents didn't refuse although I think my father would have preferred to call me Bill."

"You must be a very wealthy man."

"Yes, I reckon I am. You're not poor yourself, are you?"

"No—but there are degrees of wealth."

"Mine's old money, it came out in bundles from England and the Australian Liddels made more. My brother runs the property near Scone —he's married, no kids."

"Are you married?"

"No—" He put back his head and guffawed. "I don't like being tied to anything except this—" He gestured to the trees and the sky. "She's hard to please and she was all I wanted until I saw your face in the sky. Driving up William Street and suddenly—above me against the clouds."

We sat silently and I tried to think, but everything except the wine in my mouth and the glistening black eyes of the possums slipped from my head. It was as if I were being kept in an everlasting present, content to be held in mindless feeling, undisturbed by intellect or memory.

"I could live with you," he said. "I knew that when I saw you at the races."

Rosalia drifted across my mind and I remembered her saying that no spell was stronger than time. I knew with absolute certainty that this fragrant night and the man I loved so passionately would disappear, but not yet— not soon—I prayed.

Kurt would have mocked at our lovemaking because we had no tricks or games to arouse the senses; it was, instead, a guileless locking of flesh that was like nothing I had ever experienced or will again. Time is like God, as Rosalia said, and there is a time when a king comes into your life who may be just another man at a different time when the order of senses is changed.

We spent three days at Avalon, swimming out beyond the breaking surf and riding the great waves in to the shore, lying in the garden, watching the life of the bush come down to the rock pools, and drinking until Taps said quietly at my shoulder one evening, "Don't—please don't get started, Miss Harcourt. There's no end to it—"

He drove us back to the city on Thursday when Beau said he had to see his horses.

"If you'd decided to marry that little twit on a Saturday, someone else would have had to rescue you." He grinned. "Saturday is sacred to horses."

If Beau had any occupation, it was racing, and he kept one of the largest stables in Sydney. He rocked with laughter when I told him about Dolfi's horses.

"Those weren't horses he bought. They were goats with long legs. Everyone said you could sell Danny Burns a broken rocking horse."

When I walked into Trelawney, McGregor greeted me as if I had been away for a hundred years, and I felt like someone who had fallen asleep in a fairy ring and woken in a different world. Terry ran towards me and hugged me, crying and laughing at the same time. After being held by Beau, this was like a bird in my arms.

"My God! Where have you been? What have you been doing? You look as though you were shipwrecked."

The reflection in the Florentine mirror showed a wild woman with tangled black hair falling over her shoulders, barefoot, wearing a man's shirt held at the waist with a piece of string.

"I've been in Avalon. Beau has a house there," I replied simply.

"I'll run your bath and get some supper on the table. I hope you can persuade Mr Mapes to eat something," McGregor said as I poured myself a whisky.

"You're all right?" Terry's voice was anxious, his face drawn with fatigue and lack of sleep.

"Yes," I replied slowly, "I think I'm becoming someone else and I'm not sure who it is. If Bessie were here—"

Only Bessie remained fixed in my mind and I remember one morning—was it that first time I went to Avalon, or was it another?—when I was lazily making a wall against the sea and I told Beau about Bessie.

"If you saw her now, you probably wouldn't know her," he said bluntly.

"That's not true! I would always know her."

"Ah, but you lost her when you were kids. What's happened to her since? She may be fat with a pack of kids—"

"She could be dead," I said quietly.

"No, she'll come back to you," he said firmly. "But you must be careful to recognize her, because she'll be different."

Terry was speaking and I struggled to concentrate.

"Some people say he should be certified. If he didn't have so much money, he'd be locked up."

"I'm in love with him, Terry."

"There's nothing I can say then except—"

"Not even that. What's happening at the studio?"

"Oh, we're recording just the same. There'll be auditions next week. Of course, we'll never be able to replace Dolfi."

His eyes filled with tears as he spoke and he jerked his narrow shoulders irritably and grimaced.

"I shouldn't be so selfish. After all, this is what I always wanted for him—fame and fortune in Hollywood."

"Is that really what you imagine is going to happen?"

"Dolfi is a genius. He—"

"Dolfi was wandering around the docks starving when you found him and made him Danny Burns. What do you think his father will do for him? Can you see Carmelo Rossi and his two sisters managing a film star?"

And what, I wondered, would Dolfi's next role be?

"Dolfi spoke to me before he left. It was awful, Gwen. He accused me of arranging that stunt with the brewery wagon."

"Oh, let him imagine what he likes. Terry, we're partners now, but—I may often be at Avalon with Beau."

If I concentrated on Bessie I could hold the pattern of my mind that always slipped and blurred whenever I saw Beau and felt the riot and joy of his love.

"Oh, I can manage for a while. Athol wants to help produce and I think I can find some more writers."

"Dolfi thought—" I doubled over laughing.

"Yes, he told me that you were betrothed to him when you were children. He seemed to think that once you were married all the property would be shared as it is in Sicily."

"His father's advice, no doubt."

We sat together on the balcony and I tried to make Terry eat.

"Nothing has any taste—when I'm working, the pain is not so bad. I really shouldn't be here, Gwen, but I haven't had time to find a flat."

"I want you to stay here, Terry. I shall be with Beau—wherever he lives in Sydney."

It was an old sprawling red-brick house in Randwick set up high above the road on a corner overlooking the racecourse, and half a mile from Wes Tidgett's stables where Beau kept his string of horses. Steep white marble steps led up from the street to a tiled veranda where Beau had a chair and his binoculars. "In case I'm too drunk to get to the course," he said genially. But he was not drinking so heavily these days and Taps continually said what a good influence I was on him.

"Looking after Mr Liddel is not just a job," Taps said. "It's more like a vocation. You never know what he'll get up to next. Every time he takes a brewery wagon he explains to the magistrate that it will never happen again if they'll only give him back his licence to drive a car. So he pays the fine and the magistrate says that if he's even seen in the front seat of a car it will be a prison sentence."

Everybody told me I was making a fool of myself and I laughed at them because I loved Beau as I never have any other man. Granted, I may have been mad at that time, but it was a madness fraught with moments of vatic insight.

"Do you know why I'm different from other men?" he once asked me. "Because I know that I'm an animal and I don't deny my nature. Sometimes

I look at them, prancing along with high collars and bow ties, and they remind me of performing seals with clowns' hats and frills around their necks. That's when I have to strip off and walk like an animal with other animals who know what they are."

And there was always laughter—

Billy Garvin discovered the house in Randwick and one morning when I went down to the car I found him squatting outside the front gate with a photographer spitting leisurely into the garden.

"You are going to let us have a story, aren't you? I mean—you and Beau Liddel—when are you getting married?"

I pushed past him cursing, but the following Sunday I was on the front page of *Truth* with a luridly titillating account of my past.

"What can you see in this Liddel *vishcrob*?" Minna cried and Joel raised his hands and shook his head.

"Watch your step," Florrie and Norma said to me in unison and Florrie added that everyone knew Beau Liddel was crazy.

One evening, after Beau and I had been to the course watching his horses train, Alan came to the house in Randwick. His shoulders were hunched and I could see the concern in his eyes when he looked at me.

"You read the newspapers, don't you?" he said tersely. "Menzies wants to ship pig iron to Japan that will undoubtedly be delivered back to us as bullets."

"Yes—yes, I heard something about it," I said vaguely.

"Do you mind if I speak honestly to you—"

"When have you ever done anything else, Alan?" I smiled.

"First, I'd like to ask you if you're taking drugs."

"No—" I laughed. "I'm probably drinking more than I should but—"

"You couldn't do anything else with Beau Liddel."

"We're going to be married—"

"When?"

"Oh, soon—"

"I don't doubt that he loves you, Gwen. That isn't difficult, but I know Beau. We were at school together. He was a larrikin then and he hasn't changed now. Beau Liddel wasn't just a juvenile vandal, there were dozens of those. No, there was something odd about him that made most of the boys a little afraid of him. A streak of the irrational. Boys run wild, that's expected, but they don't throw a master through a window. That's what Beau did."

"I hope it wasn't a high window." I giggled.

For a moment he stared at me, anger drawing taut lines in his face. In that instant I wanted to put out my hand to draw him to me, yet it was no more than a thought and instantly I felt a dreaming fill my head and comfort my heart.

"What is he doing to you, Gwen—you never sounded like this before."

Beau came in and stood frowning at Alan and then his face lit up.

"God almighty, it's young Alan Gilchrist. I haven't seen you for years."

"No, we never had the same interests until now, Beau."

A note of laconic calm was in Alan's voice but he did not smile as Beau grasped his hand.

"He was a regular little swot at Grammar," Beau chuckled. "Always carting off an armload of cups at speech day. Well—" He paused. "Are you here to try and knock me down?"

"I'm a lawyer, remember," Alan said drily.

"That's a pity." Beau sighed. "You had all the makings of an honest man. Seriously though, I wouldn't mind hiring you when I'm next in trouble. You'd help me if I needed you, wouldn't you?"

"Is this what you want?" Alan said to me, gesturing at Beau.

"With all my heart," I replied.

The one person who approved wholeheartedly of Beau was Angelica and she was so often at the Randwick house that we gave her a room at the back with her own entrance.

"Aren't you sharing a flat with Sheila any more?" I asked her.

"Sheila? I haven't seen her for ages," Angelica replied. "I saw her once last year and she's even fatter than she was before. Can you imagine? I wouldn't be seen dead walking down the street with her."

"You're still engaged to Jack, aren't you?"

"Oh yes, I suppose so," she said offhandedly. "But he's teaching down the South Coast and he can't afford to get up here often. I've told him that we can't talk about marriage for ages. After all, I have my stage career now."

I noticed that she was wearing a medal on a gold chain and I suddenly recognized St Rosalia.

"Did your aunt send you that?" I asked.

Angelica flushed scarlet and pushed the medal down into her blouse.

"My aunt? Don't make a cat laugh. She wouldn't give me the time of day. No, one of my friends in the chorus gave it to me. I took it because it's—" She faltered and then said cheekily, "It's supposed to keep your lover faithful to you so I won't have to worry about Jack, will I?"

Taps detested her and told me that she was always running up to the shops at the corner.

"To buy herself some food when we're away," I said.

"I'm not so sure. Mrs Corcoran comes in regular every day and the pantry's always full."

"She probably buys chocolate and crisps and things like that."

"She could be selling our groceries up there," he muttered darkly.

"Taps! Don't be absurd."

"Just the same, I'm going to ask Mrs Corcoran to keep a sharp eye out for anything missing from the pantry."

As it was, we hardly saw Angelica because our time was divided between the stables, Avalon and Beau's own property near his brother's at Scone. I went to the opening night of every production she was in at the Theatre Royal, however, and proudly saw her name, Angela Scarf, listed as a member of the chorus. She was never close to me—and if I had been honest I would have said that I did not particularly care for her—but *destino* had made her part of my life and I had not failed her as I once did Margaret Moglen. I daresay that gave me some peculiar satisfaction even though I did not really know her or try to look behind her pat phrases and silly affectations. She was always borrowing money and always gushing her undying affection for me, yet I think that she meant less to me than a pet dog. I was not responsible for what happened to Angelica, but sometimes I wonder if I could have discovered the terrible power in that small body had I studied her as my parents taught me to examine everything. Still, I was pleased that she had done well for herself when she kicked her way across the stage with eleven other girls who were exactly the same height and looked the same as she did. Beau said she reminded him of a dancing flea and promptly went to sleep on my shoulder to the audible annoyance of a stout little woman behind us.

Those months made me feel as if I had found the land of the Lotus Eaters, except that with Beau the passions were urgent and every convention was flouted. We talked about marriage and once Beau pulled me out of bed and said we were going to get it over and done with and I drove him down to the registry office. Blearily, we looked around, wondering why there was so little traffic, realizing suddenly that it was a bank holiday and all government offices were closed.

We sat in the car laughing and Beau said, "You will be my wife, won't you?"

When I reminded him that I was barren he chuckled and said that he would give me a child.

"How?"

"Don't you know by now?" He laughed.

"You'll have to think of something different," I retorted, and Beau put his hand under my chin and turned my face to his.

"You are going to have a kid—"

Because I had no memory at that time and nothing really disturbed my blissful content, I told him I would like to have the child soon.

"You're on," he said, and we drove back to Randwick and had brandy flips for breakfast.

Billy Garvin was still following us and every Sunday there was another instalment of the life of Miss Paris Rose, Miss Gwenadalina and now the "very special friend of socialite punter and pastoralist, Beau Liddel."

A few days after Garvin's last effusion, I came down to the car where Beau was waiting for me to drive him round to the stable.

"I've got a surprise for you," he said.

There was a thumping and a banging in the back of the car and I was about to pull over to the side and stop.

"I think I've hit something," I said.

"It's nothing, keep going—"

The thumps and bangs continued all the way to the stable. As soon as we were in the yard, Beau jumped out and lifted up the boot. Billy Garvin was lying there in a crumpled heap.

"I'll finish you for this, Liddel," he screamed. "You won't be able to live in this country. You don't realize the power of the press."

"You don't appreciate the power of shit," Beau retorted, dragging Billy out by the scruff of his neck.

In the corner of the yard there was a vast steaming mound of manure and rank hay that had just been swept out of the stables. Roaring with laughter, Beau swung Billy up into the air and dropped him into the middle of it. Every time he came up for air, Beau pushed him down with his foot until Tobbo, the stable hand, said he thought that Billy was done for. Everyone stood back and after a few minutes, Billy slowly crawled out on his hands and knees.

"That," Beau said genially, "was just the hors d'oeuvre. You have no idea what I have in mind for the main course."

Billy was cowed and Beau walked the filly that he had just bought me around the yard.

"I've called her Gwen's Girl and she'll win her first race for you in two weeks' time."

The chestnut filly had a golden mane and bright intelligent eyes that seemed to approve of me. I put out my hand to her and she nuzzled her soft nose into my palm.

"Yes, I fell for her too when I first saw her," Beau said quietly and we stood together, stroking the horse that bright June morning.

Forty-One

Madness can only end in sanity or death, and sometimes I think death may well be the easier resolution. In the beginning, when Beau and I were lovers, I was always intoxicated with passion, riot and liquor. I drank with him, not glass for glass, for no one could match Beau, but in those first months I was always tipsy. "People grieve in different ways," I remember Joel once saying to me at their house. "This is not the best way." Yet with Beau I felt exalted, as though we stood in a circle of light where nothing had any meaning unless we'd drunk a toast to it: the rest of the world was huddled outside in the shadows of sober logic and drab reason. Above all, when Beau was with me, it was as if I had no memory. Occasionally, people from that other world intruded and I remember it was in July of 1938 that Terry came to me looking more bedraggled and harassed than ever.

"Someone has to go to Melbourne to see the sponsors and sell the new serials. Thank heavens, Valmai and Henry are more popular than ever, but the shows won't sell themselves. Can you—?"

I was irritated by his request because I guiltily knew that I had done nothing for the Radio Theatre for weeks.

"Oh—when do you want me to go?"

"Next week. Please, Gwen, there's so much to do. Athol and I can manage the production side but we've never handled the selling. You know the sponsors—"

"All right." I yawned. "Beau won't like it. My horse is racing on the following Saturday. I'll have to be back by then."

I saw the same expression in Terry's face that I had seen reflected in so many of my friends.

"You—you're all right, aren't you?" he asked gently.

"Why is everyone so concerned about me? You all behave as if some old witch, a *magara*, had made a wax doll of me and stuck pins into its head."

"No—no, it's just that you seem—possessed."

"Have you forgotten what it was like to be in love?" I laughed and Terry flinched as if I had struck him.

Beau raged when I told him I was going to Melbourne.

"Damn you!" he shouted, throwing a bottle against the wall. "I want you with me! God! You're the only woman I've been able to stand for more than ten minutes. Do you think I want you wandering off around the bush selling those flaming serials? How much is that rotten little business of yours worth? I'll write you a cheque for it now."

"It's not what it means to me, it's for Terry—he's my friend."

"Bloody little fairy."

"Wouldn't you help a mate if he needed you?"

That, I knew, was the appeal no Australian could ever refuse.

"I—oh well, if you have to go—but remember, Saturday at 2.15, Gwen's Girl is going to break all records in the maiden handicap. What we need now is to get that old Shylock, Joel Aaron, to set decent odds and you'll be making more money on that one race than you would in a year selling serials."

Taps drove me to the station and told me he'd keep an eye on Beau.

"By the way, Mrs Corcoran says that your niece has been seeing a fellow. When we were at Avalon she—"

"It's probably her fiancé. He's a schoolteacher down the South Coast."

"I'm just warning you."

I hardly listened to him because I needed a drink and wondered whether to get one at the station or wait until I was on the train. It was not easy selling the serials without Danny Burns as our star, but once the sponsors heard the records and realized that radio drama could flourish without Dolfi, they all renewed their contracts. Besides, Terry had found a young actor from Tasmania who could give an eerily accurate imitation of Dolfi, and he was now playing Dino in our top comedy.

"I wonder how long it will take people to forget Danny Burns," one man said to me. "Out of sight, out of mind. That's show business. Have you had any news from him?"

"None," I replied.

"Funny—I would have thought they'd be getting out the publicity on his new Hollywood film by now."

When Beau was not with me, I saw with different eyes and, as I was hurrying down Collins Street, it occurred to me how many Europeans there were in the crowd. Their long overcoats and briefcases set them apart from the Australians, and when I stood beside two of them and heard them speaking, I remembered Kurt and it was as if someone had thrust a knife into my stomach. Why hadn't I thought about Kurt and wondered where he was? Where had I been these last weeks? The two Austrian Jews were lost and trying to read the street signs through the rain. Haltingly, they asked a passing man for help but he scowled, told them to learn bloody English, and walked on. I did what I could for them, then realized I had minutes to catch my train.

Nothing troubled me when I was with Beau, I assured myself, settling back into my seat and sipping a brandy. The express would get me to Albury by midnight and then I could sleep on the *Spirit of Progress* until I woke in Sydney in time to drive to Randwick and the races. Beau stood at the portals of my mind and defended it against memory, and I was no longer carried to the grotto when I slept.

Rain beat against the windows; through the sound of the engine and the wheels, thunder echoed like a battle being fought across the mountains. The jolting halt sent me sprawling across the opposite seat as I dazedly tried to see where we were. All the lights in the train had gone out. People were running up and down the corridors and the door to my compartment was jerked open by a guard with a lantern.

"There's going to be a delay, miss," he said. "The line's up ahead and all the power's out."

"I must be in Sydney by noon tomorrow," I said.

"Not a hope. We haven't heard if they're going to hold the *Progress* at Albury."

It was a little before seven o'clock in the evening when the taxi left me at Randwick and I ran up the steps laughing and calling for Beau; at the station, I had glimpsed the list of winners and prices on a placard and Gwen's Girl had won at six to one.

"Oh my God, miss—"

Taps was at the door, shaking, his face ashen.

"If you'd only been here—"

"Where is he?"

"He's here," a barely intelligible voice responded. I realized that the whole house had been wrecked. Broken chairs littered the hallway and china lay in fragments on the floor. Beau was leaning against the door, holding a bottle, and I had never seen him so drunk.

"Where the bloody hell were you?" he yelled.

"Trying to get here," I shouted.

"You—you weren't here," he moaned and began to sob, falling against the wall.

Angelica peered round the corner, trembling.

"He's mad," she said. "Taps should have phoned for the police. I had him here on my own and I thought he was going to murder me!"

"Why don't you get lost," Taps shouted at her. "I can manage him."

"Just because a horse died—" Angelica sniffed. "Oh Christ, I'll be late for the show," she squeaked and vanished.

"I had to shoot you. Gwen, I killed you—bare hands—killed you," Beau groaned and tried to stand, but fell forwards on his knees.

"Gwen's Girl came in first," Taps gabbled, "she was two full strides past the winning post and suddenly, it was like a gunshot . . . They say you could hear the crack at the back of the stands. She was down on her side and screaming. I never heard a horse sound like that—her cannon bone had snapped. Every time she tried to get up, she struggled and fell back screaming. The vet said she had to be put down because she'd never be able to stand again and they brought out the screens, but Mr Liddel said he'd do it himself. After that, he went mad. I drove him back here and left him on the bed. I thought he'd passed out, and I went back to the racecourse to make sure the horse wasn't carted off for dogs' meat. Then I decided I might need some help moving him and there's a couple of chaps at the pub who come round and give me a hand when he has one of his really bad turns. I waited for them, only they didn't turn up so I left a message for them and drove straight back here. I heard him when I was half way up the steps. He was tearing the house apart and your niece was screeching her head off. Fat lot of good she was."

Beau was huddled against the wall sobbing, arms wrapped around his head. I bent down and tried to comfort him, but he pushed me away.

"I killed you, Gwen. I killed you," he kept saying over and over.

"There's only one thing to do now," Taps said and poured a tumbler full of whisky. "This will knock him right out."

The whisky dribbled down his chin, but he swallowed it in gulps and then his eyes turned up and he fell on his back.

"Let's get him to bed," I said, and Taps wryly told me to look in our bedroom.

Every piece of furniture in it was broken; Beau must have smashed the bed with an iron bar because the wood was splintered and even the frame had been bent out of shape. The mattress was torn and shredded, the clothes from my wardrobe ripped and tossed among the wreckage.

"Would you mind if we took him to your flat?" Taps said.

"No, he'll feel better if he wakes up at Avalon. He's always happiest there."

I was still trembling when Taps' friends arrived. They managed to push Beau into the back seat of the Rolls, and I held his head in my lap while Taps drove through the northern suburbs, talking in low whispers to the older of the men who had come along with us. Beau's breathing was so stertorous that I thought he was choking and I was terrified he might swallow his tongue. I turned his head to one side: he vomited over my knees.

The old man had been a wrestler and he carried Beau down to the house on his back, knees cracking, grunting at every step. They washed him down in the shower and put him to bed.

"I'd have a wash myself if I was you," Taps said, wrinkling his nose and bustling past me to the kitchen.

"First, I need a drink—" I said, and poured a brandy. The glass was in my hand and then slowly I walked out on to the veranda and poured it into the garden.

"I'll make it up to you," Beau said to me the next day on the beach. "Just don't leave me again—"

"Beau, I have a business to run and I can't be with you every minute of the day—"

"I need you!" he said imploringly.

Patiently, I explained that I loved him but I was part owner of the Danny Burns Radio Theatre and I intended to manage the sales and contracts as I had before.

"Would it make any difference if we were married?" he asked.

"No."

"You're a hard woman, Gwen."

"I'm a Sicilian."

He was still staggering as we walked, but he had not had a drink since Taps and I helped him out of bed in the morning. It was cold in the July sun with a tingling wind that felt like ice crystals against my face as we walked along the beach through mats of torn brown seaweed. There was a steely cast to the sky and a wall of dark cloud to the south.

"Storm's rising," Beau said and laughed.

I remembered how the fishermen's wives would hurry down to the *tonnara* and pray to St Cosimo and St Damiano to bring their men back safely. Sometimes you heard them wailing and keening as they carried a husband or a son through the streets of the town to their home and my mother used to say that in their grief they were observing rites that were as old as Homer. Beau's delight in the rising wind seemed to be taunting the Furies that ride the storm and I shivered and told him I was cold and hungry.

He left the beach reluctantly and after breakfast he filled his empty coffee cup with brandy.

"Just to keep the cold out." He winked at me.

He drank all day, watching the sky grow dark at noon with clouds scudding across the sky like breakers. The wind veered in the middle of the afternoon and thunder shook the house so violently that all the plates rattled and every glass chimed. Lightning slashed through the clouds as if they were being raked and torn. Behind the clouds the sky loomed a livid yellow in tatters of light that made the air smoulder; we smelt burning eucalyptus from a nearby tree that was struck by lightning and had burst into smoking flames. Gulls screamed from every direction, beating their way inland, and Beau was in a mood that I had never seen before as he laughed at the storm and told me stories of driving through floods and riding a wild horse that had never known a bridle.

"You have to challenge yourself," he said, and I reminded him that all the animals of the bush had taken cover and the birds were seeking shelter.

"We're the one animal that claims all the elements as its own—up there in the sky, out there in the water. Do you think the fish are worried, so why should we be afraid?"

I tried to reason with him and divert his attention but he was standing on the veranda and drinking, buffeted by the wind, pointing to the ocean.

"See—the waves are coming in at an angle now and look at that rip. My God, you could ride out in that for half a mile and come back on a wave that would bring you in faster than a locomotive."

Battle and death, honour and valour: these were the virtues of the paladins as they clashed arms in the *opera di pupei*, vanquishing Turks and dragons with their magic swords. I never understood the fascination the marionettes held for me until I came to love Beau Liddel. The puppet is not like an actor playing a role, he has only the purity of his part and knows no other. We are all torn between different selves that memory stitches irregularly and inconsequentially together, but the puppet has only one self and a spirit that is never compromised by time. Beau was a paladin like the Orlando that I had almost given my heart to when I was a child. There were no conflicts within him, all his battles were with the elements and with his enemies. His was a simplicity so inviolate that it was almost inhuman.

"Come and surf with me," he shouted.

I followed him down to the beach where earth and water were churned into a welter of blown weed and branches. The sound of the waves was like mountains crashing and if Beau shouted something to me I did not hear him. He pointed to the sea and when I shook my head, I think he laughed and strode out into a tumult of water and sand, not diving through the waves as he did when we swam together but thrusting against them with the full weight of his body, his arms held high above his head like a boxer in victory. His clothes were at my feet and as I bent to pick them up the wind caught and plucked them from my hand.

I saw him dive through the first breaker and realized that the god of time was watching us. His head appeared twice, then I lost sight of him as the fleering yellow light was blown into darkness.

Weed struck and stung my face. I knew the Furies were whipping me but if I did not have the courage to follow Beau into that foaming cauldron, I had the strength to stand against them. A clammy strand wrapped around my thighs and I jerked it loose, cursing and straining for a glimpse of Beau. He was gone. The sea had swallowed him.

I don't remember who or what I prayed to then but I know I begged the sea to give him back to me and all the shapes and sounds of Trapani returned and clamoured round me. When I shouted and screamed, the words were pushed back into my mouth by the wind and I fell sideways on to the weed and sand. I know I called to my mother who belonged to the sea and it seemed that she was standing upright in her coffin at the heart of the storm, frowning at me as she did when I lost my temper or spoke impetuously.

"Give him back to me!" I cried.

There was a moving bulk in the water and I ran screaming into the surf; the tide pulled back and I almost fell across it. In that instant I knew that something dead was in my hands. The surge pushed me over and my feet went from under me—the following wave washed it on top of me. Once there must have been a horse, but this thing had been shredded and devoured by the creatures of the sea and what was left was bloated into a nightmare. Thousands of little blue crabs scuttled over and through it and two were climbing my arm as I staggered back, rubbing my hands on the sand to clean them.

"You have always been my enemy," I screamed at my mother. "Always denying me love—my father, then Alan and Kurt—"

The next wave washed the carcass back into the water but it left a horde of crabs behind it.

I held my head in my hands and moaned because everything had been taken from me and in that same moment I heard him. He was almost bent double, pushing his way through the waves, and I ran down and helped him beyond their reach. He sat with his head on his knees gasping and holding the side of his face.

"I was half way back when it hit me," he said brokenly. "A bloody great tree trunk smashed into me."

There on the sand with the weed lashing us I knelt beside him and cradled him like a child or an old man. The dream was over and I was back in the world that divides and parts. Oh, I still loved him, but the rapture and madness were at an end and neither of us could ever hope to be more than ordinary human beings again. In my brain I almost felt the cogs and wheels falling back into place and starting to turn again to mundane laws. No one spends the gold of sunlight or drinks at a mirage.

I held him to me and he rested his head on my shoulder.

"I've never felt so crook," he said and when he tried to stand I saw he was limping.

"If I'd seen it coming I would have dodged it," he grumbled, leaning on me as we made our way slowly back to the house. Taps came down and helped me up the steps; we both saw that he was dragging his left leg, and his voice was slurred.

The doctor came that evening and told us that it was a stroke, but I had known that long before he came out of the bedroom frowning and closing his bag.

"A stroke!" Beau shouted after him. "You bloody old fool! I was belted out of my senses by a bloody great tree trunk."

"Just rest and no alcohol," the doctor said. He seemed no wiser than Dr Polcari in Trapani.

The next day Beau insisted on getting up and going for a walk and it did appear that his limp was not so bad, even though his voice had changed. Unlike my mother, he said he wanted me near him always, that he had no life without me.

"Could you try to be sober?" I asked.

"I'll do my best—" he replied and that afternoon he insisted that we go down to the beach and see what the storm had left behind.

"No swimming," I cried.

"Are you kidding?" he said. "Next time I might run into a house out there."

Near the rocks we found a gigantic cedar, shattered and with its bark shredded.

"That's what hit me!" Beau shouted triumphantly. "I told you how big it was. Only a bloody fool doctor would call a belt from that a stroke."

Every leaf had been torn from the tree but there were no marks on Beau.

We spent the next three days at Avalon and Beau seemed oblivious of his changed voice and his limp. When he stumbled going across the sand, he pointed to the tree and laughed ruefully. We fished from the rocks and after the wind dropped, he built a fire on the beach and taught me how to grill bream and snapper on green sticks. Both of us knew that we were changed, but neither of us spoke of it.

The house at Randwick was clean when we drove back and smelled of paint and varnish.

"Decorate it any way you like," he said to me.

"I'll ask my friend Norma to come round. She has a better eye for colour and fabrics than I."

"Pay her what you like—"

Even though Norma hired interior decorators and the house became an English country home with floral chintzes and bowls of flowers in Delft pots, I was never really happy there.

"If it weren't for the bloody view of the racecourse, I'd sell it," Beau grumbled.

Angelica came in one afternoon and held out her wrist to me. She was wearing a gold watch with a mother-of-pearl face.

"Is that a present from Jack?" I asked absently.

"Beau told me to buy it." Angelica smiled. "He's sorry he scared the living daylights out of me that Saturday when the horse died."

The glittering little watch irritated me and I forced myself to return her smile.

"Angelica—"

"Angela—" She corrected me.

"If Jack is coming up here to see you, don't feel that you have to hide him. I'd like very much to see him again."

Her face went scarlet and she blurted, "I don't know what you're talking about. I'm not seeing anyone here. Who told you I was? I bet it was that rotten little poofter, Taps."

I was astonished by her vehemence.

"He's tried to touch me up a couple of times. I had to remind him that I was the wrong sex for him."

"Nobody was criticizing you, Angela."

"If you want me to, I'll swear on a Bible that I have never, never had a man in that room of mine. Of course, if you're making this an excuse to get rid of me—" Hysterical tears followed her accusation and I told her that everyone must have been mistaken. When the false Angelica was accused of spreading discord among the paladins and lying, she first burst into tears and begged forgiveness before she took her own life with a silver dagger. But I was to remember that much later.

We saw very little of her. She was out every night at the theatre and on Wednesday and Saturday afternoons for the matinée performances, but both Mrs Corcoran and Taps continued to complain about her. Norma took me aside and through a mouthful of pins said, "You watch that girl. Smickering little puss. She walked in here as bold as brass and told me she thought chintz was old-fashioned."

"She's very young," I replied and wanted to add, but didn't, that Angelica was not very intelligent and had never shown any sign of ever wanting to be anything more than a chorus girl.

"Deep—very deep," was Norma's response and I laughed.

It was not easy for me to laugh because I was watching Beau. No one took more pride in his strength than Beau and now he complained of weakness.

"I wish I'd known that tree was going to hit me," he often said. "I would have found it in the bush and taken an axe to it."

The doctor's words were always in my head—"This is the first stroke, there'll be others."

Beau was trying not to drink and for days he would be sober and then I'd find him carousing with some of his racing friends, Taps hovering nervously in the background.

"You shouldn't ought to leave him for a moment," Taps whispered on one of these riotous occasions. "He's all right if you're with him."

That should have irritated me but I rejoiced in Beau's need for me and we were never apart for more than a few hours after that.

Beau was still drinking, but when he drank whisky, I drank water and Taps was jubilant.

"Oh, I can see the change in him," he said to me more than once. "You've made such a difference. It used to be a bottle with his breakfast, now he doesn't touch it till after lunch."

One afternoon I asked Beau if he'd like to come with me to Mount of Angels to see Mother George. She had sent a note saying that the cardinal was setting up a board of enquiry into the circumstances of my cousin's death and I would be called upon to give evidence.

"Betty Trevanion that was?" Beau grinned. "My dad had a crush on her. She could have been my mother."

Taps wore his new uniform for the occasion and the Rolls was iridescent with polish. Beau always seemed to reflect the sunlight from his dark red hair and tawny skin and, as we walked slowly up to the main entrance of the convent, I did not wonder when two little novices who were passing us stopped, peered back covertly at him and sighed. I took his arm and deliberately looked away from the place among the rows of little white stones where Edith was buried.

Mother George's laughter could fill a room with sound but she was subdued that day and there was a rasp to her voice that I had never heard before. Sister Joseph fidgeted on her chair by the door, cracking her knuckles with excitement.

"Beau Liddel," Mother George said drily, "I've heard a great deal about you."

Beau smiled and told her he could see why his father had fallen for her, at which Sister Joseph coughed peremptorily and Mother George asked her to show him round the gardens because she wanted to speak to me privately.

"I'll come straight back," Sister Joseph said quickly and ushered Beau out. His limp was so slight that day it was barely perceptible.

"The circumstances of your cousin's death were very strange," Mother George said slowly, "and stranger things have been happening since."

I sat silently and waited for her to continue.

"When the coffin was exhumed for the second time at the bishop's request, there were no visible signs of decay in the body. Oh, there are medical reasons why such a thing could occur, and they were noted, but— Later, two of our sisters claimed that after praying at Sister Catherine's grave they were cured, one of rheumatism and the other of a skin rash that had afflicted her ever since she entered the order."

Was this how miracles came about? And was it conceivable that my cousin Edith was now a saint with the power to save people from sickness and disease?

"Yes," she went on, "I fancy I know what you're thinking. Believe me, I've asked myself the same questions and had the same doubts. You see, I disliked her and doubted the sincerity of her vocation from the beginning. She bought her way into this order; I was forced to accept her and nothing in her demeanour when she was here led me to believe that she was—Oh, dear God, I am guilty of the sin of pride! It is my arrogance to assume I know more than God!"

She bent over her clasped hands and I felt her anguish.

"If this is a miracle, I cannot bring myself to believe it!" she murmured.

People will always believe what they want to believe, I was tempted to say, but I remained silent.

"Who am I to dictate the will of God, to say which of us deserves His love and how He should manifest that love? This is my sin—"

"She died, Mother George, because I didn't speak honestly to you when she decided to enter the convent."

"Yes! You were the instrument!" Sister Joseph cried, her hands outstretched at the door. "The ways of God are wonderful and mysterious." She paused and I saw the emotions pucker her face. "I can only wonder why you were chosen—you're not a Catholic. But perhaps—your parents?"

"My father was baptised in the Roman Catholic Church."

"Ah—I knew it." Sister Joseph was jubilant. "Your father meant this to be a sign that you should join him in the one true faith."

"My father was a Communist and detested the Church," I said bluntly.

Sister Joseph stared blankly at me, her hands pressed to her mouth.

"There is no explanation," Mother George said quietly. "Explanations are our attempt to interpret the will of God and we always lie or deceive ourselves. The act has no meaning of itself and words are always false currency when we use them to buy truth. However, Holy Mother Church will investigate and determine the nature of Sister Catherine's death. Gwen, if you are called by this panel of experts, will you give evidence?"

"My evidence won't help the Church make her a saint."

"Gwen, God may already have made that decision. It is for us to try and understand His will and obey it."

If God has decided to make my cousin Edith a saint, I thought as I went to find Beau, then He is the author of comedy and melodrama with trick and coincidence thrown in to baffle and confuse us. Perhaps it's not the priest who reflects the will of God, but the gambler.

Beau was in the rose garden discussing horses with old Pat, the gardener.

"I won't forget, Mr Liddel sir, Coronation in the third and Willie Winkie in the fifth. You're a real gentleman, Mr Liddel sir."

"What was all that about?" Beau asked as we walked back to the car.

"They think my cousin Edith may be a saint," I replied.

September the fifteenth was the day I had been asked to give evidence before an ecclesiastical panel at St Mary's Cathedral. I spent the morning at the studio and went on to an advertising agency where two of the clients were unhappy about the way all our serials were making the Nazis seem blackguards and criminals.

"All they're asking for is balance," Ned Fisk said plaintively. "Just give us a couple of good Nazis."

"There are none," I retorted. "Tell them to sponsor Dino if it's fantasy they want."

The committee appointed to investigate the circumstances of Edith's death astonished me because I had expected devout clerics arguing about the disposition of the relics. Instead, they seemed like shrewd businessmen and lawyers more inclined to scepticism than faith. None of them were shocked when I spoke to them frankly about Edith Wigram as I had known her except that, when I was leaving, an old sharp-eyed priest said quietly that it was often the greatest sinners who made the greatest saints. Even as he spoke, I remembered that Edith had once said the same thing to me.

The moment I opened the gate at Randwick my skin prickled and I wondered involuntarily what spirits had taken possession of the house in my absence. Rosalia always said a prayer when she returned to the house, but I had forgotten the words she used and even the kind of spirits that had to be appeased. My first thought was that Beau had suffered another stroke.

Forty-Two

The front door was open and as I sensed the tension in the air and felt my skin prickling, I saw Angelica standing in the middle of the living room, staring vacantly at her fingernails.

"There's something wrong," I said involuntarily. "Where's Beau?"

"How would I know?" she replied. "Taps has gone after him."

"What happened?"

"You might ask what's wrong with me? But no one's ever given a damn about me. I had tonsillitis once and all Aunt Rafaella was worried about was Rocco and whether he'd catch it from me. She made me sleep in the shed with the chickens, but when he caught it she kept him in bed and slept on the floor beside him and never stopped rousing on me." She stopped and chewed a fragment of cuticle from her thumb.

"Well?"

She began to sniffle.

"Tell me what's wrong and I'll help you."

"I'm in the club."

"What—"

"And it's his kid. I kept my word. I never mentioned a syllable of it to you and I always heard that drunks couldn't knock you up because even if they can do it, nothing comes of it. And he was terribly drunk that afternoon. You know he was."

"What in God's name are you saying?" I screamed.

"I'm carrying Beau's child and you might show a little concern for me. Look at me—I'm fat—you can see the little bastard."

She turned sideways to me but it was as if I had been struck blind and for a moment I struggled to focus.

"I tried to keep on as long as I could but that Tally Winters has eyes like a bloody hawk and he told me to see Mrs Flynn in Redfern or lose my place in the chorus. I can't go to her—she's a bloody old butcher! If I'd noticed after the first month—only I kept telling myself that a drunk can't give you a kid—"

"I don't believe this—you're making it up."

"Am I? Well, suppose you tell me what came over him—I reckon he thought I was you, because all the time he was on top of me he kept calling me Gwen."

"You're lying," I said finally.

"I knew you'd say that," she whimpered. "All right, why don't you ask him? He remembers all right. Why do you think he gave me that?"

She held out her wrist with the glittering watch on it.

"Christ! Do you think I want to get all fat and ugly like a pig with my belly sticking out in front of me? Aunt Rafaella always said I'd end up like this, but I don't think she expected that I'd be raped by your boyfriend."

The phone rang and automatically I lifted the receiver. Florrie's voice crackled on the line. If I didn't come round and pick up Beau she'd have to send for the police. He was challenging every wharfie who wanted to fight him.

Beau was standing in blood, exchanging punches with a burly man in a blue singlet, surrounded by a crowd of cheering onlookers. The wharfie caught him with a punch to the ear and Beau went down into the gutter as the crowd began to count. Another man poured a jug of beer over his head.

"Not on my head—in my mouth," he shouted, and the crowd roared.

Florrie was standing on the pub steps with arms folded. When I arrived she told me bleakly that she'd just called the police.

"I'll help you get him out of here before they arrive," she said.

Everyone stood back when Florrie shouldered her way through the mob, threatening to bar anyone who tried to stop her. I stood in front of Beau and realized that he could barely see through the blood pulsing from a cut on his forehead.

"You shouldn't have left me, Gwen," he said and his words were so blurred he could have been speaking from the bottom of a well.

"I won't leave you alone again."

"I've got to marry her—it's my kid."

"We'll talk about it when we get home."

Taps was waiting for us when I drove back to Randwick and we shouldered him up the stairs and into the house.

"Now, before Taps cleans you up, I want to know one thing for certain. Did you rape Angelica that Saturday when the horse was killed?"

"I—for God's sake, Gwen—she's a little girl—"

His tongue seemed suddenly too large for his mouth and he swallowed, his mouth twisting uncontrollably.

"I know you'll tell me the truth," I said slowly.

"I came to in bed—she was alongside me naked and crying her heart out . . ."

I tried to speak but despair choked me.

"If I did it, I thought it was you, Gwen. I wanted you. Christ, I tried to tear that room apart. It was—it happened in our bed."

Every word was like a grotesque echo of his voice.

"He's got to marry me," Angelica sniffled outside the door. "I'm not going to have a bastard. I'll kill myself first."

"I have to marry her, Gwen. Afterwards, I'll give her whatever she wants, and we'll be together—"

I told him to sleep but he wouldn't let go of my hand.

"Swear you won't leave me, Gwen. You're my life."

Always I had chosen, and always it had been the wrong choice. Oh, my mother called me Boadicea, but if I had commanded armies, I would have led them all to bitter defeat. I could have stayed with Alan but I refused to wait a year and came to Sydney, then Kurt asked me to marry him but again I would not go to Vienna and I would not live with him here as his mistress. Kurt was probably dead, or "relocated" now by the Nazis. God knows what relocation meant. And now Beau had been taken from me. His left hand was fluttering and I held it tightly in my own. This time, I would not choose—like Job I'd rail against fate, I'd curse and cry out but I would do whatever Beau wanted. If the gods were punishing me for my actions then I would not do what pride and reason dictated—I would not walk out of that house and leave Beau to die. There was a trickle of saliva running from the side of his mouth and I wiped it away as my father did for my mother. I felt Angelica standing behind me and I turned and looked at her—

"I didn't want it to happen," she whined. "He's years too old for me. I don't want this kid."

Beau was moaning and I wondered when the doctor would arrive. He was running a fever and his hand was so hot I could feel it burning my skin.

"Don't leave me, Gwen. Don't leave me," he mumbled.

"I'll stay with you, Beau. No matter what happens, I'll be near."

Beau married Angelica at the registry office the following Saturday and I do not know how he was able to stand, but he dragged himself from bed and Taps and I dressed him. Angelica was very quiet, saying only that she hoped the baby wouldn't turn out to be a drunk too. Florrie and I were witnesses. We thought that no one saw us arriving, but someone must have called the papers because when we came out we were met by a throng of reporters and photographers. Taps and two of his friends managed to push Beau into the car. A photographer yelled at him, "Drunk at your wedding, Beau?" And another laughed, "Never seen him sober, have you?"

"Can't they see he's dying?" Taps whispered to me.

The marriage was featured in all the Sunday papers. *Truth* had a special feature article in which I was described as being jilted in favour of a younger woman—my niece. There were some very flattering pictures of Theatre Royal chorine Miss Angela Scarf, now Mrs Beaufort Liddel of Randwick and Gulthorpe near Scone.

Often I've wished to be English that understanding might come to me through those muted griefs, the subtle nuances and discreet gestures of the drawing room. The chink of a teaspoon, a word spoken too soon or not at all can change the English soul. But I am Sicilian and I have lived for almost thirty years in a tragic carnival, a *festa* of despair and macabre farce. For the Sicilian, saints dance in the air, blood feuds and blood marriages are the stuff of everyday life, Christ and His Mother greet each other in the street, and paladins wage endless battle against the Turks. Yet behind the panoplied dramas and the twists of violent fate there is never resolution but mystery. The great events of one's life should be revelations but I never discovered what happened to Miki and Rosalia, or where my mother lay at rest. Clerics argued over Edith's death but would I ever know if she was a saint or the psychotic Kurt had diagnosed? Was Kurt alive and drinking May wine in the Vienna Woods or was he in another and terrible place? Dolfi—will I ever meet him again or learn of that reunion with Frau Brunner in Miami? I don't think so. Imagine the opening number of a musical extravaganza: the well-dressed satisfied audience contemplating a stage where the chorus is drawn up on either side all singing and pointing to that place on the top of the stairs where the star will appear. The music reaches a crescendo, the voices rise in acclamation, all is expectation, but on the staircase there is only emptiness, a vacant silence that grows, spreading such horror that the audience flees in terror, the musicians cast aside their instruments and the chorus disappears in tumbled disarray.

Everything in my life has come with whirlwinds and thunderbolts and has ended in silence. Especially Bessie—Ah, if I could have found Bessie I think I would have seen more clearly and understood myself.

We drove back from the registry office to Randwick with Angelica in a mood of scowling resentment, glaring out of the window and refusing to speak. It was hardly a wedding party even though Florrie and Norma tried to be cheerful. Taps and his mate helped Beau back to bed and suddenly Angelica stamped and pointed after him, her voice shrill with anger.

"It's the DTs now, isn't it? Dead drunk at his own wedding. Well, I don't want to set eyes on him and if he ever tries to touch me or come near me I'll have him bound over. This is my house just as much as his and I'm giving the orders here now and I tell you straight, I don't want him around—not in that state, or any other way. Why don't you take him to your place?" she said to me.

"Angelica, he's very ill," I replied and she scoffed.

"Of course he's ill—it's the DTs. Soon he'll start seeing pink elephants and he'll never get better, he'll be like that for years and years, drinking himself into the loony house."

I tried to explain what had happened to Beau but she would not listen.

"And don't imagine that I'm going to hang around here waiting for the odd fiver that you feel like handing out, Gwen. I'm his legal wife and I want a proper allowance—I know what my rights are."

She seemed mollified when I assured her that Beau would give her whatever she wanted and I asked Taps and his mate, the old wrestler, to help me get Beau to Trelawney.

That was the irony. Only a handful of people knew that Beau had suffered a stroke. Everyone believed he was drunk, as Angelica did, when he was seen being carried out to the car. Beau Liddel had really drunk himself into the DTs this time they all said, and when we took him to the races one Saturday afternoon and Taps and I walked out and received the prizes for two of his horses while he watched from a chair in the Members', a wag in the crowd shouted that he should try to steal a water wagon next time.

If I was mad before, everyone told me I was crazy now to stay with him. Where was my pride? they all said and reminded me that Beau had married Angelica.

Possibly I couldn't have borne it if Angelica had decided to play the part of the triumphant wife, but after throwing out the furniture at Randwick and replacing it with Louis-Quinze white and gold and acres of pink satin and ordering a wardrobe of furs and jewellery that cost thousands, she decided to entertain her own friends. Every night she had the carpets rolled back and invited the cast of the Theatre Royal out to dance and drink.

"You can tell Beau I never want to set eyes on him as long as I live," she told me whenever I spoke to her.

"It's a stroke, and there'll be others." I tried to explain. Her response was to jeer.

"Oh yes, that's a nice way to put it, isn't it. My mum used to say that Dad was just having a turn when he came home blind drunk and beat her up because she couldn't give him a son."

Beau used to sit on the veranda at Trelawney watching the Harbour and only Taps and I could understand him now when he spoke. Every word was difficult for him. He kept a pad and pencil at his side for the strokes had taken all the strength from his left side just as they had my mother. He could still use his right hand when speech became too painful for him and sometimes there would be a drift of crumpled paper beside his chair. Every second sheet had a message of love for me scribbled on it.

I remembered how my mother used to thrust me aside when she was sick and after her death my father lived only for her memory. When I took Beau's head in my hands and kissed him, it was my name he murmured and I could see myself reflected in his eyes.

Abruptly, Angelica announced that she didn't want to see her friends any more and called me to drive to Randwick immediately. My hands were clammy on the wheel as I parked the car in front of the house. Did she want Beau? Was she going to insist that it was her place as his wife to care for him? Whatever she had decided, I was determined not to relinquish Beau to her. I found her standing in front of a cheval mirror in her bedroom, tears flooding from her eyes.

"Beau is getting weaker," I said to her awkwardly for she didn't turn her head when I stood behind her.

"Are you asking me to feel sorry for that drunk? What about me? How would you like to be chucking up every morning? Waking up to vomit—that's my life. And you expect me to worry about Beau because he has the DTs?" she cried. "Look at me! I'm hideous!"

She was swelling like a flower before it blooms, her belly like a waxing moon.

"I can't bear it inside me!" she screamed. "It's there—I can feel it moving round in my stomach!"

"I'm sure that's natural."

"It's eating me—inside. I'm going to die," she wailed.

"The doctor says you're well and the baby is healthy too."

I was irritated by her complaints and wanted to return to Beau.

"I should have gone to Mrs Flynn when I had the chance. It's too late now and I'm going to die anyway. I'd sooner have died with my figure its right shape than looking like this."

She threw herself on the bed and screamed and kicked her heels. Suddenly, she twisted over on her back, her hands to her stomach.

"There—feel it! It's there—"

I placed my hand where she told me and it was as though an electric shock ran up my arm—I fell back, gasping for breath. Every nerve in my body responded to that touch, a tide of rapture overwhelmed my senses like, but surpassing, the melting ecstasy of sexual passion.

"Yes, that's how it makes me feel too," Angelica moaned, misreading my emotion. "There it is again!" she wailed.

With that touch I understood love as the source of all the dancing saints and Rosalia's charms, the flowers that appeared overnight on the slopes of Mount Giuliano and the sea that burned with its own luminous fire. I felt it locking, twining, binding all into one power of being as vast as the bounds of the universe and as small as the life stirring in her body. And I knew in one flash of piercing insight that this was the greatest love and my parents had turned their backs on it. Now I leaned back, panting like a spent animal, with only the pulse of that responsive emotion throbbing in me.

"It's all very well for you to take on like that," she moaned, "but I've got it inside me all the time."

"Angelica, you have a god in you," I whispered.

"Oh, for Christ's sake, don't come on like one of those bloody old nuns at the convent! They'd tell you that I had a bastard in my belly. I wasn't married in church, you know. A registry marriage isn't a real marriage for a Catholic."

There was an odd note of satisfaction in her last words that I caught but did not comprehend. If I thought anything at all, it was that she was making a covert accusation against Beau. Besides, all I wanted at that moment was to place my hand over the ecstatic life that had made my hand tremble—

"It is a boy, isn't it?" she asked nervously. "I wouldn't want to go through all this for a girl. Boys always kick more than girls, don't they?"

"What does it matter? It's a child," I said with longing.

"A girl? Who the hell wants a girl? No, it's a boy. I'm sure it's a boy. Nobody would suffer this bloody misery for a girl."

When I returned to Trelawney, Beau was in his chair on the veranda and I tried to explain to him what had happened to me. There were no words to describe that exultation and the joy that had made me feel supernal and when I was finished we sat together in silence. I saw him reaching for his pad and I placed it on his knee. He wrote one word—"Ours," and from that day on it was our child.

Taps bristled with disapproval whenever I mentioned the baby or said that I was driving over to Randwick to see Angelica.

"You should never have let him marry the little bitch," Taps muttered to me. "What about that fellow who was coming to the house?"

"She denied it."

"Mrs Corcoran saw someone—"

"Angelica said that Billy Garvin often came round and talked to her—"

"Garvin!"

"He was always remarkably well informed."

The only time Beau was content to be apart from me was when I went to see Angelica and she was now insisting that I drive to Randwick every day. Yet if I tried to tell her about Beau she would strike her belly with her fist and scream that he had made her like this and she never wanted to hear his name.

"If he hadn't been drunk, this wouldn't have happened to me," she wailed. "And do you think I care that he's crazy with the DTs now? That's what everyone says about him, and it's true."

The sex of the baby had become an obsession with Angelica as her tiny body swelled with that miraculous freight. Only when I told her that she was disturbing her son would she be calm. At other times she screamed that she was a freak and later she refused to leave the house altogether.

"You know what Tally used to call me," she cried. "He said I was a pocket Venus. Now look at me! I'm a pig, a fat pig."

She begged me to leave Beau and stay with her and when I suggested writing to her aunt, she told me that she'd like to spit on Rafaella's grave.

I was being torn between the two of them, Beau needing me to be constantly with him, Angelica begging me not to leave her. If all she had wanted was to be alone, it would not have been so difficult, but what she really wanted was not to be seen by her friends. It was like trying to reason with a stupid child as I told her a thousand times that she would not be deformed after the baby was born, and yes, she would be as pretty as ever.

"My waist was twenty inches. Only one girl in the chorus had a smaller waist than mine. Do you think I'll ever be that size again?" she cried.

From the moment I felt the life inside her, I yearned for the child with such a hunger, such an agony of desire, that I could have torn her apart and dragged it from her. Sexual longing I have known, but this was torture compounded with rapture.

In my dreams, I felt the child stirring in me and woke crying to feel my stomach flat, and empty like a shell. Once, Angelica crept into my bedroom and burst into shrieks of laughter. I had stuffed a pillow under my skirt and was standing, staring at myself in the mirror as she so often did.

"You're mad! Mad!" she screamed. "Here—" and she tore at her belly. "I wish I could cut it out and give it to you. Look at me—Oh, my God, do you think I'll ever get my figure back again?"

She was an enormous size and when her legs began to bulge in a web of purple veins, she shrieked hysterically and refused to leave her bed. I hired nurses to be with her night and day and then I had a little respite. Her only consolation was that she knew she was carrying a boy because one of those nurses, a garrulous woman from the bush, assured her that she could tell just by looking if it was a boy, and she had never seen anything more like the mother of a son than Angelica.

It was Joel Aaron who brought me the news about my cousin, Frederick.

He handed me a copy of the London *Times* open to the third page. There was a photo of Frederick Wigram, noted journalist and political writer, and the account of his death at Saragossa in Spain.

"It is beginning," Joel said. "Soon the pages will be full of the dead, just as they were in the last war."

I closed my eyes because I could see Rosalia dipping the lockets in my blood and I knew that they were all dead now and her prophecy had been fulfilled. Instinctively, I reached up and touched the coral horn at my neck for protection.

"He was a fine journalist. I wish we had a few like him in Australia instead of these blind fools who can only parrot whatever Menzies tells them." Joel added that there was a long obituary in the *Economist*.

Rosalia once said, with the tarot cards laid out in front of her, that I must walk through graves with death at my side. Only if I could pass through that ordeal would I find what I had lost. Was that what she told me? Find myself? Or was it love? I couldn't remember any longer as I read about the cousin whose articles I had so often studied but had never met. A week later, a letter arrived from my Aunt Eleanor.

"My son is dead and God in His Wisdom has gathered him to His everlasting rest. My despair is unimaginable and I would gladly have given my life and that of a thousand others to save my beloved Frederick. Oh God, I cry, why hast thou forsaken me? (*Mark* 15:33) Have I not been afflicted enough with a daughter who made herself subject to the Scarlet Woman of Rome (*Revelation* 17) and who died a papist to the everlasting shame of a family that fought and died for the Protestant cause when the Harcourts pledged their swords to the last man for Oliver Cromwell of blessed memory. My grief is like Job's. I am an old woman now and all around me is grief. (*Lamentations* 2) My son, my beloved Frederick is dead. Yesterday they brought his body back home to Russell Morton and he was laid to rest with his ancestors."

Not my mother, I thought bitterly. You turned her away and now she rocks in the tides off the coast of Sicily.

"I have been afflicted, and must now accept that God has willed it that you will inherit Russell Morton and all the fortunes of this family. Our solicitors will be writing to you. There are no Wigrams, no Harcourts left on this earth except this poor vessel of clay which must soon be summoned to her divine maker and you. Of course, you must return to England immediately. I particularly want you to observe that certain effects your mother felt were her possessions have been kept faithfully and noted in the household inventory, including the Nonsuch chest. The solicitors will send you a ticket for the flying boat which, they tell me, is the fastest way for you to return to England. I shall give you the keys of Russell Morton when you arrive. All that is here is yours. I have very little time left to me. I am an old woman sorely afflicted by a stern God—my heart is broken."

I gave the letter to Beau and he read it slowly and then I saw him reaching for his pad.

"Don't leave me—" he scrawled and underneath it I wrote, "Never" and underlined it so heavily that the paper split.

"I don't think I shall bother replying to her," I added and I never did. There was blood between us and not even the gift of the Nonsuch chest could atone for that.

The next day Angelica was a little more cheerful, admiring a dozen different layettes spread out on her bed. Every one of them was a different shade of blue.

"He's going to be a handsome big boy," the old nurse said and winked at me.

"The best-dressed baby boy in the world," Angelica crooned, fingering the satin ribbons and tracing the embroidered yokes with her finger.

When I returned to Trelawney, I heard voices in the dining room and Taps told me that Beau and all his lawyers were in there.

"He wanted everything settled by the time you came back," Taps whispered conspiratorially.

I heard one voice that I recognized and I knew I must be mistaken because Alan was in the country campaigning for his father's old seat in the House. Even the *Herald* and the *Telegraph* were accusing him of being a warmonger: the *Herald* had just published a recent address by Alan alongside one of his father's famous speeches in which he had proclaimed himself a pacifist at the outset of the Great War. It could not be Alan, I told myself, but as I walked through the half-open doors I saw him at one end of the table and Beau at the other propped up with cushions. In between there were several clerks and men who looked like lawyers. Beau was trying to speak and I noticed a young clerk raise his eyebrow as he placed the pad in front of him. Alan looked up at me and smiled quickly.

"Beau has made a new will," he said evenly, "and he's asked me to be an executor."

"I thought you were in the country—the election—" I said.

"Beau asked me to come and I'm here," he replied and I could tell that Beau was smiling.

"His main concern, of course, is to provide for his child. The entire estate, with some exceptions, goes to his legal issue by Angelica Liddel and the income from a third of it to the said Angelica Liddel after his death until such time as she remarries."

Beau was listening intently and nodding as Alan spoke.

"He requests that you be made guardian of his child. Is that agreeable?"

I could only nod then for I was struck as mute as Beau.

"His horses, a quantity of shares that are itemized here and the house at Avalon are to be yours."

Alan was staring at me and I saw the compassion in his eyes. So much wealth was falling into my lap as if to deride me for the poverty of my heart and the opulent rags of my life.

I walked out on to the veranda and tried to follow the pattern of the rain scudding across the Harbour in silver flurries. Without turning, I knew that Alan was at my shoulder.

"It was for you, Gwen, as well as for Beau," he said quietly.

"Nothing—" I remember saying, "I hoped for so much and it was all taken away from me. Russell Morton, my home with Bessie—and you—"

His hand was on mine and I felt the strength of his grasp. It was not easy for me to look into his face for I was accustomed to seeing controlled anger there. Now I saw pity.

"Call me and I'll come to you," he said.

"Alan, I love you," I said simply and it was possible for me to speak because the serpent was dead. It had taken me so long to learn to be loved and now it was too late, for Beau had claim to my love and I knew that if he lived forever I would care for him to the end.

Alan's grip on my hand was so tight that I flinched and then one of the lawyers spoke to him and I went back to Beau.

Laboriously he had scribbled a note to me and I took it from his hand.

"Daughter—want a daughter," I read and I couldn't see any more because I was crying and not just for Beau, but for myself and what I had lost.

Throughout those last weeks Angelica lay in bed almost motionless, grumbling when the nurses washed her and exercised her legs and arms.

"It's got to come soon. I can't get any bigger. I'll die," she said monotonously. "It's eating me up—I can feel it."

"The moment the water breaks, we'll have you off to hospital in a flash," the nurse said briskly.

"No, I want to stay here at home," she cried.

"If there are any complications, you'll be better off in hospital. Besides, the doctor insists—"

The month before the baby was due to be born, we took Beau down to Avalon. It had not been easy to understand what he wanted but I managed to make out the letters A and V on his pad, and when I said Avalon, he nodded. Taps and his mate carried him down to the house in a chair, and this time they supported him with ease because he had become so thin. I noticed that he was finding it difficult to breathe and he had lost the strength in his right hand. It was midsummer and the air was noisy with the racket of cicadas and the thrumming of bees shaking pollen from the gum blossoms.

"Perhaps when we die we'll come back as one of the animals here," I said that evening as a possum nibbled a piece of fruit from his fingers.

I was troubled by a dragging pain in my stomach, yet I did not feel ill and when I checked my temperature, it was normal. Nonetheless, if I closed my eyes, I could see my stomach swelling like a ripe melon and feel that mysterious presence inside me.

"I would give anything to be carrying Angelica's baby!" I cried suddenly.

Beau nodded and smiled and I knew his expressions so well that I laughed.

"Yes, I feel as though I'm pregnant," I said.

Taps and his mate carried him down to the rocks and we watched children build walls against the tide and decorate them with shells just as Bessie and I had done on the beach at Trapani. There was only a rippling surf that day as smoothly varied in shades of blue as the little dresses I had seen spread out on Angelica's bed. Between the rocks the water was like Sicilian amber that reflects every tone from indigo to purple when you turn it to the light so that you can never hold more than one colour in your eye for more than a moment.

We sat there and I told Beau about Trapani, the people I had known there and the people I had imagined, for it was difficult to recall Roger without thinking of Gano di Magonza who betrayed Orlando at Roncisvalle, and a single white cloud on the horizon reminded me of Alcina's magic island where Astolfo was imprisoned in a myrtle bush. Memory chooses its own cloth and time stitches strange robes for us to wear and I was not sure whether the Sicily I remembered had ever existed or whether it was like the Elymian city that lay beneath the stones of Trapani.

A squat brown child was standing in front of us staring at Beau.

"Is he dead?" the child asked.

"No—he's dreaming," I replied and the little boy turned and ran away shouting to his playmates.

Taps was waving from the bottom of the steps and I heard him say that there was a message from Randwick. As he spoke I felt a pain that struck me like a wave and I bent double, grinding my teeth to stop myself screaming.

Forty-Three

It was not a difficult birth, the Matron and doctor both told me that, and one of the sisters said they'd given Angelica twilight sleep, not because of the pain but to spare the other patients her shrieks. The matron glanced from Beau to me and unlike everyone else, even the porter at the hospital gate who'd winked knowingly, she did not immediately assume that he was drunk. Instead she told me that he should be in a hospital bed, not propped up in a wheelchair. While she was speaking I detected the tremor of resentment from Beau and I said firmly that he was still capable of making his own decisions. Instantly I felt a faint pressure from his hand in mine and I smiled at him.

"Well, I suppose you want to see the baby, Mr Liddel," she said dubiously.

She disappeared and came back like a priestess with a cloaked bundle on her arm.

"I think you'd better take her," she said brusquely to me.

"It's not a boy?" I whispered, for this was a miracle.

"I get very tired of all this nonsense of wanting this or that when what you should be grateful for is that you have a healthy baby," the Matron retorted sharply.

I couldn't speak and I think my joy must have mollified her because she said I could have her for five minutes and then she would be taken back to the nursery.

Gently, I knelt and placed her on Beau's lap and with an effort that drew the muscles of his face taut, he lifted a finger and touched her face. Suddenly I felt that I was being released from the rack to which I'd been bound for endless years—all pain left me. Her eyes were of a blue so dark they were almost black and it was only when she blinked that I realized my tears were wetting her face. Beau was trying to speak and I bent down to listen.

"Name—" he said slowly.

It came without thinking.

"Elizabeth, like the English princess, and we can call her Bessie."

I was holding her to me and as she stirred against my breast, I felt my flesh respond and close around her in a surge of happiness.

The matron was reaching out for her and I protested that I wanted to keep her a little longer, but the priestess in her white starched crown was adamant.

I followed her down the corridor to the entrance to the nursery where she turned and I thought she was going to let me hold Bessie again; instead she passed her to another nurse and frowned at me.

"Mr Liddel is gravely ill. You know that, don't you?"

"Yes—"

"He should be in hospital."

"No—I'm taking him home now."

The Matron stiffened. "God help that child. I hope there's someone who'll look after her."

"I will," I cried and she smiled thinly.

"You're Gwen, aren't you?"

"Yes—"

"Then you're the one Mrs Liddel is asking for. I wouldn't bring Mr Liddel into her room if I were you. She's disturbed enough as it is. I can't make it out."

I asked Taps to take Beau down to the car but he moved his head and I realized he wanted to go to the nursery. I left him there in front of the long window.

Bessie—I had held Bessie in my arms. That was my only thought and no concern for Angelica entered my mind. It was when I was in her room that I guiltily remembered her longing for a son. She had told me a thousand times over when she was pregnant that she wanted a boy and I had listened and nodded and tried to reassure her. Of course, it was true that I seldom paid much attention to anything she said. Angelica never really argued, she simply repeated her demand and seemed incapable of holding more than one thought in her head. When she was pregnant, I always found it easier to agree than to try and reason with her. I knew she would be disappointed, but I was sure that when she saw that miraculous child her heart would melt as mine had.

"Angela," I said quietly and she squinted up at me, frowning. Her face was blotched and swollen as I placed my hand on her forehead and stroked her hair. The twilight sleep was still clouding her and I saw her trying to focus.

"It's a boy, isn't it?" she said slowly.

I shook my head.

She stared at me in disbelief for a moment, then began to utter little sharp screams like a flogged puppy.

A nurse came in carrying Bessie and stopped short when she saw Angelica.

"Oh, this won't do. This won't do at all," she said.

I tried to take the baby from her, but she had turned on her heel and was gone. Two minutes later Matron came in creaking with starch and anger.

"Mrs Liddel! Mrs Liddel!" she said sharply. "We've had more than enough of your tantrums. You have a beautiful healthy daughter and you're going to nurse her and be a good, loving mother."

Angelica pulled herself up on her elbows and glared with such ferocity that even the Matron stepped back and I was startled by the change: it was not a young woman before us, it was not the Angelica that I knew but a Fury, her face contorted with rage, her hair in spikes around her head.

"I wanted a son!" she screamed. "A son! A son! Not a little bitch that no one needs."

"You don't mean a word of that because you're still feeling groggy from the anaesthesia. Now, I'm going to take your pulse and then you're going to nurse your baby like a good girl," the Matron said, taking hold of her wrist.

"Bring me my son!" Angelica shrieked and clawed the Matron's face. "If you bring that bitch near me I'll smash her against that wall! I'll kill her. I swear I will."

"Well, Doctor had better deal with you," Matron said and stalked past us, dabbing the bloody streaks on her cheek, her eyebrows almost disappearing under the peak of her cap.

Doctors examined her and argued with her, the matron bullied her, but Angelica was implacable; she would not even have the baby in the same room with her.

The following day I took Bessie home to Randwick. Angelica had furnished a nursery there in blue silk and everything was ready for her son but Bessie did not seem disturbed by the sky-blue muslin over her cradle. I wondered why blue should always symbolize the male in this country when in Sicily it was the colour of Aphrodite and the Madonna.

Taps and his mate made up a bed for Beau in a room at the corner of the house where they could carry him out on to the veranda in the late afternoon. You could hear the roar of the racecourse there and that Saturday, when his new colt won the six furlongs in record time, a crowd gathered on the road and cheered him. His racing friends came and people often said there was a bigger mob on Beau Liddel's veranda than you'd ever find in the Members'. He liked to have a radio by his side and I remember that once he motioned everyone to be silent: the latest election news was being broadcast. The bookies were offering seven to one against Alan winning his father's old seat.

Doctors and specialists harangued Angelica but all she did was fall into a frenzy and demand that they give her back her son. When I saw her she accused me of lying to her, of stealing her baby, of destroying her life, and I turned helplessly away. One afternoon the doctor told me that Angelica was not recovering as a young woman of her age should and asked me if she had any burden on her mind.

"She wanted a son," was all I could say.

I went into her room and she was flushed, her hair hanging in tangles round her face.

"All right! Stare at me! I know what I look like."

I tried to calm her, but I did not speak about Bessie or tell her how every day she was growing more beautiful. Whenever I mentioned the baby Angelica would scream and then mutter that there had been another woman in the hospital, a special friend of one of the doctors, and when her baby died, they had given her Angelica's son.

I listened as the stories grew more fabulous and tried to disparage her inventions by talking about Terry's new detective serial and film stars, anything that would divert her. It was useless so finally I sat in silence, forcing myself to appear sympathetic as she wailed, and thinking all the time of the baby that I had left sleeping in her blue cradle. Bessie filled my mind and if I thought of her for an instant, her presence would flood through my body in coursing tides of joy. It was as if I could feel her even as I was contemplating her mental image. She was imprinted on my soul.

"Look at me!" Angelica shrieked and, startled, I realized that she had pushed back the sheet and pulled her nightgown up to her chin.

"Look at that and tell me if any man would want to touch that."

Her body was crumpled like an empty sack with sagging welts across her stomach, her legs still swollen with rope-like veins.

"That's what the little bitch did to me!"

It was only when Angelica looked at her body that she remembered her daughter.

"You'll change, Angela. You'll be prettier than you were before."

"I suppose you're blissfully happy with that old drunk," she said sourly.

"Beau's a little better, I think."

Angelica snorted and told me she wanted to die.

Everything in the house at Randwick turned upon Bessie and Beau seemed happiest when I placed her on his lap and she clasped one of his fingers with her hand. I used to sit beside him for hours while she slept in my arms and sometimes I would be half asleep myself when Norma or Florrie came in and took her from me.

They were there every day and quarrelled constantly.

"It's not as if you ever had a kid of your own," Norma said, her voice rising. "You seem to forget that I've raised three, Florrie."

"The only reason I never had any of my own was because I was the eldest of nine and my mother suffered from nerves, so I had to look after the whole bloody lot of them."

I was still laughing when they finally agreed on the temperature of the bottle and brought it out to me.

"It is a pretty baby," they both agreed, and only Taps refused to admire her.

The following day I went to see Angelica and the Matron stopped me in the corridor.

"It's a miracle," she said. "I really think we'll be able to discharge her if she continues making such progress."

It was indeed a transformation for a freshly bleached and professionally painted young woman had taken Angelica's place in the bed. Gold curls floated against a collar of maribou feathers and her nails were a brilliant scarlet.

"You're not going to stay long, are you?" she said querulously. "I'm expecting company."

"Angela, you look wonderful!"

"Oh, my head is all right, and if I keep the sheet up, no one will see my figure."

Fear suddenly buffeted me—this could only mean that Angelica, now sane again, would demand Bessie. But Bessie was not her child, she was mine! Rage followed fear and I realized that Angelica was staring at me.

"Are you having a turn or something?" she asked.

"Bessie—"

"Bessie be damned! When I get out of this bloody dump I'm going to call the police and they'll find my son. I daren't mention it here because that old Matron would poison me. But I've been making enquiries and I have a pretty fair idea where my son is right now."

I was shaking my head more with relief than to deprecate her accusations.

"You're not going to stay much longer, are you?" she said again, glancing at her watch. "My friend will be here soon."

I was deaf to everything except the warning cry in my head that Angelica was Bessie's mother and that she had every right in nature and law to take her from me. Later I remembered and knew the friend she spoke of was death.

Beau listened intently as I poured out my fears to him but when I looked up at him, I realized that he was smiling. His lips were trying to shape a word and I heard one syllable that I knew was "Ours."

It was a little after three when the phone rang and Taps told me I was wanted at the hospital urgently. Nothing could have happened to Angelica, I was sure of that, and I wondered if she had discovered some new culprit in the conspiracy of theft she daily wove like a crazed quilt. Again I was buffeted with fear because I was certain that Angelica was now well enough to leave the hospital and the urgency must be the Matron's desire to get rid of her as quickly as possible. She would return to the house in Randwick, to Beau, and my baby would no longer be mine but hers, despite all her threats and accusations. Anxiety and dread made me hurry down the corridor and I was about to open Angelica's door when the Matron spoke to me.

"She's very ill," she said and told me that Angelica was now running a fever and the doctors were sure she had septicaemia.

"Is that possible? She was so well this morning."

"She couldn't have contracted it here. I wouldn't put it past her to make herself ill."

The Matron glared around her and breathed deeply of air that rasped the throat with the odour of Lysol.

"She was looking forward to seeing friends today," I added with my thoughts floundering in conflicting directions.

"A woman and a young man came to see her a little after eleven—that's all. Perhaps you can talk some sense into her."

Angelica was staring blindly when I walked over to the bed and at first she did not seem aware of my presence as I reached out and touched her hand. Her face was stained with tears and the gold ringlets of the morning were tattered.

"What has happened?" I asked her.

It was some moments before she recognized my voice and then she turned slowly to me as if her flesh was wooden and it was only with difficulty that she could move.

"He won't marry me," she said slowly.

"You are married," I replied, and I couldn't avoid the edge of bitterness to the statement.

"Not a proper marriage. I told him that. In the eyes of the Church I'm not married at all."

Somewhere she must have said this many times because it came out by rote.

"I told him we'd find our son, but she laughed at that too."

"I don't understand," I said slowly and wondered if this were some new fantasy she had created.

Suddenly she leaned forward as if in agony and clutched the sheet.

"He's going to be married! She's arriving next month—they showed me her photograph. Younger than me with black hair—not pretty as I could be, but a virgin. A virgin—"

The last word choked her and she dragged the sheet up to her sobbing face.

"I don't understand what you're saying, I don't know who you're talking about, Angela."

Slowly and with an expression of puzzled irritation she lifted her head and looked at me.

"Rocco—Rocco, my lover."

They were walking up the dusty path to Giacopo's house, all the Sciafas, and with them a dark-haired boy holding a little barefoot girl by the hand. Rafaella pulled her forward and the girl began to cry. The boy wiped away her tears with a rag and murmured something to her that I could not hear.

"I never knew, never suspected—" I said lamely.

"Of course you didn't."

Her cheeks were flushed and she began to titter with her head to one side.

"I fooled everyone, especially that fat bitch, Sheila. The old nuns said I was stupid and all my brains were in my feet."

She was laughing uncontrollably now and I leaned forward to restrain her but she pushed my hand away.

"Sheila would have done anything for me. I used to see Rocco every holiday and when you went to Randwick with that old drunk and Rocco was working at the fruit shop, I knew it was *destino*! Oh, he loves me, I saw it today, but he won't marry me!" she wailed.

"If Rocco was your lover then who is Bessie's father?" I cried.

"I'm not stupid, you are. Everyone saying how smart you were but I was running rings round you."

"Beau remembers—"

She was laughing so wildly now that I took her by the shoulders and shook her.

"*Furba*—that's what Rafaella said about me, and she was right. But I'm not going to sleep with the chickens this time," she added furiously.

"Is Beau the child's father?" I repeated the question slowly and she smiled.

"I was in bed with him," she said archly. "He was lying there blind drunk and I took my clothes off and got in alongside him. When he started to come round I began yelling. He was drunk. He didn't know any different. *Furba!*" and she burst out laughing again.

Once before I had been deceived like this and I suddenly saw Mrs Chambers pirouetting with the letter in her hand.

Angelica's voice was a whisper. Just as it had for me, memory had summoned up the past and now it stood mockingly in front of her.

"He said he couldn't marry me because I wasn't a virgin and his mother was going to send to Sicily for a bride. Rafaella called me a *puttana* and threw me out. She said her son was going to marry a virgin, but Rocco was the one who took my *verginitá*. I was never with anyone else but him. We loved each other from as long as I can remember. I can't remember anything before I loved him."

I sat silently with a horror in my mind as her words came out discordantly, in fragments.

"I thought I could make him marry me. It's worked for other girls. I told him I was pregnant and he said he still couldn't marry me, but I knew if it was a boy that he'd kill that old drunk for his son."

She hammered the bed with her fists and then she was quiet and staring at me.

"Rafaella laughed when I told her that my son had been stolen. She pushed the photograph in front of me and said this virgin had six brothers and she would give Rocco many sons." She paused and when she looked at me again her eyes were half closed as if she were sleepy. "I'm going to die. There's nothing else for me now. Dead, I'll curse their bed and make her barren."

Two doctors and a nurse were at my shoulder and she looked up at them and laughed.

"I'm going to die," she said and turned her head from side to side, wailing, "Rocco, *ti amo*. Rocco, *ti amo*," the same words over and over again.

I know one of the doctors spoke to me and as I was leaving the Matron said something else to me, but I can recall nothing until I parked my car in front of the shops in Alison Road that were clustered at the corner. A grocery shop, another that sold hardware, and at the corner, the Sicilian greengrocer's where the windows were filled with rich triangles of peaches, apricots and scarlet plums. I walked into a humid dark and the aroma reminded me of the harvest in Griffith when the carts and trucks were unloading at the factory. A beaded curtain hung across a doorway to the back of the shop but all I could hear were the flies beating against the window. Nobody came in, yet I knew that I was being watched. I did not move and suddenly I felt an old terror reaching out for me as the shop filled with a gathering darkness.

The curtain jangled, I turned and saw a woman dressed in black, her hands folded under a black shawl just as Rosalia used to stand and wait for me outside the museum in Trapani.

Neither of us spoke and the darkness pressed in upon me.

"What do you want?"

The voice seemed to come from the depths of a cave.

"Rafaella?"

She nodded.

"Then you know why I'm here. Angelica is dying. She's calling for Rocco."

The woman shrugged.

"Angelica is dead."

"Rocco is the father of her child."

With what anguish I said that.

"Angelica died many years ago."

The past was claiming me now and I struggled vainly to be free.

"You saw her in the hospital today, Rafaella. You were there with Rocco."

At the corner of my eye I saw a thin, dark-haired boy peering through the bead curtain.

"Let me speak to him," I said, but Rafaella pointed at me, her face glowering with anger.

"Rocco's *fidanzata* will soon be here and when they are married they will have Giacopo's farm. Benno does not want it. He has three trucks now and he will soon have more. There is no future for Rocco here working in my brother's shop."

Rafaella seemed annoyed at having told me what did not concern me and was about to turn away when I felt myself trembling with anger and fear. I tried to keep my voice firm, to sound like my mother, but when I spoke I heard a child's voice.

"You must let Rocco see Angelica. They have loved each other since they were children. He's the father of her baby."

"How can a dead woman give birth? Tell me that!" she shouted.

"She's your niece, you cared for Angelica when her parents died. She's your family."

"Angelica died when she lost her honour."

"No! No, you can't bury her. This is not Sicily and the old ways are gone."

"If her own mother, my dear sister Nina, had been alive and seen her daughter's shameless ways, she would have killed her with her own hands, and I would have helped her."

Carrying the drugged girl on their shoulders, treading the winding path to the grotto where she would wake in stone.

My breath was coming short and I drove my nails into my palms.

"Let me speak to Rocco. He knows what his duty is."

"Duty!" She put back her head and guffawed and I saw that the broken teeth were now capped with gold.

She stepped forward and thrust her face into mine.

"My son made use of her as any man will a *puttana*, but now he is going to be married and a young and pretty wife will keep him at home. She will give him her honour unstained and he will be satisfied."

"Rocco took Angelica when she was a virgin!"

"Because she was a *puttana*—like you!" and she spat on the floor in front of me. "We read in the papers about you—one man and then another, but not one of them will ever marry you. You are *disgraziata* and you have shamed your family."

"I may be all of those things and more, but I am not dead. You were never able to bury me alive!" I shouted.

"*Disgraziata, puttana* and *ladra*!" she responded. "Wasn't it enough to rob poor Benno in Sicily? No, you came to us and stole Giacopo's fortune. What good did it do you? Did that young lawyer marry you? Never—he had more sense. And then we read about some Austrian who ran back to his own country and now this—" She put her head back and laughed. "The young *puttana* stole the prize from the old one."

Every word she said was a knife in my flesh but I did not turn away.

"You must let Rocco see Angelica before she dies."

"She died when she sacrificed her honour. What should a fine young man do with a corpse? Play with the bones?"

There was nothing more I could say to her, but I could not make myself turn away from her. It was Rafaella who decided for me, taking hold of my elbow and pushing me towards the door. As I stumbled out to the pavement I could still hear her laughing.

What she had said about me was true and I thought bitterly about my life. My mother had hoped I would become a classical archaeologist and Frau Brunner had told me that one day I would run a fine hotel. Instead, I was twenty-nine and all I had amassed was money. Instead of respect, I had notoriety and now that Beau was stricken, I was certain that Billy Garvin would take great delight in reminding his public of my colourful past and my present desolation. Yet how many times I had sought for a settled way; I remembered the ring that Alan had given me with its four diamonds. My hands were bare now and I knew that they would remain so.

At the bottom of the steps I reached out and grasped the gate involuntarily as a thought more frightful than all the rest took possession of my mind. Beau believed that Bessie was his child, treasured because she shared his flesh, even though he knew that she was the fruit of a drunken rape. I resolved to tell him that he was mistaken, that Angelica had lied to us all and he was not guilty of any wrong. And if I freed him from that guilt, I would rob him of a joy that made him smile every time I placed Bessie on his knees. Ah, in that same instant I remembered the strange picture on the fragment of pottery that showed a man strangling himself to escape from the pain of the cords that bound his neck to his heels.

Norma was on the veranda and I became aware that she must have been speaking for some time before I heard her.

"Much worse, the Matron said. I said I'd go with you, Gwen."

"Please—yes, I don't think I can bear any more on my own."

Norma was at my side and then I heard her distinctly.

"The Matron says it's the fever, but she keeps asking for someone called Rocco. Do you know who it is?"

"Oh yes, it's a relation of hers," I replied evenly. "She must be delirious. Rocco died years ago."

Coda

The child of a great love is always an orphan. Everything in life is subject to time and the love that declares it will last forever and never change, is death. And what odd, frail and unexpected vessels carry this doomed freight. If all the great lovers of history were set down before us, they would probably be as strange as Angelica and my parents. Some would seem monsters. It was small comfort to remember that even though my parents regarded me as an intruder, a stranger trespassing in their garden of love, they never rejected me as Angelica had her child. Rosalia once said that I would walk among graves and I wondered if that path had been chosen for me, or whether I had deliberately followed it because I was seeking the deathly love of my parents. Rafaella's words still echoed in my head. If I had not been driven by that inexorable quest, I would probably have been married to Alan now and my name would not be one of scandal and disrepute. I had shamed my family. But what family did I have? Dolfi was gone and Edith was dead. All I had left were Beau and the child in my arms. Neither was related to me nor they to each other and yet we were all part of a whole bound together by a law that only I could interpret.

Bessie, that secret is ours. People always confuse Italians with Sicilians and imagine we are frank and open-hearted, when the true Sicilian is a creature of silence and oblique utterance. Perhaps Beau should have known the truth—and then I would see him smile when I placed Bessie on his lap and measured against that happiness, truth was less than a trifle.

Every day brought fresh despair as I saw him slowly drawn towards death, yet no one seemed more content to watch the strength of his body dwindle and his senses fail than Beau. Once at Avalon he had said that he hoped he could die like an animal and I thought he wanted some violent end, but I knew now what he meant. Beau welcomed death as he had life and when I took his head between my hands and kissed him, it was as if I had given him the treasures of the world and everlasting life. I felt the weight and the power of his love and it was almost more than I could bear.

The specialist was very cheerful and said he thought Beau's condition had stabilized and he might last for some time, but I remembered my mother and I could read the signs. Bessie was my strength and when I held her to me she was like a mighty fortress protecting me from memory and grief. All the imperious force of life was in that tiny body.

My friends were troubled and Minna said that I had not done well for myself, but it was Florrie who voiced their general concern.

"Gwen, it doesn't make any sense, love. You've got to pull yourself together and face the facts: you're looking after a kid that isn't yours for a man that isn't even your husband. For a man who dumped you for that little —well, I won't speak ill of the dead, but we all know what she was like. I can understand you taking to the baby, that's natural in a woman, but you're not much more than a kid yourself, and yet sometimes you act as though you were ninety and the next step will put you in the grave."

I had no answers except to say that Beau loved me, and then Florrie said that I deserved the love of a man my own age. Everything she said was rational, and I rejected every part of it.

It was Billy Garvin's next article in the Sunday *Truth* that made me weep as I never had before. Billy had discovered that I was once engaged to Alan and, piecing together what he had found out in Griffith, embroidering it with details of Kurt and Beau, he had presented it to his readers under the title of "Warmonger's Lurid Past." Billy Garvin was now the dove of peace, charging Alan with deliberately trying to introduce conscription so that young Australians could be sacrificed in a futile and unnecessary struggle. The *Bulletin* was more restrained, but even there it was mentioned that he was the son of Valmai Vitale and had once been engaged to the notorious Gwen Harcourt.

Valmai Vitale was the creation of the Danny Burns Radio Theatre and we had all let her grow into a profitable monster for us and an enduring embarrassment for Alan. Now, I was to be the final straw that would sink his hopes of being elected. Garvin reported that the electorate was turning against him, that when he spoke in one small town, a bucket of red paint had been thrown at the platform. Everyone in the world except Menzies and his followers knew there was going to be another war, but Australians seemed to think that if it did come it would be confined to Europe, and only militarists like Alan Gilchrist wanted to send our men off to another Gallipoli.

Once Alan had rebuked me because all I wanted to do was talk about Kurt and myself, oblivious to the world around us, and now the one man who was trying to make his country see the danger from Japan was being cut down by my scandalous past.

My body ached and my breasts were swollen and as hard as stones. Perhaps I too was dying and would follow Beau as surely as my father had my mother. Every day I planned to write to Alan and ask him to forgive me but I didn't know what he should forgive me for except for being what I was. Day followed day in misery as I swore not to read the paper and then I found myself with it in front of me, torturing myself with another diatribe from the crusader for peace and justice in the world. Menzies had laughed when he was asked what he thought about Alan's chances of winning the election and said that they were slim, very slim indeed, and all the journalists had laughed with him.

The only moments of calm I knew came when I held Bessie or sat with Beau. The summer was drawing to an end and a cold December had become a March of bushfires and blazing heat. The windows were open in Beau's room and I sat there in the early morning breeze while Bessie drank. Powers and currents of feeling were inside me that I did not understand and when she moved sleepily, the milk filming her lips, I felt my breasts throbbing. Bessie was turning her face towards me and I opened my dress and held her to me. Her mouth closed on my breast and I almost cried out with the piercing joy. Angelica's great love had become death, but this was life and renewal, hope and all the blessings of *fortuna muliebris*. She rustled drowsily and her eyelids were fluttering. On my breast there was a pearl of milk like the tear that fell from Bradamante's eye.

Norma shook her head when I told her and said I should see a doctor.

"False pregnancy—you have all the symptoms—everything except the baby."

"But I have a baby, Norma. She's mine."

"Gwen, you've been under a lot of strain but you know as well as I do who Bessie's mother is—was. Remember, you were having a turn like this when I first met you on the train to Griffith. What you want is a nice new outfit and a pretty hat that I'll make for you and a bit of fun at the races."

The following day was the fifth of March with a heatwave and a pall of red dust blown in from the outback. I placed a fan by Bessie's cradle and Norma helped me hang wet sheets across the windows of Beau's room and the nursery.

"I learned how to cope with heat like this on the farm," she said and told me to spray the sheets and leave bowls of ice on every window ledge.

The specialist had been and gone, and this time his cheery manner was put aside and he said quietly that he did not think Beau would last the day. Taps flew into a tantrum and denounced all doctors as gravedigging ghouls but we both knew that he had spoken the truth. I brought Bessie to Beau's side and placed his hand against her face, but he did not stir, and when I knelt and kissed his forehead, his skin was cold. I understood then what must be done. I asked Taps to turn his bed so that the foot was facing the door and when he asked me why, I could not give him any reason except that I knew this was what must be done for the dying. I found a loaf of bread and a candle in the kitchen and placed them on a chair against the door.

There was no breeze that evening, even though the radio said we could expect a cool change before morning. People stood out on their verandas and front steps, faces turned towards the Harbour, waiting for the Southerly Buster.

Bessie was fretful and I bathed her in cool water and watched her stretch her legs as if she were dreaming of swimming. If Beau was still breathing it was less than a whisper of air, but I knew he was aware of us beside him. Later, it grew dark, and I lit the white candle and rocked Bessie to sleep in her cradle.

The house was very still. Taps brought me a tray of food but I wasn't hungry and shook my head when he told me I should eat something.

"I'm going to call a few of your friends," he said. "I'll get in touch with the racing crowd later."

"Friends? Now?" I asked bewildered.

"It's time," he replied and pointed to the guttering candle. "They'd all want to be here," Taps said. "I think he enjoyed your friends more than his own. Even Terry and—Henry. And Mr Gilchrist. He won his father's old seat. It just came over the radio. By a landslide too. Just goes to show you shouldn't believe what you read in the papers."

When I heard that Alan had triumphed I was jubilant, then I despaired because I knew the pain I had caused him.

"You'd like me to call him, wouldn't you?" Taps asked.

"Yes, Taps, please—tell him I need him," I said, knowing that if reason had any authority in Alan's life, he would plead political business and I would never see him again.

I heard the clock by the front door chime midnight and occasionally a door opened and was closed, and there was a stirring in the house and the murmur of voices. Beau's hand was in mine and as life left him, it grew heavier. Suddenly, just after midnight, the windows clattered and the lid of a garbage tin rattled clanging down the street. The Southerly Buster arrived with gusting rain and the heat was drawn from the house.

A thread of light filtered across the room, no more, when I woke and realized that someone was in the chair opposite me.

Bessie was there in the white pleated bonnet and pinafore she had worn when I first saw her on the beach at Trapani. I could hear Assunta telling me that this was a little English girl who would be my friend and then she slowly handed me her spade and showed me how to make a wall against the tide.

I sat there, scarcely breathing, because I could see the sand on her feet and the sweet gravity of her face. Beau stirred and I felt his hand convulse in mine. When I looked back to the chair, Bessie was gone and Beau was dead.

The air had been washed clean and smelt of salt as I stood on the veranda with Bessie in my arms watching the gulls wheel across to the racecourse, listening to all the sounds of the house behind me.

So many voices were there that morning. Was it my mother I could hear complaining about her roses and Frau Brunner denouncing the Sicilians? Surely that was Dolfi's laughter as he made fun of Miki and that soft deliberate voice was my father's.

Alan's voice was not an echo and when I heard him arguing with Joel, the sounds of the past were silenced. He had come to me and I could still feel the strength of his arms around me.

Mother George and Florrie were helping Norma sort ribbons in the living room.

"Keep the different colours in separate balls," she was saying.

"Waste of time," Florrie muttered. "You should junk the lot."

"Those scraps will make some of the prettiest hats you ever saw," Norma retorted. "You've worn a few of them yourself, Florrie."

"We should be doing something more useful than this," Florrie argued.

"It's very soothing and we can't do anything more now."

"Ah, now there's a fine length of gold."

That was Mother George's voice.

"When it's as long as that, cut it into scraps, Mother. Makes it easier to work with."

"No, it would be a waste—such a length of gold ribbon."

Alan's step in the hall again and saying something to Taps. Sister Joseph had taken charge of the funeral just as she had for Angelica, and now she was telling McGregor that the Presbyterian minister was a disgrace to the Christian faith and not fit to bury a dog. I know that when the time comes for me to find the pale forest, Sister Joseph will be there to show me the way.

The road was still shining from the rain but the sun was rising and the asphalt began to steam. Bessie moved sleepily in my arms and I rocked her gently. Across the road a thin dark boy stared at me but I did not speak, and after a few moments, he hunched his shoulders and walked up towards the greengrocer's shop on the corner.

"Ah Bessie—my love—" I murmured and turned to carry her into the house.

Alan was behind me and he put out his hand to steady me.

"Come," he said quietly. "It's time you got some rest."

"Rest? Oh no," I said joyfully. "I can go back now and change everything."

Wondering, I looked down and saw the thread of scarlet on my leg reaching for the earth.